文
景

Horizon

追风筝的人

[美] 卡勒德·胡赛尼 著　李继宏 译

THE
KITE RUNNER

上海人民出版社

评论

　　巧妙、惊人的情节交错，让这部小说值得瞩目，这不仅是一部政治史诗，也是一个关于童年选择如何影响我们成年生活的极度贴近人性的故事。单就书中的角色刻画来看，这部初试啼声之作就已值得一读。从敏感、缺乏安全感的阿米尔到他具有多层次性格的父亲，直到阿米尔回到阿富汗之后才逐步揭露父亲的牺牲与丑闻，也才了解历史在美国和中东的分岔……这些内容缔造了一部完整的文学作品，将这个过去不引人注意、在新千年却成为全球政治焦点的国家的文化呈现在世人面前。同时兼具时代感与高度文学质感，极为难能可贵。

——《出版商周刊》

　　凡夫俗子在历史狂涛里的独力奋斗，一部非比寻常的小说。

——《人物》

　　本书偏重个人的情节，从阿米尔与他父亲仆人儿子哈桑的亲密友谊开始，这段感情成为贯穿全书的脉络。这两个男孩所放的风筝，象征了他们之间关系的脆弱，在往日生活消逝之际，备受考验。作者笔下的阿富汗温馨闲适，却因为不同种族之间的摩擦而现紧张。书中充满令人回萦难忘的景象：一个为了喂饱孩子的男人在市场上出售他的义腿；足球赛中场休息时间，一对通奸的情侣在体育场上活活被石头砸死；一个涂脂抹粉的男孩被迫出卖身体，跳着以前街头手风琴艺人的猴子表演的舞步。

——《纽约时报》

极为动人的作品……没有虚矫赘文，没有无病呻吟，只有精练的篇章……细腻勾勒家庭与友谊、背叛与救赎，无须图表与诠释就能打动并启发吾人。作者对祖国的爱显然与造成它今日沧桑的恨一样深……故事娓娓道来，轻笔淡描，近似川端康成的《千只鹤》，而非马哈福兹的《开罗三部曲》。作者描写缓慢沉静的痛苦尤其出色。

——《华盛顿邮报》

敏锐，真实，能引起人们的共鸣。《追风筝的人》最伟大的力量之一是对阿富汗人与阿富汗文化的悲悯描绘。作者以温暖、令人欣羡的亲密笔触描写阿富汗和当地人民，一部生动且易读的作品。

——《芝加哥论坛报》

一鸣惊人之作。一对阿富汗朋友的故事，也是关于文化的不可思议的故事。真正荡气回肠的经典小说。

——《旧金山纪事报》

一部美丽的小说，2005年写作最佳也最震撼人心的作品。一段没有前景的友谊，一个令人心碎的故事……这部感人非凡的作品也描写了父与子、人与上帝、个人与国家之间脆弱的关系。忠诚与血缘串连这些故事，使之成为2005年最抒情、最动人，也最出人意料的一本书。

——《丹佛邮报》

不算是中东政治的故事，而是在一个在分崩离析的美丽国家里生活的故事。透过扣人心弦，甚至有时令人极度不安的角色与情节安排，作者以自身的文化与他挚爱的祖国的历史为我们提供借鉴。

——《圣安东尼快报》

生命的节奏是这个故事的架构。这部小说以1970年代的阿富汗与之后的美国为背景，文采飞扬，雅俗共赏。小说的高潮如此残忍又如此美丽，令人不忍揭露，作者以恩典与救赎勾勒生命圆满循环的功力展露无遗。一部极具疗愈力量的恢弘文学作品。

——《水牛城新闻》

作者以极其敏锐的笔触让他的祖国栩栩如生。他深入描绘阿富汗移民在哀悼失去祖国、努力融入美国生活之际、仍然根深蒂固的传统与风俗。此书是一部睿智并发人深思的小说：赎罪并不必然等同幸福。

——《休斯敦纪事报》

既表现出对说故事的热爱，也展现文学写作的功力，具备获奖特质的大气之作。这部小说最吸引人的部分之一是简单的记述文体。就像哈金那部描写爱情、政治与阶级问题的小说《等待》一样，本书以真实的故事洗涤读者的心灵。

——《克利夫兰平原经销商》

一部扣人心弦的感人作品，给人带来意想不到的收获：了解并悲悯阿富汗的人民。这本书的力量来自于作者让文化在书页上栩栩如生的功力，让人爱不释手。

——《爱荷华城市新闻》

生动描绘三十年前的阿富汗。

——《华尔街日报》

作者以相同的沉着笔调处理温情与恐怖、加州美梦与喀布尔梦魇……非常出色的故事与道德寓言。

——《加拿大环球邮报》

一位现居美国的阿富汗作家的一鸣惊人之作。这部缠绕着背叛与赎罪的小说以阿富汗近代的悲剧为骨架，不仅仅是一个关于成长或移民的辛酸故事，作者把这两个元素都融入到得之不易的个人救赎宏景之中。所有的这些，加上丰富的阿富汗文化风情：魅力难挡。

——《科克斯书评》

生动描绘阿富汗在过去四分之一个世纪以来的生活。阿米尔和他父亲的角色，他们的关系，以及哈桑与阿米尔的关系，都描写且发展得极为缜密，具有说服力。现于加州行医的作者可能是惟一一位以英文写作的阿富汗作家，他的第一部小说值得推荐。

——《图书馆杂志》

谨以此书献给哈里斯和法拉，他们是我的眼睛之光。献给所有阿富汗的孩子。

前言

　　如同《追风筝的人》中的阿米尔，我在上个世纪 70 年代的喀布尔开始写作，当时还是孩子。虽然我用来写作的语言已经变了——从法尔西文、法文，到如今的英文，但有个因素却始终未变：我向来只为一个读者写作——我自己。某个特定的人物或者场景激起我的兴趣，我坐下来，强迫自己将其完成。《追风筝的人》正是这样写就的。我脑海中有两个男孩，其中一个在感情和道德上不知何去何从，摇摆不定；另外一个单纯、忠诚，生性纯良正直。我知道这两个男孩的友谊前景暗淡，两人的决裂对他们的生活影响巨大。内中缘由是促使我在 2001 年 3 月开始创作这本书的原因。我必须将其找出来，因为到头来，于我而言，写作总是服务于我自己，是一种把故事告诉我自己的行动。

　　我从不曾想过还有别的人会真的阅读这本书。也不尽然。我知道我的妻子罗雅会看。我的父母、兄弟和姻亲也会。我想或许还能哄骗一两个表亲来看。在我脑海中，我会说出阿米尔的故事，然后书稿将会安放在储藏室的书架上。

　　我开始创作这本小说的六个月后，双子塔倒塌了。

不久之后，我的妻子建议——实际上是要求——我把手稿投出去。当时我完成了差不多三分之二，而我每写出一章，罗雅便读一章。我反对将这本书投给出版商。首先，我根本不知道它是否够好。更重要的是，我认为全美国没有人会听一个阿富汗人的诉说，不过这个想法似乎错得更加厉害。你们一定理解的，当时那次袭击发生未久，伤口尚新，民愤高涨。现在阿富汗人备受歧视，我对罗雅说。就算我接受这个滑稽的假设，认为我的书有可能出版，但人们干吗要买它呢？那些在美国的土地上制造了有史以来最大惨案的人就在某人的祖国进行训练，人们干吗要把钱放进他的口袋呢？况且，我还担心，当时把书稿投出去会有机会主义的嫌疑，好像我在利用一个悲剧——尽管我创作这本书早在阿富汗人成为国际社会关注点之前。

罗雅不赞同。她认为这是我获得更多读者的机会。她信心十足，费了好大劲说服我。她觉得当时实际上是向世界讲一个阿富汗故事的良机。那些日子——很悲哀，直到如今——关于阿富汗人的文章多数围绕着塔利班、本·拉登和反恐战争展开。到处是对阿富汗人的误解和偏见。你的书能让他们看到阿富汗人的另一面，罗雅说。我虽然犹豫，但不得不认可她的部分观点。《追风筝的人》很大部分发生在20世纪70年代，苏联战争之前的时期，对很多西方读者来说，实际上是个盲点。甚至还有相当多的篇幅谈到流亡美国的阿富汗人，而至少是在小说界，这些人很少被提起。罗雅最后的也是产生作用的理由是：他们妖魔化，你可以人性化。

情况并非全然如此，我们两人都知道。随着时间的流逝，我们已经见到多数美国人民不再妖魔化阿富汗人。他们的憎恶直接发泄向塔利班——而人们无法妖魔化那些已经是魔鬼的人。此外，她对这未完稿的前景的估计，我认为很善意，但过于乐观。尽管如此，我明白了她的意思。

2002年6月，我把书稿寄到纽约，给一位可爱的女士，名字是伊莲·科斯特，是个文学经纪人。7月的一个炎热下午，她给我打电话，说的话跟几个月前罗雅说过的差不多。那年夏天快结束的时候，她给《追风筝的人》找到了家。这本书于2003年6月在美国出版。

这本书自出版之后在全世界范围内备受欢迎，你们能想象得到我有多么吃惊。别忘了，我写下它的时候，意识中的读者只是我自己；所以，能收到印度、南非、特拉维夫、悉尼、伦敦、阿肯色的读者来信，表达他们对我的感情，我非常地惊讶。很多人想捐钱给阿富汗人。有些人甚至还告诉我，他们想收养阿富汗孤儿。在这些信中，我看到小说作品独有的联结人们的力量，我还看到了人类的体验有多么普遍：羞耻、负疚、后悔、爱情、友谊、宽宥和赎罪。

对我来说，这些读者来信是巨大的满足感的来源，也不断提醒我，我娶了一位贤妻，没有她，这本书可能还摆放在我的储藏室里。身为作家，若读者对这个故事、对里面的人物和他们的艰苦、对情节的纠缠转折有所触动，我感到激动。身为阿富汗人，当读者告诉我，阅读这本小说让他们对阿富汗人有了具体的认识，他们再也不把我的祖国看作仅仅是一片不幸、麻烦不断、灾难深重的土地，对此我深感光荣。

我希望你们也这样。

谢谢你们阅读这本书，愿你们的风筝飞得又远又高。

卡勒德·胡赛尼

第一章

2001 年 12 月

我成为今天的我，是在 1975 年某个阴云密布的寒冷冬日，那年我十二岁。我清楚地记得当时自己趴在一堵坍塌的泥墙后面，窥视着那条小巷，旁边是结冰的小溪。许多年过去了，人们说陈年旧事可以被埋葬，然而我终于明白这是错的，因为往事会自行爬上来。回首前尘，我意识到在过去二十六年里，自己始终在窥视着那荒芜的巷子。

今年夏季的某天，朋友拉辛汗从巴基斯坦打来电话，要我回去探望他。我站在厨房里，听筒贴在耳朵上，我知道电话线连着的，并不只是拉辛汗，还有我过去那些未曾赎还的罪行。挂了电话，我离开家门，到金门公园北边的斯普瑞柯湖边散步。晌午的骄阳照在波光粼粼的水面上，数十艘轻舟在和风的吹拂中漂行。我抬起头，望见两只红色的风筝，带着长长的蓝色尾巴，在天空中冉冉升起。它们舞动着，飞越公园西边的树林，飞越风车，并排飘浮着，如同一双眼睛俯视着旧金山，这个我现在当成家园的城市。突然间，哈桑的声音在我脑中响起：**为你，千千万万遍**。哈桑，那个兔唇的哈桑，那个追风筝的人。

我在公园里柳树下的长凳坐下，想着拉辛汗挂电话前说的那句意味深长的话。*那儿有再次成为好人的路。*我抬眼看看那比翼齐飞的风筝。我忆起哈桑。我缅怀爸爸。我想到阿里。我思念喀布尔。我想起曾经的生活，想起 1975 年那个改变了一切的冬天。那造就了今天的我。

第二章

　　小时候，爸爸的房子有条车道，边上种着白杨树，哈桑和我经常爬上去，用一块镜子的碎片把阳光反照进邻居家里，惹得他们很恼火。在那高高的枝丫上，我们相对而坐，没穿鞋子的脚丫晃来荡去，裤兜里满是桑葚干和胡桃。我们换着玩那破镜子，边吃桑葚干，边用它们扔对方，忽而吃吃逗乐，忽而开怀大笑。我依然能记得哈桑坐在树上的模样，阳光穿过叶子，照着他那浑圆的脸庞。他的脸很像木头刻成的中国娃娃，鼻子大而扁平，双眼眯斜如同竹叶，眼珠在不同光线下会显现出金色、绿色，甚至是宝石蓝。我依然能看到他长得较低的小耳朵，还有突出的下巴，肉乎乎的，看起来像是一团后来才加上去的附属物。他的嘴唇从中间裂开，兴许是那个制作中国娃娃的工匠手中的工具不慎滑落，又或者只是由于他的疲倦和心不在焉。

　　有时在树上我还会怂恿哈桑，让他用弹弓将胡桃射向邻家那独眼的德国牧羊犬。哈桑从无此想法，但若是我要求他，真的要求他，他不会拒绝。哈桑从未拒绝我任何事情。弹弓在他手中可是致命的武器。哈桑的父亲阿里常常逮到我们，像他那样和蔼的人，也被我们气得要疯了。

他会挥舞双手，要我们从树上下来。他会将镜子拿走，并告诉我们，他的妈妈说魔鬼也用镜子，用它们照那些正在做礼拜的穆斯林，让他们分心。"他这么做的时候会哈哈大笑。"他总是加上这么一句，并对他的儿子怒目相向。

"是的，爸爸。"哈桑会咕哝着，低头看自己的双脚。但他从不告发我，从来不提镜子、用胡桃射狗其实都是我的鬼主意。

那条通向两扇锻铁大门的红砖车道两旁植满白杨。车道延伸进两扇铁门，再进去就是我父亲的地盘了。砖路的左边是房子，尽头则是后院。

人人都说我父亲的房子是瓦兹尔·阿克巴·汗区最华丽的屋宇，甚至有人认为它是全喀布尔最美观的建筑。它坐落于喀布尔北部这个繁华的新兴城区，入口通道甚为宽广，两旁种着蔷薇；房子开间不少，铺着大理石地板，还有很大的窗户。爸爸亲手在伊斯法罕[1]选购了精美的马赛克瓷砖，铺满四个浴室的地面，还从加尔各答[2]买来金丝织成的挂毯，用于装饰墙壁，拱形的天花板上挂着水晶吊灯。

楼上是我的卧房，爸爸的卧室，还有他的书房，书房也被称为"吸烟室"，总是弥漫着烟草和肉桂的气味。在阿里的服侍下用完晚膳之后，爸爸跟他的朋友躺在书房的黑色皮椅上。他们填满烟管——爸爸总说是"喂饱烟管"，高谈阔论，总不离三个话题：政治，生意，足球。有时我会求爸爸让我坐在他们身边，但爸爸会堵在门口。"走开，现在就

---

[1] Isfahan，伊朗中部城市。——译者注，下同

[2] Calcutta，印度城市。

走开，"他会说，"这是大人的时间。你为什么不回去看你自己的书本呢？"他会关上门，留下我独自纳闷：何以他总是只有大人的时间？我坐在门口，膝盖抵着胸膛。我坐上一个钟头，有时两个钟头，听着他们的笑声，他们的谈话声。

楼下的起居室有一面凹壁，摆着专门定做的橱柜。里面陈列着镶框的家庭照片：有张模糊的老照片，是我祖父和纳迪尔国王[1]的合影，拍于 1931 年，就在国王遇刺前两年。他们穿着及膝的长靴，肩膀上扛着来复枪，站在一头死鹿前。有张是在我父母新婚之夜拍的，爸爸穿着黑色的西装，朝气蓬勃，脸带微笑的妈妈穿着白色礼服，宛如公主。还有一张照片，爸爸和他最好的朋友和生意伙伴拉辛汗站在我们的房子外面，两人都没笑，我在照片中还是婴孩，爸爸抱着我，看上去疲倦而严厉。我在爸爸怀里，手里却抓着拉辛汗的小指头。

凹壁有门通往餐厅，餐厅正中摆着红木餐桌，坐下三十人绰绰有余。由于爸爸热情好客，确实几乎每隔一周就有这么多人坐在这里用餐。餐厅的另一端有高大的大理石壁炉，每到冬天总有橙色的火焰在里面跳动。

拉开一扇玻璃大滑门，便可走上一个半圆形的露台；下面是占地两英亩的后院和几排樱桃树。爸爸和阿里在东边的围墙下辟了个小菜园，种着西红柿、薄荷和胡椒，还有一排从未结实的玉米。哈桑和我总是叫它"病玉米之墙"。

---

[1] Nadir Shah（1883~1933），阿富汗国王，1929 年登基，1933 年 11 月 8 日被刺杀。

花园的南边种着枇杷树，树荫之下便是仆人的住所了。那是一座简陋的泥屋，哈桑和他父亲住在里面。

在我母亲因为生我死于难产之后一年，也即1964年冬天，哈桑诞生在那个小小的窝棚里面。

我在家里住了十八年，但进入阿里和哈桑房间的次数寥寥无几。每当日落西山，玩了一天的哈桑和我就分开了。我穿过那片蔷薇，回到爸爸的广厦去；哈桑则回到他的寒庐，他在那儿出世，在那儿度过一生。我记得它狭小而干净，点着两盏煤油灯，光线昏暗。屋里两端各摆着一床褥子，一张破旧的赫拉特[1]出产的地毯四边磨损，摆在中间。屋角还有一把三脚凳，一张木头桌子，哈桑就在那上面画画。此外四壁萧然，仅有一幅挂毯，用珠子缀着"Allah-u-akbar"（真主伟大）的字样。那是爸爸某次去麦什德[2]旅行时给阿里买的。

1964年某个寒冷的冬日，正是在这间小屋，哈桑的母亲莎娜芭生下了哈桑。我的妈妈因为生产时失血过多而弃世，哈桑则在降临人世尚未满七日就失去了母亲。而这种失去她的宿命，在多数阿富汗人看来，简直比死了老娘还要糟糕：她竟然跟着一群江湖艺人跑了。

哈桑从未提及他的母亲，仿佛她从未存在过。我总是寻思他会不会在梦里见到她，会不会梦见她长什么样子，去了哪里。我还寻思他会不会渴望见到她。他会为她心痛吗，好比我为自己从未见过的妈妈难过一样？有一天，为了看一部新的伊朗电影，我们从爸爸家里朝萨纳博电影

---

[1] Herati，阿富汗西部城市。
[2] Mashad，伊朗城市。

院走去。我们抄了近路，穿过独立中学旁边的军营区——爸爸向来不许
我们走那条捷径，但当时他跟拉辛汗在巴基斯坦。我们跨过围绕着军营
的藩篱，跳过一条小溪，闯进那片开阔的泥地，那儿停放着积满尘灰的
废旧坦克。数个士兵聚集在一辆坦克的影子下抽烟玩牌。有个士兵发现
了我们，用手肘碰碰身边的家伙，冲哈桑嚷嚷。

"喂，你！"他说，"我认识你。"

我们跟他素不相识。他又矮又胖，头发剃得很短，脸上还有黑乎乎
的胡茬。他脸带淫亵，朝我们咧嘴而笑，我心下慌乱。"继续走！"我
低声对哈桑说。

"你！那个哈扎拉[1]小子！看着我，我跟你说话呐！"那士兵咆哮
着。他把香烟递给身边那个家伙，用一只手的拇指和食指围成圆圈，另
外一只手的中指戳进那个圈圈，不断戳进戳出。"我认识你妈妈，你知
道吗？我和她交情不浅呢。"

众士兵轰然大笑，有个还发出一声尖叫。我告诉哈桑继续走，继
续走。

那士兵边说边跟其他人握手，哈哈大笑。后来，电影开始了，我在
黑暗中听到坐在身边的哈桑低声啜泣，看到眼泪从他脸颊掉下来。我从
座位上探过身去，用手臂环住他，把他拉近。他把脸埋在我的肩膀上。
"他认错人了，"我低语，"他认错人了。"

据说莎娜芭抛家弃子的时候，没有人感到奇怪。熟背《古兰经》的
阿里娶了比他年轻 19 岁的莎娜芭，这个女人美貌动人，可是不洁身自

---

[1] Hazara，阿富汗民族，主要分布在该国中部省份。

爱，向来声名狼藉。人们对这桩婚事大皱眉头。跟阿里一样，她也是什叶派穆斯林[1]，也是哈扎拉族人。她还是他的表妹，因而他们天生就应该是一对。但除了这些，至少在他们的外表上，阿里和莎娜芭毫无共同之处。风传莎娜芭那善睐的绿眼珠和俏皮的脸蛋曾诱得无数男人自甘堕落，阿里则半边脸罹患先天麻痹，因此他无法微笑，总是一副阴鸷的脸色。要判断石头脸的阿里究竟高兴还是难过可不是容易的事情，因为只有从他眯斜的棕色眼睛，才能判断其中是欢乐的闪烁，还是哀伤的涌动。人们说眼睛是心灵的窗口，用在阿里身上再贴切不过，他只能在眼神中透露自己。

我听说莎娜芭步履款款，双臀摇摆，那诱人的身姿令众多男人跟他们的爱人同床异梦。但阿里得过小儿麻痹症，右腿萎缩，菜色的皮肤包着骨头，夹着一层薄如纸的肌肉。我记得八岁那年，有一天阿里带我到市场去买馕饼[2]。我走在他后面，嘴里念念有词，学着他走路的样子。我看见他提起那条嶙峋的右腿，摇晃着划出一道弧形；看见他那条腿每次踏下，身体不由自主地往右边倾低。他这样蹒跚前进而又能不摔倒，不能不说是个小小的奇迹。我学着他走路，差点摔进水沟，忍不住咯咯笑起来。阿里转过身，看到我正学着他，他什么也没说。当时没说，以后也一直没说，他只是继续走。

_____

[1] 伊斯兰教分为逊尼（Sunni）和什叶（Shi'a）两大派系。两派的分别主要在于对于穆罕默德继承人的合法性的承认上。按什叶派的观点，只有阿里及其直系后裔才是合法的继承人，而逊尼派承认艾布·伯克尔、欧麦尔、奥斯曼、阿里四大哈里发的合法性。
[2] Naan，阿富汗日常主食，将面团抹在烤炉上烘焙而成。

阿里的脸庞和步伐吓坏了某些邻居的小孩。但真正麻烦的是那些较大的少年。每逢他走过，他们总在街道上追逐他，作弄他。有些管他叫"巴巴鲁"，也就是专吃小孩的恶魔。"喂，巴巴鲁，今天你吃了谁啊？"他们一起欢乐地叫喊，"你吃了谁啊，塌鼻子巴巴鲁？"

他们管他叫"塌鼻子"，因为阿里和哈桑是哈扎拉人，有典型的蒙古人种外貌。很长一段时间内，我对哈扎拉人的了解就这么多：他们是蒙古人的后裔，跟中国人稍微有些相似。学校的教材对他们语焉不详，仅仅提到过他们的祖先。有一天，我在爸爸的书房翻阅他的东西，发现有本妈妈留下的旧历史书，作者是伊朗人，叫寇拉米。我吹去蒙在书上的尘灰，那天晚上偷偷将它带上床，吃惊地发现里面关于哈扎拉人的故事竟然写了满满一章。整整一章都是关于哈扎拉人的！我从中读到自己的族人——普什图人[1]曾经迫害和剥削哈扎拉人。它提到19世纪时，哈扎拉人曾试图反抗普什图人，但普什图人"以罄竹难书的暴行镇压了他们"。书中说我的族人对哈扎拉人妄加杀戮，迫使他们离乡背井，烧焚他们的家园，贩售他们的女人。书中认为，普什图人压迫哈扎拉人的原因，部分是由于前者是逊尼派穆斯林，而后者是什叶派。那本书记载着很多我不知道的事情，那些事情我的老师从未提及，爸爸也缄口不谈。它还诉说着一些我已经知道的事情，比如人们管哈扎拉人叫"吃老鼠的人"、"塌鼻子"、"载货蠢驴"等。我曾听到有些邻居的小孩这么辱骂哈桑。

随后那个星期，有天下课，我把那本书给老师看，指着关于哈扎拉

---

[1] Pashtuns，阿富汗人口最多的民族，其语言普什图语为阿富汗官方语言。

人那一章。他翻了几页，嗤之以鼻地把书还给我。"这件事什叶派最拿手了，"他边收拾自己的教案边说，"把他们自己送上西天，还当是殉道呢。"提到什叶派这个词的时候，他皱了皱鼻子，仿佛那是某种疾病。

虽说同属一族，甚至同根所生，但莎娜芭也加入到邻居小孩取笑阿里的行列里去了。据说她憎恶阿里的相貌，已经到了尽人皆知的地步。

"这是个丈夫吗？"她会冷笑着说，"我看嫁头老驴子都比嫁给他好。"

最终，人们都猜测这桩婚事是阿里和他舅舅——也就是莎娜芭的父亲之间的某种协定。他们说阿里娶他的表妹，是为了给声名受辱的叔叔恢复一点荣誉，尽管阿里五岁痛失怙恃，也并无值得一提的财物或遗产。

阿里对这些侮辱总是默默以待，我认为这跟他畸形的腿有关：他不可能逮到他们。但更主要的是，这些欺辱对他来说毫不见效，在莎娜芭生下哈桑那一刻，他已经找到他的快乐、他的灵丹妙药。那真是足够简单的事情，没有产科医生，也没有麻醉师，更没有那些稀奇古怪的仪器设备。只有莎娜芭躺在一张脏兮兮的褥子上，身下什么也没垫着，阿里和接生婆在旁边帮手。她根本就不需要任何帮助，因为，即使在降临人世的时候，哈桑也是不改本色——他不会伤害任何人。几声呻吟，数下推动，哈桑就出来了。脸带微笑地出来了。

先是爱搬弄是非的接生婆告诉邻居的仆人，那人又到处宣扬，说莎娜芭看了一眼阿里怀中的婴儿，瞥见那兔唇，发出一阵凄厉的笑声。

"看吧，"她说，"现在你有了这个白痴儿子，他可以替你笑了！"她不愿抱着哈桑，仅仅五天之后，她离开了。

爸爸雇佣了那个喂过我的奶妈给哈桑哺乳。阿里跟我们说她是个蓝眼睛的哈扎拉女人，来自巴米扬[1]，那座城市有巨大的佛陀塑像。"她唱歌的嗓子可甜了！"他常常这么说。

她唱什么歌呢？哈桑跟我总是问，虽然我们已经知道——阿里已经告诉过我们无数次了，我们只是想听阿里唱。

他清了清喉咙，放声唱起来：

我站在高高的山上

呼唤阿里的名字，神灵的狮子

啊～阿里，神灵的狮子，凡人的国王

给我悲伤的心灵带来喜悦

然后他会提醒我们，喝过同样的乳汁长大的人就是兄弟，这种亲情连时间也无法拆散。

哈桑跟我喝过同样的乳汁。我们在同一个院子里的同一片草坪上迈出第一步。还有，在同一个屋顶下，我们说出第一个字。

我说的是"爸爸"。

他说的是"阿米尔"。我的名字。

如今回头看来，我认为1975年冬天发生的事情——以及随后所有的事情——早已在这些字里埋下根源。

---

[1] Bamiyan，阿富汗城市，在喀布尔西北150公里处。

第三章

　　传说我父亲曾经在俾路支[1]赤手空拳，和一只黑熊搏斗。如果这是个关于别人的故事，肯定有人会斥之为笑话奇谈。阿富汗人总喜欢将事物夸大，很不幸，这几乎成了这个民族的特性。如果有人吹嘘说他儿子是医生，很可能是那孩子曾经在高中的生物学测验中考了个及格的分数。但凡涉及爸爸的故事，从来没人怀疑它们的真实性。倘使有人质疑，那么，爸爸背上那三道弯弯曲曲的伤痕就是证据。记不清有多少次，我想象着爸爸那次搏击的场面，甚至有时连做梦也梦到了。而在梦中，我分不清哪个是爸爸，哪个是熊。

　　有一次拉辛汗管爸爸叫"飓风先生"，这随后变成远近闻名的绰号。这个绰号可是名副其实。爸爸是典型的普什图人，身材高大，孔武有力，留着浓密的小胡子，卷曲的棕色头发甚是好看，跟他本人一样不羁；他双手强壮，似乎能将柳树连根拔起；并且，就像拉辛汗经常说的那样，黑色的眼珠一瞪，会"让魔鬼跪地求饶"。爸爸身高近两米，每

---

[1]　Baluchistan，巴基斯坦最大的省。

当他出席宴会，总是像太阳吸引向日葵那样，把注意力引到自己身上。

爸爸即使在睡觉的时候，也是引人注目。我常在耳朵里面塞上棉花球，用毯子盖住头，但爸爸的鼾声宛如轰轰作响的汽车引擎，依然穿墙越壁而来，而我们的房间中间还隔着客厅呢。妈妈如何能跟他睡在同一个房间？我不得而知。要是能见到我的妈妈，我还有一长串问题要她解答呢。

在1960年代晚期，我五六岁的样子，爸爸决定建造一座恤孤院。故事是拉辛汗告诉我的。他说爸爸亲自设计施工图，尽管他根本没有半点建筑经验。人们对此表示怀疑，劝他别犯傻，雇个建筑师得了。当然，爸爸拒绝了，人们大摇其头，对爸爸的顽固表示不解。然而爸爸成功了，人们又开始摇头了，不过这次是带着敬畏，对他成功的法门称赞不已。恤孤院楼高两层，位于喀布尔河南岸，在雅德梅湾大道旁边，所耗资费均由父亲自己支付。拉辛汗说爸爸独力承担了整个工程，工程师、电工、管道工、建筑工，这些人的工钱都是爸爸支付的。城里的官员也抽了油水，他们的"胡子得上点油"。

恤孤院工程耗时三年，盖好的那年我八岁。我记得恤孤院落成前一天，爸爸带我去喀布尔以北几英里远的喀尔卡湖。他让我叫上哈桑，但我撒谎，说哈桑有事情要做。我要爸爸全属我一人。再说，有一次哈桑和我在喀尔卡湖畔打水漂，他的石头跳了八下，我用尽力气，也只能跳五下。爸爸在旁边看着我们，他伸手拍拍哈桑的后背，甚至还用手臂搂住他的肩膀。

我们在湖边的野餐桌旁边坐下来，只有爸爸跟我，吃着水煮蛋和肉丸夹饼——就是馕饼夹着肉丸和腌黄瓜。湖水澄蓝，波平如镜，阳光照在湖上熠熠生辉。每逢周五，总有很多家庭到湖边，在阳光下度过假期。但那天不是周末，那儿只有我们——爸爸和我，还有几个留着胡子和长发的游客，我听说他们叫"嬉皮士"。他们坐在码头上，手里拿着钓鱼竿，脚板在水里晃荡。我问爸爸，为什么那些人留着长头发，但爸爸没有回答，只哼了一声。他正准备翌日的演讲，翻阅着一叠手稿，不时用铅笔做些记号。我吃一口鸡蛋，告诉爸爸，学校里面有个男孩说，要是吃下鸡蛋壳，就得将它尿出来。我问爸爸这是不是真的，爸爸又哼了一声。

我咬一口夹饼。有个黄头发的游客放声大笑，用手拍拍另外一人的后背。远处，在湖那边，一辆卡车蹒跚着转过山路的拐角处，它的观后镜反射出闪闪的阳光。

"我想我得了癌症。"我说。和风吹拂着那些手稿，爸爸抬头，告诉我可以自行去拿些苏打水，我所能做的，便只有去搜寻那轿车的行李箱。

翌日，在恤孤院外面，椅子没有来客多。很多人只好站着观看落成庆典。那天刮风，新建筑的大门外面搭了个礼台，爸爸坐在上面，我坐在他后面。爸爸身穿绿色西装，头戴羔羊皮帽。演讲当中，风把他的帽子吹落，人们开怀大笑。他示意我替他把帽子捡回来，我很高兴，因为当时人人可以看到他是我的父亲，我的爸爸。他转过身，对着麦克风说，他希望这座房子比他的皮帽来得牢靠，人们又大笑起来。爸爸演讲结束的时候，大家站起来，欢呼致意，掌声经久不息。接着，来宾与他握手。有些人摸摸我的头发，也跟我握手。我为爸爸自豪，为我们骄傲。

虽说爸爸事业兴旺，人们总是说三道四。他们说爸爸没有经商的天分，应该像爷爷那样专研法律。所以爸爸证明他们统统错了：他不仅经营着自己的生意，还成了喀布尔屈指可数的巨贾。爸爸和拉辛汗创办了一家日进斗金的地毯出口公司，两家药房，还有一家餐厅。

当时人们嘲弄爸爸，说他不可能有桩好婚事——毕竟他没有皇族血统，但他娶了我妈妈，索菲亚·阿卡拉米。妈妈受过良好教育，无论人品还是外貌，都被公认是喀布尔数得上的淑女。她在大学教授古典法尔西语[1]文学，祖上是皇亲贵胄。这让爸爸十分高兴，总在那些对他有所怀疑的人面前称呼她"我的公主"。

父亲随心所欲地打造他身边的世界，除了我这个明显的例外。当然，问题在于，爸爸眼里的世界只有黑和白。至于什么是黑，什么是白，全然由他说了算。他就是这么一个人，你若爱他，也必定会怕他，甚或对他有些恨意。

我上五年级的时候，上伊斯兰课的毛拉[2]叫法修拉，个子矮小粗壮，脸上满是青春痘的疤痕，声音嘶哑。他教导我们，让我们知道施天课[3]的益处，还有朝觐的责任。他还教给我们每天五次礼拜[4]的复杂仪式，要我们背诵《古兰经》。他从不替我们翻译经文，总是强调——有时还会用上一根柳树条——我们必须准确地念出那些阿拉伯字眼，以便真主

---

[1]　Farsi，即波斯语。

[2]　Mullah，某些国家穆斯林对老师、先生、学者的敬称。

[3]　伊斯兰教有五大功：念、礼、斋、课、朝。天课（zakat），即伊斯兰教法定的施舍，或称"奉主命而定"的宗教赋税，又称"济贫税"。

[4]　穆斯林每天要进行五次礼拜，在黎明、中午、下午、日落和晚上各进行一次。

能听得更清楚。一天，他说在伊斯兰教义里面，喝酒是极大的罪过，那些嗜酒的家伙将会在接受超度那一天（审判日）得到惩罚。当年喀布尔饮酒的人比比皆是，没有人会公然加以谴责。不过那些爱小酌几杯的阿富汗人也只敢阳奉阴违，从不在公开场合喝酒。人们把烈酒称为"药"，到特定的"药店"购买，用棕色纸袋包着。他们将袋子扎好，以免被看到；然而有时在路上仍不免被人偷眼斜睨，因为知道这些商店在兜售什么玩意儿的人可不少。

我们在楼上，爸爸的书房——那个吸烟室——里面，我告诉他法修拉毛拉在课堂上讲的话。爸爸走到那个他造在屋角的吧台，自斟了一杯威士忌。他边听边点头，不时从他的酒杯小啜一口。接着他坐在皮沙发上，把酒杯放下，把我抱在他的膝盖上。我觉得自己好像坐在一对树干上。他用鼻子深深吸一口气，又呼出来，气息嘶嘶作响，穿过他的胡子，似乎永无止境。我不知道自己是该拥抱他呢，还是该害怕得从他膝盖上跳下来。

"我知道，你被学校教的功课和在生活中学到的东西搞糊涂了。"他那浑厚的声音说。

"可是，如果他说的是真的，那你岂不是罪人了吗，爸爸？"

"嗯。"爸爸咬碎嘴里的冰块，"你想知道自己的父亲怎么看待罪行吗？"

"想。"

"那我会告诉你，"爸爸说，"不过首先，你得知道一件事情，阿米尔，那些白痴大胡子不会教给你任何有价值的东西。"

"你是说法修拉毛拉吗？"

爸爸拿起酒杯，冰块叮咚作响。"我是说他们全部，那些自以为是的猴子，应该在他们的胡子上撒尿。"

我咯咯笑起来。想到爸爸在猴子的胡子上撒尿，不管那猴子是否自以为是，那场面太搞笑了。

"除了用拇指数念珠，背诵那本根本就看不懂的经书，他们什么也不会。"他喝了一口，"要是阿富汗落在他们手里，所有人都得求真主保佑了。"

"可是法修拉毛拉人很好。"我忍住发笑。

"成吉思汗也很好，"[1] 爸爸说，"够了，不说这个了。你问我对罪行的看法，我会告诉你。你在听吗？"

"是的。"我说，试着抿紧嘴唇，但笑声从鼻孔冒出来，发出一阵鼻息的声响，惹得我又咯咯笑起来。

爸爸双眼坚定地看着我的眼睛，仅仅这样，我就止住了笑声。"我的意思是，像男人跟男人说话那样跟你谈谈。你觉得你做得到吗？"

"是的，亲爱的爸爸。"我低声说，不止一次，爸爸只用几个字就能刺痛我，这真是叫人惊奇。我们有过一段短暂的美好时光——爸爸平时很少跟我说话，更别提把我抱在膝盖上——而我这个笨蛋，竟然白白将其浪费了。

"很好，"爸爸说，但眼睛仍透露出怀疑的神色，"现在，不管那个毛拉怎么说，罪行只有一种，只有一种。那就是盗窃，其他罪行都是盗

---

[1] 公元 1219 年至 1221 年，成吉思汗的西征大军入侵阿富汗地区（当时属花剌子模王朝），屠杀了许多无辜百姓，因而在阿富汗，成吉思汗是恶魔的代名词。

窃的变种。你明白吗？”

“不，亲爱的爸爸。”我说，我多希望自己能懂，我不想再让他失望。

爸爸不耐烦地叹了一口气，那又刺痛我了，因为他不是没耐心的人。他总是直到夜幕降临才回家，留我独自吃饭，每一次我都记得清清楚楚。我问阿里“爸爸在哪儿，什么时候回来”，虽然我知道他在建筑工地，看看这儿，检查那儿。难道那不需要耐心吗？我一度恨上他建造的那所恤孤院里面的孩子，有时甚至希望他们统统随着父母一起死掉。

“当你杀害一个人，你偷走一条性命，”爸爸说，“你偷走他妻子身为人妇的权利，夺走他子女的父亲。当你说谎，你偷走别人知道真相的权利。当你诈骗，你偷走公平的权利。你懂吗？”

我懂。爸爸六岁那年，有个窃贼在深夜溜进爷爷的房子。我的爷爷，一个万众景仰的法官，发现了他，但那个贼割开他的喉咙，立刻要了他的命——夺走了爸爸的父亲。翌日午前，当地居民抓住了那个凶手，人们发现他是来自昆都士[1]地区的流浪汉。在晌礼开始之前两个小时，凶手被吊死在橡树上。告诉我这件往事的，不是爸爸，而是拉辛汗。我总是从他人口里得知爸爸的事情。

“没有比盗窃更十恶不赦的事情了，阿米尔。”爸爸说，“要是有人拿走不属于他的东西，一条性命也好，一块馕饼也好，我都会唾弃他。要是我在街上碰到他，真主也救不了。你明白吗？”

我发现爸爸痛击窃贼这个主意让我既兴奋又害怕。“我明白，

---

[1] Kunduz，阿富汗北部省份。

爸爸。"

"如果说有什么真主的话，我希望他有其他更重要的事情做，而不是来关注我喝烈酒。好了，下去吧。说了这么多关于罪行的看法，我又渴了。"

我看着他在吧台斟满酒杯，心里想着，要再过多久我们才能再次这样交谈呢？因为真相摆在那儿，我总觉得爸爸多少有点恨我。为什么不呢？毕竟，是我杀了他深爱着的妻子，他美丽的公主，不是吗？我所能做的，至少应该是试图变得更像他一点。但我没有变得像他，一点都没有。

上学时，我们常常玩一种连句的游戏，也就是诗歌比赛。教授法尔西语课的老师从中主持，规则大抵是这样的：你背一句诗，你的对手有六秒钟的时间可以回答，但必须是以你背出来那句诗最后一个字开头的诗句。班里人人都想跟我一组，因为那时十一岁的我已经能背出迦亚谟[1]、哈菲兹[2]的数十篇诗歌，也能诵得鲁米著名的《玛斯纳维》。[3]有一次，我代表全班出战，并且旗开得胜。那天夜里我告诉爸爸，他只是点点头，咕哝了一声："不错。"

为了逃避爸爸的冷漠，我埋首翻阅故去的母亲留下的书本。此外，

---

　　[1]　Khayyám（1048~1122），古代波斯诗人，代表作为《鲁拜集》（*Rubaiyat of Omar Khayyám*）。

　　[2]　Shamseddin Mohammad Hafez（约1320~约1388），古代波斯诗人。

　　[3]　Mowlana Jalaluddin Rumi（1207~1273），古代波斯诗人，《玛斯纳维》（*Masnavi*）是他的叙事诗。

当然还有哈桑。我什么都读，鲁米，哈菲兹，萨迪[1]，维克多·雨果，儒勒·凡尔纳，马克·吐温，伊恩·弗莱明[2]。读完妈妈的遗藏——我从来不碰那些枯燥的历史书，只看小说和诗歌——之后，我开始用零花钱买书。我每周到"电影公园"边上的书店买一本书，直到书架放不下了，就放在硬纸箱里面。

当然，跟诗人结婚是一回事，但生个喜欢埋首诗书多过打猎的儿子……这么说吧，那可不是爸爸所希望看到的，我想。真正的男人不看诗——真主也禁止他们创作呢。真正的男人——真正的男孩——应该像爸爸小时候那样踢足球去，那才是值得付出热情的玩意儿。1970年，爸爸暂停了恤孤院的工程，飞往德黑兰，在那儿停留一个月：由于阿富汗当时还没有电视，他只好去那边看世界杯足球赛。为了激起我对足球的热情，他替我报名参加球队。但我这个可怜虫变成球队的负担，不是传丢了球，就是愚蠢地挡住队友的进攻路线。我瘦弱的双腿跌跌撞撞地在球场上奔跑，声嘶力竭，球却不会滚到我脚下来。我越是喊得起劲，双手在头顶尽力挥舞，高声大喊"传给我，传给我！"，队友越是对我视若不见。但爸爸从不放弃。等到他没有将任何运动天分遗传给我的事实昭然若揭之后，他又开始试着把我变成一个热情的观众。当然，我能做得到，不是吗？我尽量装得兴致勃勃。我跟他一起，每逢喀布尔队跟坎大哈[3]队比赛，就大喊大叫；每逢我们的球队遭到判罚，就咒骂裁判。但爸爸察觉到我并非真心实意，只好黯然放弃，接受这个悲惨的事实：

---

[1]　Mosleh al-Din Saadi Shirazi（约1210~约1290），古代波斯诗人。

[2]　Ian Fleming（1908~1964），英国小说家，撰写了007系列小说。

[3]　Kandahar，阿富汗南部城市。

他的儿子非但不喜欢玩足球，连当观众也心不在焉。

我记得有个新年，爸爸带我去看一年一度的比武竞赛。比武竞赛在春季的第一天举行，至今仍是阿富汗举国热爱的赛事。技艺精熟的骑士通常会得到大亨的赞助，他必须在混战中夺得一只屠宰后的羊或牛，驮着它全速绕看台疾跑，然后将其丢进得分圈。在他后面，会有另外一群骑士追逐着他，竭尽所能——脚踢、手抓、鞭打、拳击——试图将牛羊夺过来。那天，骑士在战场上高声叫喊，横冲直撞，激起重重尘雾；观众则沸反盈天，兴奋异常，马蹄嘚嘚，震得大地抖动。我们坐在看台的座位上，看着那些骑士在我们面前呼啸而过，他们的坐骑则白沫横飞。

爸爸指着某个人："阿米尔，你看到坐在那边的家伙吗，身边围着很多人那个？"

我说："看到了。"

"那是亨利·基辛格。"

"哦。"我不知道基辛格是何许人，兴许随口问了。但在那个关头，我见到一件恐怖的事情：有个骑士从鞍上跌落，数十只马蹄从他身上践踏而过。他的身体像个布娃娃，在马蹄飞舞间被拉来扯去。马队飞奔而过，他终于跌落下来，抽搐了一下，便再也没有动弹；他的双腿弯曲成不自然的角度，大片的血液染红了沙地。

我放声大哭。

我一路上哭着回家。我记得爸爸的手死死抓住方向盘，一会儿抓紧，一会儿放松。更重要的是，爸爸开车时沉默不语，厌恶溢于言表，我永远都不会忘记。

那天夜里，我路过爸爸的书房，偷听到他在跟拉辛汗说话。我将耳朵贴在门板上。

"……谢天谢地，他身体健康。"拉辛汗说。

"我知道，我知道，可他总是埋在书堆里，要不就在家里晃晃悠悠，好像梦游一般。"

"那又怎样？"

"我可不是这个样子。"爸爸丧气地说，声音中还有些愤怒。

拉辛汗笑起来。"孩子又不是图画练习册，你不能光顾着要涂上自己喜欢的色彩。"

"我是说，"爸爸说，"我根本不是那个样子的。跟我一起长大的孩子也没有像他那样的。"

"你知道，有时你是我认识的人中最自以为是的了。"拉辛汗说。在我认识的人中，只有他敢这么跟爸爸说话。

"跟这个没有任何关系。"

"没有吗？"

"没有。"

"那跟什么有关系？"

我听到爸爸挪动身子，皮椅吱吱作响。我合上双眼，耳朵更加紧贴着门板，又想听，又不想听。"有时我从这扇窗望出去，我看到他跟邻居的孩子在街上玩。我看到他们推搡他，拿走他的玩具，在这儿推他一下，在那儿打他一下。你知道，他从不反击，从不。他只是……低下头，然后……"

"这说明他并不暴戾。"拉辛汗说。

"我不是这个意思，拉辛，你知道的。"爸爸朝他嚷着，"这孩子身上缺了某些东西。"

"是的，缺了卑劣的性格。"

"自我防卫跟卑劣毫不搭边。你知道事情总是怎么样的吗？每当那些邻居的孩子欺负他，总是哈桑挺身而出，将他们挡回去。这是我亲眼见到的。他们回家之后，我问他，'哈桑脸上的伤痕是怎么回事？'他说：'他摔了一跤。'我跟你说，拉辛，这孩子身上缺了某些东西。"

"你只消让他找到自己的路。"拉辛汗说。

"可是他要走去哪里呢？"爸爸说，"一个不能保护自己的男孩，长大之后什么东西都保护不了。"

"你总是将问题过度简化了。"

"我认为不是的。"

"你生气，是因为你害怕他不会接管你的生意。"

"现在谁在简化问题？"爸爸说，"看吧，我知道你跟他关系很好，这我很高兴。我是说，我有些妒忌，但很高兴。他需要有人……有人能理解他，因为真主知道我理解不了。可是阿米尔身上有些东西让我很烦恼，我又说不清楚，它像是……"我能猜到他在寻觅，在搜寻一个恰当的字眼。他放低了声音，但终究还是让我听到了。"要不是我亲眼看着大夫把他从我老婆肚子里拉出来，我肯定不相信他是我的儿子。"

次日清晨，哈桑在替我准备早餐，他问我是不是有什么烦心的事情。我朝他大吼，叫他别多管闲事。

至于那卑劣的性格，拉辛汗错了。

第四章

　　爸爸生于 1933 年，同年查希尔国王 [1] 开始了他对阿富汗长达 40 载的统治。就在那年，一对来自喀布尔名门望族的年轻兄弟，开着他们父亲的福特跑车一路狂飙。他们抽了大麻，喝了法国葡萄酒，醉意醺然，又有些亢奋，在去往帕格曼 [2] 的途中撞死了一对哈扎拉夫妇。警察逮到了这两个略带悔意的青年，连同罹难夫妻那个五岁的遗孤，带到爷爷跟前。爷爷是位德高望重的法官，听完那对兄弟辩说来龙去脉之后，爷爷不顾他们父亲的哀求，判决那两个年轻人立即到坎大哈去，充军一年。此前他们家里已经不知用了什么手段，免去他们服役的义务。他们的父亲有所申辩，然而不是太激烈，最终，人人都赞同这样的判罚，认为也许有些严厉，却不失公正。至于那个孤儿，爷爷将他收养在自己家里，让仆人教导他，不过得对他和蔼一些。那个孤儿就是阿里。

　　阿里和爸爸一起长大，他们小时候也是玩伴——至少直到小儿麻痹

---

[1]　Mohammed Zahir Shah（1914~2007），阿富汗前国王，1933~1973 年在位。
[2]　Paghman，阿富汗城市。

症令阿里腿患残疾，就像一个世代之后哈桑和我共同长大那样。爸爸总是跟我们说起他和阿里的恶作剧，阿里会摇摇头，说："可是，老爷，告诉他们谁是那些恶作剧的设计师，谁又是可怜的苦工。"爸爸会开怀大笑，伸手揽住阿里。

不过爸爸说起这些故事的时候，从来没有提到阿里是他的朋友。

奇怪的是，我也从来没有认为我与哈桑是朋友。无论如何，不是一般意义上的朋友。虽然我们彼此学习如何在骑自行车的时候放开双手，或是用硬纸箱制成功能齐备的相机。虽然我们整个冬天一起放风筝、追风筝。虽然于我而言，阿富汗人的面孔就是那个男孩的容貌：骨架瘦小，理着平头，耳朵长得较低，那中国娃娃似的脸，那永远燃着微笑的兔唇。

无关乎这些事情，因为历史不会轻易改变，宗教也是。最终，我是普什图人，他是哈扎拉人，我是逊尼派，他是什叶派，这些没有什么能改变得了。没有。

但我们是一起蹒跚学步的孩子，这点也没有任何历史、种族、社会或者宗教能改变得了。十二岁以前，我大部分时间都在跟哈桑玩耍。有时候回想起来，我的整个童年，似乎就是和哈桑一起度过的某个懒洋洋的悠长夏日，我们在爸爸院子里那些交错的树木中彼此追逐，玩捉迷藏，玩警察与强盗，玩牛仔和印第安人，折磨昆虫——我们拔掉蜜蜂的尖刺，在那可怜的东西身上系根绳子，每当它想展翅飞走，就把它拉回来，这带给我们无与伦比的快乐。

我们还追逐过路的游牧部落，他们经由喀布尔，前往北方的层峦叠嶂。我们能听到他们的牧群走近的声音：绵羊咪咪，山羊咩咩，还有那叮当作响的驼铃。我们会跑出去，看着他们的队伍在街道上行进，男人满身尘灰，脸色沧桑，女人披着长长的、色彩斑斓的肩巾，挂着珠链，手腕和脚踝都戴着银镯子。我们朝他们的山羊投掷石头，拿水泼他们的骡子。我让哈桑坐在"病玉米之墙"，拿弹弓用小圆石射他们的骆驼的屁股。

我们第一次看西部电影也是两个人，在与那家我最喜欢的书店一街之隔的电影公园，看的是约翰·韦恩的《赤胆屠龙》。我记得当时我求爸爸带我们到伊朗去，那样我们就可以见到约翰·韦恩了。爸爸爆发出一阵爽朗的狂笑——与汽车引擎加速的声音颇为相像，等他能说得出话的时候，告诉我们电影配音是怎么回事。哈桑跟我目瞪口呆，愣住了。原来约翰·韦恩不是真的说法尔西语，也不是伊朗人！他是美国人，就像那些我们经常看到的男男女女一样，他们神情友善，留着长发，吊儿郎当地穿着五颜六色的衣服，在喀布尔城里游荡。我们看了三遍《赤胆屠龙》，但我们最喜欢的西部片是《七侠荡寇志》，看了十三遍。每次电影快结束的时候，我们哭着观看那些墨西哥小孩埋葬查尔斯·勃朗森——结果他也不是伊朗人。

我们在喀布尔新城那个弥漫着难闻气味的市场闲逛。新城叫沙里诺区，在瓦兹尔·阿克巴·汗区以西。我们谈论刚刚看完的电影，走在市场熙熙攘攘的人群中。我们在商人和乞丐中蜿蜒前进，穿过那些小店云集的拥挤过道。爸爸每周给我们每人十块阿富汗尼[1]的零花钱，我们用来买温热的可口可乐，还有撒着开心果仁的玫瑰香露雪糕。

---

[1] Afghanis，阿富汗货币名称。

上学那些年，我们每日有固定的程式。每当我从床上爬起来，拖拖沓沓走向卫生间，哈桑早已洗漱完毕，跟阿里做完早晨的祈祷，帮我弄好早餐：加了三块方糖的热红茶，一片涂着我最爱吃的樱桃酱的馕饼，所有这些整整齐齐地摆在桌子上。我边吃边抱怨功课，哈桑收拾我的床铺，擦亮我的鞋子，熨好我那天要穿的衣服，替我放好课本和铅笔。我听见他在门廊边熨衣服边唱歌，用他那带鼻音的嗓子唱着古老的哈扎拉歌曲。然后，爸爸和我出发，开着他的福特野马轿车——会引来艳羡的目光，因为当时有部叫《警网铁金刚》的电影在电影院已经上映了半年，主角史蒂夫·麦奎因在影片中就开这种车。哈桑留在家里，帮阿里做些杂务：用手将脏衣服洗干净，然后在院子里晾干；拖地板；去市场买刚出炉的馕饼；为晚餐准备腌肉；浇灌草坪。

放学后，我跟哈桑碰头，抓起书本，一溜小跑，爬上瓦兹尔·阿克巴·汗区爸爸房子北边的那座碗状山丘。山顶有久已废弃的墓园，各条小径灌木丛生，还有成排成排的空白墓碑。多年的风霜雨雪锈蚀了墓园的铁门，也让那低矮的白色石墙摇摇欲坠。墓园的入口边上有株石榴树。某个夏日，我用阿里厨房的小刀在树干刻下我们的名字："阿米尔和哈桑，喀布尔的苏丹。"这些字正式宣告：这棵树属于我们。放学后，哈桑和我爬上它的枝丫，摘下一些血红色的石榴果实。吃过石榴，用杂草把手擦干净之后，我会念书给哈桑听。

哈桑盘腿坐着，阳光和石榴叶的阴影在他脸上翩翩起舞。我念那些他看不懂的故事给他听，他心不在焉地摘着地上杂草的叶片。哈桑长大后，会跟阿里和多数哈扎拉人一样，自出生之日起，甚至自莎娜芭不情不愿地怀上他那天起，就注定要成为文盲——毕竟，仆人要读书识字干吗呢？但尽管他目不识丁，兴许正因为如此，哈桑对那些谜一样的文字十分入迷，那个他无法接触的世界深深吸引了他。我给他念诗歌和故事，有时也念谜语——不过后来我不念了，因为我发现他解谜语的本领远比我高强。所以我念些不那么有挑战性的东西，比如装腔作势的纳斯鲁丁毛拉和他那头驴子出洋相的故事。我们在树下一坐就是几个钟头，直到太阳在西边黯淡下去，哈桑还会说，日光还足够亮堂，我们可以多念一个故事、多读一章。

给哈桑念故事的时候，碰到某个他无法理解的字眼，我就十分高兴，我会取笑他，嘲弄他的无知。有一次，我给他念纳斯鲁丁毛拉的故事，他让我停下来。"那个词是什么意思？"

"哪个？"

"梼昧。"

"你不知道那是什么意思吗？"我一脸坏笑地说着。

"不知道，阿米尔少爷。"

"可是这个词很常见啊。"

"不过我还是不懂。"就算他听到我话中带刺，他也是不露声色地微笑着。

"这么说吧，在我们学校，人人都认识这个词。"我说，"让我看看，'梼昧'，它的意思是聪明、机灵。我可以用它来给你造句。'在读书识字方面，哈桑够梼昧。'"

"啊哈。"他点头说。

后来我总是对此心怀愧疚。所以我试着弥补，把旧衬衣或者破玩具送给他。我会告诉自己，对于一个无关紧要的玩笑来说，这样的补偿就足够了。

哈桑最喜欢的书是《列王纪》，一部描写古代波斯英雄的 10 世纪的史诗。他通篇都喜欢，他喜欢那些垂垂老矣的国王：费里敦、扎尔，还有鲁达贝。但他最喜欢的故事，也是我最喜欢的，是"罗斯坦和索拉博"，讲的是神武的战士罗斯坦和他那匹千里马拉克什的故事。罗斯坦在战斗中，给予他的强敌索拉博以致命一击，最终却发现索拉博是他失散多年的儿子。罗斯坦强忍悲恸，听着他儿子的临终遗言：

若汝果为吾父，血刃亲子，名节有亏矣。此乃汝之专横所致也。汝持先母信物，吾报汝以爱，呼汝之名，然汝心难回，吾徒费唇舌，此刻命赴黄泉……

"再念一次吧，阿米尔少爷。"哈桑会这么说。有时我给他念这段话的时候，他泪如泉涌，我总是很好奇，他到底为谁哭泣呢，为那个泪满衣襟、埋首尘灰、悲恸难当的罗斯坦，还是为即将断气、渴望得到父爱的索拉博呢？在我看来，罗斯坦的命运并非悲剧。毕竟，每个父亲的内心深处，不是都有想把儿子杀掉的欲望吗？

1973 年 7 月某天，我开了哈桑另外一个玩笑。我念书给他听，接着突然不管那个写好的故事。我假装念着书，像平常那样翻着书，可是我说的跟书本毫无关系，而是抛开那个故事，自己杜撰一个。当然，哈桑对此一无所知。对他而言，书页上的文字无非是一些线条，神秘而不知所云。文字是扇秘密的门，钥匙在我手里。完了之后，我嘴里咯咯笑着，问他是否喜欢这个故事，哈桑拍手叫好。

"你在干吗呢？"我说。

"你很久没念过这么精彩的故事了。"他说，仍拍着双手。

我大笑："真的吗？"

"真的。"

"太奇妙了。"我喃喃说道。我是说真的，这真是……完全意料不到。"没骗我吧，哈桑？"

他仍在鼓掌："太棒了，阿米尔少爷。你明天可以多念一些给我听吗？"

"太奇妙了。"我又说了一遍，有些喘不过气，好比有个男人在自家后院发现了一处宝藏。下山的时候，各种念头在我脑海炸开来，如同在察曼大道燃放的烟花。**你好久没念过这么精彩的故事了。**他这么说。哈桑在问我问题。

"什么？"我说。

"'奇妙'是什么意思？"

我哈哈大笑，给了他一个拥抱，在他脸上亲了一下。

"干吗这样啊？"他红着脸，吃吃地说。

我友善地推了他一把，微笑着说："你是王子，哈桑。你是王子，我爱你。"

当天夜里，我写了自己第一篇短篇小说，花了我半个小时。那是个悲伤的小故事，讲的是有个男人发现了一个魔法杯，得知如果他对着杯子哭泣，掉进杯里的眼泪会变成珍珠。可尽管一贫如洗，他却是个快乐的家伙，罕得流泪。于是他想方设法，让自己悲伤，以便那些眼泪会变成他的财富。珍珠越积越多，他越来越贪婪。小说的结尾是，那男人坐在一座珠宝山上，手里提着刀，怀中抱着他深爱着的妻子死于非命的尸体，无助地将眼泪滴进魔法杯。

入夜之后，我爬上楼，走进爸爸的吸烟室，手里拿着两张稿纸，上面写着我的故事。我进去的时候，爸爸和拉辛汗边抽大烟边喝白兰地。

"那是什么，阿米尔？"爸爸说，他斜靠在沙发上，双手放在脑后。蓝色的烟雾环绕着他的脸庞，他的眼光让我唇干舌燥。我清清喉咙，告诉他我创作了一篇小说。

爸爸点点头，那丝微笑表明他对此并无多大兴趣。"挺好的，你写得很好吧，是吗？"他说，然后就没有话了，只是穿过缭绕的烟雾望着我。

也许我在那儿站了不到一分钟，但时至今日，那依旧是我生命中最漫长的一分钟。时间一秒一秒过去，而一秒与一秒之间，似乎隔着永恒。空气变得沉闷，潮湿，甚至凝固，我呼吸艰难。爸爸继续盯着我，丝毫没有要看一看的意思。

一如既往，仍是拉辛汗救了我。他伸出手，给我一个毫不造作的微笑："可以让我看看吗，亲爱的阿米尔？我会很高兴能读你写的故事。"爸爸称呼我的时候，几乎从来不用这个表示亲昵的"亲爱的"。

爸爸耸耸肩，站起来。他看上去浑身轻松，仿佛拉辛汗也解放了他。"这就对了，把它给拉辛汗。我要上楼去准备了。"他扔下这句话，转身离开。在我生命的大部分时光，我对爸爸敬若神明。可是那一刻，我恨不得能扯开自己的血管，让他那些该死的血统统流出我的身体。

过了一个钟头，夜色更加黯淡了。他们两个开着爸爸的轿车去参加派对。拉辛汗快出门的时候，在我身前蹲下来，递给我那篇故事，还有另外一张折好的纸。他亮起微笑，还眨眨眼。"给你，等会儿再看。"然后他停下来，加了一个词：**太棒了！** 就鼓励我写作而言，这个词比如今任何编辑的恭维给了我更多的勇气。

他们离开了，我坐在自己的床上，心里想要是拉辛汗是我父亲就好了。随后我想起爸爸，还有他宽广的胸膛，他抱着我的时候，靠着它感觉多好啊。我想起每天早晨他身上甜甜的酒味，想起他用胡子扎我的脸蛋。一阵突如其来的罪恶感将我淹没，我跑进卫生间，在水槽里吐了。

那夜稍晚的时候，我蜷缩在床上，一遍遍读着拉辛汗的字条。他写道：

亲爱的阿米尔：

我非常喜欢你的故事。我的天，真主赋予你独特的天分。如今你的责任是磨炼这份天才，因为将真主给予的天分白白浪费的人是蠢驴。你写的故事语法正确，风格引人入胜。但最令人难忘的是，你的故事饱含讽刺的意味。你也许还不懂得讽刺是什么，但你以后会懂的。有些作家奋斗终生，对它梦寐以求，然而徒唤奈何。你的第一篇故事已经达到了。

我的大门永远为你开着，亲爱的阿米尔。我愿意倾听你诉说的任何故事。太棒了！

你的朋友，
拉辛

拉辛汗的字条让我飘飘然，我抓起那篇故事，直奔楼下而去，冲到门廊。阿里和哈桑睡在那儿的地毯上。只有当爸爸外出,阿里不得不照看我的时候,他们才会睡在屋子里。我把哈桑摇醒,问他是否愿意听个故事。

他揉揉惺忪的睡眼,伸伸懒腰:"现在吗?几点了?"

"别问几点了。这个故事很特别,我自己写的。"我不想吵醒阿里,低声说。哈桑脸上神色一振。

"那我一定要听听。"他拉开盖在身上的毛毯,说。

我在客厅里的大理石壁炉前面念给他听。这次可没有开玩笑,不是照本宣科了,这次是我写的故事!就很多方面而言,哈桑堪称完美的听众。他全然沉浸在故事中,脸上的神情随着故事的情节变化。我念完最后一句话,他鼓起掌来,不过没发出声音。

"我的天啦!阿米尔少爷,太棒了!"哈桑笑逐颜开。

"你喜欢它吗?"我说。得到第二次称赞,真是太甜蜜了。

"安拉保佑,你肯定会成为伟大的作家。"哈桑说,"全世界的人都读你的故事。"

"你太夸张了,哈桑。"我说,不过很高兴他这么认为。

"我没有。你会很伟大、很出名。"他坚持自己的观点。接着他停了一下,似乎还想说些什么,他想了想,清清喉咙,"可是,你能允许我问个关于这故事的问题吗?"他羞涩地说。

"当然可以。"

"那好……"他欲言又止。

"告诉我,哈桑。"我说。我脸带微笑,虽然刹那间我这个作家心中惴惴,不知道是否想听下去。

"那好吧,"他说,"如果让我来问,那男人干吗杀了自己的老婆呢?实际上,为什么他必须感到悲伤才能掉眼泪呢?他不可以只是闻闻洋葱吗?"

我目瞪口呆。这个特别的问题,虽说它显然太蠢了,但我从来没有想到过,我无言地动动嘴唇。就在同一个夜晚,我学到了写作的目标之一:讽刺;我还学到了写作的陷阱之一:情节破绽。芸芸众生中,唯独哈桑教给我。这个目不识丁、不会写字的哈桑。有个冰冷而阴暗的声音在我耳边响起:他懂得什么,这个哈扎拉文盲?他一辈子只配在厨房里打杂。他胆敢批评我?

"很好……"我开口说,却无法说完那句话。

因为突然之间,阿富汗一切都变了。

第五章

不知道什么东西发出一阵雷鸣般的声响，接着大地微微抖动，我们听见"砰——砰——砰"的枪声。"爸爸！"哈桑大声叫喊。我们拔腿跑出起居室，看见阿里跛着脚在走廊狂奔。

"爸爸！那是什么声音？"哈桑大叫，伸开双臂朝阿里奔过去。阿里伸手揽住我们。一道白光闪起，夜空亮起银辉。又是一道白光，随后是暴风骤雨般的枪声。

"他们在猎杀野鸭。"阿里嘶哑地说，"他们在夜里猎鸭子，别害怕。"

远处传来警报声。不知道从什么地方传来玻璃破裂的声音，还有人高声叫嚷。我听见人们从睡梦中惊醒，跑到街道上，也许身上还穿着睡衣，披头散发，睡眼惺忪。哈桑在哭，阿里将他抱紧，轻轻地抚摸着他。后来我告诉自己，我没有妒忌哈桑，一点都没有。

我们就那样哆嗦地抱成一团，直到天快破晓。枪声和爆炸声还没一个钟头就结束，可是把我们吓坏了，因为我们从来没听过街道上会有枪响。当时这些声音对我们来说太奇怪了。那些耳朵里面除了枪响再没有其他声音的阿富汗孩子当时还没出世。在餐厅里，我们挤成一堆，等待太阳升起，没有人意识到过去的生活方式已然告终。我们的生活方式，即使尚未全然终结，那也是苟延残喘。终结，正式的终结是在 1978 年 4 月，其时政变发生，接着是 1979 年 12 月，俄国坦克行进在我和哈桑玩耍的街道上，给我过去认识的阿富汗带来死亡，开启了绵延至今的，流血冲突的时代。

太阳快升起的时候，爸爸的轿车驶进车道。他重重地关上车门，匆忙的脚步在台阶上发出沉重的声音。接着他在门口出现，我看见他脸色挂着某种神情，那种脸色我一时辨认不出来，因为此前从未在他身上见过：恐惧。"阿米尔！哈桑！"他大喊，张开双臂朝我们跑过来，"他们封锁了所有的道路，电话又坏了，我很担心。"

我们停在他怀里，有那么一会儿，我竟然发疯似的觉得很高兴，而不管当晚究竟发生了什么事情。

他们根本不是在猎杀野鸭。真相终于大白：1973 年 7 月 17 日夜里，他们根本就没有对什么东西开枪。翌日清晨，大梦初醒的喀布尔发现君主制已然成为历史。查希尔国王远在意大利，他的堂兄达乌德汗 [1] 趁他不在，发动了政变，没有多加杀戮，就终结了他四十年来的统治。

我记得隔日早上，爸爸和拉辛汗喝着红茶，听着喀布尔广播电台播送的有关政变的最新消息，我跟哈桑躲在爸爸的书房外面。

---

[1] Mohammed Daoud Khan（1909~1978），1973 年起任阿富汗共和国总统，直到 1978 年被刺杀。

"阿米尔少爷?"哈桑低声说。

"怎么啦?"

"什么是'共和'?"

我耸耸肩:"我不懂。"爸爸的收音机一遍又一遍地传出"共和"这个词。

"阿米尔少爷?"

"怎么啦?"

"'共和'是不是要我和爸爸离开这里?"

"我觉得不是。"我低声回答。

哈桑想了想,说:"阿米尔少爷?"

"什么呀?"

"我不想他们把我跟爸爸送走。"

我露出微笑:"好啦,你这头驴子,没有人会送走你们。"

"阿米尔少爷?"

"什么呀?"

"你想去爬我们的树吗?"

我笑得更开心了。这也是哈桑的本领,他总是懂得在恰当的时间说恰当的事情——收音机的新闻实在是太闷了。哈桑回到他那寒碜的屋子去做准备,我跑上楼抓起一本书。接着我到厨房去,往口袋里塞一把松子,然后跑出去,哈桑在外面等我。我们穿过前门,朝那座山头进发。

我们穿过住宅区,在一片通往山丘的荒芜空地上跋涉前进。突然间,一块石头击中了哈桑的后背。我们转过身,我的心一沉。阿塞夫和他的两个狐朋狗友,瓦里和卡莫,正朝我们走过来。

阿塞夫的父亲叫马赫穆德，我爸爸的朋友，是个飞机驾驶员。他家位于一处豪华的住宅区，深院高墙，棕榈环绕，就在我们家南边，只隔了几条街。住在喀布尔瓦兹尔·阿克巴·汗区的小孩，人人都知道阿塞夫和他那臭名昭著的不锈钢拳套，谁都不愿意尝尝它的滋味。由于父亲是阿富汗人，母亲是德国人，蓝眼睛的阿塞夫头发金黄，身材比其他孩子都要高大。他凶残成性，恶名远播，人们总是避之唯恐不及。他身旁有群为虎作伥的党羽，走在附近的街道上，宛如可汗在阿谀逢迎的部属陪伴下，视察自己的领地。他说的话就是法律，如果你需要一点法律教育，那么他那不锈钢拳套无疑是最好的教具。我曾见过他用那拳套折磨一个卡德察区的小孩。我永远都不会忘记阿塞夫蓝色的眼睛中闪烁的近乎疯狂的光芒，还有他那邪恶的笑脸——那可怜的孩子被他痛击得不省人事，他竟然咧嘴大笑。瓦兹尔·阿克巴·汗区某些儿童给他起了个花名，叫"吃耳朵的阿塞夫"。当然，没有人胆敢当面这样称呼他，除非他们想亲身体会那个可怜孩子的下场：他跟阿塞夫争夺一只风筝，结果之后在路边的臭水沟打捞自己的右耳。多年以后，我学到了一个英文单词，在法尔西语找不到对应的字眼，可以用来形容阿塞夫那样的人渣：反社会分子。

在那些折磨阿里的男孩中，阿塞夫远比其他人来得恶毒。实际上，人们用"巴巴鲁"来嘲弄阿里，他正是始作俑者。喂，巴巴鲁，你今天吃了谁啊？哦？来吧，巴巴鲁，朝我们笑一笑。在那些他觉得特别来劲的日子，他会加油添醋：喂，你这个塌鼻子巴巴鲁，今天吃了谁啊？告诉我们，你这头细眼睛的驴子！

眼下他正双手放在背后，用那双胶底运动鞋踢起尘灰，朝我们走来。

"早上好，苦哈哈！"阿塞夫说，摆摆手。"苦哈哈"是另外一个阿塞夫喜欢用来侮辱人的词语。他们三个都比我们大，看到他们走近，哈桑躲在我后面。他们站在我们面前，三个穿着牛仔裤T恤的高大男生。阿塞夫身材最魁梧，双臂抱胸，脸上露出凶残的笑容。我已经不止一次觉得阿塞夫不太像个正常人。幸运的是，我有爸爸这样的父亲，我相信正是因为这个，阿塞夫对我不敢太过放肆造次。

他朝哈桑扬起下巴。"喂，塌鼻子，"他说，"巴巴鲁可好吗？"

哈桑一言不发，在我身后又退了一步。

"你们听到消息了吗，小子？"阿塞夫说，脸上还是带着那副邪恶的笑容，"国王跑掉了，跑得好！总统万岁！我爸爸跟达乌德汗相熟。你认识他吗，阿米尔？"

"我爸爸跟他也熟。"我说，实际上连我自己都不知道那是不是真的。

"好吧，达乌德汗去年还在我家吃过晚饭。"阿塞夫继续说，"怎么样啊，阿米尔？"

我在想，如果我们在这片荒地高声求救，会不会有人听到？爸爸的房子距这儿足足有一公里。要是我们留在家里就好了！

"你知道下次达乌德汗到我们家里吃晚饭我会对他说什么吗？"阿塞夫说，"我会跟他稍作交谈，男人和男人的交谈。将我跟妈妈说过的那些告诉他，关于希特勒的。现在我们有位伟大的领袖，伟大的领袖，一个志向远大的男人。我会告诉达乌德汗，提醒他记住，要是希特勒完成他那未竟的事业，这个世界会变得比现在更好。"

"我爸爸说希特勒是个疯子，他下令杀害了很多无辜的人。"我来不及用手捂住嘴巴，这话已经脱口而出。

阿塞夫不屑地说："他说的跟我妈妈一样。她是德国人，她本来应该更清楚。不过他们要你这么认为，是吗？他们不想让你知道真相。"

我不知道"他们"是谁，也不知道他们隐瞒了什么真相，我也根本不想去知道。我希望我什么也没说，我又希望我抬起头就能看见爸爸朝山上走来。

"但是你得读读那些学校里面看不到的书。"阿塞夫说，"我读了，令我茅塞顿开。现在我有个抱负，我要将它告诉我们的总统。你想知道那是什么吗？"

我摇摇头。他终究还是说了，阿塞夫总是自问自答。

他那双蓝眼睛望着哈桑："阿富汗是普什图人的地盘，过去一直是，将来也永远是。我们是真正的阿富汗人，纯种的阿富汗人，这个塌鼻子不是。他们这种人污染了我们的土地、我们的国家，他们弄脏我们的血脉。"他挥舞双手，做了个夸张的姿势，"普什图人的阿富汗，我说，这就是我的抱负。"

阿塞夫又看着我，他看起来像是刚从美梦中醒来。"希特勒生不逢时，"他说，"但我们还来得及。"

他伸手去牛仔裤的后兜摸索某样东西，"我要恳求总统完成从前国王没做的事情，派军队清除所有这些垃圾，这些肮脏的哈扎拉人。"

"放我们走，阿塞夫，"我说，对自己颤抖的声音感到厌恶，"我们没有碍着你。"

"哦，你们碍着我了。"阿塞夫说。看到他从裤兜里掏出那个东西，我的心开始下沉。当然，他掏出来的是那黄铜色的不锈钢拳套，在阳光下闪闪发亮。"你们严重地碍着我。实际上，你比这个哈扎拉小子更加碍着我。你怎么可以跟他说话，跟他玩耍，让他碰你？"他的声音充满了嫌恶。瓦里和卡莫点头以示同意，随声附和。阿塞夫双眉一皱，摇摇头。他再次说话的时候，声音显得跟他的表情一样困惑。"你怎么可以当他是'朋友'？"

可是他并非我的朋友！我几乎冲口说出。我真的想过这个问题吗？当然没有，我没有想过。我对哈桑很好，就像对待朋友，甚至还要更好，像是兄弟。但如果这样的话，那么何以每逢爸爸的朋友带着他们的孩子来拜访，我玩游戏的时候从来没喊上哈桑？为什么我只有在身边没有其他人的时候才和哈桑玩耍？

阿塞夫戴上他的不锈钢拳套，冷冷瞟了我一眼。"你也是个问题，阿米尔。如果没有你和你父亲这样的白痴，收容这些哈扎拉人，我们早就可以清除他们了。他们全都应该去哈扎拉贾特[1]，在那个属于他们的地方烂掉。你是个阿富汗败类。"

我看着他那狂妄的眼睛，看懂了他的眼色，他是真的要伤害我。阿塞夫举起拳头，向我走来。

我背后传来一阵急遽的活动声音。我眼角一瞄，看见哈桑弯下腰，迅速地站起来。阿塞夫朝我身后望去，吃惊地瞪大了眼睛。我看见瓦里和卡莫也看着我身后，眼里同样带着震惊的神色。

---

[1] Hazarajat，阿富汗中部山区，为哈扎拉人聚居地。

我转过身，正好看到哈桑的弹弓。哈桑把那根橡皮带满满拉开，弓上是一块核桃大小的石头。哈桑用弹弓对着阿塞夫的脸，他用尽力气拉着弹弓，双手颤抖，汗珠在额头上渗出来。

"请让我们走，少爷。"哈桑语气平静地说。他称呼阿塞夫为少爷，有个念头在我脑里一闪而过：带着这种根深蒂固的意识，生活在一个等级分明的地方，究竟是什么滋味？

阿塞夫咬牙切齿："放下来，你这个没有老娘的哈扎拉小子。"

"请放过我们，少爷。"哈桑说。

阿塞夫笑起来："难道你没有看到吗？我们有三个人，你们只有两个。"

哈桑耸耸肩。在外人看来，他镇定自若，但哈桑的脸是我从小就看惯了的，我清楚它所有细微的变化，他脸上任何一丝颤动都躲不过我的眼睛。我看得出他很害怕，非常害怕。

"是的，少爷。但也许你没有看到，拉着弹弓的人是我。如果你敢动一动，他们会改掉你的花名，不再叫你'吃耳朵的阿塞夫'，而是叫你'独眼龙阿塞夫'。因为我这块石头对准你的左眼。"他泰然自若地说着，就算是我，也要费尽力气才能听得出他平静的声音下面的恐惧。

阿塞夫的嘴巴抽搐了一下。瓦里和卡莫看到强弱易势，简直无法置信，有人在挑战他们的神，羞辱他。更糟糕的是，这个家伙居然是个瘦小的哈扎拉人。阿塞夫看看那块石头，又看看哈桑。他仔细看着哈桑的脸，他所看到的，一定让他相信哈桑并非妄言恫吓，因为他放下了拳头。

"你应该对我有所了解，哈扎拉人。"阿塞夫阴沉着脸说，"我是个非常有耐心的人。今天这事可没完，相信我。"他转向我，"我跟你也没完，阿米尔。总有一天，我会亲自让你尝尝我的厉害。"阿塞夫退了一步，他的跟班也是。

"你的哈扎拉人今天犯了大错，阿米尔。"他说，然后转身离开。我看着他们走下山，消失在一堵墙壁之后。

哈桑双手颤抖，努力把弹弓插回腰间。他的双唇弯起，或是想露出一个安心的微笑吧。他试了五次，才把弹弓系在裤子上。我们脚步沉重地走回家，深知阿塞夫和他的朋友很可能在某个拐角处等着收拾我们，没有人开口说话。他们没有，那应该让我们松一口气。但是我们没有，根本就没有。

随后几年，喀布尔的人们不时将"经济发展"、"改革"之类的词挂在嘴边。君主立宪制被废除了，取而代之的是共和国总统领导下的共和制。有那么一阵，这个国家焕发出勃勃生机，也有各种远大目标，人们谈论着妇女权利和现代科技。

对于大多数人来说，尽管喀布尔的皇宫换了新主人，生活仍和过去并无二致。人们依旧从周六到周四上班，依旧每逢周五聚集在公园、喀尔卡湖边或者帕格曼公园野餐。五颜六色的公共汽车和货车载满乘客，在喀布尔狭窄的街道上川流不息，司机的助手跨坐在后面的保险杠上，用口音浓重的喀布尔方言大声叫嚷，替司机指引方向。到了为期三天的开斋节，斋月 [1] 之后的节日，喀布尔人穿上他们最新、最好的衣服，相

---

[1] 伊斯兰教历的第九个月为斋月。

互拜访。人们拥抱，亲吻，互祝"开斋节快乐"。儿童拆开礼物，玩着染色的水煮蛋。

1974 年初冬，有一天哈桑和我在院子里嬉闹，用雪堆一座城堡。这时阿里唤他进屋："哈桑，老爷想跟你说话！"他身穿白色衣服，站在门口，双手缩在腋下，嘴里呼出白气。

哈桑和我相视而笑。我们整天都在等他的传唤：那天是哈桑的生日。"那是什么，爸爸？你知道吗？可以告诉我们吗？"哈桑说，眼里洋溢着快乐。

阿里耸耸肩："老爷没有告诉我。"

"别这样嘛，阿里，跟我们说说。"我催他，"一本图画册吗？还是一把新手枪？"

跟哈桑一样，阿里也不善说谎。每年我们生日，他都假装不知道爸爸买了什么礼物。每年他的眼神都出卖他，我们都能从他口里将礼物套出来。不过这次他看来似乎真的不知道。

爸爸从来不会忘记哈桑的生日。曾经，他经常问哈桑想要什么，但后来他就不问了，因为哈桑要的东西太过细微，简直不能被称之为礼物，所以每年冬天爸爸自行挑选些东西。有一年他给买了一套日本的玩具车。上一年，爸爸让哈桑喜出望外，给他买了一顶毛皮牛仔帽，克林特·伊斯特伍德戴着这种帽子演出了《黄金三镖客》——这部电影取代了《七侠荡寇志》，成为我们最喜爱的西部片。整整一个冬天，哈桑和我轮流戴那顶帽子，唱着那首著名的电影主题曲，爬上雪堆，打雪仗。

我们在前门脱掉手套，擦掉靴子上的雪。我们走进门廊，看到爸爸坐在炭火熊熊的铁炉前面，旁边坐着一个矮小的秃头印度人，他穿着棕色西装，系着红领带。

"哈桑，"爸爸说，脸上带着不好意思的微笑，"来见见你的生日礼物。"

哈桑和我茫然对视。那儿没有见到任何包着礼物的盒子，没有袋子，没有玩具，只有站在我们后面的阿里，还有爸爸，和那个看上去像数学老师的印度人。

身穿棕色西装的印度人微笑着，朝哈桑伸出手。"我是库玛大夫，"他说，"很高兴见到你。"他的法尔西语带着浓厚的印度卷舌音。

"你好。"哈桑惴惴说。他礼貌地点点头，但眼睛却望向站在他后面的父亲。阿里上前一步，把手放在哈桑肩膀上。

爸爸望着哈桑迷惑不解的眼睛："我从新德里请来库玛大夫，库玛大夫是名整容外科医生。"

"你知道那是什么吗？"那个印度人——库玛大夫说。

哈桑摇摇头。他带着询问的眼色望向我，但我耸耸肩。我只知道，人们要是得了阑尾炎，就得去找外科医生医治。我之所以知道，是因为此前一年，有个同学死于阑尾炎，我们老师说他拖了太久才去找外科医生。我们两个齐齐望向阿里，但从他那里当然也得不到答案。跟过去一样，他仍是木无表情，但眼神变得严肃一些。

"这么说吧，"库玛大夫说，"我的工作是修理人们的身体，有时是人们的脸庞。"

"噢，"哈桑说，他看看库玛大夫，看看爸爸，又看看阿里，伸手遮住上唇。"噢。"他又说。

"这不是份寻常的礼物，我知道。"爸爸说，"也许不是你想要的，但这份礼物会陪伴你终生。"

"噢，"哈桑说，他舔舔嘴唇，清清喉咙，说，"老爷，这……这会不会……"

"别担心，"库玛大夫插嘴说，脸上带着微笑，"不会让你觉得很痛的。实际上，我会给你用一种药，你什么都不会记得。"

"噢。"哈桑说。他松了一口气，微笑着，但也只是松了一口气。"我不是害怕，老爷，我只是……"哈桑也许是个傻瓜，我可不是。我知道要是医生跟你说不会痛的时候，你的麻烦就大了。我心悸地想起去年割包皮的情形，医生也是这么对我说，安慰说那不会很痛。但那天深夜，麻醉药的药性消退之后，感觉像有人拿着又红又热的木炭在烫我的下阴。爸爸为什么要等到我十岁才让我割包皮呢？我百思不得其解，这也是我永远无法原谅他的事情之一。

我希望自己身上也有类似的残疾，可以乞换来爸爸的怜悯。太不公平了，哈桑什么都没干，就得到爸爸的爱护，他不就是生了那个愚蠢的兔唇吗？

手术很成功。他们刚解掉绷带的时候，我们多少都有点吃惊，但还是像库玛大夫先前交代的那样保持微笑。但那并不容易，因为哈桑的上唇看起来又肿又怪，没有表皮。护士递给哈桑镜子的时候，我希望他哭起来。哈桑深深地看着镜子，若有所思，阿里则紧紧握住他的手。他咕哝了几句，我没听清楚。我把耳朵凑到他唇边，他又低声说了一遍。

"谢谢。"

接着他的嘴唇扭曲了，当时，我完全知道他在干什么。他在微笑。就像他从母亲子宫里出来时那样微笑着。

随着时间的过去，肿胀消退，伤口弥合。不久，他的嘴唇上就只剩下一道弯弯曲曲的缝合线。到下一个冬天，它变成淡淡的伤痕。说来讽刺，正是从那个冬天之后，哈桑便不再微笑了。

第六章

冬天。

每年下雪的第一天，我都会这样度过：一大清早我穿着睡衣，走到屋子外面，双臂环抱抵御严寒。我发现车道、爸爸的轿车、围墙、树木、屋顶还有山丘，统统覆盖着一英尺厚的积雪。我微笑。天空一碧如洗，万里无云。白晃晃的雪花刺痛我的眼睛。我捧起一把新雪，塞进嘴里，四周静谧无声，只有几声乌鸦的啼叫传进耳里。我赤足走下前门的台阶，把哈桑叫出来看看。

冬天是喀布尔每个孩子最喜欢的季节，至少那些家里买得起一个温暖铁炉的孩子是这样的。理由很简单：每当天寒地冻，学校就停课了。于我而言，冬天意味着那些复杂的除法题目的结束，也不用去背保加利亚的首都，可以开始一连三个月坐在火炉边跟哈桑玩扑克，星期二早晨去电影公园看免费的俄罗斯影片，早上堆个雪人之后，午餐吃一顿甜芜菁拌饭。

当然还有风筝。放风筝。追风筝。

对于某些可怜的孩子来说，冬天并不代表学期的结束，还有种叫自愿冬季课程的东西。据我所知，没有学生自愿去参加那些课程，当然是父母自愿送他们去。幸运的是，爸爸不是这样的家长。我记得有个叫艾哈迈德的家伙，住的地方跟我家隔街相望。他的父亲可能是个什么医生，我想。艾哈迈德患有癫痫，总是穿着羊毛内衣，戴一副黑框眼镜——阿塞夫经常欺负他。每天早晨，我从卧室的窗户看出去，他们家的哈扎拉佣人把车道上的雪铲开，为那辆黑色的欧宝清道。我看着艾哈迈德和他的父亲上车，艾哈迈德穿着羊毛内衣和冬天的外套，背着个塞满课本和铅笔的书包。我穿着法兰绒睡衣，看他们扬长而去，转过街道的拐角，然后钻回我的床上去。我将毛毯拉到脖子上，透过窗户，望着北边白雪皑皑的山头。望着它们，直到再次入睡。

我喜欢喀布尔的冬天。我喜欢夜里满天飞雪轻轻敲打我的窗户，我喜欢新霁的积雪在我的黑色胶靴下吱嘎作响，我喜欢感受铁炉的温暖，听寒风呼啸着吹过街道、吹过院子。但更重要的是，每逢林木萧瑟，冰雪封路，爸爸和我之间的寒意会稍微好转。那是因为风筝。爸爸和我生活在同一个屋顶之下，但我们生活在各自的区域，风筝是我们之间薄如纸的交集。

每年冬天，喀布尔的各个城区会举办风筝比赛。如果你是生活在喀布尔的孩子，那么比赛那天，无疑是这个寒冷季节最令人振奋的时候。每次比赛前夜我都会失眠，我会辗转反侧，双手借着灯光在墙上投射出动物形状的影子，甚至裹条毛毯，在一片漆黑中到阳台上呆坐。我像是个士兵，大战来临前夜试图在战壕里入睡。其实也差不多，在喀布尔，斗风筝跟上战场有点相像。

跟任何战争一样，你必须为自己做好准备。有那么一阵，哈桑和我经常自己制作风筝。秋天开始，我们每周省下一点零用钱，投进爸爸从赫拉特买来的瓷马里面。到得寒风呼啸、雪花飞舞的时候，我们揭开瓷马腹部的盖子，到市场去买竹子、胶水、线、纸。我们每天花几个小时，打造风筝的骨架，剪裁那些让风筝更加灵动的薄棉纸。再接着，我们当然还得自己准备线。如果风筝是枪，那么缀有玻璃屑的线就是膛里的子弹。我们得走到院子里，把五百英尺线放进一桶混有玻璃屑的胶水里面，接着把线挂在树上，让它风干。第二天，我们会把这为战斗准备的线缠绕在一个木轴上。等到雪花融化、春雨绵绵，喀布尔每个孩子的手指上，都会有一些横切的伤口，那是斗了一个冬天的风筝留下的证据。我记得开学那天，同学们挤在一起，比较各自的战伤。伤口很痛，几个星期都好不了，但我毫不在意。我们的冬天总是那样匆匆来了又走，伤疤提醒我们怀念那个最令人喜爱的季节。接着班长会吹口哨，我们排成一列，走进教室，心中已然渴望冬季的到来，但招呼我们的是又一个幽灵般的漫长学年。

但是没隔多久，事实证明我和哈桑造风筝实在不行，斗风筝倒是好手。我们设计的风筝总是有这样或那样的问题，难逃悲惨的命运。所以爸爸开始带我们去塞弗的店里买风筝。塞弗是个近乎瞎眼的老人，以替人修鞋为生，但他也是全城最著名的造风筝高手。他的小作坊在拥挤的雅德梅湾大道上，也就是喀布尔河泥泞的南岸那边。爸爸会给我们每人买三个同样的风筝和几轴玻璃线。如果我改变主意，求爸爸给我买个更大、更好看的风筝，爸爸会买给我，可是也会给哈桑买一个。有时我希望他别给哈桑买，希望他最疼我。

斗风筝比赛是阿富汗古老的冬日风俗。比赛一大清早就开始，直到仅剩一只胜出的风筝在空中翱翔才告结束。我记得有一年，比赛到了天黑还没终结。人们在人行道上，在屋顶上，为自家的孩子鼓劲加油。街道上满是风筝斗士，手里的线时而猛拉、时而速放，目不转睛地仰望天空，力图占个好位置，以便割断敌手的风筝线。每个斗风筝的人都有助手，帮忙收放风筝线。我的助手是哈桑。

有一次，有个多嘴的印度小孩，他家最近才搬到附近，告诉我们，在他的家乡，斗风筝必须严格遵守一些规则和规定。"你必须在指定的区域放风筝，并且你必须站在风向成直角的地方。"他骄傲地说，"还有，你不能用铝来做玻璃线。"

哈桑和我对望了一眼。让你吹吧。这个印度小孩很快会学到的，跟英国人在这个世纪之初以及俄国人在 1980 年代晚期学到的如出一辙：阿富汗人是独立的民族。阿富汗人尊重风俗，但讨厌规则，斗风筝也是这样。规则很简单：放起你的风筝，割断对手的线，祝你好运。

不仅如此，若有风筝被割断，真正的乐趣就开始了。这时，该追风筝的人出动，那些孩子追逐那个在随风飘扬的风筝，在邻近的街区奔走，直到它盘旋着跌落在田里，或者掉进某家的院子里，或挂在树上，或停在屋顶上。追逐十分激烈：追风筝的人蜂拥着漫过大街小巷，相互推搡，像西班牙人那样。我曾看过一本书，说起他们在斗牛节时被公牛追赶的景象。有一年某个邻居的小孩爬上松树，去捡风筝，结果树枝不堪重负，他从三十英尺高的地方跌下来，摔得再也无法行走，但他跌下来时手里还抓着那只风筝。如果追风筝的人手里拿着风筝，没有人能将它拿走。这不是规则，而是风俗。

对追风筝的人来说，最大的奖励是在冬天的比赛中捡到最后掉落的那只风筝。那是无上的荣耀，人们会将其挂在壁炉架之下，供客人欢欣赞叹。每当满天风筝消失得只剩下最后两只，每个追风筝的人都厉兵秣马，准备摘取此项大奖。他们会朝向那个他们预计风筝跌落的地方，绷紧的肌肉蓄势待发，下巴抬起，眼睛眯着，斗志昂扬。当最后一只风筝被割断，立即一片骚动。

多年过去，我曾见到无数家伙参与追风筝，但哈桑是我见过的人中最精于此道的高手。十分奇怪的是，在风筝跌落之前，他总是等在那个它将要跌落的地方，似乎他体内有某种指南针。

我记得有个阴暗的冬日，哈桑和我追着一只风筝。我跟着他，穿过各处街区，跳过水沟，侧身跑过那些狭窄的街道。我比他大一岁，但哈桑跑得比我快，我落在后面。

"哈桑，等等我。"我气喘吁吁地大喊，有些恼怒。

他转过身，挥挥手："这边！"说完就冲进另外一个拐角处。我抬头一看，那个方向与风筝跌落的方向恰好相反。

"我们追不到它了！我们跑错路了！"我高声叫道。

"相信我！"我听见他在前面说。我跑到拐角处，发现哈桑低首飞奔，根本就没有抬头看看天空，汗水浸透了他后背的衣服。我踩到一块石头，摔了一跤——我非但跑得比哈桑慢，也笨拙得多，我总是羡慕他与生俱来的运动才能。我站起身来，瞥见哈桑又拐进了另一条巷子。我艰难地追着他，摔破的膝盖传来阵阵剧痛。

我看到我们最终停在一条车辙纵横的泥土路上，就在独立中学旁边。路边有块田地，夏天会种满莴苣；路的另外一边有成排的酸樱桃树。

只见哈桑盘起双腿,坐在其中一棵树下,吃着手里的一捧桑葚干。

"我们在这干吗呢?"我上气不接下气,胃里翻江倒海,简直要吐出来。

他微笑:"在我这边坐下,阿米尔少爷。"

我在他旁边颓然倒下,躺在一层薄薄的雪花上,喘着气。"你在浪费时间。它朝另外一边飞去了,你没看到吗?"

哈桑往嘴里扔了一颗桑葚:"它飞过来了。"我呼吸艰难,而他一点都不累。

"你怎么知道?"我问。

"我知道。"

"你是怎么知道的?"

他朝我转过身,有些汗珠从他额头流下来,"我骗过你吗,阿米尔少爷?"

刹那间我决定跟他开开玩笑:"我不知道。你会骗我吗?"

"我宁愿吃泥巴也不骗你。"他带着愤愤的表情说。

"真的吗?你会那样做?"

他疑惑地看了我一眼:"做什么?"

"如果我让你吃泥巴,你会吃吗?"我说。我知道自己这样很残忍,好像以前,我总是拿那些他不懂的字眼来戏弄他,但取笑哈桑有点好玩——虽然是病态的好玩,跟我们折磨昆虫的游戏有点相似。不过现在,他是蚂蚁,而拿着放大镜的人是我。

他久久看着我的脸。我们坐在那儿,两个男孩,坐在一棵酸樱桃树下,突然间我们看着,真的看着对方。就在那时,哈桑的脸又变了。也许没有变，不是真的变了，但我瞬间觉得自己看到了两张脸，一张是我认得的，我从小熟悉的；另外一张，第二张，就隐藏在表层之下。我曾经看到过他的脸色变化——总是吓我一跳，它每次出现不过惊鸿一瞥，但足以让我疑惑不安，觉得自己也许曾在什么地方见到过。随后，哈桑眨眨眼，他又是他了，只是哈桑了。

"如果你要求，我会的。"他终于说，眼睛直看着我。我垂下眼光，时至今日，我发现自己很难直视像哈桑这样的人，这种说出的每个字都当真的人。

"不过我怀疑，"他补充说，"你是否会让我这么做。你会吗，阿米尔少爷？"就这样，轮到他考验我了。如果我继续戏弄他，考验他的忠诚，那么他会戏弄我，考验我的正直。

要是我没有开始这场对话就好了！我勉强露出一个笑脸，"别傻了，哈桑，你知道我不会的。"

哈桑报我以微笑，不过他并非强颜欢笑。"我知道。"他说。这就是那些一诺千金的人的作风，以为别人也和他们一样。

"风筝来了。"哈桑说，指向天空，他站起身来，朝左边走了几步。我抬头，望见风筝正朝我们一头扎下来。我听见脚步声，叫喊声，一群追风筝的人正闹哄哄向这边跑来。但他们只是白费时间。因为哈桑脸带微笑，张开双手，站在那儿等着风筝。除非真主——如果他存在的话——弄瞎了我的眼，不然风筝一定会落进他张开的臂弯里。

1975 年冬天，我最后一次看到哈桑追风筝。

通常，每个街区都会举办自己的比赛。但那年，巡回赛由我所在的街区，瓦兹尔·阿克巴·汗区举办，几个其他的城区——卡德察区、卡德帕湾区、梅寇拉扬区、科德桑吉区——也应邀参加。无论走到哪里，都能听见人们在谈论即将举办的巡回赛，据说这是二十五年来规模最大的风筝比赛。

那年冬天的一个夜里，距比赛还有四天，爸爸和我坐在书房里铺满毛皮的椅子上，烤着火，边喝茶边交谈。早些时候，阿里服侍我们用过晚餐——土豆、咖喱西兰花拌饭，回去跟哈桑度过漫漫长夜。爸爸塞着他的烟管，我求他讲那个故事给我听，据说某年冬天，有一群狼从山上下来，游荡到赫拉特，迫使人们在屋里躲了一个星期。爸爸划了一根火柴，说："我觉得今年你也许能赢得巡回赛，你觉得呢？"

我不知道该怎么想，或者该怎么说。我要接过他的话头吗？他这是递给我一把钥匙吗？我是斗风筝的好手，实际上，是非常出色的好手。好几次我差点赢得冬季巡回赛——有一次，我还进了前三名。但差点儿和赢得比赛是两回事，不是吗？爸爸从来不差点儿，他只是获胜，获胜者赢得比赛，其他人只能回家。爸爸总是胜利，赢得一切他想赢得的东西。难道他没有权利要求他的儿子也这样吗？想想吧，要是我赢得比赛……

爸爸吸着烟管，跟我说话。我假装在听，但我听不进去，有点心不在焉，因为爸爸随口一说，在我脑海埋下了一颗种子：赢得冬季巡回赛是个好办法。我要赢得比赛，没有其他选择。我要赢得比赛，我的风筝要坚持到最后。然后我会把它带回家，带给爸爸看。让他看看，他的儿子终究非同凡响，那么也许我在家里孤魂野鬼般的日子就可以结束。我让自己幻想着：我幻想吃晚饭的时候，充满欢声笑语，而非一言不发，只有银餐具偶尔的碰撞声和几声"嗯哦"打破寂静。我想象星期五爸爸开着车带我去帕格曼，中途在喀尔卡湖稍作休憩，吃着炸鳟鱼和炸土豆。我们会去动物园看看那只叫"玛扬"的狮子，也许爸爸不会一直打哈欠，偷偷看着他的腕表。也许爸爸甚至还会看看我写的故事，我情愿为他写一百篇，哪怕他只挑一篇看看。也许他会像拉辛汗那样，叫我"亲爱的阿米尔"。也许，只是也许，他最终会原谅我杀了他的妻子。

爸爸告诉我有一天他割断了十四只风筝的线。我不时微笑，点头，大笑，一切恰到好处，但我几乎没有听清他在说什么。现在我有个使命了，我不会让爸爸失望。这次不会。

巡回赛前夜大雪纷飞。哈桑和我坐在暖炉桌前玩一种叫做"番吉帕"的扑克游戏，寒风吹着树枝，打在窗户上嗒嗒作响。当天早些时候，我要阿里替我们布置暖炉桌——在一张低矮的桌子下面，摆放电暖片，然后盖上厚厚的棉毯。他在桌旁铺满地毯和坐垫，足够供二十个人坐下，把腿伸进桌子下面。每逢下雪，哈桑和我经常整天坐在暖炉桌边，下棋或者打牌，主要是玩"番吉帕"。

我杀了哈桑两张方块10，打给他两条J和一张6。隔壁是爸爸的书房，他和拉辛汗在跟几个人谈生意。其中有个我认得是阿塞夫的父亲。隔着墙，我能听到喀布尔新闻广播电台沙沙的声音。

哈桑杀了6，要了两条J。达乌德汗在收音机中宣布有关外国投资的消息。

"他说有一天喀布尔也会拥有电视。"我说。

"谁？"

"达乌德汗，你这个家伙，我们的总统。"

哈桑咯咯笑起来，"我听说伊朗已经有了。"他说。

我叹了一口气："那些伊朗人……"对多数哈扎拉人来说，伊朗是个避难所，我猜想也许是因为多数伊朗人跟哈扎拉人一样，都是什叶派穆斯林。但我记得夏天的时候有个老师说起伊朗人，说他们都是笑面虎，一边用手拍拍你的后背示好，另一只手却会去掏你的口袋。我将这个告诉爸爸，爸爸说我的老师不过是个嫉妒的阿富汗人，他嫉妒，因为伊朗在亚洲声望日隆，而世界上多数人看世界地图的时候还找不到阿富汗在哪里。"这样说很伤感情，"他说，耸着肩，"但被真相伤害总比被谎言安慰好。"

"有一天我会给你买的。"我说。

哈桑笑逐颜开："电视机？真的吗？"

"当然，还不是黑白的那种。到时我们也许都是大人了，不过我会给我们买两台。一台给你，一台给我。"

"我要把它放在我画画的桌子上。"哈桑说。

他这么说让我觉得很难过。我为哈桑的身份、为他居住的地方难过。他长大之后，将会像他父亲一样，住在院子里那间破房子，而他对此照单全收，让我觉得难过。我抽起最后一张牌，给他一对 Q 和一张10。

哈桑要了一对 Q，"你知道吗，我觉得你明天会让老爷觉得很骄傲。"

"你这样想啊？"

"安拉保佑。"他说。

"安拉保佑。"我回应，虽然这句"安拉保佑"从我嘴里说出来有些口不由心。哈桑就是这样，他真是纯洁得该死，跟他在一起，你永远觉得自己是个骗子。

我杀了他的 K，扔给他最后一张牌：黑桃 A。他必须吃下。我赢了，不过在洗牌的时候，我怀疑这是哈桑故意让我赢的。

"阿米尔少爷？"

"怎么啦？"

"你知道……我喜欢我住的地方。"他总是这样，能看穿我的心事，"它是我的家。"

"不管怎样，"我说，"准备再输一局吧。"

第七章

次日早晨，哈桑在泡早餐红茶，他告诉我他做了一个梦。"我们在喀尔卡湖，你，我，爸爸，老爷，拉辛汗，还有几千个人。"他说，"天气暖和，阳光灿烂，湖水像镜子一样清澈。但是没有人游泳，因为他们说湖里有个鬼怪。它在湖底潜伏着，等待着。"

他给我倒了一杯茶，加了糖，吹了几下，把它端给我。"所以大家都很害怕，不敢下水。突然间你踢掉鞋子，阿米尔少爷，脱掉你的衣服。'里面没有鬼怪，'你说，'我证明给你们看看。'大家还来不及阻止你，你一头扎进湖里，游开了。我跟着你，我们都游着。"

"可是你不会游泳。"

哈桑哈哈大笑："那是在梦里啊，阿米尔少爷，你能做任何事情。每个人都尖声叫唤：'快起来！快起来！'但我们只是在冰冷的湖水里面游泳。我们游到湖中央，停下来。我们转向湖岸，朝人们挥手。他们看起来像小小的蚂蚁，但我们能听到他们的掌声。现在他们知道了，湖里没有鬼怪，只有湖水。随后他们给湖改了名字，管它叫'喀布尔的苏丹阿米尔和哈桑之湖'。我们向那些到湖里游泳的人收钱。"

"这梦是什么意思呢？"我说。

他替我烤好馕饼，涂上甜果酱，放在盘子里。"我不知道，我还指望你告诉我呢。"

"好吧，那是个愚蠢的梦而已，没有什么含义。"

"爸爸说梦总是意味着某种东西。"

我喝着茶，"那么你为什么不去问他呢？他多聪明呀。"我的不耐烦简直出乎自己意料。我彻夜未眠，脖子和后背像绷紧的钢丝，眼睛刺痛。即使这样，我对哈桑也太刻薄了。我差点向他道歉，但是没有。哈桑明白我只是精神紧张。哈桑总是明白我。

楼上，我听见从爸爸的卫生间传来一阵水流的声音。

街上新霁的积雪银光闪闪，天空蓝得无可挑剔。雪花覆盖了每一个屋顶，矮小的桑葚树在我们这条街排开，树枝上也堆满了积雪。一夜之间，雪花塞满了所有的裂缝和水沟。哈桑和我走出锻铁大门时，雪花反射出白晃晃的光芒，照得我睁不开眼。阿里在我们身后关上门。我听见他低声祈祷——每次他儿子外出，他总是要祈祷。

我从来没有见到街上有这么多人。儿童在打雪仗，拌嘴，相互追逐，咯咯笑着。风筝斗士和帮他们拿卷轴的人挤在一起，做最后的准备。周围的街道传来欢声笑语，各处屋顶已经挤满了看客，他们斜躺在折叠椅上，暖水壶里的红茶热气腾腾，录音机传出艾哈迈德·查希尔[1]喧闹的音乐。风靡全国的艾哈迈德·查希尔改进了阿富汗音乐，给传统

---

[1] Ahmad Zahir（1946~1979），阿富汗歌星。

的手鼓和手风琴配上电吉他、小号和鼓，激怒了那些保守的教徒。无论在台上表演还是开派对，他都避免像老歌手们那样严肃且近乎阴郁地演出，而是边唱边微笑——有时甚至对女人微笑。我朝自家的屋顶看去，发现爸爸和拉辛汗坐在一张长凳上，两人都穿着羊毛衫，喝着茶。爸爸挥挥手，我不知道他究竟是跟我还是跟哈桑打招呼。

"我们得开始了。"哈桑说。他穿着一双黑色的橡胶雪靴，厚厚的羊毛衫和褪色的灯芯绒裤外面，罩着绿色的长袍。阳光照在他脸上，我看到他唇上那道粉红色的伤痕已经弥合得很好了。

突然间我想放弃，把东西收起来，转身回家。我在想什么呢？我既然已经知道结局，何必还要让自己来体验这一切呢？爸爸在屋顶上，看着我。我觉得他的眼光像太阳那样热得令人发烫。今天，即使是我，也必定难逃惨败。

"我有点不想在今天放风筝了。"我说。

"今天是个好日子。"哈桑说。

我转动双脚，试图让眼光离开我们家的屋顶。"我不知道，也许我们该回家去。"

接着他上前一步，低声说了一句让我有些吃惊的话。"记住，阿米尔少爷，没有鬼怪，只是个好日子。"我对他脑海盘桓的念头常常一无所知，可是我在他面前怎么就像一本打开的书？到学校上学的人是我，会读书写字的人是我，聪明伶俐的也是我。哈桑虽然看不懂一年级的课本，却能看穿我。这让人不安，可是有人永远对你的需求了如指掌，毕竟也叫人宽心。

"没有鬼怪。"我低声说，出乎意料的是我竟然觉得好些了。

他微笑:"没有鬼怪。"

"你确定?"

他闭上双眼,点点头。

我看着那些在街道蹿上蹿下打雪仗的孩子,"今天是个好日子,对吧?"

"我们来放风筝吧。"他说。

当时我觉得哈桑那个梦可能是他编出来的。那可能吗?我确定不是,哈桑没那么聪明,我也没那么聪明。但不管是否是编造的,那个愚蠢的梦缓解了我的焦虑。兴许我该除去衣服,到湖里去游一游。为什么不呢?

"我们来放。"我说。

哈桑神色一振:"好啊!"他举起我们的风筝:红色的风筝,镶着黄边,在竖轴和横轴交叉的地方,有塞弗的亲笔签名。他舔舔手指,把它举起,测试风向,然后顺风跑去。我们偶尔也在夏天放风筝,他会踢起灰尘,看风吹向什么方位。我手里的卷轴转动着,直到哈桑停下来,大约在五十英尺开外。他将风筝高举过顶,仿佛一个奥运会的田径运动员高举获得的金牌。按照我们往常的信号,我猛拉两次线,哈桑放开了风筝。

虽说爸爸和学校的老师诲我不倦,我终究无法对真主死心塌地。可是当时,从教义答问课程学到的某段《古兰经》涌上嘴边,我低声念诵,然后深深吸气,呼气,跟着拉线跑开。不消一分钟,我的风筝扶摇直上,发出宛如鸟儿拍打翅膀的声音。哈桑拍掌称好,跑在我身后。我把卷轴交给他,双手拉紧风筝线,他敏捷地将那松弛的线卷起来。

空中已经挂着至少二十来只风筝，如同纸制的鲨鱼，巡游搜猎食物。不到一个钟头，这个数字翻了一番，红色的、蓝色的、黄色的风筝在苍穹来回飞舞，熠熠生辉。寒冷的微风吹过我的头发。这风正适宜放风筝，风速不大，恰好能让风筝飘浮起来，也便于操控。哈桑在我身旁，帮忙拿着卷轴，手掌已被线割得鲜血淋漓。

顷刻间，割线开始了，第一批被挫败的风筝断了线，回旋着跌落下来。它们像流星那样划过苍天，拖着闪亮的尾巴，散落在邻近的街区，给追风筝的人带来奖赏。我能听得见那些追风筝的人，高声叫嚷，奔过大街小巷。有人扯开喉咙，报告说有两条街上爆发冲突了。

我偷眼望向爸爸，看见他和拉辛汗坐在一起，寻思他眼下在想些什么。他在为我加油吗？还是希望我的失败给他带来愉悦？放风筝就是这样的，思绪随着风筝高低起伏。

风筝纷纷坠下，而我的仍在翱翔。我仍在放着风筝，双眼不时瞟向爸爸，紧紧盯着他的羊毛衫。我坚持了这么久，他是不是很吃惊？**你的眼睛没有看着天上，你坚持不了多久啦**。我将视线收回空中。有只红色的风筝正在飞近——我发现它的时间恰到好处。我跟它对峙了一会儿，它失去耐心，试图从下面割断我，我将它送上了不归路。

街头巷尾满是凯旋的追风筝者，他们高举追到的战利品，拿着它们在亲朋好友面前炫耀。但他们统统知道最好的还没出现，最大的奖项还在飞翔。我割断了一只带有白色尾巴的黄风筝，代价是食指又多了一道伤口，血液汩汩流入我的掌心。我让哈桑拿着线，把血吸干，在牛仔裤上擦擦手指。

又过了一个钟头，天空中幸存的风筝，已经从约莫五十只剧减到十来只。我的是其中之一，我杀入前十二名。我知道巡回赛到了这个阶段，会持续一段时间，因为那些家伙既然能活下来，技术实在非同小可——他们可不会掉进简单的陷阱里面，比如哈桑最喜欢用的那招，古老的猛升急降。

到下午三点，阴云密布，太阳躲在它们后面，影子开始拉长，屋顶那些看客戴上围巾，穿上厚厚的外套。只剩下六只风筝了，我仍是其中之一。我双腿发痛，脖子僵硬。但看到风筝一只只掉落，心里的希望一点点增大，就像堆在墙上的雪花那样，一次一片地累积。

我的眼光转向一只蓝风筝，在过去那个钟头里面，它大开杀戒。

"它干掉几只？"我问。

"我数过了，十一只。"哈桑说。

"你知道放风筝的人是谁吗？"

哈桑吧嗒一下舌头，仰起下巴。那是哈桑的招牌动作，表示他不知道。蓝风筝割断一只紫色的大家伙，转了两个大圈。隔了十分钟，它又干掉两只，追风筝的人蜂拥而上，追逐它们去了。

又过了半个小时，只剩下四只风筝了。我的风筝仍在飞翔，我的动作无懈可击，仿佛阵阵寒风都照我的意思吹来。我从来没有这般胜券在握，这么幸运，太让人兴奋了！我不敢抬眼望向那屋顶，眼光不敢从天空移开，我得聚精会神，聪明地操控风筝。又过了十五分钟，早上那个看起来十分好笑的梦突然之间触手可及：只剩下我和另外一个家伙了，那只蓝风筝。

局势紧张得如同我流血的手拉着的那条玻璃线。人们纷纷顿足、拍掌、尖叫、欢呼。"干掉它！干掉它！"我在想，爸爸会不会也在欢呼呢？音乐震耳欲聋，蒸饺子和油炸菜饼的香味从屋顶和敞开的门户飘出来。

但我所能听到的——我迫使自己听到的——是脑袋里血液奔流的声音。我所看到的，只是那只蓝风筝。我所闻到的，只是胜利的味道。获救。赎罪。如果爸爸是错的，如果真像他们在学校说的，有那么一位真主，那么他会让我赢得胜利。我不知道其他家伙斗风筝为了什么，也许是为了在人前吹嘘吧。但于我而言，这是唯一的机会，让我可以成为一个被注目而非仅仅被看到、被聆听而非仅仅被听到的人。倘若真主存在，他会引导风向，让它助我成功，我一拉线，就能割断我的痛苦，割断我的渴求，我业已忍耐得太久，业已走得太远。刹那之间，就这样，我信心十足。我会赢。只是迟早的问题。

结果比我预想的要快。一阵风拉升了我的风筝，我占据了有利的位置。我卷开线，让它飞高。我的风筝转了一个圈，飞到那只蓝色家伙的上面，我稳住位置。蓝风筝知道自己麻烦来了，它绝望地使出各种花招，试图摆脱险境，但我不会放过它，我稳住位置。人群知道胜负即将揭晓。"干掉它！干掉它！"的齐声欢呼越来越响，仿佛罗马人对着斗士高喊"杀啊！杀啊！"。

"你快赢了，阿米尔少爷，快赢了！"哈桑兴奋得直喘气。

那一刻来临了。我合上双眼，松开拉着线的手。寒风将风筝拉高，线又在我手指割开一个创口。接着……不用听人群欢呼我也知道，我也不用看。哈桑抱着我的脖子，不断尖叫。

"太棒了！太棒了！阿米尔少爷！"

我睁开眼睛，望见蓝风筝猛然扎下，好像轮胎从高速行驶的轿车脱落。我眨眨眼，疲累不堪，想说些什么，却没有说出来。突然间我腾空而起，从空中望着自己。黑色的皮衣，红色的围巾，褪色的牛仔裤。一个瘦弱的男孩，肤色微黄，身材对于十二岁的孩子来说显得有些矮小。他肩膀窄小，黑色的眼圈围着淡褐色的眼珠，微风吹起他淡棕色的头发。他抬头望着我，我们相视微笑。

然后我高声尖叫，一切都是那么色彩斑斓、那么悦耳动听，一切都是那么鲜活、那么美好。我伸出空手抱着哈桑，我们跳上跳下，我们两个都笑着、哭着。"你赢了，阿米尔少爷！你赢了！"

"我们赢了！我们赢了！"我只说出这句话。这是真的吗？在过去的日子里，我眨眨眼，从美梦中醒来，起床，下楼到厨房去吃早餐，除了哈桑没人跟我说话。穿好衣服。等爸爸。放弃。回到我原来的生活。然后我看到爸爸在我们的屋顶上，他站在屋顶边缘，双拳挥舞，高声欢呼，拍掌称快。就在那儿，我体验到有生以来最棒的一刻，看见爸爸站在屋顶上，终于以我为荣。

但他似乎在做别的事情，双手焦急地摇动。于是我明白了，"哈桑，我们……"

"我知道，"他从我们的拥抱中挣脱，"安拉保佑，我们等会儿再庆祝吧。现在，我要去帮你追那只蓝风筝。"他放下卷轴，撒腿就跑，他穿的那件绿色长袍的后褶边拖在雪地上。

"哈桑！"我大喊，"把它带回来！"

他的橡胶靴子踢起阵阵雪花，已经飞奔到街道的拐角处。他停下来，转身，双手放在嘴边，说："为你，千千万万遍！"然后露出一脸哈桑式的微笑，消失在街角之后。再一次看到他笑得如此灿烂，已是二十六年之后，在一张褪色的宝丽来照片上。

人群涌上来向我道贺，我开始把风筝收回来。我跟他们握手，向他们道谢。那些比我更小的孩童望着我的眼神充满敬畏，我是个英雄。人们伸手拍拍我的后背，摸摸我的头发。我边拉着线，边朝每个人微笑，但我的心思在那个蓝风筝上。

最后，我收回了自己的风筝。我捡起脚下的卷轴，把松弛的线收好，其间又握了几双手，接着走回家。走到那扇锻铁大门时，阿里在门后等着，他从栅栏伸出手，"恭喜。"

我把风筝和卷轴给他，握握他的手，"谢谢你，亲爱的阿里。"

"我一直为你祈祷。"

"继续祈祷吧，我们还没全赢呢。"

我匆忙走回街上。我没向阿里问起爸爸，我还不想见到他。在我脑里，一切都计划好了：我要班师回朝，像一个英雄，用鲜血淋漓的手捧着战利品。我要万头攒动，万众瞩目，罗斯坦和索拉博彼此打量，此时无声胜有声。然后年老的战士会走向年轻的战士，抱着他，承认他出类拔萃。证明。获救。赎罪。然后呢？这么说吧……之后当然是永远幸福。还会有别的吗？

瓦兹尔·阿克巴·汗区的街道不多，彼此成直角纵横交错，像个棋盘。当时它是个新城区，仍在蓬勃发展中，已建成的住宅区有八英尺高的围墙，在它们之间，街道上有大量的空地和尚未完工的房子。我跑遍每条街巷，搜寻哈桑的踪迹。到处都是忙着收起折叠椅的人们，在整天的狂欢之后，收起食物和器皿。有些还坐在他们的屋顶上，高声向我道贺。

在我们家南边第四条街，我碰到奥马尔，他父亲是工程师，也是爸爸的朋友。他正在自家门前的草坪上，跟他弟弟玩足球。奥马尔是个不错的家伙。我们是四年级的同学，有次他送给我一支水笔，配有抽取式墨水盒那种。

"听说你赢了，阿米尔，"他说，"恭喜恭喜。"

"谢谢，你见到哈桑了吗？"

"你的哈扎拉人？"

我点点头。

奥马尔用头将足球顶给他弟弟，"我听说他追风筝可厉害了。"他弟弟将足球顶回来，奥马尔伸手抓住，拍上拍下。"不过我总是奇怪他是怎么追到的。我的意思是说，他的眼睛那么小，怎么能看到任何东西呢？"

他弟弟哈哈大笑，随后又要回足球，奥马尔没理他。

"你见到他了吗？"

奥马尔伸出拇指，朝肩膀后指了指西南边的方向："刚才我看见他朝市场那边跑过去。"

"谢谢。"我赶忙跑开。

我到达市场那边时，太阳已经快下山了，粉红色和紫色的晚霞点缀着天空。再走几条街就是哈吉·雅霍清真寺，毛拉在那儿高声呼喊，号令那些朝拜者铺开毯子，朝西边磕头，诚心礼拜。每日五次的礼拜哈桑从不错过，就算我们在玩，他也会告退，从院子里的深井汲起一桶水，清洗完毕，消失在那间破屋子里面。隔几分钟，他就会面带微笑走出来，发现我坐在墙上，或者坐在树枝上。可是，他今晚就要错过礼拜了，那全因为我。

市场不一会儿就空荡荡的，做生意的人都打烊了。我在一片泥泞中奔走，两边是成排的、挤得紧紧的小店，人们可以在一个血水横流的摊前买刚宰好的野鸡，而隔壁的小店则出售电子计算器。我在零落的人群中寻路前进，步履维艰的乞丐身上披着一层又一层的破布，小贩肩上扛着毛毯，布料商人和出售生鲜的屠夫则在关上铺门。我找不到哈桑的踪迹。

我停在一个卖干果的小摊前面，有个年老的商人戴着蓝色的头巾，把一袋袋松子和葡萄干放到驴子身上。我向他描述哈桑的相貌。

他停下来，久久看着我，然后开口说："兴许我见过他。"

"他跑哪边去了？"

他上下打量着我："像你这样的男孩，干吗在这个时候找一个哈扎拉人呢？"他艳羡地看着我的皮衣和牛仔裤——牛仔穿的裤子，我们总是这样说。在阿富汗，拥有任何不是二手的美国货，都是财富的象征。

"我得找到他，老爷。"

"他是你的什么人？"他问。我不知道他干吗要这样问，但我提醒自己，不耐烦只会让他缄口不言。

"他是我家仆人的儿子。"我说。

那老人扬了扬灰白的眉毛："是吗？幸运的哈扎拉人，有这么关心他的主人。他的父亲应该跪在你跟前，用睫毛扫去你靴子上的灰尘。"

"你到底告不告诉我啊？"

他将一只手放在驴背上，指着南边："我想我看见你说的那个男孩朝那边跑去。他手里拿着一只风筝，蓝色的风筝。"

"真的吗？"我说。**为你，千千万万遍。**他这样承诺过。好样的，哈桑。好样的，可靠的哈桑。他一诺千金，替我追到了最后那只风筝。

"当然，这个时候他们也许已经逮住他了。"那个老人咕哝着说，把另一个箱子搬到驴背上。

"什么人？"

"其他几个男孩。"他说，"他们追着他，他们的打扮跟你差不多。"他抬眼看看天空，叹了口气，"走开吧，你耽误了我做礼拜。"

但我已经朝那条小巷飞奔而去。

有那么几分钟，我徒劳无功地在市场中搜寻着。兴许那个老人看走了眼，可是他看到了蓝色的风筝。想到亲手拿着那只风筝……我探头寻找每条通道，每家店铺。没有哈桑的踪迹。

我正在担心天就快黑了，听到前面传来一阵声响。我来到一条僻静、泥泞的小巷。市场被一条大路分成两半，它就在那条大路的末端，成直角伸展开去。小巷车辙宛然，我走在上面，随着声音而去。靴子在泥泞中吱嘎作响，我呼出的气变成白雾。这狭窄的巷道跟一条冻结小溪平行，要是在春天，会有溪水潺潺流淌。小巷的另外一边是成排的柏树，枝头堆满积雪，散落在一些窄巷交错的平顶黏土房屋之间——那些房子比土屋茅舍好不了多少。

我又听见那声音，这次更响了，从某条小巷传出。我悄悄走进巷口，屏住呼吸，在拐角处窥探。

那小巷是死胡同，哈桑站在末端，摆出一副防御的姿势：拳头紧握，双腿微微张开。在他身后，有一堆破布瓦砾，摆着那只蓝风筝。那是我打开爸爸心门的钥匙。

挡住哈桑去路的是三个男孩，就是达乌德汗发动政变隔日，我们在山脚遇到、随后又被哈桑用弹弓打发走的那三个。瓦里站在一边，卡莫在另外一边，阿塞夫站在中间。我感到自己身体收缩，一阵寒意从脊背升起。阿塞夫神态放松而自信，他正在戴上他的不锈钢拳套。其他两个家伙紧张地挪动着双脚，看看阿塞夫，又看看哈桑，仿佛他们困住某种野兽，只有阿塞夫才能驯服。

"你的弹弓呢，哈扎拉人？"阿塞夫说，玩弄着手上的拳套，"你说过什么来着？'他们会管你叫独眼龙阿塞夫。'很好，独眼龙阿塞夫。太聪明了，真的很聪明。再说一次，当人们手里握着上了膛的武器，想不变得聪明也难。"

我觉得自己无法呼吸。我慢慢地、安静地呼着气，全身麻木。我看见他们逼近那个跟我共同长大的男孩，那个我懂事起就记得他的兔唇的男孩。

"但你今天很幸运，哈扎拉人。"阿塞夫说。他背朝我，但我敢打赌他脸上一定挂着邪恶的笑容。"我心情很好，可以原谅你。你们说呢，小子们？"

"太宽宏大量了，"卡莫喊道，"特别是考虑到他上次对我们那样粗鲁无礼。"他想学着阿塞夫的语调，可是声音里面有些颤抖。于是我明白了：他害怕的不是哈桑，绝对不是。他害怕，是因为不知道阿塞夫在打什么主意。

阿塞夫做了个解散的手势。"原谅你，就这样。"他声音放低一些，"当然，这个世界没有什么是免费的，我的原谅需要一点小小的代价。"

"很公平。"卡莫说。

"没有什么是免费的。"瓦里加上一句。

"你真是个幸运的哈扎拉人。"阿塞夫说，朝哈桑迈上一步。"因为今天，你所有付出的代价只是这个蓝风筝。公平的交易，小子们，是不是啊？"

"不止公平呢。"卡莫说。

即使从我站的地方，我也能看到哈桑眼里流露的恐惧，可是他摇摇头。"阿米尔少爷赢得巡回赛，我替他追这只风筝。我公平地追到它，这是他的风筝。"

"忠心的哈扎拉人，像狗一样忠心。"阿塞夫说。

卡莫发出一阵战栗、紧张的笑声。

"但在你为他献身之前，你想过吗？他会为你献身吗？难道你没有觉得奇怪，为什么他跟客人玩总不喊上你？为什么他总是在没有人的时候才理睬你？我告诉你为什么，哈扎拉人。因为对他来说，你什么都不是，只是一只丑陋的宠物。一种他无聊的时候可以玩的东西，一种他发怒的时候可以踢开的东西。别欺骗自己了，别以为你意味着更多。"

"阿米尔少爷跟我是朋友。"哈桑红着脸说。

"朋友？"阿塞夫大笑说，"你这个可怜的白痴！总有一天你会从这小小的幻想中醒来，发现他是个多么好的朋友。听着，够了，把风筝给我们。"

哈桑弯腰捡起一块石头。

阿塞夫一愣，他开始退后一步，"最后的机会了，哈扎拉人。"

哈桑的回答是高举那只抓着石头的手。

"不管你想干吗。"阿塞夫解开外套的纽扣，将其脱下，慢条斯理地折叠好，将它放在墙边。

我张开嘴，几乎喊出来。如果我喊出来，我生命中剩下的光阴将会全然改观。但我没有，我只是看着，浑身麻木。

阿塞夫挥挥手，其他两个男孩散开，形成半圆，将哈桑包围在小巷里面。

"我改变主意了，"阿塞夫说，"我不会拿走你的风筝，哈扎拉人。你会留着它，以便它可以一直提醒你我将要做的事情。"

然后他动手了，哈桑扔出石块，击中了阿塞夫的额头。阿塞夫大叫着扑向哈桑，将他击倒在地。瓦里和卡莫一拥而上。

我抓紧拳头，合上双眼。

一段记忆：

"你知道哈桑跟你喝着同一个胸脯的奶水长大吗？你知道吗，阿米尔少爷？萨吉娜，乳母的名字。她是个漂亮的哈扎拉女人，有双蓝眼睛，从巴米扬来，她给你们唱古老的婚礼歌谣。人们说同一个胸脯喂大的人就是兄弟。你知道吗？"

一段记忆：

"每人一个卢比，孩子们。每人只要一个卢比，我就会替你们揭开命运的帷幕。"那个老人倚墙而坐，黯淡无光的双眼像滑溜溜的银子，镶嵌在一双深深的火山洞口中。算命先生弯腰拄着拐杖，从消瘦的脸颊下面伸出一只嶙峋的手，在我们面前做成杯状。"每人一个卢比就可知道命运，不贵吧？"哈桑放了个铜钿在他粗糙的手掌上，我也放了一个。"以最仁慈、最悲悯的安拉之名。"那位老算命先生低声说。他先是拿起哈桑的手，用一只兽角般的指甲，在他掌心转了又转，转了又转。跟着那根手指飘向哈桑的脸庞，慢慢摸索着哈桑脸颊的曲线、耳朵的轮廓，发出干燥的刮擦声。他的手指生满老茧，轻轻拂着哈桑的眼睑。手停在那儿，迟疑不去。老人脸上掠过一抹阴影，哈桑和我对望了一眼。老人抓起哈桑手，把那个卢比还给他。"让我看看你怎么样，小朋友？"他说。墙那边传来公鸡的叫声。老人伸手来拉我的手，我抽回来。

一个梦境：

我在暴风雪中迷失了方向。寒风凛冽，吹着雪花，刺痛了我的双眼。我在白雪皑皑中跋涉。我高声求救，但风淹没了我的哭喊。我颓然跌倒，躺在雪地上喘息，茫然望着一片白茫茫，寒风在我耳边呼啸，我看见雪花抹去我刚踩下的脚印。我现在是个鬼魂，我想，一个没有脚印的鬼魂。我又高声呼喊，但希望随着脚印消逝。这当头，有人闷声回应。我把手架在眼睛上，挣扎着坐起来。透过风雪飞舞的帘幕，我看见人影摇摆，颜色晃动。一个熟悉的身影出现了。一只手伸在我面前，我望见手掌上有深深的、平行的伤痕，鲜血淋漓，染红了雪地。我抓住那只手，瞬间雪停了。我们站在一片原野上，绿草如茵，天空中和风吹着白云。我抬眼望去，但见万里晴空，满是风筝在飞舞，绿的、黄的、红的、橙的。它们在午后的阳光中闪耀着光芒。

小巷堆满了破铜烂铁，废弃的自行车轮胎、标签剥落的玻璃瓶子、卷边的杂志、发黄的报纸，所有这些，散落在一堆砖头和水泥板间。墙边有个锈蚀的铁火炉，炉洞像血盆大口般张开。但在那些垃圾之间，有两件东西让我无法移开目光：一件是蓝风筝，倚在墙边，紧邻铁炉；另一件是哈桑的棕色灯芯绒裤，丢在那堆碎砖块上面。

"我不知道，"瓦里说，"我爸爸说那是犯罪。"他的声音自始至终充满了怀疑、兴奋、害怕。哈桑趴在地上。卡莫和瓦里一人抓住他一只手，将其从手肘扭转，压在哈桑背后。阿塞夫站在他们上方，用雪靴的后跟踩着哈桑的脖子后面。

"你爸爸不会发现。"阿塞夫说，"给这头无礼的蠢驴一点教训，跟犯罪有什么关系？"

"我不知道。"瓦里咕哝着。

"随便你。"阿塞夫说，他转向卡莫，"你怎么说呢？"

"我……好吧……"

"他只是个哈扎拉人。"阿塞夫说，但卡莫把眼睛望向别处。

"好吧，"阿塞夫不满地说，"你们这些懦夫，帮我把他按住就好了。你们能做到吗？"

瓦里和卡莫点点头，看上去如释重负。

阿塞夫在哈桑身后跪倒，双手放在哈桑的臀部，把他光光的屁股抬起。他一手伸在哈桑背上，另外一只手去解开自己的皮带。他脱下牛仔裤，脱掉内裤。他在哈桑身后摆好位置。哈桑没有反抗，甚至没有呻吟。他稍稍转过头，我瞥见他的脸庞，那逆来顺受的神情。之前我也见过这种神色，这种羔羊的神色。

第二天是教历最后一个月的第十天，为期三天的宰牲节[1]从这天开始。人们在这一天纪念先知易卜拉欣为真主牺牲了他的儿子。这一年，爸爸又亲手挑选了一只绵羊，粉白色的绵羊，有着弯弯的黑色耳朵。

我们全部人站在院子里，哈桑，阿里，爸爸，还有我。毛拉背诵经文，转动他的念珠。爸爸咕哝着，"快了结吧。"他低声说。他对这分肉的仪式和无止境的礼拜感到厌烦。爸爸对宰牲节起源的故事不以为然，就像他对所有宗教事务不以为然一样。但他尊重宰牲节的风俗，这个风俗要求人们把肉分成三份，一份给家人，一份给朋友，一份给穷人。每年爸爸都会把肉全给穷人。"有钱人已经足够肥了。"他说。

毛拉完成了礼拜。谢天谢地。他拿起一柄刀锋长长的菜刀。风俗要求不能让绵羊看见刀。阿里喂给绵羊一块方糖——这也是风俗，让死亡变得甜蜜些。那羊伸脚乱踢，但不是太激烈。毛拉抓住它的下巴，刀锋在它脖子上一割。就在他精熟的刀法施加在绵羊喉咙之上的前一刻，我看见了羊的眼睛。好几个星期，我总是在梦里见到那双眼睛。我不知道自己为什么每年都要在院子里观看这个仪式，即使草地上的血污消退得不见痕迹，我的噩梦仍会继续。但我总是去看。我去看，是为了那只动物眼里无可奈何的神色。荒唐的是，我竟然想象它能理解。我想象它知道，那迫在眉睫的厄运，是为了某个崇高的目的……

我停止了观看，转身离开那条小巷。有种温热的东西从我手腕流淌下来。我眨眨眼，看见自己依旧咬着拳头，咬得很紧，从指节间渗出血

---

[1] 伊斯兰教重要节日，也称古尔邦节。

来。我意识到还有别的东西。我在流泪。就从刚才那个屋角，传来阿塞夫仓促而有节奏的呻吟。

我仍有最后的机会可以作决定，一个决定我将成为何等人物的最后机会。我可以冲进小巷，为哈桑挺身而出——就像他过去无数次为我挺身而出那样——接受一切可能发生在我身上的后果。或者我可以跑开。

结果，我跑开了。

我逃跑，因为我是懦夫。我害怕阿塞夫，害怕他折磨我。我害怕受到伤害。我转身离开小巷、离开哈桑的时候，心里这样对自己说。我试图让自己这么认为。说真的，我宁愿相信自己是出于软弱，因为另外的答案，我逃跑的真正原因，是觉得阿塞夫说得对：这个世界没有什么是免费的。为了赢回爸爸，也许哈桑只是必须付出的代价，是我必须宰割的羔羊。这是个公平的代价吗？我还来不及抑止，答案就从意识中冒出来：他只是个哈扎拉人，不是吗？

我沿着来路跑回去，回到那个空无一人的市场。我跌撞上一家小店铺，斜倚着那紧闭的推门。我站在那儿，气喘吁吁，汗水直流，希望事情并没有变成这个样子。

约莫隔了十五分钟，我听到人声，还有脚步声。我躲在那家小店，望着阿塞夫和那两个人走过，笑声飘过空荡荡的过道。我强迫自己再等十分钟。然后我走回到那条和冰封的小溪平行、满是车辙的小巷。我在昏暗的光芒中眯起眼睛，看见哈桑慢慢朝我走来。在河边一棵光秃秃的桦树下，我和他相遇。

他手里拿着那只蓝风筝，那是我第一眼看到的东西。时至今日，我无法扯谎说自己当时没有查看风筝是否有什么裂痕。他的长袍前方沾满泥土，衬衣领子下面开裂。他站着，双腿摇摇晃晃，似乎随时都会倒下。接着他站稳了，把风筝递给我。

"你到哪里去了？我在找你。"我艰难地说，仿佛在吞嚼一块石头。

哈桑伸手用衣袖擦擦脸，抹去眼泪和鼻涕。我等待他开口，但我们只是静静地站在那儿，在消逝的天光中。我很感谢夜幕降临，遮住了哈桑的脸，也掩盖了我的面庞。我很高兴我不用看着他的眼睛。他知道我知道吗？如果他知道，我能从他眼里看到什么呢？埋怨？耻辱？或者，愿真主制止，我最怕看到的：真诚的奉献。所有这些里，那是我最不愿看到的。

他开始说些什么，但他有点哽咽。他闭上嘴巴，张开，又闭上，往后退了一步，擦擦他的脸。就在当时，我几乎就要和哈桑谈论起在小巷里头发生的事情来。我原以为他会痛哭流涕，但，谢天谢地，他没有，而我假装没有听到他喉咙的哽咽。就像我假装没有看到他裤子后面深色的污渍一样。也假装没有看到从他双腿之间滴下的血滴，它们滴下来，将雪地染成黑色。

"老爷会担心的。"他就说了这么一句。他转过头，蹒跚着走开。

事情就如我想象的那样。我打开门，走进那烟雾缭绕的书房。爸爸和拉辛汗在喝茶，听着收音机传出的噼里啪啦的新闻。他们转过头，接着爸爸嘴角亮起一丝笑容，他张开双手，我把脸埋在他温暖的胸膛上，哭起来。爸爸紧紧抱着我，不断抚摸着我的后背。在他怀里，我忘了自己的所作所为。那感觉真好。

第八章

有一个星期，我几乎没有看见哈桑。我起床，发现面包已经烤好，茶已经泡好，还有个水煮蛋，统统放在厨房的桌子上。我当天要穿的衣服已经熨好叠好，摆在门廊的藤椅上，过去哈桑就在那儿熨衣服。他总是等我坐下来吃早餐才熨——这样我们就有机会谈谈心了。过去他还唱歌，在熨斗的嘶嘶声中，哼着那些古老的哈扎拉民谣，歌唱那郁金香盛开的原野。现在迎接我的，只有叠好的衣服，此外，还有那顿我已经吃不下去的早餐。

某个阴天的早晨，我正在拨弄着餐盘里的水煮蛋。阿里背着一捆劈好的柴走进来，我问他哈桑到哪里去了。

"他回去睡觉了。"阿里说，他在火炉前跪低，拉开那个小方门。

"哈桑今天会陪我玩吗？"

阿里怔了怔，手里拿着一根木头，脸上掠过一丝担忧。"迟些吧，看起来他只想睡觉。他把活干完——我看着他做完——可是之后他就只愿意裹在毛毯下面了。我能问你一些事情吗？"

"你问吧。"

"风筝比赛过后，他回家的时候有点流血，衬衣也破了。我问他发生什么事情了，他说没事，只是在争风筝的时候跟几个小孩发生了冲突。"

我什么也没说，只是继续在盘子里拨弄着那个鸡蛋。

"他到底怎么了，阿米尔少爷？他对我隐瞒了什么吗？"

我耸耸肩："我哪里知道？"

"你会告诉我的，对吗？安拉保佑，如果你知道发生了什么事，你会告诉我吗？"

"就像我说的，我哪里知道他出了什么问题？"我不耐烦地说，"也许他生病了。人们总是会生病的，阿里。看吧，你想冻死我呢，还是准备给炉子点火？"

当天夜里，我问爸爸可不可以在星期五带我去贾拉拉巴德[1]。他坐在办公桌后面的皮转椅上，看着报纸。他把报纸放下，摘下那副我很讨厌的老花镜。爸爸又不老，一点都不老，还有好多年可以活，可是他干吗要戴那副愚蠢的眼镜啊？

"当然可以！"他说。最近，爸爸对我有求必应。不止这些，两个晚上之前，他还问我要不要去亚雅纳电影院看查尔顿·赫斯顿主演的《万世英雄》。"你想让哈桑跟着去贾拉拉巴德吗？"

为什么爸爸总是如此扫兴呢？"他不舒服。"我说。

"真的？"爸爸仍坐在椅子上，"他怎么啦？"

[1]　Jalalabad，阿富汗东部城市。

我耸耸肩，在火炉边的沙发坐下来。"他可能感冒了或者什么吧。阿里说他每天总是在睡觉。"

"这几天我很少见到哈桑。"爸爸说，"仅仅是这样吗？感冒？"看到他双眉紧蹙，忧虑溢于言表，我十分不满。

"只是感冒而已啦，我们星期五去，是吗，爸爸？"

"是，是，"爸爸说，推着书桌站起来，"哈桑不能去，太糟糕了。我想他要是能去，你会更加开心的。"

"好吧，我们两个也可以很开心啊。"我说。

爸爸笑着，眨眨眼，"穿暖和些。"

本来就应该只有我们两个——我就希望这样——但星期三那夜，爸爸设法邀请了另外二十来个人。他打电话给他表弟霍玛勇——实际上他是爸爸的远房表弟——说星期五会到贾拉拉巴德去。霍玛勇曾在法国进修机械工程，如今在贾拉拉巴德有座房子，他说欢迎大家都去，他会带上他的孩子和两个老婆。还有，雪菲嘉表姐和家人从赫拉特到访，目前还在，或许她也想一起去。而这次雪菲嘉来喀布尔住在表哥纳德家，所以也得邀请他们一家，虽然霍玛勇跟纳德向来不和。倘使邀请了纳德，自然也得请他的哥哥法拉克，要不就伤害到他的感情了，并且下个月他们的女儿结婚，可能会因此不邀请霍玛勇……

我们坐满了三辆旅行车。我跟爸爸、拉辛汗、霍玛勇"卡卡"搭一辆车——小时候爸爸教我管男性长辈叫"卡卡"，也就是叔叔伯伯，管女性长辈叫"卡哈拉"，也就是姑姑阿姨。霍玛勇叔叔的两个老婆也跟我们一起——较老那个满脸皱纹，手上长着肉瘤；较年轻那个则浑身散发着香水的味道，跳舞的时候老闭着眼睛——还有霍玛勇叔叔那对双胞胎女儿。我坐在最后一排，晕车并且头昏眼花，被那对双胞胎夹在中间，她们不停地越过我的膝盖，相互拍打。通往贾拉拉巴德的是条盘旋的山路，要两个小时的颠簸才能走完，车每次急转都会让我的胃翻江倒海。车里每个人都在说话，同时大声说话，近乎叫喊，这是阿富汗人交谈的方式。我问了双胞胎中的一个——法茜拉或者卡丽玛，我总是分不清她们谁是谁——问她愿不愿意让我换到窗边的位置去，因为我晕车，需要呼吸一点新鲜空气。她伸了伸舌头，说不。我告诉她无所谓，不过我也许会呕吐，弄脏她的新衣服。隔了一会儿，我把头伸出车窗外面。我看见路面坑坑洼洼，高低起伏，盘旋着消失在山那边；数着从我们车边经过的货车，它们五颜六色，载满喧哗的乘客，蹒跚前进。我试图合上双眼，让风扑打我的脸颊；我张开嘴巴，大口大口吸着干净的空气，但仍没有觉得好一些。有人用手指戳了我一下，是法茜拉或者卡丽玛。

"干吗？"我说。

"我刚把风筝比赛的事情跟大家说了！"爸爸坐在驾驶座上说。霍玛勇叔叔和他两个老婆坐在中间那排，朝我微笑。

"那天天上一定有一百只风筝吧？"爸爸说，"对吗，阿米尔？"

"我想应该有的。"我喃喃说。

"一百只风筝，亲爱的霍玛勇，不是吹牛。那天最后一只还在天上飞的风筝，是阿米尔放的。他还得到最后那只风筝，把它带回家，一只漂亮的蓝风筝。哈桑和阿米尔一起追回来的。"

"恭喜恭喜。"霍玛勇叔叔说。他的第一个老婆，手上生瘤那个，拍起掌来："哇，哇，亲爱的阿米尔，我们都为你感到骄傲！"年轻的老婆也加入了，然后他们全都鼓掌，欢喜赞叹，告诉我他们有多么以我为荣。只有拉辛汗，坐在副驾驶的位子上，紧邻着爸爸，一言不发。他只是奇怪地看着我。

"请停一停，爸爸。"我说。

"干吗？"

"我晕车。"我喃喃说，倒在座位上，靠着霍玛勇叔叔的女儿。

法茜拉或卡丽玛脸色一变。"快停，叔叔！他脸色都黄了！我可不希望他弄脏我的新衣服！"她尖叫道。

爸爸开始刹车，但我没能撑住。隔了几分钟，我坐在路边的一块石头上，他们让风吹散车里的气味。爸爸吸着烟，跟霍玛勇叔叔在一起，他正在安慰法茜拉或者卡丽玛，要她别哭泣，说到了贾拉拉巴德再给她另买一套新衣服。我合上双眼，把脸对着太阳。眼睑后面出现一小片阴影，好像用手在墙上玩影子那样，它们扭曲着，混合着，变成一幅画面：哈桑的棕色灯芯绒裤子，扔在那条小巷的一堆旧砖头上面。

霍玛勇叔叔在贾拉拉巴德的白色房子楼高两层，带有阳台，从上面可以看到一个大花园，有围墙环绕，种着苹果树和柿子树。那儿还植有树篱，到了夏天，园丁会将其剪成动物形状。此外还有个铺着翡翠绿瓷砖的游泳池。游泳池没有水，底部积着一层半融的雪，我坐在池边，双脚在池里晃荡。霍玛勇叔叔的孩子在院子的另外一端玩捉迷藏。妇女在厨房做饭，我闻到炒洋葱的味道，听到高压锅扑哧扑哧的声音，还有音乐和笑声。爸爸、拉辛汗、霍玛勇叔叔、纳德叔叔坐在阳台上抽烟。霍玛勇叔叔说他带了投影机，可以放他在法国的幻灯片给大家看。他从巴黎回来已经十年了，还在炫耀那些愚蠢的幻灯片。

　　事情本来不应该是这样的。爸爸和我终于变成朋友了，几天前我们去了动物园，看那头叫"玛扬"的狮子，我趁没人注意，还朝熊扔了一块石头。之后，我们去电影公园对面那家"达克达"烤肉店吃饭，点了烤羊肉和从那个印度烤炉取下来的馕饼。爸爸跟我说他去印度和俄罗斯的故事，给我讲他碰到的人，比如说他在孟买[1]看到一对夫妇，没手没脚，结婚已经四十七年，还养了十一个孩子。跟爸爸这样过上一天，听他讲故事，太有趣了。我终于得到了我多年来梦寐以求的东西。可是现在我得到了，却觉得十分空虚，跟这个我在里面摇晃双腿的游泳池一样。

　　黄昏的时候，诸位太太和女儿张罗着晚餐——米饭、馕饼肉丸，还有咖喱鸡肉。我们按照传统的方式用膳，在地面铺上桌布，坐在遍布房间的坐垫上，每四人或者五人共用一个大浅盘，用手抓着东西吃。我不饿，不过还是坐下了，跟爸爸、法拉克，还有霍玛勇叔叔的两个儿子一起。爸爸在晚饭前喝了一点烈酒，还在跟他们吹嘘风筝比赛，活灵活现地描述我如何将其他人统统打败，如何带着最后那只风筝回家。人们从大浅盘抬起头来，纷纷向我道贺，法拉克叔叔用他那只干净的手拍拍我的后背。我感觉好像有把刀子刺进眼睛。

　　后来，午夜过后，爸爸和他的亲戚玩了几个小时的扑克，终于在我们吃饭那间房子倒下，躺在平行摆放的地毯上呼呼入睡。妇女则到楼上去。过了一个钟头，我仍睡不着。各位亲戚在睡梦中或咕哝，

---

[1]　Mumbai，印度城市。

或叹气，或打鼾，我翻来覆去。我坐起身，一缕月光穿过窗户，弥漫进来。

"我看着哈桑被人强暴。"我自说自话。爸爸在梦里翻身，霍玛勇叔叔在说吃语。有一部分的我渴望有人醒来听我诉说，以便我可以不再背负着这个谎言度日。但没有人醒来，在随后而来的寂静中，我明白这是个下在我身上的咒语，终此一生，我将背负着这个谎言。

我想起哈桑的梦，那个我们在湖里游泳的梦。**那儿没有鬼怪。他说，只有湖水。**但是他错了。湖里有鬼怪，它抓住哈桑的脚踝，将他拉进暗无天日的湖底。我就是那个鬼怪。

自从那夜起，我得了失眠症。

又隔了半个星期，我才开口跟哈桑说话。当时我的午餐吃到一半，哈桑在收拾碟子。我走上楼梯，回房间去，哈桑问我想不想去爬山。我说我累了。哈桑看起来也很累——他消瘦了，双眼泡肿，下面还有灰白的眼圈。但他又问了一次，我勉为其难地答应了。

我们爬上那座山，靴子踩在泥泞的雪花上吱嘎吱嘎响。没有人开口说话。我们坐在我们的石榴树下，我知道自己犯了个错误。我不应到山上来。我用阿里的菜刀在树干上刻下的字迹犹在：阿米尔和哈桑，喀布尔的苏丹……现在我无法忍受看到这些字。

他求我念《列王纪》给他听，我说我改变主意了。告诉他我只想走回自己的房间去。他望着远方，耸耸肩。我们沿着那条来路走下，没有人说话。我生命中第一次渴望春天早点到来。

　　1975 年冬天剩下的那些日子在我记忆里面十分模糊。我记得每当爸爸在家，我就十分高兴。我们会一起吃饭，一起看电影，一起拜访霍玛勇叔叔或者法拉克叔叔。有时拉辛汗来访，爸爸也会让我在书房里喝茶。他甚至还让我念些自己写的故事给他听。一切都很美好，我甚至相信这会永恒不变。爸爸也这么想，我认为。我们彼此更加了解。至少，在风筝大赛之后的几个月里，爸爸和我相互抱有甜蜜的幻想，以某种我们过去从未有过的方式相处。我们其实在欺骗自己，居然认为一个用棉纸、胶水和竹子做的玩具，能弥合两人之间的鸿沟。

　　可是，每当爸爸不在——他经常不在家——我便将自己锁在房间里面。我几天就看完一本书，写故事，学着画马匹。每天早晨，我会听见哈桑在厨房忙上忙下，听见银器碰撞的叮当声，还有茶壶烧水的嘶嘶声。我会等着，直到他把房门关上，我才会下楼吃饭。我在日历上圈出开学那天，开始倒数上课的日子。

　　让我难堪的是，哈桑尽一切努力，想恢复我们的关系。我记得最后一次，我在自己的房间里，看着法尔西语节译本的《劫后英雄传》[1]，他来敲我的门。

　　"谁？"

　　"我要去烤馕店买馕饼，"他在门外说，"我来……问问要不要一起去。"

　　"我觉得我只想看书。"我说，用手揉揉太阳穴。后来，每次哈桑在

---

　　[1]　*Ivanhoe*，苏格兰作家瓦尔特·司各特（Sir Walter Scott, 1771~1832）著，讲述中世纪英格兰的骑士故事。

我身边，我就头痛。

"今天阳光很好。"他说。

"我知道。"

"也许出去走走会很好玩。"

"你去吧。"

"我希望你也去。"他说。停了一会儿，不知道什么东西又在撞着门，也许是他的额头。"我不知道自己做错了什么，阿米尔少爷。希望你告诉我，我不知道为什么我们不再一起玩了。"

"你没有做错任何事情，哈桑，你走开。"

"你可以告诉我，我会改的。"

我将头埋在双腿间，用膝盖挤着太阳穴。"我会告诉你我希望你别做什么。"我说，双眼紧紧闭上。

"你说吧。"

"我要你别再骚扰我，我要你走开。"我不耐烦地说。我希望他会报复我，破门而入，将我臭骂一顿——这样事情会变得容易一些，变得好一些。但他没有那样做，隔了几分钟，我打开门，他已经不在了。我倒在自己的床上，将头埋在枕上，眼泪直流。

自那以后，哈桑搅乱了我的生活。我每天尽可能不跟他照面，并以此安排自己的生活。因为每当他在旁边，房间里的氧气就会消耗殆尽。我的胸口会收缩，无法呼吸；我会站在那儿，被一些没有空气的泡泡包围，喘息着。可就算他不在我身边，我仍然感觉到他在，他就在那儿，在藤椅上那些他亲手浆洗和熨烫的衣服上，在那双摆在我门外的温暖的便鞋里面，每当我下楼吃早餐，他就在火炉里那些熊熊燃烧的木头上。无论我走到哪儿，都能看见他忠心耿耿的信号，他那该死的、毫不动摇的忠心。

那年早春，距开学还有几天，爸爸和我在花园里种郁金香。大部分积雪已经融化，北边的山头开始露出一片片如茵绿草。那是个寒冷、阴沉的早晨，爸爸在我身旁，一边说话，一边掘开泥土，把我递给他的球茎种下。他告诉我，有很多人都以为秋天是种植郁金香的最好季节，然而那是错的。这当头，我问了他一个问题："爸爸，你有没有想过请新的佣人？"

他扔下球茎，把铲子插在泥土中，扔掉手里的工作手套，看来我让他大吃一惊，"什么？你刚才说什么？"

"我只是想想而已，没别的。"

"为什么我要那样做？"爸爸粗声说。

"你不会，我想。那只是一个问题而已。"我说，声音降低了。我已经后悔自己那样说了。

"是因为你和哈桑吗？我知道你们之间有问题，但不管那是什么问题，应该处理它的人是你，不是我。我会袖手旁观。"

"对不起，爸爸。"

他又戴上手套。"我和阿里一起长大。"他咬牙切齿地说，"我爸爸将他带回家，他对阿里视如己出。阿里待在我家四十年了，整整四十年。而你认为我会将他赶走？"他转向我，脸红得像郁金香一样，"我不会碰你一下，阿米尔，但你要是胆敢再说一次……"他移开眼睛，摇摇头，"你真让我觉得着耻。至于哈桑……哈桑哪里也不去。你知不知道？"

我望着地面，手里抓起一把冷冷的泥土，任由它从我指缝间滑落。

"我说，你知不知道？"爸爸咆哮了。

我害怕了："我知道，爸爸。"

"哈桑哪儿都不去，"爸爸愤怒地说，他拿起铲子，在地上又掘了一个坑，用比刚才更大的力气将泥土铲开，"他就在这儿陪着我们，他属于这儿。这里是他的家，我们是他的家人。以后别再问我这样的问题！"

"不会了，爸爸，对不起。"

他闷声把剩下的郁金香都种完。

第二个星期，开学了，我如释重负。学生分到了新的笔记本，手里拿着削尖的铅笔，在操场上聚集在一起，踢起尘土，三五成群地交谈，等待班长的哨声。爸爸的车开上那条通向校门的土路。学校是座两层的古旧建筑，窗户漏风，鹅卵石砌成的门廊光线阴暗，在剥落的泥灰之间，还可以看见它原来土黄色油漆。多数男孩走路上课，爸爸黑色的野马轿车引来的不仅仅是艳羡的眼光。本来他开车送我上学，我应该觉得很骄傲——过去的我就是这样——但如今我感到的只是有些尴尬，尴尬和空虚。爸爸连声"再见"都没说，就掉头离开。

我没有像过去那样，跟人比较斗风筝的伤痕，而是站到队伍中去。钟声响起，我们鱼贯进入分配的教室，找座位坐好，我坐在教室后面。法尔西语老师分发课本的时候，我祈祷有做不完的作业。

上学给了我长时间待在房间里头的借口。并且，确实有那么一阵，我忘记了冬天发生的那些事，那些我让它们发生的事。接连几个星期，我满脑子重力和动力，原子和细胞，英阿战争，不去想着哈桑，不去想他的遭遇。可是，我的思绪总是回到那条小巷。总是想到躺在砖头上的哈桑的棕色灯芯绒裤，想到那些将雪地染成暗红色、几乎是黑色的血滴。

那年初夏，某个让人昏昏欲睡的午后，我让哈桑跟我一起去爬山。告诉他我要给他念一个刚写的故事。他当时在院子里晾衣服，他手忙脚乱把衣服晾好的样子让我看到他的期待。

我们爬上山，稍作交谈。他问起学校的事情，问起我在学什么，我谈起那些老师，尤其是那个严厉的数学老师，他惩罚那些多话的学生，将铁棍放在他们的指缝间，然后用力捏他们的手指。哈桑吓了一跳，说希望我永远不用被惩罚。我说我到目前为止都很幸运，不过我知道那和运气没什么关系。我也在课堂上讲话，但我的爸爸很有钱，人人认识他，所以我免受铁棍的刑罚。

我们坐在墓园低矮的围墙上，在石榴树的树影之下。再过一两个月，成片的焦黄野草会铺满山坡，但那年春天雨水绵绵，比往年持续得久，到了初夏也还不停地下着，杂草依然是绿色的，星星点点的野花散落其间。在我们下面，瓦兹尔·阿克巴·汗区的房子平顶白墙，被阳光照得闪闪发亮；院子里的晾衣线挂满衣物，在和风的吹拂中如蝴蝶般翩翩起舞。

我们从树上摘了十来个石榴。我打开带来的那本故事书，翻到第一页，然后又把书放下。我站起身来，捡起一个熟透了的跌落在地面的石榴。

"要是我拿这个打你，你会怎么做啊？"我说，石榴在手里抛上抛下。

哈桑的笑容枯萎了。他看起来比我记得的要大，不，不是大，是老。怎么会这样呢？皱纹爬上他那张饱经风吹日晒的脸，爬过他的眼角，他的唇边。也许那些皱纹，正是我亲手拿刀刻出来的。

"你会怎么做呢？"我重复。

他脸无血色。我答应要念给他听的那本故事书在他脚下，书页被微风吹得噼啪响。我朝他扔了个石榴，打中他的胸膛，爆裂出红色的果肉。哈桑又惊又痛，放声大哭。

"还手啊！"我咆哮着。哈桑看看胸前的污渍，又看看我。

"起来！打我！"我说。哈桑站起来了，但他只是站在那儿，露出茫然失措的表情，好比一个男人，刚才还在海滩愉快地散步，此刻却被浪花卷到大洋中间。

我又扔出一个石榴，这次打在他的肩膀上，果汁染上他的脸。"还手！"我大喊，"还手，你这个该死的家伙！"我希望他还击。我希望他满足我的愿望，好好惩罚我，这样我晚上就能睡着了。也许到时事情就会回到我们以前那个样子。但哈桑纹丝不动，任由我一次又一次扔他。"你是个懦夫！"我说，"你什么都不是，只是个该死的懦夫！"

我不知道自己击中他多少次。我所知道的是，当我终于停下来，筋疲力尽，气喘吁吁，哈桑浑身血红，仿佛被一队士兵射击过那样。我双足跪倒，疲累不堪，垂头丧气。

然后哈桑捡起一个石榴。他朝我走来，将它掰开，在额头上磨碎。"那么，"他哽咽着，红色的石榴汁如同鲜血一样从他脸上滴下来。"你满意了吧？你觉得好受了吗？"他转过身，朝山下走去。

我任由泪水决堤，跪在地上，身体前后摇晃。"我该拿你怎么办，哈桑？我该拿你怎么办？"但等到泪痕风干，我脚步沉重地走回家，我找到了答案。

我的十三岁生日在 1976 年夏天。这是阿富汗最后一段平静的和平岁月。我和爸爸的关系再度冷却了。我想这都是因为在我们种郁金香那天我所说的那句愚蠢的话，关于请新仆人的那句话。我后悔说了那句话——真的很后悔——但我认为即使我没说，我们这段短短的快乐插曲也会告终。也许不会这么快，但终究会结束。到夏天结束的时候，勺子和叉子碰撞盘子的声音又取代了晚餐桌上的交谈，爸爸开始在晚饭后回到书房去，并把门关上。我则回去翻看哈菲兹和迦亚谟的书，咬指甲咬到见皮，写故事。我将故事放在床底的架子上，将它们保留起来，以备万一爸爸会跟我要去看，虽然我怀疑他不会。

爸爸举办宴会的座右铭是：如果没请来全世界的人，就不算是个宴会。我记得生日之前一个星期，我看着那份邀请名单，发现在近四百人中，至少有四分之三我并不认识——包括那些将要送我生日礼物以祝贺我活过十三个年头的叔伯姑姨。然后我意识到他们并非真的因我而来。那天是我的生日，但我知道谁才是宴会上的天皇巨星。

一连数天，屋子里挤满了爸爸请来的帮手。有个叫萨拉胡丁的屠夫拖来一头小牛和两只绵羊，拒绝收下哪怕一分钱。他亲自在院子里的白杨树下宰了那些畜生。"用血浇灌对树有好处。"我记得鲜血染红树下的青草时，他这么说。有些我不认识的男人爬上橡树，挂上成串的灯泡和长长的电线。其他人在院子里摆出几十张桌子，逐一披上桌布。盛宴开始之前一夜，爸爸的朋友德尔－穆罕默德带来几袋香料，他在沙里诺区开了一间烧烤店。跟屠夫一样，德尔－穆罕默德——爸爸管他叫"德罗"——也拒绝收钱。他说爸爸已经帮了他家里太多忙了。德罗在腌肉的时候，拉辛汗低声告诉我，德罗开餐厅的钱是爸爸借给他的，并且没有要他还钱。直到有一天，德罗开着奔驰轿车，来到我家门口，说要是爸爸不收钱他就不走，爸爸这才收下。

我想从各个方面来说，或者至少从评价宴会的标准来说，我的生日盛宴称得上极为成功。我从来没有见到屋子里有那么多人。来宾或是手拿酒杯，在门廊聊天，或是在台阶上吸烟，或是倚着门口。他们找到空位就坐下，厨房的柜台上，门廊里面，甚至楼梯下面都坐满了人。院子里，蓝色的、红色的、绿色的灯泡在树上闪闪发光，人们聚集在下面，四处点燃的煤油灯照亮他们的脸庞。爸爸把舞台设在俯览花园的阳台上，但扬声器布满整个院子。艾哈迈德·查希尔拉着手风琴，唱着歌，人们在舞台下面跳舞。

我不得不逐一跟来宾打招呼——爸爸这么要求，他可不希望翌日有人乱嚼舌头，说他养了个不懂礼貌的儿子。我亲了几百个脸颊，和所有的陌生人拥抱，感谢他们的礼物。我的脸因为僵硬的微笑而发痛。

我跟爸爸站在院子里的酒吧前面，这当头有人说："生日快乐，阿米尔。"是阿塞夫，还有他的父母。阿塞夫的父亲马赫穆德是矮个子，又矮又瘦，皮肤黝黑，脸部狭小。他的妈妈谭雅是个小妇人，神经兮兮，脸带微笑，不停眨眼。如今阿塞夫就站在他们两个之间，咧嘴笑着，居高临下，双手搂着他们的肩膀。他带着他们走过来，好像拎着他们过来一样，似乎他才是父亲，他们是孩子。我感到一阵眩晕。爸爸对他们的莅临表示感谢。

"我亲自给你挑选了礼物。"阿塞夫说。谭雅的脸抽动，眼光从阿塞夫身上移到我身上。她微笑着，显得有些勉强，眨着眼。我怀疑爸爸有没有看到。

"还玩足球吗，亲爱的阿塞夫？"爸爸说，他一直希望我跟阿塞夫交朋友。

阿塞夫微笑，他甜蜜的笑容显得纯真无瑕，真叫人不寒而栗。"当然，亲爱的叔叔。"

"我记得你踢右路？"

"是的，我今年改踢中场了。"阿塞夫说，"那样我就可以多进一些球了。我们下个星期跟梅寇拉扬队比赛。那会很精彩，他们有几个球员很棒。"

爸爸点点头："你知道，我年轻的时候也踢中场。"

"我敢打赌，现在你要是愿意，也能踢。"阿塞夫说，他一脸天真地眨眨眼，拍爸爸的马屁。

爸爸也朝他眨眼："我看你老爸已经把他举世闻名的拍马屁技术传给你了。"他用手肘碰碰阿塞夫的父亲，差点把那个小家伙撞倒。马赫穆德的笑声就像谭雅的微笑那样虚伪。突然之间，我在想，也许从某种程度上说，他们害怕自己的儿子。我试图装出一个笑容，但我所能做到的，只是勉强让嘴角往上翘了翘——看到爸爸和阿塞夫这么投机，我的胃翻动着。

阿塞夫把眼光移向我。"瓦里和卡莫也来了，他们怎么也不会错过你的生日。"他皮笑肉不笑地说。我默默点头。

"我们打算明天在我家玩排球，"阿塞夫说，"也许你可以来一起玩，如果你愿意，也可以带上哈桑。"

"听起来很有趣。"爸爸说，双眼放光。"你觉得呢，阿米尔？"

"我真的不喜欢排球。"我喃喃说，看到爸爸眼里的光芒消失了，接着是一阵令人不适的沉默。

"很抱歉，亲爱的阿塞夫。"爸爸说，耸耸肩。他竟然替我道歉！那刺痛了我。

"不，没关系。"阿塞夫说，"不过大门随时为你开放，亲爱的阿米尔。不管怎样，我听说你喜欢看书，所以我给你带了一本，我最喜欢的。"他将一份包扎好的礼物递给我，"生日快乐。"

他穿着棉布衬衣、蓝色裤子，系着红色领带，脚上是一双闪亮的黑色皮鞋。他身上散发着古龙水的香味，金黄色的头发整齐地梳向后面。就外表而言，他是每个父母梦想中的儿子：强壮，高大，衣冠楚楚，举止得体，英俊得令人吃惊，还富有才华，更不用说还能机智地跟大人打趣。但在我看来，他的眼睛出卖了他。我看着他的眼睛，看穿他虚有其表，有一种疯狂隐藏在他身内。

"怎么不收下，阿米尔？"爸爸说。

"嗯？"

"你的礼物啊，"他不耐烦地说，"亲爱的阿塞夫给你送礼物呢。"

"哦。"我说，从阿塞夫手里接过那个盒子，放低视线。要是我能独自在房间里，陪着我的书，远离这些人就好了。

"喂？"爸爸说。

"什么？"

爸爸放低了声音，每次我当众给他难堪，他就会这样，"你不谢谢亲爱的阿塞夫吗？他太周到了。"

　　我希望爸爸别那样叫他，他叫过我几次"亲爱的阿米尔"呢？"谢谢。"我说。阿塞夫的母亲看着我，欲言又止。我意识到阿塞夫的双亲还没说过一句话。为了不再让我自己和爸爸难堪——但主要是因为不想看到阿塞夫和他的笑脸——我走开了。"谢谢你来。"我说。

　　我从拥挤的宾客中走出来，偷偷溜出那扇锻铁大门。我们家往下两座房子，有一片很大的空地。我听爸爸告诉拉辛汗，有个法官买下了那片地，建筑师正在设计蓝图。现在，那块地皮是荒芜的，只有泥土、石块和野草。

　　我扯开阿塞夫的礼物外面那层包装纸，借着月光端详书的封面。那是一本希特勒自传。我将它扔在杂草中。

　　我倚着邻居的墙壁，滑坐在地上，只是在黑暗中坐一会儿，膝盖抵着胸膛，抬眼望着星星，等着夜晚结束。

　　"你不用去陪你的客人吗？"一个熟悉的声音说，拉辛汗沿着墙壁朝我走来。

　　"他们不用我陪。爸爸在那边呢，你忘了？"我说。拉辛汗酒杯中的冰块叮咚响，他坐在我身边。"我不知道原来你也喝酒。"

　　"我喝酒，"他说，高兴地用手肘撞了我一下，"不过只有在重要的场合才喝。"

　　我微笑："谢谢。"

　　他朝我举举杯，喝了一口。他点起一根香烟，没有过滤嘴的巴基斯坦香烟，他和爸爸总是抽这种。"我有没有告诉过你我差点就结婚了？"

　　"真的吗？"我说，想到拉辛汗也结婚，不由微微笑着。我一直当他是爸爸寡言的知交，我的写作导师，我的朋友，当他是那个每次到国外旅行总不忘给我买点小礼物的人。但是丈夫？父亲？

他点点头："真的。那年我十八岁。她的名字叫荷麦拉。她是哈扎拉人，我家邻居仆人的女儿。她像仙女一样好看，淡棕色的头发，褐色的大眼睛……她总是这样笑……我有时还能听到她的笑声。"他晃晃酒杯，"我们经常在我父亲的苹果园里幽会，总是在夜阑人静的时候。我们在树下聊天，我拉着她的手……我让你不好意思了吗，阿米尔？"

"有一点点。"我说。

"那对你无害的。"他说，又喝了一口。"不管怎样，我们有着这样的幻想。我们会有一个盛大的、梦幻般的婚礼，从坎大哈和喀布尔请亲朋好友来参加。我会给我们盖一座大房子，白色的，露台铺着瓷砖，窗户很大。我们会在花园里种果树，还有各种各样的花儿，有一个草坪，我们的孩子在上面玩耍。星期五，在清真寺做过礼拜之后，每个人会到我们家里吃午饭，我们在花园用膳，在樱桃树下，从井里打水喝。然后我们喝着茶，吃着糖果，看着我们的孩子跟亲戚的小孩玩……"

他喝了一大口烈酒，咳嗽。"可惜你看不到我把这件事告诉我爸爸时他脸上的表情。我妈妈完全昏厥了，我的姐妹用冷水扑打她的脸，她们对着她扇风，仿佛我用刀子割了她的喉咙。要不是我爸爸及时阻止，我哥哥雅拉尔真的会去抓来他的猎枪。"拉辛汗说，带着痛苦的笑声，"我跟荷麦拉对抗着整个世界。并且我告诉你，亲爱的阿米尔，到了最后，总是这个世界赢得胜利。就这么回事。"

"后来怎样呢？"

"就在那天，我爸爸将荷麦拉和她的家人赶上一辆货车，送他们去哈扎拉贾特。我再也没有见到过她。"

"真遗憾。"我说。

"不过这也许是最好的结果了，"拉辛汗说，耸耸肩，"她会受辱的。我的家人将永远不会平等对待她。你不会下令让某人替你擦鞋子，而当天晚些时候管她叫'姐妹'。"他看着我，"你知道，你可以告诉我任何你想说的事情，亲爱的阿米尔，任何时候。"

"我知道，"我惴惴地说。他久久看着我，似乎在等待；他黑色的眼睛深洞无底，隐藏着我们之间一个没有说出的秘密。那一刻，我差点就告诉他了，差点把什么都对他说，可是到时他会怎么看待我？他会恨我，而且合情合理。

"给你，"他递给我某件东西，"我差点忘记了，生日快乐。"那是个棕色的皮面笔记本。我伸出手指，摸索着它镶着金线的边缘，闻到皮革的味道。"给你写故事用的。"他说。我刚要向他道谢，有些东西爆炸了，在天空中燃起火焰。

"烟花！"

我们匆忙赶回家，发现所有的宾客都站在院子里，望着天空。每次爆裂和呼啸升空的声音，都会引来孩子们大声尖叫。每次火焰嘶嘶作响，爆裂开来，变成花束，都会引起人们欢呼，拍掌称好。每隔几秒钟，后院就会被突然爆发的火光点亮，有红的、绿的、黄的。

在一次短暂的闪光中，我看到永世不会忘记的情景：哈桑端着银盘，服侍阿塞夫和瓦里喝酒。那阵光芒消失了，又是一声嘶嘶，一声爆裂，接着是一道橙色的火光：阿塞夫狞笑着，用一根指节敲打着哈桑的胸膛。

然后，天可怜见，什么都看不到了。

第九章

隔日清早，我坐在房间中间，拆开一个又一个礼品盒子。我不知道自己为何如此费劲，因为我总是兴味索然地看上一眼，就将礼物丢到屋角去。它们在那边积成一堆：宝丽来相机，变频收音机，精巧的电动列车组合玩具——还有几个装着现金的信封。我知道自己永远不会花那些钱，不会听那个收音机，而那辆电动列车也不会在我房间中爬上它的轨道。我不想要这些东西——这些全都是血腥钱；而且，若非我赢得风筝大赛，爸爸根本就不会替我举办那么一场宴会。

爸爸给了我两件礼物。一辆崭新的施温·斯丁格雷[1]，自行车之王，毫无疑问会让邻近的小孩垂涎三尺，喀布尔拥有新斯丁格雷的孩子寥寥无几，如今我也跻身其中了。它的车把高高升起，握柄由黑色橡胶制成，还有个蜚声久远的香蕉形车座，轮辐是金色的，钢做的车身是红色的，赭红色，像鲜血那样。换成别的孩子，恐怕会立即跳上去，骑着它招摇过市。几个月前的我也许会这么做。

---

[1] Schwinn Stingray，美国著名高档自行车品牌。

"你喜欢吗？"爸爸斜倚在我房间门口问。我露出温顺的笑容，匆
匆说了声"谢谢"。我多希望我能多说几句话。

"我们可以去骑骑。"爸爸说。他在邀请我，不过并非真心实意。

"再说吧，我有点累了。"

"好的。"爸爸说。

"爸爸？"

"怎么？"

"谢谢你的烟花。"我说。我在感谢他，不过并非真心实意。

"好好休息吧。"爸爸说，朝他房间走去。

爸爸给我的另一件礼物——他甚至不愿意等我打开它——是手表。
表面是蓝色的，金色的指针呈闪电状。我甚至都没试着戴一下，就将其
扔到角落那堆玩具中去。唯一没有被扔到那堆东西里去的礼物是拉辛汗
的皮面笔记本，只有它不像是血腥钱。

我坐在自己的床沿，双手打开笔记本，想着拉辛汗提起荷麦拉的故
事，被他父亲逐走是她最好的下场。*她会受苦的*。好比霍玛勇叔叔的投
影机被同一面幻灯片卡住，总有个画面在我脑中挥之不去：哈桑，他低
着头，端饮料服侍阿塞夫和瓦里。兴许那是最好的结局，既可减少他的
伤痛，也可缓和我的苦楚。不管怎样，事情变得清楚起来：我们有一个
必须离开。

那天午后，我第一次，也是最后一次骑上那辆施温自行车。我绕着
那个街区骑了好几圈，然后回家。我骑上那条车道，通向后院，哈桑和
阿里正在那儿打扫昨夜宴会留下的一片狼藉。院子里到处是纸杯、揉成
一团的纸巾，还有空空如也的汽水瓶。阿里正把椅子折叠起来，放到墙

边去。他看见我，招招手。

"你好，阿里。"我挥着手说。

他举起一只手指，让我稍等，接着走进他住的那间屋子。片刻之后，他手里拿着某些东西走出来。"昨晚我和哈桑找不到机会把这份礼物给你，"他说着交给我一个盒子，"它太普通，配不上你，阿米尔少爷。不过我们还是希望你喜欢它。生日快乐。"

我喉咙一哽。"谢谢你，阿里。"我说。我宁愿他们什么也没给我买。我打开盒子，看到一本崭新的《列王纪》，硬皮的，每页的下方附有精美的彩色插图。这张是菲兰吉凝望她刚出世的儿子凯寇斯劳；那张是阿佛拉西雅手执利剑，胯骑骏马，领军前进。当然还有罗斯坦给他儿子，勇士索拉博以致命一击。"真漂亮。"我说。

"哈桑说你那本又旧又破，还掉了一些书页。"阿里说，"这本书里面全部图画都是用钢笔和墨水手绘的。"他骄傲地补充说，望着这本他和他的儿子都看不懂的书。

"它很可爱。"我说。确实很可爱。甚至也不便宜，我怀疑。我想告诉阿里，书没有配不上我，是我配不上他们的礼物。我重新跳上那辆自行车。"替我谢谢哈桑。"我说。

我终究将这本书扔在屋角那堆礼物上面。可是我的眼睛总是忍不住看向它，所以我将它埋在下面。那夜睡觉之前，我问爸爸有没有看到我的新手表。

翌日清早，我在房间里等着阿里清理完厨房用过早餐的桌子。等着他把盘碗洗好，把灶台抹净。我倚窗等着，直到望见阿里和哈桑推着那辆空的独轮车，到市场去购买杂货。

然后，我从那堆礼物中拣起数个装着钞票的信封和那个手表，蹑手蹑脚走出去。路过爸爸书房时，我停下来听听动静。整个早上他都在那儿打电话，现在他正跟某人说话，有一批地毯预计下星期到达。我走下楼梯，穿过院子，从枇杷树后进入阿里和哈桑的房间。我掀起哈桑的毛毯，将新手表和一把阿富汗尼钞票塞在下面。

我又等了半个小时，然后敲敲爸爸的房门，说了那个谎——我希望这是一长串可耻的谎话中最后一个。

透过卧房的窗户，我看见阿里和哈桑推着独轮车，载满牛肉、馕饼、水果、蔬菜，推上车道。我看见爸爸从屋子里出现，朝阿里走过去。他们的嘴巴说着我听不见的话，爸爸指了指屋子，阿里点点头。他们分开。爸爸走回屋子，阿里随着哈桑走进他们的斗室。

隔了几分钟，爸爸敲敲我的房门。"到我的办公室来，"他说，"我们得坐下来，把这件事处理好。"

我走到爸爸的书房，坐在一只皮沙发上。约莫过了三十分钟，哈桑和阿里也来了。

他们双眼红肿，我敢肯定他们一定哭过。他们手拉手站在爸爸面前，而我则寻思自己究竟在什么时候具有造成这种痛苦的能力。

爸爸开门见山，问道："钱是你偷的吗？你偷了阿米尔的手表吗，哈桑？"

哈桑的回答简单得只有一个字，以他嘶哑孱弱的声音说："是。"

我身体紧缩，好似被人扇了个耳光。我的心一沉，真话差点脱口而出。我随即明白：这是哈桑最后一次为我牺牲。如果他说"不是"，爸爸肯定相信，因为我们都知道哈桑从来不骗人。若爸爸相信他，那么矛头就转向我了，我不得不辩解，我的真面目终究会被看穿，爸爸将永远永远不会原谅我。这让我明白了另外的事情：哈桑知道。他知道我看到了小巷里面的一切，知道我站在那儿，袖手旁观。他明知我背叛了他，然而还是再次救了我，也许是最后一次。那一刻我爱上了他，爱他胜过爱任何人，我只想告诉他们，我就是草丛里面的毒蛇，湖底的鬼怪。我不配他作出的牺牲，我是撒谎蛋，我是骗子，我是小偷。我几乎就要说出来，若非心里隐隐有高兴的念头。高兴是因为这一切很快就要终结了，爸爸会赶走他们，也许会有些痛苦，但生活会继续。那是我所想要的，要继续生活，要遗忘，要将过去一笔勾销，从头来过。我想要能重新呼吸。

然而爸爸说出了让我震惊的话："我原谅你。"

原谅？可是盗窃是不能被原谅的罪行啊，是所有罪行的原型啊。当你杀害一个人，你偷走一条性命，你偷走他妻子身为人妇的权利，夺走他子女的父亲。当你说谎，你偷走别人知道真相的权利。当你诈骗，你偷走公平的权利。没有比盗窃更十恶不赦的事情了。难道爸爸没有将我抱在膝盖上，对我说出这番话吗？那么他对哈桑怎么可以只是原谅了事？而且，如果爸爸肯原谅这样的事情，那么他为何不肯原谅我，仅仅是因为我没有成为他所期许的儿子？为什么……

"我们要走了，老爷。"阿里说。

"什么？"爸爸脸色大变。

"我们没法在这里生活下去了。"阿里说。

"可是我原谅他了，阿里，你没听到吗？"爸爸说。

"我们不可能在这里过日子了，老爷。我们要走了。"阿里把哈桑拉到身旁，伸臂环住他儿子的肩膀。这是个保护的动作，我知道阿里对哈桑的保护是在抵御什么人的伤害。阿里朝我瞟来，带着冷冷的、不可谅解的眼神，我明白哈桑告诉他了。他把一切都告诉他了，关于阿塞夫和他的朋友对他所做的事情，关于那只风筝，关于我。奇怪的是，我很高兴终于有人识破我的真面目，我装得太累了。

"我不在乎那些钱或者那个手表。"爸爸说，他手掌朝上，张开双臂，"我不知道你为什么这样做……你说'不可能'是什么意思？"

"很抱歉，老爷。可是我们的行李已经收拾好了，我们已经决定了。"

爸爸站起身来，悲伤的神情溢于言表："阿里，我给你的还不够多吗？我对你和哈桑不好吗？我没有兄弟，你就是我的兄弟，阿里，你知道的。请别这样做。"

"我们已经很为难了，别让事情变得更难，老爷。"阿里说。他嘴巴抽搐，我看见了他痛楚的表情，正是那个时候，我才明白自己引起的痛苦有多深，才明白我给大家带来的悲伤有多浓，才明白甚至连阿里那张麻痹的脸也无法掩饰他的哀愁。我强迫自己看看哈桑，但他低着头，肩膀松垮，手指缠绕着衬衫下摆一根松开的线。

现在爸爸哀求着："告诉我为什么，我得知道！"

阿里没有告诉爸爸，一如哈桑承认偷窃，没有丝毫抗辩。我永远不会知道那究竟是为什么，但我能够想象，他们两个在那间昏暗的斗室里面，抹泪哭泣，哈桑求他别揭发我。但我想象不出，是什么样的自制力才会让阿里缄口不言。

"你可以送我们去汽车站吗？"

"我不许你这么做！"爸爸大喊，"你听到了吗？我不许你这么做！"

"尊敬的老爷，你不能禁止我任何事情了，"阿里说，"我们不再为你工作了。"

"你们要去哪儿？"爸爸问，他的声音颤抖着。

"哈扎拉贾特。"

"去你表亲家？"

"是的，你可以送我们去汽车站吗，老爷？"

接着我看到爸爸做了我之前从未见过的事情：号啕大哭。见到大人哭泣，我被吓了一跳。我从未想到爸爸也会哭。"求求你。"爸爸说。可是阿里已经走到门口，哈桑跟在他后面。我永远不会忘记爸爸说出那话的神情，那哀求中透露的痛苦，还有恐惧。

喀布尔的夏天罕得下雨，天空一碧如洗，阳光像烙铁般灼痛后颈。整个春天我和哈桑在溪流打水漂，到了夏天它们也干涸了。三轮摩托车嗒嗒走过，扬起阵阵灰尘。午间祈祷时分，人们到清真寺去行十次"晌礼"，跟着随便找个阴凉的地方躲进去，等待傍晚的凉意。夏天意味着漫长的学校生活，坐在密不透风的拥挤教室里面，浑身大汗地学着背诵《古兰经》的经文，和那些饶舌而奇怪的阿拉伯单词作斗争；夏天意味着听毛拉念念有词，用手掌拍死苍蝇；意味着一阵和风吹过，带来操场那边厕所的粪便气味，在那形影相吊的歪斜篮球架旁边吹起尘雾。

但爸爸送阿里和哈桑去车站那天下午，天下雨了。雷轰电闪，天空灰沉沉的。顷刻之间，大雨倾盆而至，哗哗的雨声在我耳边回荡。

爸爸本来要亲自送他们到巴米扬，但阿里拒绝了。隔着我的卧房那扇被雨水湿透的模糊窗户，我看见阿里拖着个孤零零的箱子，里面装着他们全副身家，走向爸爸停在大门外的轿车。哈桑的毯子紧紧卷起来，用绳子系住，背在他身后。他把所有的玩具都留在那间四壁萧然的斗室了，隔天我发现它们堆在屋角，如同我房间里面的生日礼物。

雨珠刷刷流下我的窗户。我看见爸爸将后备厢的门摔上。他浑身湿透，走向驾驶座那边，斜倚着身子，向后座的阿里说些什么，也许是作最后的努力，以便让他回心转意。他们那样交谈了片刻，爸爸身上湿淋淋的，弯下腰，一只手放在轿车的顶篷上。但当他站起身来，我从他松垮的肩膀看出，我与生俱来的那种熟悉的生活已经一去不返了。爸爸上车，车前灯亮起，在雨水中照出两道灯光。如果这是哈桑跟我过去常看的印度电影，在这个时候，我应该跑出去，赤裸的双脚溅起雨水。我应该追逐着轿车，高声叫喊，让它停下来。我应该把哈桑从后座拉出来，告诉他我很抱歉，非常抱歉，我的眼泪会跟雨水混在一起。我们会在如注大雨中拥抱。可这不是印度电影。我很抱歉，但我不会哭喊，不会追逐那辆轿车。我看着爸爸的轿车驶离路边，带走那个人，那个平生说出的第一个字是我名字的人。我最后一次模糊地瞥见哈桑，他瘫坐在后座，接着爸爸转过街角，那个我们曾无数次玩弹珠的地方。

我退后，眼里只见到玻璃窗外的雨水，看上去好像熔化的白银。

第十章

1981 年 3 月

　　有个年轻的妇女坐在我们对面。她穿着一身橄榄绿服装，黑色的披肩将面部包得严严实实，以抵御深夜的寒意。每逢卡车急刹或颠簸过路面的凹陷，她就会出声祈祷，每次汽车的高低起伏总伴随着她的"奉安拉之名"。她的丈夫身材矮壮，穿着破旧的裤子、天蓝色的长袍，一手抱着婴儿，空出来的那只手用拇指转动着念珠。他嘴唇开合，默默祈祷。同行的还有其他人，总共十来个，包括爸爸跟我，行李箱放在我们两腿之间，盘膝坐在被帆布包起来的后斗上，跟这些陌生人挤在一起，搭乘这辆破旧的俄国卡车。

　　我们凌晨两点离开喀布尔，自那时起我的内脏就已经翻江倒海。虽然爸爸没有说什么，但我知道在他眼里，晕车是孱弱无能的表现——这可以从他的脸色看出来，有好几次，我的胃收缩得厉害，忍不住呻吟，他的表情很尴尬。那个拿着念珠的矮壮男人——在祈祷的那个妇女的丈夫——问我是不是要吐了，我说可能是。爸爸把头别开。那男人掀起帆布的一角，敲敲驾驶室的窗门，要求司机停下来。司机卡林是个黑瘦的汉子，一张老鹰般的脸上留着小胡子，他摇摇头。

"我们离喀布尔太近了，"他大喊，"让他撑住。"

爸爸低声咕哝了几句。我想告诉他我很抱歉，但刹那间我满嘴唾液，喉底尝到胆汁的苦味。我转过身，揭起帆布，在行进的卡车一边呕吐起来。在我身后，爸爸正向其他乘客赔不是，仿佛晕车是犯罪，仿佛人们到了十八岁就不应该晕车。我又吐了两次，卡林这才同意停车，大部分原因还是因为担心我弄脏他的车，他赖以谋生的工具。卡林是个蛇头，从被俄国人占领的喀布尔，将人们偷偷运到相对安全的巴基斯坦，这在当时可是日进斗金的生意。他把我们载往喀布尔西南 170 公里外的贾拉拉巴德，他的堂兄图尔在那边接应，负责再送逃难的人一程，他有一辆更大的卡车，会载着我们通过开伯尔山口 [1]，去往白沙瓦 [2]。

卡林把车停在路旁，这时我们在玛希帕瀑布以西数公里的地方。玛希帕——它的意思是"飞翔的鱼儿"——是一处山峰，壁立千仞，俯览着下面 1967 年德国人为阿富汗援建的水电站。数不清有多少次，爸爸跟我路过那座山峰，前往贾拉拉巴德，那个遍地柏树和甘蔗的城市是阿富汗人过冬的胜地。

我从卡车后面跳下去，跌跌撞撞走到路边布满尘灰的护栏。我嘴里涨满了唾液，那是快要呕吐的征兆。我蹒跚着走近悬崖边，下面的深渊被黑暗吞噬了。我弯下腰，双手撑在膝盖上，做好呕吐的准备。在某个地方传来树枝噼啪作响的声音，还有猫头鹰的叫声。寒风微微拂动树枝，吹过山坡上的灌木丛。而下面，水流在山谷淌动，传来阵阵微弱的

---

[1]　Khyber Pass，阿富汗通往巴基斯坦的重要山口，长 60 公里。

[2]　Peshawar，巴基斯坦中部城市。

声音。

我站在路肩上，想起我们如何离开家园，那个我生活了一辈子的地方。仿佛我们只是外出下馆子：厨房的洗碗盆堆放着沾有肉丸夹饼残渣的盘子，盛满衣物的柳条篮子摆在门廊，被褥还没叠好，衣橱里挂着爸爸做生意穿的西装。起居室的墙上仍挂着壁毯，我妈妈的图书仍拥挤地占据着爸爸书房里的架子。我们出逃的迹象很微妙：我父母的结婚照不见了，爷爷跟纳迪尔国王站在死鹿之前合影的那张老照片杳然无踪。衣橱里少了几件衣服。五年前拉辛汗送我的那本皮面笔记本也消失了。

早晨，贾拉鲁丁——五年来的第七个仆人——兴许会以为我们出去散步或者兜风。我们没有告诉他。在喀布尔，你再不能相信任何人——为了获得悬赏或者因为受到威胁，人们彼此告密：邻居告发邻居，儿童揭发父母，兄弟陷害兄弟，仆人背叛主人，朋友出卖朋友。我想起歌手艾哈迈德·查希尔，他在我 13 岁生日那天弹奏手风琴。他和几个朋友开车去兜风，随后有人在路边发现他的尸体，有颗子弹射中他的后脑。那些人无所不在，他们将喀布尔人分成两派：告密的和没有告密的。最麻烦的是，没有人知道谁属于哪一派。裁缝给你量身时，你几句无心快语可能会让你身处波勒卡其区的黑牢。对卖肉的老板抱怨几句宵禁，你的下场很可能是在牢栏之后望着俄制步枪的枪管。甚至在吃晚饭的桌子上，在自家的屋子里，人们说话也得深思熟虑——教室里面也有这样的人，他们教小孩监视父母，该监听些什么，该向谁告发。

我三更半夜在这路边干什么呢？我应当躺在床上，盖着毯子，身旁放着一本毛边的旧书。这肯定是一场梦，肯定是。明天早晨，我会醒来，朝窗外望出去：人行道上没有那些阴沉着脸的俄国士兵在巡逻；没有坦克在我的城市里面耀武扬威，它们的炮塔活像责难的手指那样转动；没有断壁残垣，没有宵禁，没有俄国军队的运兵车在市场上迂回前进。这时，我听到爸爸和卡林在我身后讨论到了贾拉拉巴德的安排，持续了一根烟的时间。卡林一再向爸爸保证，他的兄弟有辆"很棒的、质量一流的"大卡车，到白沙瓦去可谓轻车熟路。"他闭上眼也能把你们送到那儿。"卡林说。我听见他跟爸爸说，他和他的兄弟认识把守关卡的俄国和阿富汗士兵，他们建立了一种"互惠互利"的关系。这不是梦。一架米格战斗机突然从头顶呼啸而过，仿佛在提醒这一切都是真的。卡林扔掉手里的香烟，从腰间掏出一把手枪，指向天空，做出射击的姿势，他朝那架米格吐口水，高声咒骂。

我想知道哈桑在哪里。跟着，不可避免地，我对着杂草丛吐出来，我的呕吐声和呻吟声被米格震耳欲聋的轰鸣淹没了。

过了二十分钟，我们停在玛希帕的检查站。司机没熄火，跳下车去问候走上前来的声音。鞋子踏上沙砾。短促的低声交谈。火机打火的声音。"谢谢。"有人用俄语说。

又一声打火的火机声。有人大笑，一阵令人毛骨悚然的噼啪声让我跳起来。爸爸伸手按住我的大腿。发笑的那个男人哼起歌来，带着厚厚的俄国口音，含糊走调地唱着一首古老的阿富汗婚礼歌谣：

慢慢走，我心爱的月亮，慢慢走。

鞋子踏上柏油路。有人掀开悬挂在卡车后面的帆布，探进三张脸。

一张是卡林，其他是两个士兵，一个阿富汗人，另外一个是咧嘴而笑的俄国佬，脸庞像牛头犬，嘴巴叼着香烟。在他们身后，一轮明月高悬在空中。卡林和那个阿富汗士兵用普什图语谈了几句。我听到一点——有关图尔和他的霉运。俄国士兵把头伸进卡车的后斗，他哼着那首婚礼歌谣，手指敲打着卡车的后挡板。虽然月色昏暗，我还是能看到他的炯炯目光，扫视过一个又一个的乘客。尽管天气寒冷，他的额头仍有汗珠渗出。他的眼光落在那个戴着黑色披肩的妇女身上，他眼睛死死盯着她，朝卡林说了几句俄语。卡林用俄语简略地回答。那士兵听了之后转过身，更简略地咆哮了一下。阿富汗士兵也开口说话，声音低沉，晓之以理。但俄国士兵高声说了几句，他们两个畏缩了。我能感到身旁的爸爸变得紧张起来。卡林假咳几声，低下脑袋，他说俄国士兵想与那位女士单独在卡车后面相处半个钟头。

那年轻的妇女拉下披肩，盖住脸，泪如泉涌。她丈夫膝盖上那个婴孩也哭喊起来。那个丈夫的脸色变得跟天上的月亮一样苍白，他跟卡林说，求求那个"士兵老爷"发发善心，也许他也有姐妹，也有母亲，也许他还有妻子。俄国佬听卡林说完，连珠炮般叫嚣了几句。

"这是他放我们通过的代价。"卡林说，他不敢正视那丈夫的眼光。

"但我们已经付出可观的报酬，他得到了一大笔钱。"丈夫说。

卡林跟俄国士兵交谈。"他说……他说任何代价都有一点附加税费。"

那当头，爸爸站起身。这回轮到我用手按住他的大腿了，可是爸爸将其抹开，拔起腿来，他站立的身影挡住了月光。"我要你跟这个家伙说几句，"爸爸说，他在跟卡林说话，但眼睛直望着那个俄国兵，"你问他的羞耻到哪里去了。"

他们交谈。"他说这是战争。战争无所谓羞耻。"

"跟他说他错了。战争不会使高尚的情操消失，人们甚至比和平时期更需要它。"

你每次都得充好汉不可吗？我想，心怦怦跳。你就不能忍哪怕一次吗？但我知道他不会——忍气吞声不是他的本性。问题是，他的本性正要送我们上西天。

俄国兵对卡林说了什么，嘴角露出一丝邪笑。"老爷，"卡林说，"这些俄国佬跟我们不同，他们不懂得尊重、荣誉是什么。"

"他说什么？"

"他说在你脑袋射颗子弹一定很爽，就像……"卡林说不下去，但朝那个被士兵看中的女人努努嘴。那士兵弹掉手里还没吸完的香烟，取下他的手枪。看来爸爸要死在这里了，我想，事情就会这么发生。在我的脑海里，我念了一段从课堂上学来的祷文。

"告诉他，我就算中了一千颗子弹，也不会让这龌龊下流的事情发生。"爸爸说。我的心思一闪，回到六年前那个冬天。我，在小巷的拐角处窥视。卡莫和瓦里把哈桑按在地上，阿塞夫臀部的肌肉收紧放松，他的屁股前后晃动。我算哪门子英雄？只担心风筝。有时我也怀疑自己究竟是不是爸爸的亲生儿子。

脸庞像牛头犬的俄国兵举起他的枪。

"爸爸，坐下吧，求求你，"我说，拉着他的衣袖，"他真的会朝你开枪。"

爸爸将我的手打开。"我什么也没教过你吗？"他生气地说，转向那个一脸坏笑的士兵，"告诉他最好一枪就把我打死，因为如果我没有倒下，我会把他撕成碎片。操他妈的。"

听完翻译，俄国兵狞笑依然。他打开保险栓，将枪口对准爸爸的胸膛。我的心快要跳出喉咙，用双手把脸掩住。

枪声响起。

完了，完了。我十八岁，孤身一人，在这世上举目无亲。爸爸死了，我得埋葬他。把他埋在哪里呢？埋完之后我该去哪里呢？

但我睁开眼睛，看到爸爸仍站着，脑里这些盘旋的念头停止了。我看见又一个俄国兵，还有其他人。他的枪口朝天，冒出一阵烟雾。那个要射杀爸爸的士兵已经把他的武器收好，立正敬礼。我从未像此刻一样，又想笑又想哭。

第二个俄国军官头发灰白，身材魁梧，用一口破法尔西语对我们说话。他为他手下的所作所为道歉，"俄国送他们来这里为战斗，"他说，"但他们只是孩子，一来到这里，他们就迷上了毒品。"他恨恨地望着那个年轻的士兵，如同严父被儿子的行为不端激怒。"这个家伙现在药性发作。我会试试阻止他……"他挥手让我们离开。

顷刻之后，我们的车开走了。我听到一声大笑，跟着传来第一个士兵的声音，含混而走调地唱着那古老的婚礼歌谣。

我们在路上默默行进了十五分钟，那年轻妇女的丈夫突然站起来，做了一件在他之前我曾见到很多人做过的事情：他亲了爸爸的手。

图尔的霉运。在玛希帕那边，我不是从短暂的交谈中听到过这句话吗?

大约在太阳上山之前一个钟头，我们驶进了贾拉拉巴德。卡林匆匆将我们从卡车领进一座房子。那是单层的平房，位于两条土路的交叉处，路的两边是平房，还有没开门的商店，种着合欢树。我们拖着行李走进屋子里头，我拉起衣领，以抵御严寒。不知道为什么，我记得有萝卜的味道。

我们刚进入那间昏暗且一无所有的房间，卡林就把前门锁上，拉上那代替窗帘的破布。跟着他深深吸了一口气，告诉我们坏消息。他的兄弟图尔没法送我们去白沙瓦。上个星期，他那卡车的发动机坏了，图尔还在等零件。

"上星期?"有人叫道，"要是你知道这事情，为什么还把我们带到这里来?"

我用眼角的余光瞥见一阵急遽的动作。随后有个模糊的身影穿过房间，接下来我看到的事情是，卡林猛然撞在墙上，爸爸的双手掐住他的脖子。

"我来告诉你们为什么，"爸爸愤怒地说，"因为他要赚这一程的车费，他只在乎这个。"卡林发出哽咽的声音，唾液从嘴角流出来。

"把他放下来，老爷，你会杀了他的。"有个乘客说。

"我正要这么做。"爸爸说。这个屋子里面其他人所不知道的是，爸爸并非在开玩笑。卡林脸色涨红，双脚乱踢。爸爸仍掐着他，直到那个年轻的妈妈，被俄国兵看中的那个，求他放手。

爸爸终于放手，卡林瘫倒在地板上，翻滚喘气，房间安静下来。不到两个钟头之前，为了一个素昧平生的女子的清白，爸爸甘愿吃一颗子

弹。而如今，若非同一个女人的求情，他会毫不犹豫地将一个汉子
掐死。

隔壁传来一阵敲打的声音。不，不是隔壁，是地下。

"那是什么？"有人问。

"其他人，"卡林呼吸艰难地喘息着，"在地下室。"

"他们等多久了？"爸爸说，眼睛盯着卡林。

"两个星期。"

"我记得你说过那辆卡车是上星期坏的。"

卡林揉揉脖子，"应该是再上一个星期的事情。"

"多久？"

"什么？"

"要过多久零件才会到？"爸爸咆哮了。卡林身子一缩，但哑口无
言。我很高兴身边漆黑一片，我可不想看到爸爸杀气腾腾的凶相。

卡林打开门，门后是通往地下室的破楼梯，一股像霉菌的潮湿臭味
扑鼻而来。我们一个个下去，楼梯被爸爸压得吱嘎作响。站在寒冷的地
下室里面，我感到黑暗中有很多双一眨一眨的眼睛在看着我们。我看见
房间到处有人蜷缩着，两盏昏暗的煤油灯将他们的身影投射在墙上。地
下室的人窃窃私语，除此之外，不知道从什么地方传来滴水的声音，还
有刮擦声。

爸爸在我身后叹了口气，把行李包扔下。

卡林告诉我们，应该再过几天，卡车就可以修好了。那时我们便可
前往白沙瓦，奔上那通往自由和安全的旅途。

接下来那个星期，地下室就是我们的家；到了第三晚，我发现了刮擦声的来源：老鼠。

待得眼睛适应了黑暗，我数出地下室里面约莫有三十个难民。我们肩挨着肩，倚墙而坐，吃着饼干、面包，配以椰枣和苹果。第一天夜里，所有的男人在一起礼拜，当中有个问爸爸为什么不加入，"真主会拯救我们所有人，你怎么不向他祈祷呢？"

爸爸重重哼了一声，伸伸他的双腿。"能够救我们的是八个汽缸和一个好的化油器。"这句话让其他人说不出话来，再也不提真主的事。

第一天夜里稍晚的时候，我发现卡莫和他父亲藏身在我们这群人之间。看到卡莫坐在地下室里面，距我只有数尺之遥，这太让我吃惊了。但当他和他的父亲走到我们这边来的时候，我看见了卡莫的脸，真的看见了……

他枯萎了——显然没有其他词可以代替这个。他双眼空洞地看着我，丝毫没有认出我。他耷拉着肩膀，脸颊凹陷，似乎已经厌倦了附在下面的骨头上。他的父亲在喀布尔有座电影院，正在跟爸爸诉苦，三个月前，他的妻子在寺里，被一颗流弹击中，当场毙命。然后他跟爸爸说起卡莫，我零星听到一点：不该让他一个人去的……你知道，他那么俊美……他们有四个人……他试图反抗……真主……血从那儿流下来……他的裤子……不再说话……目光痴呆……

我们在地下室与老鼠做伴一个星期之后，卡林说没有卡车了，卡车没法修。

"还有另外的选择。"卡林说，在一片哀叹之中，他提高了声音。他的堂兄有辆油罐车，曾经用它偷运过几次旅客。它就在这里，在贾拉拉巴德，也许可以装下我们所有人。

除了一对老年夫妻，其他人都决定上路。

那晚我们离开，爸爸和我，卡莫和他的父亲，还有其他人。卡林和他的堂兄阿吉兹，一个方脸秃顶的汉子，帮助我们进入油罐。汽车发动了，停在那里，我们挨个爬上油罐车的后踏板，爬上后面那条梯子，滑进油罐。我记得爸爸爬到一半，从梯子一跃而下，从口袋里掏出烟盒。他把盒子清空，从土路中央抓起一把灰泥。他亲吻泥土，把它放进盒子，把盒子放进胸前的口袋，贴着他的心。

惊惶。

你张开嘴巴，张得大大的，连腭骨都咯咯作响。你下令自己的肺吸进空气，如今，你需要空气，现在就要。但是你肺里的气道不听使唤，它们坍塌，收紧，压缩，突然之间，你只能用一根吸管呼吸。你的嘴巴闭上，嘴唇抿紧，你所能做的，只是发出一阵窒息的咳嗽。你双手抽搐，晃动。身体里似乎某个地方有座水坝决堤，冰冷的汗水汹涌而出，浸湿你的身体。你想哭喊。如果你能，一定喊出声来。可是你必须吸气才能哭喊。

惊惶。

地下室已经够暗了，油罐更是不见天日。我右看，左看，上看，下看，伸手在眼前挥动，可是什么也见不到。我眨眼，再眨眼，不见五指。空气不对劲，它太厚重了，几乎是固态的。空气不应该是固态的。我很想伸出手，把空气捏成碎片，把它们塞进我的气管。还有汽油的味道，油气刺痛我的眼睛，好像有人拉开我的眼皮，拿个柠檬在上面摩擦。每次呼吸都让我的鼻子火辣辣的。我会死在这样的地方，我想。尖叫就要来了，来了，来了……

接着出现了小小的神迹。爸爸卷起我的衣袖，有个东西在黑暗中发出绿光。光芒！爸爸送的手表。我的眼睛盯着那萤绿的指针。我害怕会失去它们，我不敢眨眼。

慢慢地，我对周边的景况有所知觉。我听到呻吟声，还有礼拜声。我听到一个婴儿哭喊，母亲在低声安抚。有人作呕，有人咒骂俄国佬。卡车左右摇晃，上下颠簸。大家的头撞上金属板。

"想着一些美好的事情，"爸爸在我耳边说，"快乐的事情。"

美好的事情，快乐的事情。我放任自己思绪翻飞，浮现出来的是：

星期五下午，在帕格曼。一片开阔的草地，上面有繁花满枝头的桑葚树。哈桑和我坐在浅及脚踝的野草上，我拉着线，卷轴在哈桑长满老茧的手里滚动，我们的眼睛望着天空中的风筝。我们默默无声，但并非因为我们无话可说，而是因为我们之间无需交谈——那些自出世就认识、喝着同样奶水长大的人就是这样。和风拂过草丛，哈桑放着线。风筝旋转，降下，又稳定了。我们的影子双双在波动的草丛上跳舞。草地那端，越过那低矮的砖墙，某个地方传来谈话声、笑声，和泉水的潺潺声。还有音乐，古老而熟悉的曲调，我想那是雷巴布琴[1]演奏的《莫拉曲》。墙那边有人喊我们的名字，说到时间喝茶吃点心了。

我不记得那是何年何月的事情。我只知道记忆与我同在，将美好的

---

[1] Rubab，阿富汗民族乐器。

往事完美地浓缩起来，如同一笔浓墨重彩，涂抹在我们那已经变得灰白单调的生活画布上。

剩下的路程只在脑海里留下零零碎碎、时隐时现的记忆，多数跟声音和味道有关：米格战斗机在头顶轰鸣；断断续续的枪声；旁边有驴子昂昂叫；一阵铃铛的声音和羊群的咩咩叫，车轮压上沙砾的响声；黑暗中婴孩的哭号；汽油、呕吐物和粪便的臭味。

接下来我还记得的，是爬出油罐之后清早耀眼的光线。我记得自己抬脸向天，眯着眼睛，大口呼吸，仿佛世间的空气即将用完。我躺在泥土路一边，下面是怪石嶙峋的坑壑，我望着清晨灰蒙蒙的天空，为空气感恩，为光芒感恩，为仍活着感恩。

"我们在巴基斯坦，阿米尔。"爸爸说，他站在我身边，"卡林说他会唤来巴士，把我们送到白沙瓦。"

我翻过身，仍趴在冰冷的泥土上，看到爸爸脚下两边放着我们的行李箱。从他双腿间的三角形望去，我看到油罐车停在路边，其他逃难的人正从后面的梯子下来。更远处，大地在灰蒙的天空下宛如铅板，土路伸延而去，消失在一排碗状的山丘之后。有座小小的村落沿着马路，悬挂在向阳的山坡上。

我把眼光转回我们的行李箱，它们让我替爸爸感到难过。在他打造、谋划、奋斗、烦恼、梦想了一切之后，他的生命只剩下这么点东西：一个不争气的儿子和两个手提箱。

有人在哭喊。不，不是哭喊，是哀号。我看到旅客围成一团，听到他们焦急的声音。有人说了一个字："油气。"有人也说了。哀号变成撕心裂肺的惨叫。

爸爸跟我匆忙走到那堆围观者身边，推开他们，走上前去。卡莫的父亲盘腿坐在围观的人群中间，身体前后摇晃，亲吻着他儿子死灰的脸。

"他没气了！我的儿子没气了！"他哭喊着。卡莫毫无生气的身体躺在他父亲的膝盖上，他的右手软软垂着，随着他父亲的哭泣来回抖动。"我的孩子！他没气了！安拉，帮帮他，让他活过来！"

爸爸在他身边跪下，伸手搅住他的肩膀。但卡莫的父亲把他推开，冲向跟他堂兄站在旁边的卡林。接着发生的事情太快、太短，甚至不能称之为扭打。卡林吃惊地大叫，朝后退去。我看见一只手挥舞，一只脚踢出。过了一会儿，卡莫的父亲手里拿着卡林的手枪站着。

"别杀我！"卡林哭喊。

但我们所有人还来不及说什么或者做什么，卡莫的父亲将枪口伸进自己的嘴里。我永远不会忘记那声回荡的枪响，不会忘记那一道闪光和溅出的血红。

我又弯下腰，在路边干呕。

第十一章

爸爸爱美国的理想。

正是在美国生活，让他得了溃疡。

我记得我们两个走过几条街道，在弗里蒙特的伊丽莎白湖公园散步，看着男孩练习挥棒，女孩在游戏场的秋千上咯咯娇笑。爸爸会利用步行的机会，长篇大论对我灌输他的政治观点。"这个世界上只有三个真正的男人，阿米尔，"他说，他伸出手指数着，"美国这个鲁莽的救世主，英国，还有以色列。剩下那些……"通常他会挥挥手，发出不屑的声音，"他们都像是饶舌的老太婆。"

他关于以色列的说法惹恼了弗里蒙特的阿富汗人，他们指责他亲近犹太人，而这实际上就是反对伊斯兰。爸爸跟他们聚会，喝茶，吃点心，用他的政治观念将他们气疯。"他们所不明白的是，"后来他告诉我，"那跟宗教毫无关系。"在爸爸眼里，以色列是"真正的男人"居住的岛屿，虽然处在阿拉伯海洋的包围之下，可是阿拉伯人只顾着出卖石油赚钱，毫不关心自家人的事情。"以色列干这个，以色列干那个，"爸爸会模仿阿拉伯人的语气说，"那做些事情啊！行动啊！你们这些阿拉伯人，那么去帮巴勒斯坦啊！"

他讨厌吉米·卡特，管他叫"大牙齿的蠢货"。早在 1980 年，我们还在喀布尔，美国宣布抵制在莫斯科举办的奥运会。"哇！哇！"爸爸充满厌恶地说，"勃列日涅夫入侵阿富汗，那个捏软柿子的家伙居然只说我不去你家的泳池游泳。"爸爸认为卡特不知不觉间为共产主义做的要比勃列日涅夫多。"他不配掌管这个国家。这好像让一个连自行车都不会骑的小孩去驾驶一辆崭新的凯迪拉克。"美国，乃至世界需要的是一个强硬的汉子，一个会被看得起、会采取行动而非一筹莫展的人。罗纳德·里根就是这样的硬汉。当里根在电视现身，将俄国称为"邪恶帝国"，爸爸跑出去，买回一张照片：总统微笑着竖起拇指。他把照片裱起来，挂在入门的墙上，将它钉在一张黑白的老照片右边，在那张照片里面，他系着领带，跟查希尔国王握手。我们在弗里蒙特的邻居多数是巴士司机、警察、加油站工人、靠救济金生活的未婚妈妈，确切地说，全都是被里根的经济政策压得喘不过气来的蓝领工人。爸爸是我们那栋楼唯一的共和党员。

但交通的浓雾刺痛他的眼睛，汽车的声响害他头痛，还有，花粉也让他咳嗽。水果永远不够甜，水永远不够干净，所有的树林和原野到哪里去了？开头两年，我试着让爸爸参加英语培训班的课程，提高他那口破英语，但他对此不屑一顾。"也许我会把'cat'拼出来，然后老师会奖给我一颗闪闪发光的星星，那么我就可以跑回家，拿着它向你炫耀了。"他会这么咕哝。

1983 年春季的某个星期天，我走进一家出售平装旧书的小店，旁边是家印度电影院，往东是美国国家铁路和弗里蒙特大道交界的地方。

我跟爸爸说等我五分钟，他耸耸肩。他当时在弗里蒙特某个加油站上班，那天休假。我看到他横跨弗里蒙特大道，走进一家杂货便利店，店主是一对年老的越南夫妻，阮先生和他的太太。他们白发苍苍，待人友善，太太得了帕金森症，先生则换过髋骨。"他现在看起来像《无敌金刚》了。"她总是这么笑着对我说，张开没有牙齿的嘴巴。"记得《无敌金刚》吗，阿米尔？"接着阮先生会学着李·梅杰斯，怒眉倒竖，以缓慢的动作假装正在跑步。

我正在翻阅一本破旧的麦克·汉默[1]悬疑小说，这当头传来一声尖叫，还有玻璃碎裂的声音。我放下书，匆匆穿过马路。我发现阮先生夫妇在柜台后面，脸如死灰，紧贴墙壁，阮先生双手抱着他的太太。地板上散落着橙子，翻倒的杂志架，一个装牛肉干的破罐子，爸爸脚下还有玻璃的碎片。

原来爸爸买了橙子，身上却没有现金。他给阮先生开了支票，阮先生想看看他的身份证。"他想看我的证件，"爸爸用法尔西语咆哮，"快两年了，我在这里买这些该死的水果，把钱放进他的口袋，这个狗杂碎居然要看我的证件！"

"爸爸，这又不是针对你。"我说，朝阮氏夫妇挤出微笑，"他们理应查看证件的。"

"我不欢迎你在这里，"阮先生说，站在他妻子身前，他用拐杖指着爸爸，然后转向我，"你是个很好的年轻人，但是你爸爸，他是个疯子。

---

[1] Mike Hammer，美国作家迈克·斯毕兰（Mickey Spillane，1918~2006）创作的系列恐怖小说主角。

这里再也不欢迎他。"

"他以为我是小偷吗？"爸爸抬高了声音说，外面围满了旁观的人，"这是个什么国家？没有人相信任何人！"

"我叫警察。"阮太太说，她探出脸来，"你走开，要不我喊警察。"

"求求你，阮太太，别叫警察。我把他带回家，请别叫警察，好不好？求求你。"

"好的，你带他回家，好主意。"阮先生说。他戴着金丝眼镜，眼睛一直望着爸爸。我隔着门去拉爸爸，他出来的时候踢飞一本杂志。我说服他别再走进去，然后转身到店里向阮氏夫妇道歉，告诉他们爸爸处境艰难。我把家里的电话和地址给了阮太太，告诉她估计一下损失了多少东西。"算好之后请打电话给我，我会赔偿一切的，阮太太，我很抱歉。"阮太太从我手里接过纸片，点点头。我看到她的手比平时抖得更厉害，那让我很生爸爸的气，他把一个老太太吓成这样。

"我爸爸仍在适应美国的生活。"我解释着说。

我想告诉他们，在喀布尔，我们折断树枝，拿它当信用卡。哈桑和我会拿着那根木头到烤馕店去。店主用刀在木头上刻痕，划下一道，表示他从火焰升腾的烤炉取给我们一个馕饼。每到月底，爸爸按照树枝上的刻痕付钱给他。就是这样。没有问题，不用身份证。

但我没告诉他们。我谢谢阮先生没叫警察，带爸爸回家。我炖鸡脖子饭的时候，他在阳台抽烟生闷气。我们自白沙瓦踏上波音飞机，到如今已经一年半了，爸爸仍在适应期。

那晚我们默默吃饭。爸爸吃了两口，把盘子推开。

我的眼光越过桌子，望着他，他的指甲开裂，被机油弄得脏兮兮的，他的手指刮伤了，衣服散发出加油站的味道——尘灰、汗水和汽油。爸爸像个再婚的鳏夫，可是总忍不住想起故去的妻子。他怀念贾拉拉巴德的甘蔗地，还有帕格曼的花园。他怀念那些在他屋里进进出出的人，怀念索尔市集拥挤的通道，他走在那里，和他打招呼的人认得他，认得他的父亲，认得他的祖父，那些跟他同一个祖宗的人，他们的过去交织在一起。

对我来说，美国是个埋葬往事的地方。

对爸爸来说，这是个哀悼过去的地方。

"也许我们应该回到白沙瓦。"我说，盯着在玻璃杯里面的水上浮动的冰块。我们在那里度过了半年的光阴，等待移民局核发签证。我们那间满是尘灰的房子散发出脏袜子和猫粪的气味，但住在我们周围的全是熟人——至少爸爸认得他们。他会邀请整条走廊的邻居到家里吃晚饭，他们中多数都是等待签证的阿富汗人。当然，有人会带来手鼓，也有人带手风琴。茶泡好了，嗓子还可以的人会高歌一曲，直到太阳升起，直到蚊子不再嗡嗡叫，直到鼓掌的手都酸了。

"你在那边更开心，爸爸，那儿更有家的感觉。"我说。

"白沙瓦对我来说是好地方，但对你来说不是。"

"你在这儿工作太辛苦了。"

"现在还好啦。"他说，他的意思是自升任加油站日班经理之后。但在天气潮湿的日子，我总能见到他忍痛揉着手腕。也见过他在饭后，头冒冷汗去拿止痛药瓶子的模样。"再说，我又不是为了自己才让我们两个来到这里的，你知道吗？"

我把手伸过桌子，握住他的手。我的是学生哥儿的手，干净柔软；

他的是劳动者的手，肮脏且长满老茧。我想起在喀布尔时，他给我买的所有那些卡车、火车玩具，还有那些自行车。如今，美国是爸爸送给阿米尔的最后一件礼物。

我们到美国仅一个月之后，爸爸在华盛顿大道找到工作，在一个阿富汗熟人开的加油站当助理——他从我们到美国那天就开始找工作了。每周六天，每天轮班十二小时，爸爸给汽车加油、收银、换油、擦洗挡风玻璃。有好几次，我带午饭给他吃，发现他正在货架上找香烟，油污斑斑的柜台那端，有个顾客在等着，在明亮的荧光映衬下，爸爸的脸扭曲而苍白。每次我走进去，门上的电铃会"叮咚叮咚"响，爸爸会抬起头，招招手，露出微笑，他的双眼因为疲累而流泪。

被聘请那天，爸爸和我到圣何塞[1]去找我们的移民资格审核官杜宾斯太太。她是个很胖的黑人妇女，眼睛明亮，笑起来露出两个酒窝。有一回她跟我说她在教堂唱歌，我相信——她的声音让我想起热牛奶和蜂蜜。爸爸将一叠食物券放在她的柜台上。"谢谢你，可是我不想要。"爸爸说，"我一直有工作。在阿富汗，我有工作；在美国，我有工作。非常感谢，杜宾斯太太，可是我不喜欢接受施舍。"

杜宾斯太太眨眨眼，把食物券捡起来，看看我，又看看爸爸，好像我们在开她玩笑，或者像哈桑经常说的"耍她一下"。"我干这行十五年了，从来没人这么做过。"她说。就是这样，爸爸结束了在收银台用食物券支付的屈辱日子，也消除了他最担心的事情之一：被阿富汗人看到他用救济金买食物。爸爸走出福利办公室时，好像大病初愈。

---

[1] San Jose，美国加利福尼亚州城市。

1983 年那个夏天，我 20 岁，高中毕业。那天在橄榄球场上掷帽子的人中，要数我最老了。我记得球场上满是蓝色袍子，学生的家人、闪光的镜头，把爸爸淹没了。我在二十码线附近找到他，双手插袋，相机在胸前晃荡。我们之间隔着一群人，一会儿把他挡住，一会儿他又出现。穿蓝色衣服的女生尖叫着，相互拥抱，哭泣；男生和他们的父亲拍掌庆贺。爸爸的胡子变灰了，鬓边的头发也减少了，还有，难道他在喀布尔更高？他穿着那身棕色西装——他只有这么一套，穿着它参加阿富汗人的婚礼和葬礼——系着他五十岁生日时我送的红色领带。接着他看到我，挥挥手，微笑。他示意我戴上方帽子，以学校的钟楼为背景，替我拍了张照片。我朝他微笑着——在某种意义上，那日子与其说是我的，毋宁说是他的。他朝我走来，伸手揽住我的脖子，亲吻了我的额头。"我很骄傲，阿米尔。"他说。他说话的时候眼睛闪亮，那样的眼光望着的是我，让我很高兴。

那晚，他带我到海沃德[1]的阿富汗餐厅，点了太多的食物。他跟店主说，他的儿子秋天就要上大学了。毕业之前，我就上大学的事情跟他稍稍争论过，告诉他我想工作，补贴家用，存些钱，也许次年才上大学。但他恨铁不成钢地盯了我一眼，我只好闭嘴。

晚饭后，爸爸带我去饭店对面的酒吧。那地方光线阴暗，墙壁上散发着我素来不喜欢的啤酒酸味。男人们头戴棒球帽，身穿无袖上衣，玩着撞球，绿色的桌子上烟雾升腾，袅袅绕着荧光灯。爸爸穿着棕色西装，我穿着休闲长裤和运动外套，显得格外引人注目。我们在吧台找到

---

[1] Hayward，美国加利福尼亚州城市，近弗里蒙特。

位子，坐在一个老人身边。老人头上有个麦克罗啤酒的商标，发出蓝光，将他那张沧桑的脸照得病恹恹的。爸爸点了根香烟，给我们要了啤酒。"今晚我太高兴了！"他自顾自地向每个人宣布，"今晚我带我的儿子来喝酒。来，请给我的朋友来一杯。"他的手拍在那个老人背上。老头抬抬帽子，露出微笑，他没有上排的牙齿。

爸爸三口就喝完了他的啤酒，又要了一杯。我强迫自己，还没喝完四分之一，他已经干掉三杯了。他请那个老头一杯苏格兰烈酒，还请那四个打撞球的家伙一大罐百威。人们同他握手，用力拍他的后背。他们向他敬酒，有人给他点烟。爸爸松了松领带，给那个老人一把二毛五分的硬币，指指电唱机。"告诉他，来几首他最拿手的。"他对我说。老人点点头，向爸爸敬礼。不久就响起乡村音乐，就像这样，爸爸开始宴会了。

酒到酣处，爸爸站起来，举起酒杯，将它摔在遍地锯屑的地板，高声喊叫。"操他妈的俄国佬！"酒吧里爆发出一阵笑声，大家高声附和，爸爸又给每个人买啤酒。

我们离开的时候，大家都舍不得他走。喀布尔，白沙瓦，海沃德。爸爸还是爸爸，我想，微笑着。

我开着爸爸那辆土黄色的旧别克世纪轿车，驶回我们家。爸爸在路上睡着了，鼾声如电钻。我在他身上闻到烟草的味道，还有酒精味，甜蜜而辛辣。但我在停车的时候，他醒过来，嘶哑的嗓音说："继续开，到街道那边去。"

"干吗，爸爸？"

"只管开过去，"他让我停在街道的南端。他把手伸进外衣的口袋，掏给我一串钥匙，"那边。"他指着停在我们前面的一辆轿车。那是一辆旧款的福特，又长又宽，车身很暗，在月光下我辨认不出是什么颜色。"它得烤漆，我会让加油站的伙计换上新的避震器，但它还能开。"

我看着钥匙，惊呆了。我看看他，看看轿车。

"你上大学需要一辆车。"他说。

我捧起他的手，紧紧握住。泪水从我眼里涌出来，我庆幸阴影笼罩了我们的面庞。"谢谢你，爸爸。"

我们下车，坐进福特车。那是一辆"大都灵"。"海军蓝。"爸爸说。我绕着街区开，试试刹车、收音机、转向灯。我把它停在我们那栋楼的停车场，熄了引擎。"谢谢你，亲爱的爸爸。"我说。我意犹未尽，想告诉他，他慈祥的行为让我多么感动，我多么感激他过去和现在为我所做的一切。但我知道那会让他不好意思，"谢谢。"我只是重复了一次。

他微微一笑，靠在头枕上，他的前额几乎碰到顶篷。我们什么也没说，静静坐在黑暗中，听着引擎冷却的"嘀嘀"声，远处传来一阵警笛的鸣叫。然后爸爸将头转向我，"要是哈桑今天跟我们在一起就好了。"

听到哈桑的名字，我的脖子好像被一对铁手掐住了。我把车窗摇下，等待那双铁手松开。

毕业典礼隔日，我告诉爸爸，秋天我就要去专科学校注册了。他正在喝冷却的红茶，嚼着豆蔻子，他自己用来治头痛的偏方。

"我想我会主修英文。"我说，内心忐忑，等着他的回答。

"英文？"

"创作。"

他想了想，啜他的红茶，"故事，你是说，你要写故事？"我低头看着自己的双脚。

"写故事能赚钱吗？"

"如果你写得好，"我说，"而且又被人发掘的话。"

"被人发掘？机会有多大？"

"有机会的。"我说。

他点点头。"那你在写得好和被人发掘之前准备干什么呢？你怎么赚钱？要是结婚了，你怎么撑起自己的家庭？"

我不敢看着他的眼睛，"我会……找份工作。"

"哦！"他说，"哇！哇！这么说，如果我没理解错，你将会花好几年，拿个学位，然后你会找一份像我这样卑微的工作，一份你今天可以轻易找到的工作，就为渺茫的机会，等待你拿的学位也许某天会帮助你……被人发掘。"他深深呼吸，啜他的红茶，咕哝地说着什么医学院、法学院，还有"真正的工作"。

我脸上发烧，一阵罪恶感涌上心头。我很负疚，我的放纵是他的溃疡、黑指甲和酸痛的手腕换来的。但我会坚持自己的立场，我决定了。我不想再为爸爸牺牲了。这是最后一次了，我咒骂自己。

爸爸叹气，这一次，扔了一大把豆蔻子到嘴里。

有时，我会开着我的福特，摇下车窗，一连开几个钟头，从东湾到南湾，前往半岛区，[1]然后开回来。我会驶过弗里蒙特附近那些纵横交

---

[1]　东湾（East Bay）、南湾（South Bay）和半岛区（Penisula）是加州湾区不同区域。

错、棋盘似的街道，这里的人们没有和国王握过手，住在破旧的平房里面，窗户破损；这里的旧车跟我的一样，滴着油，停在柏油路上。我们附近那些院子都被铅灰色的铁丝栅栏围起来，乱糟糟的草坪上到处扔着玩具、汽车内胎、标签剥落的啤酒瓶子。我驶过散发着树皮味道的林荫公园，驶过巨大的购物广场，它们大得足以同时举办五场马上比武竞赛。我开着这辆都灵，越过罗斯·阿托斯的山丘，滑行过一片住宅区，那儿的房子有景观窗，银色的狮子守护在锻铁大门之外，塑有天使雕像的喷泉在修葺完善的人行道排开，停车道上没有福特都灵。这里的房子使我爸爸在喀布尔的房子看起来像仆人住的。

有时候，在星期六我会早起，朝南开上17号高速公路，沿着蜿蜒的山路前往圣克鲁斯。我会在旧灯塔旁边停车，等待太阳升起，坐在我的轿车里面，看着雾气在海面翻滚。在阿富汗，我只在电影里面见过海洋。在黑暗中，挨哈桑坐着，我总是寻思，我在书上看到，说海水闻起来有盐的味道，那是不是真的？我常常告诉哈桑，有朝一日，我们会沿着海藻丛生的海滩散步，让我们的脚陷进沙里，看着海水从我们的脚趾退去。第一次看到太平洋时，我差点哭起来。它那么大，那么蓝，跟我孩提时在电影银幕上看到的一模一样。

有时候，夜幕初降，我会把车停好，爬上横跨高速公路的天桥。我的脸压着护栏，极目远望，数着那缓缓移动的闪闪发亮的汽车尾灯，宝马，绅宝，保时捷，那些我在喀布尔从来没见过的汽车，在那儿，人们开着俄国产的伏尔加，破旧的欧宝，或者伊朗出产的培康。

我们来到美国几乎快两年了，我仍为这个国家辽阔的幅员惊叹不已。高速公路之外，还有高速公路，城市之外还有城市，山脉之外还有峰峦，峰峦之外还有山脉，而所有这些之外，还有更多的城市，更多的人群。

早在俄国佬的军队入侵阿富汗之前，早在乡村被烧焚、学校被毁坏之前，早在地雷像死亡的种子那样遍布、儿童被草草掩埋之前，对我来说，喀布尔就已成了一座鬼魂之城，一座兔唇的鬼魂萦绕之城。

美国就不同了。美国是河流，奔腾前进，往事无人提起。我可以蹚进这条大川，让自己的罪恶沉在最深处，让流水把我带往远方，带往没有鬼魂、没有往事、没有罪恶的远方。

就算不为别的，单单为了这个，我也会拥抱美国。

接下来那个夏天，也就是 1984 年夏天——那年夏天我满 21 岁——爸爸卖掉他的别克，花了 550 美元，买了一辆破旧的 1971 年出厂的大众巴士，车主是阿富汗的老熟人了，先前在喀布尔教高中的科学课程。那天下午，巴士轰鸣着驶进街道，"突突"前往我们的停车场，邻居都把头转过来。爸爸熄了火，让巴士安静地滑进我们的停车位。我们坐在座椅上，哈哈大笑，直到眼泪从脸颊掉下来，还有，更重要的是，直到我们确信没有任何邻居在观望，这才走出来。那辆巴士是一堆废铁的尸体，黑色的垃圾袋填补破裂的车窗，光秃秃的轮胎，弹簧从座椅下面露出来。但那位老教师一再向爸爸保证，引擎和变速器都没有问题，实际上，那个家伙没有说谎。

每逢星期六，天一亮爸爸就喊我起来。他穿衣的时候，我浏览本地报纸的分类广告栏，圈出车库卖场的广告。我们设定线路——先到弗里蒙特、尤宁城、纽瓦克和海沃德，接着是圣何塞、米尔皮塔斯、桑尼维尔，如果时间许可，则再去坎贝尔。爸爸开着巴士，喝着保温杯里面的热红茶，我负责引路。我们停在车库卖场，买下那些原主不再需要的二手货。我们搜罗旧缝纫机，独眼的芭比娃娃，木制的网球拍，缺弦的吉他，还有旧伊莱克斯吸尘器。下午过了一半，我们的大众巴士后面就会塞满这些旧货。然后，星期天清早，我们开车到圣何塞巴利雅沙跳蚤市场，租个档位，加点微薄的利润把这些垃圾卖出去：我们前一天花二毛五分买来的芝加哥唱片也许可以卖到每盘一元，或者五盘四元；一台花十元买来的破旧辛格牌缝纫机经过一番讨价还价，也许可以卖出二十五元。

到得那个夏天，阿富汗人已经在圣何塞跳蚤市场占据了一整个区域。二手货区域的通道上播放着阿富汗音乐。在跳蚤市场的阿富汗人中间，有一套心照不宣的行为规范：你要跟通道对面的家伙打招呼，请他吃一块土豆饼或一点什锦饭，你要跟他交谈。要是他家死了父母，你就好言相劝；要是生了孩子你就道声恭喜；当话题不可避免地转到阿富汗人和俄国佬，你就悲伤地摇摇头。但是你得避免说起星期六的事情，因为对面那人很可能就是昨天在高速公路出口被你超车挡住、以致错过一桩好买卖的家伙。

在那些通道里，唯一比茶更流行的是阿富汗人的流言。跳蚤市场是这样的地方，你可以喝绿茶，吃杏仁饼，听人说谁家女儿背弃婚约，跟美国男友私奔去了，她男友以前在喀布尔是个"旗帜派"党员；谁用黑钱买了座房子，却还领救济金。茶，政治，丑闻，这些都是跳蚤市场的阿富汗星期天必备的成分。

有时我会看管摊位，爸爸则沿着过道闲逛。他双手庄重地放在胸前，跟那些在喀布尔认识的熟人打招呼：机械师和裁缝兜售有擦痕的自行车头盔和旧羊毛衫，过道两边是原来的外交官、找不到工作的外科医生和大学教授。

1984 年 7 月某个星期天清早，爸爸在清理摊位，我到贩卖处买了两杯咖啡，回来的时候，发现爸爸在跟一位上了年纪、相貌出众的先生说话。我把杯子放在巴士后面的保险杠上，紧邻里根和布什竞选 1984 年总统的宣传画。

"阿米尔，"爸爸说，示意我过去，"这是将军大人，伊克伯·塔赫里先生，原来住在喀布尔，得过军功勋章，在国防部上班。"

塔赫里。这个名字怎么如此熟悉？

将军哈哈干笑，通常在宴会上，每当重要人物说了不好笑的笑话，人们就会听到这样的笑声。他一头银发整齐地梳向后面，露出平滑的黄铜色前额，浓密的眉毛中有撮撮白色。他身上闻起来有古龙水的香味，穿着铁灰色的三排扣套装，因为洗熨了太多次而泛着亮光，背心上面露出一根怀表的金链子。

"这样的介绍可不敢当。"他说，他的声音低沉而有教养。"你好，我的孩子。"

"你好，将军大人。"我说，跟他握手。他的手貌似瘦弱，但握得很有力，好像那油亮的皮肤下面藏着钢条。

"阿米尔将会成为一个了不起的作家。"爸爸说。我愣了一下才反应过来。"他刚念完大学一年级，考试门门都得优。"

"是专科学校。"我纠正他。

"安拉保佑。"塔赫里将军说，"你会写我们国家的故事吗，也许可以写写历史？经济？"

"我写小说。"我说着想起了自己写在拉辛汗送的皮面笔记本里面那十来个故事，奇怪自己为什么在这个人面前突然有些不自在。

"啊，讲故事的。"将军说，"很好，人们在如今这样的艰苦岁月需要故事来分散注意力。"他把手伸在爸爸的肩膀上，转向我。"说到故事，有一年夏天，你爸爸跟我到贾拉拉巴德去猎野鸡，"他说，"那次真叫人称奇。如果我没记错，你爸爸打猎跟他做生意一样，都是一把好手。"

爸爸正在用鞋尖踢着摆在我们的帆布上的一把木制网球拍。"有些生意而已。"

塔赫里将军露出一丝礼貌而哀伤的微笑，叹了口气，轻轻拍拍爸爸的肩膀。"生活总会继续。"他把眼光投向我，"我们阿富汗人总是喜欢夸大其词，孩子，我听过无数人愚蠢地使用'了不起'这个词。但是，你的爸爸属于少数几个配得上这个形容词的人。"这番短短的话在我听来，跟他的衣服如出一辙：用的场合太多了，闪亮得有些造作。

"你在奉承我。"爸爸说。

"我没有。"将军说，他侧过头，把手放在胸前表示尊敬，"男孩和女孩得知道他们父亲的优点。"他转向我，"你崇敬你的爸爸吗，我的孩子？你真的崇敬他吗？"

"当然，将军大人，我崇敬他。"我说，要是他别叫我"我的孩子"就好了。

"那么，恭喜你，你已经快要长成一位男子汉了。"他说，口气没有半点幽默，没有讽刺，只有不卑不亢的恭维。

"亲爱的爸爸，你忘了你的茶。"一个年轻女子的声音。她站在我们后面，是个身材苗条的美人，天鹅绒般的黑发，手里拿着一个打开的保温杯和一个塑料杯。我眨眨眼，心跳加快。她的眉毛又黑又浓，中间连在一起，宛如飞翔的鸟儿张开的双翅，笔挺的鼻子很优雅，活像古代波斯公主——也许像拓敏妮，《列王纪》书中罗斯坦的妻子，索拉博的妈妈。她那长长睫毛下面胡桃色的眼睛跟我对望了一会儿，移开了视线。

"你真乖，我亲爱的。"塔赫里将军说，从她手里接过杯子。在她转身离去之前，我见到她光滑的皮肤上有个镰状的棕色胎记，就在左边下巴上。她走过两条通道，把保温杯放在一辆货车里面。她跪在装着唱片和平装书的盒子中间，秀发倾泻在一旁。

"我的女儿，亲爱的索拉雅。"塔赫里将军说。他深深吸了一口气，看来想换个话题了，他掏出金怀表，看了看时间。"好啦，到时间了，我得去整理整理。"他和爸爸相互亲吻脸颊，用双手跟我握别。"祝你写作顺利。"他盯着我的眼睛说，浅蓝色的双眼没有透露出半点他心里的想法。

在那天剩下的时间里，我总忍不住望向那辆灰色的货车。

在我们回家的路上，我想起来了。塔赫里，我知道我以前听过这个名字。

"是不是有过关于塔赫里将军女儿的流言蜚语啊？"我假装漫不经心地问爸爸。

"你知道我的，"爸爸说，他开着巴士，在跳蚤市场出口长长的车队中缓慢前进，"每当人们说三道四我都会走开。"

"可是有过，是吗？"我说。

"你为什么要问呢？"他犹疑地看着我。

我耸耸肩，挤出微笑："好奇而已，爸爸。"

"真的吗？真是这样吗？"他说，眼光露出一丝狡狯，看着我的眼睛，"你该不是对她有意思了吧？"

我把眼光移开，"拜托，老爸。"

他微微一笑，驱车离开跳蚤市场。我们朝 680 号公路前进。有那么一会儿，我们并没有说话。"我所听到的是她有过一个男人，而且事情……不是太好。"他神情严肃地说，好像跟我说她得了乳癌一样。

"哦。"

"我听说她是个淑女，工作卖力，待人也不错。但自那以后，再也没有媒人敲响将军的家门。"爸爸叹气，"这也许不公平，但几天内发生的事情，有时甚至是一天内发生的事情，也足以改变一生，阿米尔。"

那晚我辗转反侧，老想着索拉雅·塔赫里的镰状胎记，想着她那优雅的笔挺鼻子，想着她明亮的眼睛跟我对望的情景。我的思绪在她身上迟疑不肯离去。索拉雅·塔赫里，我的跳蚤市场公主。

第十二章

在阿富汗，雅尔达是教历中嘉帝月的第一夜，也是冬天的第一夜，一年之中最长的夜晚。按照风俗，哈桑和我会熬到深夜，我们把脚藏在火炉桌下面，阿里将苹果皮丢进炉子，给我们讲苏丹和小偷的古老传说，度过漫漫长夜。正是从阿里口中，我得知了雅尔达的故事，知道了飞蛾扑火是因为着魔，还知道狼群爬山是要寻找太阳。阿里发誓说，要是在雅尔达那夜吃到西瓜，翌年夏天就不会口渴。

稍大一些之后，我从诗书中读到，雅尔达是星光黯淡的夜晚，恋人彻夜难眠，忍受着无边黑暗，等待太阳升起，带来他们的爱人。遇到索拉雅之后那个星期，对我来说，每个夜晚都是雅尔达。等到星期天早晨来临，我从床上起来，索拉雅·塔赫里的脸庞和那双棕色的明眸已然在我脑里。坐在爸爸的巴士里面，我暗暗数着路程，直到看见她赤足坐着，摆弄那些装着发黄的百科全书的纸箱，她的脚踝在柏油路的映衬下分外白皙，柔美的手腕上有银环叮当作响。一头秀发从她背后甩过，像天鹅绒幕布那样垂下来，我望着她的头发投射在地上的影子怔怔出神。索拉雅，我的交易会公主，我的雅尔达的朝阳。

我制造各种各样的借口——爸爸显然知道，但只露出戏谑的微笑——沿着那条过道走下去，经过塔赫里的摊位。我会朝将军招招手，而他，永远穿着那身熨得发亮的灰色套装，会挥手应答。有时他从那张导演椅站起来，我们会稍作交谈，提及我的写作、战争、当天的交易。而我不得不管住自己的眼睛别偷看，别总是瞟向坐在那里读一本平装书的索拉雅。将军和我会彼此告别，而我走开的时候，得强打精神，掩饰自己心中的失望。

有时将军到其他过道去跟人攀交情，留她一人看守摊位，我会走过去，假装不认识她，可是心里想认识她想得要死。有时陪着她的还有个矮胖的中年妇女，染红发，肤色苍白。我暗下决心，在夏天结束之前一定要跟她搭讪，但学校开学了，叶子变红、变黄、掉落，冬天的雨水纷纷洒洒，折磨爸爸的手腕，树枝上吐出新芽，而我依然没有勇气、没有胆量，甚至不敢直望她的眼睛。

春季学期在 1985 年 5 月底结束。我所有的课程都得了优，这可是个小小的神迹，因为我人在课堂，心里却总是想着索拉雅柔美而笔挺的鼻子。

然后，某个闷热的夏季星期天，爸爸跟我在跳蚤市场，坐在我们的摊位，用报纸往脸上扇风。尽管阳光像烙铁那样火辣辣，那天市场人满为患，销售相当可观——才到 12 点半，我们已经赚了 160 美元。我站起来，伸伸懒腰，问爸爸要不要来杯可口可乐。他说来一杯。

"当心点，阿米尔。"我举步离开时他说。

"当心什么，爸爸？"

"我不是蠢货，少跟我装蒜。"

"我不知道你在说什么啊。"

"你要记住,"爸爸指着我说,"那家伙是个纯正的普什图人,他有名誉和尊严。"这是普什图人的信条,尤其是关系到妻子或者女儿的贞节时。

"我不过是去给我们买饮料。"

"别让我难看,我就这点要求。"

"我不会的,天啦,爸爸。"

爸爸点了根烟,继续扇着风。

起初我朝贩卖处走去,然后在卖衬衫的摊位左转。在那儿,你只消花五块钱,便可以在白色的尼龙衬衫上印上耶稣、猫王或者吉姆·莫里森的头像,或者三个一起印。马里亚奇[1]的音乐在头顶回响,我闻到腌黄瓜和烤肉的味道。

我看见塔赫里灰色的货车,和我们的车隔着两排,紧挨着一个卖芒果串的小摊。她单身一人,在看书,今天穿着长及脚踝的白色夏装,凉鞋露出脚趾,头发朝后扎,梳成郁金香形状的发髻。我打算跟以前一样只是走过,我以为可以做到,可是突然之间,我发现自己站在塔赫里的白色桌布边上,越过烫发用的铁发夹和旧领带,盯着索拉雅。她抬头。

"你好,"我说,"打扰了,对不起。我不是故意打扰你的。"

"你好。"

"将军大人今天不在吗?"我说。我的耳朵发烧,无法正视她的

---

[1] Mariachi,墨西哥传统音乐乐团,主要使用乐器有小号、曼陀铃、吉他、竖琴以及小提琴等,所演唱歌曲风格通常较为热烈。

明眸。

"他去那边了。"她说，指着右边，绿色镶银的手镯滑落至她的胳膊肘。

"你可不可以跟他说，我路过这里，问候他一下。"我说。

"可以。"

"谢谢你。"我说，"哦，我的名字叫阿米尔。这次你需要知道，才好跟他说。说我路过这里，向他……问好。"

"好的。"

我挪了挪脚，清清喉咙，"我要走了，很抱歉打扰到你。"

"没有，你没有。"她说。

"哦，那就好。"我点点头，给她一个勉强的微笑。"我要走了。"好像我已经说过了吧？"再见。"

"再见。"

我举步离开。停下，转身。趁着勇气还没有消失，我赶忙说："我可以知道你在看什么书吗？"

她眨眨眼。

我屏住呼吸。刹那间，我觉得跳蚤市场里面所有的眼睛都朝我们看来。我猜想四周似乎突然寂静下来，话说到一半戛然而止。人们转过头，饶有兴致地眯起眼睛。

这是怎么回事？

直到那时，我们的邂逅可以解释成礼节性的问候，一个男人问起另外一个男人。但我问了她问题，如果她回答，我们将会……这么说吧，我们将会聊天。我，一个单身的青年男子，而她是个未婚的少女。

她有过一段历史，这就够了。我们正徘徊在风言风语的危险边缘，毒舌会说长道短，而承受流言毒害的将会是她，不是我——我十分清楚阿富汗人的双重标准，身为男性，我占尽便宜。不是"你没见到他找她聊天吗？"而是"哇，你没看到她舍不得他离开吗？多么不知道廉耻啊！"

按照阿富汗人的标准，我的问题很唐突。问出这句话，意味着我无所遮掩，对她的兴趣再也毋庸置疑。但我是个男人，我所冒的风险，顶多是尊严受伤罢了，受伤了会痊愈，可是名誉毁了不再有清白。她会接受我的挑战吗？

她翻过书，让封面对着我。《呼啸山庄》。"你看过吗？"她说。

我点点头。我感到自己的心怦怦跳。"那是个悲伤的故事。"

"好书总是跟悲伤的故事有关。"她说。

"确实这样。"

"听说你写作？"

她怎么知道？我寻思是不是她父亲说的，也许她曾问过他。我立即打消了这两个荒谬的念头。父亲跟儿子可以随心所欲地谈论妇女。但不会有阿富汗女子——至少是有教养的阿富汗淑女——向她父亲问起青年男子。而且，没有父亲，特别是一个有名誉和尊严的普什图男人，会跟自己的女儿谈论未婚少男，除非这个家伙是求爱者，已经做足体面的礼节，请他父亲前来提亲。

难以置信的是，我听见自己说："你愿意看看我写的故事吗？"

"我愿意。"她说。现在我从她的神情感觉她有些不安，她的眼睛开始东瞟西看，也许是看看将军来了没有。我怀疑，要是让他看到我跟他女儿交谈了这么久，他会有什么反应呢？

"也许改天我会带给你，"我说。我还想说些什么，那个我曾见到跟索拉雅在一起的女人走进过道。她提着塑料袋，里面装满水果。她看到我们，滴溜溜的眼珠看着我和索拉雅，微笑起来。

"亲爱的阿米尔，见到你真高兴。"她说，把袋子放在桌布上。她的额头泛出丝丝汗珠，一头红发看上去像头盔，在阳光下闪闪发亮——在她头发稀疏的地方露出点点头皮。她有双绿色的小眼睛，埋藏在那圆得像卷心菜的脸蛋上，牙齿镶金，短短的手指活像香肠。她胸前挂着一条金色安拉项链，链子在她皮肤的褶皱和脖子的肥肉间忽隐忽现。"我叫雅米拉，亲爱的索拉雅的妈妈。"

"你好，亲爱的阿姨。"我说，有些尴尬，我经常身处阿富汗人之间，他们认得我是什么人，我却不知道对方姓甚名谁。

"你爸爸还好吗？"她说。

"他很好，谢谢。"

"你认识你的爷爷伽兹老爷吗？他是个法官。喏，他的叔叔跟我爷爷是表亲。"她说，"所以你看，我们还是亲戚呢。"她微笑着露出一口金牙，我注意到她右边的嘴角有点下垂。她的眼睛又在我和索拉雅之间转起来。

有一次，我问爸爸，为什么塔赫里将军的女儿还没有嫁出去。"没有追求者，"爸爸说，"没有门当户对的追求者。"他补充说。但他再也不说了——爸爸知道这种致命的闲言碎语会给少女未来的婚姻造成什么样的影响。阿富汗男人，尤其是出身名门望族的那些人，都是见风使舵的家伙。这儿几句闲话，那儿数声诋毁，他们就会像惊鸟般落荒而逃。所以不断有婚礼举行，可是没人给索拉雅唱"慢慢走"，没有人在她手掌涂指甲花，没有人把《古兰经》摆放在她头巾上，每个婚礼上，陪着她跳舞的，总是塔赫里将军。

而如今，这个妇女，这个母亲，带着令人心碎的渴望，讨好微笑，对眼中的希望不加掩饰。我对自己所处的有利地位感到畏怯，而这全都因为，我赢得了那场决定我性别的基因博彩。

我从来没能看穿将军的双眸，但我从他妻子眼里懂得的可就多了：如果我在这件事情上——不管这件事情是什么——会遇到对手，那绝对不是她。

"请坐，亲爱的阿米尔。"她说，"索拉雅，给他一张椅子，我的孩子。洗几个桃子，它们又甜又多汁。"

"不用了，谢谢。"我说，"我得回去了，爸爸在等我。"

"哦？"塔赫里太太说，显然，她被我礼貌的婉拒她的得体举止打动了。"那么，给你，至少带上这个。"她抓起一把猕猴桃，还有几个桃子，放进纸袋，坚持要我收下。"替我问候你爸爸，常来看看我们。"

"我会的，谢谢你，亲爱的阿姨。"我说，我用眼角的余光看到索拉雅正望着别处。

"我还以为你去买可乐了呢。"爸爸说，从我手里接过那袋桃子。他看着我，神情既严肃，又戏谑。我开始找说词，但他咬了一口桃子，挥挥手："别费劲了，阿米尔。只要记得我说的就行。"

那天夜晚，躺在床上，我想着闪烁的阳光在索拉雅眼里舞动的样子，想着她锁骨上方那美丽的凹陷。我在脑里一遍又一遍回放着我们的对话。她说的是"我听说你是个作家"还是"我听说你写作"？是哪句呢？我捂紧被子，盯着天花板，痛苦地想起，要度过连续六个漫漫的雅尔达之夜，我才能再次见到她。

好几个星期都是如此这般。我等到将军散步离开，然后走过塔赫里的货摊。如果塔赫里太太在，她会请我喝茶、吃饼干，我们会谈起旧时在喀布尔的光景，那些我们认识的人，还有她的关节炎。她显然注意到我总是在她丈夫离开的时候出现，但她从不揭穿。"哦，你家叔叔刚刚才走开。"她会说。我真的喜欢塔赫里太太在那儿，并且不仅是由于她和善的态度，还因为有她母亲在场，索拉雅会变得更放松、更健谈。何况她在也让我们之间的交往显得正常——虽然不能跟塔赫里将军在场相提并论。有了塔赫里太太的监护，我们的约会就算不能杜绝风言风语，至少也可以少招惹一些。不过她对我套近乎的态度明显让索拉雅觉得尴尬。

某天，索拉雅跟我单独在他们的货摊上交谈。她正告诉我学校里的事情，她如何努力学习她的通选课程，她在弗里蒙特的"奥龙专科学校"就读。

"你打算主修什么呢？"

"我想当老师。"她说。

"真的吗？为什么？"

"这是我一直梦想的。我们在弗吉尼亚生活的时候，我获得了英语培训证书，现在我每周有一个晚上到公共图书馆教书。我妈妈过去也是教师，她在喀布尔的高级中学教女生法尔西语和历史。"

一个大腹便便的男人头戴猎帽，出价三块钱，想买一组五块钱的烛架，索拉雅卖给他。她把钱丢进脚下那个小小的糖果罐，羞涩地望着我。"我想给您讲个故事，"她说，"可是我有点难为情。"

"讲来听听。"

"它有点傻。"

"告诉我吧。"

她笑起来，"好吧，在喀布尔，我四年级的时候，我爸爸请了个打理家务的佣人，叫兹芭。她有个姐妹在伊朗的马夏德。因为兹芭不识字，每隔不久，她就会求我给她姐妹写信。每当她姐妹回信，我会念给兹芭听。有一天，我问她想不想读书识字。她给我一个大大的微笑，双眼放光，说她很想很想。所以，我完成自己的作业之后，我们就坐在厨房的桌子边，我教她认字母。我记得有时候，我作业做到一半，抬起头，发现兹芭在厨房里，搅搅高压锅里面的牛肉，然后坐下，用铅笔做我前一天夜里给她布置的字母表作业。

"反正不到一年，兹芭能读儿童书了。我们坐在院子里，她给我念达拉和沙拉的故事——念得很慢，不过全对。她开始管我叫'索拉雅老师'。"她又笑起来，"我知道这听起来很孩子气，但当兹芭第一次自己写信，我就知道自己除了教书，别的什么都不想做。我为她骄傲，觉得自己做了些真正有价值的事情。您说呢？"

"是的。"我说谎。我想起自己如何愚弄不识字的哈桑，如何用他不懂的晦涩字眼取笑他。

"我爸爸希望我去念法学院，我妈妈总是暗示我选择医学院。但我想要成为教师。虽然在这里收入不高，但那是我想要的。"

"我妈妈也是教师。"我说。

"我知道,"她说,"我妈妈跟我说过。"接着因为这句话,她脸上泛起红晕。她的答案暗示着,我不在的时候,她们曾经"谈起阿米尔"。我费了好大劲才忍住让自己不发笑。

"我给你带了些东西,"我从后裤兜掏出一卷订好的纸张,"实现诺言。"我递给她一篇自己写的小故事。

"哦,你还记得。"她说,笑逐颜开,"谢谢你!"我没有时间体会她第一次用"你"而非用较正式的"您"称呼我到底意味着什么,因为突然间她的笑容消失了,脸上的红晕退去,眼睛盯着我身后。我转过身,跟塔赫里将军面对面站着。

"亲爱的阿米尔,抱负远大的说故事的人,很高兴见到你。"他说,挂着淡淡的微笑。

"你好,将军大人。"我嗫嚅着说。

他从我身旁走过,迈向货摊。"今天天气很好,是吗?"他说,拇指搭在他那件背心的上袋,另一只手伸向索拉雅。她把纸卷给了他。

"他们说整个星期都会下雨呢。很难相信吧,是吗?"他把那卷纸张丢进垃圾桶。转向我,轻轻地把手放在我的肩膀上,我们并排走了几步。

"你知道,我的孩子,我相当喜欢你。你是个有教养的孩子,我真的这么认为,但是……"他叹了口气,挥挥手,"……即使有教养的男孩有时也需要提醒。所以,我有责任提醒你,你是在跳蚤市场的众目睽睽之下做事情。"他停住,他那不露喜怒的眸子直盯着我双眼,"你知道,这里每个人都会讲故事。"他微笑,露出一口整整齐齐的牙齿,"替我向你爸爸问好，亲爱的阿米尔。"

他把手放下，又露出微笑。

"怎么回事？"爸爸说，接过一个老妇人买木马的钱。

"没事。"我说。我坐在一台旧电视机上。不过还是告诉他了。

"唉，阿米尔。"他叹气。

结果，刚才发生的事情没有让我烦恼太久。

因为那个星期稍晚一些时候，爸爸感冒了。

开始只是有点咳嗽和流鼻涕。他的流鼻涕痊愈了，可是咳嗽还是没好。他会咳在手帕上，把它藏在口袋里。我不停地求他去检查，但他会挥手叫我走开。他讨厌大夫和医院。就我所知，爸爸唯一去医院那次，是在印度染上疟疾。

然后，过了两个星期，我撞见他正把一口带血丝的痰咳到马桶里面去。

"你这样多久了？"我说。

"晚饭吃什么？"他说。

"我要带你去看大夫。"

虽说爸爸已经是加油站的经理，但老板却没有给他提供医疗保险，而爸爸满不在乎，没有坚持。于是我带他去圣何塞的县立医院。有个面带菜色、双眼浮肿的大夫接待了我们，自我介绍说是第二年的住院医师。"他看起来比你还年轻，但比我病得还重。"爸爸咕哝说。那住院医师让我们下楼去做胸部 X 光扫描。护士喊我们进去的时候，医师正在填一张表。

"把这张表带到前台。"他说，匆匆写着。

"那是什么？"我问。

"转诊介绍。"他写啊写。

"干吗用？"

"给肺科。"

"那是什么？"

他瞥了我一眼，推了推眼镜，又开始写起来。"他肺部的右边有个黑点，我想让他们复查一下。"

"黑点？"我说，房间突然之间变得太小了。

"癌症吗？"爸爸若无其事地加上一句。

"也许是，总之很可疑。"医生咕哝道。

"你可以多告诉我们一些吗？"我问。

"没办法，需要先去做 CAT 扫描，然后去看肺科医生。"他把转诊单递给我。"你说过你爸爸吸烟，对吧？"

"是的。"

他点点头，眼光又看看我，看看爸爸，又收回来。"两个星期之内，他们会给你打电话。"

我想质问他，带着"可疑"这个词，我怎么撑过这两个星期？我怎么能够吃饭、工作、学习？他怎么可以用这个词打发我回家？

我接过那张表格，交了上去。那晚，我等到爸爸入睡，然后叠起一条毛毯，把它当成礼拜用的褥子。我把头磕在地面，暗暗念诵那些记不太清楚的《古兰经》——在喀布尔的时候毛拉要求我们背诵的经文——

求求真主大发善心，虽则我不知道他是否存在。那时我很羡慕那个毛拉，羡慕他的信仰和坚定。

两个星期过去了，我们没有接到电话。我打电话过去，他们告诉我说找不到那张转诊单，问我究竟有没有把它交上去。他们说再过三个星期，会打电话来。我勃然作色，经过一番交涉，把三个星期改为一个星期内做 CAT，两个星期内看医生。

接诊的肺科医师叫施内德，开头一切都好，直到爸爸问他从哪里来，他说俄国。爸爸当场翻脸。

"对不起，大夫。"我说，将爸爸拉到一旁。施内德大夫微笑着站起来，手里还拿着听诊器。

"爸爸，我在候诊室看过施内德大夫的简历。他的出生地是密歇根，密歇根！他是美国人，远比你和我更美国。"

"我不在乎他在哪儿出生，他是俄国佬。"爸爸说，做出扭曲的表情，仿佛那是个肮脏的字眼。"他的父母是俄国佬，他的祖父母是俄国佬。我当着你妈妈的面发誓，要是他胆敢再碰我一下，我就扭断他的手。"

"施内德大夫的父母从俄国逃亡出来，你懂吗？他们逃亡！"

但爸爸一点都没听进去。有时我认为，爸爸唯一像爱他妻子那样深爱着的，是阿富汗，他的故国。我差点儿抓狂大叫，但我只是叹口气，转向施内德医师。"对不起，大夫，没有办法。"

第二个肺科医师叫阿曼尼，是伊朗人，爸爸同意了。阿曼尼大夫声音轻柔，留着弯曲的小胡子，一头银发。他告诉我们，他已经看过 CAT 扫描的结果，接下来他要做的，是进行一项叫支气管镜检查的程序，取下一片肺块做病理学分析。他安排下个星期进行。我搀扶爸爸走出诊室，向大夫道谢，心里想着如今我得带着"肺块"这个词过一整个星期了，这个字眼甚至比"可疑"更不吉利。我希望索拉雅能在这儿陪着我。

就像魔鬼一样，癌症有各种不同的名字。爸爸患的叫"燕麦细胞恶性肿瘤"。已经扩散。没法开刀。爸爸问起病况，阿曼尼大夫咬咬嘴唇，用了"严重"这个词。"当然，可以做化疗。"他说，"但那只是治标不治本。"

"那是什么意思？"爸爸问。

阿曼尼叹气说："那就是说，它无法改变结果，只能延迟它的到来。"

"这个答案清楚多了，阿曼尼大夫，谢谢你。"爸爸说，"但请不要在我身上做化疗。"他露出如释重负的神情，一如那天在杜宾斯太太的柜台上放下那叠食物券。

"可是，爸爸……"

"别在公众场合跟我顶嘴，阿米尔，永远不要。你以为你是谁？"

塔赫里将军在跳蚤市场提到的雨水姗姗来迟了几个星期，但当我们走出阿曼尼大夫的诊室，过往的车辆令地面上的积水溅上人行道。爸爸点了根烟。我们回家的路上，他一直在车里抽烟。

就在他把钥匙插进楼下大门的锁眼时，我说："我希望你能考虑一下化疗，爸爸。"

爸爸将钥匙放进口袋，把我从雨中拉进大楼破旧的雨棚之下，用拿着香烟的手戳戳我的胸膛："住口！我已经决定了。"

"那我呢，爸爸？我该怎么办？"我说，泪如泉涌。

一抹厌恶的神色掠过他那张被雨水打湿的脸。在我小时候，每逢我摔倒，擦破膝盖，放声大哭，他也会给我这种脸色。当时是因为哭泣让他厌恶，现在也是因为哭泣惹他不快。"你二十二岁了，阿米尔！一个成年人！你……"他张开嘴巴，闭上，再次张开，重新思索。在我们头顶，雨水敲打着帆布雨棚。"你会碰到什么事情，你说？这些年来，我一直试图教你的，就是让你永远别问这个问题。"

他打开门，转身对着我。"还有，别让人知道这件事情，听到没有？别让人知道。我不需要任何人的怜悯。"然后他消失在昏暗的大厅里。那天剩下的时间里，他坐在电视机前，一根接一根抽烟。我不知道他藐视的是什么，或者是谁。我？阿曼尼大夫？或者也许是他从来都不相信的真主？

有那么一阵，即使是癌症也没能阻止爸爸到跳蚤市场去。我们星期六仍搜罗各处车库卖场，爸爸当司机，我指路，并且在星期天摆摊。铜灯。棒球手套。坏了拉链的滑雪夹克。爸爸跟在那个古老的国家就认识的人互致问候，我和顾客为一两块钱讨价还价。仿佛一切如常。仿佛我成为孤儿的日子并没有随着每次收摊渐渐逼近。

塔赫里将军和他的太太有时会逛到我们这边来。将军仍是一派外交官风范，脸带微笑跟我打招呼，用双手跟我握手。但是塔赫里太太的举止显得有些冷漠，但她会趁将军不留神，偷偷低头朝我微笑，投来一丝歉意的眼光。

　　我记得那段岁月出现了很多"第一次"：我第一次听到爸爸在浴室里呻吟。第一次发现他的枕头上有血。执掌加油站三年以来，爸爸从未请过病假。又是一个第一次。

　　等到那年万圣节，星期六的下午刚过一半，爸爸就显得疲累不堪，我下车去收购那些废品时，他留在车上等待。到了感恩节，还没到中午他就吃不消了。待得雪橇在屋前草坪上出现，假雪洒在花旗松的枝丫上，爸爸待在家里，而我独自开着那辆大众巴士，穿梭在半岛地区。

　　在跳蚤市场，阿富汗人偶尔会对爸爸的消瘦议论纷纷。起初，他们阿谀奉承，问及爸爸饮食有何秘方。可是询问和奉承停止了，爸爸的体重却继续下降。磅数不断减少，再减少。他脸颊深陷，太阳穴松塌，眼睛深深凹进眼眶。

　　接着，新年之后不久，在一个寒冷的星期天早晨，爸爸在卖灯罩给一个壮硕的菲律宾人，我在大众巴士里面东翻西找，寻找一条毛毯盖住他的腿。

　　"喂，小子，这个家伙需要帮忙！"菲律宾人焦急地喊道。我转过身，发现爸爸倒在地上，四肢抽搐。

　　"救命！"我大喊，"来人啊！"我奔向爸爸。他口吐白沫，流出的泡泡浸湿了胡子。他眼珠上翻，只见一片白。

　　大家都朝我们涌过来。我听见有人说发作了，另外有人说"快打911！"，我听见一阵跑步声。人群围过来，天空变得阴暗。

　　爸爸的泡沫变红了，他在咬自己的舌头。我跪在他身旁，抓住他的手臂，说我在这里爸爸，我在这里，你会好的，我就在这里。好像如此这般，我就能减缓他的病痛，让它们不再烦我爸爸。我感到膝盖一片

潮湿。爸爸小便失禁了。嘘，亲爱的爸爸，我在这里。你的儿子就在
这里。

那个白胡子的大夫头顶油光可鉴，把我拉出病房。"我想跟你一起
看看你爸爸的 CAT 扫描。"他说。他把菲林放在走廊的灯箱上，用铅笔
带橡皮擦的那头指着爸爸的癌症所在的图片，好像警察将凶手的大头像
展示给罹难者的家属看。在那些照片上，爸爸的大脑看起来像个胡桃的
切面，点缀着几个网球状的灰色阴影。

"正如你看到的，癌症转移了。"他说，"他必须服用类固醇，以便
缩减他大脑里的肿块，还得吃抗中风的药物。我建议做放射线治疗，你
明白我意思吗？"

我说我明白。我已经熟悉癌症的相关术语了。

"那就好，"他说，看看他的寻呼机，"我得走了，不过如果你有任
何问题，可以给我打传呼。"

"谢谢你。"

那天晚上，我彻夜坐在爸爸床边的椅子上。

翌日早晨，走廊那端的候诊室挤满了阿富汗人，有纽瓦克来的屠
夫，爸爸建造恤孤院时的工程师。他们纷纷走进来，语调沉痛地向爸
爸表达他们的敬意，祝福他尽早康复。那时爸爸已经醒了，他虚弱而疲
倦，但清醒。

早晨过了一半，塔赫里将军和他太太也来了。索拉雅跟在后面，我
们对望了一眼，同时将眼光移开。"你好吗，老朋友。"塔赫里将军说，

捂着爸爸的手。

爸爸示意他看着臂上的输液管，露出孱弱的微笑。将军回以微笑。

"你们不应如此麻烦的，你们大家。"爸爸呻吟着说。

"这不麻烦。"塔赫里太太说。

"一点都不麻烦。更重要的是，你需要什么吗？"塔赫里将军说，"什么都行，请把我当成你的兄弟。"

我记得有一次爸爸跟我说起普什图人的事情。我们也许头脑顽固，我知道我们太过骄傲，可是，在危难的时刻，相信我，你会宁愿在身边的是普什图人。

爸爸在枕上摇摇头："你能到这里来已经叫我很高兴了。"将军脸现微笑，捏捏爸爸的手。"你怎么样？亲爱的阿米尔？你需要什么东西吗？"

他竟然那样看着我，眼中充满慈爱……"不，谢谢，将军大人。我……"我喉咙一哽，泪水止不住掉下来，冲出病房。

我站在走廊的灯箱边上哭泣，就在那儿，前一天晚上，我看到了凶手的真面目。

爸爸的门开了，索拉雅从他的病房走出来。她站在我身边，穿着灰色的长衫和牛仔裤。她的头发倾泻而下。我想在她怀里寻求安慰。

"我很抱歉，阿米尔。"她说，"我们大家都知道事情很糟糕，但却拿不出什么主意。"

我用衣袖擦擦眼睛："他不想让任何人知道。"

"你需要什么吗？"

"不。"我挤出微笑。她把手放在我的手上。这是我们第一次碰触。

我捧起她的手，拉到我的脸上，眼睛上，然后任她抽走。"你最好还是回到里面去，不然你爸爸会出来找的。"

她笑着点点头，"那我回去。"她转身离开。

"索拉雅？"

"怎么啦？"

"我很高兴你来了。这对我……意味着一切。"

隔了两天，他们让爸爸出院。他们请来一位放射线肿瘤学专家，游说爸爸接受放射线治疗。爸爸拒绝了。他们试图让我也加入到游说的行列中去。但我见到爸爸脸上的表情，对他们表达谢意，在他们的表格上签名，用那辆福特都灵将爸爸带回家。

那晚爸爸躺在沙发上，身上盖着一条羊毛毯。我给他端来热红茶和烤杏仁，把手伸在他背后，轻而易举地将他扶上来。他的肩侧在我手中感觉就像鸟儿的翅膀。我把毛毯拉到他的胸膛上，那儿瘦骨嶙峋，肤色很差。

"需要我为你做些什么吗，爸爸？"

"不用，我的孩子，谢谢你。"

我坐在他身旁："我想你能不能替我办点事情，如果你身体还撑得过去的话。"

"什么事？"

"我想你帮我提亲，我想你到塔赫里将军家里去，向他提亲。"

爸爸的干嘴唇绽放出微笑，宛如枯萎的树叶上的一点绿色。"你想好了吗？"

"我从来没有这么清楚过。"

"你仔细考虑了吗？"

"当然，爸爸。"

"那把电话给我，还有我那本小笔记本。"

我眨眨眼："现在？"

"不然还等什么时候？"

我微笑："好的。"我把电话给他，还有爸爸用来记录他那些阿富汗朋友的电话号码的本子。他找到塔赫里的号码。拨号。把听筒提到耳边。我的心脏在胸口怦怦跳。

"亲爱的雅米拉？晚上好。"他说，他表明身份。停下。"好多了，谢谢你。你去看望我，真是太谢谢了。"他听了一会儿，点点头，"我会记住的，谢谢。将军大人在家吗？"停下。"谢谢。"

他的眼光射向我。不知何故我直想发笑，或者尖叫。我的手握成拳头，塞在嘴里，咬着它。爸爸轻轻哼笑。

"将军大人，晚上好……是的，好多了好多了……好的……你太好了。将军大人，我打电话来，是想问，明天早上我可不可以去拜访你和塔赫里太太，有件很荣誉的事情……是的……十一点刚刚好。到时见。再见。"

他挂上电话。我们看着对方。我突然笑起来，爸爸也跟着加入。

爸爸弄湿头发，将其朝后梳。我帮他穿上干净的白衬衫，替他打好领带，发现领口的纽扣和爸爸的脖子之间多出了两英寸的空间。我在想当爸爸逝去，该留下多大的虚空。我强迫自己想别的。他没逝去，还没有，今天应该想些美好的事情。他那套棕色西装的上衣，我毕业那天他穿着那件，松松垮垮挂在他身上——爸爸消瘦得太厉害了，再也不合身了。我只好把袖子卷起来。我弯腰替他绑好鞋带。

塔赫里一家住在一座单层的平房里面，那一带是弗里蒙特知名的阿富汗人聚居地。那房子有凸窗，斜屋顶，还有个围起的门廊，我看见上面有几株天竺葵。

我扶爸爸下福特车，再溜回车里。他倚着副驾驶座的车窗："回家去吧，过一个小时我打电话给你。"

"好的，爸爸。"我说，"好运。"

他微笑。

我驱车离开。透过观后镜，爸爸正走上塔赫里家的车道，尽最后一次为人父的责任。

我在我们住所的客厅走来走去，等待爸爸的电话。客厅长15步，宽10步半。如果将军拒绝怎么办？要是他讨厌我那又如何？我不停走进厨房，查看烤炉上的时钟。

快到中午的时候电话响起。是爸爸。

"怎么样？"

"将军同意了。"

我松了一口气。坐下，双手颤抖。"他同意了？"

"是的。不过亲爱的索拉雅在阁楼她的房间里面，她想先跟你谈谈。"

"好的。"

爸爸对某个人说了几句话，接着传来两下按键声，他挂了电话。

"阿米尔？"索拉雅的声音。

"你好。"

"我爸爸同意了。"

"我知道。"我说，换手握住听筒。我在微笑。"我太高兴了，不知道说什么。"

"我也很高兴，阿米尔。我……我无法相信这是真的。"

我大笑："我知道。"

"听着，"她说，"我想告诉你一些事情。一些你必须事先知道的事情……"

"我不在乎那是什么。"

"你必须知道。我不想我们一开始就有秘密，而且我宁愿亲口告诉你。"

"如果那会让你觉得好一些，你就告诉我吧。但是它不会改变任何事情。"

电话那端沉默了好久。"我们在弗吉尼亚生活的时候，我跟一个阿富汗人私奔了。那时我十八岁……很叛逆……愚蠢……他吸毒……我们同居了将近一个月。弗吉尼亚所有的阿富汗人议论纷纷。

"最后爸爸找到我们。他站在门口……要我回家。我歇斯底里，哭喊，尖叫，说我恨他……

"不管怎样，我回家了，并且……"她在哭，"对不起。"我听见她放低话筒，擦着鼻子。"对不起，"她又开始了，声音有点嘶哑，"我回到家里，发现妈妈中风了，她右半边脸麻痹……我觉得很内疚。她本来不会这样的。

"过后不久，爸爸就举家搬到加利福尼亚来了。"跟着一阵沉默。

"你和你爸爸现在怎么样？"我说。

"我们一直有分歧，现在还有，但我很感激他那天去找我。我真的相信他救了我。"她停顿，"那么，我所说的让你为难吗？"

"有一点。"我说。这次我对她说了真话。我不能欺骗她，在听到她跟男人上床之后，说我的尊严毫发无伤是假的，毕竟我从来没把女人带上床。这让我非常为难，但在让爸爸替我求婚之前，我已经想了好几个星期。而每次到最后，总是回到同一个问题：我凭什么去指责别人的过去？

"你很为难，要改变主意吗？"

"不，索拉雅。没那么严重。"我说，"你无论说什么，都不会改变任何事情。我想娶你。"

她又哭起来。

我妒忌她。她的秘密公开了，说出来了，得到解决了。我张开嘴巴，差点告诉她，我如何背叛了哈桑，对他说谎，把他赶出家门，还毁坏了爸爸和阿里四十年的情谊。但我没有。我怀疑，在很多方面，索拉雅·塔赫里都比我好得多。勇气只是其中之一。

第十三章

隔日早晨，我们到塔赫里家里，完成"定聘"的仪式，我不得不把福特停在马路对面。他们的车道挤满了轿车。我穿着海军蓝西装，昨天我把前来提亲的爸爸接回家之后，去买了这身衣服。我对着观后镜摆了摆领带。

"你看上去很帅。"爸爸说。

"谢谢你，爸爸。你还好吗？你觉得撑得住吗？"

"撑得住？今天是我有生以来最高兴的一天，阿米尔。"他说，露出疲累的微笑。

我能听见门那边的交谈声、欢笑声，还有轻柔的阿富汗音乐——听起来像乌斯塔德·萨拉汉[1]的情歌。我按门铃。一张脸从前窗的窗帘露出来，又缩回去。"他们来了。"我听见有个女人说。交谈声戛然而止，有人关掉音乐。

---

[1] Ustad Sarahang（1924~1983），阿富汗歌星。

塔赫里太太打开门。"早上好。"她说，眼里洋溢着喜悦。我见她做了头发，穿着一件长及脚踝的黑色衣服。我跨进门廊，她眼睛湿润。"你还没进屋子我就已经哭了，亲爱的阿米尔。"她说。我在她手上吻了一下，跟爸爸前一天夜里教我那样如出一辙。

她领着我们，走过被灯光照得通明的走廊，前往客厅。我看见镶木板的墙上挂着照片，照片中的人都将成为我的亲人：年轻的塔赫里太太头发蓬松，跟将军在一起，背景是尼亚加拉大瀑布；塔赫里太太穿着无缝外套，将军穿着窄领外套，系着细领带，头发又黑又密；索拉雅正要登上过山车，挥手微笑，阳光照得她银色的牙套闪闪发亮。还有张照片是将军全套戎装，跟约旦国王侯赛因[1]握手。另一张是查希尔国王的画像。

客厅约莫有二十来个客人，坐在靠墙边的椅子上。爸爸走进去时，全部人起立。我们绕屋走着，爸爸慢慢领路，我跟在后边，和各位宾客握手问好。将军仍穿着他的灰色西装，跟爸爸拥抱，彼此轻拍对方的后背。他们用严肃的语气，相互说"你好"。

将军抱住我，心照不宣地微笑着，仿佛在说："喏，这就对了，按照阿富汗人的方式，我的孩子。"我们互相亲吻了三次脸颊。

我们坐在拥挤的房间里，爸爸和我一边，对面是塔赫里将军和他的太太。爸爸的呼吸变得有点艰难，不断擦去额头上的汗水，掏出他的手帕咳嗽。他看见我在望着他，挤出勉强的笑容。"我还好。"他低声说。

遵从传统风习，索拉雅没出场。

---

[1] Hussein bin Talal（1935~1999），1953 年至 1999 年在位。

　　大家谈了几句，就随意闲聊起来，随后将军假咳了几声。房间变得安静，每个人都低头看着自己的手，以示尊重。将军朝爸爸点点头。

　　爸爸清清喉咙。他开口说话，然而总要停下来喘气，才能把话说完整。"将军大人，亲爱的雅米拉……今天，我和我的儿子怀着敬意……到你家来。你们是……有头有面的人……出身名门望族……血统尊荣。我今天带来的，没有别的，只有无上的崇敬……献给你，你的家族，还有……对你先人的缅怀。"他歇了一会儿，等呼吸平息，擦擦额头。"亲爱的阿米尔是我唯一的儿子……唯一的儿子，他一直是我的好儿子。我希望他……不负你的慈爱。我请求你赐亲爱的阿米尔和我以荣幸……接纳我们成为你的亲人。"

　　将军礼貌地点点头。

　　"像你这样的男人的儿子成为我们的家人，我们很荣幸。"他说，"你声誉卓著，在喀布尔，我就是你谦卑的崇拜者，今天也是如此。你家和我家结成姻亲，这让我们觉得荣幸。

　　"亲爱的阿米尔，至于你，我欢迎你到我的家里来，你是我们的女婿，是我掌上明珠的丈夫。今后我们休戚与共。我希望你能够将亲爱的雅米拉和我当成你的父母，我会为你和亲爱的索拉雅祈祷，愿你们幸福。我们祝福你们俩。"

　　每个人鼓起掌来，在掌声中，人们把头转向走廊。那一刻我等待已久。

　　索拉雅在那端出现。她穿着酒红色的传统阿富汗服装，长长的袖子，配着黄金镶饰，真是惊艳夺目。爸爸紧紧抓着我的手。塔赫里太太又哭了。索拉雅慢慢地向我们走来，身后跟着一群年轻的女性亲戚。

她亲了亲爸爸的手。终于坐在我身边，眼光低垂。

掌声响起。

根据传统，索拉雅家里会举办订婚宴会，也就是所谓"食蜜"仪式。之后是订婚期，一连持续几个月。随后是婚礼，所有费用将由爸爸支付。

我们全部人都同意索拉雅和我省略掉"食蜜"仪式。原因大家都知道，虽然没人真的说出来：爸爸没几个月好活了。

在筹备婚礼期间，索拉雅和我从无独处的机会——因为我们还没有结婚，甚至连订婚都没有，那于礼不合。所以我只好满足于跟爸爸一起，到塔赫里家用晚餐。晚餐桌上，索拉雅坐在我对面。我想象着她把头放在我胸膛上，闻着她的秀发，那该是什么感觉呢？我想象着亲吻她，跟她做爱。

为了婚礼，爸爸花了三万五千美元，那几乎是他毕生的积蓄。他在弗里蒙特租了个很大的阿富汗宴会厅，老板是他在喀布尔的旧识，给了他优惠的折扣。爸爸请来了乐队，给我挑选的钻石戒指付款，给我买燕尾服，还有在誓约仪式要穿的传统绿色套装。

在为婚礼之夜所做的全部乱糟糟的准备——幸好多数由塔赫里太太和她的朋友帮忙——中，我只记得屈指可数的几件事。

我记得我们的誓约仪式。大家围着一张桌子坐下，索拉雅和我穿着绿色的衣服——伊斯兰的颜色，但也是春天和新起点的颜色。我穿着套装，索拉雅（桌子上唯一的女子）蒙着面，穿长袖衣服。爸爸、塔赫里将军（这回他穿着燕尾服），还有索拉雅几个叔伯舅舅也坐在桌子上。

索拉雅和我低着头，表情神圣而庄重，只能偷偷斜视对方。毛拉向证人提问，读起《古兰经》。我们发誓，在结婚证书上签名。索拉雅的舅舅，塔赫里太太的兄弟，来自弗吉尼亚，站起来，清清他的喉咙。索拉雅曾告诉过我，他在美国生活已经超过二十年。他在移民局工作，娶了个美国老婆。他还是个诗人，个子矮小，鸟儿似的脸庞，头发蓬松。他念了一首献给索拉雅的长诗，那是草草写在酒店的信纸上。"哇！哇！亲爱的沙利夫！"他一念完，每个人都欢呼起来。

我记得走向台上的情景，当时我穿着燕尾服，索拉雅蒙着面，穿着白色礼服，我们挽着手。爸爸紧挨着我，将军和他太太在他们的女儿那边，身后跟着一群亲戚，我们走向宴会厅。两旁是鼓掌喝彩的宾客，还有闪个不停的镜头。我和索拉雅并排站着，她的表弟，亲爱的沙利夫的儿子，在我们头上举起《古兰经》。扬声器传来婚礼歌谣，慢慢走，就是爸爸和我离开喀布尔那天晚上，玛希帕检查站那个俄国兵唱的那首。

　　将清晨化成钥匙，扔到水井去
　　慢慢走，我心爱的月亮，慢慢走
　　让朝阳忘记从东方升起
　　慢慢走，我心爱的月亮，慢慢走

我记得我们坐在沙发上，舞台上那对沙发好像王位，索拉雅拉着我的手，大约三百位客人注视着我们。我们举行另外的仪式。在那儿，人们拿给我们一面镜子，在我们头上覆上一条纱巾，留下我们两个凝望彼此在镜子中的容颜。看到镜子中索拉雅笑靥如花，我第一次低声对她说我爱她。一阵指甲花般的红晕在她脸庞绽放。

我记得各色佳肴，有烤肉，炖肉饭，野橙子饭。我看见爸爸夹在我们两个中间，坐在沙发上，面带微笑。我记得浑身大汗的男人围成一圈，跳着传统舞蹈，他们跳跃着，在手鼓热烈的节拍之下越转越快，直到有人精疲力竭，退出那个圆圈。我记得我希望拉辛汗也在。

并且，我还记得，我寻思哈桑是不是也结婚了。如果是的话，他蒙着头巾，在镜子中看到的那张脸是谁呢？他手里握着那涂了指甲花的手是谁的？

2点左右，派对从宴会厅移到爸爸的寓所。又上一轮茶，音乐响起，直到邻居叫来警察。一直到了很晚，离日出不到一个小时，才总算曲终人散，索拉雅和我第一次并排躺着。终我一生，周围环绕的都是男人。那晚，我发现了女性的温柔。

索拉雅亲自提议她搬过来，跟我和爸爸住在一起。

"我还以为你要求我们住到自己的地方去。"我说。

"扔下生病的叔叔不顾？"她回答说。她的眼睛告诉我，那并非她为人妻之道。我亲吻她："谢谢你。"

索拉雅尽心照料我的爸爸。早上，她替他准备好面包和红茶，帮助他起床。她递给他止痛药，浆洗他的衣服，每天下午给他读报纸的国际新闻报道。她做他最爱吃的菜，杂锦土豆汤，尽管他每次只喝几勺子。她还每天带着他在附近散步。等到他卧床不起，她每隔一个小时就帮他翻身，以免他得褥疮。

某天，我去药房给爸爸买吗啡回家。刚关上门，我看见索拉雅匆匆把某些东西塞到爸爸的毛毯下面。"喂，我看见了。你们两个在干什么？"我说。

"没什么。"索拉雅微笑说。

"骗人。"我掀起爸爸的毛毯。"这是什么？"我说，虽然我刚一拿起那本皮面的笔记本，心里就知道了。我的手指抚摸着那挑金线的边缘。我记得拉辛汗把它送给我那夜，我13岁生日那夜，烟花嘶嘶升空，绽放出朵朵的火焰，红的，绿的，黄的。

"我简直无法相信你会写这些东西。"索拉雅说。

爸爸艰难地从枕上抬起头："是我给她的，希望你别介意。"

我把笔记本交回给索拉雅，走出房间。爸爸不喜欢见到我哭泣。

婚礼之后一个月，塔赫里夫妇、沙利夫和他的妻子苏丝，还有索拉雅几个阿姨到我们家吃晚饭。索拉雅用白米饭、菠菜和羊肉招待客人。晚饭后，大家都喝着绿茶，四人一组打扑克牌。索拉雅和我在咖啡桌上跟沙利夫两口子对垒，旁边就是沙发，爸爸躺在上面，盖着毛毯。他看着我和沙利夫开玩笑，看着索拉雅和我勾指头，看着我帮她掠起一丝滑落的秀发。我能见到他发自内心的微笑，辽阔如同喀布尔的夜空，那些白杨树沙沙响、蟋蟀在花园啾啾叫的夜晚。

快到午夜，爸爸让我们扶他上床睡觉。索拉雅和我将他的手臂架在我们的肩膀上，我们的手搭在他背后。我们把他放低，他让索拉雅关掉床头灯，叫我们弯下身，分别亲了我们一下。

"我去给你倒杯水，带几片吗啡，亲爱的叔叔。"索拉雅说。

"今晚不用了。"他说，"今晚不痛。"

"好的。"她说。她替他盖好毛毯。我们关上门。

爸爸再也没有醒来。

他们填满了海沃德清真寺的停车场。在那座建筑后面光秃秃的草坪上，乱七八糟地停放着众多轿车和越野车。人们不得不朝清真寺以北开上三四条街，才能找到停车位。

清真寺的男人区是个巨大的正方形房间，铺着阿富汗地毯，薄薄的褥子井然有序地排列着。男人们把鞋脱在门口，鱼贯进入房间，盘膝坐在褥子上。有个毛拉对着麦克风，诵读《古兰经》的章节。根据风俗，我作为死者的家人坐在门边。塔赫里将军坐在我身边。透过洞开的大门，我看见轿车越停越多，阳光在它们的挡风玻璃上闪耀。从车上跳下乘客，男人穿着黑色的西装，女眷身穿黑色的衣服，头部则笼罩白色面纱。

《古兰经》的经文在屋子里回荡，我想起爸爸在俾路支赤手空拳和黑熊搏斗那个古老的传说。爸爸毕生都在和熊搏斗。痛失正值芳年的妻子；独自把儿子抚养成人；离开他深爱的家园，他的祖国；遭受贫穷、屈辱。而到了最后，终于来了一只他无法打败的熊。但即便这样，他也绝不妥协。

每轮祈祷过后，成群的哀悼者排着队，他们在退出的时候安慰我。我尽人子之责，和他们握手。他们之中大多数人我素未晤面。我不失礼节地微笑，感谢他们的祝愿，倾听他们提到爸爸时的言语。

"……帮我在泰曼尼盖了房子……"

"……保佑他……"

"……我走投无路，他借钱给我……"

"……他与我一面之缘，帮我找到工作……"

"……他就像我的兄弟……"

听到这些，我才明白自己的生活、身上的秉性有多少是来自爸爸，才知道他在人们的生命中留下的烙印。终我一生，我是"爸爸的儿子"。如今他走了。爸爸再也不会替我引路了，我得自己走。

想到这个，我不由害怕。

早些时候，在公共墓地那块小小的穆斯林墓区，我看着他们将爸爸放到墓穴里面。毛拉和另外一个男人开始争论，在下葬的时候究竟该引用哪段《古兰经》经文才算正确。若非塔赫里将军插手，他们一定闹得不可开交。毛拉选了一段经文，将其诵读出来，鄙夷地望着那个人。我看着他们将第一铲泥土丢进爸爸墓穴，然后走开。我走到墓园的另一边，坐在一株红枫树的阴影下面。

最后一批哀悼者已经致哀完毕，清真寺人去楼空，只有那个毛拉在收起麦克风，用一块绿布裹起《古兰经》。将军和我走进黄昏的阳光中。我们走下台阶，走过一群吸烟的男人。我零星听到他们谈话，下个周末在尤宁城有场足球赛，圣克拉拉新开了一家阿富汗餐厅。生活已然在前进，留下爸爸在后面。

"你怎么样，我的孩子？"塔赫里将军说。

我咬紧牙齿，将忍了一整天的泪水咽下。"我去找索拉雅。"我说。

"好的。"

我走进清真寺的女人区。索拉雅和她妈妈站在台阶上，还有几个我似乎在婚礼上见过的女士。我朝索拉雅招招手。她跟母亲说了几句话，向我走来。

"可以陪我走走吗？"

"当然。"她拉起我的手。

我们沿着一条蜿蜒的碎石路，默默前行，旁边有一排低矮的篱笆。我们坐在长凳上，看见不远处有对年老夫妇，跪在墓前，将一束雏菊放在墓碑上。"索拉雅？"

"怎么了？"

"我开始想他了。"

她把手放在我的膝盖上。爸爸的戒指在她手上闪闪发亮。我能看到，在她身后，那些前来哀悼爸爸的人们驾车离开，驶上传教大道。很快，我们也会离开，第一次，也是永远，留下爸爸孤独一人。

索拉雅将我拉近，泪水终于掉下来。

由于我和索拉雅没有经历过订婚期，我对塔赫里一家的了解，多半是来自婚后。例如，将军患有严重的偏头痛，每月发作一次，持续将近一个星期。当头痛难忍的时候，将军到自己的房间去，脱光衣服，关掉电灯，把门锁上，直到疼痛消退才走出来。他不许任何人进去，不许任何人敲门。他终究会出来，穿着那身灰色的西装，散发着睡眠和床单的气味，血红的双眼浮肿。我从索拉雅口中得知，自她懂事起，将军就和塔赫里太太分房睡。我还知道他有时很小气，比如说他妻子把菜肴摆在他面前，他会尝一口，就叹着气把它推开。"我给你做别的。"塔赫里太太会说。但他不理不睬，阴沉着脸，只顾吃面包和洋葱。这让索拉雅很恼怒，让她妈妈哭起来。索拉雅告诉我，说他服用抗抑郁的药物。我了解到他靠救济金生活，而他到了美国之后还没工作过，宁愿用政府签发的支票去换现金，也不愿自贬身份，去干那些与他地位不配的活儿。至于跳蚤市场的营生，在他看来只是个爱好，一种可以跟他的阿富汗朋友交际的方式。将军相信，迟早有一天，阿富汗会解放，君主制会恢复，而当权者会再次征召他服役。所以他每天穿上那身灰色套装，捂着怀表，等待时来运转。

我了解到塔赫里太太——现在我管她叫雅米拉阿姨——在喀布尔时，一度以美妙的歌喉闻名。虽然她从不曾得到专业训练，但她有唱歌的天赋——我听说她会唱民歌、情歌，甚至还会唱"拉格"[1]，这可通常是男人才唱的。可是，尽管将军非常喜欢听音乐——实际上，他拥有大量阿富汗和印度歌星演唱的经典情歌磁带，他认为演唱的事情最好还是留给那些地位低下的人去做。他们结婚的时候，将军的条款之一就是，她永远不能在公开场合唱歌。索拉雅告诉我，她妈妈本来很想在我们的婚礼上高歌一曲，只唱一首，但将军冷冷地盯了她一眼，这事就不了了之。雅米拉阿姨每周买一次彩票，每晚看约翰尼·卡森[2]的节目。白天她在花园里劳动，照料她的蔷薇、天竺葵、土豆藤和胡姬花。

我和索拉雅结婚之后，花草和约翰尼·卡森不再那么受宠了。我成了雅米拉阿姨生活中的新欢。跟将军防人之心甚强的外交手腕——我继续喊他"将军大人"，他甚至都没纠正我——不同，雅米拉阿姨毫不掩

---

[1] Raga，印度的一种传统音乐。
[2] Johnny Carson（1925~2005），美国著名电视节目主持人。

饰她有多么喜欢我。首先，她细数身上病痛的时候，我总是专心聆听，而将军对此充耳不闻。索拉雅告诉我，自从她母亲中风之后，每次心悸都是心脏病，每一处关节疼痛都是风湿关节炎发作，每一次眼跳都是中风。我记得第一次，雅米拉阿姨给我看她脖子上的肿块。"明天我会逃课，带你去看医生。"我说。将军笑着说："那么，你干脆退学不去上课算了，我的孩子，你阿姨的病历就像鲁米的著作，厚厚好几册呢。"

但她发现，我不仅是听她诉说病痛的好听众。我深信不疑，就算我抓起来复枪杀人越货，也依然能得到她对我毫不动摇的怜爱。因为我治愈了她最大的心病，我使她免受折磨，摆脱了每个阿富汗母亲最大的恐惧：没有门户光彩的人来向她的女儿提亲。那她的女儿就会独自随着年华老去，无夫无子，无依无靠。凡是女人都需要丈夫，即使他扼杀了她唱歌的天赋。

并且，从索拉雅口中，我得知了在弗吉尼亚发生的事情的细节。

我们去参加婚礼。索拉雅的舅舅，沙利夫，在移民局工作那位，给他儿子娶了个纽瓦克的阿富汗女孩。婚礼举行的宴会厅，就是半年前我和索拉雅成百年之好的地方。我们站在一群宾客之中，看着新娘从新郎家人手中接过戒指。其时我们听到两个中年妇女在谈话，她们背对着我们。

"多么可爱的新娘啊，"她们中一个说，"看看她，那么美丽，就像月亮一般。"

"是的，"另外一个说，"而且还纯洁呢，品德良好，没有谈过男朋友。"

"我知道，我告诉你，男孩最好别和他表姐那样的女人结婚。"

回家路上，索拉雅放声大哭。我把福特驶向路边，停在弗里蒙特大道的一盏路灯下面。

"事情已经过去了，"我说，撩拨着她的秀发，"谁在乎呢？"

"这太他妈的不公平了。"她嚎叫道。

"忘掉就好。"

"她们的儿子晚上到酒吧鬼混，寻欢作乐，搞大女朋友的肚子，未婚生子，没有人会说半句闲话。哦，他们只是找乐子的男人罢了。我不过犯了一次错，而突然之间，所有人都开始谈论清白和尊严，我一辈子将不得不背负这个罪名，抬不起头来。"

我伸出拇指，从她下巴抹去一颗泪珠，就在她的胎记上方。

"我没跟你说，"索拉雅说，眼里泛着泪花，"那天夜里，我爸爸掏出一把枪。他告诉……那人……说枪膛里有两颗子弹，如果我不回家，他就一枪打死他，然后自杀。我尖叫着，用各种各样的话骂我爸爸，跟他说他无法将我锁上一辈子，告诉他我希望他去死。"她又哭起来，泪水沾满嘴唇，"我真的对他那么说，说我希望他去死。

"他把我带回家时，我妈妈伸臂抱住我，她也哭起来了。她在说话，可是我一句也没听清，因为她口齿不清，说话含混。于是我爸爸将我带回我的房间，令我坐在化妆镜前面，给我一把剪刀，不动声色地叫我把头发都剪下来。我剪的时候，他就在旁边看着。

"一连好几个星期，我都没有出门。而当我走出去的时候，无论走到哪里，我都能听到有人窃窃私语，或者那是想象出来的。四年过去了，那个地方离这儿三千英里，而我还能听到这些话。"

"让他们去死。"我说。

她破涕为笑，说："提亲那夜，我在电话里把事情告诉你，原以为你会改变主意。"

"没有什么能改变，索拉雅。"

她微笑起来，握住我的手。"能够找到你我真幸运。你和我遇到的阿富汗男人都不同。"

"让我们永远别提这个了，好吗？"

"好的。"

我亲亲她的脸颊，驶离路边。我边开车边寻思自己何以与众不同。也许那是因为我在男人堆中长大，在我成长的时候，身旁没有女人，从未切身体会到阿富汗社会有时对待女人的双重标准。也许那是因为爸爸，他是非同寻常的阿富汗父亲，依照自己规则生活的自由人士，他总是先看社会规范是否入情入理，才决定遵从还是拒绝。

但我认为，我不在乎别人的过去，很大一部分原因，是由于我自己也有过去。我全都知道，但悔恨莫及。

爸爸死后不久，索拉雅和我搬进弗里蒙特一套一居室的房子，离将军和雅米拉阿姨的寓所只有几条街。索拉雅的双亲给我们买了棕色的沙发，还有一套日本产的三笠瓷器[1]，作为乔迁之礼。将军还额外送我一份礼物，崭新的 IBM 打字机。他用法尔西语写了一张字条，塞在箱子里面：

———————————

[1] Mikasa，日本出产的高档瓷器品牌。

亲爱的阿米尔：

　　我希望你从这键盘上发现很多故事。

伊克伯·塔赫里将军

　　我卖掉爸爸的大众巴士，时至今日，我再也没回到跳蚤市场去。每逢周五，我会开车到墓地去，有时，我发现墓碑上摆着一束新鲜的小苍兰，就知道索拉雅刚刚来过。

　　索拉雅和我的婚姻生活变得波澜不兴，像例行公事。我们共用牙刷和袜子，交换着看晨报。她睡在床的右边，我喜欢睡在左边。她喜欢松软的枕头，我喜欢硬的。她喜欢像吃点心那样干吃早餐麦片，然后用牛奶送下。

　　那年夏天，我接到圣何塞州立大学的录取通知，主修英文。我在桑尼维尔找到一份保安工作，轮班看守太阳谷某家家具仓库。工作极其无聊，但也带来相当的好处：下午六点之后，人们统统离开，仓库的沙发堆至天花板，一排排盖着塑料覆膜，阴影爬上它们之间的通道，我掏出书本学习。正是在家具仓库那间弥漫着松香除臭剂的办公室，我开始创作自己的第一本小说。

　　第二年，索拉雅也跟着进了圣何塞州立大学，主修教育，这令她父亲大为光火。

　　"我搞不懂你干吗要这样浪费自己的天分，"某天用过晚饭后，将军说，"你知道吗，亲爱的阿米尔，她念高中的时候所有课程都得优秀？"他转向她，"像你这样的聪明女孩，应该去当律师，当政治科学家。并且，奉安拉之名，阿富汗重获自由之后，你可以帮忙起草新的宪法。像你这样聪明的年轻阿富汗人大有用武之地。他们甚至会让你当大臣，旌表你的家族。"

我看到索拉雅身子一缩，绷紧了脸。"我又不是女孩，爸爸。我是结了婚的妇女。还有，他们也需要教师。"

"谁都可以当教师。"

"还有米饭吗，妈妈？"索拉雅说。

在将军找借口去海沃德看望朋友之后，雅米拉阿姨试着安慰索拉雅。"他没有恶意，"她说，"他只是希望你出人头地。"

"那么他便可以跟他的朋友吹牛啦，说他有个当律师的女儿。又是一个军功章。"索拉雅说。

"胡说八道！"

"出人头地，"索拉雅不屑地说，"至少我不喜欢他，当人们跟俄国佬干仗，他只是坐在那儿，干等尘埃落地，他就可以趁机而入，去要回他那个一点也不高贵的官职。教书也许清贫，但那是我想做的！那是我所喜爱的，顺便说一下，它比领救济金好得太多了。"

雅米拉阿姨欲说还休："要是他听到你这么说，以后再也不会跟你搭腔了。"

"别担心，"索拉雅不耐烦地说，将纸巾丢在盘子里，"我不会伤害他那宝贝的尊严。"

1988 年夏季，俄国人从阿富汗撤军之前约莫半年，我完成第一部小说，讲述父与子的故事，背景设在喀布尔，大部分是用将军送的打字机写出来的。我给十几家出版机构寄去征询信。8 月某天，我打开信箱，看到有个纽约的出版机构来函索取完整的书稿，我高兴得呆住了。次日我把书稿寄出。索拉雅亲了那包扎妥当的书稿，雅米拉阿姨坚持让我们将它从《古兰经》下穿过。她说要是我书稿被接受，她就会替我感谢真主，宰一头羊，把肉分给穷人。

"拜托，别宰羊，亲爱的阿姨。"我说，亲了亲她的脸颊。"只要把钱分给有需要的人就好了，别杀羊。"

隔了六个星期，有个叫马丁·格林瓦特的家伙从纽约给我打电话，许诺当我的出版代理。我只告诉了索拉雅："仅仅有了代理机构，并不意味着我的书能够出版。如果马丁把小说卖掉，我们到时再庆祝不迟。"

一个月后，马丁来电话，说我就要成为一名有作品出版的小说家。我告诉索拉雅，她尖叫起来。

那天晚上，我们做了丰盛的晚饭，请来索拉雅的父母，以示庆祝。雅米拉阿姨做了肉丸——米饭配肉丸——和杏仁布丁。将军眼里泛着泪花，说他为我感到骄傲。塔赫里将军和他妻子离开之后，我拿出一瓶回家路上买的昂贵干红葡萄酒，索拉雅和我举杯相庆。将军不赞同女人喝酒，他在的时候索拉雅滴酒不沾。

"你让我感到很骄傲，"她说，举杯和我碰了一下，"叔叔也一定会为你骄傲。"

"我知道。"我说，想起爸爸，希望他地下有灵。

等到夜阑人静，索拉雅入睡——酒精总是让她睡意蒙眬——之后，我站在阳台，吸着冰凉的夏夜空气。我想起拉辛汗，还有那鼓励我写作的字条，那是他读了我写的第一个故事之后写下的。我想起哈桑。总有

*一天，奉安拉之名，你会成为了不起的作家。他曾经说。全世界的人都
会读你的故事。*我生命中有过这么多美好的事情，这么多幸福的事情，
我寻思自己究竟哪点配得上这些。

小说在第二年，也就是 1989 年夏天出版，出版社让我到五个城市
签售。就在那年，俄国佬的军队从阿富汗撤得干干净净。那本来应该是
阿富汗人的光荣。可是，战乱继续，这次是内战，人民圣战者组织 [1] 和
纳吉布拉 [2] 傀儡政权之间的斗争。阿富汗难民依旧如潮水般涌向巴基斯
坦。就在那一年，冷战结束，柏林墙倒塌。在所有这些之中，阿富汗被
人遗忘。而塔赫里将军，俄国人撤军曾让他燃起希望，又开始给他的怀
表上发条了。

也就是在那一年，我和索拉雅打算生个孩子。

想到自己要当父亲，我心中像打翻了五味瓶。我又害怕又开心，又
沮丧又兴奋。我在想，自己会成为什么样的父亲呢？我既想成为爸爸那
样的父亲，又希望自己一点都不像他。

但一年过去了，什么都没发生。随着月经一次次如期而至，索拉
雅越来越沮丧，越来越焦躁，越来越烦恼。等到那时，原先只是旁敲侧
击的雅米拉阿姨也变得不耐烦了。"好啦！我什么时候能给我的孙子唱
摇篮曲啊？"将军永远不失普什图人风范，从来不过问——提起这些问
题，意味着试探他女儿和一个男人的性生活，尽管这个男人跟他女儿结

---

[1] Mujahedin，1979 年在美国的帮助下成立的民族激进组织，抗击苏联军队；
后来成长为阿富汗重要的政治势力。

[2] Mohamed Najibullah（1947~1996），1987 年出任阿富汗总统，1992 年辞职。

婚已经超过四年之久。但每当雅米拉阿姨问起孩子，让我们难为情的时候，他总是眼睛一亮。

"有时生孩子需要花一点时间。"某天夜里我对索拉雅说。

"一年了，可不是一点时间，阿米尔！"她冷冷说，声音完全像变了一个人，"肯定有问题，我知道。"

"那么我们去看看大夫。"

罗森大夫大腹便便，脸蛋圆润，一口细牙齿相当整齐，说话稍微带点东欧口音，有些像斯拉夫人。他对火车情有独钟——他的办公室到处都是跟铁路历史有关的书籍、火车头模型，还有各种照片：铁轨上的火车穿过如黛青山或者桥梁。他的桌子上方悬挂着一条标语：生命如火车，请上车。

他替我们出谋划策。我先做检查。"男人简单些。"他说，手指在红木办公桌上轻轻敲打。"男人的管道就像他的头脑：简单，很少出人意料。你们女士就不同了……这么说吧，上帝造你们的时候花了很多心思。"我怀疑他是不是碰到每对夫妇，都要扯这套管道理论。

"我们真幸运。"索拉雅说。

罗森大夫大笑，不过笑声听上去很假。他给我一张测试纸和一个塑料罐，要求索拉雅定期做血检。我们握手作别。"欢迎上车。"他说，请我们出去。

我通过了测试。

接下来几个月，索拉雅不断做检查：基础体温，抽血检查每一种所能想象得到的荷尔蒙，某种叫"子宫黏液测试"的检查，超声波，更多的血检，更多的尿检。索拉雅还接受了"宫腔镜"检查——罗森大夫将显微镜插进索拉雅的阴道，进行检视，他没发现异常。"管道很干净。"他一边脱掉橡胶手套，一边宣布。我希望他别这样称呼——我们又不是浴室！检查统统结束之后，他解释说他无法解释为什么我们怀不上小孩。而且，很显然，这并不罕见。这叫"原因不明性不孕症"。

接下来是治疗期。我们服用一种叫"克罗米芬"的药物，索拉雅还定期给自己注射"尿促性素"。这些全没效，罗森大夫建议我们考虑体外受孕。我们收到一封来自"健康维护组织"[1]的信函，措辞礼貌，祝我们好运，并说恕不替我们支付那笔费用。

我们动用我那本小说的预付金支付了治疗费用。体外受孕繁琐冗长，令人沮丧，最终也没有成功。好几个月在候诊室翻阅诸如《时尚好管家》、《读者文摘》之类的杂志之后，穿过无数纸袍、走进一间点着荧光灯的冰冷无菌检查室之后，一次次屈辱地跟素昧平生的人谈论我们性生活的每一个细节之后，无数次注射、探针和采集精子之后，我们回去找罗森大夫和他的火车。

他坐在我们对面，用手指敲着桌子，第一次用了"收养"这个字眼。索拉雅一路上哭着回家。

我们最后一次去拜访罗森大夫之后那个周末，索拉雅把这惊人的消

---

[1] Health Maintenance Organization，美国的预付费医疗组织，最初出现于20世纪三四十年代之间，1973年美国通过《健康维护法案》，自此这种医疗保障制度得到全国性的法律支持。参与HMO的人通常预先支付若干费用，即可得到免费医疗和康复服务，但某些特殊的病情除外，如小说中的体外受孕。

息告诉她父母。我们坐在塔赫里家后院的烧烤椅子上，烤着鳟鱼，喝着酸奶。那是 1991 年 3 月的某个黄昏。雅米拉阿姨已经给她的蔷薇和新种的金银花浇过水，它们的芳香混杂着烤鱼的味道。她已经两次从椅子上伸出手，去抚摸索拉雅的头发。"只有真主最清楚。我的孩子，也许事情不是这样的。"

索拉雅一直低头看着她的双手。我知道她很疲累，厌倦了这一切。"大夫说我们可以收养一个。"她低声说。

听到这个，塔赫里将军抬起头来，给烤炉盖上盖子。"他真的这么说？"

"他说那是个选择。"索拉雅说。

在家里我们已经就收养交换过意见，索拉雅并不想那么做。"我知道这很蠢，也许还有些虚荣，"在去她父母家的途中，她说，"可是我止不住这个念头。我总是梦想，我可以把孩子拥在怀里，知道我用血水养了他九个月，我梦想有一天，我看着他的眼睛，吃惊地看到你或我的影子。我梦想那婴儿会长大成人，笑起来像你或者像我。如果没有……这有错吗？"

"没有。"我说。

"我很自私吗？"

"不，索拉雅。"

"因为如果你真的想那么做……"

"不，"我说，"如果我们打算那么做，我们根本就不应该有任何动摇，并且，我们的意见必须一致。要不然对孩子不公平。"

她把头靠在车窗上，在剩下的路程中一言不发。

当时将军坐在她身旁："我的孩子，关于收养……这件事，我不知道对我们阿富汗人来说是否合适。"索拉雅疲惫地看着我，幽幽叹气。

"首先，他们长大成人，想要知道亲生父母是谁，"他说，"你们对此不能抱怨。你们操劳多年，所做全为了他们，有时候，他们会离家出走，去寻找给他们生命的人。血缘是最重要的，我的孩子，千万不能忘记。"

"我不想再谈论这个话题了。"索拉雅说。

"我再说一件事。"他说。我察觉到他激动起来了，我们听到将军的一番高谈阔论："这里就拿亲爱的阿米尔来说吧。我们都认得他的父亲，我在喀布尔之时，便认得他的祖父是什么人，还认得他的曾祖父。如果你们问起，我可以坐下来，细数他好几代祖先。这就是为什么他的爸爸——真主保佑他安息——前来提亲，我不假思索就应承的原因。而且，相信我，如果他的爸爸不了解你祖上的历史，也不会要你当他的媳妇。血缘是最重要的，我的孩子，你们收养别人的时候，根本不知道将谁的血带进家门。

"现在，如果你们是美国人，这不成问题。这里的人们为了爱情结合，家族和祖辈根本不起作用。他们收养孩子也是这样的，只要婴儿健康，每个人都很高兴。但我们是阿富汗人，我的孩子。"

"鱼烤好了吗？"索拉雅说。塔赫里将军眼睛盯着她，他拍拍她的膝盖。"高兴点吧，就为你身体健康，还有个好丈夫。"

"你怎么想呢，亲爱的阿米尔？"雅米拉阿姨问。

我把酒杯放到架子上，上面一排天竺葵滴着水。"我同意将军大人的看法。"

将军很满意，点点头，走回烤架去。

我们都有不收养的理由。索拉雅有她的理由，将军有他的理由，而我的理由是：也许在某个地方，有某个人，因为某件事，决定剥夺我为人父的权利，以报复我曾经的所作所为。也许这是我的报应，也许这样是罪有应得。**也许事情不是这样的。**雅米拉阿姨说。或者，也许事情注定是这样的。

几个月后，我们用我第二部小说的预付款作为最低首期付款，买下一座漂亮的维多利亚式房子，有两个卧房，位于旧金山的巴诺尔山庄。它有尖尖的屋顶，硬木地板，还有个小小的后院，尽头处有一个晒台和一个火炉。将军帮我重新擦亮晒台，粉刷墙壁。雅米拉阿姨抱怨我们搬得这么远，开车要一个半小时，特别是她认为索拉雅需要她全心全意的爱护和支持——殊不知正是她的好意和怜悯让索拉雅难以承受，这才决定搬家。

有时候，索拉雅睡在我身旁，我躺在床上，听着纱门在和风吹拂下开开关关，听着蟋蟀在院子里鸣叫。我几乎能感知到索拉雅子宫里的虚空，它好像是个活着的、会呼吸的东西。它渗进我们的婚姻，那虚空，渗进我们的笑声，还有我们的交欢。每当夜阑人静，我会察觉到它从索拉雅身上升起，横亘在我们之间。像新生儿那样，睡在我们中间。

第十四章

我把话筒放回座机，久久凝望着它。阿夫拉图的吠声吓了我一跳，我这才意识到房间变得多么安静。索拉雅消掉了电视的声音。

"你脸色苍白，阿米尔。"她说，坐在沙发上，就是她父母当成我们第一套房子的乔迁之礼的沙发。她躺在那儿，阿夫拉图的头靠在她胸前，她的脚伸在几个破旧的枕头下面。她一边看着公共电视台关于明尼苏达濒危狼群的特别节目，一边给暑期学校的学生改作文——六年来，她在同一所学校执教。她坐起来，阿夫拉图从沙发跳下。给我们这只长耳软毛猎犬取名的是将军，名字在法尔西语里面的意思是柏拉图，因为，他说，如果你长时间观察那只猎犬朦胧的黑眼睛，你一定会发现它在思索着哲理。

索拉雅白皙的下巴稍微胖了些。逝去的十年使得她臀部的曲线变宽了一些，在她乌黑的秀发渗进几丝灰白。然而她仍是个公主，脸庞圆润，眉毛如同小鸟张开的翅膀，鼻子的曲线像某些古代阿拉伯书籍中的字母那样优雅。

"你脸色苍白。"索拉雅重复说，将那叠纸放在桌子上。

"我得去一趟巴基斯坦。"

她当即站起来:"巴基斯坦?"

"拉辛汗病得很厉害。"我说着这话的时候内心绞痛。

"叔叔以前的合伙人吗?"她从未见过拉辛汗,但我提及过他。我点点头。

"哦,"她说,"我很难过,阿米尔。"

"过去我们很要好。"我说,"当我还是孩子的时候,他是第一个被我当成朋友的成年人。"我描述起来,说到他和爸爸在书房里面喝茶,然后靠近窗户吸烟,和风从花园带来阵阵蔷薇的香味,吹得两根烟柱袅袅飘散。

"我记得你提到过。"索拉雅说。她沉默了一会儿,"你会去多久?"

"我不知道,他想看到我。"

"那儿……"

"是的,那儿很安全。我会没事的,索拉雅。"她想问的是这个问题——十五年的琴瑟和鸣让我们变得心有灵犀。"我想出去走走。"

"要我陪着你吗?"

"不用,我想一个人。"

我驱车前往金门公园,独自沿着公园北边的斯普瑞柯湖边散步。那是个美丽的星期天下午,太阳照在波光粼粼的水面上,数十艘轻舟在旧金山清新的和风吹拂中漂行。我坐在公园的长椅上,看着一个男人将橄榄球扔给他的儿子,告诉他不可横臂投球,要举过肩膀。我抬起头,望见两只红色的风筝,拖着蓝色的长尾巴。它们越过公园西端的树林,越过风车。

我想起挂电话之前拉辛汗所说的一句话。他不经意间提起，却宛如经过深思熟虑。我闭上眼，看见他在嘈杂的长途电话线那端，看见他歪着头，嘴唇微微分合。再一次，他深邃莫测的黑色眼珠中，有些东西暗示着我们之间未经说出的秘密。但是此刻我知道他知道。我这些年来的怀疑是对的。他知道阿塞夫、风筝、钱，还有那个指针闪光的手表的事情。他一直都知道。

"来吧。这儿有再次成为好人的路。"拉辛汗在挂电话之前说了这句话。不经意间提起，却宛如经过深思熟虑。

再次成为好人的路。

我回到家中，索拉雅在跟她妈妈打电话。"不会太久的，亲爱的妈妈。一个星期吧，也许两个……是的，你跟爸爸可以来陪我住……"

两年前，将军摔断了右边髋骨。那时他的偏头痛又刚刚发作过，他从房间里出来，眼睛模糊昏花，被地毯松脱的边缘绊倒。听到他的惨叫，雅米拉阿姨从厨房跑出来。"听起来就像是一根扫把断成两半。"她总是喜欢那么说，虽然大夫说她不太可能听到那样的声音。将军摔断髋骨之后出现了诸多并发症状，有肺炎、败血症，在疗养院度过不少时日，雅米拉阿姨结束长期以来对自身健康状况的自怜自艾，而开始对将军的病况喋喋不休。她遇到人就说，大夫告诉他们，他的肾功能衰退了。"可是他们从来没有见过阿富汗人的肾，是吧？"她骄傲地说。至于将军住院的那些日子，我印象最深刻的是，雅米拉阿姨如何在将军身边轻轻哼唱，直到他入眠，在喀布尔的时候，那些歌谣也曾从爸爸那个嘶嘶作响的破旧变频收音机里传出来。

将军的病痛——还有时间——缓和了他和索拉雅之间的僵局。他们会一起散步，周六出去下馆子，而且，将军偶尔还会去听她讲课。他身穿那发亮的灰色旧西装，膝盖上横摆着拐杖，微笑着坐在教室最后一排。他有时甚至还做笔记。

那天夜里，索拉雅和我躺在床上，她的后背贴着我的胸膛，我的脸埋在她秀发里面。我记得过去，我们总是额头抵额头躺着，缠绵拥吻，低声呻吟，直到我们的眼睛不知不觉间闭上，细说着她那纤细弯曲的脚趾、第一次微笑、第一次交谈、第一次散步。如今我们偶尔也会这样，不过低语的是关于学校、我的新书，也为某人在宴会穿了不得体的衣服咯咯发笑。我们的性生活依然很好，有时甚至可以说是很棒。但有的夜晚，做完爱之后，我的全部感觉只是如释重负：终于做完了，终于可以放任思绪飘散了，至少可以有那么一时半会儿，忘记我们适才所做的竟然是徒劳无功。虽然她从没提起，但我知道有时索拉雅也有这样的感觉。在那些夜晚，我们会各自蜷缩在床的两边，让我们的恩人来解救我们。索拉雅的恩人是睡眠，我的永远是一本书。

拉辛汗打电话来那晚，我躺在黑暗中，眼望月光刺穿黑暗、在墙壁上投射出来的银光。也许快到黎明的某一刻，我昏昏睡去。梦见哈桑在雪地奔跑，绿色长袍的后摆拖在他身后，黑色的橡胶靴子踩得积雪吱吱响。他举臂挥舞：**为你，千千万万遍**！

一周之后，我上了巴基斯坦国际航空公司的飞机，坐在靠窗的位置，看着两个地勤人员把挡住机轮的东西搬开。飞机滑行，离开航站楼，很快，我们腾空而上，刺穿云层。我将头靠在窗子上，徒劳地等着入眠。

第十五章

　　我乘坐的航班在白沙瓦着陆三个小时之后，我坐在一辆弥漫着烟味的破旧的士后座上。汗津津的司机个子矮小，一根接一根抽着烟，自我介绍说他叫戈蓝。他开起车来毫无顾忌，横冲直撞，每每与其他车辆擦身而过，一路上滔滔不绝的话语片刻不停地从他口中涌出来：

　　"……你的祖国发生的一切太恐怖了，真的。阿富汗人和巴基斯坦人就像兄弟，我告诉你，穆斯林必须帮助穆斯林，所以……"

　　我不搭腔，带着礼貌点头称是。1981年，爸爸和我在这里住过几个月，脑海里依然认得白沙瓦。现在我们在雅姆鲁德路往西开着，路过兵站，还有那些高墙耸立的豪宅。这喧嚣的城市匆匆后退，让我想起记忆中的喀布尔，比这里更繁忙、更拥挤，特别是鸡市，哈桑和我过去常常去那儿，买酸辣酱腌过的土豆和樱桃水。街路上挤满了自行车、摩肩接踵的行人，还有冒出袅袅蓝烟的三轮摩托车，所有这些，都在迷宫般的狭窄巷道穿来插去。拥挤的小摊排成一行行，留着胡子的小贩在地面摆开一张张薄薄的褥子，兜售兽皮灯罩、地毯、绣花披肩和铜器。这座城市喧闹非凡，小贩的叫卖声、震耳欲聋的印度音乐、三轮摩托车的突突声、马车的叮叮当当声，全都混在一起，在我耳边回荡。还有各种各样的味道，香的臭的，炸蔬菜的香辣味、爸爸最喜爱的炖肉味、柴油机的烟味，还有腐烂物、垃圾、粪便的臭味，纷纷飘进车窗，扑鼻而来。

驶过白沙瓦大学的红砖房子之后不久，我们进入了一个区域，那个饶舌的司机称之为"阿富汗城"。我看到了糖铺、售卖地毯的小贩、烤肉摊，还有双手脏兮兮的小孩在兜售香烟，窗户上贴着阿富汗地图的小餐馆，厕身其中的是众多救助机构。"这个地区有你很多同胞，真的。他们做生意，不过多数很穷。"他"啧"了一声，叹了口气，"反正，我们就快到了。"

我想起最后一次见到拉辛汗的情景，那是在 1981 年。我和爸爸逃离喀布尔那晚，他前来道别。我记得爸爸和他在门廊拥抱，轻声哭泣。爸爸和我到了美国之后，他和拉辛汗保持联系。他们每年会交谈上那么四五次，有时爸爸会把听筒给我。最后一次和拉辛汗说话是在爸爸去世后不久。死讯传到喀布尔，他打电话来。我们只说了几分钟，电话线就断了。

司机停在一座房子前，这房子位于两条蜿蜒街道的繁忙交叉路口。我付了车钱，提起仅有的一个箱子，走进那雕刻精美的大门。这座建筑有木板阳台和敞开的窗户，窗外多数晾着衣服。我踩上吱嘎作响的楼梯，登上二楼，转右，走到那昏暗走廊最后一扇门。我看看手里那张写着地址的信纸，敲敲门。

然后，一具皮包骨的躯体伪装成拉辛汗，把门打开。

圣何塞州立大学有位创作老师经常谈起陈词滥调："应该像逃瘟疫

那样避开它们。"然后他会为自己的幽默笑起来。全班也跟着他大笑，可是我总觉得这种对陈词滥调的指责毫无价值。因为它们通常准确无误。但是因为人们把这些说法当成陈词滥调，它们的贴切反而无人提及。例如，"房间里的大象"[1] 这句话，用来形容我和拉辛汗重逢那一刻再也贴切不过了。

我们坐在墙边一张薄薄的褥子上，对面是窗口，可以看到下面喧闹的街道。阳光照进来，在门口的阿富汗地毯上投射出三角形的光影。两张折叠椅倚在墙上，对面的屋角摆放着一个小小的铜壶。我从它里面倒出两杯茶。

"你怎么找到我？"我问。

"要在美国找一个人并不难。我买了张美国地图，打电话查询北加利福尼亚城市的资料。"他说，"看到你已经长大成人，感觉真是又奇怪又美好。"

我微笑，在自己的茶杯中放了三块方糖。我记得他不喜欢加糖。"爸爸来不及告诉你我十五年前就结婚了。"真相是，当时爸爸脑里的肿瘤让他变得健忘，忽略了。

"你结婚了？和谁？"

"她的名字叫索拉雅·塔赫里。"我想起她在家里，替我担忧。我很高兴她并非孤身一人。

"塔赫里……她是谁的女儿？"

我告诉他。他眼睛一亮："哦，没错，我想起来了。塔赫里将军是

---

[1] 指大家都知道，但避而不谈的事情。

不是娶了亲爱的沙利夫的姐姐？她的名字叫……"

"亲爱的雅米拉。"

"对！对！"他说，微笑着，"我在喀布尔认识亲爱的沙利夫，很久以前了，那时他还没搬去美国。"

"他在移民局工作好多年了，处理了很多阿富汗案子。"

"哎，"他叹气说，"你和亲爱的索拉雅有孩子吗？"

"没有。"

"哦。"他啜着茶，不再说什么。在我遇到的人中，拉辛汗总是最能识破人心那个。

我向他说了很多爸爸的事情，他的工作，跳蚤市场，还有到了最后，他如何在幸福中溘然长辞。我告诉他我上学的事情，我出的书——如今我已经出版了四部小说。他听了之后微微一笑，说他对此从未怀疑。我跟他说，我在他送我那本皮面笔记本上写小故事，但他不记得那笔记本。

话题不可避免地转向塔利班[1]。

"不是我听到的那么糟糕吧？"我说。

"不，更糟，糟得多。"他说，"他们不会把你当人看。"他指着右眼上方的伤疤，弯弯曲曲地穿过他浓密的眉毛。"1998年，我坐在伽兹体

---

[1] Taliban，阿富汗政治组织，主要由普什图人组成，1994年在坎大哈成立，推行原教旨主义，禁止电视、录像、音乐、跳舞等，随后于1996年执政，直到2001年被美国军队击溃。为了行文简洁和阅读方便起见，译文同时用塔利班来指称塔利班组织和塔利班党人。

育馆里面看足球赛。我记得是喀布尔队和马扎里沙里夫[1]队，还记得球员被禁止穿短衣短裤。我猜想那是因为裸露不合规矩。"他疲惫地笑起来。"反正，喀布尔队每进一球，坐在我身边的年轻人就高声欢呼。突然间，一个留着胡子的家伙向我走来，他在通道巡逻，样子看起来最多十八岁。他用俄制步枪的枪托撞我的额头。'再喊我把你的舌头割下来，你这头老驴子！'他说。"拉辛汗用骨节嶙峋的手指抹抹伤疤。"我老得可以当他爷爷了，坐在那里，血流满面，向那个狗杂碎道歉。"

我给他添茶。拉辛汗说了更多。有些我已经知道，有些则没听说过。他告诉我，就像他和爸爸安排好那样，自1981年起，他住进了爸爸的屋子——这个我知道。爸爸和我离开喀布尔之后不久，就把房子"卖"给拉辛汗。爸爸当时的看法是，阿富汗遇到的麻烦是暂时的，我们被打断的生活——那些在瓦兹尔·阿克巴·汗区的房子大摆宴席和去帕格曼野炊的时光毫无疑问会重演。所以直到那天，他把房子交给拉辛汗托管。

拉辛汗告诉我，在1992年到1996年间，北方联盟[2]占领了喀布尔，不同的派系管辖喀布尔不同的地区。"如果你从沙里诺区走到卡德帕湾区去买地毯，就算你能通过所有的关卡，也得冒着被狙击手枪杀或者被火箭炮炸飞的危险，事情就是这样。实际上，你从一个城区到另外的城区去，都需要通行证。所以人们留在家里，祈祷下一枚火箭炮别击中他们的房子。"他告诉我，人们如何穿墙凿壁，在家里挖出洞来，以便能

[1] Mazar-i-Sharif，阿富汗西部城市。
[2] Northern Alliance，主要由三支非普什图族的军事力量于1992年组成，得到美国等西方国家的支持，1996年被塔利班推翻。

避开危险的街道，可以穿过一个又一个的墙洞，在邻近活动。在其他地区，人们还挖起地道。

"你干吗不离开呢？"我说。

"喀布尔是我的家园。现在还是。"他冷笑着说，"还记得那条从你家通向独立中学旁边那座兵营的路吗？"

"记得。"那是条通往学校的近路。我记得那天，哈桑和我走过去，那些士兵侮辱哈桑的妈妈。后来哈桑还在电影院里面哭了，我伸手抱住他。

"当塔利班打得联军节节败退、撤离喀布尔时，我真的在那条路上跳起舞来。"拉辛汗说，"还有，相信我，雀跃起舞的不止我一个。人们在夏曼大道、在德马赞路庆祝，在街道上朝塔利班欢呼，爬上他们的坦克，跟他们一起摆姿势拍照片。人们厌倦了连年征战，厌倦了火箭炮、炮火、爆炸，厌倦了古勒卜丁[1]和他的党羽朝一切会动的东西开枪。联军对喀布尔的破坏比俄国佬还厉害。他们毁掉你爸爸的恤孤院，你知道吗？"

"为什么？"我说，"他们干吗要毁掉一个恤孤院呢？"我记得恤孤院落成那天，我坐在爸爸后面，风吹落他那顶羔羊皮帽，大家都笑起来，当他讲完话，人们纷纷起立鼓掌。而如今它也变成一堆瓦砾了。那些爸爸所花的钱，那些画蓝图时挥汗如雨的夜晚，那些在工地悉心监工，确保每一块砖头、每一根梁子、每一块石头都没摆错的心血……

"城门失火，殃及池鱼罢了，"拉辛汗说，"你不忍知道的，亲

---

[1]　Gulbuddin Hekmatyar（1947~　　），1993 年至 1996 年任阿富汗总理。

爱的阿米尔，那在恤孤院的废墟上搜救的情景，到处是小孩的身体碎片……"

"所以当塔利班刚来的时候……"

"他们是英雄。"拉辛汗说。

"至少带来了和平。"

"是的，希望是奇怪的东西。至少带来了和平。但代价是什么呢？"拉辛汗剧烈地咳嗽起来，瘦弱的身体咳得前后摇晃。他掏出手帕，往里面吐痰，立刻将它染红。我想这当头，说一头汗流浃背的大象跟我们同在这小小的房间里面，那再也贴切不过。

"你怎么样？"我说，"别说客套话，你身体怎样？"

"实际上，来日无多了。"他用沙哑的声音说，又是一轮咳嗽。手帕染上更多的血。他擦擦嘴巴，用袖子从一边塌陷的太阳穴抹向另一边，抹去额头上的汗珠，匆匆瞥了我一眼。他点点头，我知道他读懂了我脸上的疑问。"不久了。"他喘息着。

"多久？"

他耸耸肩，再次咳嗽。"我想我活不到夏天结束。"他说。

"跟我回家吧。我给你找个好大夫。他们总有各种各样的新疗法。那边有新药，实验性疗法，我们可以让你住进……"我知道自己在信口开河。但这总比哭喊好，我终究可能还是会哭的。

他发出一阵咔咔的笑声，下排牙齿已经不见了。那是我有生以来听到最疲累的笑声。"我知道美国给你灌输了乐观的性子，这也是她了不起的地方。那非常好。我们是忧郁的民族，我们阿富汗人，对吧？我们总是陷在悲伤和自恋中。我们在失败、灾难面前屈服，将这些当成生活的实质，甚至视为必须。我们总是说，生活会继续的。但我在这里，没有向命运投降，我看过几个很好的大夫，他们给的答案都一样。我信任他们，相信他们。像这样的事情，是真主的旨意。"

"只有你想做和不想做的事情罢了。"我说。

拉辛汗大笑。"你刚才的口气可真像你父亲。我很怀念他。但这真的是真主的旨意，亲爱的阿米尔。这真的是。"他停下。"另外，我要你来这里还有另一个原因。我希望在离开人世之前看到你，但也还有其他缘故。"

"什么原因都行。"

"你们离开之后，那些年我一直住在你家，你知道吧？"

"是的。"

"那些年我并非都是一人度过，哈桑跟我住在一起。"

"哈桑？"我说。我上次说出这个名字是什么时候？那些久远的负疚和罪恶感再次刺痛了我，似乎说出他的名字就解除了一个魔咒，将它们释放出来，重新折磨我。刹那间，拉辛汗房间里面的空气变得太厚重、太热，带着太多街道上传来的气味。

"之前我想过写信给你，或者打电话告诉你，但我不知道你想不想听。我错了吗？"

而真相是，他没有错。说他错了则是谎言。我选择了模糊其词："我不知道。"

他又在手帕里面咳出一口血。他弯腰吐痰的时候，我看见他头皮上有结痂的疮口。"我要你到这里来，是因为有些事情想求你。我想求你替我做些事情。但在我求你之前，我会先告诉你哈桑的事情，你懂吗？"

"我懂。"我低声说。

"我想告诉你关于他的事，我想告诉你一切。你会听吗？"

我点点头。

然后拉辛汗又喝了几口茶，把头靠在墙上，开始说起来。

第十六章

　　1986 年，有很多原因促使我到哈扎拉贾特寻找哈桑。最大的一个，安拉原谅我，是我很寂寞。当时，我多数朋友和亲人若不是死于非命，便是离乡背井，逃往巴基斯坦或者伊朗。在喀布尔，那个我生活了一辈子的城市，我再也没几个熟人了。大家都逃走了。我会到卡德帕湾区散步——你记得吗，过去那儿经常有叫卖甜瓜的小贩出没，看到的都是不认识的人。没有人可以打招呼，没有人可以坐下来喝杯茶，没有人可以说说话，只有俄国士兵在街头巡逻。所以到了最后，我不再在城里散步。我会整天在你父亲的房间里面，上楼到书房去，看看你妈妈那些旧书，听听新闻，看看电视上那些宣传。然后我会做礼拜，煮点东西吃，再看看书，又是礼拜，上床睡觉。早上我会醒来，礼拜，再重复前一天的生活。

　　因为患了关节炎，照料房子对我来说越来越难。我的膝盖和后背总是发痛——早晨我起床之后，至少得花上一个小时，才能让麻木的关节活络起来，特别是在冬天。我不希望你父亲的房子荒废，我们在这座房子有过很多美好的时光，有很多记忆，亲爱的阿米尔。你爸爸亲自设计了那座房子，它对他来说意义重大，除此之外，他和你前往巴基斯坦的时候，我亲口应承他，会把房子照料好。如今只有我和这座房子……我尽力了，我尽力每隔几天给树浇水，修剪草坪，照料花儿，钉牢那些需要固定的东西，但，就算在那个时候，我也已经不再是个年轻人了。

可是即使这样，我仍能勉力维持。至少可以再过一段时间吧。但当我听到你爸爸的死讯……在这座屋子里面，我第一次感到让人害怕的寂寞。还有无法忍受的空虚。

于是有一天，我给别克车加油，驶向哈扎拉贾特。我记得阿里从你家离开之后，你爸爸告诉我，说他和哈桑搬到一座小村落，就在巴米扬城外。我想起阿里在那儿有个表亲。我不知道哈桑是否还在那儿，不知道是否有人认识，或者知道他在哪里。毕竟，阿里和哈桑离开你爸爸的家门已经十年了。1986 年，哈桑已经是个成年人了，应该是 22 岁，或者 23 岁，如果他还活着的话，就是这样的——俄国佬，但愿他们因为在我们祖国所做的一切，在地狱里烂掉，他们杀害了我们很多年轻人。这些我不说你也知道。

但是，感谢真主，我在那儿找到他。没费多大劲就找到了——我所做的，不过是在巴米扬问了几个问题，人们就指引我到他的村子去。我甚至记不起那个村子的名字了，也不知道它究竟有没有名字。但我记得那是个灼热的夏天，我开车驶在坑坑洼洼的泥土路上，路边除了被晒蔫的灌木、枝节盘错而且长着刺的树干、稻秆般的干草之外，什么也没有。我看见路旁有头死驴，身体开始发烂。然后我拐了个弯，看到几间破落的泥屋，在右边那片空地中间，它们后面什么也没有，只有广袤的天空和锯齿似的山脉。

　　在巴米扬，人们说我会很容易就找到他——整个村庄，只有他住的屋子有垒着围墙的花园。那堵泥墙很短，有些墙洞点缀在上面，围住那间小屋——那真的比一间破茅舍好不了多少。赤着脚的孩子在街道上玩耍，用棒子打一个破网球，我把车停在路边，熄了火，他们全都看着我。我推开那扇木门，走进一座院子，里头很小，一小块地种着干枯的草莓，还有株光秃秃的柠檬树。院子的角落种着合欢树，树荫下面摆着烤炉，我看见有个男人站在旁边。他正在把生面团涂到一把木头抹刀上，用它拍打着烤炉壁。他一看到我就放下生面团，捧起我的手亲个不停。

　　"让我看看你。"我说。他退后一步。他现在可高了——我踮起脚尖，仍只是刚刚有他下巴那么高。巴米扬的阳光使他的皮肤变得更坚韧了，比我印象中黑得多，他有几颗门牙不见了，下巴上长着几撮稀疏的毛。除此之外，他还是那双狭窄的绿眼睛，上唇的伤痕还在，还是那张圆圆的脸蛋，还是那副和蔼的笑容。你一定会认出他的，亲爱的阿米尔，我敢肯定。

　　我们走进屋里。里面有个年轻的哈扎拉女人，肤色较淡，在屋角缝披肩。她显然怀孕了。"这是我的妻子，拉辛汗。"哈桑骄傲地说，"她是亲爱的法莎娜。"她是个羞涩的妇人，很有礼貌，说话声音很轻，只比耳语大声一点，她淡褐色的美丽眼睛从来不和我的眼光接触。但她那样看着哈桑，好像他坐在皇宫内的宝座上。

　　"孩子什么时候出世？"参观完那间泥砖屋之后，我问。屋里一无所有，只有磨损的褥子，几个盘子，两张坐垫，一盏灯笼。

　　"奉安拉之名，这个冬天，"哈桑说，"我求真主保佑，生个儿子，给他取我父亲的名字。"

"说到阿里，他在哪儿？"

哈桑垂下眼光。他告诉我说，阿里和他的表亲——这个屋子是他的——两年前被地雷炸死了，就在巴米扬城外。一枚地雷。阿富汗人还有其他死法吗，亲爱的阿米尔？而且我荒唐地觉得，一定是阿里的右脚——他那患过小儿麻痹的废脚——背叛了他，踩在地雷上。听到阿里去世，我心里非常难过。你知道，你爸爸和我一起长大，从我懂事起，阿里就陪伴着他。我还记得那年我们都很小，阿里得了小儿麻痹症，差点死掉。你爸爸整天绕着屋子走来走去，哭个不停。

法莎娜用豆子、芜菁、土豆做了蔬菜汤，我们洗手，抓起从烤炉取下的新鲜馕饼，浸在汤里——那是我几个月来吃过的最好的一顿。就在那时，我求哈桑搬到喀布尔，跟我住一起。我把屋子的情况告诉他，跟他说我再也不能独力打理。我告诉他我会给他可观的报酬，让他和他的妻子过得舒服。他们彼此对望，什么也没说。饭后，我们洗过手，法莎娜端给我们葡萄。哈桑说这座村庄现在就是他的家，他和法莎娜在那儿自食其力。

"而且离巴米扬很近，我们在那儿有熟人。原谅我，拉辛汗。我请求你的原谅。"

"当然，"我说，"你不用向我道歉，我知道。"

喝完蔬菜汤又喝茶，喝到一半，哈桑问起你来。我告诉他你在美国，但其他情况我也不清楚。哈桑问了很多跟你有关的问题。你结婚了吗？你有孩子吗？你多高？你还放风筝吗？还去电影院吗？你快乐吗？他说他跟巴米扬一个年老的法尔西语教师成了朋友，他教他读书写字。

如果他给你写一封信，我会转交给你吗？还问我，你会不会回信？我告诉他，我跟你爸爸打过几次电话，从他口里得知你的情况，但我不知道该怎么回答他。接着他问起你爸爸。我告诉他时，他双手掩着脸，号啕大哭。那天晚上，他像小孩一样，抹了整夜的眼泪。

他们执意留我过夜。我在那儿住了一晚。法莎娜给我弄了个铺位，给我一杯井水，以便渴了可以喝。整个夜里，我听见她低声跟哈桑说话，听着他哭泣。

翌日早晨，哈桑跟我说，他和法莎娜决定搬到喀布尔，跟我一起住。

"我不该到这里来，"我说，"你是对的，亲爱的哈桑，这儿有你的生活。我到这里来，要求你放弃一切，真是太冒失了。需要得到原谅的人是我。"

"我们没有什么可以放弃的，拉辛汗。"哈桑说，他的眼睛仍是又红又肿。"我们会跟你走，我们会帮你照料屋子。"

"你真的想好了吗？"

他点点头，把头垂下。"老爷待我就像父亲一样……真主保佑他安息。"

他们把家当放在几块破布中间，绑好那些布角。我们把那个包袱放在别克车里。哈桑站在门槛上，举起《古兰经》，我们都亲了亲它，从下面穿过。然后我们前往喀布尔。我记得我开车离开的时候，哈桑转过头，最后一次看了他们的家。

到了喀布尔之后，我发现哈桑根本没有搬进屋子的意思。"可是所有这些房间都空着，亲爱的哈桑，没有人打算住进来。"我说。

但他不听。他说那关乎尊重。他和法莎娜把家当搬进后院那间破屋子，那个他出生的地方。我求他们搬进楼顶的客房，但哈桑一点都没听进去。"阿米尔少爷会怎么想呢？"他对我说，"要是战争结束，有朝一日阿米尔少爷回来，发现我鸠占鹊巢，他会怎么想？"然后，为了悼念你的父亲，哈桑穿了四十天黑衣服。

我并不想要他们那么做，但他们两个包办了所有做饭洗衣的事情。哈桑悉心照料花园里的花儿，松土，摘掉枯萎的叶子，种植蔷薇篱笆。他粉刷墙壁，把那些多年无人住过的房间抹干净，把多年无人用过的浴室清洗整洁。好像他在打理房间，等待某人归来。你记得你爸爸种植的那排玉米后面的那堵墙吗，亲爱的阿米尔？你和哈桑怎么称呼它？"病玉米之墙"？那年初秋某个深夜，一枚火箭炮把那墙统统炸塌了。哈桑亲手把它重新建好，垒起一块块砖头，直到它完整如初。要不是有他在那儿，我真不知道该怎么办。

那年深秋，法莎娜生了个死产的女婴。哈桑亲吻那个婴儿毫无生气的脸，我们将她葬在后院，就在蔷薇花丛旁边，我们用白杨树叶盖住那个小坟堆。我替她祈祷。法莎娜整天躲在小屋里面，凄厉地哭喊。母亲的哀号。我求安拉，保佑你永远不会听到。

在那屋子的围墙之外，战争如火如荼。但我们三个，在你爸爸的房子里，我们自己营造了小小的天堂。自1980年代晚期开始，我的视力就衰退了，所以我让哈桑给我读你妈妈的书。我们会坐在门廊，坐在火炉边，法莎娜在厨房煮饭的时候，哈桑会给我念《玛斯纳维》或者《鲁拜集》。每天早晨，哈桑总会在蔷薇花丛那边小小的坟堆上摆一朵鲜花。

1990年年初，法莎娜又怀孕了。也是在这一年，盛夏的时候，某天早晨，有个身披天蓝色长袍的女人敲响前门，她双脚发抖，似乎羸弱得连站都站不稳。我问她想要什么，她沉默不语。

"你是谁？"我说。但她一语不发，就在那儿瘫下，倒在车道上。我把哈桑喊出来，他帮我把她扶进屋子，走进客厅。我们让她躺在沙发上，除下她的长袍。长袍之下是个牙齿掉光的妇女，蓬乱的灰白头发，手臂上生着疮。她看上去似乎很多天没有吃东西了。但更糟糕的是她的脸。有人用刀在她脸上……亲爱的阿米尔，到处都是刀痕，有一道从颧骨到发际线，她的左眼也没有幸免。太丑怪了。我用一块湿布拍拍她的额头，她睁开眼。"哈桑在哪里？"她细声说。

"我在这里。"哈桑说，他拉起她的手，紧紧握住。

她那只完好的眼打量着他。"我走了很久很远，来看看你是否像我梦中见到那样英俊。你是的。甚至更好看。"她拉着他的手，贴近她伤痕累累的脸庞。"朝我笑一笑，求求你。"

哈桑笑了，那个老妇人流出泪水。"你的笑是从我这里来的，有没有人告诉过你？而我甚至没有抱过你。愿安拉宽恕我，我甚至没有抱过你。"

自从莎娜芭 1964 年刚生下哈桑不久就跟着一群艺人跑掉之后，我们再也没人见过她。你从来没见过她，阿米尔，但她年轻的时候，她是个美人。她微笑起来脸带酒窝，步履款款，令男人发狂。凡是在街上见到她的人，无论是男的还是女的，都会忍不住再看一眼。而现在……

哈桑放下她的手，冲出房子。我跟着他后面，但他跑得太快了。我看见他跑上那座你们两个以前玩耍的山丘，他的脚步踢起阵阵尘土。我任他走开。我整天坐在莎娜芭身边，看着天空由澄蓝变成紫色。夜幕降临，月亮在云层中穿梭，哈桑仍没回来。莎娜芭哭着说回来是一个错误，也许比当年离家出走错得更加厉害。但我安抚她。哈桑会回来的，我知道。

隔日早上他回来了，看上去疲累而憔悴，似乎彻夜未睡。他双手捧起莎娜芭的手，告诉她，如果她想哭就哭吧，但她不用哭，现在她在家里了，他说，在家里和家人在一起。他抚摸着她脸上的伤疤，把手伸进她的头发里面。

在哈桑和法莎娜照料下，她康复了。他们喂她吃饭，替她洗衣服。我让她住在楼上一间客房里面。有时我会从窗户望出去，看见哈桑和他母亲跪在院子里，摘番茄，或者修剪蔷薇篱笆，彼此交谈。他们在补偿所有失去的那些岁月，我猜想。就我所知，他从来没有问起她到哪里去了，或者为什么要离开，而她也没有说。我想有些事情不用说出来。

1990年冬天，莎娜芭把哈桑的儿子接生出来。那时还没有下雪，但冬天的寒风呼啸着吹过院子，吹弯了苗圃里的花儿，吹落了树叶。我记得莎娜芭用一块羊毛毯抱着她的孙子，将他从小屋里面抱出来。她站在阴暗的灰色天空下，喜悦溢于言表，泪水从她脸上流下，刺人的寒风吹起她的头发，她死死抱着那个孩子，仿佛永远不肯放手。这次不会了。她把他交给哈桑，哈桑把他递给我，我在那个男婴耳边，轻轻唱起《古兰经》的经文。

他们给他起名索拉博，那是《列王纪》里面哈桑最喜欢的英雄，你知道的，亲爱的阿米尔。他是个漂亮的小男孩，甜蜜得像糖一样，而性子跟他爸爸毫无二致。你应该看看莎娜芭带那个孩子，亲爱的阿米尔。他变成她生活的中心，她给他缝衣服，用木块、破布和稻秆给他做玩具。他要是发热，她会整晚睡不着，斋戒三天。她在锅里烧掉一本教历，说是驱走魔鬼的眼睛。索拉博两岁的时候，管她叫"莎莎"。他们两个形影不离。

她活到他四岁的时候，然后，某个早晨，她再也没有醒来。她神情安详平静，似乎死得无牵无挂。我们在山上的墓地埋了她，那座种着石榴树的墓地，我也替她祈祷了。她的去世让哈桑很难过——得到了再失去，总是比从来就没有得到更伤人。但小索拉博甚至更加难过，他不停地在屋里走来走去，找他的"莎莎"，但你知道，小孩就是那样，他们很快就忘了。

那时——应该是1995年——俄国佬已经被赶走很久了，喀布尔依次落在马苏德[1]、拉巴尼[2]和人民圣战者组织手里。不同派系间的内战十分激烈，没有人知道自己是否能活到一天结束。我们的耳朵听惯了炮弹落下、机枪嗒嗒的声音，人们从废墟爬出来的景象也司空见惯。那些日子里的喀布尔，亲爱的阿米尔，你在地球上再也找不到比这更像地狱的地方了。瓦兹尔·阿克巴·汗区没有遭受太多的袭击，所以我们的处境不像其他城区一样糟糕。

在那些炮火稍歇、枪声较疏的日子，哈桑会带索拉博去动物园看狮子"玛扬"，或者去看电影。哈桑教他射弹弓，而且，后来，到了他八岁的时候，弹弓在索拉博手里变成了一件致命的武器：他可以站在阳台

---

[1] Ahmad Shah Massoud（1953~2001），20世纪80年代组织游击队在阿富汗潘杰希尔谷地抗击苏联游击队，1996年后为北方联盟领导人之一。
[2] Burhanuddin Rabbani（1940~2011），阿富汗政治家，1992年至1996年任阿富汗总统。

上，射中院子中央水桶上摆放着的松果。哈桑教他读书识字——以免他的儿子长大之后跟他一样是个文盲。我和那个小男孩越来越亲近——我看着他学会走路，听着他牙牙学语。我从电影公园那边的书店给索拉博买童书——现在它们也被炸毁了——索拉博总是很快看完。他让我想起你，你小时候多么喜欢读书，亲爱的阿米尔。有时，我在夜里讲故事给他听，和他猜谜语，教他玩扑克。我想他想得厉害。

冬天，哈桑带他儿子追风筝。那儿再也没有过去那么多风筝大赛了——因为缺乏安全，没有人敢在外面待得太久——但零星有一些。哈桑会让索拉博坐在他的肩膀上，在街道上小跑，追风筝，爬上那些挂着风筝的树。你记得吗，亲爱的阿米尔，哈桑追风筝多么在行？他仍和过去一样棒。冬天结束的时候，哈桑和索拉博会把他们整个冬天追来的风筝挂在门廊的墙上，他们会像挂画像那样将它们摆好。

我告诉过你，1996 年，当塔利班掌权，结束日复一日的战争之后，我们全都欢呼雀跃。我记得那晚回家，发现哈桑在厨房，听着收音机，神情严肃。我问他怎么了，他只是摇摇头："现在求真主保佑哈扎拉人，拉辛汗老爷。"

"战争结束了，哈桑，"我说，"很快就会有和平，奉安拉之名，还有幸福和安宁。再没有火箭炮，再没有杀戮，再没有葬礼！"但他只是关掉收音机，问我在他睡觉之前还需要什么。

几个星期后，塔利班禁止斗风筝。隔了两年，在 1998 年，他们开始在马扎里沙里夫屠杀哈扎拉人。

第十七章

　　拉辛汗慢慢地伸开双腿，斜倚在光秃秃的墙上，他的举止是那样小心翼翼，仿佛每个动作都会带来剧痛。外面有头驴子叫起来，有人用乌尔都语[1]不知道喊了些什么。太阳开始下山，那些摇摇欲坠的房子的裂缝中，渗出闪闪的红色斜晖。

　　我在那年冬天、以及随后那个夏天所犯下的罪恶，再次向我袭来。那些名字在我脑海回荡：哈桑、索拉博、阿里、法莎娜，还有莎娜芭。听着拉辛汗提起阿里的名字，恍如找到一个尘封多年的老旧唱机，那些旋律立即开始演奏：**你今天吃了谁啊，巴巴鲁。你吃了谁啊，你这个斜眼的巴巴鲁？**我努力想起阿里那张冰冷的脸，想真的见到他那双安详的眼睛，但时间很贪婪——有时候，它会独自吞噬所有的细节。

　　"哈桑现在仍住那间屋子吗？"

　　拉辛汗把茶杯举到他干裂的唇边，啜了一口，接着从他背心的上袋掏出一封信，递给我。"给你的。"

---

　　[1]　巴基斯坦国语。

　　我撕开贴好的信封，里面有张宝丽来相片，和一封折叠着的信。我盯着那张照片，足足看了一分钟。

　　一个高高的男子，头戴白色头巾，身穿绿色条纹长袍，和一个小男孩站在一扇锻铁大门前面。阳光从左边射下，在他那张圆脸投下半边阴影。他眯眼，对着镜头微笑，显示出缺了两个门牙。即使在这张模糊的宝丽来照片上，这个戴着头巾的男人也给人自信、安适的感觉。这可以从他站立的样子看出来：他双脚微微分开，手臂舒适地在胸前交叉，他的头稍微有些倾向太阳。但更多的是体现在他的微笑上。看着这张照片，人们一定会想，这个男人认为世界对他来说很美好。拉辛汗说得对：如果我碰巧在街头见到他，一定能认出他来。那个小男孩赤足站着，一只手抱着那男人的大腿，剃着短发的头靠在他爸爸的臀部上。他也是眯眼微笑着。

　　我展开那封信。用法尔西语写的，没有漏写的标点，没有遗忘的笔画，没有模糊的字词——字迹整洁得近乎孩子气。我看了起来：

以最仁慈、最悲悯的安拉之名

我最尊敬的阿米尔少爷：

　　亲爱的法莎娜、索拉博和我祈望你见信安好，蒙受安拉的恩宠。请替我谢谢拉辛汗老爷，将这封信带给你。我希望有朝一日，我能亲手捧着你的来信，读到你在美国的生活。也许我们还会有幸看到你的照片。我告诉亲爱的法莎娜和索拉博很多次，那些我们过去一起长大、玩游戏、在街上追风筝的事情。听到我们过去的恶作剧，他们会大笑起来！

　　阿米尔少爷，你少年时的那个阿富汗已经死去很久了。这个国度不再有仁慈，杀戮无从避免。在喀布尔，恐惧无所不在，在街道上，在体育馆中，在市场里面；在这里，这是生活的一部分，阿米尔少爷。统治我们祖国的野蛮人根本不顾人类的尊严。有一天，我陪着亲爱的法莎娜到市场去买土豆和馕饼。她问店主土豆多少钱，但他充耳不闻，我以为他是个聋子。所以她提高声音，又问了一句。突然间有个年轻的塔利班跑过来，用他的木棒打她的大腿。他下手很重，她倒了下去。他朝她破口大骂，说"道德风化部"禁止妇女高声说话。她腿上浮出一大块淤肿，好几天都没消，但我除了束手无策地站在一旁看着自己的妻子被殴打之外，还能做什么呢？如果我反抗，那个狗杂碎肯定会给我一颗子弹，并洋洋自得。那么我的索拉博该怎么办？街头巷尾已经满是饥肠辘辘的孤儿，每天我都会感谢安拉，让我还活着，不是因为我怕死，而是为了我的妻子仍有丈夫，我的儿子不致成为孤儿。

我希望你能见到索拉博，他是个乖孩子。拉辛汗老爷和我教他读书识字，所以他长大成人之后，不至于像他父亲那样愚蠢。而且他还会射弹弓！有时我带索拉博到喀布尔游玩，给他买糖果。沙里诺区那边仍有个耍猴人，如果我们到他那儿去，我会付钱给他，让猴子跳舞给索拉博看。你应该见到他笑得多么开心！我们两个常常走上山顶的墓地。你还记得吗，过去我们坐在那儿的石榴树下面，念着《列王纪》的故事？旱灾令山上变得很干，那株树已经多年没有结果实了，但索拉博和我仍坐在树下，我给他念《列王纪》。不用说你也知道，他最喜欢的部分是他名字的来源，罗斯坦和索拉博的故事。很快他就能够自己看书了。我真是个非常骄傲和非常幸运的父亲。

阿米尔少爷，拉辛汗老爷病得很重。他整天咳嗽，他擦嘴的时候，我见到他袖子上有血迹。他消瘦得厉害，亲爱的法莎娜给他做米饭和蔬菜汤，我希望他能多吃一些，但他总是只吃一两口，即使这样，我相信也是出于他对亲爱的法莎娜的尊重。我很为这个令人敬爱的男人担忧，每天为他祈祷。再过几天，他就要去巴基斯坦看医生了，奉安拉之名，他会带着好消息归来。亲爱的法莎娜和我告诉索拉博，说拉辛汗老爷会好起来。我们能做什么呢？他只有十岁，对拉辛汗老爷十分敬爱。他们两个很要好。拉辛汗老爷过去经常带他去市场，给他买气球和饼干，但他现在太虚弱了，再也做不来。

后来我常常做梦，阿米尔少爷。有些是噩梦，比如说梦到足球场上挂着腐烂的尸体，草地血迹斑斑。我会很快惊醒，喘着气，浑身大汗。但是，我梦到的事情多数是美好的，为此得感谢安拉。我梦到拉辛汗老爷身体好起来了。我梦到我的儿子长大成人，成为一个好人，一个自由的人，还是一个重要人物呢。我梦到花儿再次在喀布尔街头盛开，音乐再次在茶屋响起，风筝再次在天空飞翔。我梦到有朝一日，你会回到喀布尔，重访这片我们儿时的土地。如果你回来，你会发现有个忠诚的老朋友在等着你。

愿安拉永远与你同在。

哈桑

我将这封信看了两次，把信纸折好，拿起照片，又看了一分钟。我把它们放进口袋，"他现在怎样？"我问。

"信是半年前写的，我到白沙瓦去之前几天。"拉辛汗说，"离开之前我用宝丽来拍了这张照片。到达白沙瓦一个月后，我接到一个喀布尔邻居的电话。他告诉我这么一件事：我离开之后不久，有个谣言迅速传开，说一个哈扎拉家庭独自住在瓦兹尔·阿克巴·汗区的豪宅里面，大约是塔利班放出的风声。两个塔利班官员前来调查，逮捕了哈桑。哈桑告诉他们，他跟我住在一起，虽然有很多邻居作证，包括打电话给我那个，但他们指控他说谎。塔利班说他像所有哈扎拉人那样，是骗子，是小偷，勒令他全家在天黑之前搬离那座房子。哈桑抗议。但我的邻居说那些塔利班的党羽觊觎那座大房子，就像——他怎么说来着？——是了，就像'饿狼看见羊群'。他们告诉哈桑，为了保障它的安全，他们会搬进来，直到我回去。哈桑又抗议。所以他们将他拉到街上……"

"不。"我喘气说。

"……下令他跪下……"

"不！天啦，不。"

"……朝他后脑开枪。"

"不。"

"……法莎娜尖叫着跑出来，扑打他们……"

"不。"

"……也杀了她。自我防卫，他们后来宣称……"

但我所能做的，只是一次又一次地低声说着："不。不。不。"

我想着1974年那天，在医院的病房里面，哈桑刚刚做完补唇手术。爸爸、拉辛汗、阿里和我围在哈桑床前，看着他举起一面镜子，察看他的新嘴唇。如今，除我之外，那个房间的人要么已经死去，要么即将死去。

接着我还看到其他东西：一个男人穿着人字形背心，将他那把俄制步枪的枪口抵在哈桑脑后。枪声在我父亲房子那条街道上回荡。哈桑扑倒在柏油路上，他那不求回报的忠贞生命，像他以前经常追逐的断线风筝那样，从他身上飘走。

"塔利班搬进了那座房子，"拉辛汗说，"他们托词赶走非法占有他人财产的人，杀害哈桑和法莎娜被法庭当成自我防卫，宣布无罪。没有人说一句话。我想主要是出于对塔利班的恐惧。但也是因为，不会有人为了一对哈扎拉仆人去冒什么风险。"

"他们怎么处置索拉博？"我问。我觉得劳累不堪，精疲力竭。一阵咳嗽袭击了拉辛汗，持续了好长时间。当他最终抬起头时，他的脸涨得通红，双眼充血。"我听说他在卡德帕湾区某个恤孤院里面。亲爱的阿米尔……"接着他又咳起来。咳嗽停止后，他看上去比刚才要老一些，似乎每声咳嗽都催他老去。"亲爱的阿米尔，我呼唤你到这里来，因为我在死之前想看看你，但这并非全部。"

我一语不发。我想我已经知道他接下来要说什么。

"我要你到喀布尔去，我要你把索拉博带到这里。"他说。

我搜肠刮肚，寻找恰当的词汇。我还来不及接受哈桑已然死去的事实。

"请听我说。我认识一对在白沙瓦的夫妇，丈夫叫约翰，妻子叫贝蒂·卡尔德威。他们是基督徒，利用私人募捐来的钱，开设了一个小小的慈善机构。他们主要收容和抚养失去双亲的阿富汗儿童。那儿又干净又安全，儿童得到很好的照料，卡尔德威先生和太太都是好人。他们已经告诉我，欢迎索拉博到他们家去，而且……"

"拉辛汗，你不是说真的吧？"

"儿童都很脆弱，亲爱的阿米尔。喀布尔已经有太多身心残缺的孩子，我不希望索拉博也变成其中之一。"

"拉辛汗，我不想去喀布尔，我不能去！"我说。

"索拉博是个有天分的小男孩。在这里我们可以给他新的生活、新的希望，这里的人们会爱护他。约翰老爷是个善良的人，贝蒂太太为人和善，你应该去看看她如何照料那些孤儿。"

"为什么是我？你干吗不花钱请人去呢？如果是因为经济问题，我愿意出钱。"

"那和钱没有关系，阿米尔！"拉辛汗大怒，"我是个快死的人了，我不想被侮辱！在我身上，从来没有钱的问题，你知道的。至于为什么是你？我想我们都知道，为什么一定要你去，是吗？"

我不想明白他话中的机锋，但是我清楚，我太清楚了。"我在美国有妻子、有房子、有事业、有家庭。喀布尔是个危险的地方，你知道的，你要我冒着失去一切的危险，就为了……"我停住不说。

"你知道吗，"拉辛汗说，"有一次，你不在的时候，你爸爸和我在说话。而你知道他在那些日子里最担心的是什么。我记得他对我说，'拉辛，一个不能为自己挺身而出的孩子，长大之后只能是个懦夫。'我在想，难道你变成这种人了吗？"

我垂下眼光。

"我所哀求的，是要你满足一个老人的临终遗愿。"他悲伤地说。

他把宝押在那句话上，甩出他最好的牌。或者这仅是我的想法。他话中带着模棱两可的意思，但他至少知道说些什么。而我，这个房间里的作家，仍在寻找合适的字眼。最终，我吐出这样的句子："也许爸爸说对了。"

"你这么想让我很难过，阿米尔。"

我无法看着他，"你不这样想吗？"

"如果我这么想，我就不会求你到这儿来。"

我拨弄着指上的结婚戒指："你总是太过抬举我了，拉辛汗。"

"一直以来，你对自己太严苛了。"他犹疑着说，"但还有些事情，还有些你所不知道的事情。"

"拜托，拉辛汗……"

"莎娜芭不是阿里的第一个妻子。"

现在我抬起头。

"他之前结过一次婚，跟一个雅荷里来的哈扎拉女人。那是早在你出生之前的事情。他们的婚姻持续了三年。"

"这跟什么事情有关系吗？"

"三年后，她仍没生孩子，抛弃了阿里，去科斯特跟一个男人结婚。她给他生了三个女儿。这就是我想告诉你的。"

我开始明白他要说什么，但我实在不想听下去了。我在加利福尼亚有美好的生活，有座带尖顶的漂亮房子，婚姻幸福，是个前程远大的作家，岳父岳母都很爱我。我不需要这些乱七八糟的事。

"阿里是个不育的男人。"拉辛汗说。

"不，他不是的。他跟莎娜芭生了哈桑，不是吗？他们有哈桑……"

"不，哈桑不是他们生的。"

"是的，是他们生的！"

"不，不是他们，阿米尔。"

"那么是谁……"

"我想你知道是谁。"

我觉得自己好像堕入万丈深渊，拼命想抓住树枝和荆棘的藤蔓，却什么也没拉到。突然之间天旋地转，房间左摇右晃。"哈桑知道吗？"这话仿佛不是从我口中说出来的。拉辛汗闭上眼睛，摇摇头。

"你这个混蛋，"我喃喃说，站起来，"你们这群该死的混蛋！"我大叫，"你们全部，你们这群该死的说谎的混蛋！"

"请你坐下。"拉辛汗说。

"你们怎么可以瞒着我？瞒着他？"我悲愤地说。

"拜托你想想，亲爱的阿米尔。这是丢人的事情，人们会说三道四。那时，男人所能仰仗的全部就是他的声誉、他的威名，而如果人们议论纷纷……我们不能告诉任何人，你一定也知道。"他伸手来摸我，但我推开他的手，埋头奔向门口。

"亲爱的阿米尔，求求你别走。"

我打开门，转向他，"为什么？你想对我说什么？我今年三十八岁了，我刚刚才发现我一辈子活在一个他妈的谎言之下！你还想说些什么，能让事情变好？没有！没有！"

我扔下这些话，嘭嘭冲出公寓。

第十八章

太阳已经快下山了，天空布满紫色的、红色的晚霞。我沿着那条繁忙而狭窄的街道步行，将拉辛汗的寓所撇在后面。那条街是嘈杂的小巷，和那些迷宫似的深巷里间交织在一起，挤满了行人、自行车和三轮摩托车。它的拐角处竖着各式各样的布告牌，粘贴着可口可乐和香烟的广告；还有罗丽坞[1]的电影海报，展示着一片开满万寿菊的原野，卖弄风情的女演员和古铜色皮肤的英俊男人翩翩起舞。

我走进一间烟雾弥漫的茶室，要了一杯茶。我朝后仰，让折叠椅的前脚离地，双手抹着脸。如坠深渊的感觉渐渐消失，但取而代之的是，我好像睡在自己的家中，一觉醒来，发现所有的家具都被重新摆设过，原先习以为常的每一个角落、每一处裂缝，现在全然陌生了。我茫然失措，只好重新审时度势，重新找到自己的方向。

我怎会如此熟视无睹呢？自始至终，迹象一直都在我眼前，它们现在飞回来了：爸爸请库玛大夫修补哈桑的兔唇。爸爸从来不会忘记哈桑

---

[1]　Lollywood，指巴基斯坦拉合尔的电影业。

的生日。我想起我们种郁金香那天，我问爸爸他能否考虑请新的仆人。**哈桑哪里都不去！**他勃然作色，**他就在这儿陪着我们，他属于这里。这里是他的家，我们是他的家人。**当阿里宣布他和哈桑要离开我们时，他流泪了，流泪了！

服务生把一个茶杯摆在我面前的桌子上。桌脚交叉成 X 状的地方有一圈胡桃大小的铜球，有个铜球松了，我弯下腰，把它拧紧。我希望我也能这般轻而易举地拧紧自己的生活。我喝了一口数年来喝过的最浓的茶，试图想着索拉雅，想着将军和亲爱的雅米拉阿姨，想着我未完成的小说。我试图看着街上过往的车辆，看着行人在那些小小的糖铺进进出出。试图听着邻桌客人收音机播放的伊斯兰教音乐。任何东西都可以。但我总是想起我毕业那天晚上，爸爸坐在那辆他刚买给我的福特车上，身上散发着啤酒的气味，他说，**要是哈桑今天跟我们在一起就好了！**

这么多年来，他怎么可以一直欺骗我？欺骗哈桑？我很小的时候，有一次他抱我坐在他的膝盖上，眼睛直勾勾看着我，并说，**世间只有一种罪行，那就是盗窃……当你说谎，你剥夺了某人得知真相的权利。**难道他没有亲口对我说那些话吗？而现在，在我葬了他十五年之后，我得知爸爸曾经是一个贼！还是最坏那种，因为他偷走的东西非常神圣：于我而言，是得知我有兄弟的权利；对哈桑来说，是他的身份。他还偷走了阿里的荣誉。他的荣誉。他的尊严。

我不禁想起这些问题：爸爸如何能够面对阿里的眼睛？阿里倘若得知他的妻子被他的主人以阿富汗人最不齿的方式侮辱，他如何能够每天在屋子里进进出出？爸爸穿着那身棕色旧西装、踏上塔赫里家的车道、向索拉雅提亲的形象在我脑海记忆犹深，我如何才能将它和这个新形象结合起来？

这儿又有一句为我的创作老师所不屑的陈词滥调：有其父必有其子。但这是真的，不是吗？结果证明，我和爸爸的相似超乎原先的想象。我们两个都背叛了愿意为我们付出生命的人。我这才意识到，拉辛汗传唤我到这里来，不只是为了洗刷我的罪行，还有爸爸的。

拉辛汗说我一直在苛求自己。但我怀疑。是的，我没有让阿里的右脚踩上地雷，没有把塔利班的人带到家里，射杀哈桑。可是我把阿里和哈桑赶出家门。若非我那么做，事情也许会变得全然不同，这样的想法不算太牵强吧？也许爸爸会带着他们到美国。也许在那个没有人在意他是哈扎拉人、人们甚至不知道哈扎拉人是什么意思的国度，哈桑会拥有自己的家、工作、亲人、生活。也许不会。但也许会。

我不能去喀布尔。我刚才对拉辛汗说，我在美国有妻子、房子、事业，还有家庭。但也许正是我的行为断送了哈桑拥有这一切的机会，我能够这样收拾行囊、掉头回家吗？

我希望拉辛汗没有打过电话给我。我希望他没有把真相告诉我。但他打了电话，而且他所揭露的事情使一切面目全非。让我明白我的一生，早在1975年冬天之前，回溯到那个会唱歌的哈扎拉女人还在哺乳我的时候，种种谎言、背叛和秘密，就已经开始轮回。

那儿有再次成为好人的路。他说。

一条终结轮回的路。

带上一个小男孩。一个孤儿。哈桑的儿子。在喀布尔的某个地方。

我雇了三轮摩托车，在回拉辛汗寓所的路上，我想起爸爸说过，我的问题是，总有人为我挺身而出。如今我三十八岁了，我的头发日渐稀疏，两鬓开始灰白，最近我发现鱼尾纹开始侵蚀我的眼角。现在我老了，但也许还没有老到不能为自己挺身而出的地步。尽管最终发现爸爸说过很多谎言，但这句话倒是实情。

我再次看着宝丽来照片上的圆脸，看着阳光落在它上面。我弟弟的脸。哈桑曾经深爱过我，以前无人那样待我，日后也永远不会有。他已经走了，但他的一部分还在。在喀布尔。

等待。

我发现拉辛汗在屋角做礼拜。我只见到在血红色的天空下，一个黑色的身影对着东方朝拜。我等待他结束。

然后我告诉他要去喀布尔，告诉他明天早上给卡尔德威打电话。

"我会为你祈祷，亲爱的阿米尔。"他说。

第十九章

再次晕车。当时我们驶过一块带着弹孔的标牌，上面写着"开伯尔山口欢迎你"，我的嘴里开始冒水，胃里有些东西翻滚绞动。司机法里德冷冷看了我一眼，眼里毫无同情。

"我们可以把车窗摇下来吗？"我问。

他一只手抓着方向盘，另外一只手仅有的两根手指夹着点燃的香烟。他黑色的眼睛仍望着前方，弯下腰，拿起放在脚边的螺丝刀，递给我。我把它插进车门的一个小洞里面，那里原先有个摇柄，把我这边的车窗摇下来。

法里德又鄙夷地看着我，眼中的嫌恶不加掩饰，然后收回目光，继续抽烟。自从我们离开雅姆鲁德堡垒以来，他跟我说的，只有寥寥数语。

"谢谢。"我低声说，把头伸出车窗，让午后的寒风猎猎吹过我的脸庞。马路穿过开伯尔山口的部落领地，蜿蜒在页岩和石灰岩的悬崖峭壁间，一如我记得的那样——1974年，爸爸和我曾驾车驶过这片崎岖的地带。那些贫瘠而壮丽的山脉坐拥深沟大壑，峰峦高高耸起。峭壁之上，有座座泥墙砌成的堡垒，年久失修，崩塌倾颓。我试图让眼光盯牢在北方兴都库什山脉[1]白雪皑皑的峰顶，但每次我的胃稍微平息一些，卡车便来个转弯，让我又是一阵恶心。

"吃个柠檬试试。"

"什么？"

"柠檬。对晕车很有效。"法里德说，"每次开这条路我都会带一个。"

"不用，谢谢你。"我说。光是想到要我吃下酸的东西，就够我反胃的了。法里德冷冷一笑，"它不像美国药丸那样灵妙，我知道，不过是我妈妈告诉我的古老药方罢了。"

我后悔白白放过这个和他套近乎的机会，"要是那样的话，也许你可以给我一些。"

他从后座抓起一个纸袋，拿出半个柠檬。我咬一口，等上几分钟。"你说得对，我感觉好多了。"我说谎。身为阿富汗人，我深知宁可遭罪也不可失礼，我挤出孱弱的微笑。

"古老的土方，用不上玄妙的药丸。"他说，语气不再乖戾。他弹去烟灰，自我感觉良好地从观后镜看着自己。他是塔吉克人，皮肤黝黑，高高瘦瘦，满脸风霜；他肩膀不宽，脖子细长，转头的时候，人们可以窥见那长长的胡子后面突起的喉结。他穿得跟我一样多，但我想附近的人应该不是这样的：他穿着一件背心和灰色的棉袍，外面还罩着粗毛线

---

[1] Hindu Kush Mountains，东起帕米尔高原南缘，向西南经巴基斯坦延伸至阿富汗境内。山势雄伟，有"阿富汗的脊梁"之称。

织成的羊毛毯。他头戴棕色的毡帽，稍微斜向一旁，好像塔吉克的英雄艾哈迈德·沙阿·马苏德——塔吉克人称之为"潘杰希尔[1]雄狮"。

在白沙瓦，拉辛汗介绍我认识法里德。他告诉我，法里德二十九岁，不过他那机警的脸满是皱纹，看上去要老二十岁。他生于马扎里沙里夫，在那儿生活，直到十岁那年，他父亲举家搬到贾拉拉巴德。十四岁，他和他父亲加入了人民圣战者组织，抗击俄国佬。他们在潘杰希尔峡谷抗战了两年，直到直升机的炮火将他父亲炸成碎片。法里德娶了两个妻子，有五个小孩。"他过去有七个小孩。"拉辛汗眼露悲哀地说，但在早几年，就在贾拉拉巴德城外，地雷爆炸夺走了他两个最小的女儿；那次爆炸还要去了他的脚趾以及他左手的三个手指。在那之后，他带着妻子和小孩搬到白沙瓦。

"关卡。"法里德不满地说。我稍稍瘫在座位上，双臂抱胸，暂时忘却了眩晕的感觉。但我不用担心，两个阿富汗民兵朝我们这辆破旧的陆地巡洋舰走来，匆匆看了一眼车内，挥手让我们走。

在拉辛汗为我准备的清单中，法里德是第一项，清单还包括把美元换成卡尔达[2]和阿富汗尼钞票，我的长袍和毡帽——讽刺的是，真正在阿富汗生活的那些年，这两件东西我统统没穿过——哈桑和索拉博的宝丽来合影，最后，也许是最重要的是：一副黑色假胡子，长及胸膛。表示对伊斯兰教——至少是塔利班眼中的伊斯兰教——的友好。拉辛汗认得白沙瓦几个精于此道的家伙，有时他们替那些前来报道战争的西方记

---

[1]　Panjsher，阿富汗中部峡谷。

[2]　Kaldar，巴基斯坦货币名称。

者服务。

拉辛汗曾要求我多陪着他几天，计划得更详尽些。但我知道自己得尽快启程。我害怕自己会改变主意。我害怕自己会犹豫不决，瞻前顾后，寝食难安，寻找理由，说服自己不要前去。我害怕来自美国生活的诱惑会将我拉回去，而我再也不会蹚进这条大河，让自己遗忘，让这几天得知的一切沉在水底。我害怕河水将我冲走，将我冲离那些当仁不让的责任，冲离哈桑，冲离那正在召唤我的往事，冲离最后一次赎罪的机会。所以我在这一切都还来不及发生之前就出发了。至于索拉雅，我没有告诉她我回阿富汗其实是明智之举。因为如果我那么做，她会给自己订票，坐上下一班飞往阿富汗的客机。

我们已经越过国境，触目皆是贫穷的迹象。在路的两旁，我看见村落一座连一座，如同被丢弃的玩具般，散落在岩石间；而那些残破的泥屋和茅舍，无非是四根木柱，加上屋顶的破布。我看见衣不蔽体的孩子在屋外追逐一个足球。再过几里路，我看到有群男人弓身蹲坐，如同一群乌鸦，坐着的是被焚毁的破旧俄军坦克，寒风吹起他们身边毛毯的边缘，猎猎作响。他们身后，有个穿着棕色长袍的女子，肩膀上扛着大陶罐，沿着车辙宛然的小径，走向一排泥屋。

"真奇怪。"我说。

"什么？"

"我回到自己的祖国，却发现自己像个游客。"我说。路边有个牧人，领着几只干瘦的山羊在赶路。

法里德冷笑，扔掉烟蒂，"你还把这个地方当成祖国？"

"我想有一部分的我永远会这么认为。"我说，我的戒备之心出乎自己意料。

"在美国生活了二十年之后？"他说，打着方向盘，避开路上一个海滩球那么大的洞。

我点点头："我在阿富汗长大。"

法里德又冷笑。

"你为什么这样？"

"没什么。"

"不，我想知道。你干吗这样？"

借着他那边的观后镜，我见到他眼里有神色闪动。"你想知道？"他嗤之以鼻，"我来想象一下，老爷。你也许生活在一座两层或者三层的楼房，有个漂亮的后院，你的园丁给它种满花草和果树。当然，门都锁上了。你父亲开美国车。你有仆人，估计是哈扎拉人。你的父母请来工人，装潢他们举办宴会的房间，好让他们的朋友前来饮酒喝茶，吹嘘他们在美国和欧洲的游历。而我敢拿我大儿子的眼睛打赌，这是你第一次戴毡帽。"他朝我咧嘴而笑，露出一口过早蛀蚀的牙齿，"我说的没错吧？"

"你为什么要说这些呢？"我说。

"因为你想知道，"他回嘴说。他指着一个衣衫褴褛的老人，背着装满柴草的麻袋，在泥土路上跋涉前进。"那才是真正的阿富汗人，老爷，那才是我认识的阿富汗人。你？在这里，你一直无非是个过客而已，只是你自己不知道罢了。"

拉辛汗警告过我，在阿富汗，别指望那些留下来战斗的人会给我好脸色看。"我为你父亲感到难过，"我说，"我为你女儿感到难过，我为你的手感到难过。"

"那对我来说没有意义。"他摇摇头说，"为什么无论如何，你们总是要回到这里呢？卖掉你们父亲的土地？把钱放进口袋，跑回美国找你们的妈妈？"

"我妈妈在生我的时候死了。"我说。

他叹气，又点一根烟，一语不发。

"停车。"

"什么？"

"停车，该死。"我说，"我要吐了。"车还没在路边的沙砾上停稳，我就吐了出来。

接近黄昏的时候，地形变了，从烈日灼烤的山峰和光秃秃的悬崖变成一派更翠绿的田园风光。大路从蓝地科托下降，穿过新瓦里地区，直达蓝地卡纳。我们从托尔坎进入阿富汗。[1] 夹道相送的柏树比我记忆中少多了，但在经历开伯尔山口那段乏味的旅途之后，再次看到树木，还是神情一振。我们正在接近贾拉拉巴德，法里德有个兄弟在那儿，我们会在他家过夜。

我们驶进贾拉拉巴德的时候，太阳还没完全下山。这座城市是楠格哈尔省[2]的首府，过去以温和的气候和水果闻名。法里德驶过市中心的楼宇和石头房子。那儿的棕榈树也没记忆中多，有些房子已经变成

---

[1] 蓝地科托（Landi Kotal）、新瓦里（Shinwari）、蓝地卡纳（Landi Khana）和托尔坎（Torkham）均是开伯尔山口沿途小镇。

[2] Nangarhar，阿富汗省份。

几堵没有屋顶的墙壁、几堆杂乱的泥土。

法里德驶上一条土路，将陆地巡洋舰停在干涸的水沟旁边。我从他的车上溜出来，伸展拳脚，深深吸了一口气。从前，和风拂过贾拉拉巴德富饶的平原，农民种满甘蔗，城里的空气弥漫着甜蜜的香味。我闭上眼睛，搜索香味，可是没有找到。

"我们走吧。"法里德不耐烦地说。我们踏上那条土路，经过几株光秃秃的白杨和一排残破的泥墙。法里德将我领到一座破落的平房，敲敲木板门。

有个用白色头巾蒙住脸的少女探出头来，露出海蓝色的眼睛。她先看到我，身子一缩，然后看到法里德，眼睛亮起来。"你好，法里德叔叔。"

"你好，亲爱的玛丽亚。"法里德回答说，给了她一种他整天都没给我的东西：一个温暖的微笑。他亲了她的额头。少女让出路，有点紧张地看着我随法里德走进那座小小的房子。

泥砖屋顶很低，四面泥墙空空如也，赖以照明的是屋角两盏提灯。草席盖住地面，我们脱掉鞋子，踏上去。三个年轻的男孩盘膝坐在一堵墙下的垫子上，下面铺着卷边的毛毯。有个留着胡子的高个子男人站起来迎接我们。法里德和他拥抱，亲吻彼此的脸颊。法里德介绍说他叫瓦希德，是他哥哥。"他从美国来。"他对瓦希德说，翘起拇指着我，然后丢下我们，自行去跟那些男孩打招呼。

瓦希德和我倚着墙，坐在那些男孩对面，他们跟法里德开玩笑，爬上他的肩膀。尽管我一再推辞，瓦希德令其中一个男孩去给我拿毛毯，以便我坐得舒服些，又让玛丽亚给我端茶。他问起从白沙瓦来的旅途，问起路过开伯尔山口的情况。

"我希望你们没有碰到任何强盗。"他说。与开伯尔山口同样远近闻名的是，强盗利用那里的地形打劫过往旅客。我还没有回答，他就眨眨眼，大声说:"当然，没有任何强盗会打我兄弟那辆破车的主意。"

法里德将最小那个孩子抱倒在地，用那只完好的手去挠他的肋骨。那孩子咯咯大笑，双脚乱踢。"最少我还有一辆车，"法里德气喘吁吁地说，"你那头驴子最近怎样？"

"我的驴子骑起来比坐你的车好。"

"骑驴才知驴难骑。"法里德回敬说。他们全都笑起来，我也笑了。我听见隔壁传来女人的声音。从我坐的地方，可以看到那间屋子的一半。玛丽亚和蒙着棕色面纱的妇女低声交谈，从一个大水壶往茶壶里面倒茶。那女人年纪较大，应该是她妈妈。

"你在美国干什么呢，老爷？"瓦希德问。

"我是个作家。"我说，法里德听到之后轻声一笑。

"作家？"瓦希德说，显然颇有好感。"你写阿富汗吗？"

"这么说吧，我写过，但现在没有。"我说。我最后一本小说叫《此情可待成追忆》[1]，写的是一个大学教授的故事，他发现妻子跟他的学生上床之后，追随一群吉卜赛人而去。这本书不错。有些评论家说它是本"好"书，有一个甚至还用了"引人入胜"这样的评语。但突然之间，它让我很难为情。我希望瓦希德不会问起它的内容。

"也许你应该再写写阿富汗。"瓦希德说，"将塔利班在我们国家的

[1] 原文为 *A Season for Ashes*，这里为意译。

所作所为告诉世界其他角落的人们。”

“嗯，我不是……我不算是那种作家。”

“哦，”瓦希德说，点点头，有点脸红，“你知道得最清楚，当然。我不该建议你……”

就在那时，玛丽亚和另一个妇女走进来，端着一个小盘子，上面有茶壶和两个茶杯。我毕恭毕敬地站起来，双手交叉放在胸前，弯身鞠躬。“你好。”我说。

那妇女放下面纱，遮住下半边脸，也鞠躬。“你好。”她的声音细不可闻。我们不看对方的眼睛。她倒茶水的时候我站立着。

那妇人将热气腾腾的茶杯放在我面前，退出房间。离开的时候，她赤裸的双脚没有发出任何声音。我坐下，喝起那杯浓浓的红茶。瓦希德终于打破那之后令人不安的沉默。

“是什么让你回到阿富汗呢？”

“是什么让他们这些人回到阿富汗呢，亲爱的哥哥？”法里德说，他在跟瓦希德说话，鄙夷的眼光却一直看着我。

“住口！”瓦希德怒道。

“总是同样的事情。”法里德说，“卖掉土地，卖掉房子，收钱，像老鼠那样跑开。回到美国去，用那笔钱带上家人去墨西哥度假。”

“法里德！”瓦希德咆哮。他的孩子，甚至还有法里德都害怕起来。“你的礼貌哪里去了？这是我的房子！阿米尔老爷今晚是我的客人，我不容许你这样给我丢脸！”

法里德张开口，几乎就要说出些什么，想了想又没说出来。他颓然倚着墙，无声说着些什么，将那只残疾的脚放在完好的脚上面，鄙薄的眼光一直盯着我。

"原谅我们，阿米尔老爷。"瓦希德说，"打小时候起，我弟弟的嘴巴就比脑袋快两步。"

"那是我的错，真的。"我说，试图在法里德的逼视之下露出笑脸。"我没觉得被冒犯了。我应该把我到阿富汗来的任务跟他说。我不是来卖田产的，我要去喀布尔找个小男孩。"

"小男孩？"瓦希德重复说。

"是的。"我从衬衣的口袋掏出宝丽来照片。再次看到哈桑的照片，再次让我的心因为他的死揪痛起来。我不得不将眼光移开，把它递给瓦希德。他端详着那张照片，抬眼望望我，又看回去。"这个男孩？"

我点点头。

"这个哈扎拉男孩？"

"是的。"

"他对你很重要吗？"

"他的父亲对我来说很重要，就是照片中那个男人，现在他死了。"

瓦希德眨眨眼："他是你的朋友？"

我内心想说是，仿佛在心灵深处，我想保守爸爸的秘密。可是谎言已经足够多了，"他是我同父异母的兄弟。"我压制着情绪说，又加上一句，"我的私生弟弟。"我转过茶杯，把弄着杯柄。

"我不是想要刺探你的隐私。"

"你没有。"我说。

"你会怎么安置他呢？"

"把他带到白沙瓦，那儿有人会好好照料他。"

瓦希德把照片还给我，厚厚的手掌放在我肩膀上。"你是条让人尊敬的汉子，阿米尔老爷。一个真正的阿富汗人。"

我暗自汗颜。

"你今晚来我家做客，让我很骄傲。"瓦希德说。我跟他客气了几句，偷眼看向法里德。现在他低着头，玩弄着草席残破的边缘。

隔了一会儿，玛丽亚跟她妈妈端来两碗热气腾腾的蔬菜汤，还有两片面包。"很抱歉，没有肉。"瓦希德说，"现在只有塔利班才能吃上肉。"

"这看起来很棒。"我说，它确实很棒。我让他跟小孩也吃些，但瓦希德说他们在我们来之前刚吃过。法里德和我卷起衣袖，手抓面包，浸在蔬菜汤里面，吃了起来。

吃的时候，我看着瓦希德的儿子，他们三个都很瘦，脸上脏兮兮的，棕色的头发剪得很短，戴着无边草帽，不时偷偷看着我的电子手表。最小那个在他哥哥耳边说了些什么，他哥哥点点头，眼神一直没离开我的手表。最大那个男孩——我猜想他大概十二岁——摇晃着身体，眼光也落在我的手表上。吃完之后，玛丽亚端来一陶罐水，我洗过手，问瓦希德我能不能送点礼物给他儿子。他不许，但我执意要送，他勉强同意了。我把手表脱下来，交给三个男孩中最小那个。他怯生生地说了句"谢谢"。

"它可以告诉你世界任何城市的时间。"我告诉他。孩子们礼貌地点点头，将手表传来传去，轮流试戴。但他们很快就不感兴趣了，将手表扔在草席上。

"你本来可以告诉我。"法里德后来说。瓦希德的妻子替我们铺好草席，我们两个躺在一起。

"告诉你什么？"

"你到阿富汗的原因。"他的声音没有了那种自遇到他以来一直听到的锋芒。

"你没问。"我说。

"你应该告诉我。"

他翻过身，脸朝着我，屈手垫在头下。"也许我会帮你找到这个男孩。"

"谢谢你，法里德。"我说。

"我错了，不该瞎猜。"

我叹气："别烦了。你是对的，只是你不知道而已。"

他双手被绑在身后，粗粗的绳索勒进他的手腕，黑布蒙住他的眼睛。他跪在街头，跪在一沟死水边上，他的头耷拉在两肩之间。他跪在坚硬的地面上，他礼拜，身子摇晃，鲜血浸透了裤子。天色已近黄昏，他长长的身影在沙砾上来回晃动。他低声说着什么。我踏上前。千千万万遍，他低声说，为你，千千万万遍。他来回摇晃。他扬起脸，我看到上唇有道细微的疤痕。

并非只有我们两个。

我先是看到枪管，接着看到站在他身后那个人。他很高，穿着人字形背心和黑色长袍。他低头看着身前这个被蒙住眼睛的男人，眼中只有无尽的空虚。他退后一步，举起枪管，放在那个跪着的男人脑后。那时，黯淡的阳光照在那金属上，闪耀着。

来复枪发出震耳欲聋的响声。

我顺着枪管向上的弧形，看见枪口冒着袅袅烟雾，看见它后面那张脸。我就是那个穿着人字背心的人。

我惊醒，尖叫卡在喉咙中。

我走到外面。明月半弯，银光黯淡，我伫立，抬头望着星辰遍布的夜空。蟋蟀隐身黑暗中啾啾鸣叫，风拂过树梢。我赤裸的脚下大地寒凉，刹那间，自我们穿过国境后，我初次感到我回来了。度过所有这些年月，我又回来了，站在祖辈的土地上。正是在这片土地上，我的曾祖父在去世前一年娶了第三个妻子。1915 年那场横扫喀布尔的霍乱要了他的命。最后，她给他生了前两个妻子所未能生出的：一个儿子。正是在这片土地上，我的祖父跟纳迪尔国王一起狩猎，射杀一头鹿。我妈妈死在这片土地上。也是在这片土地上，我曾为了得到父亲的爱苦苦奋斗。

我倚着那屋子的一堵泥墙坐下。突然间，我觉得自己和这片古老的土地血脉相连……这让我很吃惊。我的离开很久远了，久远得足以遗忘，也足以被遗忘。我在大地某处有个家，对于那些睡在我倚着这面墙那边的人们来说，那地方或许遥远如另外一个星系。我曾以为我忘了这片土地。但是我没忘。而且，在皎洁的月光中，我感到在我脚下的阿富汗发出低沉的响声。也许阿富汗也没有把我遗忘。

我朝西望去，觉得真是奇妙，在峰峦那边的某处，喀布尔依然存在。它真的存在，不只是久远的记忆，不只是《旧金山纪事报》第十五版上某篇美联社报道的标题。西方的山脉那边某个地方有座沉睡的城市，我的兔唇弟弟和我曾在那里追过风筝。那边某个地方，我梦中那个蒙着眼的男人死于非命。曾经，在山那边，我作过一个抉择。而如今，时隔四分之一个世纪，正是那个抉择让我重返这片土地。

我正打算回去，听到屋里传出说话声。我认得有个是瓦希德的嗓音。

"……没有什么留给孩子吃的了。"

"我们是很饿，但我们不是野蛮人！他是客人！你说我该怎么办？"他的声音很疲累。

"……明天去找些东西，"她哭泣着说，"我拿什么来养……"

我蹑手蹑脚走开。现在我明白为什么那些男孩对手表毫无兴趣了。他们根本就不是在看着手表，他们看着的是我的食物。

我们在隔日早上道别。就在我爬上陆地巡洋舰之前，我谢谢瓦希德的热情招待。他指着身后那座小小的房子。"这里是你的家。"他说。他三个儿子站在门口，看着我们。最小那个戴着手表——它在他瘦小的手腕上荡来荡去。

我们离开的时候，我看着侧视镜。瓦希德被他的儿子环绕着，站在一阵车轮卷起的尘雾中。我突然想起，要是在另外的世界，这些孩子不会饿得连追逐汽车的力气都没有。

那天早些时候，我确信无人注意，做了一件二十六年前就已经做过的事情：将一把皱皱的钞票塞在草席下面。

第二十章

　　法里德警告过我。他警告过，可是，到头来，他不过是白费唇舌。

　　我们沿着弹坑密布的道路，从贾拉拉巴德，一路蜿蜒驶向喀布尔。我上一次踏上这条征途，是在盖着帆布的卡车中，往相反的方向而去。爸爸差点被那个嗑了毒品的、唱着歌曲的俄国兵射杀——那晚爸爸真让我抓狂，我吓坏了，而最终为他感到骄傲。喀布尔到贾拉拉巴德的车程非常崎岖，道路在山岩之间逶迤颠簸，足以震得人们的骨头咔咔响。如今沿途景象荒凉，正是两次战争遗下的残迹。二十年前，我目睹了第一场战争的一部分。路边散落的东西无情地提醒着它的存在：焚毁的旧俄军坦克残骸、锈蚀的倾覆的军车，还有一辆陷在山脚被撞得粉碎的俄军吉普。至于第二次战争，我曾在电视上见过，现在正透过法里德的眼睛审视着它。

　　法里德驾轻就熟地避开那条破路上的坑洞。他显然是个性情中人。自从我们在瓦希德家借宿之后，他的话多起来了。他让我坐在副驾驶的位置，说话的时候看着我。他甚至还微笑了一两次。他用那只残疾的手熟练地把着方向盘，指着路边座座泥屋组成的村落，说多年以前，他就认得那里的村民，他们中多数不是死了，就是聚集在巴基斯坦的难民营。"有时候死掉的那些反而更幸运一些。"他说。

他指着一座遭受祝融之灾的小村落，现在它只是一些黑色的墙壁，没有屋顶。我看见有条狗睡在那些墙壁之下。"我在这里有过一个朋友，"法里德说，"他修理自行车的手艺很棒，手鼓也弹得不错。塔利班杀了他全家，放火烧掉这座村子。"

我们驶过焚毁的村子，那条狗一动不动。

记得从前，贾拉拉巴德到喀布尔只要两个小时的车程，也许多一些。法里德和我开了四个小时才抵达喀布尔。而当我们到达……我们刚驶过玛希帕水库的时候，法里德便警告我。

"喀布尔不是你记忆中那样了。"他说。

"我听说过。"

法里德看了我一眼，仿佛在说听见和看到不是一回事。他是对的。因为当我们最终驶进喀布尔，我敢肯定，绝对肯定，他一定开错路了。法里德肯定见到我目瞪口呆的表情，也许在累次载人进出喀布尔之后，他对这种久违了喀布尔的人脸上出现的神情早已习以为常。

他拍拍我的肩头，"欢迎你回来。"他忧郁地说。

废墟和乞丐，触目皆是这种景象。我记得从前也有乞丐——爸爸身上总是额外带着一把阿富汗尼硬币，分发给他们；我从不曾见过他拒绝乞讨的人。可是如今，街头巷尾都能见到他们，身披破麻布，伸出脏兮兮的手，乞讨一个铜板。而且如今乞食的多数是儿童，瘦小，脸色冷漠，有些不超过五六岁。妇女裹着长袍，坐在繁忙街道的水沟边，膝盖上是她们的儿子，一遍遍念着："行行好，行行好！"还有别的，某种我一开始没有注意到的事情：几乎见不到有任何成年男子在他们身边——战争把父亲变成阿富汗的稀缺物品。

我们开在一条朝西通往卡德察区的街道上，我记得在 1970 年代，这可是主要的商业街：雅德梅湾。干涸的喀布尔河就在我们北边。那边的山麓之上，耸立着残破的旧城墙。它东边紧邻的巴拉·希萨堡垒——1992 年军阀杜斯塔姆[1]一度占领这座古代城堡——坐落在雪达瓦扎山脉上。1992 年到 1996 年间，人民圣战者组织的火箭炮如雨点般从那座山脉射出来，落进喀布尔城里，造成如今摆在我眼前的浩劫。雪达瓦扎山脉朝西逶迤而去。我记得，"午炮"也是从这些山峦中发出来的，它每天响起，宣告中午来临；在斋月期间，它也是一声信号，意味着白天的禁食可以结束了。那些天，整座城市都能听见午炮的轰鸣。

"我小时候常常路过这儿，前往雅德梅湾。"我喃喃说，"过去这儿商店宾馆林立，遍地食肆和霓虹灯。我经常向一个叫做塞弗的老人买风筝。他在旧警察局旁边开了间小小的风筝铺。"

"警察局还在那儿。"法里德说，"这座城市不缺警察。但你在雅德梅湾，或者喀布尔任何地方，再也找不到风筝或者风筝铺了。那样的日子已经结束。"

雅德梅湾业已变成一座巨大的废墟。那些尚未被彻底摧毁的屋宇赤条条竖在那儿，屋顶破了大洞，墙壁嵌满火箭炮的弹片。整个街区已经化为瓦砾。我看见一个带着弹孔的招牌斜斜埋在一堆残骸中，上面写着

---

[1] Abdul Rashid Dostum（1954~ ），北方联盟领导人之一。

"请喝可口可……"。我看见在那些犬牙交错的砖石废墟中,有座没有窗户的破房子,儿童在里面玩耍。自行车和骡车在孩子、流浪狗和一堆堆废物中穿梭。城市上方是灰蒙蒙的尘雾,河那边,一道青烟袅袅升上天空。

"那些树呢?"我说。

"冬天的时候被人们砍成柴火了。"法里德说,"俄国佬也砍了不少。"

"为什么?"

"树上经常躲着狙击手。"

一阵悲哀向我袭来。重返喀布尔,犹如去拜访一个多年未遇的老朋友,却发现他潦倒凄戚,发现他无家可归、身无分文。

"我爸爸过去在沙里诺区盖了个恤孤院,旧城那边,就在这里南面。"我说。

"我有印象,"法里德说,"它在几年前被毁了。"

"你可以停车吗?"我说,"我想在这里走走,很快就好。"

法里德把车停在一条小巷,旁边有座摇摇欲坠的房子,没有门。"那过去是间药房。"我们下车时法里德咕哝着说。我们走上雅德梅湾,转右,朝西走去。"什么味道?"我说。某些东西熏得我眼泪直流。

"柴油。"法里德回答说,"这座城市的发电厂总是出毛病,用电得不到保证,人们烧柴油。"

"柴油。你记得从前这条街道散发着什么味道吗?"

法里德笑着说:"烤肉。"

"烤羊羔肉。"我说。

"羊羔肉。"法里德说，舔了舔嘴唇。"现在喀布尔城里只有塔利班吃得上羊羔肉啦。"他拉拉我的衣袖，"说起……"

一辆汽车朝我们开来。"大胡子巡逻队。"法里德低声说。

那是我第一次见到塔利班。我在电视上、互联网上、杂志封面上、报纸上见过他们。但如今我站在这里，离他们不到五十英尺，告诉自己心里突然涌起的并非纯粹的赤裸裸的恐惧；告诉自己我的血肉没有突然之间压着我的骨头，我的心跳没有加速。他们来了，趾高气扬。

红色的丰田皮卡慢慢驶过我们。几个脸色严峻的青年人蹲在车斗上，肩膀扛着俄制步枪。他们全都留着大胡子，穿着黑色长袍。有个皮肤黝黑的家伙，看上去二十出头，皱着一双浓眉，手中挥舞着鞭子，有节奏地甩打车身一侧。他溜转的眼睛看见我，和我对望。终我一生，我从未觉得自己如此无遮无拦。接着那个塔利班吐了一口沾有烟丝的口水，眼睛移开。我发现自己又能呼吸了。皮卡沿雅德梅湾驶去，在车后卷起一阵尘雾。

"你怎么回事？"法里德嘘声说。

"什么？"

"永远不要瞪着他们！你听到了吗？永远不要！"

"我不是故意的。"我说。

"你的朋友说得对，老爷。好像你不该用棍子去捅一条疯狗。"有人说。声音来自一个老乞丐，赤足坐在一座弹印斑斑的建筑的台阶上。他身上的旧衣磨得破烂不堪，戴着肮脏的头巾。他左边眼眶空空如也，眼皮耷拉。他举起患关节炎的手，指着红色皮卡驶去的方向。"他们开着车，四处寻找。希望找到那些激怒他们的人，他们迟早会找到，然后那些疯狗就有的吃了，整天的沉闷终于被打破，每个人都高呼'真主至尊！'而在那些没人冒犯他们的日子里，嗯，他们就随便发泄。对吧？"

"塔利班走近的时候，你的眼睛要看着地面。"法里德说。

"你的朋友提了个好建议。"老乞丐插嘴说。他咳了一声，把痰吐在油污的手帕上。"原谅我，你能施舍几个阿富汗尼吗？"他喘着气说。

"别理他。我们走。"法里德说，拉着我的手臂。

我给了那个老人一张十万阿富汗尼的钞票，大约相当于三美元。他倾着身子过来取钱，身上的臭气——好像酸牛奶和几个星期没洗的臭脚——扑鼻而来，令我作呕。他匆忙把钱塞在腰间，独眼滴溜溜转。"谢谢你的慷慨布施，老爷。"

"你知道卡德察的恤孤院在哪里吗？"我问。

"它不难找，就在达鲁拉曼大道西端。"他说，"自从火箭炮炸毁老恤孤院之后，孩子们就搬到那边去了。真是才脱狼群，又落虎口。"

"谢谢你，老爷。"我说，转身走开。

"你这是第一次吗？"

"什么？"

"你第一次看到塔利班。"

我一语不发。老乞丐点点头，露出微笑。嘴里剩下的牙齿屈指可数，泛黄且弯曲。"我还记得第一次看到他们席卷喀布尔的情景，那天多么高兴！"他说，"杀戮结束了！哇，哇！但就像诗人说的：'爱情看似美好，但带来麻烦。'"

我脸上绽出笑容，"我知道那首诗，哈菲兹写的。"

"对对，是他写的。"那老人回答说，"我知道。我过去在大学教过它。"

"你教大学？"

老人咳嗽，"从 1958 年到 1996 年。我教哈菲兹、迦亚谟、鲁米、贝德尔[1]、雅米[2]、萨迪。我甚至还在德黑兰开过讲座，那是在 1971 年，关于神秘的贝德尔。我还记得他们都起立鼓掌。哈！"他摇摇头，"但你看到车上那些年轻人。你认为在他们眼里，苏非主义[3]有什么价值？"

"我妈妈也在大学教书。"我说。

"她叫什么名字？"

"索菲亚·阿卡拉米。"

他那患白内障的眼睛闪出光芒："'大漠荒草生息不绝，反教春花盛放凋零。'她那么优雅，那么高贵。真是悲剧啊。"

"你认识我妈妈？"我问，在他身边蹲下。

"是的，我认识。"老乞丐说，"过去下课后我们常坐在一起交谈。最后一次是下雨天，隔天就期末考试，我们分享一块美味的杏仁蛋糕。杏仁蛋糕，热茶，还有蜂蜜。那时她肚子很大了，变得更加美丽。我永远不会忘记她那天对我说的话。"

"那是什么？请告诉我。"爸爸每次向我提起妈妈，总是很含混，比

---

[1] Abdul Qader Baydel（1644~1720），印度诗人，出生于今天的印度比哈尔邦，大多数诗作用波斯语写成。原书作 Beydel，有误。

[2] Ahmad Jami（1048~1141），古代波斯诗人。

[3] Sufism，伊斯兰教一个奉行神秘主义的派别。

如"她是个了不起的女人"。但我一直渴望知道细节，比如，她的秀发在阳光下是什么样子，她最喜爱的冰淇淋是什么口味，她最喜欢哼唱的歌是哪一首，她也咬指甲吗？爸爸关于妈妈的记忆，已经随着他长埋地下。也许提起她的名字会唤起他心中的负疚，为她死后他犯下的事情。抑或是因为失去她的伤痛太深，他不忍再度提及。也许两种原因都有。

"她说，'我很害怕。'我问，'为什么？'她说，'因为我深深地感到快乐，拉索尔博士，快乐成这样，真叫人害怕。'我问她为什么，她说，'他们只有准备要剥夺你某种东西的时候，才会让你这么快乐。'我说，'快别胡说。这种想法太蠢了。'"

法里德拉我的手臂。"我们该走了，阿米尔老爷。"他轻声说。我将手臂挣脱出来，"还有呢？她还说什么了？"

老人露出柔和的神情。"我希望我能替你记起来。可是我不记得了。你妈妈走得太久了，我的记忆四散崩塌，像这些房子。对不起。"

"可是哪怕一件小事也好，任何事情都好。"

老人微笑，"我会想想看。这是承诺，记得回来找我。"

"谢谢你。"我说，"太谢谢你了。"我是说真的。现在我知道妈妈曾经喜欢涂了蜂蜜的杏仁蛋糕，还有热红茶，知道她用过"深深地"这个词，知道她曾为快乐烦恼过。我对妈妈的了解，从这个街头老人身上得到的，甚至比从爸爸身上知道的还要多。

露宿街头的老乞丐恰好认识我妈妈，这在多数非阿富汗人眼里，也许会是匪夷所思的巧合，但我们对此只字不提，默默走回那辆汽车。因为我们知道，在阿富汗，特别是在喀布尔，这样的荒唐事情司空见惯。爸爸过去说过："把两个素昧平生的阿富汗人关在同一间屋子里，不消十分钟，他们就能找出他们之间的亲戚关系。"

我们离开了坐在那座房子台阶上的老人。我原想带他到他的办公室去，看看他能否想起更多关于我妈妈的事情。但我再也没有见到他。

我们发现新恤孤院在卡德察区北边，紧邻干涸的喀布尔河河堤。那是一座平房，军营式建筑，墙上有裂缝，窗户用木板封上。前去的途中，法里德告诉我说，在喀布尔各个城区中，卡德察区受战争破坏最严重，而当我们下车，证据太明显了。立在满是弹坑的街道两旁的，只有比废墟好不了多少的破落建筑，以及久无人烟的房子。我们走过一具锈蚀的轿车残骸，看到一台半截埋在碎石堆里面、没有荧屏的电视机，一堵涂着黑色"塔利班万岁"标语的墙壁。

应门的是个秃顶男人，矮矮瘦瘦，留着蓬松的灰白胡子。他穿着旧斜纹呢夹克，戴着无边便帽，眼镜挂在鼻尖上，有块镜片已经碎裂。眼镜后面，黑豆似的眼珠在我和法里德身上扫来扫去。"你好。"他说。

"你好，"我说，把宝丽来照片给他看，"我们在找这个男孩。"

他匆匆瞥了一眼照片，"对不起，我从没见过他。"

"你还没仔细看看那张照片呢，老弟，"法里德说，"为什么不好好看看呢？"

"麻烦你。"我补上一句。

门后的男人接过相片，端详着，把它还给我。"不，对不起。我只认得这所机构里面的每一个孩子，但这个看起来很面生。现在，如果你们没别的事情，我得去工作了。"他关上门，上闩。

我用指节敲门："老爷，老爷，麻烦你开门。我们对他没有恶意。"

"我跟你说过，他不在这里。"门那边传来他的声音，"现在，请你们走开。"

法里德上前几步，把前额贴在门上。"老弟，我们没带塔利班的人来。"他小心翼翼，低声说，"这个男人是想把那孩子带到安全的地方。"

"我从白沙瓦来。"我说，"我有个好朋友认识一对美国夫妇，在那儿开设恤孤院。"我感到那人就在门后。知道他站在那儿，倾听着，犹豫不决，在希望和怀疑之间来回挣扎。"你看，我认识索拉博的父亲，"我说，"名字叫哈桑。他妈妈的名字叫法莎娜。他管他奶奶叫莎莎。他能读书写字，弹弓打得很好。那儿有孩子的希望，老爷，一条生路。麻烦你开门。"

门后只有沉默。

"我是他伯伯。"我说。

隔了一会儿，传来开锁的声音，门缝又露出那张窄窄的脸。他看看我和法里德，对我说："有件事你说错了。"

"哪件？"

"他的弹弓射得很了不起！"

我笑了。

"那东西跟他形影不离。他无论走到哪儿，都会将它塞在裤带上。"

那人放我们进去，自我介绍，他叫察曼，恤孤院的负责人。"我带你们去我的办公室。"他说。

我们跟着他，穿过阴暗污秽的走廊，孩子们穿着残破的羊毛衫，赤着脚走来走去。我们走过一些房间，没有一间铺着地毯，窗子蒙着塑料膜。房间塞满铁床，但多数没有被褥。

"这里有多少个孤儿？"法里德问。

"多到我们都装不下了，大概两百五十个。"察曼回头说，"但他们并非全都无亲无故。有很多人因为战争失去了父亲，母亲无法抚养他们，因为塔利班不许女人工作。所以她们把孩子送到这里。"他用手做了抹眼泪的动作，伤心地补充道："这个地方总比街头好，但也好不了多少。这座房子本来就不是给人住的——它过去是仓库，用来存放地毯。所以这里没有热水器，他们留下的井也干了。"他放低声音，"我求过塔利班，跟他们要钱，用来掘一眼更深的井，次数多得记不清了，他们只是转动念珠，告诉我他们没有钱。没有钱。"他冷笑。

他指着墙边的一排床铺。"我们的床不够，已经有的床也缺少褥子。更糟糕的是，我们没有足够的毛毯。"他让我们看着一个在跳绳的女孩，有两个孩子陪着她。"你们见到那个女孩吗？上个冬天，孩子们不得不共用毛毯。她哥哥被冻死了。"他继续走，"上次我检查的时候，发现仓库里面只有不到够一个月吃的大米了，等用完之后，这些孩子的早饭和晚饭只有面包和红茶可吃了。"我注意到他没提起午饭。

他站住，转向我："这里提供的庇护少得可怜，几乎没有食物，没有衣服，没有干净的水。我这里大量过剩的是那些失去童年的孩子。但可悲的是，这些孩子算是幸运的了。我们负荷过重，每天我都要拒绝带着孩子到这里来的母亲。"他朝我走上一步，"你说索拉博还有希望？我祈望你没有说谎，老爷。可是……也许你来得太迟了。"

"什么意思？"

察曼移开眼光。"跟我来。"

负责人的办公室是这么一间房子：四面空荡荡的开裂墙壁，一张地毯，一张桌子，两张折叠椅。察曼和我坐下的时候，我看见一只灰色的老鼠从墙洞探出头来，窜过房间。它嗅嗅我的鞋子，我身体一缩，接着它去嗅察曼的鞋子，这才奔出洞开的门。

"你刚才说太迟了是什么意思？"我说。

"你们想喝茶吗？我可以去弄一些。"

"不了，谢谢。我们还是谈谈。"

察曼身子倒在座椅上，双臂抱胸，"我要告诉你的是不愉快的事情，更别提可能还很危险。"

"谁危险？"

"你，我。当然还有索拉博，如果还不算太迟的话。"

"我需要知道。"

他点点头："好的。但我首先想问你一个问题。你有多渴望想找到你的侄儿？"

我想起童年时代，我们在街头和人打架，每次都是哈桑为我挺身而出，一个打两个，有时是三个。我畏缩旁观，心里想帮忙，但总是望而却步，总是被不知道什么东西拉退。

我望着走廊，看见一群孩子，围成一圈跳舞。有个小女孩，左腿从膝盖以下不见了，她坐在破旧的垫子上观望，微笑着，和其他孩子一起拍着手。我看见法里德也在看着那些孩子，他残疾的手就挂在身边。我想起瓦希德的儿子……我恍然省悟：如果没有找到索拉博，我绝不离开阿富汗。"告诉我他在哪儿。"我说。

察曼凝望着我，然后他点点头，捡起一支铅笔，在手指间转动。"别说是我告诉你的。"

"我答应你。"

他用铅笔敲桌子，"尽管你答应了，我想我也许会后悔一辈子，不过，也许那样也好。反正我很该死。但如果能帮到索拉博什么……我会告诉你，因为我相信你。看起来你像个负责任的人。"他沉默了好久。"有个塔利班官员，"他低声说，"他每隔一两个月就来一次，带着钱，虽然不多，但总比什么也没有好。"他滑溜溜的眼睛看着我，又转开，"通常他会带走一个女孩，但不总是这样。"

"你居然同意？"法里德在我身后说。他冲向桌子，接近察曼。

"我能有什么选择呢？"察曼回嘴说，他推着桌子站起来。

"你是这里的负责人。"法里德说，"你的工作是照料这些孩子。"

"我根本没有能力阻止它发生。"

"你卖掉孩子！"法里德大怒。

"法里德，坐下！让他说！"但已经太迟了，因为突然间法里德跳上桌子。他纵身而下，将察曼的椅子踢飞，把他按倒在地。察曼在法里德身下挥舞着手，发出声声闷叫。他的脚踢掉一个抽屉，纸片散落在地面。

我跑到桌子那边，这才发现察曼的叫声为何闷住：法里德扼住他的脖子。我双手抓住法里德的肩膀，使劲拉。他挣脱我。"够了！"我大喊。但法里德的脸涨得通红，张口狂叫："我要杀了他！你不能阻止我！我要杀了他！"他冷笑。

"放开他！"

"我要杀了他！"他的叫声让我明白，如果我不尽快采取行动，就只好目睹有生以来见到的第一场谋杀了。

"孩子们在看着，法里德。他们在看着。"我说。他肩膀的肌肉在我手中缩紧，那当头，我以为他不管怎样都会扼着察曼的脖子不放。然而他回头，看到了孩子们。他们默默站在门外，手拉手，有的还哭起来。我觉得法里德的肌肉松弛了，他放手站起来，低头看着察曼，在他脸上吐了一口口水。然后他走到门边，把门关上。

察曼挣扎着站起身，用袖子去擦血淋淋的嘴唇，擦掉脸上的口水。他咳嗽、喘息，戴好便帽和眼镜，看到两块镜片都破了，又把眼镜摘下。他双手掩脸。好长一段时间，我们谁也没说话。

"一个月前，他带走了索拉博。"终于，察曼哽咽着说。手仍掩着脸。

"你还说自己是负责人？"

察曼放下手："我已经有六个月没有收入了。我破产了，因为我毕生的积蓄，都投在这个恤孤院。我卖掉一切财产和遗产，来维持这个凄凉的地方。你以为我没有家人在巴基斯坦和伊朗吗？我完全可以像其他人那样一走了之。但我没有，我留下。我留下来，全是为了他们。"他指着门，"如果我拒绝给他一个孩子，他会带走十个。所以我让他带走，让安拉来作决定。我忍气吞声，拿过他那些该死的、肮脏的臭钱，然后到市场去，给孩子买食物。"

法里德垂下眼睛。

"被他带走的孩子会怎样？"我问。

察曼用食指和拇指揉揉眼睛："有时他们会回来。"

"他是谁？我们怎样才能找到他？"

"明天到伽兹体育馆去，中场休息的时候你会看到他，他就是那个戴着黑色太阳镜的人。"他捡起他的破眼镜，在手里翻转，"我要你们现在就离开，孩子吓坏了。"

他送我们出去。

车开走的时候，我从侧视镜看到察曼，他站在门口，一群孩子围在他身边，拉着他松开的衬衣下摆。我看见他戴上那副破眼镜。

第二十一章

我们过河，向北驶去，穿过拥挤的普什图广场，从前爸爸常带我到那儿的开伯尔餐馆吃烤肉。那屋宇依然挺立，只是大门上了挂锁，窗户破裂，招牌上不见了"K"和"R"两个字母。

在餐馆附近，我见到一具尸体。那儿行过绞刑，有个年轻人被吊起来，绳索末端绑在横梁上，他脸庞青肿，寿终那日，他穿着残破的衣服，染着血迹。人们对他视而不见。

我们默默驶过广场，直奔瓦兹尔·阿克巴·汗区。我目光所及，见到的总是一座尘雾笼罩的城市，还有生砖垒成的建筑。在普什图广场往北几条街，法里德指着两个男人，他们在繁忙的街角相谈甚欢。其中有个金鸡独立，他另外那条腿从膝盖以下不见了，怀里抱着一根义肢。"你知道他们在干什么吗？就那条腿讨价还价呢。"

"他要卖掉他的腿？"

法里德点头："在黑市可以卖个好价钱，足以喂饱你的孩子好几个星期。"

让我意外的是，瓦兹尔·阿克巴·汗区的房子多数依然有屋顶，墙壁依然完整。实际上，它们保存完好。墙头仍有树枝伸出来，街道也不像卡德察区那样，到处是废墟垃圾。褪色的指路牌虽说偶有弯曲和弹孔，仍指引着方向。

"这儿不算太糟。"我评论说。

"别奇怪，现在多数重要人物住在这里。"

"塔利班？"

"他们也是。"法里德说。

"还有谁？"

我们驶上一条宽广的街道，两边是相当干净的人行道，还有高墙耸立的住宅。"塔利班背后的人，政府的真正首脑，你也可以这么叫他们：阿拉伯人，车臣人，巴基斯坦人。"法里德说，他指着西北方向："那边的十五号街叫迎宾大道。他们在这儿的尊号就是这个，宾客。我想有朝一日，这些贵宾会在地毯上到处撒尿。"

"我想就是它！"我说，"在那边！"我指着一处地标，小时候，我常靠着它认路。如果你迷路了，爸爸过去说，记得在我们街道的尽头，有一座粉红色的房子。从前，附近只有这座屋顶高耸的房子是粉红色的。现在还是这样。

法里德转上那条街。我立即看到爸爸的房子。

我们在院子里的蔷薇花丛后面找到那只小乌龟。我们不知道它怎么会在那里，而我们太高兴了，顾不上关心这个。我们把它涂成鲜红色，哈桑的主意，也是个好主意：这样，我们永远不会在灌木丛中找不到它。我们扮成两个孤胆英雄，在某处遥远的丛林，发现一只巨大的史前怪兽，我们将它带回来，让世人开开眼界。去年冬天，阿里造了一辆木车，送给哈桑当生日礼物。我们假装它是巨大的铁笼，将乌龟放在上面。抓住那只喷火的怪兽了！我们在草丛中游行，背后拖着木车，周围是苹果树和樱桃树，它们变成高耸入云的摩天大厦，人头从成千上万的窗户探出来，争睹楼下的奇观。我们走过爸爸在无花果树林边上搭建的那座小拱桥，它变成连接城市的巨大吊桥；而它下面的小水塘则是波涛汹涌的大海。烟花在壮观的桥塔上方绽放，两边有荷枪实弹的士兵朝我们敬礼，还有巨大的桥索射向天空。小乌龟在车上颠来颠去，我们拖着木车，沿红砖车道穿出锻铁大门，全世界的领导人起立鼓掌，我们报以敬礼。我们是哈桑和阿米尔，著名的冒险家，无人可以匹敌的探险家，正要接受一枚表彰我们丰功伟绩的勋章……

我小心翼翼地走上那条车道，太阳晒得砖块色泽黯淡，砖缝之间杂草丛生。我站在我爸爸房子的大门外面，形同路人。我把手放在锈蚀的铁栅上，回忆起儿童年代，为了一些现在看来微不足道、但当时觉得至关重要的事情，我曾成千上万次跑过这扇大门。我望进去。

车道从大门伸进院子，当年夏天，我和哈桑就在这里轮流学骑自行车，先后摔倒，它看起来没有我记忆中那么宽。柏油路裂开闪电状的缝隙，从中长出更多的野草。多数白杨树已经被伐倒——过去哈桑和我常常爬上那些树，用镜子将光线照进邻居家，那些仍伫立着的树如今叶子稀疏。病玉米之墙仍在那儿，然而我没有看到玉米，无论病的还是健康的。油漆已经开始剥落，有数处已然整块掉下。草坪变成棕色，跟弥漫在这座城市上空的尘雾一样，点缀着几处裸露的泥土，上面根本没有东西生长。

车道上停了一辆吉普，看上去全然错了：爸爸的黑色野马属于那儿。很多年前，野马的八个汽缸每天早晨轰轰作响，将我唤醒。我看见吉普下面漏着油，滴在车道上，活像一块大大的墨渍。吉普车后面，一辆空空的独轮车侧倾倒地。车道左边，我看不到爸爸和阿里所种的蔷薇花丛，只有溅上柏油的泥土和杂草。

法里德在我背后揿了两次喇叭。"我们该走了，老爷。我们会惹人疑心。"他喊道。

"再给我一分钟就好。"我说。

房子本身远不是我自童年起便熟悉的宽敞白色房子。它看上去变小了，屋顶塌陷，泥灰龟裂。客厅、门廊，还有楼顶客房的浴室，这些地方的窗户统统破裂，被人漫不经心地补上透明的塑料片，或者用木板钉满窗框。曾经光鲜的白漆如今黯淡成阴森的灰色，有些已经蜕落，露出下面层层砖块，前面的台阶已经倾颓。和喀布尔其他地方如此相似，我爸爸的房子一派繁华不再的景象。

我看到自己那间旧卧房的窗户，在二楼，房间的主楼梯以南第三个窗户。我踮起脚，除了阴影，看不见窗户后面有任何东西。二十五年前，我曾站在同一扇窗户后面，大雨敲打窗片，我呼出的气在玻璃上结成雾。我目睹哈桑和阿里将他们的行囊放进爸爸轿车的后备厢。

"阿米尔老爷。"法里德又喊了。

"我来了。"我回他一句。

发疯似的，我想进去。想踏上前门的台阶，过去阿里经常在那儿，要我和哈桑脱掉雪靴。我想走进门廊，闻闻橙皮的香味，阿里总是将它们扔到炉里，跟锯屑一起燃烧。我想坐在厨房的桌子边，喝茶，吃一片馕饼，听哈桑唱古老的哈扎拉歌谣。

又是一声喇叭。我走回停在路边的陆地巡洋舰。法里德在车里吸烟。

"我得再去看一件东西。"我跟他说。

"你能快点吗？"

"给我十分钟。"

"那么，去吧。"接着，我正要转身离开，"都忘了吧，让它容易一些。"

"让什么容易一些？"

"活下去。"法里德说，他将烟蒂弹出车窗，"你还要看多少东西？让我替你省下麻烦吧。你记得的东西，没有一件存下来。最好都忘了。"

"我不想再遗忘了，"我说，"等我十分钟。"

当我们爬上爸爸房子北边那座山的时候，我们，我和哈桑，几乎一点汗都没出。我们在山顶奔走嬉闹，彼此追逐，或者坐在倾斜的山脊上，在那儿可以将远处的机场尽收眼底。我们看着飞机起降，又嬉闹起来。

如今，当我爬上崎岖的山顶，气息粗重，仿佛要喷出火来，脸上汗水直流。我站着喘了好一会儿，身子一阵刺痛。然后我去看那废弃的墓园，没费多少时间就找到了，它仍在那儿，那株苍老的石榴树也在。

我再次倚着墓园的灰色石门，哈桑就在里面埋葬了他母亲。过去那扇折叶松脱的铁门已经不见了，浓密的杂草已经占领这片土地，几乎将墓碑全然掩埋。两只乌鸦栖息在墓园低矮的围墙上。

哈桑在信中提到，石榴树已经多年没有结果实了。看着那枯萎凋零的树木，我怀疑它是否能够再次开花结果。我站在它下面，想起我们无数次爬上去，坐在枝丫上，双腿摇晃，斑驳的阳光穿越过树叶，在我们脸上投射出交错的光和影。我嘴里涌起强烈的石榴味道。

我屈膝蹲下，双手抚摸着树干。我见到我所要找的，刻痕模糊，几乎全然消退，但它仍在："阿米尔和哈桑，喀布尔的苏丹。"我用手指顺着每个字母的笔画，从那些细微的裂缝刮下一点点树皮。

我盘膝坐在树下，朝南眺望这座我童年的城市。遥想当年，家家户户的围墙都有树梢探出来，天空广袤而澄蓝，在阳光下闪闪发亮的晾衣线挂满衣物。如果你仔细听，兴许你甚至能听到来自瓦兹尔·阿克巴·汗区的叫卖声，兜售水果的小贩高喊：樱桃！杏子！葡萄！日暮时分，你还可以听到钟声，来自沙里诺区的清真寺，召唤人们前去礼拜。

我听见喇叭声，看到法里德朝我招手。是该走的时候了。

我们又朝南驶去，回到普什图广场。我们和好几辆红色的皮卡擦身而过，车斗上挤满荷枪实弹、留着大胡子的年轻人。每次遇到他们，法里德都会低声咒骂。

我付钱住进了普什图广场附近一间小旅馆。三个小女孩穿着统一的黑色服装，戴着白色头巾，紧贴着柜台后面那个瘦小的四眼佬。他索价75美元，那地方相当破落，这个价格简直匪夷所思，但我并不在乎。

为了给夏威夷海边的房子付款漫天要价是一回事，为了养活孩子这么做又是一回事。

　　房间没有热水，破旧的厕所无法冲水。只有一张铁床，一张破褥子，一条旧毛毯，角落摆着只木椅。正对广场的窗户破了，还没修补。我放下行李箱，发现床后的墙壁上有块干了的血迹。

　　我给法里德钱，让他出去买吃的。他带回四串热得嗞嗞响的烤肉，刚出炉的馕饼，还有一碗白米饭。我们坐在床上，埋头大吃。毕竟，喀布尔还有一样没有改变的事情：烤肉依然如我记忆中那般丰腴美味。

　　那天晚上，我睡床，法里德睡地板，我额外付了钱，让老板取来一条毛毯，给法里德裹上。除了月色从破窗倾泻进来，再无其他光线。法里德说老板告诉过他，喀布尔停电两天了，而他的发电机需要修理。我们谈了一会儿。他告诉我他在马扎里沙里夫长大的故事，在贾拉拉巴德的故事。他告诉我说，在他和他爸爸加入圣战者组织，在潘杰希尔峡谷抗击俄国佬之后不久，他们粮草告罄，只好吃蝗虫充饥。他跟我说起那天直升机的炮火打死了他父亲，说起那天地雷索走他两个女儿的命。他问我美国的情况。我告诉他，在美国，你可以走进杂货店，随意选购十五或者二十种不同的麦片。羔羊肉永远是新鲜的，牛奶永远是冰冻的，有大量的水果，自来水很干净。每个家庭都有电视，每个电视都有遥控器，如果你想要的话，可以安装卫星接收器，能看到超过五百个电视台。

　　"五百个？"法里德惊叹。

　　"五百个。"

　　我们沉默了一会儿。我刚以为他睡着，法里德笑起来。"老爷，你听过纳斯鲁丁毛拉的故事吗？他女儿回家，抱怨丈夫打了她，你知道纳斯鲁丁怎么做吗？"我能感到他在黑暗中脸带微笑，而我脸上也泛起笑容。关于那个装腔作势的毛拉有很多笑话，世界各地的每个阿富汗人多多少少知道一些。

"他怎么说？"

"他也揍了她，然后让她回家告诉她丈夫，说毛拉可不是蠢货：如果哪个混蛋胆敢揍他的女儿，毛拉会揍他的妻子以示报复。"

我大笑。部分是因为这个笑话，部分是由于阿富汗人的幽默从不改变。战争发动了，互联网发明了，机器人在火星的表面上行走，而在阿富汗，我们仍说着纳斯鲁丁毛拉的笑话。"你听说过这个故事吗？有一次毛拉骑着他的驴子，肩膀上扛着一个重重的袋子。"我说。

"没有。"

"有个路人问，你为什么不把袋子放在驴背上呢？他说：'那太残忍了，我已经压得这可怜的东西不堪重负。'"

我们轮流说着纳斯鲁丁毛拉的笑话，全都讲完之后，我们再次陷入了沉默。

"阿米尔老爷？"法里德说，惊醒睡意蒙眬的我。

"怎么？"

"你为什么到这里来呢？我是说，你为什么真的到这里来呢？"

"我告诉过你。"

"为了那个男孩？"

"为了那个男孩。"

法里德在地上翻身，"真叫人难以相信。"

"有时候，我也无法相信自己竟然来到这里。"

"不……我想问的是，为什么是那个男孩？你从美国漂洋过海，就为了……一个什叶派信徒？"

这句话让我再也笑不出来，睡意全消。"我累了。"我说，"我们睡觉吧。"

法里德的鼾声很快在空荡荡的房间响起。我睡不着，双手交叉放在胸前，透过那扇破窗，望着星光闪闪的夜空，想起人们对阿富汗的评论，也许那是对的。也许它确实是一个没有希望的地方。

我们走进伽兹体育馆入口通道的时候，喧哗的人群正在纷纷入座。阶梯状的水泥看台上挤满了几千人。儿童在过道嬉闹，上下追逐。空气中散发着辣酱鹰嘴豆的味道，还有动物粪便和汗水的臭味。法里德和我走过那些兜售香烟、松子和饼干的小贩。

有个骨瘦如柴的男孩身穿斜纹呢夹克，抓住我的胳膊，在我耳边低语。他问我要不要买些"性感的图片"。

"非常诱人，老爷。"他说，机警的眼睛四下扫视——让我想起一个女孩，早几年的时候，在旧金山田德龙区街头，她竭力劝我买毒品。那男孩拉开夹克的一边，让我匆匆看一眼他的性感图片：印度电影的明信片，上面是媚眼如丝的女演员，穿着全套衣服，躺在男人怀里。"多么性感。"他重复说。

"不了，谢谢。"我说，把他推开，继续走。

"他要是被抓住，他们会用鞭子打得他父亲从坟里醒过来。"法里德低声说。

当然，票上没有座位号码，没有人礼貌地指引我们到哪一区、哪一排就座。从来就是这样，即使在旧时君主制的那些岁月。我们找到一个视线很好的位置坐下，就在中场左边，不过法里德那边有点挤，推推搡搡的。

我记得在1970年代，爸爸常带我到这里看足球赛，那时球场上的草多么绿啊。现在则是一团糟。到处都是洞和弹坑，特别引人注意的是，南边球门门柱后面，地上有两个很深的洞，球场根本没有草，只有泥土。等到两支队伍各自入场——虽然天气很热，所有人都穿着长裤——开始比赛，球员踢起阵阵尘雾，很难看到球在哪里。年轻的塔利班挥舞着鞭子，在过道来回巡视，鞭打那些喊得太大声的观众。

中场的哨声吹响之后，他们将球员清走。一对红色的皮卡开进来，跟我来这城市之后到处都看见的一样，它们从大门驶进体育馆。一个妇女穿着蓝色的蒙头长袍，坐在一辆皮卡的后斗上。另外一辆上面有个蒙住眼睛的男子。皮卡慢慢绕着场边的跑道开动，似乎想让观众看得清楚些。它收到了想要的效果：人们伸长脖子，指指点点，踮着脚站起。在我身旁，法里德低声祈祷，喉结上下蠕动。

红色卡车并排驶进球场，卷起两道尘雾，阳光在它们的轮毂上反射出来。在球场末端，它们和第三辆车相遇。这一辆的车斗载着的东西，让我突然明白了球门后面那两个洞究竟起何作用。他们将第三辆卡车上的东西卸下来。意料之中，人群窃窃私语。

"你想看下去吗？"法里德悲哀地说。

"不。"我说，有生以来，我从未有过如此强烈地想离开一个地方的渴望，"但我们必须留下来。"

两个塔利班肩头扛着俄制步枪，将第一辆车上蒙着眼的男子揪下来，另外两个去揪穿着长袍的妇女。那个女人双膝一软，跌倒在地。士兵将她拉起来，她又跌倒。他们试图抬起她，她又叫又踢。只要我还有一口气在，就永远不会忘记那声惨叫。那是跌进陷阱的动物试图把被夹住的脚挣脱出来的惨叫。又来两个塔利班，帮着将她塞进深没胸口的洞。另外一边，蒙着眼的男子安静地让他们将他放进那个为他而掘的洞里。现在，地面上只有那对被指控的躯体突出来。

有个矮胖的男人站在球门附近，他胡子花白，穿着灰色教袍，对着麦克风清清喉咙。他身后那个埋在洞里的女人仍不停惨叫。他背诵了《古兰经》上某段长长的经文，体育馆里面的人群突然鸦雀无声，只有他鼻音甚重的声音抑扬顿挫。我记得很久以前，爸爸对我说过一段话：*那些自以为是的猴子，应该在他们的胡子上撒尿。除了用拇指数念珠，背诵那本根本就看不懂的经书，他们什么也不会。要是阿富汗落在他们手里，我们全部人就得求真主保佑了。*

当祈祷结束，毛拉清清喉咙。"各位兄弟姐妹！"他用法尔西语说，声音响彻整个体育馆，"今天，我们在这里执行伊斯兰教法。今天，我们在这里秉持正义。今天，我们在这里，是出于安拉的意愿，也是因为先知穆罕默德的指示，愿他安息，在阿富汗，我们深爱的家园，依然存在，得到弘扬。我们倾听真主的意旨，我们服从他，因为我们什么也不是，在伟大的真主面前，我们只是卑微的、无力的造物。而真主说过什么？我问你们！真主说过什么？真主说，对每种罪行，都应量刑，给予恰如其分的惩罚。这不是我说的，也不是我的兄弟说的。这是真主说的！"他那空出来的手指向天空。我脑里嗡嗡响，觉得阳光太过毒辣了。

"对每种罪行，都应量刑，给予恰如其分的惩罚！"毛拉对着麦克风，放低声音，慢慢地、一字一句地、紧张地重复了一遍。"各位兄弟姐妹，对于通奸，应该处以什么样的刑罚？对于这些亵渎了婚姻的神圣的人，我们应该怎么处置？我们该怎么对待这些朝真主吐口水的人？若有人朝真主房间的窗丢石头，我们应该有什么反应？我们应该把石头丢回去！"他关掉麦克风。低沉的议论声在人群中迅速传开。

我身边的法里德摇摇头，"他们也配称穆斯林。"他低声说。

接着，有个肩膀宽大的高个子男人从皮卡车走出来。他的出现在围观人群中引起了几声欢呼。这一次，没有人会用鞭子抽打喊得太大声的人。高个子男人穿着光鲜的白色服装，在午后的阳光下闪闪发光。他的衬衣露在外面，下摆在和风中飘动。他像耶稣那样张开双臂，慢慢转身一圈，向人群致意。他的脸转向我们这边时，我看见他戴着黑色的太阳镜，很像约翰·侬戴的那副。

"他一定就是我们要找的人。"法里德说。

戴墨镜的高个子塔利班走过几堆石头，那是他们适才从第三辆车上卸载的。他举起一块石头，给人群看。喧闹声静下来，取而代之的是阵阵嗡嗡声，在体育馆起伏。我看看身边的人，大家都啧啧有声。那个塔利班，很荒唐的，看上去像个站在球板上的棒球投手，把石头扔向埋在洞里那个蒙着眼的男子，击中了那人的头部，那个妇女又尖叫起来。人群发出一声"啊！"的怵叫。我闭上眼，用手掩着脸。每块投出的石头都伴随着人群的惊呼，持续了好一会儿。他们住口不喊了，我问法里德是不是结束了，法里德说还没。我猜想人们叫累了。我不知道自己掩

着脸坐了多久，我只知道，当我听到身边人们问"死了吗？死了吗？"，
这才重新睁开眼睛。

洞里那个男子变成一团模糊的血肉和破布。他的头垂在前面，下巴
抵在胸前。戴着约翰·列侬墨镜的塔利班看着蹲在洞边的另一个男子，
手里一上一下抛掷石头。蹲下那个男子耳朵挂着听诊器，将另外一端压
在洞里男子的胸前。他把听诊器摘离耳朵，朝戴墨镜的塔利班摇摇头。
人群哀叹。

"约翰·列侬"走回投球板。

一切都结束之后，血肉淋漓的尸体各自被草草丢到红色皮卡车的后
面，数个男人用铲子匆匆把洞填好。其中有个踢起尘土，盖在血迹上，
勉强将其掩住。不消几分钟，球队回到场上。下半场开始了。

我们的会见被安排在下午三点钟。这么快就得到接见，实在出乎我
意料。我原以为会拖一段时间，至少盘问一番，也许还要检查我们的证
件。但这提醒我，在阿富汗，直到今天，官方的事情仍是如此不正式：
法里德所做的，不过是告诉一个手执鞭子的塔利班，说我们有些私人事
情要跟那个穿白色衣服的男子谈谈。法里德和他说了几句。带鞭子那人
点点头，用普什图语朝球场上某个年轻人大喊，那人跑到南边球门，戴
太阳镜的塔利班在那儿跟刚才发言的毛拉聊天。他们三个交谈。我看见
戴太阳镜那个家伙抬起头。他点点头，在传讯人耳边说话。那个年轻人
把消息带给我们。

就这么敲定。三点钟。

第二十二章

    法里德驾驶陆地巡洋舰，缓缓开上瓦兹尔·阿克巴·汗区一座大房子的车道。那座院子在十五号街，迎宾大道，柳树的枝条从围墙上伸出来，法里德把车停在柳荫下。他熄了火，我们坐了那么一分钟，听着发动机嘀嘀的冷却声，没有人说话。法里德在座位上转动身子，拨弄那把还挂在点火锁孔的钥匙。我知道他心里有话要对我说。

    "我想我会留在车里等你。"他最后说，语气有点抱歉。他没有看着我，"这是你的事情。我……"

    我拍拍他的手臂。"你替我做的事情，比我付钱请你做的还多。我没想过要你陪我进去。"但我希望自己不用独自进去。尽管已经知道爸爸的真面目，我还是希望他现在就站在我身边。爸爸会昂首挺胸走进前门，要求去见他们的头目，在那些胆敢拦住去路的人胡子上撒尿。可是爸爸死去很久了，长埋在海沃德一座小小墓园的阿富汗区。就在上个月，索拉雅和我还在他的坟头摆了一束雏菊和小苍兰。我只有靠自己了。

    我下车，走向那房子高高的木头大门。我按下门铃，但没有反应——还在停电，我只好嘭嘭敲门。片刻之后，门后传来短促的应声，两个扛着俄制步枪的男人打开门。

我看了看坐在车里的法里德，大声说："我会回来的。"但心里却是忐忑不安。

持着枪械的家伙搜遍我全身，拍拍我的腿，摸摸我的胯下。其中一个用普什图语说了几句，他们两个哈哈大笑。我们穿过前门。那两个卫兵护送着我，走过一片修剪齐整的草坪，经过一排植在墙边的天竺葵和茂密的灌木丛。远处，在院子尽头，有一泵摇井。我记得霍玛勇叔叔在贾拉拉巴德的房子也有这样的水井——那对双胞胎，法茜拉和卡丽玛，还有我，经常往里面丢石头，听它落水的声音。

我们走上台阶，进入一座装潢精美的大房子。我们穿过门廊——墙上挂着一面巨大的阿富汗国旗，那两个男人带我上楼，走进一间房子，里面摆放着一对翠绿色的沙发，一台大屏幕电视摆在距离颇远的屋角。墙上钉着绣有麦加地图的礼拜毯。年纪较大那人用枪管指指沙发。我坐下。他们离开房间。

我跷起脚，又放下。我坐在那儿，双手冒着汗水，放在膝盖上。这让我看起来很紧张吧？我合起手掌，觉得这样更糟糕，干脆横抱在胸前。血液在我的太阳穴里面涌动。我感到深深的孤独。思绪在我脑海翻飞，但我根本不想去思考，因为我体内清醒的那部分知道，我是发疯了，才会让自己陷进这一切。我远离妻子几千英里，坐在感觉像地牢的房间里面，等待一个凶手，我刚刚才亲眼看到他杀死两个人。这一定是疯了。甚至更糟糕，这还很不负责任。非常可能的是，我即将让年方三十六岁的索拉雅成为寡妇。**这不是你，阿米尔。**我体内有个声音说，你懦弱，这是你的天性。这并非什么坏事，因为你从不强装勇敢，这是你的优点。只要三思而后行，懦弱并没有错。可是，当一个懦夫忘了自己是什么人……愿真主保佑他。

沙发前面摆着一张咖啡桌，底座是 X 状的，金属桌脚交叉的地方，拴着一环胡桃大小的铜球。我之前见过这样的桌子。在哪里？我突然想起来：在白沙瓦那家拥挤的茶馆里面，那天傍晚我出去闲逛时走进去的那家。桌上摆着一盘红色的葡萄，我摘下一个，丢进嘴里。我得找件事来想着，任何事情都行，这样才能让脑子里的声音安静下来。葡萄很甜，我又吃了一个，完全没有想到在接下来很长一段时间里面，这是我吃下的最后一口固体食物。

门打开，那两个持枪的男人回来，他们中间是那个穿白色衣服的高个子塔利班，依然戴着约翰·列侬式的墨镜，看上去有点像某个神秘的新世纪巫师。

他坐在我对面，双手放在沙发的扶手上。好长一段时间，他一语不发，只是坐在那儿，看着我，一手拍打着沙发套，一手捻着青绿色的念珠。现在，他在白色的衬衣外面加了件黑色的背心，戴着金表。我看见他左袖有一小块干涸的血迹。他没换掉早些时候行刑的衣服，这对我来说竟然有些病态的魔力。

他那没拿念珠的手不时抬起，厚厚的手指在空气中做拍打状，慢慢地，上下左右拍打着，仿佛他在摸着一只隐形的宠物。他的袖子后缩，我见到他前臂上有吸毒的标记——同样的标记，我也曾在旧金山那些生活在污秽小巷的流浪汉身上见过。

他的皮肤比其他两个白得多，白得近乎病态，他的前额，就在黑色头巾边缘之下，有颗汗珠渗出来。他的胡子跟其他人一样，长到胸前，也是颜色较浅。

"你好。"他说。

"你好。"

"现在可以弄掉那个了，你知道。"他说。

"什么？"

他朝一个持枪的家伙做了个手势。嘶嘶。刹那间我脸颊发痛，那个卫兵咯咯发笑，手里拿着我的假胡子丢上丢下。那个塔利班狞笑："这是我最近见过的最好的假胡子。但我认为现在这样更好一些，你说呢？"他摩着手指，压得它们咯咯响，不断握着拳头，又张开。"好了，安拉保佑，你喜欢今天的表演吗？"

"那是表演吗？"我抚着脸颊说，唯求声音别暴露我心里极大的恐惧。

"杀鸡儆猴是最好的表演，老兄。如同一出戏剧，充满悬念。但，最重要的是，教育大众。"他打了个响指，较年轻的那个卫兵给他点上香烟。塔利班哈哈大笑，喃喃自语，双手颤抖，香烟差点掉下来。"但如果你想看看真正的表演，你应该随着我到马扎[1]去，1998年8月，那才叫精彩。"

"没听明白。"

"你知道的，我们将他们留给狗吃。"

----

[1] Mazar，即前文提到的马扎里沙里夫中的"马扎"，Mazar-i-Sharif在波斯语中意为"马扎和沙里夫"，由马扎和沙里夫两个地区组成。

我明白他在说什么了。

他站起来，绕着沙发走了一圈，两圈，又坐下。"我们挨家搜索，把男人和男孩抓出来。我们就在那儿，当着他们家人的面，把他们干掉，给他们颜色看，让他们记得自己是谁，属于哪里。"他现在几乎是在喘气，"有时候，我们破门而入，走进他们的屋子。而我……我拿着冲锋枪，在屋子里一通扫射，直到烟雾弥漫，挡住我的视线。"他倾向我，似乎要跟我分享什么大秘密。"如果你没那么干过，一定不知道'解放'是什么意思。站在到处是靶子的屋子里面，让子弹纷飞，忘掉负疚和悔恨，知道你自己品德良好，善良，高尚，知道你自己在替天行道。真叫人兴奋。"他亲吻念珠，转过头，"你还记得吗，贾维德？"

"记得，老爷。"年轻那个卫兵回答说，"我怎么会忘记呢？"

我在报纸上看过有关马扎里沙里夫的哈扎拉人遭到屠杀的新闻。那在塔利班攻陷马扎之后就发生了。马扎是几个最后沦陷的城市之一。我记得早餐后，索拉雅给我看那篇报道，她面无血色。

"挨家过户。我们只有吃饭和礼拜的时候才停手。"塔利班说。他说的时候神情愉悦，好像一个男人在描绘他参加过的盛宴。"我们将尸体扔在街道上，如果他们的家人试图偷偷将他拉回家，我们就连他们一块干掉。我们将他们扔在街道上好多天，把他们留给狗吃，狗肉应该留给狗。"他吸了一口烟，用颤抖的手揉揉眼睛。"你从美国来？"

"是的。"

"那个婊子近来如何？"

我突然想尿尿，祈祷尿意会消失。"我在找一个男孩。"

"谁不是呢？"他说。持枪那两个人哈哈大笑，露出被鼻烟熏成绿色的牙齿。

"我知道他在这里，跟你在一起。"我说，"他的名字叫索拉博。"

"我要问你，你投奔那个婊子干什么呢？你为什么不留在这里，跟你的穆斯林兄弟在一起，保卫你的国家？"

"我离开很久了。"我只想得出这么一句话。我头脑发涨，紧紧压住膝盖，忍住尿意。

塔利班转向那两个站在门口的男子，"这算是答案吗？"他问。

"不算，老爷。"他们笑着齐声说。

他把眼光转向我，耸耸肩，"这不算答案，他们说。"他吸一口烟，"在我生活的圈子里面，人们认为，在祖国需要的时候离开，跟叛国一样可恶。我可以用叛国的罪名逮捕你，甚至将你干掉，你害怕吗？"

"我来这里只是要找那个男孩。"

"你害怕了吗？"

"是的。"

"那是应该的。"他说，回身靠着沙发，吸烟。

我想起索拉雅。这让我镇定。我想起她镰刀状的胎记，脖子优雅的曲线，还有明亮的眼睛。我想起婚礼那夜，我们在绿色头巾之下，看着彼此在镜里的容貌，对她说我爱她。我记得我们两个在一首古老的阿富汗歌谣伴奏下翩翩起舞，转了一圈又一圈，大家看着，鼓掌称好，满世界都是花朵、西服、燕尾服，还有笑脸。

塔利班在说话。

"什么？"

"我问你是不是想见见他，见见我的男孩？"说到最后两个字时，他上唇卷起，发出一声冷笑。

"是的。"

卫兵离开房间。我听见一扇摇晃的门打开的声音，听见卫兵声音严厉，用普什图语说了些什么，然后是脚步声，每一步都伴有铃铛的响声。它让我想起过去，我和哈桑经常在沙里诺区追逐的那个耍猴人。我们常常从零用钱中给他一个卢比的硬币，猴脖子上的铃铛就发出同样的声音。

然后门打开，卫兵走进来。他肩膀上扛着个立体声放音机，他后面跟着个男孩，身穿宽松的天蓝色棉袍。

相似得令人心碎、令人迷惑。拉辛汗的宝丽来照片拍得并不像。

那男孩有他父亲那张满月似的脸庞，翘起的下巴，扭曲的海贝般的耳朵，还有同样瘦削的身形。它是那张我童年见到的中国娃娃脸，那张冬天时看着呈扇子状展开的扑克牌的脸，那张我们夏天睡在爸爸房子的屋顶上时躲在蚊帐后面的脸。他剃着平头，眼睛被睫毛膏涂黑，脸颊泛出不自然的红色。他在房子中央停住，套在他脚踝上的铃铛也不再发出声响。

他眼光落在我身上，打量着，然后移开，看着他自己赤裸的双足。

有个卫兵按下按钮，房间里响起普什图音乐。手鼓，手风琴，还有如泣如诉的雷布巴琴。我猜想，音乐只要传进塔利班的耳朵，就不算是罪恶。那三个男人开始鼓掌。

"哇！哇！太棒了！"

索拉博抬起手臂，缓缓转身。他踮起脚尖，优雅地旋转，弯身触碰膝盖，挺直，再次旋转。他的小手在手腕处转动，打着响指，而他的头像钟摆那样来回摇动。他的脚踩着地板，铃铛的响声完美地和手鼓声融合在一起。他始终闭着双眼。

"真棒！"他们欢呼，"跳得好！太棒了！"两个卫兵吹着口哨，哈哈大笑。穿白衣的塔利班身子随着音乐前后晃动，嘴角挂着淫亵的笑容。

索拉博绕着圆圈跳舞，闭着眼睛跳啊跳，直到音乐停止。他的脚随最后一个音符顿在地上，铃铛响了最后一次。他维持半转的姿势。

"好啊，好啊，我的孩子。"塔利班说，把索拉博喊过去。索拉博低头走过去，站在他两腿之间。那个塔利班伸臂抱住索拉博，"多么有天分啊，不是吗，我的哈扎拉孩子！"他说。他的手在孩子背后滑落，然后摸起，停在他的腋窝下面。一个卫兵用手肘撞了另外那个，偷偷发笑。塔利班让他们退下。

"是，老爷。"他们说完退出去。

塔利班扳过男孩的身子，让他面对着我。他把手停在索拉博的小腹上，下巴抵着他的肩膀。索拉博低头看着脚，但不停用羞涩的眼神偷偷看着我。那男人的手在男孩的小腹上下移动、上下抚摸，慢慢地，温柔地。

"我一直在想，"塔利班说，他血红的双眼在索拉博肩膀上看着我，"那个老巴巴鲁后来怎么样了？"

这个问题问得我眼冒金星。我觉得脸上冒出冷汗，双脚渐渐变冷，变麻木。

他哈哈大笑："你想干什么呢？以为挂上一副假胡子我就认不出你来？我敢说，我身上有一点你从来不知道：我从来不会忘记人们的脸，从来不会。"他用嘴唇去擦索拉博的耳朵，眼睛看着我。"我听说你父亲死了，啧啧，我一直想跟他干上一架，看来，我只好解决他这个没用的儿子了。"说完他将太阳镜摘下，血红的眼睛逼视着我。

我想呼吸，但不能。我想眨眼，但不能。那一刻多么虚幻——不，不是虚幻，是荒唐。它让我无力呼吸，让我身边的世界停止转动。我脸上发烧。那句关于烂钱的谚语 [1] 怎么说来着？往事就是如此，总是会回来。他的名字从深处冒出来，我却不愿意提及，仿佛一说出来，他就会现身。但这许多年过去以后，他已经在这里了，活生生的，坐在离我不到十英尺的地方。我脱口说出他的名字："阿塞夫。"

"亲爱的阿米尔。"

"你在这里干什么？"我说，明知自己这个问题蠢得无以复加，可是想不出有其他可说的。

"我？"阿塞夫眉毛一扬，"这里是我的地盘，问题是，你在这里干什么？"

"我已经告诉过你了。"我说，声音颤抖。我希望话不是这么说出口，希望自己没有浑身发抖。

"这个男孩？"

"是的。"

"为什么？"

"我可以为了他付钱给你，"我说，"我可以汇钱给你。"

"钱？"阿塞夫说，忍不住狂笑起来。"你听说过洛金汉吗？在澳

---

[1] 英语中有句俗语，"A bad penny always turns up"，意思是坏人总是会回来。

大利亚西部，天堂般的地方。你应该去看看，沙滩连绵不绝，绿色的海水，蓝色的天空。我父母在那儿，住在海滨别墅里面。别墅后面有高尔夫球场，有个小小的湖泊。爸爸每天打高尔夫球，我妈妈比较喜欢网球——爸爸说她打得很棒。他们开着一家阿富汗餐厅、两家珠宝店，生意非常兴隆。"他拣起一颗葡萄，慈爱地放进索拉博口里。"所以，如果我需要钱，我会让他们汇给我。"他亲吻索拉博脖子的侧边。男孩身子稍微一缩，又闭上双眼。"再说，我跟俄国佬干仗不是为了钱。加入塔利班也不是为了钱。你想知道我为什么加入他们吗？"

我嘴唇已经变干了，舔了舔，这才发现舌头也变干了。

"你口渴吗？"阿塞夫说，满脸坏笑。

"不。"

"我认为你很渴。"

"还好。"我说。事情的真相是，房间突然之间变热了——汗水从我的毛孔冒出来，浸湿我的皮肤。这是真的吗？我真的坐在阿塞夫对面吗？

"随便你，"他说，"不管怎么说，我讲到哪里了？哦，对了，我为什么加入塔利班。嗯，也许你还记得，我过去不是那么虔诚。但有一天，我看到真主显灵了，在监狱里看到。你想听吗？"

我默默无语。

"很好，我来告诉你。"他说，"我在监狱里面度过了一段时间，在波勒卡其区，1980 年，就在巴布拉克·卡尔迈勒[1] 掌权之后不久。我被

---

[1]　Babrak Karmal（1929~1996），1979 年至 1986 年任阿富汗总统。

逮捕那天晚上，一群"旗帜派"士兵冲进我家，用枪口指着父亲和我，勒令我们跟他们走。那些混蛋连个理由都没说，也不回答我母亲的问题。那也不算什么秘密，人人都知道共产主义者不分阶级。他们出身贫贱，就是这些狗，俄国佬打进来之前连舔我的鞋子都不配，现在用枪口指着我，向我下令。他们衣领上别着旗帜徽章，胡言乱语说什么有钱人统统该死，仿佛他们翻身的日子到了一样。到处都是这样的事情，冲进富人家里，将他们投入监狱，给志同道合者树立起榜样。

"不管怎么说，我们六人一组，被塞在冰箱大小的牢房里。每天晚上，有个军官，一个半哈扎拉、半乌兹别克的东西，身上发出烂驴子的臭味，会将一个犯人拖出牢房，恣意殴打，直到那张肥脸滴着汗水方才罢休。然后他会点香烟，舒展筋骨，走出监狱。进去那夜，他选了别人。有一晚，他挑中我。真是糟糕透顶，我那时得了肾结石，尿了三天血。如果你没得过肾结石，请相信我，那是你所能想象到的痛苦中最厉害的一种。我妈妈过去也得过，我记得有一次，她对我说，她宁愿生孩子，也好过得肾结石。但是，我能做什么呢？他们将我拖出去，他开始踢我。他穿有铁鞋尖的及膝长靴，每天晚上都到这里来玩踢人游戏。他也用它们踢我。他不断踢，我不断惨叫，突然之间，他踢中我的左肾，结石被挤出来了。就是那样！啊，解脱！"阿塞夫大笑，"我高喊'真主伟大'，他踢得更加厉害了，我开始哈哈大笑。他气得发疯，使劲踢我；但他踢得越重，我笑得越响。他们将我扔回牢房的时候，我仍在发笑。我笑个不停，因为突然之间，我得到了真主的指示：他就在我身上。他要我为了某个目标活下去。

"你知道吗，隔了几年，我在战场撞见那个军官——真主的行为真是幽默。我在梅曼那[1]附近的战壕找到他，胸口插着一块弹片，流血不止。他还是穿着那双靴子。我问记不记得我，他说不记得了。我把刚才告诉你的跟他说了，我从来不会忘记人们的脸。我开枪射他的睾丸。自那以后，我就有了使命。"

"什么使命？"我听见自己说，"对偷情的人扔石头？强奸儿童？鞭打穿高跟鞋的妇女？屠杀哈扎拉人？而这一切都以伊斯兰的名义？"突然间，始料不及的是，我还没来得及勒住缰绳，这些话就统统跑出来。我希望我能将它们抓回来，吞下肚。但它们跑出来了。我越线了，活着走出这间房子的希望随着这些话溜走。

诧异的神情在阿塞夫脸上一闪而过。"我觉得这毕竟算是享受。"他冷笑着说，"但是，有些事情，像你这样的叛国之徒永远不会懂。"

"比如说？"

阿塞夫眉头一锁："比如为你的人民、你的习俗、你的语言骄傲。阿富汗就像一座到处扔着垃圾的美丽大厦，得有人把垃圾清走。"

"那就是你在马扎挨门挨户所做的？清走垃圾？"

"准确无误。"

"在西方，人们有另外一个说法，"我说，"他们管这个叫种族清洗。"

"真的吗？"阿塞夫神色一亮，"种族清洗。我喜欢它。我喜欢它的发音。"

"我只想要这个孩子。"

---

[1]　Meymanah，阿富汗西北部省份法里亚布（Faryab）首府。

"种族清洗。"阿塞夫喃喃自语,品味着这个词组。

"我要这个孩子。"我又说了一遍。索拉博的眼睛望着我,那是一双任人宰杀的羔羊的眼睛,甚至还有眼影——我记得,宰牲节那天,我家院子里面,毛拉在割断绵羊的喉咙之前,涂黑它的眼睛,给它吃一块糖。我认为我从索拉博眼中看到了哀求。

"告诉我为什么。"阿塞夫说。他的牙齿轻轻咬着索拉博的耳垂,在上面游走。他的额头流出汗珠。

"那是我的事情。"

"你想要他干什么呢?"他说,然后露出猥亵的微笑,"或者,想要对他做什么?"

"真恶心。"我说。

"你怎么知道?你试过了吗?"

"我会带他到一个更好的地方去。"

"告诉我为什么。"

"那是我的事情。"我说。我不知道自己何以变得如此强硬,也许是临死一搏吧。

"我真奇怪,"阿塞夫说,"我真的很奇怪,为何你那么老远来?阿米尔,为什么你那么老远来,就为了一个哈扎拉人?你为什么来这儿?你来这里的真正原因是什么?"

"我有我的理由。"我说。

"那么很好。"阿塞夫冷笑着说。他按着索拉博的背,将他推向桌子右边。索拉博的屁股碰到桌子,将其撞翻,葡萄掉了一地。他迎面跌倒在葡萄上,上衣被葡萄汁染成紫色。穿着一圈铜球的桌脚现在指向天花板。

"那么，给你。"阿塞夫说。我把索拉博扶起来，压碎的葡萄沾在他裤子上，如同海贝吸附在码头上，我帮他抹掉。

"去吧，带上他。"阿塞夫指着门说。

我拉起索拉博的手。他很小，皮肤干燥，长着茧。他手指挪动，跟我扣在一起。我又看见宝丽来照片上的索拉博了，看到他的手臂抱着哈桑的大腿、头靠在他父亲臀部上的那种神情，看到他们两个微笑着。我们穿过房间，铃铛叮当叮当响。

我们走到门边。

"当然，"阿塞夫在身后说，"我没有说这是免费的。"

我转过身："你想要什么？"

"你必须自己赢得他。"

"你想要什么？"

"我们还有些没了结的账，你和我。"阿塞夫说，"你记得的，对吧？"

他无须担心。我永世不会忘记达乌德汗推翻国王那天。成年之后，每当我听到达乌德汗的名字，就能想起哈桑举起弹弓，瞄准阿塞夫的脸，哈桑说人们会叫他独眼龙阿塞夫，而不是吃耳朵的阿塞夫。我记得自己对哈桑的勇气钦羡不已。阿塞夫退开，发誓说他会给我们教训。他已经在哈桑身上实现了誓言。现在轮到我了。

"好吧。"我找不到其他话可说。我不想求饶，那只会让他更加痛快。

阿塞夫把卫兵唤进屋里。"我要你们听着。"他对他们说，"再过一会儿，我会关上门。然后他和我会处理一点陈年烂账。你们无论听到什么，都别进来！听到没有？别进来！”

卫兵点着头，看看阿塞夫，看看我。"是，老爷。"

"完了之后，我们只有一个能活着走出这间房子，"阿塞夫说，"如果是他，那么他就赢得自由，你们放他走，明白了吗？"

年纪较大的卫兵不安地说："可是老爷……"

"如果他走出去，你们放他走！"阿塞夫大叫。那两个卫兵吓得连连点头。他们转身离开，有个去拉索拉博。

"让他留下，"阿塞夫说，狞笑着，"让他看看。学点教训对孩子有好处。"

卫兵离开。阿塞夫放下念珠，把手伸进黑色背心的上袋。他掏出来的东西，我早就料到了：不锈钢拳套。

那人的头发涂着啫喱水，厚厚的嘴唇上面留着克拉克·盖博那样的小胡子。啫喱水浸透了绿色的手术纸帽，弄出非洲地图似的污迹。我记得他黑色的脖子上挂着一条安拉金链。他俯视着我，连珠炮似的说出一种我听不懂的语言，乌尔都语，我想。我的眼睛盯在他的喉结，看着它上上下下，我想问他究竟多大年纪——他看上去太年轻，像外国肥皂剧里面某个演员。但我说出口的只是，我要狠狠揍他一顿，我要狠狠揍他一顿。

我不知道自己有没有狠狠揍阿塞夫一顿。我想没有吧，怎么可能呢？那是我第一次跟人打架。我长这么大了，还没朝人挥过一拳呢。

在我记忆中，跟阿塞夫打架的情景栩栩如生，真叫人吃惊：我记得阿塞夫在戴上拳套之前打开了音乐。在某个时刻，长方形的礼拜毯，织着麦加地图那张，从墙上松落，掉在我头上，它上面的泥土弄得我打喷嚏。我记得阿塞夫抓起葡萄磨着我的脸，他咬牙切齿，滚动着血红的眼睛。在某个时刻，阿塞夫的头巾脱落，露出几缕长及肩膀的金色头发。

还有结局，当然。结局我看得一清二楚。我想我会永远记得。

我记得的大体是这样的：他的拳套在午后的阳光中闪亮，他第一次击中我时，我浑身发冷，但很快，我的鲜血就温暖了他的拳套。我被甩到墙壁，一颗本来可能挂着画的钉子刺进我的后背。我听到索拉博的尖叫，还有手鼓、手风琴、雷布巴琴演奏的乐声。身子撞到墙壁上，拳套击打我的下巴。被自己的牙齿噎住，将它们吞下去，我想起自己曾花了无数时间刷牙、清牙缝。被摔倒墙上。倒在地板上，血从破裂的上唇流出来，滴污了淡紫色的地毯，腹部阵阵剧痛起伏，想着我什么时候才能再次呼吸。我的肋骨断裂，声音跟折断树枝一样，从前哈桑和我经常拿折断的树枝当剑，像旧电影里面的辛巴德那样决斗。听到索拉博的尖叫。我的侧脸撞上电视柜的一角。又是一声断裂，这次正中我左眼下面。我听到音乐声，索拉博的尖叫声。手指抓着我的头发，拖着我向后，不锈钢闪闪发亮，它们挥击过来，断裂声再次响起，这次是我的鼻子。咬牙忍痛，发现我的牙齿已经不像过去那样齐整了。被踢中。索拉博不断尖叫。

我不知道自己何时开始发笑，但我笑了。笑起来很痛，下巴、肋骨、喉咙统统剧痛难忍。但我不停笑着。我笑得越痛快，他就越起劲地踢我、打我、抓我。

"什么事这样好笑？"阿塞夫不断咆哮，一拳拳击出。他的口水溅上我的眼睛。索拉博尖叫。

"什么事这样好笑？"阿塞夫怒不可遏。又一根肋骨断裂，这次在左边胸下。好笑的是，自1975年冬天以来，我第一次感到心安理得。我大笑，因为我知道，在我大脑深处某个隐蔽的角落，我甚至一直在期待这样的事情。我记得那天，在山上，我用石榴扔哈桑，试图激怒他。他只是站在那儿，一动不动，红色的果汁染在他衬衣上，跟鲜血一样。然后他从我手里拿过一个石榴，在自己额头上磨碎。现在你满意了吗？他凄然说，你觉得好受一些了吗？我从不曾觉得高兴，从不曾觉得好受一些，根本就没有过。但我现在感觉到了。我体无完肤——我当时并不清楚有多糟糕，后来才知道——但心病已愈。终于痊愈了，我大笑。

接着是结局，我就算埋在坟里也会记得。

我躺在地上哈哈大笑，阿塞夫坐在我胸膛，一张发疯似的脸被缕缕晃动的头发围绕着，离我的脸只有几英寸。他一只手掐着我的喉咙，另外一只戴着拳套，作势悬在肩上，他举起拳头，准备再次击落。

接着，"别打了。"一个微弱的声音响起。

我们都看着。

"求求你，别再打了。"

我想起在恤孤院的时候，负责人给我和法里德开门，说了一句话。他叫什么名字来着？察曼？那东西跟他形影不离。他说，他无论走到哪儿，都会将它塞在裤带上。

"别再打了。"

　　眼影混着泪珠，在他脸上冲出两道黑色的痕迹，弄糊了胭脂。他下唇颤抖着，流着鼻涕，"别打了。"他哽咽道。

　　弹弓被拉满，他的手高举过肩，握着橡皮筋末端的弓杯。弓杯里面有个东西，黄色的，闪闪发光。我将血从眼上眨落，看到那是一个铜球，从桌子的底座取下来的。索拉博将弹弓瞄准阿塞夫的脸。

　　"别再打了，老爷。"他说，嘶哑的声音颤抖着，"别再伤害他。"

　　阿塞夫的嘴巴无言地扭曲，欲言又止。"你知道你自己在干什么吗？"最后他说。

　　"求求你，停下来。"索拉博说，泪水又从绿色的眼睛涌出，和眼影混在一起。

　　"把它放下，哈扎拉人。"阿塞夫气急败坏，"把它放下，不然我会处置你，相比之下，我刚才对他做的，不过是温柔地拧拧耳朵罢了。"

　　泪水流个不停。索拉博摇摇头。"求求你，老爷，"他说，"停下来。"

　　"放下。"

　　"别再伤害他了。"

　　"放下。"

　　"求求你。"

　　"把它放下！"

　　"别打了。"

　　"把它放下！"阿塞夫放开我的喉咙，朝索拉博扑去。

　　索拉博松开弓杯，弹弓发出嘶嘶的声音。接着阿塞夫惨叫起来，用

手掩着片刻之前还是左眼所在的地方。血渗出他的指缝。血，还有其他
东西，像啫喱水一样的白色的东西。**那叫玻璃状液，我清楚地想起来。
我在某个地方读到过，玻璃状液。**

阿塞夫在地毯上打滚，翻来覆去，不断惨叫，双手仍掩着血淋淋的
眼眶。

"我们走！"索拉博说，他拉起我的手，把我扶起来。我被痛击过
的身体每一寸都在发痛。阿塞夫在我们后面叫着。

"出去！滚出去！"他高声尖叫。

我跌跌撞撞打开门。卫兵看到我的时候，眼睛睁得大大的，我在
想自己像什么样子，每次呼吸都带来胃痛。有个卫兵用普什图语说了
几句，接着飞也似的跑过我们，奔进房间。阿塞夫仍在里面不停喊着
"出去！"。

"快走，"索拉博说，拉着我的手，"我们走。"

我拉着索拉博的小手，挣扎着走下门厅。我回头看了最后一眼，卫
兵在阿塞夫身边乱成一团，朝他脸上做着什么。我恍然大悟：铜球还嵌
在他空洞的眼眶里。

我觉得天旋地转，倚着索拉博，蹒跚走下楼梯。楼上传来阿塞夫声
声惨叫，如同受伤野兽的哀号。我们走出来了，走进阳光中，我的手臂
压在索拉博肩膀上，然后我看见法里德朝我们跑来。

"奉安拉之名！奉安拉之名！"他说，眼睛大大地瞪着我。他将我
的手臂摔在肩膀，背起我，朝卡车飞奔而去。我想我尖叫了。我看见他
的拖鞋嘭嘭蹭着地面，甩打着他粗黑的后脚跟。呼吸很痛。然后我看到
了陆地巡洋舰的车顶，被放进后座，看到发皱的米色坐垫，听见车门

打开的叮叮叮声音。一阵跑步声绕过车身，法里德和索拉博匆匆谈了几句，车门用力关上，引擎发动。车子猛然前冲，我感到额头上有只小手。我听见街道上的声音，几声呼喝，看见窗外的模糊的树朝后退去。索拉博在哭泣，法里德仍不停重复着："奉安拉之名！奉安拉之名！"

大约在那时，我昏了过去。

第二十三章

迷迷糊糊间，我看见一些面孔，停留，又退去。他们弯身望着我，问我问题。他们统统在问。我知道我自己是谁吗？我身上哪里发痛吗？我知道我是谁，我浑身发痛。我想告诉他们这些，可是痛得无法开口。这些我从前就知道了，也许是一年前，也许是两年前，也许是十年前。我想和一个脸抹胭脂、眼涂黑影的男孩说话。那个孩子。是的，我现在看见他了。我们似乎在轿车里面，那个孩子和我，而我知道开车的不是索拉雅，因为她从来不开这么快。我想跟那个孩子说话——似乎跟他说话是顶要紧的事情。但我忘了自己想说什么，或者为什么跟他说话那么重要。也许我想告诉他，让他别哭了，现在一切都会好起来。也许不是。由于某种我说不上来的原因，我想谢谢那个孩子。

面孔。他们全都戴着绿色帽子。他们进进出出。他们说话很快，说的语言我不懂。我听见别的声音，别的噪声、哔哔声和警笛声。总有更多的面孔，俯视下来。我谁也记不清了，只忆起一张面孔，头发和克拉克·盖博式的胡子上有啫喱水，帽子上有非洲地图似的污迹。肥皂剧之星。那很好笑。我现在就想笑。但发笑也会疼痛。

我昏过去。

她说她叫艾莎，"跟先知的妻子一样"。她头发有些灰白，从中间分开，扎着马尾辫；她的鼻子穿着太阳形状的扣子。她戴着眼镜，双眼看上去突出。她也穿绿色衣服，她的手很柔软。她看着我凝望她的笑容。用英语说话。有东西插进我胸膛一侧。

我昏过去。

有个男人站在我床边。我认识他。他皮肤黝黑，又高又瘦，胡子很长。他戴着帽子——这些帽子叫什么名字来着？毡帽？帽子斜斜戴在一边，像极了某个我现在想不起来的著名人物。我认识这个男人，几年前，他开车送我到某个地方，我认识他。我的嘴巴不对劲。我听到一阵泡泡的声音。

我昏过去。

我右臂灼痛。那个戴着眼镜和鼻子穿着太阳状扣子的女人弯身在我的臂膀上，插进一根透明的塑料管子。她说那是"钾"。"好像被蜜蜂叮了一下，对吧？"她说。确实是。她叫什么名字？似乎和先知有关。我也认识她好几年了。她过去常常扎着马尾辫，现在它朝后梳，挽成发髻。我和索拉雅初次交谈的时候，她也是这个发型。那是什么时候？上个星期吗？

艾莎！想起来了。

我的嘴巴不对劲。那东西插进我的胸膛。

我昏过去。

我们在俾路支的苏莱曼山，爸爸在跟一只黑熊搏斗。他是我小时候的爸爸，飓风先生，高如铁塔，孔武有力，是典型的普什图人；不是盖着毛毯那个萎靡的人，不是那个脸颊深陷、眼神空洞的人。他们，爸爸和黑熊，在一片绿草地来回翻滚，爸爸棕色的鬈发飘扬着。黑熊吼叫，或许那是爸爸的叫声。唾沫和血液飞起，熊掌和人手相击。他们倒在地上，发出巨响，爸爸坐在黑熊的前胸，手指插进它的鼻孔。他抬头望向我。他是我。我在和黑熊搏斗。

我惊醒。那个瘦长的黑汉子又在我床边。他叫法里德，我现在想起来了。我和他还有一个男孩在车里。他的脸让我想起了铃铛声。我口渴。

我昏过去。

我不断清醒了又昏过去。

原来那个有着克拉克·盖博胡子的男人叫法鲁奇大夫。他根本不是肥皂剧明星，而是一个专治颅颈的外科医师。不过我总是把他当成阿曼德，某出背景设在一个热带岛屿的肥皂剧的主角。

我在哪儿？我想问，但无法张口。我皱眉，呻吟。阿曼德笑起来，他的牙齿真白。

"还没好，阿米尔。"他说，"不过快了，拆了线就好。"他的英语带有浓厚的乌尔都语翘舌音。

线？

阿曼德双臂抱胸，他的小臂毛茸茸的，戴着一条结婚金链。"你肯定在想你在哪儿，发生什么事了。那很正常。手术后总是有这种茫然的状态。所以我会把我知道的告诉你。"

我想问他线的事情。手术后？艾莎在哪里？我想看见她的微笑，想拉着她柔软的手。

阿曼德皱眉，扬起一道眉毛，看上去有点自以为是。"你在白沙瓦的医院。你在这儿两天了。你伤得很重，阿米尔，我得对你说。要我说，你能活下来真的很幸运，我的朋友。"他一边说，一边伸出食指，像钟摆那样来回晃动。"你的脾脏破裂，幸运的是，很可能是后来才破裂的，因为你的腹腔有出血的初期症状。我那些普通外科的同事已经给你做了脾切手术。如果它破裂的时间早一些，你也许会流血致死。"他拍拍我的手臂，插着输液管那边，露出笑脸。"你还断了七根肋骨，其中有根引发气胸。"

我皱眉，试图张开嘴巴，却想起有线。

"也就是说，你的肺被刺破了。"阿曼德解释说，他拉着我左侧的一根透明塑料管，胸腔又传来阵痛。"我们用这根胸管弥合裂口。"我顺着那根管子，看见它一头插在我胸前的绷带之下，另一头插在装着半罐水柱的容器里面。泡泡的声音就是从那儿传来的。

"你身上还有很多不同的创口。也就是'伤口'。"

我想跟他说我知道那个词是什么意思，我是个作家。我想要张开嘴，又忘记缝着线了。

"最严重的创口在上唇。"阿曼德说，"冲击力让你的上唇裂成两半，从人中裂开。不过别担心，整容医师帮你缝好了，他们认为你会恢复得很好，不过那儿会有道伤痕。这可避免不了。

"你左边眶骨组织破裂，就是你左眼眶的骨头，我们也替你修好了。你下巴的线要过六个星期才能拆，"阿曼德说，"在那之前，只能吃流食和奶昔。你会消瘦一些，而且在一段很短的时间内，你说话会像电影《教父》第一部里面那个阿尔·帕西诺一样。"他笑起来，"但你今天需要完成一项工作，你知道是什么吗？"

我摇摇头。

"你今天的工作是排便。你完成之后我们才能开始喂你吃流食。不见粪便，不给食物。"他又哈哈大笑。

稍后，艾莎帮我换输液管，又善解人意地摇起床头。随后，我想起发生在自己身上的事情。脾脏破裂。牙齿脱落。肺被刺穿。眼眶裂开。当我看见窗台上有只鸽子啄食碎面包的时候，忍不住想起阿曼德或者法鲁奇大夫适才说过的话。冲击力让你的上唇裂成两半，他说，从人中裂开。从人中裂开，像兔唇那样。

隔日，法里德和索拉博前来探望。"你今天知道我们是谁吗？你记得吗？"法里德半开玩笑地说。我点头。

"赞美安拉！"他说，喜气洋洋，"不用再说废话了。"

"谢谢你，法里德。"我透过缝着线的下巴说。阿曼德说得对——我听起来确实像《教父》里面那个阿尔·帕西诺。而我的舌头让我大吃一惊：它伸过我赖以进食的牙齿原来所在的地方，却是空空荡荡。"说真的，谢谢你替我做的一切。"

他摇摇手，脸色有点尴尬："别这么说，没什么好谢的。"我转向索拉博。他穿着新衣服，淡蓝色的棉布长袍，看上去尺寸大了一些，还戴着黑色的无边便帽。他低头看着脚，手里拨弄着床边弯曲的输液管。

"我们还没好好地相互介绍呢。"我说，朝他伸出手，"我是阿米尔。"

他看着我的手，然后看着我。"你是爸爸跟我说过的阿米尔老爷吗？"他说。

"是的。"我想起哈桑信里那些话。我告诉亲爱的法莎娜和索拉博很多次，那些我们过去一起长大、玩游戏、在街上追风筝的事情。听到我们过去的恶作剧，他们会大笑起来！"我也得谢谢你，亲爱的索拉博。"我说，"你救了我一命。"

他默默不语，没跟我握手。我把手放下，"我喜欢你的新衣服。"我低声说。

"那是我儿子的。"法里德说，"这些衣服他穿不下了。我觉得它们穿在索拉博身上真好看。"他说索拉博可以跟着他，直到我们为他找到去处。"我们房间不够，但我能怎么办呢？我不能任他露宿街头。再说，我的孩子们也很喜欢索拉博。对吧，索拉博？"但那个男孩只是低着头，将线缠在手指上。

"我一直想问，"法里德有点犹疑地说，"在那座屋子里面究竟发生了什么？你和那个塔利班之间究竟发生了什么事？"

"这么说吧，我们都是罪有应得。"我说。

法里德点点头，不再追问。我突然发觉，就在我们离开白沙瓦、前往阿富汗到现在，不知什么时候起，我们已经成了朋友。"我也有一直想要问的事情。"

"什么？"

我突然不想问，我害怕听到答案。"拉辛汗。"我说。

"他走了。"

我的心一沉："他……"

"不，只是……走了。"他递给我一张折好的信纸，还有一把小钥
匙。"我前去寻他，房东把这个交给我。他说我们走后隔日，拉辛汗也
走了。"

"他去哪里？"

法里德耸耸肩："房东也不知道。他说拉辛汗留下那封信和钥匙给
你，就走了。"他看看手表，"我得走了。走吧，索拉博。"

"你能让他在这儿留一会儿吗？"我说，"迟点再来接他？"我转向
索拉博："你愿意留下来陪我一会儿吗？"

他耸耸肩，一语不发。

"当然，"法里德说，"做晚祷之前我会来接他。"

我的房间还有其他三个病人。两个年纪较大，一个脚上浇着石膏，
另外那个患有哮喘，还有个十五六岁的少年，刚割过阑尾。浇石膏那个
老家伙目不转睛地看着我们，他的眼睛来回看着我和那个坐在一张小矮
凳上的哈扎拉男孩。我室友的家人——长罩衫光鲜的老太婆、孩子、戴
无边便帽的男子——喧闹地在病房进进出出。他们带来炸蔬菜饼、馕
饼、土豆饼和印度饭。偶尔还有人只是走进屋子，比如刚刚在法里德和
索拉博来之前，有个高高的大胡子就进来过，身上裹着棕色的毛毯。艾
莎用乌尔都语问他话，他不理不睬，自顾用眼光扫射房间。我认为他看

着我的时间长得有点不对头。那护士又跟他说话，他只是转过身离开。

"你好吗？"我问索拉博。他耸耸肩，看着自己的手。

"你饿吗？那边的太太给我一盘饭，但我吃不下。"我说。我不知道跟他说什么，"你想吃吗？"

他摇摇头。

"你想说话吗？"

他又摇摇头。

我们就那样坐了一会儿，默不作声，我倚在床上，背后垫着两个枕头；索拉博坐在床边的三脚凳上。我不知不觉睡着了，醒来的时候，天色已经有点昏暗，影子变长，而索拉博仍坐在我身边。他仍在看着自己的双手。

那晚，法里德把索拉博接走之后，我展开拉辛汗的信。我尽可能慢慢看，信上写着：

亲爱的阿米尔：

安拉保佑，愿你毫发无损地看到这封信。我祈祷我没让你受到伤害，我祈祷阿富汗人对你不至于太过刻薄。自从你离开那天，我一直在为你祈祷。

这些年来，你一直在怀疑我是否知道。我确实知道。事情发生之后不久，哈桑就告诉我了。你做错了，亲爱的阿米尔，但别忘记，事情发生的时候，你还只是个孩子，一个骚动不安的小男孩。当时你对自己太过苛刻，现在你依然如此——在白沙瓦时，我从你的眼神看出来。但我希望你会意识到：没有良心、没有美德的人不会痛苦。我希望这次你到阿富汗去，能结束你的苦楚。

亲爱的阿米尔，这些年来，我们一直瞒着你，我感到羞耻。你在白沙瓦大发雷霆并没错。你有权利知道，哈桑也是。我知道这于事无补，但那些年月，我们生活的喀布尔是个奇怪的世界，在那儿，有些事情比真相更加重要。

亲爱的阿米尔，我深知在你成长过程中，你父亲对你有多么严厉。我知道你有多么痛苦，多么渴望得到他的宠爱，而我为你感到心痛。但你父亲是一个被拉扯成两半的男人，亲爱的阿米尔：被你和哈桑。他爱你们两个，但他不能公开表露对哈桑的爱，以尽人父之责。所以他将怨气发泄在你身上——你恰好相反，阿米尔，你是社会承认的一半，他所继承的财富，以及随之而来的犯罪免受刑罚的特权，统统都会再赠给你。当他看到你，他看到自己，还有他的疚恨。你现在依然愤愤不平，而我明白，要你接受这些为时尚早。但也许有朝一日，你会明白，你父亲对你严厉，也是对自己严厉。你父亲跟你一样，也是个痛苦的人，亲爱的阿米尔。

我无法向你形容，在听到你父亲的死讯之后，我心里的悲恸有多么深。我爱他，因为他是我的朋友，但也因为他是个好人，也许甚至是个了不起的人。而我想让你明白的是，你父亲的深切自责带来了善行，真正的善行。我想起他所做的一切，施舍街头上的穷人，建了那座恤孤院，把钱给有需要的朋友，这些统统是他自我救赎的方式。而我认为，亲爱的阿米尔，当罪行导致善行，那就是真正的获救。

我知道到头来，真主会宽恕。他会宽恕你父亲，宽恕我，还有你。

我希望你也一样。如果你可以的话，宽恕你父亲。如果你愿意的话，宽恕我。但，最重要的是，宽恕你自己。

我给你留下一些钱，实际上，我所能留下的，也无非就是这些了。我想你若回到这儿，兴许会有些开销，那些钱足够让你用的了。白沙瓦有个银行，法里德知道在哪里。钱存在保险箱里面，我给你留了钥匙。

至于我，是该走的时候了。我来日无多，而我希望独自度过。请别找我。这是我最后的请求。

我将你交在真主手中。

你永远的朋友
拉辛

我拉起病服的袖子，抹抹眼睛，把信折好，放在我的褥子下面。

阿米尔，你是社会承认的一半，他所继承的财富，以及随之而来的犯罪免受刑罚的特权，统统都会再赠给你。也许正是因为这样，我和爸爸在美国才能相处得那么好，我想。为了一点蝇头小利贩售旧货，我们卑微的工作，我们污秽的公寓——美国式的茅舍；也许在美国，当爸爸看到我，他也看到了哈桑的一部分。

你父亲跟你一样，也是个痛苦的人。拉辛汗这样写道。也许是吧，我们都曾犯下罪行，出卖别人。可是爸爸找到一条将负疚变成善行的路。而我所做的，除了将罪行发泄在那个被我背叛的人身上，然后试图全都忘掉之外，我还做过什么？除了让自己夜不能寐之外，我还做过什么?

我又何曾做过什么正确的事呢?

当护士——不是艾莎,而是一个我想不起名字的红发女子——拿着针筒走进来,问我要不要打一针吗啡,我说好。

次日清早,他们拿掉我的胸管,阿曼德让工作人员准备给我喝些苹果汁。艾莎在我床头的柜子上放下一杯果汁,我问她要一面镜子。她把眼镜举在额头上,拉开窗帘,让朝晖射进房间。她转过头说:"过几天会好看一些。去年我女婿骑摩托出了车祸,他那张英俊的脸摔在柏油路上,青肿得像个茄子。现在他又是那么英俊了,像罗丽坞的电影明星。"

尽管她一再安慰,望向镜子,看到它里面那个硬要说是我的脸的东西,我还是差点窒息。看上去好像有人在我脸皮下面插了根气管,然后朝里面泵气。我双眼青肿。最糟糕的是我的嘴,那一大块青紫红肿的东西,满是淤血和缝线。我试图微笑,嘴唇掠过一阵痛楚。看来我很长时间不能这么做了。我左边脸颊也缝着线,就在颧骨下面,额头上的缝口在发际线之下。

脚上打石膏那个老家伙用乌尔都语说了几句。我朝他耸耸肩,摇摇头。他指着自己的脸,轻轻拍打,嘴巴咧得大大的,露出没有牙齿的笑容。"很好,"他用英语说,"安拉保佑。"

"谢谢你。"我低声说。

我刚把镜子放下,法里德和索拉博就进来了。索拉博坐在凳子上,头倚着病床的护栏。

"你知道吗，我们越快让你离开这里越好。"

"法鲁奇大夫说……"

"我不是说出院，我是说离开白沙瓦。"

"为什么？"

"我认为你在这里待得太久不安全。"法里德降低声音说，"塔利班在这里有朋友，他们会开始搜寻你。"

"我想他们也许已经来过了。"我喃喃说。我突然想起那个留着胡子的男人，他走进房间，只是站在那儿盯着我。

法里德低声说："一旦你能走动，我会带你去伊斯兰堡 [1]。那儿也不尽安全，巴基斯坦没有安全的地方，但好过在这里。至少这能为你赢得一些时间。"

"亲爱的法里德，这会把你也拖下水的。也许你不应该被他们见到跟我在一起，你有家庭需要照顾。"

法里德摆摆手："我的儿子是还小，但他们很聪明。他们知道如何保护他们的妈妈和姐妹。"他笑着说，"再说，我又没说替你白干。"

"就算你愿意，我也不会答应啊。"我说。我忘了自己无法微笑，想挤出个笑脸，一丝血从下巴流下来。"你能再帮我一个忙吗？"

"为你，千千万万遍。"法里德说。

就这样，我哭起来。我呼吸急促，泪水从脸上冲下，刺痛嘴唇翻开的肉。

"你怎么啦？"法里德紧张地说。

---

[1] Islamabad，巴基斯坦首都。

我一只手掩着脸，一只手挡在前面。我知道整个房间都在看着我。而后，我觉得很累，很空虚。"对不起。"我说。索拉博露出担忧的神色望着我。

我又能说话的时候，跟法里德说我的要求："拉辛汗说他们住在白沙瓦。"

"也许你应该将他们的名字写下来。"法里德说，慎重地看着我，似乎在想着接下来我又会为什么而崩溃。我在一张纸巾上写下他们的名字："约翰和贝蒂·卡尔德威。"

法里德把纸巾叠好，放进口袋。"我会尽快找到他们。"他说。他转向索拉博："至于你，我今晚再来接你。别累着阿米尔老爷。"

但索拉博走到窗边，几只鸽子在窗台上来回走动，啄食着木头和面包碎片。

在我床头柜子中间的抽屉里面，我找到一本旧《国家地理》杂志，一支用过的铅笔，一把缺了些梳齿的梳子，还有我汗流满面努力伸手去拿的：一副扑克牌。早些时候我数过，出乎意料的是，那副牌竟然是完整的。我问索拉博想不想玩。我没指望他会回答，更别说玩牌了。自我们离开喀布尔之后，他一直很安静。但他从窗口转身说："我只会玩'番吉帕'。"

"真替你感到遗憾，因为我是玩番吉帕的高手，全世界都知道。"

他在我旁边的凳子上坐下，我给他发了五张牌。"当你爸爸和我像你这么大的时候，我们经常一起玩这游戏。特别是在冬季，天下雪、我们不能出去的时候，我们常常玩到太阳下山。"

他出了一张牌，从牌堆抽起一张。他望着牌思考的时候，我偷偷看着他。他很多地方都像他父亲：将牌在手里展成扇形的样子，眯眼看牌的样子，还有他很少看别人眼睛的样子。

我们默默玩着。第一盘我赢了，让他赢了第二盘，接下来五局没使诈，但都输了。"你打得跟你父亲一样好，也许还要好一些。"我输了最后一局之后说，"我过去经常赢他，不过我觉得那是他让我的。"我顿了顿，又说："你父亲和我是吃同一个女人的奶长大的。"

"我知道。"

"他……他跟你怎么说起我们？"

"他说你是他一生最好的朋友。"他说。

我捏着方块杰克上下摇动。"恐怕我没他想的那么好。"我说，"不过我想跟你交朋友。我想我可以成为你的好朋友。好不好？你愿意吗？"我轻轻将手放在他手臂上，但他身子后缩。他将牌放下，从凳子上站起来，走回窗边。太阳在白沙瓦落下，天空铺满了红色和紫色的云霞。下面的街道传来阵阵喇叭声，驴子的叫声，警察的哨声。索拉博站在红色的斜晖中，额头靠着玻璃，把手埋在腋下。

那天晚上，在艾莎和一名男性护理的帮助下，我跨了第一步。我一只手抓住装着滑轮的输液架，另一只手扶在助理的前臂上，绕了房间一圈。十分钟后，我回到床边，体内肺腑翻涌，也冒出浑身大汗。我躺在床上，喘息着，耳边听到心脏怦怦跳，心里十分想念我的妻子。

隔日，索拉博和我仍是默默无语，几乎整天都在玩"番吉帕"。又那样度过一天。我们只是玩着"番吉帕"，几乎没有说过话，我斜倚在床上，他坐在三脚凳上。除了我在房间里走动，或者到走廊尽头的卫生间去，我们一直都在打牌。那天深夜我做了个梦。我梦见阿塞夫站在病房的门口，眼眶仍嵌着铜球。"我们是同一种人，你和我。"他说，"你跟他一个奶妈，但你是我的孪生兄弟。"

第二天早晨，我告诉阿曼德我想离开。

"现在出院太早了。"阿曼德抗议说。那天他穿着的并非手术袍，而是一套海军蓝西装，系着黄色领带，头发又涂着啫喱水。"你还在静脉注射抗生素期间，还有……"

"我非走不可。"我说，"谢谢你，谢谢你们为我所做的一切。真的。但我必须离开。"

"你要去哪里？"阿曼德说。

"我不能说。"

"你几乎寸步难行。"

"我能走到走廊那边，再走回来。"我说，"我会没事的。"计划是这样的：离开医院，从保险箱里面把钱取出来，付清医药费，开车到那家恤孤院，把索拉博交给约翰和贝蒂·卡尔德威。然后前往伊斯兰堡，调整旅行计划，给我自己几天时间，等身子好一些就飞回家。

无论如何，计划就是这样，直到那天早晨法里德和索拉博来临。"你的朋友，约翰和贝蒂·卡尔德威，他们不在白沙瓦。"法里德说。

我花了十分钟才将棉袍穿上。他们在我胸膛开过插胸管的口子，我抬手的时候那儿痛得厉害；而且每次倾斜身体，总是脏腑翻动。我将一些随身物品收进一个棕色的纸袋，累得气喘吁吁。但法里德带着那个消息到来之前，我已经设法准备妥当，坐在床沿。索拉博挨着我，坐在床上。

"他们去哪儿了？"我问。

法里德摇摇头："你还不明白……"

"因为拉辛汗说……"

"我去过美国领事馆，"法里德提起我的袋子说，"白沙瓦从来没有叫约翰和贝蒂·卡尔德威的人。领事馆的人说，没有这两个人。无论如何，白沙瓦这里没有。"

索拉博在我身旁翻阅着那本旧《国家地理》。

我们到银行取钱。经理是个大腹便便的男人，腋窝下有汗渍；他不断露出笑脸，告诉我银行的人从未碰过那笔钱。"绝对没有。"他郑重地说，摇着他的食指。阿曼德也那样做过。

带着这么一大袋钱开车驶过白沙瓦，真有点胆战心惊。另外，我怀疑每个看着我的大胡子都是阿塞夫派来的塔利班杀手。而令我恐惧的是：白沙瓦有很多大胡子，他们都盯着我。

"我们该怎么安置他？"法里德说，陪着我慢慢从医院的付账办公室走回汽车。索拉博在陆地巡洋舰的后座上，摇下车窗，掌心托着下巴，望着街上过往车辆。

"他不能留在白沙瓦。"我喘着气说。

"是的，阿米尔老爷，他不能。"法里德说，他听出我言下之意，"我很抱歉，我希望我……"

"没关系的，法里德。"我说，设法挤出一个疲惫的微笑，"你还得养家糊口。"现在有条狗站在汽车旁边，用后腿支撑着身子，前爪搭在车门上，摇着尾巴。"我想他现在应该到伊斯兰堡去。"我说。

到伊斯兰堡要四个小时，我几乎一路睡过去。我梦到很多东西，而我所记得的，只有大杂烩似的景象，栩栩如生的记忆碎片如同旋转架上的名片，不断在我脑里闪过。爸爸为我十三岁生日腌制羊肉。索拉雅和我初尝云雨，太阳从东边升起，我们耳里仍有婚礼音乐的袅袅余音，她涂了指甲花的手和我十指相扣。爸爸带我和哈桑到贾拉拉巴德的草莓地——主人告诉我们，只要买四公斤，我们就可随意大吃，最后我们两个撑得肚子发痛。哈桑的血从臀部的裤子滴下来，滴在雪地上，看上去那么暗，几乎是黑色的。*血缘是最重要的，我的孩子。*雅米拉阿姨拍拍索拉雅的膝盖说，*只有真主最清楚，也许事情不是这样的。*睡在爸爸房子的屋顶上。*爸爸说唯一的罪行是盗窃。当你说谎，你偷走了人们知道真相的权利。*拉辛汗在电话里，*告诉我那儿有条再次成为好人的路。一条再次成为好人的路……*

第二十四章

如果说白沙瓦让我回忆起喀布尔过去的光景，那么，伊斯兰堡就是喀布尔将来可能成为的城市。街道比白沙瓦的要宽，也更整洁，种着成排的木槿和凤凰树。市集更有秩序，而且也没有那么多行人和三轮摩托车挡道。屋宇也更美观，更摩登，我还见到一些公园，林荫之下有蔷薇和茉莉盛开。

法里德在一条通往玛加拉山的巷道找了个小旅馆。路上，我们经过著名的费萨尔清真寺，世界上最大的清真寺，香火甚旺，耸立着巨大的水泥柱和直插云霄的尖塔。看到清真寺，索拉博神色一振，趴在车窗上，一直看着它，直到法里德开车拐了个弯。

旅馆的房间比我和法里德在喀布尔住过的那间好得太多了。被褥很干净，地毯用吸尘器吸过，卫生间没有污迹，里面有洗发水、香皂、刮胡刀、浴缸，有散发着柠檬香味的毛巾。墙上没有血迹。还有，两张单人床前面的柜子上摆着个电视机。

"看！"我对索拉博说。我用手将它打开——没有遥控器，转动旋钮。我调到一个儿童节目，两只毛茸茸的卡通绵羊唱着乌尔都语歌曲。

索拉博坐在床上，膝盖抵着胸膛。他看得入迷，绿眼珠反射出电视机里面的影像，前后晃动身子。我想起有一次，我承诺哈桑，在我们长大之后，要给他家里买台彩电。

"我要走了，阿米尔老爷。"法里德说。

"留下过夜吧，"我说，"路途遥远。明天再走。"

"谢谢你。"他说，"但我想今晚就回去。我想念我的孩子。"他走出房间，在门口停下来。"再见，亲爱的索拉博。"他说。他等着回应，但索拉博没理他，自顾摇着身子，屏幕上闪动的图像在他脸上投下银光。

在门外，我给他一个信封。打开之后，他张大了嘴。

"真不知道该怎么谢谢你，"我说，"你帮了我这么多。"

"这里面有多少钱？"法里德有点手足无措。

"将近两千美元。"

"两千……"他说，下唇稍微有点颤抖。稍后，他驶离停车道的时候，揿了两下喇叭、摇摇手。我也朝他招手。再也没有见到他。

我回到旅馆房间，发现索拉博躺在床上，身子弯成弓形。他双眼合上，但我不知道他是不是睡着了。他关掉了电视。我坐在床上，痛得龇牙咧嘴，抹去额头上的冷汗。我在想，要过多久，起身、坐下、在床上翻身才不会痛呢？我在想，什么时候才能吃固体食物呢？我在想，我该拿这个躺在床上的受伤的小男孩怎么办？不过我心里已经有了想法。

柜台上有个饮水机。我倒了一玻璃杯水，吞下两片阿曼德的药丸。水是温的，带有苦味。我拉上窗帘，慢慢躺在床上。我觉得自己的胸膛会裂开。等到痛楚稍减、我又能呼吸的时候，我拉过毛毯盖在身上，等着阿曼德的药丸生效。

醒来之后，房间变黑了。窗帘之间露出一线天光，那是即将转入黑夜的紫色斜晖。汗水浸透被褥，我脑袋昏重。我又做梦了，但忘记梦到什么。

我望向索拉博的床，发现它是空的，心里一沉。我叫他的名字，发出的嗓音吓了自己一跳。那真是茫然失措，坐在阴暗的旅馆房间，离家万里，身体伤痕累累，呼唤着一个几天前才遇到的男孩的名字。我又喊了他的名字，没听到回答。我挣扎着起床，查看卫生间，朝外面那条狭窄的走廊望去。他不见了。

我锁上房门，一只手扶在走廊的栏杆上，跌跌撞撞走到大堂的经理办公室。大堂的角落有株满是尘灰的假棕榈树，粉红的火烈鸟在壁纸上飞舞。我在塑料贴面的登记柜台后面，找到正在看报纸的经理。我向他描绘索拉博的样子，问他有没有见到过。他放下报纸，摘掉老花镜。他的头发油腻，整齐的小胡子有些灰白，身上依稀有种我叫不上名字的热带水果味道。

"男孩嘛，他们总喜欢出去玩。"他叹气说，"我有三个男孩，他们整天都跑得不见踪影，给他们母亲惹麻烦。"他用报纸扇风，看着我的下巴。

"我认为他不是出去玩，"我说，"我们不是本地人，我担心他会迷路。"

他摇摇头："你应该看好那个孩子，先生。"

"我知道，"我说，"但我睡着了，醒来他已经不见了。"

"孩子应该多加关心的，你知道。"

"是的。"我说，血气上涌。他怎么可以对我的焦急如此无动于衷？

他把报纸交在另外一只手上，继续扇风，"他们现在想要自行车。"

"谁？"

"我的孩子。"他说，"他们总在说：'爸爸，爸爸，请给我们买自行车，我们不会给你带来麻烦。求求你，爸爸。'"他哼笑一声，"自行车。他们的母亲会杀了我，我敢向你保证。"

我想象着索拉博横尸街头，或者在某辆轿车的后备厢里面，手脚被绑，嘴巴被塞住。我不想他死在我手里，不想他也因我而死。"麻烦你……"我说，皱起眉头，看见他那件短袖蓝色棉衬衫翻领上的商标，"费亚兹先生，你见过他吗？"

"那个男孩？"

我强忍怒火："对，那个男孩！那个跟我一起来的男孩。以真主的名义，你见过他吗？"

扇风停止。他眼睛一缩："别跟我来这套，老弟，把他弄丢的不是我。"

虽然他说得没错，但不能平息我的怒火。"你对，我错了，是我的错。那么，你见过他吗？"

"对不起。"他强硬地说，戴上眼镜，打开报纸，"我没见过这样的男孩。"

我在柜台站了一会儿，抑制自己别发火。我走出大厅的时候，他说："有没有想过他会去什么地方？"

"没有。"我说。我感到疲惫，又累又怕。

"他有什么爱好吗？"他说，我看见他把报纸收起来。"比如说我的孩子，他们无论如何总是要看美国动作片，特别是那个阿诺什么辛格演的……"

"清真寺！"我说，"大清真寺。"我记得我们路过的时候，清真寺让索拉博从萎靡中振奋起来，记得他趴在车窗上望着它的样子。

"费萨尔？"

"是的，你能送我去吗？"

"你知不知道它是世界上最大的清真寺？"他问。

"不知道，可是……"

"光是它的院子就可以容下四万人。"

"你能送我到那边去吗？"

"那儿距这里还不到一公里。"他说，不过他已经从柜台后站起来。

"我会付你车钱。"

他叹气，摇摇头，"在这里等着。"他走进里间，出来的时候换了一副眼镜，手里拿着串钥匙，有个披着橙色纱丽的矮胖女人跟在身后。她坐上他在柜台后面的位子。"我不会收你的钱。"他朝我吹着气，"我会载你去，因为我跟你一样，也是个父亲。"

我原以为我们会在城里四处寻找，直到夜幕降临。我以为我会看到自己报警，在费亚兹同情的目光下，给他们描绘索拉博的样子。我以为会听见那个警官疲累冷漠的声音，例行公事的提问。而在那些正式的问题之后，会来个私人的问题：不就是又一个死掉的阿富汗孩子，谁他妈的关心啊？

但我们在离清真寺约莫一百米的地方找到他，坐在车辆停满一半的停车场里面，一片草堆上。费亚兹在那片草堆停下，让我下车。"我得回去。"他说。

"好的。我们会走回去。"我说，"谢谢你，费亚兹先生，真的谢谢。"

我走出去的时候，他身子从前座探出来。"我能对你说几句吗？"

"当然。"

在薄暮的黑暗中，他的脸只剩下一副反照出微光的眼镜。"你们阿富汗的事情……这么说吧，你们有点鲁莽。"

我很累，很痛。我的下巴抖动，胸膛和腹部那些该死的伤口像鱼钩在拉我的皮肤。但尽管这样，我还是开始大笑起来。

"我……我说了……"费亚兹在说话，但我那时哈哈大笑，喉头爆发出来的笑声从我缝着线的嘴巴进出来。

"疯掉了。"他说。他踩下油门，车轮在地面打转，尾灯在黯淡的夜光中闪闪发亮。

"你把我吓坏了。"我说。我在他身旁坐下，强忍弯腰带来的剧痛。

他望着清真寺。费萨尔清真寺的外观像一顶巨大的帐篷。轿车进进出出，穿着白衣的信徒川流不息。我们默默坐着，我斜倚着树，索拉博挨着我，膝盖抵在胸前。我们听着宣礼声，看着那屋宇随日光消退而亮起成千上万的灯光。清真寺在黑暗中像钻石那样闪着光芒。它照亮了夜空，照亮了索拉博的脸庞。

"你去过马扎里沙里夫吗？"索拉博说，下巴放在膝盖上。

"很久以前去过，我不太记得了。"

"我很小的时候，爸爸带我去过那儿，妈妈和莎莎也去了。爸爸在市集给我买了一只猴子。不是真的那种，而是你得把它吹起来的那种。它是棕色的，还打着蝴蝶结。"

"我小时候似乎也有一只。"

"爸爸带我去蓝色清真寺，"索拉博说，"我记得那儿有很多鸽子，就在那个清真寺外面，它们不怕人。它们朝我们走来，莎莎给我一小片馕，我喂那些鸟儿。很快，那些鸽子都围在我身边咯咯叫。真好玩。"

"你一定很想念你的父母。"我说。我在想他有没有看到塔利班将他的父母拖到街上。我希望他没有。

"你想念你的父母吗？"他问，把脸颊放在膝盖上，抬眼看着我。

"我想念我的父母吗？嗯，我从没见过我的妈妈。我爸爸几年前死了，是的，我想念他。有时很想。"

"你记得他长什么样子吗？"

我想起爸爸粗壮的脖子，黑色的眼睛，那头不羁的棕发，坐在他大腿上跟坐在树干上一样。"我记得他长什么样子，"我说，"我还记得他身上的味道。"

"我开始忘记他们的面孔，"索拉博说，"这很糟吗？"

"不，"我说，"是时间让你忘记的。"我想起某些东西。我翻开外套的前袋，找出那张哈桑和索拉博的宝丽来合影，"给你。"

他将相片放在面前几英寸的地方，转了一下，以便让清真寺的灯光照在上面。他久久看着它。我想他也许会哭，但他只是双手拿着照片，拇指在它上面抚摸着。我想起一句不知道在什么地方看来的话，或者是从别人口里听来的：阿富汗有很多儿童，但没有童年。他伸出手，把它递给我。

"你留着吧,"我说,"它是你的。"

"谢谢你。"他又看了看照片,把它放在背心的口袋里面。一辆马车发着声响驶进停车场。马脖子上挂着很多小铃铛,随着马步叮当作响。

"我最近经常想起清真寺。"索拉博说。

"真的吗?都想些什么呢?"

他耸耸肩,"就是想想而已。"他仰起脸,看着我的眼睛。这时,他哭了起来,轻柔地,默默地。"我能问你一些问题吗,阿米尔老爷?"

"当然。"

"真主会不会……"他开始说,语声有点哽咽,"真主会不会因为我对那个人做的事情让我下地狱?"

我伸手去碰他,他身子退缩。我收回手。"不会,当然不会。"我说。我想把他拉近,抱着他,告诉他世界曾经对他不仁,他别无选择。

他的脸扭曲绷紧,试图保持平静:"爸爸常说,甚至连伤害坏人也是不对的。因为他们不知道什么是好的,还因为坏人有时也会变好。"

"不一定的,索拉博。"

他疑惑地看着我。

"那个伤害你的人,我认识他很多年。"我说,"我想这个你从我和他的对话中听出来了。我像你这样大的时候,他……他有一次想伤害我,但你父亲救了我。你父亲非常勇敢,他总是替我解决麻烦,为我挺身而出。所以有一天那个坏人伤害了你父亲,他伤得你父亲很重,而我……我不能像你父亲救过我那样救他。"

"为什么人们总是伤害我父亲?"索拉博有点喘着气说,"他从不针对任何人。"

"你说得对。你父亲是个好人。但我想告诉你的是，亲爱的索拉博，这个世界有坏人，有时坏人坏得很彻底，有时你不得不反抗他们。你对那个人所做的，我很多年前就应该对他做的。他是罪有应得，甚至还应该得到更多的报应。"

"你觉得爸爸会对我失望吗？"

"我知道他不会。"我说，"你在喀布尔救了我的命。我知道他会为你感到非常骄傲。"

他用衣袖擦脸，弄破了他嘴唇上挂着的唾液泡泡。他把脸埋在手里，哭了很久才重新说话。"我想念爸爸，也想念妈妈，"他哽咽说，"我想念莎莎和拉辛汗。但有时我很高兴他们不……他们不在了。"

"为什么？"我碰碰他的手臂，他抽开。

"因为……"他抽泣着说，"因为我不想让他们看到我……我这么脏。"他深吸一口气，然后抽泣着慢慢呼出，"我很脏，浑身是罪。"

"你不脏，索拉博。"我说。

"那些男人……"

"你一点都不脏。"

"……他们对我……那个坏人和其他两个……他们对我……对我做了某些事情。"

"你不脏，你身上没有罪。"我又去碰他的手臂，他抽开。我再伸出手，轻轻地将他拉近。"我不会伤害你，"我低声说，"我保证。"他挣扎了一下，全身放松，让我将他拉近，把头靠在我胸膛上。他小小的身体在我怀里随着每声呜泣抽动。

喝着同样的奶水长大的人之间会有亲情。如今，就在这个男孩痛苦的泪水浸湿我的衣裳时，我看到我们身上也有亲情开始生长出来。在那间房间里面和阿塞夫发生的事情让我们紧紧联系在一起，不可分开。

我一直在寻找恰当的机会、恰当的时间，问出那个萦绕在我脑里、让我彻夜无眠的问题。我决定现在就问，就在此地，就在此刻，就在照射着我们的真主房间的蓝色灯光之下。

"你愿意到美国去、跟我和我的妻子一起生活吗？"

他没有回答，他的泪水流进我的衬衣，我随他去。

整整一个星期，我们两个都没提起我所问过他的，似乎那个问题从来没被说出来。接着某天，我和索拉博坐出租车，前往"达曼尼科"——它的意思是"那座山的边缘"——观景台。它坐落在玛加拉山半腰，可以看到伊斯兰堡的全景，树木夹道的纵横街路，还有白色房子。司机告诉我们，从上面能看到总统的宫殿。"如果刚下过雨，空气清新，你们甚至能看到拉瓦尔品第[1]。"他说。我从他那边的观后镜，看见他扫视着我和索拉博，来回看个不停。我也看到自己的脸，不像过去那样浮肿，但各处消退中的淤伤在它上面留下黄色的痕迹。

我们坐在橡胶树的阴影里面，野餐区的长椅上。那天很暖和，太阳高悬在澄蓝的天空中，旁边的长椅上坐着几个家庭，在吃土豆饼和炸蔬菜饼。不知何处传来收音机播放印度音乐的声音，我想我在某部旧电影

---

[1]　Rawalpindi，伊斯兰堡附近古城。

里面听过，也许是《纯洁》[1]吧。一些孩子追逐着足球，他们多数跟索拉博差不多年纪，咯咯发笑，大声叫喊。我想起卡德察区那个恤孤院，想起在察曼的办公室，那只老鼠从我双脚之间穿过。我心口发紧，猛然升起一阵始料不及的怒火，为着我的同胞正在摧毁他们的家园。

"怎么了？"索拉博问。我挤出笑脸，跟他说没什么。

我们把一条从旅馆卫生间取来的浴巾铺在野餐桌上，在它上面玩起番吉帕。在那儿跟我同父异母兄弟的儿子一起玩牌，温暖的阳光照射在我脖子后面，那感觉真好。那首歌结束了，另外一首响起，我没听过。

"看。"索拉博说，他用扑克牌指着天空。我抬头，见到有只苍鹰在一望无垠的天空中翱翔。

"我还不知道伊斯兰堡有老鹰呢。"

"我也不知道。"他说，眼睛看着那只回旋的鸟儿，"你生活的地方有老鹰吗？"

"旧金山？我想有吧，不过我没有见过很多。"

"哦。"他说。我希望他会多问几句，但他又甩出一手牌，问是不是可以吃东西了。我打开纸袋，给他肉丸夹饼。我的午餐是一杯混合的香蕉汁和橙汁——那个星期我租了费亚兹太太的榨汁机。我用吸管吮着，满嘴甜甜的混合果汁。有些从嘴角流出来，索拉博递给我一张纸巾，看着我擦嘴唇。我朝他微笑，他也微笑。

"你父亲跟我是兄弟。"我说，自然而然地。在我们坐在清真寺附近那晚，我本来打算告诉他，但终究没说出口。可是他有权利知道，我不

---

[1]　Pakeeza，1971 年公映，巴基斯坦电影。

想再隐瞒什么事情了。"同父异母，真的。我们有共同的爸爸。"

索拉博不再吃东西了，把夹饼放下，"爸爸没说过他有兄弟。"

"那是因为他不知道。"

"他为什么不知道？"

"没人告诉他，"我说，"也没人告诉我。我最近才发现。"

索拉博眨眼，好像那是他第一次看着我，第一次真正看着我。"可是人们为什么瞒着爸爸和你呢？"

"你知道吗，那天我也问了这个问题。那儿有个答案，但不是个好答案。让我们这么说吧，人们瞒着我们，因为你父亲和我……我们不应该被当成兄弟。"

"因为他是哈扎拉人吗？"

我强迫自己看着他："是的。"

"你父亲，"他眼睛看着食物，说，"你父亲爱你和爱我爸爸一样多吗？"

我想起很久以前，有一天我们在喀尔卡湖，哈桑的石头比我多跳了几下，爸爸情不自禁拍着哈桑的后背。我想起爸爸在病房里，看着人们揭开哈桑唇上的绷带，喜形于色。"我想他对我们的爱是一样的，但方式不同。"

"他为我爸爸感到羞耻吗？"

"不，"我说，"我想他为自己感到羞耻。"

他捡起夹饼，默默地吃起来。

我们快傍晚的时候才离开，天气很热，让人疲累，不过疲累得开心。回去的路上，我觉得索拉博一直在观察我。我让司机在某间出售电话卡的商店门口停车。我给他钱还有小费，让他帮我去买电话卡。

那天晚上，我们躺在床上，看着电视上的谈话节目。两个毛拉胡子花白，穿着白袍，接听世界各地信徒打来的电话。有人从芬兰打来，那家伙叫艾优博，问他十来岁的儿子会不会下地狱，因为他穿的裤子宽大耷拉，低得露出内裤的橡皮筋勒带。

"我见过一幅旧金山的照片。"索拉博说。

"真的？"

"那儿有座红色的大桥，和一座屋顶尖尖的建筑。"

"你应该看看那些街道。"我说。

"它们是什么样的？"他现在看着我。电视上，两个毛拉正在交换意见。

"它们很陡，当你开车上坡的时候，你只能见到前面的车顶和天空。"

"听起来真吓人。"他说。他翻过身，脸朝着我，背对着电视。

"刚开始有点吓人，"我说，"不过你会习惯的。"

"那儿下雪吗？"

"不，不过有很多雾。你知道那座你看过的红色大桥吧？"

"是的。"

"有时候，早晨的雾很浓，你只能看到两座尖耸的塔顶。"

他惊奇地微笑着："哦。"

"索拉博？"

"怎么？"

"你考虑过我之前问你的问题吗？"

他的笑容不见了，翻身仰面躺着，十指交叉，放在脑后。毛拉确定了，艾优博的儿子那样穿着裤子是会下地狱的。他们说《圣训》里面提到过。"我想过了。"索拉博说。

"怎么样？"

"我很怕。"

"我知道那有点可怕，"我说，抓住那一丝渺茫的希望，"但你很快就可以学会英语，等你习惯了……"

"我不是这个意思。那也让我害怕。可是……"

"可是什么？"

他又翻身朝着我，屈起双膝，"要是你厌倦我怎么办呢？要是你妻子不喜欢我怎么办？"

我从床上挣扎起来，走过我们之间的距离，坐在他身边。"我永远不会厌倦你，索拉博。"我说，"永远不会。这是承诺。你是我的侄儿，记得吗？而亲爱的索拉雅，她是个很好的女人。相信我，她会爱上你的。这也是承诺。"我试探着伸手拉住他的手掌，他稍微有点紧张，但让我拉着。

"我不想再到恤孤院去。"他说。

"我永远不会让那发生。我向你保证。"我双手压住他的手，"跟我一起回家。"

他泪水浸湿了枕头，很长很久默不作声。然后他把手抽回去，点点头。他点头了。

拨到第四次，电话终于接通了。铃声响了三次，她接起电话。"喂？"当时在伊斯兰堡是晚上 7 点半，加利福尼亚那边差不多是早晨这个时间。那意味着索拉雅已经起床一个小时了，在为去上课做准备。

"是我。"我说。我坐在自己的床上，看着索拉博睡觉。

"阿米尔！"她几乎是尖叫，"你还好吗？你在哪儿？"

"我在巴基斯坦。"

"你为什么不早点打电话来？我担心得都生病了！我妈妈每天祈祷，还许愿！"

"我很抱歉没打电话。我现在没事了。"我曾经跟她说我会离开一个星期，也许两个星期，但我离开将近一个月了。我微笑。"跟雅米拉阿姨说不要再杀羊了。"

"你说'没事'是什么意思？你的声音怎么回事？"

"现在别担心这个。我没事，真的。索拉雅，我要告诉你一个故事，一个我早就该告诉你的故事，但我得先告诉你一件事。"

"什么事？"她放低声音说，语气谨慎一些了。

"我不会一个人回家。我会带着一个小男孩，"我顿了顿，说，"我想我们要收养他。"

"什么？"

我看看时间："这张该死的电话卡还剩下四十七分钟，我有很多话要对你说。找个地方坐下。"我听见椅脚匆匆拖过木地板的声音。

"说吧。"她说。

然后我做了结婚十五年来没做过的事：我向妻子坦白了一切事情。一切事情。我很多次设想过这一刻，害怕这一刻，可是，我说了，我感到胸口有些东西涌起来。我觉得就在提亲那夜，索拉雅跟我说起她的过去，也体验过某种非常相似的感觉。

但这一次，说故事的人是我，她在哭泣。

"你怎么想？"我说。

"我不知道该怎么想，阿米尔。你一下子告诉我太多了。"

"我知道。"

我听见她擦鼻子的声音。"但我很清楚地知道的是：你必须把他带回家。我要你这么做。"

"你确定吗？"我说，闭上双眼，微笑起来。

"我确定？"她说，"阿米尔，他是你的侄儿，你的家人，所以他也是我的侄儿。我当然确定，你不能任他流落街头。"她停顿了一会儿，"他性子怎样？"

我望向睡在床上的索拉博："他很可爱，很严肃那种。"

"谁能怪他呢？"她说，"我想见到他，阿米尔。我真的想。"

"索拉雅？"

"嗯。"

"我爱你。"

"我也爱你。"她说。我听得见她话里的笑意，"小心点。"

"我会的。还有，别告诉你父母他是谁。如果他们想知道，应该让我来说。"

"好的。"

我们挂上电话。

伊斯兰堡美国大使馆外面的草坪修剪齐整，点缀着一圈圈花儿，四周是挺直的篱笆。房子本身跟伊斯兰堡很多建筑很相像：白色的平房。我们穿过几个街区，到达那儿，三个不同的安检人员搜我的身，因为我下巴缝着的线弄响了金属探测器。我们最终从热浪中走进去，空调的冷风扑面而来，好像冰水泼在脸上。接待室的秘书是个五十来岁的金发妇女，脸庞瘦削。我自报家门，她微微一笑。她穿着米色的罩衫和黑色的休闲裤——她是我数个星期来见到的第一个没有穿着蒙脸长袍或者棉袍的女人。她在预约单上查找我的名字，用铅笔带橡皮擦那头敲着办公桌。她找到我的名字，让我坐下。

"你们想来杯柠檬汁吗？"她问。

"我不要，谢谢。"

"你儿子要吗？"

"什么？"

"那个英俊的小绅士，"她说，朝索拉博笑着。

"哦，好的，谢谢你。"

索拉博和我坐在黑色的皮沙发上，就在接待柜台对面，挨着一面高高的美国国旗。索拉博从玻璃桌面的咖啡桌挑起一本杂志。他翻阅着，心不在焉地看着图片。

"怎么啦？"索拉博说。

"什么？"

"你在微笑。"

"我在想着你的事情呢。"我说。

他露出紧张的微笑。挑起另外一本杂志，还不到三十秒就翻完了。

"别害怕。"我碰碰他的手臂说,"这些人很友善,放松点。"我自己才应该听从这个建议。我在座位上不停挪动身子,解开鞋带,又系上。秘书将一大杯混有冰块的柠檬汁放在咖啡桌上。"请用。"

索拉博羞涩一笑。"非常谢谢。"他用英语说,听起来像"灰常歇歇"。他跟我说过,他只懂得这句英语,还有"祝你今天愉快"。

她笑起来:"别客气。"她走回办公桌,高跟鞋在地板上敲响。

"祝你今天愉快。"索拉博说。

雷蒙德·安德鲁个子不高,手掌很小,指甲修剪得很好,无名指上戴着结婚戒指。他草草和我握手,感觉像捏着一只麻雀。这是一双掌握我们命运的手,我想。索拉博和我坐在他的办公桌对面。一张《悲惨世界》的海报钉在安德鲁身后的墙壁上,挨着一张美国地形图。阳光照耀的窗台上有盆番茄藤。

"吸烟吗?"他问,和他瘦弱的身形相比起来,他低沉洪亮的声音显得十分古怪。

"不,谢谢。"我说。安德鲁甚至都没看索拉博一眼,跟我说话的时候眼睛也没看着我,但我不在乎。他拉开办公桌的抽屉,从半包烟里面抽出一根点上。他还从同一个抽屉拿起一瓶液体,一边涂抹在手上,一边看窗台上的番茄藤,香烟斜斜吊在他嘴角。然后他关上抽屉,把手肘放在办公桌上,呼出一口气。"好了,"他说,在烟雾中眨眨他灰色的眼睛,"告诉我你的故事。"

我感觉就像冉·阿让坐在沙威[1]对面。我提醒自己，我如今在美国的领地上，这个家伙跟我是一边的，他领薪水，就为了帮助我这样的人。"我想收养这个孩子，将他带回美国。"我说。

"告诉我你的故事。"他重复说，用食指把烟灰在整洁的办公桌上压碎，将其扫进烟灰缸。

我把跟索拉雅通电话之后编好的故事告诉他。我前往阿富汗，带回我同父异母兄弟的儿子。我发现这个孩子处境堪忧，在恤孤院中浪费生命。我给恤孤院的负责人一笔钱，将孩子带出来。接着我把他带到巴基斯坦。

"你算是这个孩子的伯伯？"

"是的。"

他看看表，侧身转向窗台上的番茄藤，"有人能证明吗？"

"有的，但我不知道他现在在哪儿。"

他转向我，点点头。我试图从他脸上看出他的想法，但一无所获。我在想他这双小手有没有玩过扑克。

"我想，把下巴缝成这样，该不是最近时兴的证词吧。"他说。我们麻烦了，索拉博和我，我顿时明白。我告诉他我在白沙瓦被抢了。

"当然，"他说，清清喉咙，"你是穆斯林吗？"

"是的。"

"虔诚吗？"

---

[1] 冉·阿让（Jean Valjean）和沙威（Javert）都是雨果作品《悲惨世界》中的人物，前者因为偷东西入狱，后者是警察。

"是的。"实际上，我都不记得上次把头磕在地上礼拜是什么时候。然后我想起来了：阿曼尼大夫给爸爸看病那天。我跪在祈祷毯上，想起的却只有几段课堂上学到的经文。

"对你的事情有点帮助，但起不了太大作用。"他说，作势在他那蓬松的头发上搔痒。

"你是什么意思？"我问。我拉起索拉博的手，扣着他的手指。索拉博不安地看着我和安德鲁。

"有个长的答案，到了最后我会告诉你。你想先听个短的吗？"

"说吧。"我说。

安德鲁将香烟掐灭，抿着嘴，"放弃吧。"

"什么？"

"你提出的收养这个孩子的请求。放弃吧。那是我给你的建议。"

"知道了。"我说，"现在，也许你可以告诉我原因了。"

"那就是说你想听长的答案了？"他语气冷淡地说，对我不快的语气无动于衷。他合起手掌，似乎他正跪在圣母面前。"让我们假设你告诉我的故事是真的，不过我非常怀疑它是假的，或者省略掉一大部分。告诉你一声，我不关心。你在这里，他在这里，这才是要紧的事情。即使这样，你的请求面临着明显的障碍，更何况这个孩子并非孤儿。"

"他当然是。"

"从法律上来讲他不是。"

"他的父母在街上被处决了，邻居都看到了。"我说，为我们用英语交谈而高兴。

"你有死亡证明吗？"

"死亡证明？我们在说的是阿富汗，很多人甚至连出生证明都没有。"

他明亮的眼睛一眨不眨，"先生，法律不是我制定的。你生气也没用，你还是得证明他的父母确实去世了。这个男孩必须让法律承认他是孤儿。"

"可是……"

"你想要长的答案，我现在正给你呢。你的下一个问题是，你需要这个孩子出生国的合作。现在，就算在最好的情况下，这也很难，还有，引用你说过的，我们在谈论的是阿富汗。我们在喀布尔没有大使馆。这使事情极端复杂，几乎是不可能的。"

"你在说什么？我应该将他扔到街头上吗？"我说。

"我可没那么说。"

"他受过性虐待。"我说，想起索拉博脚踝上的铃铛，他眼睛上的眼影。

"听到这个我很抱歉，"安德鲁张口说，不过他望着我的样子，好像我们一直在谈论天气，"但那不会让移民局给这个小男孩放发签证。"

"你在说什么？"

"我的意思是，如果你想帮忙，可以捐钱给可靠的慈善组织，或者去难民营当义工。但在现在这样的时刻，我们非常不赞成美国公民收养阿富汗儿童。"

我站起来。"走吧，索拉博。"我用法尔西语说。索拉博倚着我，头靠在我的臀部上。我想起那张宝丽来照片，他和哈桑就这样站着。"我能问你一些问题吗，安德鲁先生？"

"可以。"

"你有孩子吗？"

这下，他第一次眨眼了。

"嗯，你有吗？随便问问而已。"

他默默无语。

"我这么认为，"我说，拉起索拉博的手，"他们应该找个知道想要孩子是什么感觉的人坐你的位置。"我转身离开，索拉博跟着我。

"我可以问你一个问题吗？"安德鲁喊道。

"说吧。"

"你承诺过这个孩子带他回家吗？"

"要是有又怎样？"

他摇摇头，"真是危险的事情，给孩子承诺。"他叹气，又打开抽屉，"你真想要这么做？"他说，翻着文件。

"我真的想这么做。"

他抽出一张名片："那么我建议你找个优秀的移民律师。奥马尔·费萨尔在伊斯兰堡工作，你可以跟他说我让你去找他。"

我从他那里拿过名片。"谢谢。"我低声说。

"祝你好运。"他说。我们走出房间的时候，我回头看了一眼。安德鲁站在长方形的阳光中，茫然地望着窗外，双手将那盆番茄藤转到阳光下，慈爱地拍打着。

"保重。"我们走过秘书的办公桌时她说。

"你老板应该礼貌一些。"我说。我以为她会转动眼珠，也许点头说

"我知道，每个人都那么说"，诸如此类。相反的是，她降低声音："可怜的雷，自从他女儿死后，他就跟变了个人似的。"

我扬起眉头。

"自杀。"她说。

在回旅馆的出租车上，索拉博头靠车窗，望着栋栋后退的房子和成排的橡胶树。他的呼吸模糊了玻璃，擦干净，又模糊了。我等待他问起会谈的情况，但他没问。

浴室的门关上，门后传来水流声。自从我们住进宾馆那天起，索拉博每晚上床之前总要洗很久的澡。在喀布尔，热自来水像父亲一样，是稀缺的产品。现在索拉博每晚几乎要用一个小时洗澡，浸在肥皂水中，不停擦着身体。我坐在床边给索拉雅打电话，看着浴室门下渗出来的光线。你觉得干净了吗，索拉博？

我将雷蒙德跟我说过的告诉索拉雅。"你现在怎么想？"

"我们得认为他错了。"她说她给几家安排国际收养的机构打过电话，她还没发现有考虑收养阿富汗孩子的机构，但她还在找。

"你父母对这个消息怎么看？"

"妈妈很为我们高兴。你知道她对你的感觉，阿米尔，在她眼里，你做什么都不会错。爸爸……嗯，跟过去一样，他有点让人猜不透。他没说太多。"

"你呢？你高兴吗？"

我听见她把听筒换到另一只手上。"我想这对你的侄儿来说是好的，但也许他也会给我们带来帮助。"

"我也这么想。"

"我知道这听起来很疯狂，可是我发现自己在想着他最喜欢吃什么菜，或者最喜欢学校里的哪门课。我设想自己在帮他做作业……"她哈哈大笑。浴室的水声停止了，我能听到索拉博在那儿，从浴缸爬出来，擦干身体。

"你真是太好了。"我说。

"啊，我差点忘了！我给沙利夫舅舅打过电话！"

我记得在我们的婚礼上，他朗诵一首写在酒店信纸上的诗歌。我和索拉雅走向舞台，朝闪光的镜头微笑的时候，他的儿子在我们头顶高举《古兰经》。"他怎么说？"

"嗯，他会帮助我们。他会给他在移民局的朋友打电话。"她说。

"真是个好消息。"我说，"我忍不住想让你快点见到索拉博。"

"我忍不住想快点见到你。"她说。

我笑着挂上电话。

几分钟后，索拉博从浴室出来。自从与安德鲁会面之后，他说过的话几乎不超过十来个单词，我每次试图跟他交谈，他总是点点头，或者用一个字回答我。他爬上床，把毯子拉到下巴。没过几分钟，他呼呼睡去。

我抹开水汽迷蒙的镜子，用旅馆的旧式刮胡刀刮脸。你得把它打开，然后把刀片装进去。接着我洗澡，躺在浴缸里面，直到冒着汽的热水变冷，让我的皮肤起鸡皮疙瘩。我躺在那儿漂浮着、思索着、想象着……

奥马尔·费萨尔皮肤很暗，矮矮胖胖，脸上有酒窝，黑色的大眼睛，还有和蔼的笑容，露出来的齿缝很大。他稀疏的头发在后面梳成马尾，穿着棕色灯芯绒西装，手肘的位置上有几块毛皮补丁，还带着个鼓鼓的破旧公文包。公文包的提手不见了，所以他将其抱在胸前。他是一见面就笑着说很多话而且过分客套的人，比如说"对不起，我将会在五点在那儿"之类的。我打电话给他，听到他的笑声，他执意要出来会晤我们。"很抱歉，这个城市里面的出租车跟鲨鱼一样，"他的英语说得很棒，没有任何口音，"一旦嗅到外国人的味道，就会多要三倍车费。"

他推开门，脸带微笑，道歉连连，稍微有点喘气和流汗。他用手帕擦额头，打开公文包，乱翻着找记事本，为把文件扔得满床都是不停道歉。索拉博盘膝坐在床上，一边看着消掉声音的电视，一边看着那个手忙脚乱的律师。那天早晨我跟他说过费萨尔要来，他点点头，似乎想问些什么，但只是走开去看一个有动物在说话的电视节目。

"找到了。"费萨尔说，翻开一本黄色的法律记事本。"就安排事务的能力而言，我希望我的孩子像他们的妈妈。很抱歉，也许这不是你所想要从你未来的律师口里听到的，对吧？"他哈哈大笑。

"嗯，雷蒙德·安德鲁对你评价很高。"

"安德鲁先生。是的，是的，那个家伙人很好。实际上，他打过电话给我，把你的事情告诉我了。"

"真的吗？"

"哦，是的。"

"那么你清楚我的情况了。"

费萨尔擦去唇边的汗水。"我清楚你告诉安德鲁先生的情况。"他说，脸上出现两个酒窝，泛起狡黠的微笑。他转向索拉博。"肯定就是这个少年惹起所有的麻烦吧？"他用法尔西语说。

"这是索拉博。"我说，"索拉博，他是费萨尔先生，我跟你说过的那个律师。"

索拉博从他的床上滑下来，跟费萨尔握手。"你好。"他低声说。

"你好，索拉博。"费萨尔说，"你知道自己的名字来自一个了不起的战士吗？"

索拉博点点头，爬回床上，继续侧身躺着看电视。

"我不知道你的法尔西语说得这么好，"我用英语说，"你在喀布尔长大吗？"

"不是，我在卡拉奇[1]出生，但在喀布尔生活了好几年。沙里诺区，靠近哈吉雅霍清真寺。"费萨尔说。"实际上，我在伯克利[2]长大。1960年代后期，我爸爸在那儿开了间唱片店。自由性爱，束发带，扎染衬衫，你能想到的我全都干过。"他身体前倾，"我在伍德斯托克[3]待过。"

"太帅了！"我说。费萨尔哈哈大笑，又开始冒汗珠了。"反正，"我继续说，"我跟安德鲁先生说得差不多了，省略掉一两件事，也许三件。我会完完整整告诉你。"

他舔了一根手指，翻到空白页，把笔帽打开。"那最好了，阿米尔。我们何不用英语交谈，免得外面的人听到？"

---

[1]　Karachi，巴基斯坦南部城市。

[2]　Berkeley，美国加州城市。

[3]　Woodstock，位于纽约州东南，每年8月举办民谣和摇滚音乐节。

"好的。"

我把发生过的一切统统告诉他：我跟拉辛汗的会面、前往喀布尔、恤孤院、伽兹体育馆的掷石头。

"天！"他低声惊呼，"很抱歉，我在喀布尔有很多美好的回忆。很难相信你刚才告诉我的竟然是同一个地方。"

"你后来回去过吗？"

"天，没有。"

"我会告诉你，那儿不是伯克利。"我说。

"继续。"

我把剩下的都告诉他了：跟阿塞夫见面、搏斗、索拉博和他的弹弓、逃回巴基斯坦。当我说完，他飞快地写下一些东西，深深呼吸，镇定地看了我一眼："好了，阿米尔，你前面有场艰苦的战斗。"

"我能打赢吗？"

他把笔帽装上。"就安德鲁的语气判断，希望渺茫。不是不可能，但是机会很小。"和蔼的笑容和戏谑的眼神不见了。

"可是像索拉博这样的孩子最需要有个家，"我说，"这些规章制度对我来说毫无意义。"

"我也心有戚戚，阿米尔。"他说，"但事实是，就当前的移民法、收养机构政策和阿富汗的政治局势看来，你的情况很不妙。"

"我真不理解，"我说，想找个东西揍一顿，"我是说，我明白，但是我不理解。"

奥马尔点头，双眉紧锁。"好了，就这样。灾难之后，不管天灾还是人祸——塔利班真是一场大灾难，阿米尔，相信我——但一个孩子是否孤儿，总是很难判断。孩子们被遗弃在难民营，或者被双亲抛弃，因为他们无法加以照料。这些情况向来都有。所以除非孩子满足孤儿的法律定义，否则移民局不会放发签证。我很抱歉，我知道这听起来很荒唐，但你需要一纸死亡证书。"

"你在阿富汗住过，"我说，"你知道这事的可能性有多大。"

"我知道，"他说，"但让我们假设现在这个孩子父母双亡的情况弄清楚了。即使那样，移民局会认为，最好由该国的人来收养这个孩子，以便他能保持本国的文化传统。"

"什么传统？"我说，"阿富汗有过的文化传统被塔利班毁掉了。你知道他们怎么对待巴米扬的大佛。"

"很抱歉，我在告诉你的是移民局怎么工作，阿米尔。"奥马尔说，碰碰我的手臂。他望向索拉博，露出微笑，然后看着我。"说到这里，一个孩子必须根据他自己国家的法规被合法地收养。但假如你碰到一个乱糟糟的国家，比如说阿富汗，政府官员会忙于处理各种突发事件，处理收养事宜不会得到优先考虑。"

我叹气，揉揉眼睛。眼睛后面突突发痛。

"但是让我们假设不管怎样，阿富汗人肯帮忙。"奥马尔说，双手交叉放在隆起的肚子上，"这次收养仍有可能被拒绝。实际上，就算是那些较为温和的穆斯林国家，对收养也不无疑虑，因为在多数这些国家中，伊斯兰教法不赞同收养。"

"你是在叫我放弃？"我问，用手压着额头。

"我在美国长大，阿米尔。如果说美国让我学到什么东西，那就是，认输简直就像在女童军[1]的柠檬水罐里面撒尿一样不可原谅。可是，身为你的律师，我必须把事实告诉你。"他说，"最后一点，收养机构会定期派人前去评估那个孩子所处的环境，而没有正常的机构会派人去阿富汗。"

我看见索拉博坐在那儿，看着电视和我们。他的坐姿跟他父亲过去一样，膝盖抵着下巴。

"我是他伯父，难道这没有用吗？"

"如果你能证明，它会起作用。很抱歉，你有什么证明文件或者什么证人吗？"

"没有文件，"我用虚脱的声音说，"没有人知道这回事。索拉博也是我说了他才知道的，而我自己也是最近才发现这个秘密。唯一知道的那个人已经走了，也许死了。"

"嗯。"

"我该怎么办，奥马尔？"

"我会坦诚相告，你的选择不多。"

"天哪，我能做什么？"

奥马尔吸气，用钢笔敲打下巴，然后把气呼出来。"你还是填一份收养申请表，期待最好的结果。你可以做独立的收养。也就是说，你得和索拉博一起生活在巴基斯坦，日复一日，挨过两年，你可以替他申请政治庇护。那是个漫长的过程，你得证明他受到政治迫害。你也可以申

---

[1] Girl Scouts，美国女童军是世界上最大的专门服务于女孩的组织，成员多为成年义工，旨在帮助女孩提高使她们终身受益的素质。

请人道主义签证。那得由检察总长审核，很难得到。"他顿了顿，"还有个选择，也许是你最好的办法了。"

"什么？"我靠近身体问。

"你可以把他重新送进这儿的恤孤院，然后填收养申请表。让他们审核你的 I-600 表格和你的家庭，把孩子留在安全的地方。"

"那是什么？"

"很抱歉，I-600 表格是移民局的官方文件。家庭评估由你选择的收养机构执行。"奥马尔说，"你知道，那是要确保你和你的妻子没有精神病。"

"我不想那么做。"我说，看了一眼索拉博，"我答应过他，不再让他进恤孤院。"

"正如我所说的，那是你最好的选择。"

我们又谈了一会儿，然后我送他上车，一辆旧大众甲壳虫。当时伊斯兰堡已近黄昏，一轮红日挂在西边。奥马尔不知道使了什么法子，居然能挤到车里去，我看见他上车的时候车身一沉。他摇下车窗："阿米尔？"

"嗯？"

"我刚才跟你说过吗？你正在努力争取的事情很了不起。"

他招招手，把车驶离。我站在宾馆房间门外，也朝他挥手。我希望索拉雅在身边陪着我。

我回到房间的时候，索拉博已经关掉电视了。我坐在自己的床沿，让他挨着我坐下。"费萨尔先生说有个办法可以让我把你带去美国。"

我说。

"真的吗？"他好几天来第一次露出微弱的笑容，"我们什么时候能走？"

"嗯，事情是这样的。可能需要一段时间，但他说可以做到，而且他会帮助我们。"我把手放在他脖子后面。外面，宣礼声响彻大街小巷。

"多久？"索拉博问。

"我不知道，一阵吧。"

索拉博耸耸肩，微笑着，这次笑得更灿烂了："我不在乎，我能等。那就像酸苹果。"

"酸苹果？"

"有一次，我很小的时候，我爬上一棵树，吃那些青青的酸苹果。我的肚子变得又肿又硬，像鼓那样，痛得厉害。妈妈说只要我等到苹果熟透，就不会生病了。所以现在，无论我真正想要什么，我都会想起她说过的关于苹果的话。"

"酸苹果，"我说，"安拉保佑，你是我见过最聪明的孩子，亲爱的索拉博。"他的耳朵红了起来。

"绝对是。"我说，"绝对是。"

"我们会开车到那些街上去吗？那些你只能看见车顶和天空的街道？"

"我们每一条都去。"我说，眼泪涌上来，我眨眼强行忍住。

"英语难学吗？"

"我敢说，不用一年，你就可以说得跟法尔西语一样流利。"

"真的吗？"

"是的，"我伸了一根手指在他下巴，把他的脸转过来，"还有一件事，索拉博。"

"什么事？"

"嗯，费萨尔先生说那会很有帮助，如果我们……如果我们能让你在一间为孩子准备的房子待上一阵。"

"为孩子准备的房间？"他的笑容消失了，"你是说孤儿院吗？"

"只是待上一阵。"

"不，"他说，"别这样，求求你。"

"索拉博，那只是很短的时间，我保证。"

"你向我保证过永远不让我去那些地方，阿米尔老爷。"他说。他声音颤抖，泪如泉涌。我一阵心痛。

"那不同的。就在这儿，在伊斯兰堡，不是在喀布尔。我会每天去探望你，直到我们能够离开，把你带去美国。"

"求求你！求求你！别这样！"他哽咽着，"我很怕那些地方。他们伤害我！我不想去。"

"没有人会伤害你。再也不会了。"

"他们会的！他们总是说他们不会，但他们说谎！他们说谎！求求你，真主啊！"

我用拇指抹去他脸上的泪痕。"酸苹果，记得吗？这就像一个酸苹果。"我轻声说。

"不，它不是。不要那些地方。天，天啦！求求你，别这样！"他浑身颤抖，涕泗俱下。

"嘘。"我把他拉近,抱着他颤抖的身体。"嘘。会没事的。我们会一起回家。你会看到的,没事的。"

他的声音被我的胸膛闷住,但我能听到话里的痛苦。"求求你答应我你不会这么做!天啊,阿米尔老爷!求求你答应我你不会!"

我如何能答应呢?我抱着他,紧紧抱着,前后摇晃。他的泪水滴进我的衣裳,直到泪流干了,直到不再颤抖了,直到惊恐的哀求变成听不清的喃喃自语。我等着,摇着他,直到他呼吸缓下来,身体松弛。我想起曾经从某个地方看来的一句话:孩子们就是这样对付恐惧:他们睡觉。

我抱他上床,把他放下。然后我躺在自己床上,望着窗外伊斯兰堡上方紫色的天空。

电话将我惊醒的时候,天已经全黑了。我揉揉眼睛,旋开床头灯。刚过晚上 10 点半,我睡了将近三个小时。我拿起话筒。"喂?"

"美国打来的电话。"费亚兹先生的声音。

"谢谢。"我说。浴室的灯光亮着,索拉博又在洗澡了。电话传来两声按键声,然后是索拉雅的声音。"你好!"她声音振奋。

"嗨。"

"你跟那个律师谈得怎样?"

我把费萨尔的建议告诉她。"好了,你可以忘了它,"她说,"我们不用那么做。"

我坐起来。"什么?为什么?怎么回事?"

"我接到沙利夫舅舅的回电了。他说关键是把索拉博送进这个国家。只要他进来,就有很多把他留下的办法。所以他给几个在移民局的朋友打了电话。他今晚给我回电，说他很有把握能替索拉博争取到人道主义签证。"

"不是开玩笑吧？"我说，"啊，谢谢真主！亲爱的沙利夫太好了！"

"我知道。不管怎样，我们可以当保证人。一切会很快的。他说那种签证有效期一年，足够我们申请收养请求了。"

"这样最好了，索拉雅。对吧？"

"看起来是的。"她说。她的声音很快乐。我说我爱她，她说她也爱我。我们挂上电话。

"索拉博！"我喊道，从床上起来，"我有个好消息。"我敲着浴室的门，"索拉博！亲爱的索拉雅刚才从加利福尼亚打电话来。我们不用把你放到恤孤院了，索拉博。我们就要去美国了，你和我。你听到吗？我们就要去美国了！"

我推开门，走进浴室。

刹那间我跪倒在地，放声大叫。我牙齿打颤，不断大叫。叫得我的喉咙快要裂开，叫得我的胸膛快要炸开。

后来，他们说救护车来了之后我还不停叫着。

第二十五章

他们不让我进去。

我看见他们推着他，穿过一些双层门，我跟在后面，冲进一扇又一扇的门，闻到碘酒和消毒水的味道，但我所来得及看到的，是两个戴着手术帽的男人和一个穿着绿色衣服的女人围在轮床之上。我看见白色床单从轮床侧面垂落，拂着污秽的花格地砖。一双鲜血淋漓的小脚从床单下面伸出来，我看见左脚大脚趾的指甲被削掉了。接着有个穿蓝色衣服的高壮汉子用手掌压住我的胸口，将我从门口往后推，我的皮肤能感觉到他那冰凉的结婚戒指。我向前挣扎，咒骂他，但他用英语说你不能留在这儿，声音礼貌而坚决。"你必须等。"他说，领着我回到等候区。现在双层门在他身后砰地关上，透过门上狭窄的长方形窗口，我只见到那个男人的手术帽。

他把我留在一条宽大的走廊上，没有窗，墙边的金属折叠椅上坐满了人，还有人坐在薄薄的破地毯上。我又想尖叫。我想起上次有这种感觉，是跟爸爸在油罐车的油罐里面，埋在黑暗和其他难民之间。我想把自己撕成碎片，离开这个地方，离开现实世界，像云朵那样升起，飘荡而去，融进湿热的夏夜，在某个遥远的地方，在山丘上方飘散。但我就在这儿，双脚沉重如水泥块，肺里空气一泻而空，喉咙发热。无法随风而去。今晚没有别的世界。我合上双眼，鼻子里塞满走廊的种种味道：汗水和氨水的气味、医用酒精和咖喱的气味。整条走廊的天花板上布满昏暗的灯管，飞蛾围绕，我听见它们拍打翅膀的声音。我听见谈话声、默默的啜泣声、擤鼻声；有人在呻吟，有人在哀叹，电梯门砰的一声打开，操作员用乌尔都语呼喊某人。

我再次睁开眼，知道自己该做些什么。我四周环顾，心脏怦怦地在胸口跳动，耳朵听得见血液流动的声音。我左边有间又暗又小的储藏室，我在里面找到自己想要的东西。用它就好了。我从一堆折叠好的白色尼龙床单中抽出一条，带回走廊。我看见护士在休息室附近和一名警察交谈。我拉拉那名护士的手肘，问她哪个方位是西边。她没听懂，眉头一皱，脸色的皱纹更深了。我喉咙发痛，汗水刺痛了双眼，每次呼吸都像在喷火，我想我在哭泣。我又问一声，苦苦哀求，警察把方向指给我。

我在地面铺开那张滥竽充数的礼拜毯，双膝跪倒，头磕在地上，泪水湿透了床单。我朝西弯下腰，那时我才想起自己已经不止十五年没礼拜过了，早已把祷词忘得一干二净。但这没有关系，我会说出依然记得的片言只语：唯安拉是真主，穆罕默德是他的使者。现在我明白爸爸错了，真主真的存在，一直存在。我看到他在这里，从这条绝望的走廊的人群眼里见到。这里才是真主真正的住所，正是在这里，而非在那些发出钻石般明亮光芒的尖塔耸立的清真寺，只有那些失去真主的人们才能找到真主。真主真的存在，他必须存在，而如今我将礼拜，我会祈祷他原谅我这些年来对他的漠然不觉，原谅我曾经背叛、说谎、作恶而未受惩罚，只有在我的危难时刻才想起他。我祈祷他如经书记载的那样慈悲、仁爱、宽宏。我朝西方磕头，亲吻地面，承诺我将会施天课，将会每天礼拜，承诺我在斋月期间将会素食，而当斋月结束，我会继续素食，我将会熟背他的圣书中每个字，我将会到沙漠中那座湿热难当的城市去朝圣，也会在天房之前磕头。我将会践行所有这些，从今日后，将会每天想起他，只要他实现我的这个愿望：我的手已经沾上哈桑的血，我祈求真主，别让它们也沾上这个小男孩的血。

我听到呜咽声，意识到正是自己发出来的，泪水从脸上汩汩而下，流过嘴唇，让我尝到咸味。我感到走廊上每个人都在看着我，而我依然朝西方磕头。我祈祷。我祈祷别以这种我向来害怕的方式惩罚我的罪行。

星光黯淡的黑夜降临在伊斯兰堡。过了数个钟头，我坐在走廊外面一间通往急诊室的小房间的地板上。在我身前是一张暗棕色的咖啡桌，上面摆着报纸和卷边的杂志——有本1996年4月的《时代》，一份巴基斯坦报纸，上面印着某个上星期被火车撞死的男孩的脸孔；一份娱乐杂志，平滑的封面印着微笑的罗丽坞男星。在我对面，有位老太太身穿碧绿的棉袍，戴着针织头巾，坐在轮椅上打瞌睡。每隔一会儿她就会惊醒，用阿拉伯语低声祈祷。我疲惫地想，不知道今晚真主会听到谁的祈祷，她的还是我的？我想起索拉博的面容，那肉乎乎的尖下巴，海贝似的小耳朵，像极了他父亲的竹叶般眯斜的眼睛。一阵悲哀如同窗外的黑夜，漫过我全身，我觉得喉咙被掐住。

我需要空气。

我站起来，打开窗门。湿热的风带着发霉的味道从窗纱吹进来——闻起来像腐烂的椰枣和动物粪便。我大口将它吸进肺里，可是它没有消除胸口的窒闷。我颓然坐倒在地面，捡起那本《时代》杂志，随手翻阅。可是我看不进去，无法将注意力集中在任何东西上。所以我把它扔回桌子，怔怔望着水泥地面上弯弯曲曲的裂缝，还有窗台上散落的死苍蝇。更多的时候，我盯着墙上的时钟。刚过四点，我被关在双层门之外已经超过五个小时，仍没得到任何消息。

我开始觉得身下的地板变成身体的一部分，呼吸越来越沉重，越来越缓慢。我想睡觉，阖上双眼，把头放低在这满是尘灰的冰冷地面，昏然欲睡。也许当我醒来，会发现我在旅馆浴室看到的一切无非是一场梦：水从水龙头滴答落进血红的洗澡水里，他的左臂垂在浴缸外面，沾满鲜血的剃刀——就是那把我前一天用来刮胡子的剃刀——落在马桶的冲水槽上，而他的眼虽仍睁开一半，但眼神黯淡。

很快，睡意袭来，我任它将我占据。我梦到一些后来想不起来的事情。

有人在拍我的肩膀。我睁开眼，看到有个男人跪在我身边。他头上戴着帽子，很像双层门后面那个男人，脸上戴着手术口罩——看见口罩上有一滴血，我的心一沉。他的传呼机上贴着一张小姑娘的照片，眼神纯洁无瑕。他解下口罩，我很高兴自己再也不用看着索拉博的血了。他皮肤黝黑，像哈桑和我经常去沙里诺区市场买的那种从瑞士进口的巧克力；他头发稀疏，浅褐色的眼睛上面是弯弯的睫毛。他用带英国口音的英语告诉我，他叫纳瓦兹大夫。刹那间，我想远离这个男人，因为我认为我无法忍受他所要告诉我的事情。他说那男孩将自己割得很深，失血很多，我的嘴巴又开始念出祷文来：

唯安拉是真主，穆罕默德是他的使者。

他们不得不输入几个单位的红细胞……

我该怎么告诉索拉雅？

两次，他们不得不让他复苏过来……

我会做礼拜，我会做天课。

如果他的心脏不是那么年轻而强壮，他们就救不活他了……

我会茹素……

他活着。

纳瓦兹大夫微笑。我花了好一会儿才弄明白刚才他所说的。然后他又说了几句，我没听到，因为我抓起他的双手，放在自己脸上。我用这个陌生人汗津津的手去抹自己的眼泪，而他没有说什么。他等着。

重症病区呈 L 形，很阴暗，充塞着很多哗哗叫的监视仪和呼呼响的器械。纳瓦兹大夫领着我走过两排用白色塑料帘幕隔开的病床。索拉博的病床是屋角最后那张，最接近护士站。两名身穿绿色手术袍的护士在夹纸板上记东西，低声交谈。我默默和纳瓦兹大夫从电梯上来，我以为我再次看到索拉博会哭。可是当我坐在他床脚的椅子上，透过悬挂着的泛着微光的塑料试管和输液管，我没流泪水。看着他的胸膛随着呼吸机的嘶嘶声有节奏地一起一伏，身上漫过一阵奇怪的麻木感觉，好像自己刚突然掉转车头，在千钧一发之际避过一场惨烈的车祸。

我打起瞌睡，醒来后发现阳光正从乳白色的天空照射进紧邻护士站的窗户。光线倾泻进来，将我的影子投射在索拉博身上。他一动不动。

"你最好睡一会儿。"有个护士对我说。我不认识她——我打盹时她们一定换班了。她把我带到另一间房，就在急救中心外面。里面没有人。她给我一个枕头，还有一床印有医院标记的毛毯。我谢过她，在屋角的塑胶皮沙发上躺下，几乎立刻就睡着了。

我梦见自己回到楼下的休息室，纳瓦兹大夫走进来，我起身迎向他。他脱掉纸口罩，双手突然比我记得的要白，指甲修剪整洁，头发一丝不苟，而我发现他原来不是纳瓦兹大夫，而是雷蒙德·安德鲁，大使馆那个抚摸着番茄藤的小个子。安德鲁抬起头，眯着眼睛。

白天，医院是一座纵横交错的走廊组成的迷宫，荧光灯在人们头顶放射出耀眼的光芒，弄得人迷迷糊糊。我弄清楚了它的结构，知道东楼电梯那颗四楼的按钮不会亮，明白同一层的男厕的门卡住了，你得用肩膀去顶才能把它打开。我了解到医院的生活有它的节奏：每天早晨换班之前匆匆忙忙，白天手忙脚乱，而深夜则寂静无声，偶然有一群医师和护士跑过，去抢救某个病患。白天我警惕地守在索拉博床前，晚上则在医院曲折的走廊游荡，倾听我的鞋跟敲击地面的声音，想着当索拉博苏醒过来我该跟他说什么。最后我会走回重症病房，站在他床边嘶嘶作响的呼吸机，依然一筹莫展。

在重症病房度过三天之后，他们撤去了呼吸管，把他换到一张低矮的病床。他们搬动他的时候我不在。那天晚上我回到旅馆，想睡一觉，最终却在床上彻夜辗转反侧。那天早晨，我强迫自己不去看浴缸。它现在干干净净，有人抹去血迹，地板上铺了新的脚踏垫，墙上也擦过了。可是我忍不住坐在它那冰凉的陶瓷边缘。我想象索拉博放满一缸水，看见他脱掉衣服，看见他转动刮胡刀的手柄，拔出刀头的双重安全插销，退出刀片，用食指和拇指捏住。我想象他滑进浴缸，躺了一会儿，闭上双眼。我在寻思他举起刀片划落的时候最后在想着什么。

我走出大堂的时候，旅馆经理费亚兹先生在身后跟上。"我很为你感到难过，"他说，"可是我要你搬离我的旅馆，拜托了。这对我的生意有影响，影响很大。"

我告诉他我能理解，退了房。他没有收取我在医院度过的那三个晚上的房钱。在大堂门口等出租车的时候，我想起那天晚上费亚兹先生对我说过的：你们阿富汗人的事情……你们有些鲁莽。我曾对他大笑，但现在我怀疑。在把索拉博最担心的消息告诉他之后，我真的睡着了吗？

坐上出租车之后，我问司机知不知道有什么波斯文书店。他说南边几公里远的地方有一家。我们去医院途中在那儿停了一会儿。

索拉博的新病房有乳白色的墙，墙上有断裂的灰色装饰嵌线，还有本来也许是白色的珐琅地砖。跟他同间病房的还有一个十来岁的旁遮普族[1]男孩，后来我从某个护士那里听到，他从一辆开动的巴士车顶跌下来，摔断了腿。他上了石膏的腿抬起，由一些绑着砝码的夹子夹住。

索拉博的病床靠近窗口，早晨的阳光从长方形的玻璃窗照射进来，落在病床的后半部上。窗边站着一个身穿制服的保安，嗑着煮过的西瓜

---

[1]　Punjabi，生活在印度和巴基斯坦一带的民族。

子——医院给索拉博安排了24小时的防自杀看护。纳瓦兹大夫跟我说过，这是医院的制度。保安看到我，举帽致意，随后离开房间。

索拉博穿着短袖的病服，仰面躺着，毛毯盖到他胸口，脸转向窗那边。我以为他睡了，但当我将一张椅子拉到他床边时，他眼睑跳动，跟着睁开。他看看我，移开视线。尽管他们给他输了很多血，他脸色依然苍白，而且在他的臂弯有一大块淤伤。

"你还好吗？"我说。

他没回答，眼望向窗外，看着医院花园里面一个围着护栏的方形沙地和秋千架。运动场旁边有个拱形的凉棚，在一排木槿的树影之下，几株葡萄藤爬上木格子。几个孩子拿着铲斗和小提桶在沙地里面玩耍。那天天空万里无云，一碧如洗，我看见一架小小的喷气式飞机，拖着两道白色的尾巴。我转向索拉博："我刚跟纳瓦兹大夫聊过，他说你再过几天就可以出院了，这是个好消息，对吧？"

我遇到的又是沉默。病房那端，旁遮普男孩睡着翻了个身，发出几声呻吟。"我喜欢你这间房，"我说，忍住不去看索拉博缠着绷带的手腕，"光线明亮，你还能看到外面的景色。"没有回应。又是尴尬的几分钟过去，丝丝汗水从我额头和上唇冒出来。他床头的柜子上摆着一碗没碰过的豌豆糊，一把没用过的塑料调羹，我指着它们说："你应该试着吃些东西，才能恢复元气。要我喂你吃吗？"

他看向我的眼睛，接着望开，脸上木无表情。我看见他的眼神依然黯淡空洞，就像我把他从浴缸里面拉出来时看到的那样。我把手伸进两腿之间的纸袋，拿出一本我在那间波斯文书店买来的《列王纪》旧书。我将封面转向索拉博。"我们还是小孩的时候，我经常读这些故事给你父亲听。我们爬上我们家后面的山丘，坐在石榴树下面……"我降低声音。索拉博再次望着窗外，我挤出笑脸。"你父亲最喜欢的是罗斯坦和索拉博的故事，你的名字就是从那儿来的，我知道你知道。"我停顿，觉得自己有点像个白痴，"反正，他在信里说你也最喜欢这个故事。所以我想我会念一些给你听，你会喜欢吗？"

索拉博闭上眼睛，将手臂放在眼睛上面，有淤伤的那只手臂。

我翻到在出租车里面折好的那页。"我们从这里开始，"我说，第一次想到，当哈桑终于能自己阅读《列王纪》，发现我曾无数次欺骗过他的时候，他的脑子里转过什么念头呢？我清清喉咙，读了起来。"请听索拉博和罗斯坦战斗的故事，不过这个故事催人泪下。"我开始了，"话说某日，罗斯坦自躺椅起身，心里闪过不祥之兆。他忆起他……"我给他念了第一章的大部分，直到年轻的斗士索拉博去找他的妈妈，萨门干王国的公主拓敏妮，要求得知他的父亲姓甚名谁。我合上书。"你想我读下去吗？接下来有战斗场面，你记得吗？索拉博带领他的军队进攻伊朗的白色城堡？要我念下去吗？"

他慢慢摇头。我把书放回纸袋，"那好。"我说，为他终于有所反应而鼓舞。"也许我们可以明天再继续。你感觉怎样？"

索拉博张开口，发出嘶哑的嗓音。纳瓦兹大夫跟我说过会有这样的情况，那是他们把呼吸管插进他的声带引发的。他舔舔嘴唇，又试一次。"厌倦了。"

"我知道，纳瓦兹大夫说过会出现这种感觉……"

他摇着头。

"怎么了，索拉博？"

他一边缩着身子，一边再次用粗哑的嗓音，声音低得几乎听不见地说："厌倦了一切事情。"

我叹气，颓然坐倒在椅子上。一道阳光照在床上，在我们两人中间，而就在那一瞬间，那张死灰的脸从光线那边看着我，它像极了哈桑的面孔，不是那个整天跟我玩弹珠直到毛拉唱起晚祷、阿里喊我们回家的哈桑，不是那个太阳没入西边的黏土屋顶时我们从山丘上追逐而下的哈桑，而是我有生最后一次见到的那个哈桑，那个我透过自己房间雨水迷蒙的窗户望着的、在夏日温暖的倾盆大雨中拖着行李走在阿里背后、将它们塞进爸爸的轿车后备厢的哈桑。

他慢慢摇着头。"厌倦了一切事情。"他重复说。

"我能做什么，索拉博？请告诉我。"

"我想要……"他开口，身子又是一缩，把手按在喉咙上，似乎要清除掉哽住他嗓音的东西。我的眼光再次落在他手腕上紧紧绑着的医用绷带上。"我想要回原来的生活。"他喘息说。

"哦，索拉博。"

"我想要爸爸和亲爱的妈妈，我想要莎莎，我想要跟拉辛汗老爷在花园玩，我想要回到我们的房子生活。"他用前臂盖住双眼，"我想要回原来的生活。"

我不知道该说什么，该看哪里，所以我望着自己双手。你原来的生活，我想，也是我原来的生活。我在同一个院子玩耍。我住在同一座房子。可是那些草已经死了，我们家房子的车道上停着陌生人的吉普车，油污滴满柏油地面。我们原来的生活不见了，索拉博，原来那些人要么死了，要么正在死去。现在只剩下你和我了。只剩下你和我。

"我没办法给你。"我说。

"我希望你没有……"

"请别那么说。"

"……希望你没有……我希望你让我留在水里。"

"别再那么说了，索拉博。"我说，身子前倾，"我无法忍受再听见你那么说。"我碰他的肩膀，他缩身抽开。我放下手，凄凉地想起我在对他食言之前的最后几天，他终于能够自在地接受我的触碰。"索拉博，我没办法把你原来的生活给你，我希望真主给我这样的力量。但我可以带你走。当时我走向浴室，就是要告诉你这个。你有前往美国跟我和我的妻子生活在一起的签证了。真的。我保证。"

他从鼻子叹出气，闭上眼睛。我要是没有说出最后三个字就好了。"你知道吗，我这一辈子做过很多后悔的事情，"我说，"也许最后悔的事情是对你出尔反尔。但那再也不会发生了，我感到非常非常对不起你。我乞求你的原谅。你能做到吗？你能原谅我吗？你能相信我吗？"我降低声音，"你会跟我一起走吗？"

等待他回答的时候，我脑里一闪，思绪回到了很久以前的某个冬日，哈桑和我坐在一株酸樱桃树下的雪地上。那天我跟哈桑开了个残酷的玩笑，取笑他，问他愿不愿意吃泥巴证明对我的忠诚。而如今，我是那个被考验的人，那个需要证明自己值得尊重的人。我罪有应得。

索拉博翻过身，背朝我。很久很久，他一语不发。接着，就在我以为他也许昏昏睡去的时候，他嘶哑地说："我很累很累。"

我坐在他床沿，直到他睡去。我和索拉博之间有些东西不见了。直到和奥马尔·费萨尔律师碰面之前，一道希望的光芒曾像怯生生的客人那样走进索拉博的眼睛。现在那光芒不见了，客人逃跑了，而我怀疑他是否有胆量回来。我寻思要再过多久才能见到索拉博的微笑，再过多久才会信任我，倘若他会的话。

于是我离开病房，走出去寻找别的旅馆，根本没有意识到我再次听到索拉博说话，已经是一年之后的事情。

结局，索拉博从来没有接受我的邀请。他也没有拒绝。当绷带拆开，脱去病服，他只是又一个无家可归的哈扎拉孤儿。他能有什么选择呢？他能去哪儿呢？所以我当他同意了，可是实际上，那更像是无言的屈服；与其说是同意，毋宁说是由于他心灰意懒、怀疑一切而来的任人摆布。他渴望的是他原来的生活，而他得到的是我和美国。从方方面面看来，这并不能说是什么凄惨的命运，可是我不能这么告诉他。倘使恶魔仍在你脑中徘徊萦绕，前程又从何谈起呢？

于是就这样，一个星期之后，穿过一片温暖的黑色停机坪，我把哈桑的儿子从阿富汗带到美国，让他飞离那业已过去的凄恻往事，降落在即将到来的未知生活之中。

某天，兴许是 1983 年或 1984 年，我在弗里蒙特一间卖录像带的商店。我站在西片区之前，身边有个家伙拿着便利店的纸杯，边喝可乐边指着《七侠荡寇志》，问我有没有看过。"看过，看了十三次。"我说，"查尔斯·勃朗森在里面死了，詹姆斯·科本和罗伯特·华恩也死了。"他狠狠盯了我一眼，好像我朝他的汽水吐口水一样。"太谢谢你啦，老兄。"他说，摇头咕哝着走开了。那时我才明白，在美国，你不能透露电影的结局，要不然你会被谴责，还得为糟蹋了结局的罪行致上万分歉意。

在阿富汗，结局才是最重要的。每逢哈桑和我在萨纳博电影院看完印度片回家，阿里、拉辛汗、爸爸或者爸爸那些九流三教的朋友——各种远房亲戚在那座房子进进出出——想知道的只有这些：电影里面那个姑娘找到幸福了吗？电影里面那个家伙胜利地实现了他的梦想吗？还是失败了，郁郁而终？

他们想知道的是结局是不是幸福。

如果今天有人问起哈桑、索拉博和我的故事结局是否圆满，我不知道该怎么说。

有人能回答吗？

毕竟，生活并非印度电影。阿富汗人总喜欢说：生活总会继续。他们不关心开始或结束、成功或失败、危在旦夕或柳暗花明，只顾像游牧部落那样风尘仆仆地缓慢前进。

我不知道如何回答那个问题。尽管上个星期天出现了小小的奇迹。

七个月前，也就是 2001 年 8 月某个温暖的日子，我们回到家里。索拉雅到机场接我们。我从未离开这么长时间，当她双臂环住我脖子的时候，我闻到她头发上的苹果香味，意识到我有多么想念她。"你仍是我的雅尔达的朝阳。"我低声说。

"什么？"

"没什么。"我亲吻她的耳朵。

随后，她将身子蹲到跟索拉博一样高，拉起他的手，笑着对他说：

"你好，亲爱的索拉博，我是你的索拉雅阿姨，我们大家一直在等你。"

我看到她朝索拉博微笑，眼噙泪水的模样，也看到假如她的子宫没有背叛主人，她该会是什么样的母亲。

索拉博双脚原地挪动，眼睛望向别处。

索拉雅已经把楼上的书房收拾成索拉博的卧房。她领他进去，他坐在床沿。床单绣着风筝在靛蓝的天空中飞翔的图案。她在衣橱旁边的墙上做了刻度尺，标记英尺和英寸，用来测量孩子日益长高的身材。我看到床脚有个装满图书的柳条篮子，一个玩具火车头，还有一盒水彩笔。

索拉博穿着纯白色衬衣，和我们离开之前我在伊斯兰堡给他新买的斜纹粗棉裤，衬衣松松垮垮地挂在他胛骨毕现的瘦削肩膀上。除了黑色的眼圈，他的面庞仍是苍白得没有其他颜色。现在他看着我们，神情冷淡，一如看着医院那些整齐地摆放在他面前的装着白米饭的盘子。

索拉雅问他喜不喜欢他的房间，我注意到她竭力避免去看他的手腕，但眼光总是瞟向那些弯曲的粉红伤痕。索拉博低下头，把手藏在大腿之间，什么也没说。接着他自顾把头倒在枕上，我和索拉雅站在门口看着他，不消五分钟，他就呼呼入睡。

我们回到床上，索拉雅头靠着我的胸膛睡去。在我们黑暗的房间中，我清醒地躺着，再次失眠。清醒、孤独地陪伴我自己的心魔。

那晚夜深人静的时候，我悄悄下床，走到索拉博的房间。我站在他身旁，望下去，看到他枕头下面有东西突出。我把它捡起来，发现是拉辛汗的宝丽来照片，那张我们坐在费萨尔清真寺附近那夜我给索拉博的照片，那张哈桑和索拉博并排站着在阳光下眯着眼睛似乎世界是个美好而有正义的地方的照片。我在想索拉博究竟躺在床上将手里拿着的这张照片翻来覆去地看了多久。

我看着那张照片。**你爸爸是被拉扯成两半的男人。**拉辛汗在信里这么说。我是有名分的那一半，社会承认的、合法的一半，不知不觉间充当了父亲疚恨的化身。我看着哈桑，阳光打在他露出缺了两个门牙的笑脸上。爸爸的另一半，没有名分、没有特权的一半，那继承了爸爸身上纯洁高贵品质的一半，也许，在爸爸内心某处秘密的地方，这是他当成自己的真正儿子的一半。

我把照片塞回刚才发现的地方，接着意识到：刚才最后那个念头居然没有让我心痛。我走向索拉博的房门，心下寻思，是否宽恕就这样萌生？它并非随着神灵显身的玄妙而来，而是痛苦在经过一番收拾之后，终于打点完毕，在深夜悄然退去，催生了它。

隔日，将军和雅米拉阿姨前来一起用晚膳。雅米拉阿姨头发剪短了，也染得比过去更红了，将一盘她买来当点心的杏仁糕递给索拉雅。看到索拉博，她喜形于色："安拉保佑！亲爱的索拉雅告诉我们你有多么英俊，但是你真人更加好看，亲爱的索拉博。"她递给他一件蓝色的圆翻领毛衣。"我替你织了这个，"她说，"到下个冬天，奉安拉之名，你穿上它会合身的。"

索拉博从她手里接过毛衣。

"你好，小伙子。"将军只说了这么一句，双手拄着拐杖，看着索拉博，似乎在研究某人房子的奇异装饰。

我一遍又一遍地回答雅米拉阿姨关于我受伤的问题——我曾让索拉

雅告诉他们我被抢了——不断向她保证，我没有受到永久性的伤害，再过一两个星期就可以拆线了，我又能吃她做的饭了，也向她保证，是的，我会在伤疤上抹大黄汁和白糖，让它消失得快一些。

索拉雅和她妈妈收拾桌子的时候，将军和我在客厅喝葡萄酒。我跟他谈起喀布尔和塔利班，他边听边点头，拐杖放在腿上。当我说起我见到那个卖假腿的家伙时，他啧啧有声。我没说到伽兹体育馆的处决，也没提及阿塞夫。他问起拉辛汗，说曾在喀布尔见过他几面，当我告诉他拉辛汗的病况时，他严肃地摇摇头。但在我们说话的时候，我注意到他的眼睛不断看向睡在沙发上的索拉博。似乎我们一直在他真正想知道的问题边缘兜圈。

兜圈终于结束了。用过晚饭之后，将军放下他的叉子，问："那么，亲爱的阿米尔，你是不是该告诉我们，你为什么要带这个男孩回来？"

"亲爱的伊克伯！这是什么问题？"雅米拉阿姨说。

"你在忙着编织毛衣的时候，亲爱的，我不得不应付邻居对我们家的看法。人们会有疑问。他们会想知道为什么有个哈扎拉男孩住在我女儿家。我怎么跟他们说？"

索拉雅放下她的调羹，转向她父亲，"你可以告诉他们……"

"没什么，索拉雅。"我说，拉起她的手，"没什么，将军说得没错，人们会有疑问。"

"阿米尔……"她说。

"没关系，"我转向将军，"你知道吗，将军大人，我爸爸睡了他仆人的老婆。她给他生了个儿子，名字叫做哈桑。现在哈桑死掉了，睡在沙发上那个男孩是哈桑的儿子。他是我的侄儿。要是有人发问，你可以这样告诉他们。"

他们全都瞪着我。

"还有，将军大人，"我说，"以后我在场的时候，请你永远不要叫他'哈扎拉男孩'。他有名字，他的名字叫索拉博。"

大家默默吃完那顿饭。

如果说索拉博很安静是错误的。安静是祥和，是平静，是降下生命音量的旋钮。

沉默是把那个按钮关掉，把它旋下，全部旋掉。

索拉博的沉默既不是来自洞明世事之后的泰然自若，也并非由于他选择了默默不语来秉持自己的信念和表达抗议，而是对生活曾有过的黑暗忍气吞声地照单全收。

他身在曹营心在汉，人跟我们共同生活，而心跟我们一起的时候少得可怜。有时候，在市场或者公园里面，我注意到人们仿佛甚至没有看到他，似乎他根本并不存在。我曾经从书本抬头，发现索拉博业已走进房间，坐在我对面，而我毫无察觉。他走路的样子似乎害怕留下脚印，移动的时候似乎不想搅起周围的空气。多数时候，他选择了睡觉。

索拉雅对索拉博的沉默也难以忍受。在巴基斯坦的国际长途电话线上，我曾听到索拉雅为索拉博准备的一切，游泳课、足球、保龄球。如今她走过索拉博的房间，投入的一瞥只见到书原封不动地摆在柳条篮里面，测量身高的标尺上没有刻痕，拼图依然散开，每一块都让人想起生活原本应该是另外一种样子，让人想起那个尚未盛放就已经凋谢的梦。但她并不孤单，我对索拉博也曾有过梦想。

索拉博沉默的时候，世界风起云涌。上个九月某个星期二早晨，双子塔大楼轰然倒塌，一夜之间，世界改变了。美国国旗突然出现在每个地方，在车水马龙中前进的黄色出租车天线上，在行色匆匆地走在拥挤人行道的行人衣襟上，甚至在那些寄身小画廊和临街商店雨篷之下的流浪汉的污秽帽子上。有一天我走过艾迪斯面前，她是个无家可归的女人，每天在萨特街和斯托克顿街的十字路口弹奏手风琴，我见到在她脚下的手风琴盒子上也贴了美国国旗。

遭到袭击之后不久，美国轰炸了阿富汗，北方联盟乘机而进，塔利班像老鼠逃回洞穴那样四处亡命。突然间，人们在杂货店排队等待收银，谈着我童年生活过的那些城市：坎大哈、赫拉特、马扎里沙里夫。我很小的时候，爸爸带我和哈桑去昆都士。关于那次旅程我已经没有什么印象了，只记得和爸爸、哈桑坐在一株金合欢树的阴影下轮流喝陶罐中的西瓜汁，比赛谁能把瓜籽吐得更远些。现在丹·拉德[1]、汤姆·布罗考[2]和那些在星巴克喝拿铁的人都在谈论昆都士的战役，那里是塔利班最后的阵地。那年12月，普什图人、塔吉克人、乌兹别克人和哈扎拉人齐集波恩，在联合国观察员的监督下，开始了一个也许有朝一日能够终结他们祖国过去二十余年来的苦难的进程。哈米德·卡尔扎伊[3]的羊皮帽和绿色长袍变得众所周知。

索拉博依然梦游般地度过这段日子。

---

[1] Dan Rather（1931~ ），美国哥伦比亚广播公司著名电视节目主持人。
[2] Tom Brokaw（1940~2021），美国国家广播公司著名电视节目主持人。
[3] Hamid Karzai（1957~ ），2001年底出任阿富汗临时政府总统，2004年当选阿富汗历史上首位民选总统。

　　索拉雅和我开始参与到阿富汗的计划中去，除了有心为故国略尽绵薄之力外，也是因为需要某些东西——任何东西都好——来填补楼上的沉默，那像黑洞般吞噬一切的沉默。我过去从未如此热心，但当有个名叫卡比尔的被派往索非亚的前阿富汗大使打电话来，问我是否愿意帮助他进行一项医疗计划，我答应了。那个小医院位于阿富汗和巴基斯坦边境，有个小小的外科手术组，治疗那些被地雷炸伤的阿富汗难民。但由于缺乏资金，它倒闭了。我成为那个计划的主持人，索拉雅是我的副手。我每天大部分时间在书房里面，给遍布世界各地的人发电子邮件，申请基金，组织募捐活动，还告诉自己把索拉博带到这儿是正确的事情。

　　那年除夕，我和索拉雅躺在沙发上，腿上盖毛毯，看着迪克·克拉克[1]主持的电视节目。当银球抛落，彩纸将荧屏变成白色，人们欢呼亲吻。在我们家，新年的开始跟上一年的结束一样，沉默无声。

　　然而，4天之前，2002年3月某个阴冷的雨天，发生了一个小小的奇迹。

　　我带索拉雅、雅米拉阿姨和索拉博参加弗里蒙特伊丽莎白湖公园的阿富汗人聚会。上个月，阿富汗终于征召将军回去履任一个大臣的职位，他两个星期前飞走——他留下了灰色西装和怀表。雅米拉阿姨计划等他安顿好之后，过一两个月再去和他团聚。她很想念他，也担心他在那边的健康状况。我们执意要她搬过来同住一阵子。

　　上个星期二是春季的第一天，过去是阿富汗的新年，湾区的阿富汗人计划在东湾和半岛举行盛大的庆祝活动。卡比尔、索拉雅和我还有另

---

[1]　Dick Clark（1929~2012），美国著名电视节目主持人。

外一个庆祝的理由：我们在拉瓦尔品第的小医院重新开张了，没有外科手术组，只是个儿科诊所。但我们一致认为这是个好的开始。

天气晴朗了好几天，但星期天早晨，我刚把脚伸出床外的时候，听到雨水沿窗户滴落的声音。阿富汗运气，我想，暗暗发笑。索拉雅还在睡觉的时候，我已经做完晨礼——我不用再求助从清真寺得来的礼拜手册了，祷文熟极而流，毫不费劲。

我们是在中午到的，发现地面插了六根柱子，上面搭了长方形的塑料布，里面有一些人。有人已经开始炸面饼；蒸汽从茶杯和花椰菜面锅冒出来。一台磁带播放机放着艾哈迈德·查希尔聒噪的老歌。我们四个人冲过那片潮湿的草地时，我微微发笑；索拉雅和我走在前面，雅米拉阿姨在中间，后面是索拉博，他穿着黄色雨衣，兜帽拍打着他的后背。

"什么事这么好笑？"索拉雅说，将一张折好的报纸举在头顶。

"你可以将阿富汗人带离帕格曼，但却无法让帕格曼离开阿富汗人。"我说。

我们站在那临时搭建的棚子下面。索拉雅和雅米拉阿姨朝一个正在炸菠菜面饼的肥胖女人走去。索拉博在雨棚下面站了一会儿，接着走回雨中，双手插进雨衣的口袋，他的头发——现在跟哈桑的头发一样，都是棕色的直发——贴在头上。他在一个咖啡色的水坑旁边停下，看着它。似乎没有人注意到他，没有人喊他进来。随着时间流逝，人们终于仁慈地不再问起我们收养这个——他的行为怪异一目了然——小男孩的问题。而考虑到阿富汗人的提问有时毫不拐弯抹角，这当真是个很大的解脱。人们不再问为什么他不说话，为什么他不和其他小孩玩。而最令人高兴的是，他们不再用夸张的同情、他们的慢慢摇头、他们的咋舌、他们的"噢，这个可怜的小哑巴"来让我们窒息。新奇的感觉不见了，索拉博就像发旧的墙纸一样融进了这个生活环境。

我跟一头银发的小个子卡比尔握手。他把我介绍给十来个男人，有个是退休教师，另外一个是工程师，有个原先是建筑师，有个目前在海沃德摆摊卖热狗的外科医师。他们都说在喀布尔就认识爸爸了，而他们谈起他的时候都很敬重。他总是以这样或那样的方式影响他们的生活。那些男人都说我有这么一个了不起的父亲真幸运。

我们谈起卡尔扎伊面对的困难，还有他那也许吃力不讨好的工作，谈起即将召开的大国民议会，还有国王在流亡二十八年之后即将重返他的家园。我记得1973年查希尔国王被他的表亲推翻的那个夜晚，我记得枪炮声和亮出银光的天空——阿里搂着我和哈桑，告诉我们别害怕，说他们只是在猎野鸭。

接着有人说了个纳斯鲁丁毛拉的笑话，我们都哈哈大笑。"你知道吗，你爸爸也是个幽默的人。"卡比尔说。

"他是的，难道不是吗？"我说，微笑着想起在我们刚来美国之后不久，爸爸开始抱怨美国的苍蝇。他拿着苍蝇拍坐在厨房里，看着苍蝇从这面墙冲到那面墙，在这儿嗡嗡叫，在那儿嗡嗡叫，飞得又快又急。"在这个国家，甚至连苍蝇都在赶时间。"他埋怨说。记得当时我哈哈大笑。现在我想起来，微笑着。

到三点的时候，雨停了，铅灰色的天空阴云密布，一阵寒风吹过公园。更多的家庭来到了。阿富汗人彼此问候，拥抱，亲吻，交换食物。有人在烧烤炉中点了木炭，很快，我闻到大蒜和烤肉的香味。我听到音乐，一些我不认识的新歌星的音乐，还有孩子们的咯咯笑。我看见索拉博依旧穿着他的黄色雨衣，斜倚着一个垃圾桶，眼光越过公园，望着那头空荡荡的击球练习区。

过了一会儿，我正在跟那个原来当外科医师的人聊天，他说他念八年级的时候跟我爸爸是同学，索拉雅拉拉我的衣袖："阿米尔，看！"

她指着天空。几只风筝高高飞翔，黄色的、红色的、绿色的，点缀在灰色的天空上，格外夺目。

"去看看。"索拉雅说，这次她指着一个在附近摆摊卖风筝的家伙。

"拿着。"我说，把茶杯递给索拉雅。我告辞离开，鞋子踩在潮湿的草地上，走到那个风筝摊。我指着一只黄色风筝。"新年快乐。"卖风筝的人说，接过二十美元，把那个风筝和一个缠着玻璃线的木轴递给我。我向他道谢，也祝他新年快乐。我试试风筝线，像过去哈桑和我经常做的那样，用拇指和食指捏着拉开。它被血染红，卖风筝那人微微发笑，我报以微笑。

我把风筝带到索拉博站着的地方，他仍倚着垃圾桶，双手抱在胸前，抬头望着天空。

"你喜欢风筝吗？"我举起风筝横轴的两端。他的眼睛从天空落到我身上，看看风筝，又望着我。几点雨珠从他头发上滴下来，流下他的脸庞。

"有一次我在书上看到，在马来西亚，人们用风筝来捉鱼。"我说，"我敢打赌你不知道。他们在风筝上绑钓鱼线，让它飞过浅水，这样它就不会投下阴影，不会吓走鱼儿。在古代中国，那些将领经常在战场放飞风筝，给他们的人传讯。这是真的，我不是在跟你开玩笑。"我把流血的拇指给他看，"这根线也没问题。"

我用眼角的余光瞥见索拉雅在帐篷那边望着我们，她双手紧张地夹在腋下。跟我不同的是，她已经慢慢放弃了亲近他的念头。那些问而不答的状况、那空洞的眼神、那沉默，所有这些太让人痛苦了。她已经转入"待命状态"，等着索拉博亮起绿灯。等待着。

我舔舔食指，将它竖起来。"我记得你父亲测风向的办法是用他的拖鞋踢起尘土，看风将它吹到哪儿。他懂得很多这样的小技巧。"我放低手指说，"西风，我想。"

索拉博擦去耳垂上的一点雨珠，双脚磨地，什么也没说。我想起索拉雅几个月前问我，他的声音听起来像什么。我告诉她我也不记得了。

"我有没有跟你说过，你爸爸是瓦兹尔·阿克巴·汗区最棒的追风筝的人？也许还是全喀布尔最棒的？"我一边说，一边将卷轴的线头系在风筝中轴的圆环上。"邻居的小孩都很妒忌他。他追风筝的时候从来不用看着天空，大家经常说他追着风筝的影子。但他们不知道我知道的事情，你爸爸不是在追什么影子，他只是……知道。"

又有几只风筝飞起来，人们开始三五成群聚在一起，手里拿着茶杯，望向天空。

"好吧。"我耸耸肩，"看来我得一个人把它放起来了。"

我左手拿稳卷轴，放开大约三英尺的线。黄色的风筝吊在线后摇晃，就在湿草地上面。"最后的机会了哦。"我说。可是索拉博看着两只高高飞在树顶之上的风筝。

"好吧，那我开始了。"我撒腿跑开，运动鞋从水洼中溅起阵阵雨水，手里抓着线连着风筝的那头，高举在头顶。我已经有很久、很多年没这么做过了，我在怀疑自己会不会出洋相。我边跑边让卷轴在我手里转开，感到线放开的时候又割伤了我的右手。风筝在我肩膀后面飞起来了，飞翔着，旋转着，我跑得更快了。卷轴迅速旋转，风筝线再次在我右掌割开一道伤痕。我站住，转身，举头，微笑。在高高的上方，我的风筝像钟摆那样从一边荡到另一边，发出那久远的"鸟儿扑打翅膀"的声音，那种总是让我联想起喀布尔冬天早晨的声音。我已经有四分之一个世纪没有放过风筝了，但刹那之间，我又变成十二岁，过去那些感觉统统涌上心头。

我感到有人在我旁边，眼睛朝下看：是索拉博。他双手深深插在雨衣口袋中，跟在我身后。

"你想试试吗？"我问。他一语不发，但我把线递给他的时候，他的手从口袋伸出来，犹疑不决，接过线。我转动卷轴把线松开，心跳加速。我们静静地并排站着，脖子仰起。

孩子在我们身边相互追逐，不断有人跌在草地上。现在有人用口琴吹奏出一曲印度老电影的音乐。一排老人在地面铺开塑料布，跪在其上做晌礼。空气散发着湿润的青草味、烟味和烤肉味。我希望时间能静止不动。

接着我看到我们有伴了。一只绿色的风筝正在靠近。我沿着线往下看，见到一个孩子站在离我们三十米外。他留着平头，身上的恤衫用粗黑字体印着"ROCK RULES"。他见到我在看他，微微发笑，招招手。我也朝他招手。

索拉博把线交还我。

"你确定吗？"我说，接过它。

他从我手里拿回卷轴。

"好的。"我说,"让我们给他一点颜色瞧瞧,教训他一下,好吧?"我俯视着他,他眼里那种模糊空洞的神色已经不见了。他的眼光在我们的风筝和那只绿色风筝之间来回转动,脸色有一点点发红,眼睛骤然机警起来。苏醒了。复活了。我在寻思,我什么时候忘了?不管怎么说,他仍只是一个孩子。

绿色风筝采取行动了。"我们等等,"我说,"我们会让它再靠近一些。"它下探了两次,慢慢朝我们挪过来。"来啊,过来啊。"我说。

绿风筝已经更近了,在我们稍高的地方拉升,对我为它布下的陷阱毫不知情。"看,索拉博,我会让你看看你爸爸最喜欢的招数,那招古老的猛升急降。"

索拉博挨着我,用鼻子急促地呼吸着。卷轴在他手中滚动,他伤痕累累的手腕上的筋腱很像雷巴布琴的琴弦。我眨眨眼,瞬间,拿着卷轴的是一个兔唇男孩指甲破裂、长满老茧的手。我听见某个地方传来牛的哞哞叫,而我抬头,公园闪闪发光,铺满的雪多么新鲜,白得多么耀眼,令我目眩神迷。雪花无声地洒落在白色的枝头上,现在我闻到了芜菁拌饭的香味,还有桑葚干、酸橙子、锯屑和胡桃的气味。一阵雪花飞舞的寂静盖住了所有声音。然后,远远地,有个声音穿透这片死寂,呼喊我们回家,是那个拖着右腿的男人的声音。

绿风筝现在就在我们正上方翱翔。"我们现在随时可以把它干掉了。"我说,眼睛在索拉博和我们的风筝间飞快地转着。

绿风筝摇摇晃晃,定住位,接着向下冲。"他玩完了!"我说。

这么多年之后,我无懈可击地再次使出那招古老的猛升急降。我松开手，猛拉着线，往下避开那只绿风筝。我侧过手臂，一阵急遽的抖动之后，我们的风筝逆时针划出一个半圆。我突然占据了上面的位置。绿色风筝现在惊惶失措，慌乱地向上攀升。但它已经太迟了，我已经使出哈桑的绝技。我猛拉着线，我们的风筝直坠而下。我几乎能听见我们的线割断他的线，几乎能听见那一声断裂。

然后，就那样，绿风筝失去控制，摇摇晃晃地摔下来。

我们身后的人们欢呼叫好，爆发出阵阵口哨声和掌声。我喘着气。上一次感到这么激动，是在 1975 年那个冬日，就在我刚刚割断最后一只风筝之后，当时我看见爸爸在我们的屋顶上，鼓着掌，容光焕发。

我俯视索拉博，他嘴角的一边微微翘起。

微笑。

斜斜的。

几乎看不见。

但就在那儿。

在我们后面，孩子们在飞奔，追风筝的人不断尖叫，乱成一团，追逐那只在树顶高高之上飘摇的断线风筝。我眨眼，微笑不见了。但它在那儿出现过，我看见了。

"你想要我追那只风筝给你吗？"

他的喉结吞咽着上下蠕动。风掠起他的头发。我想我看到他点头。

"为你，千千万万遍。"我听见自己说。

然后我转过身，我追。

它只是一个微笑，没有别的了。它没有让所有事情恢复正常。它没有让任何事情恢复正常。只是一个微笑，一件小小的事情，像是树林中的一片叶子，在惊鸟的飞起中晃动着。

　　但我会迎接它，张开双臂。因为每逢春天到来，它总是每次融化一片雪花；而也许我刚刚看到的，正是第一片雪花的融化。

　　我追。一个成年人在一群尖叫的孩子中奔跑。但我不在乎。我追，风拂过我的脸庞，我唇上挂着一个像潘杰希尔峡谷那样大大的微笑。

　　我追。

译者附记

丙戌年春节假期，我没有回广东，独自留在上海翻译《追风筝的人》。记得除夕夜半，室内灯光昏黄，窗外爆竹声声，我充耳不闻，飞快地敲击着笔记本电脑的键盘，将拉辛汗最后留给阿米尔的信一字一字打出来，等到把信译完，已是泪流满面。相信你一定明白，我流泪不是因为自己触景伤情，而是由于故事动人心弦。

但说实话，虽然翻译时入戏太深，当初我却没料到，卡勒德·胡赛尼先生这部处女作，也是我的第二部译著，竟然在随后十年里卖出数百万册，迄今仍高居各大图书畅销榜前列。当初同样没料到的是，在十年后的今天，我竟然生活在美国加州，也就是小说后半部分发生的地方。如今回想起来真是感慨万千。

自从这本书的简体版在 2006 年 5 月出版以后，几乎每周都有读者写信给我。他们大方分享阅读后的感触和生活中的故事，甚至不吝赞扬我的译笔，给我带来了极大的鼓励和满足。还有一些目光敏锐的读者，告诉我哪里也许译错了，哪里也许可以改进。如果说这次修订过的译文比原来的好，很大程度上应该感谢他们。

现在阿米尔和哈桑的故事几乎家喻户晓，相关的解读和评论多如牛毛，但我仍想在这里重复十年前写下的两段话：

在这本感人至深的小说里面，风筝是象征性的，它既可以是亲情、友情、爱情，也可以是正直、善良、诚实。对阿米尔来说，风筝隐喻他人格中必不可少的部分，只有追到了，他才能成为健全的人，成为他自我期许的阿米尔。

也许每个人心中都有一个风筝，无论它意味着什么，让我们勇敢地追。

李继宏

lijihong@hotmail.com

2016 年 7 月 2 日

文
景

Horizon

社 科 新 知　文 艺 新 潮

追风筝的人（中英双语版）

[美]卡勒德·胡赛尼 著

李继宏 译

出 品 人：姚映然
责任编辑：陈欢欢
装帧设计：奇文云海　高　熹

出　　品：北京世纪文景文化传播有限责任公司
　　　　　（北京朝阳区东土城路8号林达大厦A座4A　100013）
出版发行：上海人民出版社
印　　刷：山东临沂新华印刷物流集团有限责任公司
制　　版：北京大观世纪文化传媒有限公司
　　　　　北京大有艺彩图文设计有限公司

开 本：890mm×1240mm　1/32
印 张：23.75　字 数：393,000　插 页：4
2018年7月第1版　2025年3月第12次印刷
定 价：89.00元
ISBN：978-7-208-15184-0 / I·1721

图书在版编目（CIP）数据

追风筝的人：中文、英文 /（美）卡勒德·胡赛尼
（Khaled Hosseini）著；李继宏译. —上海：上海人
民出版社，2018
书名原文：The Kite Runner
ISBN 978-7-208-15184-0

Ⅰ.① 追… Ⅱ.① 卡…② 李… Ⅲ.① 长篇小说-美
国-现代-汉、英 Ⅳ. ① I712.45

中国版本图书馆CIP数据核字（2018）第105184号

本书如有印装错误，请致电本社更换 010-52187586

文景

Horizon

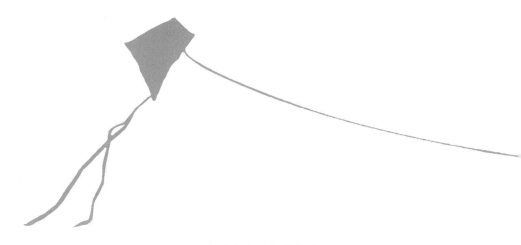

社科新知　文艺新潮

Khaled Hosseini

The Kite Runner

上海人民出版社

This book is dedicated to
Haris and Farah, both
the *noor* of my eyes,
and to the children
of Afghanistan.

FORWARD

I began writing, like Amir in The Kite Runner, as a boy, in 1970s Kabul. Though the language has changed—first it was Farsi, then French, now it's English—one factor has remained constant: I have always written for an audience of one—myself.

A given character of a situation piques my interest and I sit down to write, compelled to see it through. This was how The Kite Runner was done. I had two boys in mind: one conflicted, on unsure emotional and moral ground; the other pure, loyal, rooted in goodness and integrity.I knew that the boys' friendship was doomed, and that their falling-out would impact their lives in a profound way. The why and how were the reason, the compulsion, that led me to begin this book, in March 2001. I had to write it, because, in the end, writing for me has always been the self-serving act of telling myself a story.

It never crossed my mind that anyone else would read *The Kite Runner*. Actually, I knew my wife, Roya, would. So would my parents, sibling, and in-laws. And there might be a cousin or two who could be cajoled into it. In my mind, I would tell Amir s story, and then the pages would sit on a shelf in the garage.

Then, six months into the novel, the twin Towers came down.

Shortly after that, Roya suggested—in fact, demanded—that I submit the manuscript to a publisher. I was roughly two-thirds of the way through, and she had been reading chapters as I produced them. I was against the idea. For one thing, I wasn't sure that it was at all any good. More important, if far more erroneous, I thought no one in the United States would want to hear from an Afghan like me.

You must understand, this was in the days and weeks after the attacks. Wounds were raw and emotions ran high. Afghans were the pariah now, I remember telling Roya at the time. Even if I accepted the hypothetic, ludicrous possibility that my book would see publication, money in the pocket of someone whose country had been the training ground for those people responsible for the worst terrorist attack ever to send out the manuscript at that time, like I was capitalizing on the tragedy, even though started writing it long before Afghanistan was thrust into the international spotlight.

Roya disagreed. She thought that it was time for me to reach my audience. A lawyer by trade, she argued her case convincingly. It was the ideal time, she felt, to tell the world an Afghan story. Much of what was written about Afghanistan in those days—and, sadly, even today—revolved around bin Laden, the Taliban, and the war on terror. Preconceived notions and misconceptions about Afghanistan abounded. Your book. Roya said, can show' them a different face of Afghanistan.

In June 2002, I sent the manuscript to a lovely woman named Elaine Koster, a literary agent based in New York City. She called one hot July afternoon and more or less told me what Roya had told months before. By the end of that summer, she had found a home for *The Kite Runner*. It was published the following June, in 2003.

You can imagine my astonishment at the reception this book has received worldwide since its publication. I was the only intended audience, remember, so it amazes me to get letters from India, South Africa, Tel Aviv, Sydney, London, Arkansas; from readers who express their passion to me. Many want to send money to Afghanistan; some even want to adopt an Afghan orphan. In these letters, I see the unique ability fiction has to connect people, and I see how universal some human experiences are: shame, guilt, regret, friendship, love, forgiveness, atonement.

The letters I get from readers are a source of tremendous gratification for me, and a constant reminder that I have married the right woman, without whom this book still would be a manuscript sitting on a shelf in my garage. As a writer, I am thrilled when readers respond to the story, to the characters and their hardships, to the twists and turns in the plot. As an Afghan, I am honored when people tell me that reading this novel helped put a personal face on Afghanistan for them, that they now see my homeland as more than just another unhappy, afflicted, chronically troubled land.

I hope the same is true for you.

Thank you for reading *The Kite Runner*. And may your kites soar far and high.

Khaled Hosseini

ONE

December 2001

I became what I am today at the age of twelve, on a frigid over-cast day in the winter of 1975. I remember the precise moment, crouching behind a crumbling mud wall, peeking into the alley near the frozen creek. That was a long time ago, but it's wrong what they say about the past, I've learned, about how you can bury it. Because the past claws its way out. Looking back now, I realize I have been peeking into that deserted alley for the last twenty-six years.

One day last summer, my friend Rahim Khan called from Pakistan. He asked me to come see him. Standing in the kitchen with the receiver to my ear, I knew it wasn't just Rahim Khan on the line. It was my past of unatoned sins. After I hung up, I went for a walk along Spreckels Lake on the northern edge of Golden Gate Park. The early-afternoon sun sparkled on the wa-ter where dozens of miniature boats sailed, propelled by a crisp breeze. Then I glanced up and saw a pair of kites, red with long blue tails, soaring in the sky. They danced high above the trees on the west end of the park, over the windmills, floating side by side like a pair of eyes looking down on San Francisco, the city I now call home. And suddenly Hassan's voice whispered in my head: *For you, a thousand times over.* Hassan the harelipped kite runner.

I sat on a park bench near a willow tree. I thought about something Rahim Khan said just before he hung up, almost as an afterthought. *There is a way to be good again.* I looked up at those twin kites. I thought about Hassan. Thought about Baba. Ali. Kabul. I thought of the life I had lived until the winter of 1975 came along and changed everything. And made me what I am today.

T W O

When we were children, Hassan and I used to climb the
poplar trees in the driveway of my father's house and annoy
our neighbors by reflecting sunlight into their homes with a
shard of mirror. We would sit across from each other on a pair
of high branches, our naked feet dangling, our trouser pockets
filled with dried mulberries and walnuts. We took turns with
the mirror as we ate mulberries, pelted each other with them,
giggling, laughing. I can still see Hassan up on that tree, sunlight
flickering through the leaves on his almost perfectly round
face, a face like a Chinese doll chiseled from hardwood: his flat,
broad nose and slanting, narrow eyes like bamboo leaves, eyes
that looked, depending on the light, gold, green, even sapphire.
I can still see his tiny low-set ears and that pointed stub of a
chin, a meaty appendage that looked like it was added as a mere
afterthought. And the cleft lip, just left of midline, where the
Chinese doll maker's instrument may have slipped, or perhaps he
had simply grown tired and careless.

Sometimes, up in those trees, I talked Hassan into firing walnuts with his slingshot at the neighbor's one-eyed German

shepherd. Hassan never wanted to, but if I asked, *really* asked, he wouldn't deny me. Hassan never denied me anything. And he was deadly with his slingshot. Hassan's father, Ali, used to catch us and get mad, or as mad as someone as gentle as Ali could ever get. He would wag his finger and wave us down from the tree. He would take the mirror and tell us what his mother had told him, that the devil shone mirrors too, shone them to distract Muslims during prayer. "And he laughs while he does it," he always added, scowling at his son.

"Yes, Father," Hassan would mumble, looking down at his feet. But he never told on me. Never told that the mirror, like shooting walnuts at the neighbor's dog, was always my idea.

The poplar trees lined the redbrick driveway, which led to a pair of wrought-iron gates. They in turn opened into an extension of the driveway into my father's estate. The house sat on the left side of the brick path, the backyard at the end of it.

Everyone agreed that my father, my Baba, had built the most beautiful house in the Wazir Akbar Khan district, a new and affluent neighborhood in the northern part of Kabul. Some thought it was the prettiest house in all of Kabul. A broad entryway flanked by rosebushes led to the sprawling house of marble floors and wide windows. Intricate mosaic tiles, handpicked by Baba in Isfahan, covered the floors of the four bathrooms. Gold-stitched tapestries, which Baba had bought in Calcutta, lined the walls; a crystal chandelier hung from the vaulted ceiling.

Upstairs was my bedroom, Baba's room, and his study, also known as "the smoking room," which perpetually smelled of tobacco and cinnamon. Baba and his friends reclined on black leather chairs there after Ali had served dinner. They stuffed

their pipes—except Baba always called it "fattening the pipe"—
and dis-cussed their favorite three topics: politics, business,
soccer. Sometimes I asked Baba if I could sit with them, but
Baba would stand in the doorway. "Go on, now," he'd say. "This
is grown-ups' time. Why don't you go read one of those books
of yours?" He'd close the door, leave me to wonder why it was
always grown-ups' time with him. I'd sit by the door, knees
drawn to my chest. Sometimes I sat there for an hour, sometimes
two, listening to their laughter, their chatter.

The living room downstairs had a curved wall with custom-
built cabinets. Inside sat framed family pictures: an old, grainy
photo of my grandfather and King Nadir Shah taken in 1931,
two years before the king's assassination; they are standing
over a dead deer, dressed in knee-high boots, rifles slung over
their shoulders. There was a picture of my parents' wedding
night, Baba dashing in his black suit and my mother a smiling
young princess in white. Here was Baba and his best friend
and business partner, Rahim Khan, standing outside our house,
neither one smiling—I am a baby in that photograph and Baba
is holding me, looking tired and grim. I'm in his arms, but it's
Rahim Khan's pinky my fingers are curled around.

The curved wall led into the dining room, at the center of
which was a mahogany table that could easily sit thirty guests—
and, given my father's taste for extravagant parties, it did just that
almost every week. On the other end of the dining room was a
tall marble fireplace, always lit by the orange glow of a fire in the
wintertime.

A large sliding glass door opened into a semicircular terrace
that overlooked two acres of backyard and rows of cherry trees.
Baba and Ali had planted a small vegetable garden along the

eastern wall: tomatoes, mint, peppers, and a row of corn that never really took. Hassan and I used to call it "the Wall of Ailing Corn."

On the south end of the garden, in the shadows of a loquat tree, was the servants' home, a modest little mud hut where Hassan lived with his father.

It was there, in that little shack, that Hassan was born in the winter of 1964, just one year after my mother died giving birth to me.

In the eighteen years that I lived in that house, I stepped into Hassan and Ali's quarters only a handful of times. When the sun dropped low behind the hills and we were done playing for the day, Hassan and I parted ways. I went past the rosebushes to Baba's mansion, Hassan to the mud shack where he had been born, where he'd lived his entire life. I remember it was spare, clean, dimly lit by a pair of kerosene lamps. There were two mattresses on opposite sides of the room, a worn Herati rug with frayed edges in between, a three-legged stool, and a wooden table in the corner where Hassan did his drawings. The walls stood bare, save for a single tapestry with sewn-in beads forming the words *Allah-u-akbar*. Baba had bought it for Ali on one of his trips to Mashad.

It was in that small shack that Hassan's mother, Sanaubar, gave birth to him one cold winter day in 1964. While my mother hemorrhaged to death during childbirth, Hassan lost his less than a week after he was born. Lost her to a fate most Afghans considered far worse than death: She ran off with a clan of traveling singers and dancers.

Hassan never talked about his mother, as if she'd never existed. I always wondered if he dreamed about her, about what she looked like, where she was. I wondered if he longed to meet her. Did he ache for her, the way I ached for the mother I had never met? One day, we were walking from my father's house to Cinema Zainab for a new Iranian movie, taking the shortcut through the military barracks near Istiqlal Middle School—Baba had forbidden us to take that shortcut, but he was in Pakistan with Rahim Khan at the time. We hopped the fence that surrounded the barracks, skipped over a little creek, and broke into the open dirt field where old, abandoned tanks collected dust. A group of soldiers huddled in the shade of one of those tanks, smoking cigarettes and playing cards. One of them saw us, elbowed the guy next to him, and called Hassan.

"Hey, you!" he said. "I know you."

We had never seen him before. He was a squatty man with a shaved head and black stubble on his face. The way he grinned at us, leered, scared me. "Just keep walking," I muttered to Hassan.

"You! The Hazara! Look at me when I'm talking to you!" the soldier barked. He handed his cigarette to the guy next to him, made a circle with the thumb and index finger of one hand. Poked the middle finger of his other hand through the circle. Poked it in and out. In and out. "I knew your mother, did you know that? I knew her real good. I took her from behind by that creek over there."

The soldiers laughed. One of them made a squealing sound. I told Hassan to keep walking, keep walking.

"What a tight little sugary cunt she had!" the soldier was saying, shaking hands with the others, grinning. Later, in the dark, after the movie had started, I heard Hassan next to me, croaking. Tears were sliding down his cheeks. I reached across my seat, slung my arm around him, pulled him close. He rested his head on my shoulder. "He took you for someone else," I whispered. "He took you for someone else."

I'm told no one was really surprised when Sanaubar eloped. People *had* raised their eyebrows when Ali, a man who had memorized the Koran, married Sanaubar, a woman nineteen years younger, a beautiful but notoriously unscrupulous woman who lived up to her dishonorable reputation. Like Ali, she was a Shi'a Muslim and an ethnic Hazara. She was also his first cousin and therefore a natural choice for a spouse. But beyond those similarities, Ali and Sanaubar had little in common, least of all their respective appearances. While Sanaubar's brilliant green eyes and impish face had, rumor has it, tempted countless men into sin, Ali had a congenital paralysis of his lower facial muscles, a condition that rendered him unable to smile and left him perpetually grimfaced. It was an odd thing to see the stone-faced Ali happy, or sad, because only his slanted brown eyes glinted with a smile or welled with sorrow. People say that eyes are windows to the soul. Never was that more true than with Ali, who could only reveal himself through his eyes.

I have heard that Sanaubar's suggestive stride and oscillating hips sent men to reveries of infidelity. But polio had left Ali with a twisted, atrophied right leg that was sallow skin over bone with little in between except a paper-thin layer of muscle. I remember one day, when I was eight, Ali was taking me to the bazaar to buy some *naan*. I was walking behind him, humming, trying to imitate his walk. I watched him swing his scraggy leg in a sweeping arc, watched his whole body tilt impossibly to the right every time he planted that foot. It seemed a minor miracle he didn't tip over with each step. When I tried it, I almost fell into the gutter. That got me giggling. Ali turned around, caught me aping him. He didn't say anything. Not then, not ever. He just kept walking.

Ali's face and his walk frightened some of the younger children in the neighborhood. But the real trouble was with the older kids. They chased him on the street, and mocked him when he hobbled by. Some had taken to calling him *Babalu*, or Boogeyman. "Hey, Babalu, who did you eat today?" they barked to a chorus of laughter. "Who did you eat, you flat-nosed Babalu?"

They called him "flat-nosed" because of Ali and Hassan's characteristic Hazara Mongoloid features. For years, that was all I knew about the Hazaras, that they were Mogul descendants, and that they looked a little like Chinese people. School textbooks barely mentioned them and referred to their ancestry only in passing. Then one day, I was in Baba's study, looking through his stuff, when I found one of my mother's old history books. It was written by an Iranian named Khorami. I blew the dust off it, sneaked it into bed with me that night, and was stunned to find an entire chapter on Hazara history. An entire chapter dedicated to Hassan's people! In it, I read that my people, the Pashtuns, had persecuted and oppressed the Hazaras. It said the Hazaras had tried to rise against the Pashtuns in the nineteenth century, but the Pashtuns had "quelled them with unspeakable violence." The book said that my people had killed the Hazaras, driven them from their lands, burned their homes, and sold their women. The book said part of the reason Pashtuns had oppressed the Hazaras was that Pashtuns were Sunni Muslims, while Hazaras were Shi'a. The book said a lot of things I didn't know, things my teachers hadn't mentioned. Things Baba hadn't mentioned either. It also said some things I *did* know, like that people called Hazaras *mice-eating, flat-nosed, load-carrying donkeys.* I had heard some of the kids in the neighborhood yell those names to Hassan.

The following week, after class, I showed the book to my teacher and pointed to the chapter on the Hazaras. He skimmed through a couple of pages, snickered, handed the book back. "That's the one thing Shi'a people do well," he said, picking up his papers, "passing themselves as martyrs." He wrinkled his nose when he said the word Shi'a, like it was some kind of disease.

But despite sharing ethnic heritage and family blood, Sanaubar joined the neighborhood kids in taunting Ali. I have heard that she made no secret of her disdain for his appearance.

"This is a husband?" she would sneer. "I have seen old donkeys better suited to be a husband."

In the end, most people suspected the marriage had been an arrangement of sorts between Ali and his uncle, Sanaubar's father. They said Ali had married his cousin to help restore some honor to his uncle's blemished name, even though Ali, who had been orphaned at the age of five, had no worldly possessions or inheritance to speak of.

Ali never retaliated against any of his tormentors, I suppose partly because he could never catch them with that twisted leg dragging behind him. But mostly because Ali was immune to the insults of his assailants; he had found his joy, his antidote, the moment Sanaubar had given birth to Hassan. It had been a simple enough affair. No obstetricians, no anesthesiologists, no fancy monitoring devices. Just Sanaubar lying on a stained, naked mattress with Ali and a midwife helping her. She hadn't needed much help at all, because, even in birth, Hassan was true to his nature: He was incapable of hurting anyone. A few grunts, a couple of pushes, and out came Hassan. Out he came smiling.

As confided to a neighbor's servant by the garrulous midwife, who had then in turn told anyone who would listen, Sanaubar had taken one glance at the baby in Ali's arms, seen the cleft lip, and barked a bitter laughter.

"There," she had said. "Now you have your own idiot child to do all your smiling for you!" She had refused to even hold Hassan, and just five days later, she was gone.

Baba hired the same nursing woman who had fed me to nurse Hassan. Ali told us she was a blue-eyed Hazara woman from Bamiyan, the city of the giant Buddha statues. "What a sweet singing voice she had," he used to say to us.

What did she sing, Hassan and I always asked, though we already knew—Ali had told us countless times. We just wanted to hear Ali sing.

He'd clear his throat and begin:

> *On a high mountain I stood,*
> *And cried the name of Ali, Lion of God.*
> *O Ali, Lion of God, King of Men,*
> *Bring joy to our sorrowful hearts.*

Then he would remind us that there was a brotherhood between people who had fed from the same breast, a kinship that not even time could break.

Hassan and I fed from the same breasts. We took our first steps on the same lawn in the same yard. And, under the same roof, we spoke our first words.

Mine was *Baba*.

His was *Amir.* My name.

Looking back on it now, I think the foundation for what happened in the winter of 1975—and all that followed—was already laid in those first words.

THREE

Lore has it my father once wrestled a black bear in Baluchistan with his bare hands. If the story had been about anyone else, it would have been dismissed as *laaf,* that Afghan tendency to exaggerate—sadly, almost a national affliction; if someone bragged that his son was a doctor, chances were the kid had once passed a biology test in high school. But no one ever doubted the veracity of any story about Baba. And if they did, well, Baba did have those three parallel scars coursing a jagged path down his back. I have imagined Baba's wrestling match countless times, even dreamed about it. And in those dreams, I can never tell Baba from the bear. It was Rahim Khan who first referred to him as what eventually became Baba's famous nickname, *Toophan agha,* or "Mr. Hurricane." It was an apt enough nickname. My father was a force of nature, a towering Pashtun specimen with a thick beard, a wayward crop of curly brown hair as unruly as the man himself, hands that looked capable of uprooting a willow tree, and a black glare that would "drop the devil to his knees begging for mercy," as Rahim Khan used to say. At parties, when all six-foot-five of him thundered into the room, attention shifted to him like sunflowers turning to the sun.

Baba was impossible to ignore, even in his sleep. I used to bury cotton wisps in my ears, pull the blanket over my head, and still the sounds of Baba's snoring—so much like a growling truck engine—penetrated the walls. And my room was across the hall from Baba's bedroom. How my mother ever managed to sleep in the same room as him is a mystery to me. It's on the long list of things I would have asked my mother if I had ever met her.

In the late 1960s, when I was five or six, Baba decided to build an orphanage. I heard the story through Rahim Khan. He told me Baba had drawn the blueprints himself despite the fact that he'd had no architectural experience at all. Skeptics had urged him to stop his foolishness and hire an architect. Of course, Baba refused, and everyone shook their heads in dismay at his obstinate ways. Then Baba succeeded and everyone shook their heads in awe at his triumphant ways. Baba paid for the construction of the two-story orphanage, just off the main strip of Jadeh Maywand south of the Kabul River, with his own money. Rahim Khan told me Baba had personally funded the entire project, paying for the engineers, electricians, plumbers, and laborers, not to mention the city officials whose "mustaches needed oiling."

It took three years to build the orphanage. I was eight by then. I remember the day before the orphanage opened, Baba took me to Ghargha Lake, a few miles north of Kabul. He asked me to fetch Hassan too, but I lied and told him Hassan had the runs. I wanted Baba all to myself. And besides, one time at Ghargha Lake, Hassan and I were skimming stones and Hassan made his stone skip eight times. The most I managed was five. Baba was there, watching, and he patted Hassan on the back. Even put his arm around his shoulder.

We sat at a picnic table on the banks of the lake, just Baba and me, eating boiled eggs with *kofta* sandwiches—meatballs and pickles wrapped in *naan*. The water was a deep blue and sunlight glittered on its looking glass–clear surface. On Fridays, the lake was bustling with families out for a day in the sun. But it was midweek and there was only Baba and me, us and a couple of longhaired, bearded tourists—"hippies," I'd heard them called. They were sitting on the dock, feet dangling in the water, fishing poles in hand. I asked Baba why they grew their hair long, but Baba grunted, didn't answer. He was preparing his speech for the next day, flipping through a havoc of handwritten pages, making notes here and there with a pencil. I bit into my egg and asked Baba if it was true what a boy in school had told me, that if you ate a piece of eggshell, you'd have to pee it out. Baba grunted again.

I took a bite of my sandwich. One of the yellow-haired tourists laughed and slapped the other one on the back. In the distance, across the lake, a truck lumbered around a corner on the hill. Sunlight twinkled in its side-view mirror.

"I think I have *saratan*," I said. Cancer. Baba lifted his head from the pages flapping in the breeze. Told me I could get the soda myself, all I had to do was look in the trunk of the car.

Outside the orphanage, the next day, they ran out of chairs. A lot of people had to stand to watch the opening ceremony. It was a windy day, and I sat behind Baba on the little podium just outside the main entrance of the new building. Baba was wearing a green suit and a caracul hat. Midway through the speech, the wind knocked his hat off and everyone laughed. He motioned to me to hold his hat for him and I was glad to, because then everyone would see that he was *my* father, *my* Baba. He turned back to the microphone and said he hoped the building was sturdier than his hat, and everyone laughed again. When Baba ended his speech, people stood up and cheered. They clapped for a long time. Afterward, people shook his hand. Some of them tousled my hair and shook my hand too. I was so proud of Baba, of us.

But despite Baba's successes, people were always doubting him. They told Baba that running a business wasn't in his blood and he should study law like his father. So Baba proved them all wrong by not only running his own business but becoming one of the richest merchants in Kabul. Baba and Rahim Khan built a wildly successful carpet-exporting business, two pharmacies, and a restaurant.

When people scoffed that Baba would never marry well— after all, he was not of royal blood—he wedded my mother, Sofia Akrami, a highly educated woman universally regarded as one of Kabul's most respected, beautiful, and virtuous ladies. And not only did she teach classic Farsi literature at the university, she was a descendant of the royal family, a fact that my father playfully rubbed in the skeptics' faces by referring to her as "my princess."

With me as the glaring exception, my father molded the world around him to his liking. The problem, of course, was that Baba saw the world in black and white. And he got to decide what was black and what was white. You can't love a person who lives that way without fearing him too. Maybe even hating him a little.

When I was in fifth grade, we had a mullah who taught us about Islam. His name was Mullah Fatiullah Khan, a short, stubby man with a face full of acne scars and a gruff voice. He lectured us about the virtues of *zakat* and the duty of *hadj;* he taught us the intricacies of performing the five daily *namaz* prayers, and made us memorize verses from the Koran—and though he never translated the words for us, he did stress, sometimes with the help of a stripped willow branch, that we had to pronounce the Arabic words correctly so God would hear us better. He told us one day that Islam considered drinking a terrible sin; those who drank would answer for their sin on the day of *Qiyamat,* Judgment Day. In those days, drinking was fairly common in Kabul. No one gave you a public lashing for it, but those Afghans who did drink did so in private, out of respect. People bought their scotch as "medicine" in brown paper bags from selected "pharmacies." They would leave with the bag tucked out of sight, sometimes drawing furtive, disapproving glances from those who knew about the store's reputation for such transactions.

We were upstairs in Baba's study, the smoking room, when I told him what Mullah Fatiullah Khan had taught us in class. Baba was pouring himself a whiskey from the bar he had built in the corner of the room. He listened, nodded, took a sip from his drink. Then he lowered himself into the leather sofa, put down his drink, and propped me up on his lap. I felt as if I were sitting on a pair of tree trunks. He took a deep breath and exhaled through his nose, the air hissing through his mustache for what seemed an eternity. I couldn't decide whether I wanted to hug him or leap from his lap in mortal fear.

"I see you've confused what you're learning in school with

actual education," he said in his thick voice.

"But if what he said is true then does it make you a sinner, Baba?"

"Hmm." Baba crushed an ice cube between his teeth. "Do you want to know what your father thinks about sin?"

"Yes."

"Then I'll tell you," Baba said, "but first understand this and understand it now, Amir: You'll never learn anything of value from those bearded idiots."

"You mean Mullah Fatiullah Khan?"

Baba gestured with his glass. The ice clinked. "I mean all of them. Piss on the beards of all those self-righteous monkeys."

I began to giggle. The image of Baba pissing on the beard of any monkey, self-righteous or otherwise, was too much.

"They do nothing but thumb their prayer beads and recite a book written in a tongue they don't even understand." He took a sip. "God help us all if Afghanistan ever falls into their hands."

"But Mullah Fatiullah Khan seems nice," I managed between bursts of tittering.

"So did Genghis Khan," Baba said. "But enough about that. You asked about sin and I want to tell you. Are you listening?" "Yes," I said, pressing my lips together. But a chortle escaped through my nose and made a snorting sound. That got me giggling again.

Baba's stony eyes bore into mine and, just like that, I wasn't laughing anymore. "I mean to speak to you man to man. Do you think you can handle that for once?"

"Yes, Baba jan," I muttered, marveling, not for the first time, at how badly Baba could sting me with so few words. We'd had a fleeting good moment—it wasn't often Baba talked to me, let alone on his lap—and I'd been a fool to waste it.

"Good," Baba said, but his eyes wondered. "Now, no matter what the mullah teaches, there is only one sin, only one. And that is theft. Every other sin is a variation of theft. Do you understand that?"

"No, Baba jan," I said, desperately wishing I did. I didn't want to disappoint him again.

Baba heaved a sigh of impatience. That stung too, because he was not an impatient man. I remembered all the times he didn't come home until after dark, all the times I ate dinner alone. I'd ask Ali where Baba was, when he was coming home, though I knew full well he was at the construction site, overlooking this, supervising that. Didn't that take patience? I already hated all the kids he was building the orphanage for; sometimes I wished they'd all died along with their parents.

"When you kill a man, you steal a life," Baba said. "You steal his wife's right to a husband, rob his children of a father. When you tell a lie, you steal someone's right to the truth. When you cheat, you steal the right to fairness. Do you see?"

I did. When Baba was six, a thief walked into my grandfather's house in the middle of the night. My grandfather, a respected judge, confronted him, but the thief stabbed him in the throat, killing him instantly—and robbing Baba of a father. The townspeople caught the killer just before noon the next day; he turned out to be a wanderer from the Kunduz region. They hanged him from the branch of an oak tree with still two hours to go before afternoon prayer. It was Rahim Khan, not Baba, who had told me that story. I was always learning things about Baba from other people.

"There is no act more wretched than stealing, Amir," Baba

said. "A man who takes what's not his to take, be it a life or a loaf of *naan* … I spit on such a man. And if I ever cross paths with him, God help him. Do you understand?"

I found the idea of Baba clobbering a thief both exhilarating and terribly frightening. "Yes, Baba."

"If there's a God out there, then I would hope he has more important things to attend to than my drinking scotch or eating pork. Now, hop down. All this talk about sin has made me thirsty again."

I watched him fill his glass at the bar and wondered how much time would pass before we talked again the way we just had. Because the truth of it was, I always felt like Baba hated me a little. And why not? After all, I *had* killed his beloved wife, his beautiful princess, hadn't I? The least I could have done was to have had the decency to have turned out a little more like him. But I hadn't turned out like him. Not at all.

IN SCHOOL, we used to play a game called *Sherjangi,* or "Battle of the Poems." The Farsi teacher moderated it and it went something like this: You recited a verse from a poem and your opponent had sixty seconds to reply with a verse that began with the same letter that ended yours. Everyone in my class wanted me on their team, because by the time I was eleven, I could recite dozens of verses from Khayyám, Hãfez, or Rumi's famous *Masnawi*. One time, I took on the whole class and won. I told Baba about it later that night, but he just nodded, muttered, "Good."

That was how I escaped my father's aloofness, in my dead mother's books. That and Hassan, of course. I read everything,

Rumi, Hãfez, Saadi, Victor Hugo, Jules Verne, Mark Twain, Ian Fleming. When I had finished my mother's books—not the boring history ones, I was never much into those, but the novels, the epics—I started spending my allowance on books. I bought one a week from the bookstore near Cinema Park, and stored them in cardboard boxes when I ran out of shelf room.

Of course, marrying a poet was one thing, but fathering a son who preferred burying his face in poetry books to hunting ... well, that wasn't how Baba had envisioned it, I suppose. Real men didn't read poetry—and God forbid they should ever write it! Real men—real boys—played soccer just as Baba had when he had been young. Now *that* was something to be passionate about. In 1970, Baba took a break from the construction of the orphanage and flew to Tehran for a month to watch the World Cup games on television, since at the time Afghanistan didn't have TVs yet. He signed me up for soccer teams to stir the same passion in me. But I was pathetic, a blundering liability to my own team, always in the way of an opportune pass or unwittingly blocking an open lane. I shambled about the field on scraggy legs, squalled for passes that never came my way. And the harder I tried, waving my arms over my head frantically and screeching, "I'm open! I'm open!" the more I went ignored. But Baba wouldn't give up. When it became abundantly clear that I hadn't inherited a shred of his athletic talents, he settled for trying to turn me into a passionate spectator. Certainly I could manage that, couldn't I? I faked interest for as long as possible. I cheered with him when Kabul's team scored against Kandahar and yelped insults at the referee when he called a penalty against our team. But Baba sensed my lack of genuine interest and resigned himself to the bleak fact that his son was never going to either play or watch soccer.

I remember one time Baba took me to the yearly *Buzkashi* tournament that took place on the first day of spring, New Year's Day. Buzkashi was, and still is, Afghanistan's national passion. A *chapandaz,* a highly skilled horseman usually patronized by rich aficionados, has to snatch a goat or cattle carcass from the midst of a melee, carry that carcass with him around the stadium at full gallop, and drop it in a scoring circle while a team of other *chapandaz* chases him and does everything in its power—kick, claw, whip, punch—to snatch the carcass from him. That day, the crowd roared with excitement as the horsemen on the field bellowed their battle cries and jostled for the carcass in a cloud of dust. The earth trembled with the clatter of hooves. We watched from the upper bleachers as riders pounded past us at full gallop, yipping and yelling, foam flying from their horses' mouths.

At one point Baba pointed to someone. "Amir, do you see that man sitting up there with those other men around him?"

I did.

"That's Henry Kissinger."

"Oh," I said. I didn't know who Henry Kissinger was, and I might have asked. But at the moment, I watched with horror as one of the *chapandaz* fell off his saddle and was trampled under a score of hooves. His body was tossed and hurled in the stampede like a rag doll, finally rolling to a stop when the melee moved on. He twitched once and lay motionless, his legs bent at unnatural angles, a pool of his blood soaking through the sand.

I began to cry.

I cried all the way back home. I remember how Baba's hands clenched around the steering wheel. Clenched and unclenched. Mostly, I will never forget Baba's valiant efforts to conceal the disgusted look on his face as he drove in silence.

Later that night, I was passing by my father's study when I overheard him speaking to Rahim Khan. I pressed my ear to the closed door.

"—grateful that he's healthy," Rahim Khan was saying.

"I know, I know. But he's always buried in those books or shuffling around the house like he's lost in some dream."

"And?"

"I wasn't like that." Baba sounded frustrated, almost angry.

Rahim Khan laughed. "Children aren't coloring books. You don't get to fill them with your favorite colors."

"I'm telling you," Baba said, "I wasn't like that at all, and neither were any of the kids I grew up with."

"You know, sometimes you are the most self-centered man I know," Rahim Khan said. He was the only person I knew who could get away with saying something like that to Baba.

"It has nothing to do with that." "Nay?"

"Nay."

"Then what?"

I heard the leather of Baba's seat creaking as he shifted on it. I closed my eyes, pressed my ear even harder against the door, wanting to hear, not wanting to hear. "Sometimes I look out this window and I see him playing on the street with the neighborhood boys. I see how they push him around, take his toys from him, give him a shove here, a whack there. And, you know, he never fights back. Never. He just … drops his head and …"

"So he's not violent," Rahim Khan said.

"That's not what I mean, Rahim, and you know it," Baba shot back. "There is something missing in that boy."

"Yes, a mean streak."

"Self-defense has nothing to do with meanness. You know what always happens when the neighborhood boys tease him? Hassan steps in and fends them off. I've seen it with my own eyes. And when they come home, I say to him, 'How did Hassan get that scrape on his face?' And he says, 'He fell down.' I'm telling you, Rahim, there is something missing in that boy."

"You just need to let him find his way," Rahim Khan said.

"And where is he headed?" Baba said. "A boy who won't stand up for himself becomes a man who can't stand up to anything." "As usual you're oversimplifying."

"I don't think so."

"You're angry because you're afraid he'll never take over the business for you."

"Now who's oversimplifying?" Baba said. "Look, I know there's a fondness between you and him and I'm happy about that. Envious, but happy. I mean that. He needs someone who … understands him, because God knows I don't. But something about Amir troubles me in a way that I can't express. It's like …" I could see him searching, reaching for the right words. He lowered his voice, but I heard him anyway. "If I hadn't seen the doctor pull him out of my wife with my own eyes, I'd never believe he's my son."

THE NEXT MORNING, as he was preparing my breakfast, Hassan asked if something was bothering me. I snapped at him, told him to mind his own business.

Rahim Khan had been wrong about the mean streak thing.

FOUR

In 1933, the year Baba was born and the year Zahir Shah began his forty-year reign of Afghanistan, two brothers, young men from a wealthy and reputable family in Kabul, got behind the wheel of their father's Ford roadster. High on hashish and *mast* on French wine, they struck and killed a Hazara husband and wife on the road to Paghman. The police brought the somewhat contrite young men and the dead couple's five-year-old orphan boy before my grandfather, who was a highly regarded judge and a man of impeccable reputation. After hearing the brothers' account and their father's plea for mercy, my grandfather ordered the two young men to go to Kandahar at once and enlist in the army for one year—this despite the fact that their family had somehow managed to obtain them exemptions from the draft. Their father argued, but not too vehemently, and in the end, everyone agreed that the punishment had been perhaps harsh but fair. As for the orphan, my grandfather adopted him into his own household, and told the other servants to tutor him, but to be kind to him. That boy was Ali.

Ali and Baba grew up together as childhood playmates—at

least until polio crippled Ali's leg—just like Hassan and I grew up a generation later. Baba was always telling us about the mischief he and Ali used to cause, and Ali would shake his head and say, "But, Agha sahib, tell them who was the architect of the mischief and who the poor laborer?" Baba would laugh and throw his arm around Ali.

But in none of his stories did Baba ever refer to Ali as his friend.

The curious thing was, I never thought of Hassan and me as friends either. Not in the usual sense, anyhow. Never mind that we taught each other to ride a bicycle with no hands, or to build a fully functional homemade camera out of a cardboard box. Never mind that we spent entire winters flying kites, running kites. Never mind that to me, the face of Afghanistan is that of a boy with a thin-boned frame, a shaved head, and low-set ears, a boy with a Chinese doll face perpetually lit by a harelipped smile.

Never mind any of those things. Because history isn't easy to overcome. Neither is religion. In the end, I was a Pashtun and he was a Hazara, I was Sunni and he was Shi'a, and nothing was ever going to change that. Nothing.

But we were kids who had learned to crawl together, and no history, ethnicity, society, or religion was going to change that either. I spent most of the first twelve years of my life playing with Hassan. Sometimes, my entire childhood seems like one long lazy summer day with Hassan, chasing each other between tangles of trees in my father's yard, playing hide-and-seek, cops and robbers, cowboys and Indians, insect torture—with our crowning achievement undeniably the time we plucked the stinger off a bee and tied a string around the poor thing to yank it back every time it took flight.

We chased the *Kochi,* the nomads who passed through Kabul on their way to the mountains of the north. We would hear their caravans approaching our neighborhood, the mewling of their sheep, the *baa*ing of their goats, the jingle of bells around their camels' necks. We'd run outside to watch the caravan plod through our street, men with dusty, weather-beaten faces and women dressed in long, colorful shawls, beads, and silver bracelets around their wrists and ankles. We hurled pebbles at their goats. We squirted water on their mules. I'd make Hassan sit on the Wall of Ailing Corn and fire pebbles with his slingshot at the camels' rears.

We saw our first Western together, *Rio Bravo* with John Wayne, at the Cinema Park, across the street from my favorite bookstore. I remember begging Baba to take us to Iran so we could meet John Wayne. Baba burst out in gales of his deepthroated laughter—a sound not unlike a truck engine revving up—and, when he could talk again, explained to us the concept of voice dubbing. Hassan and I were stunned. Dazed. John Wayne didn't really speak Farsi and he wasn't Iranian! He was American, just like the friendly, longhaired men and women we always saw hanging around in Kabul, dressed in their tattered, brightly colored shirts. We saw *Rio Bravo* three times, but we saw our favorite Western, *The Magnificent Seven,* thirteen times. With each viewing, we cried at the end when the Mexican kids buried Charles Bronson—who, as it turned out, wasn't Iranian either.

We took strolls in the musty-smelling bazaars of the Shar-eNau section of Kabul, or the new city, west of the Wazir Akbar Khan district. We talked about whatever film we had just seen and walked amid the bustling crowds of *bazarris*. We snaked our way among the merchants and the beggars, wandered through narrow alleys cramped with rows of tiny, tightly packed stalls. Baba gave us each a weekly allowance of ten Afghanis and we spent it on warm Coca-Cola and rosewater ice cream topped with crushed pistachios.

During the school year, we had a daily routine. By the time I dragged myself out of bed and lumbered to the bathroom, Hassan had already washed up, prayed the morning *namaz* with Ali, and prepared my breakfast: hot black tea with three sugar cubes and a slice of toasted *naan* topped with my favorite sour cherry marmalade, all neatly placed on the dining table. While I ate and complained about homework, Hassan made my bed, polished my shoes, ironed my outfit for the day, packed my books and pencils. I'd hear him singing to himself in the foyer as he ironed, singing old Hazara songs in his nasal voice. Then, Baba and I drove off in his black Ford Mustang—a car that drew envious looks everywhere because it was the same car Steve McQueen had driven in *Bullitt,* a film that played in one theater for six months. Hassan stayed home and helped Ali with the day's chores: hand-washing dirty clothes and hanging them to dry in the yard, sweeping the floors, buying fresh *naan* from the bazaar, marinating meat for dinner, watering the lawn.

After school, Hassan and I met up, grabbed a book, and trotted up a bowl-shaped hill just north of my father's property in Wazir Akbar Khan. There was an old abandoned cemetery atop the hill with rows of unmarked headstones and tangles of brushwood clogging the aisles. Seasons of rain and snow had turned the iron gate rusty and left the cemetery's low white stone walls in decay. There was a pomegranate tree near the entrance to the cemetery. One summer day, I used one of Ali's kitchen knives to carve our names on it: "Amir and Hassan, the sultans of Kabul." Those words made it formal: the tree was ours. After school, Has-san and I climbed its branches and snatched its bloodred pomegranates. After we'd eaten the fruit and wiped our hands on the grass, I would read to Hassan.

Sitting cross-legged, sunlight and shadows of pomegranate leaves dancing on his face, Hassan absently plucked blades of grass from the ground as I read him stories he couldn't read for himself. That Hassan would grow up illiterate like Ali and most Hazaras had been decided the minute he had been born, perhaps even the moment he had been conceived in Sanaubar's unwelcoming womb—after all, what use did a servant have for the written word? But despite his illiteracy, or maybe because of it, Hassan was drawn to the mystery of words, seduced by a secret world forbidden to him. I read him poems and stories, sometimes riddles—though I stopped reading those when I saw he was far better at solving them than I was. So I read him unchallenging things, like the misadventures of the bumbling Mullah Nasruddin and his donkey. We sat for hours under that tree, sat there until the sun faded in the west, and still Hassan insisted we had enough daylight for one more story, one more chapter.

My favorite part of reading to Hassan was when we came across a big word that he didn't know. I'd tease him, expose his ignorance. One time, I was reading him a Mullah Nasruddin story and he stopped me. "What does that word mean?"

"Which one?" "'Imbecile.'"

"You don't know what it means?" I said, grinning.

"Nay, Amir agha."

"But it's such a common word!"

"Still, I don't know it." If he felt the sting of my tease, his smiling face didn't show it.

"Well, everyone in my school knows what it means," I said. "Let's see. 'Imbecile.' It means smart, intelligent. I'll use it in a sentence for you. 'When it comes to words, Hassan is an imbecile.'"

"Aaah," he said, nodding.

I would always feel guilty about it later. So I'd try to make up for it by giving him one of my old shirts or a broken toy. I would tell myself that was amends enough for a harmless prank.

Hassan's favorite book by far was the *Shahnamah,* the tenthcentury epic of ancient Persian heroes. He liked all of the chapters, the shahs of old, Feridoun, Zal, and Rudabeh. But his favorite story, and mine, was "Rostam and Sohrab," the tale of the great warrior Rostam and his fleet-footed horse, Rakhsh. Rostam mortally wounds his valiant nemesis, Sohrab, in battle, only to discover that Sohrab is his long-lost son. Stricken with grief, Rostam hears his son's dying words:

> If thou art indeed my father, then hast thou stained thy sword in the life-blood of thy son. And thou didst it of thine obstinacy. For I sought to turn thee unto love, and I implored of thee thy name, for I thought to behold in thee the tokens recounted of my mother. But I appealed unto thy heart in vain, and now is the time gone for meeting ...

"Read it again please, Amir agha," Hassan would say. Sometimes tears pooled in Hassan's eyes as I read him this passage, and I always wondered whom he wept for, the grief-stricken Rostam who tears his clothes and covers his head with ashes, or the dying Sohrab who only longed for his father's love? Personally, I couldn't see the tragedy in Rostam's fate. After all, didn't all fathers in their secret hearts harbor a desire to kill their sons?

One day, in July 1973, I played another little trick on Hassan. I was reading to him, and suddenly I strayed from the written story. I pretended I was reading from the book, flipping pages regularly, but I had abandoned the text altogether, taken over the story, and made up my own. Hassan, of course, was oblivious to this. To him, the words on the page were a scramble of codes, indecipherable, mysterious. Words were secret doorways and I held all the keys. After, I started to ask him if he'd liked the story, a giggle rising in my throat, when Hassan began to clap.

"What are you doing?" I said.

"That was the best story you've read me in a long time," he said, still clapping.

I laughed. "Really?"

"Really."

"That's fascinating," I muttered. I meant it too. This was ... wholly unexpected. "Are you sure, Hassan?"

He was still clapping. "It was great, Amir agha. Will you read me more of it tomorrow?"

"Fascinating," I repeated, a little breathless, feeling like a man who discovers a buried treasure in his own backyard. Walking down the hill, thoughts were exploding in my head like the fireworks at *Chaman*. *Best story you've read me in a long time,* he'd said. I had read him a *lot* of stories. Hassan was asking me something.

"What?" I said.

"What does that mean, 'fascinating'?"

I laughed. Clutched him in a hug and planted a kiss on his cheek.

"What was that for?" he said, startled, blushing.

I gave him a friendly shove. Smiled. "You're a prince, Hassan. You're a prince and I love you."

That same night, I wrote my first short story. It took me thirty minutes. It was a dark little tale about a man who found a magic cup and learned that if he wept into the cup, his tears turned into pearls. But even though he had always been poor, he was a happy man and rarely shed a tear. So he found ways to make himself sad so that his tears could make him rich. As the pearls piled up, so did his greed grow. The story ended with the man sitting on a mountain of pearls, knife in hand, weeping helplessly into the cup with his beloved wife's slain body in his arms.

That evening, I climbed the stairs and walked into Baba's smoking room, in my hands the two sheets of paper on which I had scribbled the story. Baba and Rahim Khan were smoking pipes and sipping brandy when I came in.

"What is it, Amir?" Baba said, reclining on the sofa and lacing his hands behind his head. Blue smoke swirled around his face. His glare made my throat feel dry. I cleared it and told him I'd written a story.

Baba nodded and gave a thin smile that conveyed little more than feigned interest. "Well, that's very good, isn't it?" he said. Then nothing more. He just looked at me through the cloud of smoke.

I probably stood there for under a minute, but, to this day, it was one of the longest minutes of my life. Seconds plodded by, each separated from the next by an eternity. Air grew heavy, damp, almost solid. I was breathing bricks. Baba went on staring me down, and didn't offer to read.

As always, it was Rahim Khan who rescued me. He held out

his hand and favored me with a smile that had nothing feigned about it. "May I have it, Amir jan? I would very much like to read it." Baba hardly ever used the term of endearment *jan* when he addressed me.

Baba shrugged and stood up. He looked relieved, as if he too had been rescued by Rahim Khan. "Yes, give it to *Kaka* Rahim. I'm going upstairs to get ready." And with that, he left the room. Most days I worshiped Baba with an intensity approaching the religious. But right then, I wished I could open my veins and drain his cursed blood from my body.

An hour later, as the evening sky dimmed, the two of them drove off in my father's car to attend a party. On his way out, Rahim Khan hunkered before me and handed me my story and another folded piece of paper. He flashed a smile and winked. "For you. Read it later." Then he paused and added a single word that did more to encourage me to pursue writing than any compliment any editor has ever paid me. That word was *Bravo.*

When they left, I sat on my bed and wished Rahim Khan had been my father. Then I thought of Baba and his great big chest and how good it felt when he held me against it, how he smelled of Brut in the morning, and how his beard tickled my face. I was overcome with such sudden guilt that I bolted to the bathroom and vomited in the sink.

Later that night, curled up in bed, I read Rahim Khan's note over and over. It read like this:

Amir jan,
I enjoyed your story very much. *Mashallah,* God has grant-ed you a special talent. It is now your duty to hone that talent, because a person who wastes his God-given talents is

a donkey. You have written your story with sound grammar and interesting style. But the most impressive thing about your story is that it has irony. You may not even know what that word means. But you will someday. It is something that some writers reach for their entire careers and never attain. You have achieved it with your first story.

My door is and always will be open to you, Amir jan. I shall hear any story you have to tell. Bravo.

Your friend,
Rahim

Buoyed by Rahim Khan's note, I grabbed the story and hurried downstairs to the foyer where Ali and Hassan were sleeping on a mattress. That was the only time they slept in the house, when Baba was away and Ali had to watch over me. I shook Hassan awake and asked him if he wanted to hear a story.

He rubbed his sleep-clogged eyes and stretched. "Now? What time is it?"

"Never mind the time. This story's special. I wrote it myself," I whispered, hoping not to wake Ali. Hassan's face brightened.

"Then I *have* to hear it," he said, already pulling the blanket off him.

I read it to him in the living room by the marble fireplace. No playful straying from the words this time; this was about me! Hassan was the perfect audience in many ways, totally immersed in the tale, his face shifting with the changing tones in the story. When I read the last sentence, he made a muted clapping sound with his hands.

"*Mashallah,* Amir agha. Bravo!" He was beaming.

"You liked it?" I said, getting my second taste—and how

sweet it was—of a positive review.

"Some day, *Inshallah,* you will be a great writer," Hassan said. "And people all over the world will read your stories."

"You exaggerate, Hassan," I said, loving him for it.

"No. You will be great and famous," he insisted. Then he paused, as if on the verge of adding something. He weighed his words and cleared his throat. "But will you permit me to ask a question about the story?" he said shyly.

"Of course."

"Well ..." he started, broke off.

"Tell me, Hassan," I said. I smiled, though suddenly the insecure writer in me wasn't so sure he wanted to hear it.

"Well," he said, "if I may ask, why did the man kill his wife? In fact, why did he ever have to feel sad to shed tears? Couldn't he have just smelled an onion?"

I was stunned. That particular point, so obvious it was utterly stupid, hadn't even occurred to me. I moved my lips soundlessly. It appeared that on the same night I had learned about one of writing's objectives, irony, I would also be introduced to one of its pitfalls: the Plot Hole. Taught by Hassan, of all people. Hassan who couldn't read and had never written a single word in his entire life. A voice, cold and dark, suddenly whispered in my ear, *What does he know, that illiterate Hazara? He'll never be anything but a cook. How dare he criticize you?*

"Well," I began. But I never got to finish that sentence. Because suddenly Afghanistan changed forever.

FIVE

Something roared like thunder. The earth shook a little and we heard the *rat-a-tat-tat* of gunfire. "Father!" Hassan cried. We sprung to our feet and raced out of the living room. We found Ali hobbling frantically across the foyer.

"Father! What's that sound?" Hassan yelped, his hands outstretched toward Ali. Ali wrapped his arms around us. A white light flashed, lit the sky in silver. It flashed again and was followed by a rapid staccato of gunfire.

"They're hunting ducks," Ali said in a hoarse voice. "They hunt ducks at night, you know. Don't be afraid."

A siren went off in the distance. Somewhere glass shattered and someone shouted. I heard people on the street, jolted from sleep and probably still in their pajamas, with ruffled hair and puffy eyes. Hassan was crying. Ali pulled him close, clutched him with tenderness. Later, I would tell myself I hadn't felt envious of Hassan. Not at all.

We stayed huddled that way until the early hours of the morning. The shootings and explosions had lasted less than an hour, but they had frightened us badly, because none of us had ever heard gunshots in the streets. They were foreign sounds to us then. The generation of Afghan children whose ears would know nothing but the sounds of bombs and gunfire was not yet born. Huddled together in the dining room and waiting for the sun to rise, none of us had any notion that a way of life had ended. *Our* way of life. If not quite yet, then at least it was the beginning of the end. The end, the *official* end, would come first in April 1978 with the communist coup d'état, and then in December 1979, when Russian tanks would roll into the very same streets where Hassan and I played, bringing the death of the Afghanistan I knew and marking the start of a still ongoing era of bloodletting.

Just before sunrise, Baba's car peeled into the driveway. His door slammed shut and his running footsteps pounded the stairs. Then he appeared in the doorway and I saw something on his face. Something I didn't recognize right away because I'd never seen it before: fear. "Amir! Hassan!" he exclaimed as he ran to us, opening his arms wide. "They blocked all the roads and the telephone didn't work. I was so worried!"

We let him wrap us in his arms and, for a brief insane moment, I was glad about whatever had happened that night.

THEY WEREN'T SHOOTING ducks after all. As it turned out, they hadn't shot much of anything that night of July 17, 1973. Kabul awoke the next morning to find that the monarchy was a thing of the past. The king, Zahir Shah, was away in Italy. In his absence, his cousin Daoud Khan had ended the king's forty-year reign with a bloodless coup.

I remember Hassan and I crouching that next morning

outside my father's study, as Baba and Rahim Khan sipped black tea and listened to breaking news of the coup on Radio Kabul.

"Amir agha?" Hassan whispered. "What?"

"What's a 'republic'?"

I shrugged. "I don't know." On Baba's radio, they were saying that word, "republic," over and over again.

"Amir agha?"

"What?"

"Does 'republic' mean Father and I will have to move away?"

"I don't think so," I whispered back.

Hassan considered this. "Amir agha?"

"What?"

"I don't want them to send me and Father away."

I smiled. "*Bas,* you donkey. No one's sending you away."

"Amir agha?"

"What?"

"Do you want to go climb our tree?"

My smile broadened. That was another thing about Hassan. He always knew when to say the right thing—the news on the radio was getting pretty boring. Hassan went to his shack to get ready and I ran upstairs to grab a book. Then I went to the kitchen, stuffed my pockets with handfuls of pine nuts, and ran outside to find Hassan waiting for me. We burst through the front gates and headed for the hill.

We crossed the residential street and were trekking through a barren patch of rough land that led to the hill when, suddenly, a rock struck Hassan in the back. We whirled around and my heart dropped. Assef and two of his friends, Wali and Kamal, were approaching us.

Assef was the son of one of my father's friends, Mahmood, an airline pilot. His family lived a few streets south of our home, in a posh, high-walled compound with palm trees. If you were a kid living in the Wazir Akbar Khan section of Kabul, you knew about Assef and his famous stainless-steel brass knuckles, hopefully not through personal experience. Born to a German mother and Afghan father, the blond, blue-eyed Assef towered over the other kids. His well-earned reputation for savagery preceded him on the streets. Flanked by his obeying friends, he walked the neighborhood like a Khan strolling through his land with his eager-toplease entourage. His word was law, and if you needed a little legal education, then those brass knuckles were just the right teaching tool. I saw him use those knuckles once on a kid from the Karteh-Char district. I will never forget how Assef's blue eyes glinted with a light not entirely sane and how he grinned, how he *grinned,* as he pummeled that poor kid unconscious. Some of the boys in Wazir Akbar Khan had nicknamed him Assef *Goshkhor,* or Assef "the Ear Eater." Of course, none of them dared utter it to his face unless they wished to suffer the same fate as the poor kid who had unwittingly inspired that nickname when he had fought Assef over a kite and ended up fishing his right ear from a muddy gutter. Years later, I learned an English word for the creature that Assef was, a word for which a good Farsi equivalent does not exist: "sociopath."

Of all the neighborhood boys who tortured Ali, Assef was by far the most relentless. He was, in fact, the originator of the Babalu jeer, *Hey, Babalu, who did you eat today? Huh? Come on, Babalu, give us a smile!* And on days when he felt particularly inspired, he spiced up his badgering a little, *Hey, you flat-nosed Babalu, who did you eat today? Tell us, you slant-eyed donkey!*

Now he was walking toward us, hands on his hips, his sneakers kicking up little puffs of dust.

"Good morning, *kunis*!" Assef exclaimed, waving. "Fag," that was another of his favorite insults. Hassan retreated behind me as the three older boys closed in. They stood before us, three tall boys dressed in jeans and T-shirts. Towering over us all, Assef crossed his thick arms on his chest, a savage sort of grin on his lips. Not for the first time, it occurred to me that Assef might not be entirely sane. It also occurred to me how lucky I was to have Baba as my father, the sole reason, I believe, Assef had mostly refrained from harassing me too much.

He tipped his chin to Hassan. "Hey, Flat-Nose," he said. "How is Babalu?"

Hassan said nothing and crept another step behind me.

"Have you heard the news, boys?" Assef said, his grin never faltering. "The king is gone. Good riddance. Long live the president! My father knows Daoud Khan, did you know that, Amir?"

"So does my father," I said. In reality, I had no idea if that was true or not.

"'So does my father,'" Assef mimicked me in a whining voice. Kamal and Wali cackled in unison. I wished Baba were there.

"Well, Daoud Khan dined at our house last year," Assef went on. "How do you like that, Amir?"

I wondered if anyone would hear us scream in this remote patch of land. Baba's house was a good kilometer away. I wished we'd stayed at the house.

"Do you know what I will tell Daoud Khan the next time he comes to our house for dinner?" Assef said. "I'm going to have a little chat with him, man to man, *mard* to *mard*. Tell him what I told my mother. About Hitler. Now, there was a leader. A great leader. A man with vision. I'll tell Daoud Khan to remember that if they had let Hitler finish what he had started, the world be a better place now."

"Baba says Hitler was crazy, that he ordered a lot of innocent people killed," I heard myself say before I could clamp a hand on my mouth.

Assef snickered. "He sounds like my mother, and she's German; she should know better. But then they want you to believe that, don't they? They don't want you to know the truth."

I didn't know who "they" were, or what truth they were hiding, and I didn't want to find out. I wished I hadn't said anything. I wished again I'd look up and see Baba coming up the hill.

"But you have to read books they don't give out in school," Assef said. "I have. And my eyes have been opened. Now I have a vision, and I'm going to share it with our new president. Do you know what it is?"

I shook my head. He'd tell me anyway; Assef always answered his own questions.

His blue eyes flicked to Hassan. "Afghanistan is the land of Pashtuns. It always has been, always will be. We are the true Afghans, the pure Afghans, not this Flat-Nose here. His people pollute our homeland, our *watan*. They dirty our blood." He made a sweeping, grandiose gesture with his hands. "Afghanistan for Pashtuns, I say. That's my vision."

Assef shifted his gaze to me again. He looked like someone coming out of a good dream. "Too late for Hitler," he said. "But not for us."

He reached for something from the back pocket of his jeans. "I'll ask the president to do what the king didn't have the *quwat* to do. To rid Afghanistan of all the dirty, *kasseef* Hazaras."

"Just let us go, Assef," I said, hating the way my voice trembled. "We're not bothering you."

"Oh, you're bothering me," Assef said. And I saw with a sinking heart what he had fished out of his pocket. Of course. His stainless-steel brass knuckles sparkled in the sun. "You're bothering me very much. In fact, you bother me more than this Hazara here. How can you talk to him, play with him, let him touch you?" he said, his voice dripping with disgust. Wali and Kamal nodded and grunted in agreement. Assef narrowed his eyes. Shook his head. When he spoke again, he sounded as baffled as he looked. "How can you call him your 'friend'?"

But he's not my friend! I almost blurted. *He's my servant!* Had I really thought that? Of course I hadn't. I hadn't. I treated Hassan well, just like a friend, better even, more like a brother. But if so, then why, when Baba's friends came to visit with their kids, didn't I ever include Hassan in our games? Why did I play with Hassan only when no one else was around?

Assef slipped on the brass knuckles. Gave me an icy look. "You're part of the problem, Amir. If idiots like you and your father didn't take these people in, we'd be rid of them by now. They'd all just go rot in Hazarajat where they belong. You're a disgrace to Afghanistan."

I looked in his crazy eyes and saw that he meant it. He *really* meant to hurt me. Assef raised his fist and came for me.

There was a flurry of rapid movement behind me. Out of the corner of my eye, I saw Hassan bend down and stand up quickly. Assef's eyes flicked to something behind me and widened with surprise. I saw that same look of astonishment on Kamal and Wali's faces as they too saw what had happened behind me.

I turned and came face to face with Hassan's slingshot. Hassan had pulled the wide elastic band all the way back. In the cup was a rock the size of a walnut. Hassan held the slingshot pointed directly at Assef's face. His hand trembled with the strain of the pulled elastic band and beads of sweat had erupted on his brow.

"Please leave us alone, Agha," Hassan said in a flat tone. He'd referred to Assef as "Agha," and I wondered briefly what it must be like to live with such an ingrained sense of one's place in a hierarchy.

Assef gritted his teeth. "Put it down, you motherless Hazara."

"Please leave us be, Agha," Hassan said.

Assef smiled. "Maybe you didn't notice, but there are three of us and two of you."

Hassan shrugged. To an outsider, he didn't look scared. But Hassan's face was my earliest memory and I knew all of its subtle nuances, knew each and every twitch and flicker that ever rippled across it. And I saw that he was scared. He was scared plenty.

"You are right, Agha. But perhaps you didn't notice that I'm the one holding the slingshot. If you make a move, they'll have to change your nickname from Assef 'the Ear Eater' to 'One-Eyed Assef,' because I have this rock pointed at your left eye." He said this so flatly that even I had to strain to hear the fear that I knew hid under that calm voice.

Assef's mouth twitched. Wali and Kamal watched this exchange with something akin to fascination. Someone had challenged their god. Humiliated him. And, worst of all, that someone was a skinny Hazara. Assef looked from the rock to Hassan. He searched Hassan's face intently. What he found in it must have convinced him of the seriousness of Hassan's intentions, because he lowered his fist.

"You should know something about me, Hazara," Assef said gravely. "I'm a very patient person. This doesn't end today, believe me." He turned to me. "This isn't the end for you either, Amir. Someday, I'll make you face me one on one." Assef retreated a step. His disciples followed.

"Your Hazara made a big mistake today, Amir," he said. They then turned around, walked away. I watched them walk down the hill and disappear behind a wall.

Hassan was trying to tuck the slingshot in his waist with a pair of trembling hands. His mouth curled up into something that was supposed to be a reassuring smile. It took him five tries to tie the string of his trousers. Neither one of us said much of anything as we walked home in trepidation, certain that Assef and his friends would ambush us every time we turned a corner. They didn't and that should have comforted us a little. But it didn't. Not at all.

FOR THE NEXT COUPLE of years, the words *economic development* and *reform* danced on a lot of lips in Kabul. The constitutional monarchy had been abolished, replaced by a republic, led by a president of the republic. For a while, a sense of rejuvenation and purpose swept across the land. People spoke of women's rights and modern technology.

And for the most part, even though a new leader lived in *Arg*— the royal palace in Kabul—life went on as before. People went to work Saturday through Thursday and gathered for picnics on Fridays in parks, on the banks of Ghargha Lake, in the gardens of Paghman. Multicolored buses and lorries filled with passengers rolled through the narrow streets of Kabul, led by the constant shouts of the driver assistants who straddled the vehicles' rear bumpers and yelped directions to the driver in their thick Kabuli accent. On *Eid,* the three days of celebration after the holy month of Ramadan, Kabulis dressed in their best and newest clothes and visited their families. People hugged and kissed and greeted each other with *"Eid Mubarak."* Happy Eid. Children opened gifts and played with dyed hard-boiled eggs.

Early that following winter of 1974, Hassan and I were playing in the yard one day, building a snow fort, when Ali called him in. "Hassan, Agha sahib wants to talk to you!" He was standing by the front door, dressed in white, hands tucked under his armpits, breath puffing from his mouth.

Hassan and I exchanged a smile. We'd been waiting for his call all day: It was Hassan's birthday. "What is it, Father, do you know? Will you tell us?" Hassan said. His eyes were gleaming.

Ali shrugged. "Agha sahib hasn't discussed it with me."

"Come on, Ali, tell us," I pressed. "Is it a drawing book? Maybe a new pistol?"

Like Hassan, Ali was incapable of lying. Every year, he pretended not to know what Baba had bought Hassan or me for our birthdays. And every year, his eyes betrayed him and we coaxed the goods out of him. This time, though, it seemed he was telling the truth.

Baba never missed Hassan's birthday. For a while, he used to ask Hassan what he wanted, but he gave up doing that because Hassan was always too modest to actually suggest a present. So every winter Baba picked something out himself. He bought him a Japanese toy truck one year, an electric locomotive and train track set another year. The previous year, Baba had surprised Hassan with a leather cowboy hat just like the one

Clint Eastwood wore in *The Good, the Bad, and the Ugly*—which had unseated *The Magnificent Seven* as our favorite Western. That whole winter, Hassan and I took turns wearing the hat, and belted out the film's famous music as we climbed mounds of snow and shot each other dead.

We took off our gloves and removed our snow-laden boots at the front door. When we stepped into the foyer, we found Baba sitting by the wood-burning cast-iron stove with a short, balding Indian man dressed in a brown suit and red tie.

"Hassan," Baba said, smiling coyly, "meet your birthday present."

Hassan and I traded blank looks. There was no gift-wrapped box in sight. No bag. No toy. Just Ali standing behind us, and Baba with this slight Indian fellow who looked a little like a mathematics teacher.

The Indian man in the brown suit smiled and offered Hassan his hand. "I am Dr. Kumar," he said. "It's a pleasure to meet you." He spoke Farsi with a thick, rolling Hindi accent.

"Salaam alaykum," Hassan said uncertainly. He gave a polite tip of the head, but his eyes sought his father behind him. Ali moved closer and set his hand on Hassan's shoulder.

Baba met Hassan's wary—and puzzled—eyes. "I have summoned Dr. Kumar from New Delhi. Dr. Kumar is a plastic surgeon."

"Do you know what that is?" the Indian man—Dr. Kumar—said.

Hassan shook his head. He looked to me for help but I shrugged. All I knew was that you went to a surgeon to fix you when you had appendicitis. I knew this because one of my classmates had died of it the year before and the teacher had told us they had waited too long to take him to a surgeon. We both looked to Ali, but of course with him you could never tell. His face was impassive as ever, though something sober had melted into his eyes.

"Well," Dr. Kumar said, "my job is to fix things on people's bodies. Sometimes their faces."

"Oh," Hassan said. He looked from Dr. Kumar to Baba to Ali. His hand touched his upper lip. "Oh," he said again.

"It's an unusual present, I know," Baba said. "And probably not what you had in mind, but this present will last you forever."

"Oh," Hassan said. He licked his lips. Cleared his throat. "Agha sahib, will it ... will it—"

"Nothing doing," Dr. Kumar intervened, smiling kindly. "It will not hurt you one bit. In fact, I will give you a medicine and you will not remember a thing."

"Oh," Hassan said. He smiled back with relief. A little relief anyway. "I wasn't scared, Agha sahib, I just ..." Hassan might have been fooled, but I wasn't. I knew that when doctors said it wouldn't hurt, that's when you knew you were in trouble. With dread, I remembered my circumcision the year prior. The doctor had given me the same line, reassured me it wouldn't hurt one bit. But when the numbing medicine wore off later that night, it felt like someone had pressed a red hot coal to my loins. Why Baba waited until I was ten to have me circumcised was beyond me and one of the things I will never forgive him for.

I wished I too had some kind of scar that would beget Baba's sympathy. It wasn't fair. Hassan hadn't done anything to earn Baba's affections; he'd just been born with that stupid harelip.

The surgery went well. We were all a little shocked when they first removed the bandages, but kept our smiles on just as Dr.

Kumar had instructed us. It wasn't easy, because Hassan's upper lip was a grotesque mesh of swollen, raw tissue. I expected Hassan to cry with horror when the nurse handed him the mirror. Ali held his hand as Hassan took a long, thoughtful look into it. He muttered something I didn't understand. I put my ear to his mouth. He whispered it again.

"*Tashakor.*" Thank you.

Then his lips twisted, and, that time, I knew just what he was doing. He was smiling. Just as he had, emerging from his mother's womb.

The swelling subsided, and the wound healed with time. Soon, it was just a pink jagged line running up from his lip. By the following winter, it was only a faint scar. Which was ironic. Because that was the winter that Hassan stopped smiling.

S I X

Winter.

Here is what I do on the first day of snowfall every year: I step out of the house early in the morning, still in my pajamas, hugging my arms against the chill. I find the driveway, my father's car, the walls, the trees, the rooftops, and the hills buried under a foot of snow. I smile. The sky is seamless and blue, the snow so white my eyes burn. I shovel a handful of the fresh snow into my mouth, listen to the muffled stillness broken only by the cawing of crows. I walk down the front steps, barefoot, and call for Hassan to come out and see.

Winter was every kid's favorite season in Kabul, at least those whose fathers could afford to buy a good iron stove. The reason was simple: They shut down school for the icy season. Winter to me was the end of long division and naming the capital of Bulgaria, and the start of three months of playing cards by the stove with Hassan, free Russian movies on Tuesday mornings at Cinema Park, sweet turnip *qurma* over rice for lunch after a morning of building snowmen.

And kites, of course. Flying kites. And running them.

For a few unfortunate kids, winter did not spell the end of the school year. There were the so-called voluntary winter courses. No kid I knew ever volunteered to go to these classes; parents, of course, did the volunteering for them. Fortunately for me, Baba was not one of them. I remember one kid, Ahmad, who lived across the street from us. His father was some kind of doctor, I think. Ahmad had epilepsy and always wore a wool vest and thick blackrimmed glasses—he was one of Assef's regular victims. Every morning, I watched from my bedroom window as their Hazara servant shoveled snow from the driveway, cleared the way for the black Opel. I made a point of watching Ahmad and his father get into the car, Ahmad in his wool vest and winter coat, his schoolbag filled with books and pencils. I waited until they pulled away, turned the corner, then I slipped back into bed in my flannel pajamas. I pulled the blanket to my chin and watched the snowcapped hills in the north through the window. Watched them until I drifted back to sleep.

I loved wintertime in Kabul. I loved it for the soft pattering of snow against my window at night, for the way fresh snow crunched under my black rubber boots, for the warmth of the cast-iron stove as the wind screeched through the yards, the streets. But mostly because, as the trees froze and ice sheathed the roads, the chill between Baba and me thawed a little. And the reason for that was the kites. Baba and I lived in the same house, but in different spheres of existence. Kites were the one paperthin slice of intersection between those spheres.

EVERY WINTER, districts in Kabul held a kite-fighting tournament. And if you were a boy living in Kabul, the day of the tourna-ment was undeniably the highlight of the cold season. I never slept the night before the tournament. I'd roll from side to side, make shadow animals on the wall, even sit on the balcony in the dark, a blanket wrapped around me. I felt like a soldier trying to sleep in the trenches the night before a major battle. And that wasn't so far off. In Kabul, fighting kites *was* a little like going to war.

As with any war, you had to ready yourself for battle. For a while, Hassan and I used to build our own kites. We saved our weekly allowances in the fall, dropped the money in a little porcelain horse Baba had brought one time from Herat. When the winds of winter began to blow and snow fell in chunks, we undid the snap under the horse's belly. We went to the bazaar and bought bamboo, glue, string, and paper. We spent hours every day shaving bamboo for the center and cross spars, cutting the thin tissue paper which made for easy dipping and recovery. And then, of course, we had to make our own string, or *tar.* If the kite was the gun, then *tar,* the glass-coated cutting line, was the bullet in the chamber. We'd go out in the yard and feed up to five hundred feet of string through a mixture of ground glass and glue. We'd then hang the line between the trees, leave it to dry. The next day, we'd wind the battle-ready line around a wooden spool. By the time the snow melted and the rains of spring swept in, every boy in Kabul bore telltale horizontal gashes on his fingers from a whole winter of fighting kites. I remember how my classmates and I used to huddle, compare our battle scars on the first day of school. The cuts stung and didn't heal for a couple of weeks, but I didn't mind. They were reminders of a beloved season that had once again passed too quickly. Then the class captain would blow his whistle and we'd march in a single file to our classrooms, longing for winter already, greeted instead by the specter of yet another long school year.

But it quickly became apparent that Hassan and I were better kite fighters than kite makers. Some flaw or other in our design always spelled its doom. So Baba started taking us to Saifo's to buy our kites. Saifo was a nearly blind old man who was a *moochi* by profession—a shoe repairman. But he was also the city's most famous kite maker, working out of a tiny hovel on Jadeh Maywand, the crowded street south of the muddy banks of the Kabul River. I remember you had to crouch to enter the prison cell–sized store, and then had to lift a trapdoor to creep down a set of wooden steps to the dank basement where Saifo stored his coveted kites. Baba would buy us each three identical kites and spools of glass string. If I changed my mind and asked for a bigger and fancier kite, Baba would buy it for me—but then he'd buy it for Hassan too. Sometimes I wished he wouldn't do that. Wished he'd let me be the favorite.

The kite-fighting tournament was an old winter tradition in Afghanistan. It started early in the morning on the day of the contest and didn't end until only the winning kite flew in the sky—I remember one year the tournament outlasted daylight. People gathered on sidewalks and roofs to cheer for their kids. The streets filled with kite fighters, jerking and tugging on their lines, squinting up to the sky, trying to gain position to cut the opponent's line. Every kite fighter had an assistant—in my case, Hassan—who held the spool and fed the line.

One time, a bratty Hindi kid whose family had recently moved into the neighborhood told us that in his hometown, kite fighting had strict rules and regulations. "You have to play in a boxed area and you have to stand at a right angle to the wind," he said proudly. "And you can't use aluminum to make your glass string." Hassan and I looked at each other. Cracked up. The Hindi kid would soon learn what the British learned earlier in the century, and what the Russians would eventually learn by the late 1980s: that Afghans are an independent people. Afghans cherish custom but abhor rules. And so it was with kite fighting. The rules were simple: No rules. Fly your kite. Cut the opponents. Good luck.

Except that wasn't all. The real fun began when a kite was cut. That was where the kite runners came in, those kids who chased the windblown kite drifting through the neighborhoods until it came spiraling down in a field, dropping in someone's yard, on a tree, or a rooftop. The chase got pretty fierce; hordes of kite runners swarmed the streets, shoved past each other like those people from Spain I'd read about once, the ones who ran from the bulls. One year a neighborhood kid climbed a pine tree for a kite. A branch snapped under his weight and he fell thirty feet. Broke his back and never walked again. But he fell with the kite still in his hands. And when a kite runner had his hands on a kite, no one could take it from him. That wasn't a rule. That was custom.

For kite runners, the most coveted prize was the last fallen kite of a winter tournament. It was a trophy of honor, something to be displayed on a mantle for guests to admire. When the sky cleared of kites and only the final two remained, every kite runner readied himself for the chance to land this prize. He positioned himself at a spot that he thought would give him a head start. Tense muscles readied themselves to uncoil. Necks craned. Eyes crinkled. Fights broke out. And when the last kite was cut, all hell broke loose.

Over the years, I had seen a lot of guys run kites. But Hassan was by far the greatest kite runner I'd ever seen. It was downright eerie the way he always got to the spot the kite would land *before* the kite did, as if he had some sort of inner compass.

I remember one overcast winter day, Hassan and I were running a kite. I was chasing him through neighborhoods, hopping gutters, weaving through narrow streets. I was a year older than him, but Hassan ran faster than I did, and I was falling behind.

"Hassan! Wait!" I yelled, my breathing hot and ragged.

He whirled around, motioned with his hand. "This way!" he called before dashing around another corner. I looked up, saw that the direction we were running was opposite to the one the kite was drifting.

"We're losing it! We're going the wrong way!" I cried out.

"Trust me!" I heard him call up ahead. I reached the corner and saw Hassan bolting along, his head down, not even looking at the sky, sweat soaking through the back of his shirt. I tripped over a rock and fell—I wasn't just slower than Hassan but clumsier too; I'd always envied his natural athleticism. When I staggered to my feet, I caught a glimpse of Hassan disappearing around another street corner. I hobbled after him, spikes of pain battering my scraped knees.

I saw we had ended up on a rutted dirt road near Isteqlal Middle School. There was a field on one side where lettuce grew in the summer, and a row of sour cherry trees on the other. I found Hassan sitting cross-legged at the foot of one of the trees, eating from a fistful of dried mulberries.

"What are we doing here?" I panted, my stomach roiling with nausea.

He smiled. "Sit with me, Amir agha."

I dropped next to him, lay on a thin patch of snow, wheezing. "You're wasting our time. It was going the other way, didn't you see?"

Hassan popped a mulberry in his mouth. "It's coming," he said. I could hardly breathe and he didn't even sound tired.

"How do you know?" I said.

"I know."

"How can you *know*?"

He turned to me. A few sweat beads rolled from his bald scalp. "Would I ever lie to you, Amir agha?"

Suddenly I decided to toy with him a little. "I don't know. Would you?"

"I'd sooner eat dirt," he said with a look of indignation.

"Really? You'd do that?"

He threw me a puzzled look. "Do what?"

"Eat dirt if I told you to," I said. I knew I was being cruel, like when I'd taunt him if he didn't know some big word. But there was something fascinating—albeit in a sick way—about teasing Hassan. Kind of like when we used to play insect torture. Except now, he was the ant and I was holding the magnifying glass.

His eyes searched my face for a long time. We sat there, two boys under a sour cherry tree, suddenly looking, *really* looking, at each other. That's when it happened again: Hassan's face changed. Maybe not *changed*, not really, but suddenly I had the feeling I was looking at two faces, the one I knew, the one that was my first memory, and another, a second face, this one lurking just beneath the surface. I'd seen it happen before— it always shook me up a little. It just appeared, this other face, for a fraction of a moment, long enough to leave me with the unsettling feeling that maybe I'd seen it someplace before. Then Hassan blinked and it was just him again. Just Hassan.

"If you asked, I would," he finally said, looking right at me. I dropped my eyes. To this day, I find it hard to gaze directly at people like Hassan, people who mean every word they say.

"But I wonder," he added. "Would you ever ask me to do such a thing, Amir agha?" And, just like that, he had thrown at me his own little test. If I was going to toy with him and challenge his loyalty, then he'd toy with me, test my integrity.

I wished I hadn't started this conversation. I forced a smile. "Don't be stupid, Hassan. You know I wouldn't."

Hassan returned the smile. Except his didn't look forced. "I know," he said. And that's the thing about people who mean everything they say. They think everyone else does too.

"Here it comes," Hassan said, pointing to the sky. He rose to his feet and walked a few paces to his left. I looked up, saw the kite plummeting toward us. I heard footfalls, shouts, an approaching melee of kite runners. But they were wasting their time. Because Hassan stood with his arms wide open, smiling, waiting for the kite. And may God—if He exists, that is—strike me blind if the kite didn't just drop into his outstretched arms.

IN THE WINTER OF 1975, I saw Hassan run a kite for the last time.

Usually, each neighborhood held its own competition. But that year, the tournament was going to be held in my neighborhood, Wazir Akbar Khan, and several other districts—Karteh-Char, Karteh-Parwan, Mekro-Rayan, and Koteh-Sangi—had been invited. You could hardly go anywhere without hearing talk of the upcoming tournament. Word had it this was going to be the biggest tournament in twenty-five years.

One night that winter, with the big contest only four days away, Baba and I sat in his study in overstuffed leather chairs by the glow of the fireplace. We were sipping tea, talking. Ali had served dinner earlier—potatoes and curried cauliflower over rice—and had retired for the night with Hassan. Baba was fattening his pipe and I was asking him to tell the story about the winter a pack of wolves had descended from the mountains in Herat and forced everyone to stay indoors for a week, when he lit a match and said, casually, "I think maybe you'll win the tournament this year. What do you think?"

I didn't know what to think. Or what to say. Was that what it would take? Had he just slipped me a key? I was a good kite fighter. Actually, a very good one. A few times, I'd even come close to winning the winter tournament—once, I'd made it to the final three. But coming close wasn't the same as winning, was it? Baba hadn't *come close*. He had won because winners won and everyone else just went home. Baba was used to winning, winning at everything he set his mind to. Didn't he have a right to expect the same from his son? And just imagine. If I did win ...

Baba smoked his pipe and talked. I pretended to listen. But I couldn't listen, not really, because Baba's casual little comment had planted a seed in my head: the resolution that I would win that winter's tournament. I was going to win. There was no other viable option. I was going to win, and I was going to run that last kite. Then I'd bring it home and show it to Baba. Show him once and for all that his son was worthy. Then maybe my life as a ghost in this house would finally be over. I let myself dream: I imagined conversation and laughter over dinner instead of silence broken only by the clinking of silverware and the occasional grunt. I envisioned us taking a Friday drive in Baba's car to Paghman, stopping on the way at Ghargha Lake for some fried trout and potatoes. We'd go to the zoo to see Marjan the lion, and maybe Baba wouldn't yawn and steal looks at his wristwatch all the time. Maybe Baba would even read one of my stories. I'd write him a hundred if I thought he'd read one. Maybe he'd call me *Amir jan* like Rahim Khan did. And maybe, just maybe, I would finally be pardoned for killing my mother.

Baba was telling me about the time he'd cut fourteen kites on the same day. I smiled, nodded, laughed at all the right places, but I hardly heard a word he said. I had a mission now. And I wasn't going to fail Baba. Not this time.

IT SNOWED HEAVILY the night before the tournament. Hassan and I sat under the *kursi* and played panjpar as wind-rattled tree branches tapped on the window. Earlier that day, I'd asked Ali to set up the *kursi* for us—which was basically an electric heater under a low table covered with a thick, quilted blanket. Around the table, he arranged mattresses and cushions, so as many as twenty people could sit and slip their legs under. Hassan and I used to spend entire snowy days snug under the *kursi*, playing chess, cards—mostly panjpar.

I killed Hassan's ten of diamonds, played him two jacks and a six. Next door, in Baba's study, Baba and Rahim Khan were discussing business with a couple of other men—one of them I recognized as Assef's father. Through the wall, I could hear the scratchy sound of Radio Kabul News.

Hassan killed the six and picked up the jacks. On the radio, Daoud Khan was announcing something about foreign investments.

"He says someday we'll have television in Kabul," I said.

"Who?"

"Daoud Khan, you ass, the president."

Hassan giggled. "I heard they already have it in Iran," he said.

I sighed. "Those Iranians ..." For a lot of Hazaras, Iran represented a sanctuary of sorts—I guess because, like Hazaras, most Iranians were Shi'a Muslims. But I remembered something my teacher had said that summer about Iranians, that they were grinning smooth talkers who patted you on the back with one hand and picked your pocket with the other. I told Baba about that and he said my teacher was one of those jealous Afghans, jealous because Iran was a rising power in Asia and most people around the world couldn't even find Afghanistan on a world map. "It hurts to say that," he said, shrugging. "But better to get hurt by the truth than comforted with a lie."

"I'll buy you one someday," I said.

Hassan's face brightened. "A television? In truth?"

"Sure. And not the black-and-white kind either. We'll probably be grown-ups by then, but I'll get us two. One for you and one for me."

"I'll put it on my table, where I keep my drawings," Hassan said.

His saying that made me kind of sad. Sad for who Hassan was, where he lived. For how he'd accepted the fact that he'd grow old in that mud shack in the yard, the way his father had. I drew the last card, played him a pair of queens and a ten.

Hassan picked up the queens. "You know, I think you're going to make Agha sahib very proud tomorrow."

"You think so?"

"Inshallah," he said.

"Inshallah," I echoed, though the "God willing" qualifier didn't sound as sincere coming from my lips. That was the thing with Hassan. He was so goddamn pure, you always felt like a phony around him.

I killed his king and played him my final card, the ace of spades. He had to pick it up. I'd won, but as I shuffled for a new game, I had the distinct suspicion that Hassan had *let* me win.

"Amir agha?"

"What?"

"You know …I *like* where I live." He was always doing that, reading my mind. "It's my home."

"Whatever," I said. "Get ready to lose again."

SEVEN

The next morning, as he brewed black tea for breakfast, Hassan told me he'd had a dream. "We were at Ghargha Lake, you, me, Father, Agha sahib, Rahim Khan, and thousands of other people," he said. "It was warm and sunny, and the lake was clear like a mirror. But no one was swimming because they said a monster had come to the lake. It was swimming at the bottom, waiting."

He poured me a cup and added sugar, blew on it a few times. Put it before me. "So everyone is scared to get in the water, and suddenly you kick off your shoes, Amir agha, and take off your shirt. 'There's no monster,' you say. 'I'll show you all.' And before anyone can stop you, you dive into the water, start swimming away. I follow you in and we're both swimming."

"But you can't swim."

Hassan laughed. "It's a dream, Amir agha, you can do anything. Anyway, everyone is screaming, 'Get out! Get out!' but we just swim in the cold water. We make it way out to the middle of the lake and we stop swimming. We turn toward the shore and wave to the people. They look small like ants, but we can hear them clapping. They see now. There is no monster, just water. They

change the name of the lake after that, and call it the 'Lake of
Amir and Hassan, Sultans of Kabul,' and we get to charge people
money for swimming in it."

"So what does it mean?" I said.

He coated my *naan* with marmalade, placed it on a plate. "I
don't know. I was hoping you could tell me."

"Well, it's a dumb dream. Nothing happens in it."

"Father says dreams always mean something."

I sipped some tea. "Why don't you ask him, then? He's so
smart," I said, more curtly than I had intended. I hadn't slept all
night. My neck and back were like coiled springs, and my eyes
stung. Still, I had been mean to Hassan. I almost apologized,
then didn't. Hassan understood I was just nervous. Hassan always
understood about me.

Upstairs, I could hear the water running in Baba's bathroom.

THE STREETS GLISTENED with fresh snow and the sky was
a blameless blue. Snow blanketed every rooftop and weighed on
the branches of the stunted mulberry trees that lined our street.
Overnight, snow had nudged its way into every crack and gutter.
I squinted against the blinding white when Hassan and I stepped
through the wrought-iron gates. Ali shut the gates behind us. I
heard him mutter a prayer under his breath—he always said a
prayer when his son left the house.

I had never seen so many people on our street. Kids were
flinging snowballs, squabbling, chasing one another, giggling.
Kite fighters were huddling with their spool holders, making
lastminute preparations. From adjacent streets, I could hear
laughter and chatter. Already, rooftops were jammed with

spectators reclining in lawn chairs, hot tea steaming from thermoses, and the music of Ahmad Zahir blaring from cassette players. The immensely popular Ahmad Zahir had revolutionized Afghan music and outraged the purists by adding electric guitars, drums, and horns to the traditional tabla and harmonium; on stage or at parties, he shirked the austere and nearly morose stance of older singers and actually smiled when he sang—sometimes even at women. I turned my gaze to our rooftop, found Baba and Rahim Khan sitting on a bench, both dressed in wool sweaters, sipping tea. Baba waved. I couldn't tell if he was waving at me or Hassan.

"We should get started," Hassan said. He wore black rubber snow boots and a bright green *chapan* over a thick sweater and faded corduroy pants. Sunlight washed over his face, and, in it, I saw how well the pink scar above his lip had healed.

Suddenly I wanted to withdraw. Pack it all in, go back home. What was I thinking? Why was I putting myself through this, when I already knew the outcome? Baba was on the roof, watching me. I felt his glare on me like the heat of a blistering sun. This would be failure on a grand scale, even for me.

"I'm not sure I want to fly a kite today," I said.

"It's a beautiful day," Hassan said.

I shifted on my feet. Tried to peel my gaze away from our rooftop. "I don't know. Maybe we should go home."

Then he stepped toward me and, in a low voice, said something that scared me a little. "Remember, Amir agha. There's no monster, just a beautiful day." How could I be such an open book to him when, half the time, I had no idea what was milling around in his head? I was the one who went to school, the one who could read, write. I was the smart one. Hassan couldn't read a firstgrade textbook but he'd read me plenty. That was a little unsettling, but also sort of comfortable to have someone who always knew what you needed.

"No monster," I said, feeling a little better, to my own surprise.

He smiled. "No monster."

"Are you sure?"

He closed his eyes. Nodded.

I looked to the kids scampering down the street, flinging snowballs. "It is a beautiful day, isn't it?"

"Let's fly," he said.

It occurred to me then that maybe Hassan had made up his dream. Was that possible? I decided it wasn't. Hassan wasn't that smart. *I* wasn't that smart. But made up or not, the silly dream had lifted some of my anxiety. Maybe I *should* take off my shirt, take a swim in the lake. Why not?

"Let's do it," I said.

Hassan's face brightened. "Good," he said. He lifted our kite, red with yellow borders, and, just beneath where the central and cross spars met, marked with Saifo's unmistakable signature. He licked his finger and held it up, tested the wind, then ran in its direction—on those rare occasions we flew kites in the summer, he'd kick up dust to see which way the wind blew it. The spool rolled in my hands until Hassan stopped, about fifty feet away. He held the kite high over his head, like an Olympic athlete showing his gold medal. I jerked the string twice, our usual signal, and Hassan tossed the kite.

Caught between Baba and the mullahs at school, I still hadn't made up my mind about God. But when a Koran *ayat* I had learned in my *diniyat* class rose to my lips, I muttered it. I took a deep breath, exhaled, and pulled on the string. Within a minute, my kite was rocketing to the sky. It made a sound like a paper bird flapping its wings. Hassan clapped his hands, whistled, and ran back to me. I handed him the spool, holding on to the string, and he spun it quickly to roll the loose string back on.

At least two dozen kites already hung in the sky, like paper sharks roaming for prey. Within an hour, the number doubled, and red, blue, and yellow kites glided and spun in the sky. A cold breeze wafted through my hair. The wind was perfect for kite flying, blowing just hard enough to give some lift, make the sweeps easier. Next to me, Hassan held the spool, his hands already bloodied by the string.

Soon, the cutting started and the first of the defeated kites whirled out of control. They fell from the sky like shooting stars with brilliant, rippling tails, showering the neighborhoods below with prizes for the kite runners. I could hear the runners now, hollering as they ran the streets. Someone shouted reports of a fight breaking out two streets down.

I kept stealing glances at Baba sitting with Rahim Khan on the roof, wondered what he was thinking. Was he cheering for me? Or did a part of him enjoy watching me fail? That was the thing about kite flying: Your mind drifted with the kite.

They were coming down all over the place now, the kites, and I was still flying. I was still flying. My eyes kept wandering over to Baba, bundled up in his wool sweater. Was he surprised I had lasted as long as I had? *You don't keep your eyes to the sky, you won't last much longer.* I snapped my gaze back to the sky. A red kite was closing in on me—I'd caught it just in time. I tangled a bit with it, ended up besting him when he became impatient and tried to cut me from below.

Up and down the streets, kite runners were returning trium-
phantly, their captured kites held high. They showed them off
to their parents, their friends. But they all knew the best was yet
to come. The biggest prize of all was still flying. I sliced a bright
yellow kite with a coiled white tail. It cost me another gash on
the index finger and blood trickled down into my palm. I had
Hassan hold the string and sucked the blood dry, blotted my
finger against my jeans.

Within another hour, the number of surviving kites dwindled
from maybe fifty to a dozen. I was one of them. I'd made it to
the last dozen. I knew this part of the tournament would take a
while, because the guys who had lasted this long were good—
they wouldn't easily fall into simple traps like the old lift-and-
dive, Hassan's favorite trick.

By three o'clock that afternoon, tufts of clouds had drifted
in and the sun had slipped behind them. Shadows started to
lengthen. The spectators on the roofs bundled up in scarves and
thick coats. We were down to a half dozen and I was still flying.
My legs ached and my neck was stiff. But with each defeated
kite, hope grew in my heart, like snow collecting on a wall, one
flake at a time.

My eyes kept returning to a blue kite that had been wreaking
havoc for the last hour.

"How many has he cut?" I asked.

"I counted eleven," Hassan said.

"Do you know whose it might be?"

Hassan clucked his tongue and tipped his chin. That was a
trademark Hassan gesture, meant he had no idea. The blue kite
sliced a big purple one and swept twice in big loops. Ten minutes later, he'd cut another two, sending hordes of kite runners

racing after them.

After another thirty minutes, only four kites remained. And I was still flying. It seemed I could hardly make a wrong move, as if every gust of wind blew in my favor. I'd never felt so in command, so lucky. It felt intoxicating. I didn't dare look up to the roof. Didn't dare take my eyes off the sky. I had to concentrate, play it smart. Another fifteen minutes and what had seemed like a laughable dream that morning had suddenly become reality: It was just me and the other guy. The blue kite.

The tension in the air was as taut as the glass string I was tugging with my bloody hands. People were stomping their feet, clapping, whistling, chanting, *"Boboresh! Boboresh!"* Cut him! Cut him! I wondered if Baba's voice was one of them. Music blasted. The smell of steamed *mantu* and fried *pakora* drifted from rooftops and open doors.

But all I heard—all I willed myself to hear—was the thudding of blood in my head. All I saw was the blue kite. All I smelled was victory. Salvation. Redemption. If Baba was wrong and there *was* a God like they said in school, then He'd let me win. I didn't know what the other guy was playing for, maybe just bragging rights. But this was my one chance to become someone who was looked at, not seen, listened to, not heard. If there was a God, He'd guide the winds, let them blow for me so that, with a tug of my string, I'd cut loose my pain, my longing. I'd endured too much, come too far. And suddenly, just like that, hope became knowledge. I was going to win. It was just a matter of when.

It turned out to be sooner than later. A gust of wind lifted my kite and I took advantage. Fed the string, pulled up. Looped my kite on top of the blue one. I held position. The blue kite knew it was in trouble. It was trying desperately to maneuver out of the jam, but I didn't let go. I held position. The crowd sensed the end was at hand. The chorus of "Cut him! Cut him!" grew louder, like Romans chanting for the gladiators to kill, kill!

"You're almost there, Amir agha! Almost there!" Hassan was panting.

Then the moment came. I closed my eyes and loosened my grip on the string. It sliced my fingers again as the wind dragged it. And then …I didn't need to hear the crowd's roar to know. I didn't need to see either. Hassan was screaming and his arm was wrapped around my neck.

"Bravo! Bravo, Amir agha!"

I opened my eyes, saw the blue kite spinning wildly like a tire come loose from a speeding car. I blinked, tried to say something. Nothing came out. Suddenly I was hovering, looking down on myself from above. Black leather coat, red scarf, faded jeans. A thin boy, a little sallow, and a tad short for his twelve years. He had narrow shoulders and a hint of dark circles around his pale hazel eyes. The breeze rustled his light brown hair. He looked up to me and we smiled at each other.

Then I was screaming, and everything was color and sound, everything was alive and good. I was throwing my free arm around Hassan and we were hopping up and down, both of us laughing, both of us weeping. "You won, Amir agha! You won!"

"*We* won! *We* won!" was all I could say. This wasn't happening. In a moment, I'd blink and rouse from this beautiful dream, get out of bed, march down to the kitchen to eat breakfast with no one to talk to but Hassan. Get dressed. Wait for Baba. Give up. Back to my old life. Then I saw Baba on our roof. He was standing on the edge, pumping both of his fists. Hollering and clapping. And that right there was the single greatest moment of my twelve years of life, seeing Baba on that roof, proud of me at last.

But he was doing something now, motioning with his hands in an urgent way. Then I understood. "Hassan, we—"

"I know," he said, breaking our embrace. "*Inshallah,* we'll celebrate later. Right now, I'm going to run that blue kite for you," he said. He dropped the spool and took off running, the hem of his green *chapan* dragging in the snow behind him.

"Hassan!" I called. "Come back with it!"

He was already turning the street corner, his rubber boots kicking up snow. He stopped, turned. He cupped his hands around his mouth. "For you a thousand times over!" he said. Then he smiled his Hassan smile and disappeared around the corner. The next time I saw him smile unabashedly like that was twentysix years later, in a faded Polaroid photograph.

I began to pull my kite back as people rushed to congratulate me. I shook hands with them, said my thanks. The younger kids looked at me with an awestruck twinkle in their eyes; I was a hero. Hands patted my back and tousled my hair. I pulled on the string and returned every smile, but my mind was on the blue kite.

Finally, I had my kite in hand. I wrapped the loose string that had collected at my feet around the spool, shook a few more hands, and trotted home. When I reached the wrought-iron gates, Ali was waiting on the other side. He stuck his hand through the bars. "Congratulations," he said.

I gave him my kite and spool, shook his hand. "*Tashakor,* Ali jan."

"I was praying for you the whole time." "Then keep praying.

We're not done yet."

I hurried back to the street. I didn't ask Ali about Baba. I didn't want to see him yet. In my head, I had it all planned: I'd make a grand entrance, a hero, prized trophy in my bloodied hands. Heads would turn and eyes would lock. Rostam and Sohrab sizing each other up. A dramatic moment of silence. Then the old warrior would walk to the young one, embrace him, acknowledge his worthiness. Vindication. Salvation. Redemption. And then? Well … happily ever after, of course. What else?

The streets of Wazir Akbar Khan were numbered and set at right angles to each other like a grid. It was a new neighborhood then, still developing, with empty lots of land and half-constructed homes on every street between compounds surrounded by eight-foot walls. I ran up and down every street, looking for Hassan. Everywhere, people were busy folding chairs, packing food and utensils after a long day of partying. Some, still sitting on their rooftops, shouted their congratulations to me.

Four streets south of ours, I saw Omar, the son of an engineer who was a friend of Baba's. He was dribbling a soccer ball with his brother on the front lawn of their house. Omar was a pretty good guy. We'd been classmates in fourth grade, and one time he'd given me a fountain pen, the kind you had to load with a cartridge.

"I heard you won, Amir," he said. "Congratulations."

"Thanks. Have you seen Hassan?"

"Your Hazara?"

I nodded.

Omar headed the ball to his brother. "I hear he's a great kite runner." His brother headed the ball back to him. Omar caught it, tossed it up and down. "Although I've always wondered how he manages. I mean, with those tight little eyes, how does he *see* anything?"

His brother laughed, a short burst, and asked for the ball.

Omar ignored him.

"Have you seen him?"

Omar flicked a thumb over his shoulder, pointing southwest. "I saw him running toward the bazaar awhile ago."

"Thanks." I scuttled away.

By the time I reached the marketplace, the sun had almost sunk behind the hills and dusk had painted the sky pink and purple. A few blocks away, from the Haji Yaghoub Mosque, the mullah bellowed *azan,* calling for the faithful to unroll their rugs and bow their heads west in prayer. Hassan never missed any of the five daily prayers. Even when we were out playing, he'd excuse himself, draw water from the well in the yard, wash up, and disappear into the hut. He'd come out a few minutes later, smiling, find me sitting against the wall or perched on a tree. He was going to miss prayer tonight, though, because of me.

The bazaar was emptying quickly, the merchants finishing up their haggling for the day. I trotted in the mud between rows of closely packed cubicles where you could buy a freshly slaughtered pheasant in one stand and a calculator from the adjacent one. I picked my way through the dwindling crowd, the lame beggars dressed in layers of tattered rags, the vendors with rugs on their shoulders, the cloth merchants and butchers closing shop for the day. I found no sign of Hassan.

I stopped by a dried fruit stand, described Hassan to an old merchant loading his mule with crates of pine seeds and raisins. He wore a powder blue turban.

He paused to look at me for a long time before answering. "I might have seen him."

"Which way did he go?"

He eyed me up and down. "What is a boy like you doing here at this time of the day looking for a Hazara?" His glance lingered admiringly on my leather coat and my jeans—*cowboy pants,* we used to call them. In Afghanistan, owning anything American, especially if it wasn't secondhand, was a sign of wealth.

"I need to find him, Agha."

"What is he to you?" he said. I didn't see the point of his question, but I reminded myself that impatience wasn't going to make him tell me any faster.

"He's our servant's son," I said.

The old man raised a pepper gray eyebrow. "He is? Lucky Hazara, having such a concerned master. His father should get on his knees, sweep the dust at your feet with his eyelashes."

"Are you going to tell me or not?"

He rested an arm on the mule's back, pointed south. "I think I saw the boy you described running that way. He had a kite in his hand. A blue one."

"He did?" I said. *For you a thousand times over,* he'd promised. Good old Hassan. Good old reliable Hassan. He'd kept his promise and run the last kite for me.

"Of course, they've probably caught him by now," the old merchant said, grunting and loading another box on the mule's back.

"Who?"

"The other boys," he said. "The ones chasing him. They were dressed like you." He glanced to the sky and sighed. "Now, run along, you're making me late for *namaz.*"

But I was already scrambling down the lane.

For the next few minutes, I scoured the bazaar in vain. Maybe the old merchant's eyes had betrayed him. Except he'd seen the blue kite. The thought of getting my hands on that kite … I poked my head behind every lane, every shop. No sign of Hassan.

I had begun to worry that darkness would fall before I found Hassan when I heard voices from up ahead. I'd reached a secluded, muddy road. It ran perpendicular to the end of the main thoroughfare bisecting the bazaar. I turned onto the rutted track and followed the voices. My boot squished in mud with every step and my breath puffed out in white clouds before me. The narrow path ran parallel on one side to a snow-filled ravine through which a stream may have tumbled in the spring. To my other side stood rows of snow-burdened cypress trees peppered among flat-topped clay houses—no more than mud shacks in most cases—separated by narrow alleys.

I heard the voices again, louder this time, coming from one of the alleys. I crept close to the mouth of the alley. Held my breath. Peeked around the corner.

Hassan was standing at the blind end of the alley in a defiant stance: fists curled, legs slightly apart. Behind him, sitting on piles of scrap and rubble, was the blue kite. My key to Baba's heart.

Blocking Hassan's way out of the alley were three boys, the same three from that day on the hill, the day after Daoud Khan's coup, when Hassan had saved us with his slingshot. Wali was standing on one side, Kamal on the other, and in the middle, Assef. I felt my body clench up, and something cold rippled up my spine. Assef seemed relaxed, confident. He was twirling his brass knuckles. The other two guys shifted nervously on their feet, looking from Assef to Hassan, like they'd cornered some kind of wild animal that only Assef could tame.

"Where is your slingshot, Hazara?" Assef said, turning the brass knuckles in his hand. "What was it you said? 'They'll have to call you One-Eyed Assef.' That's right. One-Eyed Assef. That was clever. Really clever. Then again, it's easy to be clever when you're holding a loaded weapon."

I realized I still hadn't breathed out. I exhaled, slowly, quietly. I felt paralyzed. I watched them close in on the boy I'd grown up with, the boy whose harelipped face had been my first memory.

"But today is your lucky day, Hazara," Assef said. He had his back to me, but I would have bet he was grinning. "I'm in a mood to forgive. What do you say to that, boys?"

"That's generous," Kamal blurted, "Especially after the rude manners he showed us last time." He was trying to sound like Assef, except there was a tremor in his voice. Then I understood: He wasn't afraid of Hassan, not really. He was afraid because he had no idea what Assef had in mind.

Assef waved a dismissive hand. "*Bakhshida.* Forgiven. It's done." His voice dropped a little. "Of course, nothing is free in this world, and my pardon comes with a small price."

"That's fair," Kamal said.

"Nothing is free," Wali added.

"You're a lucky Hazara," Assef said, taking a step toward Hassan. "Because today, it's only going to cost you that blue kite. A fair deal, boys, isn't it?"

"More than fair," Kamal said.

Even from where I was standing, I could see the fear creeping into Hassan's eyes, but he shook his head. "Amir agha won the tournament and I ran this kite for him. I ran it fairly. This is his kite."

"A loyal Hazara. Loyal as a dog," Assef said.

Kamal's laugh was a shrill, nervous sound.

"But before you sacrifice yourself for him, think about this: Would he do the same for you? Have you ever wondered why he never includes you in games when he has guests? Why he only plays with you when no one else is around? I'll tell you why, Hazara. Because to him, you're nothing but an ugly pet. Something he can play with when he's bored, something he can kick when he's angry. Don't ever fool yourself and think you're something more."

"Amir agha and I are friends," Hassan said. He looked flushed.

"Friends?" Assef said, laughing. "You pathetic fool! Someday you'll wake up from your little fantasy and learn just how good of a friend he is. Now, *bas!* Enough of this. Give us that kite."

Hassan stooped and picked up a rock.

Assef flinched. He began to take a step back, stopped. "Last chance, Hazara."

Hassan's answer was to cock the arm that held the rock.

"Whatever you wish." Assef unbuttoned his winter coat, took it off, folded it slowly and deliberately. He placed it against the wall.

I opened my mouth, almost said something. Almost. The rest of my life might have turned out differently if I had. But I didn't. I just watched. Paralyzed.

Assef motioned with his hand, and the other two boys separated, forming a half circle, trapping Hassan in the alley.

"I've changed my mind," Assef said. "I'm letting you keep the kite, Hazara. I'll let you keep it so it will always remind you of what I'm about to do."

Then he charged. Hassan hurled the rock. It struck Assef in the forehead. Assef yelped as he flung himself at Hassan, knocking him to the ground. Wali and Kamal followed.

I bit on my fist. Shut my eyes.

A MEMORY:

Did you know Hassan and you fed from the same breast? Did you know that, Amir agha? Sakina, her name was. She was a fair, blue-eyed Hazara woman from Bamiyan and she sang you old wedding songs. They say there is a brotherhood between people who've fed from the same breast. Did you know that?

A memory:

"A *rupia* each, children. Just one *rupia* each and I will part the curtain of truth." *The old man sits against a mud wall. His sightless eyes are like molten silver embedded in deep, twin craters.*

Hunched over his cane, the fortune-teller runs a gnarled hand across the surface of his deflated cheeks. Cups it before us. "Not much to ask for the truth, is it, a *rupia* each?" *Hassan drops a coin in the leathery palm. I drop mine too.* "In the name of Allah most beneficent, most merciful," *the old fortune-teller whispers. He takes Hassan's hand first, strokes the palm with one hornlike fingernail, round and round, round and round. The finger then floats to Hassan's face and makes a dry, scratchy sound as it slowly traces the curve of his cheeks, the outline of his ears. The calloused pads of his fingers brush against Hassan's eyes. The hand stops there. Lingers. A shadow passes across the old man's face. Hassan and I exchange a glance. The old man takes Hassan's hand and puts the* rupia *back in Hassan's palm. He turns to me.* "How about you, young friend?" *he says. On the other side of the wall, a rooster crows. The old man reaches for my hand and I withdraw it.*

A dream:

I am lost in a snowstorm. The wind shrieks, blows stinging sheets of snow into my eyes. I stagger through layers of shifting white. I call for help but the wind drowns my cries. I fall and lie panting on the snow, lost in the white, the wind wailing in my ears. I watch the snow erase my fresh footprints. I'm a ghost now, *I think,* a ghost with no footprints. *I cry out again, hope fading like my footprints. But this time, a muffled reply. I shield my eyes and manage to sit up. Out of the swaying curtains of snow, I catch a glimpse of movement, a flurry of color. A familiar shape materializes. A hand reaches out for me. I see deep, parallel gashes across the palm, blood dripping, staining the snow. I take the hand and suddenly the snow is gone. We're standing in a field of apple green grass with soft wisps of clouds drifting above. I look up and see the clear sky is filled with kites, green, yellow, red, orange. They shimmer in the afternoon light.*

A HAVOC OF SCRAP AND RUBBLE littered the alley. Worn bicycle tires, bottles with peeled labels, ripped up magazines, yellowed newspapers, all scattered amid a pile of bricks and slabs of cement. A rusted cast-iron stove with a gaping hole on its side tilted against a wall. But there were two things amid the garbage that I couldn't stop looking at: One was the blue kite resting against the wall, close to the cast-iron stove; the other was Hassan's brown corduroy pants thrown on a heap of eroded bricks.

"I don't know," Wali was saying. "My father says it's sinful." He sounded unsure, excited, scared, all at the same time. Hassan lay with his chest pinned to the ground. Kamal and Wali each gripped an arm, twisted and bent at the elbow so that Hassan's hands were pressed to his back. Assef was standing over them, the heel of his snow boots crushing the back of Hassan's neck.

"Your father won't find out," Assef said. "And there's nothing sinful about teaching a lesson to a disrespectful donkey."

"I don't know," Wali muttered.

"Suit yourself," Assef said. He turned to Kamal. "What about you?"

"I ... well ..."

"It's just a Hazara," Assef said. But Kamal kept looking away.

"Fine," Assef snapped. "All I want you weaklings to do is hold him down. Can you manage that?"

Wali and Kamal nodded. They looked relieved.

Assef knelt behind Hassan, put his hands on Hassan's hips and lifted his bare buttocks. He kept one hand on Hassan's back and undid his own belt buckle with his free hand. He unzipped his jeans. Dropped his underwear. He positioned himself behind Hassan. Hassan didn't struggle. Didn't even whimper. He moved his head slightly and I caught a glimpse of his face. Saw the resignation in it. It was a look I had seen before. It was the look of the lamb.

TOMORROW IS THE TENTH DAY of Dhul-Hijjah, the last month of the Muslim calendar, and the first of three days of Eid AlAdha, or Eid-e-Qorban, as Afghans call it—a day to celebrate how the prophet Ibrahim almost sacrificed his own son for God. Baba has handpicked the sheep again this year, a powder white one with crooked black ears.

We all stand in the backyard, Hassan, Ali, Baba, and I. The mullah recites the prayer, rubs his beard. Baba mutters, Get on with it, under his breath. He sounds annoyed with the endless praying, the ritual of making the meat halal. Baba mocks the story behind this Eid, like he mocks everything religious. But he respects the tradition of Eid-e-Qorban. The custom is to divide the meat in thirds, one for the family, one for friends, and one for the poor. Every year, Baba gives it all to the poor. The rich are fat enough already, he says.

The mullah finishes the prayer. Ameen. He picks up the kitchen knife with the long blade. The custom is to not let the sheep see the knife. Ali feeds the animal a cube of sugar—another custom, to make death sweeter. The sheep kicks, but not much. The mullah grabs it under its jaw and places the blade on its neck. Just a second before he slices the throat in one expert motion, I see the sheep's eyes. It is a look that will haunt my dreams for weeks. I don't know why I watch this yearly ritual in our backyard; my nightmares persist long after the bloodstains on the grass have faded. But I always watch. I watch because of that look of acceptance in the animal's eyes. Absurdly, I imagine the animal understands. I imagine the animal sees that its imminent demise is for a higher purpose. This is the look ...

I STOPPED WATCHING, turned away from the alley. Something warm was running down my wrist. I blinked, saw I was still biting down on my fist, hard enough to draw blood from the knuckles. I realized something else. I was weeping. From just around the corner, I could hear Assef's quick, rhythmic grunts.

I had one last chance to make a decision. One final opportunity to decide who I was going to be. I could step into that alley, stand up for Hassan—the way he'd stood up for me all those times in the past—and accept whatever would happen to me. Or I could run.

In the end, I ran.

I ran because I was a coward. I was afraid of Assef and what he would do to me. I was afraid of getting hurt. That's what I told myself as I turned my back to the alley, to Hassan. That's what I made myself believe. I actually *aspired* to cowardice, because the alternative, the real reason I was running, was that Assef was right: Nothing was free in this world. Maybe Hassan was the price I had to pay, the lamb I had to slay, to win Baba. Was it a fair price? The answer floated to my conscious mind before I could thwart it: He was just a Hazara, wasn't he?

I ran back the way I'd come. Ran back to the all but deserted bazaar. I lurched to a cubicle and leaned against the padlocked swinging doors. I stood there panting, sweating, wishing things had turned out some other way.

About fifteen minutes later, I heard voices and running footfalls. I crouched behind the cubicle and watched Assef and the other two sprinting by, laughing as they hurried down the deserted lane. I forced myself to wait ten more minutes. Then I walked back to the rutted track that ran along the snow-filled ravine. I squinted in the dimming light and spotted Hassan walking slowly toward me. I met him by a leafless birch tree on the edge of the ravine.

He had the blue kite in his hands; that was the first thing I saw. And I can't lie now and say my eyes didn't scan it for any rips. His *chapan* had mud smudges down the front and his shirt was ripped just below the collar. He stopped. Swayed on his feet like he was going to collapse. Then he steadied himself. Handed me the kite.

"Where were you? I looked for you," I said. Speaking those words was like chewing on a rock.

Hassan dragged a sleeve across his face, wiped snot and tears. I waited for him to say something, but we just stood there in silence, in the fading light. I was grateful for the early-evening shadows that fell on Hassan's face and concealed mine. I was glad I didn't have to return his gaze. Did he know I knew? And if he knew, then what would I see if I *did* look in his eyes? Blame? Indignation? Or, God forbid, what I feared most: guileless devotion? That, most of all, I couldn't bear to see.

He began to say something and his voice cracked. He closed his mouth, opened it, and closed it again. Took a step back. Wiped his face. And that was as close as Hassan and I ever came to discussing what had happened in the alley. I thought he might burst into tears, but, to my relief, he didn't, and I pretended I hadn't heard the crack in his voice. Just like I pretended I hadn't seen the dark stain in the seat of his pants. Or those tiny drops that fell from between his legs and stained the snow black.

"Agha sahib will worry," was all he said. He turned from me and limped away.

IT HAPPENED JUST THE WAY I'd imagined. I opened the door to the smoky study and stepped in. Baba and Rahim Khan were drinking tea and listening to the news crackling on the radio. Their heads turned. Then a smile played on my father's lips. He opened his arms. I put the kite down and walked into his thick hairy arms. I buried my face in the warmth of his chest and wept. Baba held me close to him, rocking me back and forth. In his arms, I forgot what I'd done. And that was good.

EIGHT

For a week, I barely saw Hassan. I woke up to find toasted bread, brewed tea, and a boiled egg already on the kitchen table. My clothes for the day were ironed and folded, left on the cane-seat chair in the foyer where Hassan usually did his ironing. He used to wait for me to sit at the breakfast table before he started ironing—that way, we could talk. Used to sing too, over the hissing of the iron, sang old Hazara songs about tulip fields. Now only the folded clothes greeted me. That, and a breakfast I hardly finished anymore.

One overcast morning, as I was pushing the boiled egg around on my plate, Ali walked in cradling a pile of chopped wood. I asked him where Hassan was.

"He went back to sleep," Ali said, kneeling before the stove. He pulled the little square door open.

Would Hassan be able to play today?

Ali paused with a log in his hand. A worried look crossed his face. "Lately, it seems all he wants to do is sleep. He does his chores—I see to that—but then he just wants to crawl under his blanket. Can I ask you something?"

"If you have to."

"After that kite tournament, he came home a little bloodied and his shirt was torn. I asked him what had happened and he said it was nothing, that he'd gotten into a little scuffle with some kids over the kite."

I didn't say anything. Just kept pushing the egg around on my plate.

"Did something happen to him, Amir agha? Something he's not telling me?"

I shrugged. "How should I know?"

"You would tell me, nay? *Inshallah,* you would tell me if something had happened?"

"Like I said, how should I know what's wrong with him?" I snapped. "Maybe he's sick. People get sick all the time, Ali. Now, am I going to freeze to death or are you planning on lighting the stove today?"

THAT NIGHT I asked Baba if we could go to Jalalabad on Friday. He was rocking on the leather swivel chair behind his desk, reading a newspaper. He put it down, took off the reading glasses I disliked so much—Baba wasn't old, not at all, and he had lots of years left to live, so why did he have to wear those stupid glasses?

"Why not!" he said. Lately, Baba agreed to everything I asked. Not only that, just two nights before, *he'd* asked *me* if I wanted to see *El Cid* with Charlton Heston at Cinema Aryana. "Do you want to ask Hassan to come along to Jalalabad?"

Why did Baba have to spoil it like that? "He's *mareez,*" I said. Not feeling well.

"Really?" Baba stopped rocking in his chair. "What's wrong with him?"

I gave a shrug and sank in the sofa by the fireplace. "He's got a cold or something. Ali says he's sleeping it off."

"I haven't seen much of Hassan the last few days," Baba said. "That's all it is, then, a cold?" I couldn't help hating the way his brow furrowed with worry.

"Just a cold. So are we going Friday, Baba?"

"Yes, yes," Baba said, pushing away from the desk. "Too bad about Hassan. I thought you might have had more fun if he came."

"Well, the two of us can have fun together," I said.

Baba smiled. Winked. "Dress warm," he said.

IT SHOULD HAVE BEEN just the two of us—that was the way I wanted it—but by Wednesday night, Baba had managed to invite another two dozen people. He called his cousin Homayoun—he was actually Baba's second cousin—and mentioned he was going to Jalalabad on Friday, and Homayoun, who had studied engineering in France and had a house in Jalalabad, said he'd love to have everyone over, he'd bring the kids, his two wives, and, while he was at it, cousin Shafiqa and her family were visiting from Herat, maybe she'd like to tag along, and since she was staying with cousin Nader in Kabul, his family would have to be invited as well even though Homayoun and Nader had a bit of a feud going, and if Nader was invited, surely his brother Faruq had to be asked too or his feelings would be hurt and he might not invite them to his daughter's wedding next month and ...

We filled three vans. I rode with Baba, Rahim Khan, Kaka

Homayoun—Baba had taught me at a young age to call any older male *Kaka,* or Uncle, and any older female, *Khala,* or Aunt. Kaka Homayoun's two wives rode with us too—the pinch-faced older one with the warts on her hands and the younger one who always smelled of perfume and danced with her eyes close—as did Kaka Homayoun's twin girls. I sat in the back row, carsick and dizzy, sandwiched between the seven-year-old twins who kept reaching over my lap to slap at each other. The road to Jalalabad is a two–hour trek through mountain roads winding along a steep drop, and my stomach lurched with each hairpin turn. Everyone in the van was talking, talking loudly and at the same time, nearly shrieking, which is how Afghans talk. I asked one of the twins—Fazila or Karima, I could never tell which was which—if she'd trade her window seat with me so I could get fresh air on account of my car sickness. She stuck her tongue out and said no. I told her that was fine, but I couldn't be held accountable for vomiting on her new dress. A minute later, I was leaning out the window. I watched the cratered road rise and fall, whirl its tail around the mountainside, counted the multicolored trucks packed with squatting men lumbering past. I tried closing my eyes, letting the wind slap at my cheeks, opened my mouth to swallow the clean air. I still didn't feel better. A finger poked me in the side. It was Fazila/Karima.

"What?" I said.

"I was just telling everyone about the tournament," Baba said from behind the wheel. Kaka Homayoun and his wives were smiling at me from the middle row of seats.

"There must have been a hundred kites in the sky that day?" Baba said. "Is that about right, Amir?"

"I guess so," I mumbled.

"A hundred kites, Homayoun jan. No *laaf*. And the only one still flying at the end of the day was Amir's. He has the last kite at home, a beautiful blue kite. Hassan and Amir ran it together."

"Congratulations," Kaka Homayoun said. His first wife, the one with the warts, clapped her hands. "Wah wah, Amir jan, we're all so proud of you!" she said. The younger wife joined in. Then they were all clapping, yelping their praises, telling me how proud I'd made them all. Only Rahim Khan, sitting in the passenger seat next to Baba, was silent. He was looking at me in an odd way.

"Please pull over, Baba," I said.

"What?"

"Getting sick," I muttered, leaning across the seat, pressing against Kaka Homayoun's daughters.

Fazila/Karima's face twisted. "Pull over, Kaka! His face is yellow! I don't want him throwing up on my new dress!" she squealed.

Baba began to pull over, but I didn't make it. A few minutes later, I was sitting on a rock on the side of the road as they aired out the van. Baba was smoking with Kaka Homayoun who was telling Fazila/Karima to stop crying; he'd buy her another dress in Jalalabad. I closed my eyes, turned my face to the sun. Little shapes formed behind my eyelids, like hands playing shadows on the wall. They twisted, merged, formed a single image: Hassan's brown corduroy pants discarded on a pile of old bricks in the alley.

KAKA HOMAYOUN'S WHITE, two-story house in Jalalabad had a balcony overlooking a large, walled garden with apple and persimmon trees. There were hedges that, in the summer, the gardener shaped like animals, and a swimming pool with emeraldcolored tiles. I sat on the edge of the pool, empty save for a layer of slushy snow at the bottom, feet dangling in. Kaka Homayoun's kids were playing hide-and-seek at the other end of the yard. The women were cooking and I could smell onions frying already, could hear the *phht-phht* of a pressure cooker, music, laughter. Baba, Rahim Khan, Kaka Homayoun, and Kaka Nader were sitting on the balcony, smoking. Kaka Homayoun was telling them he'd brought the projector along to show his slides of France. Ten years since he'd returned from Paris and he was still showing those stupid slides.

It shouldn't have felt this way. Baba and I were finally friends. We'd gone to the zoo a few days before, seen Marjan the lion, and I had hurled a pebble at the bear when no one was watching. We'd gone to Dadkhoda's Kabob House afterward, across from Cinema Park, had lamb kabob with freshly baked *naan* from the *tandoor*. Baba told me stories of his travels to India and Russia, the people he had met, like the armless, legless couple in Bombay who'd been married forty-seven years and raised eleven children. That should have been fun, spending a day like that with Baba, hearing his stories. I finally had what I'd wanted all those years. Except now that I had it, I felt as empty as this unkempt pool I was dangling my legs into.

The wives and daughters served dinner—rice, *kofta,* and chicken *qurma*—at sundown. We dined the traditional way, sitting on cushions around the room, tablecloth spread on the floor, eating with our hands in groups of four or five from common platters. I wasn't hungry but sat down to eat anyway with Baba, Kaka Faruq, and Kaka Homayoun's two boys. Baba, who'd had a few scotches before dinner, was still ranting about the kite tournament, how I'd outlasted them all, how I'd come home with the last kite. His booming voice dominated the room. People raised their heads from their platters, called out their congratulations. Kaka Faruq patted my back with his clean hand. I felt like sticking a knife in my eye.

Later, well past midnight, after a few hours of poker between Baba and his cousins, the men lay down to sleep on parallel mattresses in the same room where we'd dined. The women went upstairs. An hour later, I still couldn't sleep. I kept tossing and turning as my relatives grunted, sighed, and snored in their sleep. I sat up. A wedge of moonlight streamed in through the window.

"I watched Hassan get raped," I said to no one. Baba stirred in his sleep. Kaka Homayoun grunted. A part of me was hoping someone would wake up and hear, so I wouldn't have to live with this lie anymore. But no one woke up and in the silence that followed, I understood the nature of my new curse: I was going to get away with it.

I thought about Hassan's dream, the one about us swimming in the lake. *There is no monster,* he'd said, *just water.* Except he'd been wrong about that. There was a monster in the lake. It had grabbed Hassan by the ankles, dragged him to the murky bottom. I was that monster.

That was the night I became an insomniac.

I DIDN'T SPEAK TO HASSAN until the middle of the next week. I had just half-eaten my lunch and Hassan was doing the dishes. I was walking upstairs, going to my room, when Hassan asked if I wanted to hike up the hill. I said I was tired. Hassan looked tired too—he'd lost weight and gray circles had formed under his puffed-up eyes. But when he asked again, I reluctantly agreed.

We trekked up the hill, our boots squishing in the muddy snow. Neither one of us said anything. We sat under our pomegranate tree and I knew I'd made a mistake. I shouldn't have come up the hill. The words I'd carved on the tree trunk with Ali's kitchen knife, *Amir and Hassan: The Sultans of Kabul* ...I couldn't stand looking at them now.

He asked me to read to him from the *Shahnamah* and I told him I'd changed my mind. Told him I just wanted to go back to my room. He looked away and shrugged. We walked back down the way we'd gone up: in silence. And for the first time in my life, I couldn't wait for spring.

MY MEMORY OF THE REST of that winter of 1975 is pretty hazy. I remember I was fairly happy when Baba was home. We'd eat together, go to see a film, visit Kaka Homayoun or Kaka Faruq. Sometimes Rahim Khan came over and Baba let me sit in his study and sip tea with them. He'd even have me read him some of my stories. It was good and I even believed it would last. And Baba believed it too, I think. We both should have known better. For at least a few months after the kite tournament, Baba and I immersed ourselves in a sweet illusion, saw each other in a way that we never had before. We'd actually deceived ourselves into thinking that a toy made of tissue paper, glue, and bamboo could somehow close the chasm between us.

But when Baba was out—and he was out a lot—I closed

myself in my room. I read a book every couple of days, wrote stories, learned to draw horses. I'd hear Hassan shuffling around the kitchen in the morning, hear the clinking of silverware, the whistle of the teapot. I'd wait to hear the door shut and only then I would walk down to eat. On my calendar, I circled the date of the first day of school and began a countdown.

To my dismay, Hassan kept trying to rekindle things between us. I remember the last time. I was in my room, reading an abbreviated Farsi translation of *Ivanhoe,* when he knocked on my door.

"What is it?"

"I'm going to the baker to buy *naan,*" he said from the other side. "I was wondering if you … if you wanted to come along."

"I think I'm just going to read," I said, rubbing my temples. Lately, every time Hassan was around, I was getting a headache.

"It's a sunny day," he said. "I can see that."

"Might be fun to go for a walk."

"You go."

"I wish you'd come along," he said. Paused. Something thumped against the door, maybe his forehead. "I don't know what I've done, Amir agha. I wish you'd tell me. I don't know why we don't play anymore."

"You haven't done anything, Hassan. Just go."

"You can tell me, I'll stop doing it."

I buried my head in my lap, squeezed my temples with my knees, like a vice. "I'll tell you what I want you to stop doing," I said, eyes pressed shut.

"Anything."

"I want you to stop harassing me. I want you to go away," I snapped. I wished he would give it right back to me, break the door open and tell me off—it would have made things easier, better. But he didn't do anything like that, and when I opened the door minutes later, he wasn't there. I fell on my bed, buried my head under the pillow, and cried.

HASSAN MILLED ABOUT the periphery of my life after that. I made sure our paths crossed as little as possible, planned my day that way. Because when he was around, the oxygen seeped out of the room. My chest tightened and I couldn't draw enough air; I'd stand there, gasping in my own little airless bubble of atmosphere. But even when he wasn't around, he was. He was there in the hand-washed and ironed clothes on the cane-seat chair, in the warm slippers left outside my door, in the wood already burning in the stove when I came down for breakfast. Everywhere I turned, I saw signs of his loyalty, his goddamn unwavering loyalty.

Early that spring, a few days before the new school year started, Baba and I were planting tulips in the garden. Most of the snow had melted and the hills in the north were already dotted with patches of green grass. It was a cool, gray morning, and Baba was squatting next to me, digging the soil and planting the bulbs I handed to him. He was telling me how most people thought it was better to plant tulips in the fall and how that wasn't true, when I came right out and said it. "Baba, have you ever thought about getting new servants?"

He dropped the tulip bulb and buried the trowel in the dirt. Took off his gardening gloves. I'd startled him. "*Chi?* What did you say?"

"I was just wondering, that's all."

"Why would I ever want to do that?" Baba said curtly.

"You wouldn't, I guess. It was just a question," I said, my voice fading to a murmur. I was already sorry I'd said it.

"Is this about you and Hassan? I know there's something going on between you two, but whatever it is, you have to deal with it, not me. I'm staying out of it."

"I'm sorry, Baba."

He put on his gloves again. "I grew up with Ali," he said through clenched teeth. "My father took him in, he loved Ali like his own son. Forty years Ali's been with my family. Forty goddamn years. And you think I'm just going to throw him out?" He turned to me now, his face as red as a tulip. "I've never laid a hand on you, Amir, but you ever say that again …" He looked away, shaking his head. "You bring me shame. And Hassan … Hassan's not going anywhere, do you understand?"

I looked down and picked up a fistful of cool soil. Let it pour between my fingers.

"I said, Do you understand?" Baba roared.

I flinched. "Yes, Baba."

"Hassan's not going anywhere," Baba snapped. He dug a new hole with the trowel, striking the dirt harder than he had to. "He's staying right here with us, where he belongs. This is his home and we're his family. Don't you ever ask me that question again!"

"I won't, Baba. I'm sorry."

We planted the rest of the tulips in silence.

I was relieved when school started that next week. Students with new notebooks and sharpened pencils in hand ambled about the courtyard, kicking up dust, chatting in groups, waiting for the class captains' whistles. Baba drove down the dirt lane that led to the entrance. The school was an old two-story building with broken windows and dim, cobblestone hallways, patches of its original dull yellow paint still showing between sloughing chunks of plaster. Most of the boys walked to school, and Baba's black Mustang drew more than one envious look. I should have been beaming with pride when he dropped me off—the old me would have—but all I could muster was a mild form of embarrassment. That and emptiness. Baba drove away without saying good-bye.

I bypassed the customary comparing of kite-fighting scars and stood in line. The bell rang and we marched to our assigned class, filed in in pairs. I sat in the back row. As the Farsi teacher handed out our textbooks, I prayed for a heavy load of home-work.

School gave me an excuse to stay in my room for long hours. And, for a while, it took my mind off what had happened that winter, what I had *let* happen. For a few weeks, I preoccupied myself with gravity and momentum, atoms and cells, the An-glo-Afghan wars, instead of thinking about Hassan and what had happened to him. But, always, my mind returned to the alley. To Hassan's brown corduroy pants lying on the bricks. To the droplets of blood staining the snow dark red, almost black.

One sluggish, hazy afternoon early that summer, I asked Has-san to go up the hill with me. Told him I wanted to read him a new story I'd written. He was hanging clothes to dry in the yard and I saw his eagerness in the harried way he finished the job.

We climbed the hill, making small talk. He asked about school, what I was learning, and I talked about my teachers, es-pecially the mean math teacher who punished talkative students by sticking a metal rod between their fingers and then squeezing them together. Hassan winced at that, said he hoped I'd never have to experience it. I said I'd been lucky so far, knowing that luck had nothing to do with it. I had done my share of talking in class too. But my father was rich and everyone knew him, so I was spared the metal rod treatment.

We sat against the low cemetery wall under the shade thrown by the pomegranate tree. In another month or two, crops of scorched yellow weeds would blanket the hillside, but that year the spring showers had lasted longer than usual, nudging their way into early summer, and the grass was still green, peppered with tangles of wildflowers. Below us, Wazir Akbar Khan's whitewalled, flat-topped houses gleamed in the sunshine, the laundry hanging on clotheslines in their yards stirred by the breeze to dance like butterflies.

We had picked a dozen pomegranates from the tree. I unfolded the story I'd brought along, turned to the first page, then put it down. I stood up and picked up an overripe pomegranate that had fallen to the ground.

"What would you do if I hit you with this?" I said, tossing the fruit up and down.

Hassan's smile wilted. He looked older than I'd remembered. No, not older, *old*. Was that possible? Lines had etched into his tanned face and creases framed his eyes, his mouth. I might as well have taken a knife and carved those lines myself.

"What would you do?" I repeated.

The color fell from his face. Next to him, the stapled pages of the story I'd promised to read him fluttered in the breeze. I hurled the pomegranate at him. It struck him in the chest, exploded in a spray of red pulp. Hassan's cry was pregnant with surprise and pain.

"Hit me back!" I snapped. Hassan looked from the stain on

his chest to me.

"Get up! Hit me!" I said. Hassan *did* get up, but he just stood there, looking dazed like a man dragged into the ocean by a riptide when, just a moment ago, he was enjoying a nice stroll on the beach.

I hit him with another pomegranate, in the shoulder this time. The juice splattered his face. "Hit me back!" I spat. "Hit me back, goddamn you!" I wished he would. I wished he'd give me the punishment I craved, so maybe I'd finally sleep at night. Maybe then things could return to how they used to be between us. But Hassan did nothing as I pelted him again and again. "You're a coward!" I said. "Nothing but a goddamn coward!"

I don't know how many times I hit him. All I know is that, when I finally stopped, exhausted and panting, Hassan was smeared in red like he'd been shot by a firing squad. I fell to my knees, tired, spent, frustrated.

Then Hassan *did* pick up a pomegranate. He walked toward me. He opened it and crushed it against his own forehead. "There," he croaked, red dripping down his face like blood. "Are you satisfied? Do you feel better?" He turned around and started down the hill.

I let the tears break free, rocked back and forth on my knees. "What am I going to do with you, Hassan? What am I going to do with you?" But by the time the tears dried up and I trudged down the hill, I knew the answer to that question.

I TURNED THIRTEEN that summer of 1976, Afghanistan's next to last summer of peace and anonymity. Things between

Baba and me were already cooling off again. I think what started it was the stupid comment I'd made the day we were planting tulips, about getting new servants. I regretted saying it—I really did—but I think even if I hadn't, our happy little interlude would have come to an end. Maybe not quite so soon, but it would have. By the end of the summer, the scraping of spoon and fork against the plate had replaced dinner table chatter and Baba had resumed retreating to his study after supper. And closing the door. I'd gone back to thumbing through Hãfez and Khayyám, gnawing my nails down to the cuticles, writing stories. I kept the stories in a stack under my bed, keeping them just in case, though I doubted Baba would ever again ask me to read them to him.

Baba's motto about throwing parties was this: Invite the whole world or it's not a party. I remember scanning over the invitation list a week before my birthday party and not recognizing at least three-quarters of the four hundred–plus Kakas and Khalas who were going to bring me gifts and congratulate me for having lived to thirteen. Then I realized they weren't really coming for me. It was my birthday, but I knew who the real star of the show was.

For days, the house was teeming with Baba's hired help. There was Salahuddin the butcher, who showed up with a calf and two sheep in tow, refusing payment for any of the three. He slaughtered the animals himself in the yard by a poplar tree. "Blood is good for the tree," I remember him saying as the grass around the poplar soaked red. Men I didn't know climbed the oak trees with coils of small electric bulbs and meters of extension cords. Others set up dozens of tables in the yard, spread a tablecloth on each. The night before the big party Baba's friend

Del-Muhammad, who owned a kabob house in Shar-e-Nau, came to the house with his bags of spices. Like the butcher, Del-Muhammad—or Dello, as Baba called him—refused payment for his services. He said Baba had done enough for his family already. It was Rahim Khan who whispered to me, as Dello marinated the meat, that Baba had lent Dello the money to open his restaurant. Baba had refused repayment until Dello had shown up one day in our driveway in a Benz and insisted he wouldn't leave until Baba took his money.

I guess in most ways, or at least in the ways in which parties are judged, my birthday bash was a huge success. I'd never seen the house so packed. Guests with drinks in hand were chatting in the hallways, smoking on the stairs, leaning against doorways. They sat where they found space, on kitchen counters, in the foyer, even under the stairwell. In the backyard, they mingled under the glow of blue, red, and green lights winking in the trees, their faces illuminated by the light of kerosene torches propped everywhere. Baba had had a stage built on the balcony that overlooked the garden and planted speakers throughout the yard. Ahmad Zahir was playing an accordion and singing on the stage over masses of dancing bodies.

I had to greet each of the guests personally—Baba made sure of that; no one was going to gossip the next day about how he'd raised a son with no manners. I kissed hundreds of cheeks, hugged total strangers, thanked them for their gifts. My face ached from the strain of my plastered smile.

I was standing with Baba in the yard near the bar when someone said, "Happy birthday, Amir." It was Assef, with his parents. Assef's father, Mahmood, was a short, lanky sort with dark skin and a narrow face. His mother, Tanya, was a small, nervous woman who smiled and blinked a lot. Assef was standing between the two of them now, grinning, looming over both, his arms resting on their shoulders. He led them toward us, like *he* had brought *them* here. Like he was the parent, and they his children. A wave of dizziness rushed through me. Baba thanked them for coming.

"I picked out your present myself," Assef said. Tanya's face twitched and her eyes flicked from Assef to me. She smiled, unconvincingly, and blinked. I wondered if Baba had noticed.

"Still playing soccer, Assef jan?" Baba said. He'd always wanted me to be friends with Assef.

Assef smiled. It was creepy how genuinely sweet he made it look. "Of course, Kaka jan."

"Right wing, as I recall?"

"Actually, I switched to center forward this year," Assef said. "You get to score more that way. We're playing the Mekro-Rayan team next week. Should be a good match. They have some good players."

Baba nodded. "You know, I played center forward too when I was young."

"I'll bet you still could if you wanted to," Assef said. He favored Baba with a good-natured wink.

Baba returned the wink. "I see your father has taught you his world-famous flattering ways." He elbowed Assef's father, almost knocked the little fellow down. Mahmood's laughter was about as convincing as Tanya's smile, and suddenly I wondered if maybe, on some level, their son frightened them. I tried to fake a smile, but all I could manage was a feeble upturning of the corners of my mouth—my stomach was turning at the sight of my father bonding with Assef.

Assef shifted his eyes to me. "Wali and Kamal are here too. They wouldn't miss your birthday for anything," he said, laughter lurking just beneath the surface. I nodded silently.

"We're thinking about playing a little game of volleyball tomorrow at my house," Assef said. "Maybe you'll join us. Bring Hassan if you want to."

"That sounds fun," Baba said, beaming. "What do you think, Amir?"

"I don't really like volleyball," I muttered. I saw the light wink out of Baba's eyes and an uncomfortable silence followed.

"Sorry, Assef jan," Baba said, shrugging. That stung, his apologizing for me.

"Nay, no harm done," Assef said. "But you have an open invitation, Amir jan. Anyway, I heard you like to read so I brought you a book. One of my favorites." He extended a wrapped birthday gift to me. "Happy birthday."

He was dressed in a cotton shirt and blue slacks, a red silk tie and shiny black loafers. He smelled of cologne and his blond hair was neatly combed back. On the surface, he was the embodiment of every parent's dream, a strong, tall, well-dressed and well–mannered boy with talent and striking looks, not to mention the wit to joke with an adult. But to me, his eyes betrayed him. When I looked into them, the facade faltered, revealed a glimpse of the madness hiding behind them.

"Aren't you going to take it, Amir?" Baba was saying.

"Huh?"

"Your present," he said testily. "Assef jan is giving you a present."

"Oh," I said. I took the box from Assef and lowered my gaze. I wished I could be alone in my room, with my books, away from these people.

"Well?" Baba said.

"What?"

Baba spoke in a low voice, the one he took on whenever I embarrassed him in public. "Aren't you going to thank Assef jan? That was very considerate of him."

I wished Baba would stop calling him that. How often did he call me "Amir jan"? "Thanks," I said. Assef's mother looked at me like she wanted to say something, but she didn't, and I realized that neither of Assef's parents had said a word. Before I could embarrass myself and Baba anymore—but mostly to get away from Assef and his grin—I stepped away. "Thanks for coming," I said.

I squirmed my way through the throng of guests and slipped through the wrought-iron gates. Two houses down from our house, there was a large, barren dirt lot. I'd heard Baba tell Rahim Khan that a judge had bought the land and that an architect was working on the design. For now, the lot was bare, save for dirt, stones, and weeds.

I tore the wrapping paper from Assef's present and tilted the book cover in the moonlight. It was a biography of Hitler. I threw it amid a tangle of weeds.

I leaned against the neighbor's wall, slid down to the ground. I just sat in the dark for a while, knees drawn to my chest, looking up at the stars, waiting for the night to be over.

"Shouldn't you be entertaining your guests?" a familiar voice said. Rahim Khan was walking toward me along the wall.

"They don't need me for that. Baba's there, remember?" I said. The ice in Rahim Khan's drink clinked when he sat next to me. "I didn't know you drank."

"Turns out I do," he said. Elbowed me playfully. "But only on the most important occasions."

I smiled. "Thanks."

He tipped his drink to me and took a sip. He lit a cigarette, one of the unfiltered Pakistani cigarettes he and Baba were always smoking. "Did I ever tell you I was almost married once?"

"Really?" I said, smiling a little at the notion of Rahim Khan getting married. I'd always thought of him as Baba's quiet alter ego, my writing mentor, my pal, the one who never forgot to bring me a souvenir, a *saughat,* when he returned from a trip abroad. But a husband? A father?

He nodded. "It's true. I was eighteen. Her name was Homaira. She was a Hazara, the daughter of our neighbor's servants. She was as beautiful as a *pari,* light brown hair, big hazel eyes ... she had this laugh ... I can still hear it sometimes." He twirled his glass. "We used to meet secretly in my father's apple orchards, always after midnight when everyone had gone to sleep. We'd walk under the trees and I'd hold her hand ... Am I embarrassing you, Amir jan?"

"A little," I said.

"It won't kill you," he said, taking another puff. "Anyway, we had this fantasy. We'd have a great, fancy wedding and invite family and friends from Kabul to Kandahar. I would build us a big house, white with a tiled patio and large windows. We would plant fruit trees in the garden and grow all sorts of flowers, have a lawn for our kids to play on. On Fridays, after *namaz* at the mosque, everyone would get together at our house for lunch and we'd eat in the garden, under cherry trees, drink fresh water from the well. Then tea with candy as we watched our kids play with their cousins ..."

He took a long gulp of his scotch. Coughed. "You should have seen the look on my father's face when I told him. My mother actually fainted. My sisters splashed her face with water. They fanned her and looked at me as if I had slit her throat. My brother Jalal actually went to fetch his hunting rifle before my father stopped him." Rahim Khan barked a bitter laughter. "It was Homaira and me against the world. And I'll tell you this, Amir jan: In the end, the world always wins. That's just the way of things."

"So what happened?"

"That same day, my father put Homaira and her family on a lorry and sent them off to Hazarajat. I never saw her again."

"I'm sorry," I said.

"Probably for the best, though," Rahim Khan said, shrugging. "She would have suffered. My family would have never accepted her as an equal. You don't order someone to polish your shoes one day and call them 'sister' the next." He looked at me. "You know, you can tell me anything you want, Amir jan. Anytime."

"I know," I said uncertainly. He looked at me for a long time, like he was waiting, his black bottomless eyes hinting at an unspoken secret between us. For a moment, I almost did tell him. Almost told him everything, but then what would he think of me? He'd hate me, and rightfully.

"Here." He handed me something. "I almost forgot. Happy birthday." It was a brown leather-bound notebook. I traced my fingers along the gold-colored stitching on the borders. I smelled the leather. "For your stories," he said. I was going to thank him when something exploded and bursts of fire lit up the sky.

"Fireworks!"

We hurried back to the house and found the guests all standing in the yard, looking up to the sky. Kids hooted and screamed with each *crackle* and *whoosh*. People cheered, burst into applause each time flares sizzled and exploded into bouquets of fire. Every few seconds, the backyard lit up in sudden flashes of red, green, and yellow.

In one of those brief bursts of light, I saw something I'll never forget: Hassan serving drinks to Assef and Wali from a silver platter. The light winked out, a hiss and a crackle, then another flicker of orange light: Assef grinning, kneading Hassan in the chest with a knuckle.

Then, mercifully, darkness.

NINE

Sitting in the middle of my room the next morning, I ripped open box after box of presents. I don't know why I even bothered, since I just gave them a joyless glance and pitched them to the corner of the room. The pile was growing there: a Polaroid camera, a transistor radio, an elaborate electric train set—and several sealed envelopes containing cash. I knew I'd never spend the money or listen to the radio, and the electric train would never trundle down its tracks in my room. I didn't want any of it—it was all blood money; Baba would have never thrown me a party like that if I hadn't won the tournament.

Baba gave me two presents. One was sure to become the envy of every kid in the neighborhood: a brand new Schwinn Stingray, the king of all bicycles. Only a handful of kids in all of Kabul owned a new Stingray and now I was one of them. It had high-rise handlebars with black rubber grips and its famous banana seat. The spokes were gold colored and the steel-frame body red, like a candy apple. Or blood. Any other kid would have hopped on the bike immediately and taken it for a full block skid. I might have done the same a few months ago.

"You like it?" Baba said, leaning in the doorway to my room. I gave him a sheepish grin and a quick "Thank you." I wished I could have mustered more.

"We could go for a ride," Baba said. An invitation, but only a halfhearted one.

"Maybe later. I'm a little tired," I said. "Sure," Baba said.

"Baba?"

"Yes?"

"Thanks for the fireworks," I said. A thank-you, but only a halfhearted one.

"Get some rest," Baba said, walking toward his room.

The other present Baba gave me—and he didn't wait around for me to open this one—was a wristwatch. It had a blue face with gold hands in the shape of lightning bolts. I didn't even try it on. I tossed it on the pile of toys in the corner. The only gift I didn't toss on that mound was Rahim Khan's leather-bound notebook. That was the only one that didn't feel like blood money.

I sat on the edge of my bed, turned the notebook in my hands, thought about what Rahim Khan had said about Homaira, how his father's dismissing her had been for the best in the end. *She would have suffered.* Like the times Kaka Homayoun's projector got stuck on the same slide, the same image kept flashing in my mind over and over: Hassan, his head downcast, serving drinks to Assef and Wali. Maybe it *would* be for the best. Lessen his suffering. And mine too. Either way, this much had become clear: One of us had to go.

Later that afternoon, I took the Schwinn for its first and last spin. I pedaled around the block a couple of times and came back. I rolled up the driveway to the backyard where Hassan and

Ali were cleaning up the mess from last night's party. Paper cups, crumpled napkins, and empty bottles of soda littered the yard. Ali was folding chairs, setting them along the wall. He saw me and waved.

"*Salaam,* Ali," I said, waving back.

He held up a finger, asking me to wait, and walked to his living quarters. A moment later, he emerged with something in his hands. "The opportunity never presented itself last night for Hassan and me to give you this," he said, handing me a box. "It's modest and not worthy of you, Amir agha. But we hope you like it still. Happy birthday."

A lump was rising in my throat. "Thank you, Ali," I said. I wished they hadn't bought me anything. I opened the box and found a brand new *Shahnamah,* a hardback with glossy colored illustrations beneath the passages. Here was Ferangis gazing at her newborn son, Kai Khosrau. There was Afrasiyab riding his horse, sword drawn, leading his army. And, of course, Rostam inflicting a mortal wound onto his son, the warrior Sohrab. "It's beautiful," I said.

"Hassan said your copy was old and ragged, and that some of the pages were missing," Ali said. "All the pictures are hand-drawn in this one with pen and ink," he added proudly, eyeing a book neither he nor his son could read.

"It's lovely," I said. And it was. And, I suspected, not inexpensive either. I wanted to tell Ali it was not the book, but *I* who was unworthy. I hopped back on the bicycle. "Thank Hassan for me," I said.

I ended up tossing the book on the heap of gifts in the corner of my room. But my eyes kept going back to it, so I buried it at the bottom. Before I went to bed that night, I asked Baba if he'd seen my new watch anywhere.

THE NEXT MORNING, I waited in my room for Ali to clear the breakfast table in the kitchen. Waited for him to do the dishes, wipe the counters. I looked out my bedroom window and waited until Ali and Hassan went grocery shopping to the bazaar, pushing the empty wheelbarrows in front of them.

Then I took a couple of the envelopes of cash from the pile of gifts and my watch, and tiptoed out. I paused before Baba's study and listened in. He'd been in there all morning, making phone calls. He was talking to someone now, about a shipment of rugs due to arrive next week. I went downstairs, crossed the yard, and entered Ali and Hassan's living quarters by the loquat tree. I lifted Hassan's mattress and planted my new watch and a handful of Afghani bills under it.

I waited another thirty minutes. Then I knocked on Baba's door and told what I hoped would be the last in a long line of shameful lies.

THROUGH MY BEDROOM WINDOW, I watched Ali and Hassan push the wheelbarrows loaded with meat, *naan,* fruit, and vegetables up the driveway. I saw Baba emerge from the house and walk up to Ali. Their mouths moved over words I couldn't hear. Baba pointed to the house and Ali nodded. They separated. Baba came back to the house; Ali followed Hassan to their hut.

A few moments later, Baba knocked on my door. "Come to my office," he said. "We're all going to sit down and settle this thing."

I went to Baba's study, sat in one of the leather sofas. It was thirty minutes or more before Hassan and Ali joined us.

THEY'D BOTH BEEN CRYING; I could tell from their red, puffed-up eyes. They stood before Baba, hand in hand, and I wondered how and when I'd become capable of causing this kind of pain.

Baba came right out and asked. "Did you steal that money? Did you steal Amir's watch, Hassan?"

Hassan's reply was a single word, delivered in a thin, raspy voice: "Yes."

I flinched, like I'd been slapped. My heart sank and I almost blurted out the truth. Then I understood: This was Hassan's final sacrifice for me. If he'd said no, Baba would have believed him because we all knew Hassan never lied. And if Baba believed him, then I'd be the accused; I would have to explain and I would be revealed for what I really was. Baba would never, ever forgive me. And that led to another understanding: Hassan knew. He knew I'd seen everything in that alley, that I'd stood there and done nothing. He knew I had betrayed him and yet he was rescuing me once again, maybe for the last time. I loved him in that moment, loved him more than I'd ever loved anyone, and I wanted to tell them all that *I* was the snake in the grass, the monster in the lake. I wasn't worthy of this sacrifice; I was a liar, a cheat, and a thief. And I *would* have told, except that a part of me was glad. Glad that this would all be over with soon. Baba would dismiss them, there would be some pain, but life would move on. I wanted that, to move on, to forget, to start with a clean slate. I wanted to be able to breathe again.

Except Baba stunned me by saying, "I forgive you."

Forgive? But theft was the one unforgivable sin, the common denominator of all sins. *When you kill a man, you steal a life. You steal his wife's right to a husband, rob his children of a father. When you tell a lie, you steal someone's right to the truth. When you cheat, you steal the right to fairness. There is no act more wretched than stealing.* Hadn't Baba sat me on his lap and said those words to me? Then how could he just forgive Hassan? And if Baba could forgive that, then why couldn't he forgive me for not being the son he'd always wanted? Why—

"We are leaving, Agha sahib," Ali said.

"What?" Baba said, the color draining from his face.

"We can't live here anymore," Ali said.

"But I forgive him, Ali, didn't you hear?" said Baba.

"Life here is impossible for us now, Agha sahib. We're leaving." Ali drew Hassan to him, curled his arm around his son's shoulder. It was a protective gesture and I knew whom Ali was protecting him from. Ali glanced my way and in his cold, unforgiving look, I saw that Hassan had told him. He had told him everything, about what Assef and his friends had done to him, about the kite, about me. Strangely, I was glad that someone knew me for who I really was; I was tired of pretending.

"I don't care about the money or the watch," Baba said, his arms open, palms up. "I don't understand why you're doing this … what do you mean 'impossible'?"

"I'm sorry, Agha sahib, but our bags are already packed. We have made our decision."

Baba stood up, a sheen of grief across his face. "Ali, haven't I provided well for you? Haven't I been good to you and Hassan? You're the brother I never had, Ali, you know that. Please don't do this."

"Don't make this even more difficult than it already is, Agha sahib," Ali said. His mouth twitched and, for a moment, I thought I saw a grimace. That was when I understood the depth of the pain I had caused, the blackness of the grief I had brought onto everyone, that not even Ali's paralyzed face could mask his sorrow. I forced myself to look at Hassan, but his head was downcast, his shoulders slumped, his finger twirling a loose string on the hem of his shirt.

Baba was pleading now. "At least tell me why. I need to know!" Ali didn't tell Baba, just as he didn't protest when Hassan confessed to the stealing. I'll never really know why, but I could imagine the two of them in that dim little hut, weeping, Hassan pleading him not to give me away. But I couldn't imagine the restraint it must have taken Ali to keep that promise.

"Will you drive us to the bus station?"

"I forbid you to do this!" Baba bellowed. "Do you hear me? I forbid you!"

"Respectfully, you can't forbid me anything, Agha sahib," Ali said. "We don't work for you anymore."

"Where will you go?" Baba asked. His voice was breaking.

"Hazarajat."

"To your cousin?"

"Yes. Will you take us to the bus station, Agha sahib?"

Then I saw Baba do something I had never seen him do before: He cried. It scared me a little, seeing a grown man sob. Fathers weren't supposed to cry. "Please," Baba was saying, but Ali had already turned to the door, Hassan trailing him. I'll never forget the way Baba said that, the pain in his plea, the fear.

IN KABUL, it rarely rained in the summer. Blue skies stood tall and far, the sun like a branding iron searing the back of your neck. Creeks where Hassan and I skipped stones all spring turned dry, and rickshaws stirred dust when they sputtered by. People went to mosques for their ten *raka'ts* of noontime prayer and then retreated to whatever shade they could find to nap in, waiting for the cool of early evening. Summer meant long school days sweating in tightly packed, poorly ventilated class-rooms learning to recite *ayat*s from the Koran, struggling with those tongue-twisting, exotic Arabic words. It meant catching flies in your palm while the mullah droned on and a hot breeze brought with it the smell of shit from the outhouse across the schoolyard, churning dust around the lone rickety basketball hoop.

But it rained the afternoon Baba took Ali and Hassan to the bus station. Thunderheads rolled in, painted the sky iron gray. Within minutes, sheets of rain were sweeping in, the steady hiss of falling water swelling in my ears.

Baba had offered to drive them to Bamiyan himself, but Ali refused. Through the blurry, rain-soaked window of my bed-room, I watched Ali haul the lone suitcase carrying all of their belongings to Baba's car idling outside the gates. Hassan lugged his mattress, rolled tightly and tied with a rope, on his back. He'd left all of his toys behind in the empty shack—I discovered them the next day, piled in a corner just like the birthday presents in my room.

Slithering beads of rain sluiced down my window. I saw Baba slam the trunk shut. Already drenched, he walked to the driver's side. Leaned in and said something to Ali in the backseat, perhaps one last-ditch effort to change his mind. They talked that way awhile, Baba getting soaked, stooping, one arm on the roof of the car. But when he straightened, I saw in his slumping shoulders that the life I had known since I'd been born was over. Baba slid in. The headlights came on and cut twin funnels of light in the rain. If this were one of the Hindi movies Hassan and I used to watch, this was the part where I'd run outside, my bare feet splashing rainwater. I'd chase the car, screaming for it to stop. I'd pull Hassan out of the backseat and tell him I was sorry, so sorry, my tears mixing with rainwater. We'd hug in the downpour. But this was no Hindi movie. I *was* sorry, but I didn't cry and I didn't chase the car. I watched Baba's car pull away from the curb, taking with it the person whose first spoken word had been my name. I caught one final blurry glimpse of Hassan slumped in the backseat before Baba turned left at the street corner where we'd played marbles so many times.

I stepped back and all I saw was rain through windowpanes that looked like melting silver.

T E N

March 1981

A young woman sat across from us. She was dressed in an olive green dress with a black shawl wrapped tightly around her face against the night chill. She burst into prayer every time the truck jerked or stumbled into a pothole, her *"Bismillah!"* peaking with each of the truck's shudders and jolts. Her husband, a burly man in baggy pants and sky blue turban, cradled an infant in one arm and thumbed prayer beads with his free hand. His lips moved in silent prayer. There were others, in all about a dozen, including Baba and me, sitting with our suitcases between our legs, cramped with these strangers in the tarpaulin-covered cab of an old Russian truck.

My innards had been roiling since we'd left Kabul just after two in the morning. Baba never said so, but I knew he saw my car sickness as yet another of my array of weakness—I saw it on his embarrassed face the couple of times my stomach had clenched so badly I had moaned. When the burly guy with the beads—the praying woman's husband—asked if I was going to get sick, I said I might. Baba looked away. The man lifted his corner of the tarpaulin cover and rapped on the driver's window, asked him to stop. But the driver, Karim, a scrawny dark-skinned man with hawk-boned features and a pencil-thin mustache, shook his head.

"We are too close to Kabul," he shot back. "Tell him to have a strong stomach."

Baba grumbled something under his breath. I wanted to tell him I was sorry, but suddenly I was salivating, the back of my throat tasting bile. I turned around, lifted the tarpaulin, and threw up over the side of the moving truck. Behind me, Baba was apologizing to the other passengers. As if car sickness was a crime. As if you weren't supposed to get sick when you were eighteen. I threw up two more times before Karim agreed to stop, mostly so I wouldn't stink up his vehicle, the instrument of his livelihood. Karim was a people smuggler—it was a pretty lucrative business then, driving people out of *Shorawi*-occupied Kabul to the relative safety of Pakistan. He was taking us to Jalalabad, about 170 kilometers southeast of Kabul, where his brother, Toor, who had a bigger truck with a second convoy of refugees, was waiting to drive us across the Khyber Pass and into Peshawar.

We were a few kilometers west of Mahipar Falls when Karim pulled to the side of the road. Mahipar—which means "Flying Fish"—was a high summit with a precipitous drop overlooking the hydro plant the Germans had built for Afghanistan back in 1967. Baba and I had driven over the summit countless times on our way to Jalalabad, the city of cypress trees and sugarcane fields where Afghans vacationed in the winter.

I hopped down the back of the truck and lurched to the dusty embankment on the side of the road. My mouth filled with saliva, a sign of the retching that was yet to come. I stumbled to the edge of the cliff overlooking the deep valley that was shrouded in darkness. I stooped, hands on my kneecaps, and waited for the bile. Somewhere, a branch snapped, an owl hooted. The wind, soft and cold, clicked through tree branches and stirred the bushes that sprinkled the slope. And from below, the faint sound of water tumbling through the valley.

Standing on the shoulder of the road, I thought of the way we'd left the house where I'd lived my entire life, as if we were going out for a bite: dishes smeared with *kofta* piled in the kitchen sink; laundry in the wicker basket in the foyer; beds unmade; Baba's business suits hanging in the closet. Tapestries still hung on the walls of the living room and my mother's books still crowded the shelves in Baba's study. The signs of our elopement were subtle: My parents' wedding picture was gone, as was the grainy photograph of my grandfather and King Nader Shah standing over the dead deer. A few items of clothing were missing from the closets. The leather-bound notebook Rahim Khan had given me five years earlier was gone.

In the morning, Jalaluddin—our seventh servant in five years—would probably think we'd gone out for a stroll or a drive. We hadn't told him. You couldn't trust anyone in Kabul anymore—for a fee or under threat, people told on each other, neighbor on neighbor, child on parent, brother on brother, servant on master, friend on friend. I thought of the singer Ahmad Zahir, who had played the accordion at my thirteenth birthday. He had gone for a drive with some friends, and someone had later found his body on the side of the road, a bullet in the back of his head. The *rafiqs*, the comrades, were everywhere and they'd split Kabul into two groups: those who eavesdropped and those who didn't. The tricky part was that no one knew who belonged to which. A casual remark to the tailor while getting fitted for a suit might land you in the dungeons of Polehcharkhi. Complain about the curfew to the butcher and next thing you knew, you were behind bars staring at the muzzle end of a Kalashnikov. Even at the dinner table, in the privacy of their home, people had to speak in a calculated manner—the *rafiqs* were in the classrooms too; they'd taught children to spy on their parents, what to listen for, whom to tell.

What was I doing on this road in the middle of the night? I should have been in bed, under my blanket, a book with dog-eared pages at my side. This had to be a dream. Had to be. Tomorrow morning, I'd wake up, peek out the window: No grim-faced Russian soldiers patrolling the sidewalks, no tanks rolling up and down the streets of my city, their turrets swiveling like accusing fingers, no rubble, no curfews, no Russian Army Personnel Carriers weaving through the bazaars. Then, behind me, I heard Baba and Karim discussing the arrangement in Jalalabad over a smoke. Karim was reassuring Baba that his brother had a big truck of "excellent and first-class quality," and that the trek to Peshawar would be very routine. "He could take you there with his eyes closed," Karim said. I overheard him telling Baba how he and his brother knew the Russian and Afghan soldiers who worked the checkpoints, how they had set up a "mutually profitable" arrangement. This was no dream. As if on cue, a MiG suddenly screamed past overhead. Karim tossed his cigarette and produced a handgun from his waist. Pointing it to the sky and making shooting gestures, he spat and cursed at the MiG.

I wondered where Hassan was. Then the inevitable. I vomited on a tangle of weeds, my retching and groaning drowned in the deafening roar of the MiG.

WE PULLED UP to the checkpoint at Mahipar twenty minutes later. Our driver let the truck idle and hopped down to greet the approaching voices. Feet crushed gravel. Words were exchanged, brief and hushed. A flick of a lighter. *"Spasseba."*

Another flick of the lighter. Someone laughed, a shrill cackling sound that made me jump. Baba's hand clamped down on my thigh. The laughing man broke into song, a slurring, off-key rendition of an old Afghan wedding song, delivered with a thick Russian accent:

> *Ahesta boro, Mah-e-man, ahesta boro.*
> *Go slowly, my lovely moon, go slowly.*

Boot heels clicked on asphalt. Someone flung open the tarpaulin hanging over the back of the truck, and three faces peered in. One was Karim, the other two were soldiers, one Afghan, the other a grinning Russian, face like a bulldog's, cigarette dangling from the side of his mouth. Behind them, a bone-colored moon hung in the sky. Karim and the Afghan soldier had a brief exchange in Pashtu. I caught a little of it—something about Toor and his bad luck. The Russian soldier thrust his face into the rear of the truck. He was humming the wedding song and drumming his finger on the edge of the tailgate. Even in the dim light of the moon, I saw the glazed look in his eyes as they skipped from passenger to passenger. Despite the cold, sweat streamed from his brow. His eyes settled on the young woman wearing the black shawl. He spoke in Russian to

Karim without taking his eyes off her. Karim gave a curt reply in Russian, which the soldier returned with an even curter retort. The Afghan soldier said something too, in a low, reasoning voice. But the Russian soldier shouted something that made the other two flinch. I could feel Baba tightening up next to me. Karim cleared his throat, dropped his head. Said the soldier wanted a half hour with the lady in the back of the truck.

The young woman pulled the shawl down over her face. Burst into tears. The toddler sitting in her husband's lap started crying too. The husband's face had become as pale as the moon hovering above. He told Karim to ask "Mister Soldier Sahib" to show a little mercy, maybe he had a sister or a mother, maybe he had a wife too. The Russian listened to Karim and barked a series of words.

"It's his price for letting us pass," Karim said. He couldn't bring himself to look the husband in the eye.

"But we've paid a fair price already. He's getting paid good money," the husband said.

Karim and the Russian soldier spoke. "He says ... he says every price has a tax."

That was when Baba stood up. It was my turn to clamp a hand on his thigh, but Baba pried it loose, snatched his leg away. When he stood, he eclipsed the moonlight. "I want you to ask this man something," Baba said. He said it to Karim, but looked directly at the Russian officer. "Ask him where his shame is."

They spoke. "He says this is war. There is no shame in war."

"Tell him he's wrong. War doesn't negate decency. It *demands* it, even more than in times of peace."

Do you have to always be the hero? I thought, my heart fluttering. *Can't you just let it go for once?* But I knew he couldn't—it wasn't in his nature. The problem was, his nature was going to get us all killed.

The Russian soldier said something to Karim, a smile creasing his lips. "Agha sahib," Karim said, "these *Roussi* are not like us. They understand nothing about respect, honor."

"What did he say?"

"He says he'll enjoy putting a bullet in you almost as much as ..." Karim trailed off, but nodded his head toward the young woman who had caught the guard's eye. The soldier flicked his unfinished cigarette and unholstered his handgun. *So this is where Baba dies,* I thought. *This is how it's going to happen.* In my head, I said a prayer I had learned in school.

"Tell him I'll take a thousand of his bullets before I let this indecency take place," Baba said. My mind flashed to that winter day six years ago. Me, peering around the corner in the alley. Kamal and Wali holding Hassan down. Assef's buttock muscles clenching and unclenching, his hips thrusting back and forth. Some hero I had been, fretting about the kite. Sometimes, I too wondered if I was really Baba's son.

The bulldog-faced Russian raised his gun.

"Baba, sit down please," I said, tugging at his sleeve. "I think he really means to shoot you."

Baba slapped my hand away. "Haven't I taught you anything?" he snapped. He turned to the grinning soldier. "Tell him he'd better kill me good with that first shot. Because if I don't go down, I'm tearing him to pieces, goddamn his father!"

The Russian soldier's grin never faltered when he heard the translation. He clicked the safety on the gun. Pointed the barrel to Baba's chest. Heart pounding in my throat, I buried my face in my hands.

The gun roared.

It's done, then. I'm eighteen and alone. I have no one left in the world. Baba's dead and now I have to bury him. Where do I bury him? Where do I go after that?

But the whirlwind of half thoughts spinning in my head came to a halt when I cracked my eyelids, found Baba still standing. I saw a second Russian officer with the others. It was from the muzzle of his upturned gun that smoke swirled. The soldier who had meant to shoot Baba had already holstered his weapon. He was shuffling his feet. I had never felt more like crying and laughing at the same time.

The second Russian officer, gray-haired and heavyset, spoke to us in broken Farsi. He apologized for his comrade's behavior. "Russia sends them here to fight," he said. "But they are just boys, and when they come here, they find the pleasure of drug." He gave the younger officer the rueful look of a father exasperated with his misbehaving son. "This one is attached to drug now. I try to stop him …" He waved us off.

Moments later, we were pulling away. I heard a laugh and then the first soldier's voice, slurry and off-key, singing the old wedding song.

WE RODE IN SILENCE for about fifteen minutes before the young woman's husband suddenly stood and did something I'd seen many others do before him: He kissed Baba's hand.

TOOR'S BAD LUCK. Hadn't I overheard that in a snippet of

conversation back at Mahipar?

We rolled into Jalalabad about an hour before sunrise. Karim ushered us quickly from the truck into a one-story house at the intersection of two dirt roads lined with flat one-story homes, acacia trees, and closed shops. I pulled the collar of my coat against the chill as we hurried into the house, dragging our belongings. For some reason, I remember smelling radishes.

Once he had us inside the dimly lit, bare living room, Karim locked the front door, pulled the tattered sheets that passed for curtains. Then he took a deep breath and gave us the bad news: His brother Toor couldn't take us to Peshawar. It seemed his truck's engine had blown the week before and Toor was still waiting for parts.

"*Last* week?" someone exclaimed. "If you knew this, why did you bring us here?"

I caught a flurry of movement out of the corner of my eye. Then a blur of something zipping across the room, and the next thing I saw was Karim slammed against the wall, his sandaled feet dangling two feet above the floor. Wrapped around his neck were Baba's hands.

"I'll tell you why," Baba snapped. "Because he got paid for his leg of the trip. That's all he cared about." Karim was making guttural choking sounds. Spittle dripped from the corner of his mouth.

"Put him down, Agha, you're killing him," one of the passengers said.

"It's what I intend to do," Baba said. What none of the others in the room knew was that Baba wasn't joking. Karim was turning red and kicking his legs. Baba kept choking him until the young mother, the one the Russian officer had fancied, begged him to stop.

Karim collapsed on the floor and rolled around fighting for air when Baba finally let go. The room fell silent. Less than two hours ago, Baba had volunteered to take a bullet for the honor of a woman he didn't even know. Now he'd almost choked a man to death, would have done it cheerfully if not for the pleas of that same woman.

Something thumped next door. No, not next door, below.

"What's that?" someone asked.

"The others," Karim panted between labored breaths. "In the basement."

"How long have they been waiting?" Baba said, standing over Karim.

"Two weeks."

"I thought you said the truck broke down last week."

Karim rubbed his throat. "It might have been the week before," he croaked.

"How long?"

"What?"

"How long for the parts?" Baba roared. Karim flinched but said nothing. I was glad for the darkness. I didn't want to see the murderous look on Baba's face.

THE STENCH OF SOMETHING DANK, like mildew, bludgeoned my nostrils the moment Karim opened the door that led down the creaky steps to the basement. We descended in single file. The steps groaned under Baba's weight. Standing in the cold basement, I felt watched by eyes blinking in the dark. I saw shapes huddled around the room, their silhouettes thrown on the walls by the dim light of a pair of kerosene lamps. A low murmur buzzed through the basement, beneath it the sound of water drops trickling somewhere, and, something else, a scratching sound.

Baba sighed behind me and dropped the bags.

Karim told us it should be a matter of a couple of short days before the truck was fixed. Then we'd be on our way to Peshawar. On to freedom. On to safety.

The basement was our home for the next week and, by the third night, I discovered the source of the scratching sounds. Rats.

ONCE MY EYES ADJUSTED to the dark, I counted about thirty refugees in that basement. We sat shoulder to shoulder along the walls, ate crackers, bread with dates, apples. That first night, all the men prayed together. One of the refugees asked Baba why he wasn't joining them. "God is going to save us all. Why don't you pray to him?"

Baba snorted a pinch of his snuff. Stretched his legs. "What'll save us is eight cylinders and a good carburetor." That silenced the rest of them for good about the matter of God.

It was later that first night when I discovered that two of the people hiding with us were Kamal and his father. That was shocking enough, seeing Kamal sitting in the basement just a few feet away from me. But when he and his father came over to our side of the room and I saw Kamal's face, *really* saw it …

He had withered—there was simply no other word for it. His eyes gave me a hollow look and no recognition at all registered in them. His shoulders hunched and his cheeks sagged like they were too tired to cling to the bone beneath. His father, who'd owned a movie theater in Kabul, was telling Baba how, three months before, a stray bullet had struck his wife in the temple and killed her. Then he told Baba about Kamal. I caught only snippets of it: *Should have never let him go alone ... always so handsome, you know ... four of them ... tried to fight ... God ... took him ... bleeding down there ... his pants ... doesn't talk anymore ... just stares ...*

THERE WOULD BE NO TRUCK, Karim told us after we'd spent a week in the rat-infested basement. The truck was beyond repair.

"There is another option," Karim said, his voice rising amid the groans. His cousin owned a fuel truck and had smuggled people with it a couple of times. He was here in Jalalabad and could probably fit us all.

Everyone except an elderly couple decided to go.

We left that night, Baba and I, Kamal and his father, the others. Karim and his cousin, a square-faced balding man named Aziz, helped us get into the fuel tank. One by one, we mounted the idling truck's rear deck, climbed the rear access ladder, and slid down into the tank. I remember Baba climbed halfway up the ladder, hopped back down and fished the snuffbox from his pocket. He emptied the box and picked up a handful of dirt from the middle of the unpaved road. He kissed the dirt. Poured it into the box. Stowed the box in his breast pocket, next to his heart.

PANIC.

You open your mouth. Open it so wide your jaws creak. You order your lungs to draw air, NOW, you need air, need it NOW. But your airways ignore you. They collapse, tighten, squeeze, and suddenly you're breathing through a drinking straw. Your mouth closes and your lips purse and all you can manage is a strangled croak. Your hands wriggle and shake. Somewhere a dam has cracked open and a flood of cold sweat spills, drenches your body. You want to scream. You would if you could. But you have to breathe to scream.

Panic.

The basement had been dark. The fuel tank was pitch-black. I looked right, left, up, down, waved my hands before my eyes, didn't see so much as a hint of movement. I blinked, blinked again. Nothing at all. The air wasn't right, it was too thick, almost solid. Air wasn't supposed to be solid. I wanted to reach out with my hands, crush the air into little pieces, stuff them down my windpipe. And the stench of gasoline. My eyes stung from the fumes, like someone had peeled my lids back and rubbed a lemon on them. My nose caught fire with each breath. You could die in a place like this, I thought. A scream was coming. Coming, coming …

And then a small miracle. Baba tugged at my sleeve and something glowed green in the dark. Light! Baba's wristwatch. I kept my eyes glued to those fluorescent green hands. I was so afraid I'd lose them, I didn't dare blink.

Slowly I became aware of my surroundings. I heard groans and muttered prayers. I heard a baby cry, its mother's muted soothing. Someone retched. Someone else cursed the *Shorawi*. The truck bounced side to side, up and down. Heads banged against metal.

"Think of something good," Baba said in my ear. "Something happy."

Something good. Something happy. I let my mind wander. I let it come:

Friday afternoon in Paghman. An open field of grass speckled with mulberry trees in blossom. Hassan and I stand ankle-deep in untamed grass, I am tugging on the line, the spool spinning in Hassan's calloused hands, our eyes turned up to the kite in the sky. Not a word passes between us, not because we have nothing to say, but because we don't have to say anything—that's how it is between people who are each other's first memories, people who have fed from the same breast. A breeze stirs the grass and Hassan lets the spool roll. The kite spins, dips, steadies. Our twin shadows dance on the rippling grass. From somewhere over the low brick wall at the other end of the field, we hear chatter and laughter and the chirping of a water fountain. And music, something old and familiar, I think it's *Ya Mowlah* on *rubab* strings. Someone calls our names over the wall, says it's time for tea and cake.

I didn't remember what month that was, or what year even. I only knew the memory lived in me, a perfectly encapsulated morsel of a good past, a brushstroke of color on the gray, barren canvas that our lives had become.

THE REST OF THAT RIDE IS scattered bits and pieces of memory that come and go, most of it sounds and smells: MiGs roaring past overhead; staccatos of gunfire; a donkey braying nearby; the jingling of bells and mewling of sheep; gravel crushed under the truck's tires; a baby wailing in the dark; the stench of gasoline, vomit, and shit.

What I remember next is the blinding light of early morning as I climbed out of the fuel tank. I remember turning my face up to the sky, squinting, breathing like the world was running out of air. I lay on the side of the dirt road next to a rocky trench, looked up to the gray morning sky, thankful for air, thankful for light, thankful to be alive.

"We're in Pakistan, Amir," Baba said. He was standing over me. "Karim says he will call for a bus to take us to Peshawar."

I rolled onto my chest, still lying on the cool dirt, and saw our suitcases on either side of Baba's feet. Through the upside down *V* between his legs, I saw the truck idling on the side of the road, the other refugees climbing down the rear ladder. Beyond that, the dirt road unrolled through fields that were like leaden sheets under the gray sky and disappeared behind a line of bowl-shaped hills. Along the way, it passed a small village strung out atop a sunbaked slope.

My eyes returned to our suitcases. They made me sad for Baba. After everything he'd built, planned, fought for, fretted over, dreamed of, this was the summation of his life: one disappointing son and two suitcases.

Someone was screaming. No, not screaming. Wailing. I saw the passengers huddled in a circle, heard their urgent voices. Someone said the word "fumes." Someone else said it too. The wail turned into a throat-ripping screech.

Baba and I hurried to the pack of onlookers and pushed our way through them. Kamal's father was sitting cross-legged in the center of the circle, rocking back and forth, kissing his son's ashen face.

"He won't breathe! My boy won't breathe!" he was crying. Kamal's lifeless body lay on his father's lap. His right hand, uncurled and limp, bounced to the rhythm of his father's sobs. "My boy! He won't breathe! Allah, help him breathe!"

Baba knelt beside him and curled an arm around his shoulder. But Kamal's father shoved him away and lunged for Karim who was standing nearby with his cousin. What happened next was too fast and too short to be called a scuffle. Karim uttered a surprised cry and backpedaled. I saw an arm swing, a leg kick. A moment later, Kamal's father was standing with Karim's gun in his hand.

"Don't shoot me!" Karim cried.

But before any of us could say or do a thing, Kamal's father shoved the barrel in his own mouth. I'll never forget the echo of that blast. Or the flash of light and the spray of red.

I doubled over again and dry-heaved on the side of the road.

ELEVEN

Fremont, California. 1980s

Baba loved the *idea* of America.

It was living in America that gave him an ulcer.

I remember the two of us walking through Lake Elizabeth Park in Fremont, a few streets down from our apartment, and watching boys at batting practice, little girls giggling on the swings in the playground. Baba would enlighten me with his politics during those walks with long-winded dissertations. "There are only three real men in this world, Amir," he'd say. He'd count them off on his fingers: America the brash savior, Britain, and Israel. "The rest of them—" he used to wave his hand and make a *phht* sound "—they're like gossiping old women."

The bit about Israel used to draw the ire of Afghans in Fremont who accused him of being proJewish and, de facto, anti-Islam. Baba would meet them for tea and *rowt* cake at the park, drive them crazy with his politics. "What they don't understand," he'd tell me later, "is that religion has nothing to do with it." In Baba's view, Israel was an island of "real men" in a sea of Arabs too busy getting fat off their oil to care for their own. "Israel does this, Israel does that," Baba would say in a mock-Arabic accent. "Then do something about it! Take action. You're Arabs, help the Palestinians, then!"

He loathed Jimmy Carter, whom he called a "big-toothed cretin." In 1980, when we were still in Kabul, the U.S. announced it would be boycotting the Olympic Games in Moscow. *"Wah wah!"* Baba exclaimed with disgust. "Brezhnev is massacring Afghans and all that peanut eater can say is I won't come swim in your pool." Baba believed Carter had unwittingly done more for communism than Leonid Brezhnev. "He's not fit to run this country. It's like putting a boy who can't ride a bike behind the wheel of a brand new Cadillac." What America and the world needed was a hard man. A man to be reckoned with, someone who took action instead of wringing his hands. That someone came in the form of Ronald Reagan. And when Reagan went on TV and called the *Shorawi* "the Evil Empire," Baba went out and bought a picture of the grinning president giving a thumbs up. He framed the picture and hung it in our hallway, nailing it right next to the old black-and-white of himself in his thin necktie shaking hands with King Zahir Shah. Most of our neighbors in Fremont were bus drivers, policemen, gas station attendants, and unwed mothers collecting welfare, exactly the sort of blue-collar people who would soon suffocate under the pillow Reganomics pressed to their faces. Baba was the lone Republican in our building.

But the Bay Area's smog stung his eyes, the traffic noise gave him headaches, and the pollen made him cough. The fruit was never sweet enough, the water never clean enough, and where were all the trees and open fields? For two years, I tried to get

Baba to enroll in ESL classes to improve his broken English. But he scoffed at the idea. "Maybe I'll spell 'cat' and the teacher will give me a glittery little star so I can run home and show it off to you," he'd grumble.

One Sunday in the spring of 1983, I walked into a small bookstore that sold used paperbacks, next to the Indian movie theater just west of where Amtrak crossed Fremont Boulevard. I told Baba I'd be out in five minutes and he shrugged. He had been working at a gas station in Fremont and had the day off. I watched him jaywalk across Fremont Boulevard and enter Fast & Easy, a little grocery store run by an elderly Vietnamese couple, Mr. and Mrs. Nguyen. They were gray-haired, friendly people; she had Parkinson's, he'd had his hip replaced. "He's like Six Million Dollar Man now," she always said to me, laughing toothlessly. "Remember Six Million Dollar Man, Amir?" Then Mr. Nguyen would scowl like Lee Majors, pretend he was running in slow motion.

I was flipping through a worn copy of a Mike Hammer mystery when I heard screaming and glass breaking. I dropped the book and hurried across the street. I found the Nguyens behind the counter, all the way against the wall, faces ashen, Mr. Nguyen's arms wrapped around his wife. On the floor: oranges, an overturned magazine rack, a broken jar of beef jerky, and shards of glass at Baba's feet.

It turned out that Baba had had no cash on him for the oranges. He'd written Mr. Nguyen a check and Mr. Nguyen had asked for an ID. "He wants to see my license," Baba bellowed in Farsi. "Almost two years we've bought his damn fruits and put money in his pocket and the son of a dog wants to see my license!"

"Baba, it's not personal," I said, smiling at the Nguyens. "They're supposed to ask for an ID."

"I don't want you here," Mr. Nguyen said, stepping in front of his wife. He was pointing at Baba with his cane. He turned to me.

"You're nice young man but your father, he's crazy. Not welcome anymore."

"Does he think I'm a thief?" Baba said, his voice rising. People had gathered outside. They were staring. "What kind of a country is this? No one trusts anybody!"

"I call police," Mrs. Nguyen said, poking out her face. "You get out or I call police."

"Please, Mrs. Nguyen, don't call the police. I'll take him home. Just don't call the police, okay? Please?"

"Yes, you take him home. Good idea," Mr. Nguyen said. His eyes, behind his wire-rimmed bifocals, never left Baba. I led Baba through the doors. He kicked a magazine on his way out. After I'd made him promise he wouldn't go back in, I returned to the store and apologized to the Nguyens. Told them my father was going through a difficult time. I gave Mrs. Nguyen our telephone number and address, and told her to get an estimate for the damages. "Please call me as soon as you know. I'll pay for everything, Mrs. Nguyen. I'm so sorry." Mrs. Nguyen took the sheet of paper from me and nodded. I saw her hands were shaking more than usual, and that made me angry at Baba, his causing an old woman to shake like that.

"My father is still adjusting to life in America," I said, by way of explanation.

I wanted to tell them that, in Kabul, we snapped a tree branch and used it as a credit card. Hassan and I would take the wooden stick to the bread maker. He'd carve notches on our stick with his knife, one notch for each loaf of *naan* he'd pull for us from the *tandoor*'s roaring flames. At the end of the month, my father paid him for the number of notches on the stick. That was it. No questions. No ID.

But I didn't tell them. I thanked Mr. Nguyen for not calling the cops. Took Baba home. He sulked and smoked on the balcony while I made rice with chicken neck stew. A year and a half since we'd stepped off the Boeing from Peshawar, and Baba was still adjusting.

We ate in silence that night. After two bites, Baba pushed away his plate.

I glanced at him across the table, his nails chipped and black with engine oil, his knuckles scraped, the smells of the gas station—dust, sweat, and gasoline—on his clothes. Baba was like the widower who remarries but can't let go of his dead wife. He missed the sugarcane fields of Jalalabad and the gardens of Paghman. He missed people milling in and out of his house, missed walking down the bustling aisles of Shor Bazaar and greeting people who knew him and his father, knew his grandfather, people who shared ancestors with him, whose pasts intertwined with his.

For me, America was a place to bury my memories. For Baba, a place to mourn his.

"Maybe we should go back to Peshawar," I said, watching the ice float in my glass of water. We'd spent six months in Peshawar waiting for the INS to issue our visas. Our grimy one-bedroom apartment smelled like dirty socks and cat droppings, but we were surrounded by people we knew—at least people Baba knew. He'd invite the entire corridor of neighbors for dinner, most of them Afghans waiting for visas. Inevitably, someone would bring a set of tabla and someone else a harmonium. Tea would brew, and whoever had a passing singing voice would sing until the sun rose, the mosquitoes stopped buzzing, and clapping hands grew sore.

"You were happier there, Baba. It was more like home," I said.

"Peshawar was good for me. Not good for you."

"You work so hard here."

"It's not so bad now," he said, meaning since he had become the day manager at the gas station. But I'd seen the way he winced and rubbed his wrists on damp days. The way sweat erupted on his forehead as he reached for his bottle of antacids after meals. "Besides, I didn't bring us here for me, did I?"

I reached across the table and put my hand on his. My student hand, clean and soft, on his laborer's hand, grubby and calloused. I thought of all the trucks, train sets, and bikes he'd bought me in Kabul. Now America. One last gift for Amir.

Just one month after we arrived in the U.S., Baba found a job off Washington Boulevard as an assistant at a gas station owned by an Afghan acquaintance—he'd started looking for work the same week we arrived. Six days a week, Baba pulled twelve-hour shifts pumping gas, running the register, changing oil, and washing windshields. I'd bring him lunch sometimes and find him looking for a pack of cigarettes on the shelves, a customer waiting on the other side of the oil-stained counter, Baba's face drawn and pale under the bright fluorescent lights. The electronic bell over the door would *ding-dong* when I walked in, and Baba would look over his shoulder, wave, and smile, his eyes watering from fatigue. The same day he was hired, Baba and I went to our eligibility officer in San Jose, Mrs. Dobbins.

She was an overweight black woman with twinkling eyes and a dimpled smile. She'd told me once that she sang in church, and I believed her—she had a voice that made me think of warm milk and honey. Baba dropped the stack of food stamps on her desk. "Thank you but I don't want," Baba said. "I work always. In Afghanistan I work, in America I work. Thank you very much, Mrs. Dobbins, but I don't like it free money."

Mrs. Dobbins blinked. Picked up the food stamps, looked from me to Baba like we were pulling a prank, or "slipping her a trick" as Hassan used to say. "Fifteen years I been doin' this job and nobody's ever done this," she said. And that was how Baba ended those humiliating food stamp moments at the cash register and alleviated one of his greatest fears: that an Afghan would see him buying food with charity money. Baba walked out of the welfare office like a man cured of a tumor.

THAT SUMMER OF 1983, I graduated from high school at the age of twenty, by far the oldest senior tossing his mortarboard on the football field that day. I remember losing Baba in the swarm of families, flashing cameras, and blue gowns. I found him near the twenty-yard line, hands shoved in his pockets, camera dangling on his chest. He disappeared and reappeared behind the people moving between us: squealing blue-clad girls hugging, crying, boys high-fiving their fathers, each other. Baba's beard was graying, his hair thinning at the temples, and hadn't he been taller in Kabul? He was wearing his brown suit—his only suit, the same one he wore to Afghan weddings and funerals—and the red tie I had bought for his fiftieth birthday that year. Then he saw me and waved. Smiled. He motioned for me to wear my mortarboard, and took a picture of me with the school's clock tower in the background. I smiled for him—in a way, this was his day more than mine. He walked to me, curled his arm around my neck, and gave my brow a single kiss. "I am *moftakhir*, Amir," he said. Proud. His eyes gleamed when he said that and I liked being on the receiving end of that look.

He took me to an Afghan kabob house in Hayward that night and ordered far too much food. He told the owner that his son was going to college in the fall. I had debated him briefly about that just before graduation, and told him I wanted to get a job. Help out, save some money, maybe go to college the following year. But he had shot me one of his smoldering Baba looks, and the words had vaporized on my tongue.

After dinner, Baba took me to a bar across the street from the restaurant. The place was dim, and the acrid smell of beer I'd always disliked permeated the walls. Men in baseball caps and tank tops played pool, clouds of cigarette smoke hovering over the green tables, swirling in the fluorescent light. We drew looks, Baba in his brown suit and me in pleated slacks and sports jacket. We took a seat at the bar, next to an old man, his leathery face sickly in the blue glow of the Michelob sign overhead. Baba lit a cigarette and ordered us beers. "Tonight I am too much happy," he announced to no one and everyone. "Tonight I drinking with my son. And one, please, for my friend," he said, patting the old man on the back. The old fellow tipped his hat and smiled. He had no upper teeth.

Baba finished his beer in three gulps and ordered another. He had three before I forced myself to drink a quarter of mine. By then he had bought the old man a scotch and treated a foursome of pool players to a pitcher of Budweiser. Men shook his hand and clapped him on the back. They drank to him. Someone lit his cigarette. Baba loosened his tie and gave the old man a handful of quarters. He pointed to the jukebox. "Tell him to play his favorite songs," he said to me. The old man nodded and gave Baba a salute. Soon, country music was blaring, and, just like that, Baba had started a party.

At one point, Baba stood, raised his beer, spilling it on the sawdust floor, and yelled, "Fuck the Russia!" The bar's laughter, then its full-throated echo followed. Baba bought another round of pitchers for everyone.

When we left, everyone was sad to see him go. Kabul, Peshawar, Hayward. Same old Baba, I thought, smiling.

I drove us home in Baba's old, ochre yellow Buick Century. Baba dozed off on the way, snoring like a jackhammer. I smelled tobacco on him and alcohol, sweet and pungent. But he sat up when I stopped the car and said in a hoarse voice, "Keep driving to the end of the block."

"Why, Baba?"

"Just go." He had me park at the south end of the street. He reached in his coat pocket and handed me a set of keys. "There," he said, pointing to the car in front of us. It was an old model Ford, long and wide, a dark color I couldn't discern in the moonlight. "It needs painting, and I'll have one of the guys at the station put in new shocks, but it runs."

I took the keys, stunned. I looked from him to the car.

"You'll need it to go to college," he said.

I took his hand in mine. Squeezed it. My eyes were tearing over and I was glad for the shadows that hid our faces. "Thank you, Baba."

We got out and sat inside the Ford. It was a Grand Torino.

Navy blue, Baba said. I drove it around the block, testing the brakes, the radio, the turn signals. I parked it in the lot of our apartment building and shut off the engine. *"Tashakor,* Baba jan," I said. I wanted to say more, tell him how touched I was by his act of kindness, how much I appreciated all that he had done for me, all that he was still doing. But I knew I'd embarrass him. *"Tashakor,"* I repeated instead.

He smiled and leaned back against the headrest, his forehead almost touching the ceiling. We didn't say anything. Just sat in the dark, listened to the *tink-tink* of the engine cooling, the wail of a siren in the distance. Then Baba rolled his head toward me. "I wish Hassan had been with us today," he said.

A pair of steel hands closed around my windpipe at the sound of Hassan's name. I rolled down the window. Waited for the steel hands to loosen their grip.

I WOULD ENROLL in junior college classes in the fall, I told Baba the day after graduation. He was drinking cold black tea and chewing cardamom seeds, his personal trusted antidote for hangover headaches.

"I think I'll major in English," I said. I winced inside, waiting for his reply.

"English?"

"Creative writing."

He considered this. Sipped his tea. "Stories, you mean. You'll make up stories." I looked down at my feet.

"They pay for that, making up stories?"

"If you're good," I said. "And if you get discovered."

"How likely is that, getting discovered?"

"It happens," I said.

He nodded. "And what will you do while you wait to get good and get discovered? How will you earn money? If you marry, how will you support your *khanum*?"

I couldn't lift my eyes to meet his. "I'll ... find a job."

"Oh," he said. "*Wah wah!* So, if I understand, you'll study several years to earn a degree, then you'll get a *chatti* job like mine, one you could just as easily land today, on the small chance that your degree might someday help you get ... discovered." He took a deep breath and sipped his tea. Grunted something about medical school, law school, and "real work."

My cheeks burned and guilt coursed through me, the guilt of indulging myself at the expense of his ulcer, his black fingernails and aching wrists. But I would stand my ground, I decided. I didn't want to sacrifice for Baba anymore. The last time I had done that, I had damned myself.

Baba sighed and, this time, tossed a whole handful of cardamom seeds in his mouth.

SOMETIMES, I got behind the wheel of my Ford, rolled down the windows, and drove for hours, from the East Bay to the South Bay, up the Peninsula and back. I drove through the grids of cottonwood-lined streets in our Fremont neighborhood, where people who'd never shaken hands with kings lived in shabby, flat one-story houses with barred windows, where old cars like mine dripped oil on blacktop driveways. Pencil gray chain-link fences closed off the backyards in our neighborhood. Toys, bald tires, and beer bottles with peeling labels littered unkempt front lawns. I drove past tree-shaded parks that smelled like bark, past strip malls big enough to hold five simultaneous *Buzkashi* tournaments. I drove the Torino up the hills of Los Altos, idling past estates with picture windows and silver lions guarding the wrought-iron gates, homes with cherub fountains lining the manicured walkways and no Ford Torinos in the driveways. Homes that made Baba's house in Wazir Akbar Khan look like a servant's hut.

I'd get up early some Saturday mornings and drive south on Highway 17, push the Ford up the winding road through the mountains to Santa Cruz. I would park by the old lighthouse and wait for sunrise, sit in my car and watch the fog rolling in from the sea. In Afghanistan, I had only seen the ocean at the cinema. Sitting in the dark next to Hassan, I had always wondered if it was true what I'd read, that sea air smelled like salt. I used to tell Hassan that someday we'd walk on a strip of seaweed-strewn beach, sink our feet in the sand, and watch the water recede from our toes. The first time I saw the Pacific, I almost cried. It was as vast and blue as the oceans on the movie screens of my childhood.

Sometimes in the early evening, I parked the car and walked up a freeway overpass. My face pressed against the fence, I'd try to count the blinking red taillights inching along, stretching as far as my eyes could see. BMWs. Saabs. Porsches. Cars I'd never seen in Kabul, where most people drove Russian Volgas, old Opels, or Iranian Paikans.

Almost two years had passed since we had arrived in the U.S., and I was still marveling at the size of this country, its vastness. Beyond every freeway lay another freeway, beyond every city another city, hills beyond mountains and mountains beyond hills, and, beyond those, more cities and more people.

Long before the *Roussi* army marched into Afghanistan, long before villages were burned and schools destroyed, long before mines were planted like seeds of death and children buried in rock-piled graves, Kabul had become a city of ghosts for me. A city of harelipped ghosts.

America was different. America was a river, roaring along, unmindful of the past. I could wade into this river, let my sins drown to the bottom, let the waters carry me someplace far. Someplace with no ghosts, no memories, and no sins.

If for nothing else, for that, I embraced America.

THE FOLLOWING SUMMER, THE SUMMER of 1984— the summer I turned twenty-one—Baba sold his Buick and bought a dilap-idated '71 Volkswagen bus for $550 from an old Afghan acquaintance who'd been a high-school science teacher in Kabul. The neighbors' heads turned the afternoon the bus sputtered up the street and farted its way across our lot. Baba killed the engine and let the bus roll silently into our designated spot. We sank in our seats, laughed until tears rolled down our cheeks, and, more important, until we were sure the neighbors weren't watching anymore. The bus was a sad carcass of rusted metal, shattered windows replaced with black garbage bags, bald-ing tires, and upholstery shredded down to the springs. But the old teacher had reassured Baba that the engine and transmission were sound and, on that account, the man hadn't lied.

On Saturdays, Baba woke me up at dawn. As he dressed, I scanned the classifieds in the local papers and circled the garage sale ads. We mapped our route—Fremont, Union City, Newark, and Hayward first, then San Jose, Milpitas, Sunnyvale, and

Campbell if time permitted. Baba drove the bus, sipping hot tea from the thermos, and I navigated. We stopped at garage sales and bought knickknacks that people no longer wanted. We haggled over old sewing machines, one-eyed Barbie dolls, wooden tennis rackets, guitars with missing strings, and old Electrolux vacuum cleaners. By midafternoon, we'd filled the back of the VW bus with used goods. Then early Sunday mornings, we drove to the San Jose flea market off Berryessa, rented a spot, and sold the junk for a small profit: a Chicago record that we'd bought for a quarter the day before might go for $1, or $4 for a set of five; a ramshackle Singer sewing machine purchased for $10 might, after some bargaining, bring in $25.

By that summer, Afghan families were working an entire section of the San Jose flea market. Afghan music played in the aisles of the Used Goods section. There was an unspoken code of behavior among Afghans at the flea market: You greeted the guy across the aisle, you invited him for a bite of potato *bolani* or a little *qabuli,* and you chatted. You offered *tassali,* condolences, for the death of a parent, congratulated the birth of children, and shook your head mournfully when the conversation turned to Afghanistan and the *Roussis*—which it inevitably did. But you avoided the topic of Saturday. Because it might turn out that the fellow across the isle was the guy you'd nearly blindsided at the freeway exit yesterday in order to beat him to a promising garage sale.

The only thing that flowed more than tea in those aisles was Afghan gossip. The flea market was where you sipped green tea with almond *kolchas,* and learned whose daughter had broken off an engagement and run off with her American boyfriend, who used to be *Parchami*—a communist—in Kabul, and who had bought a house with under-the-table money while still on welfare. Tea, Politics, and Scandal, the ingredients of an Afghan Sunday at the flea market.

I ran the stand sometimes as Baba sauntered down the aisle, hands respectfully pressed to his chest, greeting people he knew from Kabul: mechanics and tailors selling hand-me-down wool coats and scraped bicycle helmets, alongside former ambassadors, out-of-work surgeons, and university professors.

One early Sunday morning in July 1984, while Baba set up, I bought two cups of coffee from the concession stand and returned to find Baba talking to an older, distinguished-looking man. I put the cups on the rear bumper of the bus, next to the REAGAN/BUSH FOR '84 sticker.

"Amir," Baba said, motioning me over, "this is General Sahib, Mr. Iqbal Taheri. He was a decorated general in Kabul. He worked for the Ministry of Defense."

Taheri. Why did the name sound familiar?

The general laughed like a man used to attending formal parties where he'd laughed on cue at the minor jokes of important people. He had wispy silver-gray hair combed back from his smooth, tanned forehead, and tufts of white in his bushy eyebrows. He smelled like cologne and wore an iron-gray three-piece suit, shiny from too many pressings; the gold chain of a pocket watch dangled from his vest.

"Such a lofty introduction," he said, his voice deep and cultured. *"Salaam, bachem."* Hello, my child.

"Salaam, General Sahib," I said, shaking his hand. His thin hands belied a firm grip, as if steel hid beneath the moisturized skin.

"Amir is going to be a great writer," Baba said. I did a double take at this. "He has finished his first year of college and earned

A's in all of his courses."

"Junior college," I corrected him.

"Mashallah," General Taheri said. "Will you be writing about our country, history perhaps? Economics?"

"I write fiction," I said, thinking of the dozen or so short stories I had written in the leather-bound notebook Rahim Khan had given me, wondering why I was suddenly embarrassed by them in this man's presence.

"Ah, a storyteller," the general said. "Well, people need stories to divert them at difficult times like this." He put his hand on Baba's shoulder and turned to me. "Speaking of stories, your father and I hunted pheasant together one summer day in Jalalabad," he said. "It was a marvelous time. If I recall correctly, your father's eye proved as keen in the hunt as it had in business."

Baba kicked a wooden tennis racket on our tarpaulin spread with the toe of his boot. "Some business."

General Taheri managed a simultaneously sad and polite smile, heaved a sigh, and gently patted Baba's shoulder. *"Zendagi migzara,"* he said. Life goes on. He turned his eyes to me. "We Afghans are prone to a considerable degree of exaggeration, *bachem,* and I have heard many men foolishly labeled great. But your father has the distinction of belonging to the minority who truly deserves the label." This little speech sounded to me the way his suit looked: often used and unnaturally shiny.

"You're flattering me," Baba said.

"I am not," the general said, tilting his head sideways and pressing his hand to his chest to convey humility. "Boys and girls must know the legacy of their fathers." He turned to me. "Do you appreciate your father, *bachem?* Do you really appreciate him?"

"Balay, General Sahib, I do," I said, wishing he'd not call me "my child."

"Then congratulations, you are already halfway to being a man," he said with no trace of humor, no irony, the compliment of the casually arrogant.

"Padar jan, you forgot your tea." A young woman's voice. She was standing behind us, a slim-hipped beauty with velvety coal black hair, an open thermos and Styrofoam cup in her hand. I blinked, my heart quickening. She had thick black eyebrows that touched in the middle like the arched wings of a flying bird, and the gracefully hooked nose of a princess from old Persia—maybe that of Tahmineh, Rostam's wife and Sohrab's mother from the *Shahnamah.* Her eyes, walnut brown and shaded by fanned lashes, met mine. Held for a moment. Flew away.

"You are so kind, my dear," General Taheri said. He took the cup from her. Before she turned to go, I saw she had a brown, sickle-shaped birthmark on the smooth skin just above her left jawline. She walked to a dull gray van two aisles away and put the thermos inside. Her hair spilled to one side when she kneeled amid boxes of old records and paperbacks.

"My daughter, Soraya jan," General Taheri said. He took a deep breath like a man eager to change the subject and checked his gold pocket watch. "Well, time to go and set up." He and Baba kissed on the cheek and he shook my hand with both of his. "Best of luck with the writing," he said, looking me in the eye. His pale blue eyes revealed nothing of the thoughts behind them.

For the rest of that day, I fought the urge to look toward the gray van.

IT CAME TO ME on our way home. Taheri. I knew I'd heard that name before.

"Wasn't there some story floating around about Taheri's daughter?" I said to Baba, trying to sound casual.

"You know me," Baba said, inching the bus along the queue exiting the flea market. "Talk turns to gossip and I walk away."

"But there was, wasn't there?" I said.

"Why do you ask?" He was looking at me coyly.

I shrugged and fought back a smile. "Just curious, Baba."

"Really? Is that all?" he said, his eyes playful, lingering on mine. "Has she made an impression on you?"

I rolled my eyes. "Please, Baba."

He smiled, and swung the bus out of the flea market. We headed for Highway 680. We drove in silence for a while. "All I've heard is that there was a man once and things … didn't go well." He said this gravely, like he'd disclosed to me that she had breast cancer.

"Oh."

"I hear she is a decent girl, hardworking and kind. But no *khastegars*, no suitors, have knocked on the general's door since." Baba sighed. "It may be unfair, but what happens in a few days, sometimes even a single day, can change the course of a whole lifetime, Amir," he said.

LYING AWAKE IN BED that night, I thought of Soraya Taheri's sickle-shaped birthmark, her gently hooked nose, and the way her luminous eyes had fleetingly held mine. My heart stuttered at the thought of her. Soraya Taheri. My Swap Meet Princess.

TWELVE

In Afghanistan, *yelda* is the first night of the month of *Jadi,* the first night of winter, and the longest night of the year. As was the tradition, Hassan and I used to stay up late, our feet tucked under the *kursi,* while Ali tossed apple skin into the stove and told us ancient tales of sultans and thieves to pass that longest of nights. It was from Ali that I learned the lore of *yelda,* that bedeviled moths flung themselves at candle flames, and wolves climbed mountains looking for the sun. Ali swore that if you ate watermelon the night of *yelda,* you wouldn't get thirsty the coming summer.

When I was older, I read in my poetry books that *yelda* was the starless night tormented lovers kept vigil, enduring the endless dark, waiting for the sun to rise and bring with it their loved one. After I met Soraya Taheri, every night of the week became a *yelda* for me. And when Sunday mornings came, I rose from bed, Soraya Taheri's brown-eyed face already in my head. In Baba's bus, I counted the miles until I'd see her sitting barefoot, arranging cardboard boxes of yellowed encyclopedias, her heels white against the asphalt, silver bracelets jingling around her slender wrists. I'd think of the shadow her hair cast on the ground when it slid off her back and hung down like a velvet curtain. Soraya. Swap Meet Princess. The morning sun to my *yelda*.

I invented excuses to stroll down the aisle—which Baba acknowledged with a playful smirk—and pass the Taheris' stand. I would wave at the general, perpetually dressed in his shiny overpressed gray suit, and he would wave back. Sometimes he'd get up from his director's chair and we'd make small talk about my writing, the war, the day's bargains. And I'd have to will my eyes not to peel away, not to wander to where Soraya sat reading a paperback. The general and I would say our good-byes and I'd try not to slouch as I walked away.

Sometimes she sat alone, the general off to some other row to socialize, and I would walk by, pretending not to know her, but dying to. Sometimes she was there with a portly middle-aged woman with pale skin and dyed red hair. I promised myself that I would talk to her before the summer was over, but schools reopened, the leaves reddened, yellowed, and fell, the rains of winter swept in and wakened Baba's joints, baby leaves sprouted once more, and I still hadn't had the heart, the *dil*, to even look her in the eye.

The spring quarter ended in late May 1985. I aced all of my general education classes, which was a minor miracle given how I'd sit in lectures and think of the soft hook of Soraya's nose.

Then, one sweltering Sunday that summer, Baba and I were at the flea market, sitting at our booth, fanning our faces with newspapers. Despite the sun bearing down like a branding iron, the market was crowded that day and sales had been strong—it was only 12:30 but we'd already made $160. I got up, stretched, and asked Baba if he wanted a Coke. He said he'd love one.

"Be careful, Amir," he said as I began to walk.

"Of what, Baba?"

"I am not an *ahmaq*, so don't play stupid with me."

"I don't know what you're talking about."

"Remember this," Baba said, pointing at me, "The man is a Pashtun to the root. He has *nang* and *namoos*." Nang. Namoos. Honor and pride. The tenets of Pashtun men. Especially when it came to the chastity of a wife. Or a daughter.

"I'm only going to get us drinks."

"Just don't embarrass me, that's all I ask."

"I won't. God, Baba."

Baba lit a cigarette and started fanning himself again.

I walked toward the concession booth initially, then turned left at the T-shirt stand—where, for $5, you could have the face of Jesus, Elvis, Jim Morrison, or all three, pressed on a white nylon T-shirt. Mariachi music played overhead, and I smelled pickles and grilled meat.

I spotted the Taheris' gray van two rows from ours, next to a kiosk selling mango-on-a-stick. She was alone, reading. White ankle-length summer dress today. Open-toed sandals. Hair pulled back and crowned with a tulip-shaped bun. I meant to simply walk by again and I thought I had, except suddenly I was standing at the edge of the Taheris' white tablecloth, staring at Soraya across curling irons and old neckties. She looked up.

"*Salaam*," I said. "I'm sorry to be *mozahem*, I didn't mean to disturb you."

"*Salaam*."

"Is General Sahib here today?" I said. My ears were burning. I couldn't bring myself to look her in the eye.

"He went that way," she said. Pointed to her right. The

bracelet slipped down to her elbow, silver against olive.

"Will you tell him I stopped by to pay my respects?" I said. "I will."

"Thank you," I said. "Oh, and my name is Amir. In case you need to know. So you can tell him. That I stopped by. To... pay my respects."

"Yes."

I shifted on my feet, cleared my throat. "I'll go now. Sorry to have disturbed you."

"Nay, you didn't," she said.

"Oh. Good." I tipped my head and gave her a half smile. "I'll go now." Hadn't I already said that? *"Khoda hafez."*

"Khoda hafez."

I began to walk. Stopped and turned. I said it before I had a chance to lose my nerve: "Can I ask what you're reading?"

She blinked.

I held my breath. Suddenly, I felt the collective eyes of the flea market Afghans shift to us. I imagined a hush falling. Lips stopping in midsentence. Heads turning. Eyes narrowing with keen interest.

What was *this*?

Up to that point, our encounter could have been interpreted as a respectful inquiry, one man asking for the whereabouts of another man. But I'd asked her a question and if she answered, we'd be ... well, we'd be chatting. Me a *mojarad,* a single young man, and she an unwed young woman. One with a *history,* no less. This was teetering dangerously on the verge of gossip material, and the best kind of it. Poison tongues would flap. And she would bear the brunt of that poison, not me—I was fully aware of the Afghan double standard that favored my gender. Not *Did you see him chatting with her?* but *Wooooy! Did you see how she wouldn't let him go? What a* lochak!

By Afghan standards, my question had been bold. With it, I had bared myself, and left little doubt as to my interest in her. But I was a man, and all I had risked was a bruised ego. Bruises healed. Reputations did not. Would she take my dare?

She turned the book so the cover faced me. *Wuthering Heights.* "Have you read it?" she said.

I nodded. I could feel the pulsating beat of my heart behind my eyes. "It's a sad story."

"Sad stories make good books," she said.

"They do."

"I heard you write."

How did she know? I wondered if her father had told her, maybe she had asked him. I immediately dismissed both scenarios as absurd. Fathers and sons could talk freely about women. But no Afghan girl—no decent and *mohtaram* Afghan girl, at least— queried her father about a young man. And no father, especially a Pashtun with *nang* and *namoos,* would discuss a *mojarad* with his daughter, not unless the fellow in question was a *khastegar,* a suitor, who had done the honorable thing and sent his father to knock on the door.

Incredibly, I heard myself say, "Would you like to read one of my stories?"

"I would like that," she said. I sensed an unease in her now, saw it in the way her eyes began to flick side to side. Maybe checking for the general. I wondered what he would say if he found me speaking for such an inappropriate length of time with his daughter.

"Maybe I'll bring you one someday," I said. I was about to

say more when the woman I'd seen on occasion with Soraya
came walking up the aisle. She was carrying a plastic bag full of
fruit. When she saw us, her eyes bounced from Soraya to me and
back. She smiled.

"Amir jan, good to see you," she said, unloading the bag on
the tablecloth. Her brow glistened with a sheen of sweat. Her
red hair, coiffed like a helmet, glittered in the sunlight—I could
see bits of her scalp where the hair had thinned. She had small
green eyes buried in a cabbage-round face, capped teeth, and
little fingers like sausages. A golden Allah rested on her chest, the
chain burrowed under the skin tags and folds of her neck. "I am
Jamila, Soraya jan's mother."

"*Salaam*, Khala jan," I said, embarrassed, as I often was around
Afghans, that she knew me and I had no idea who she was.

"How is your father?" she said.

"He's well, thank you."

"You know, your grandfather, Ghazi Sahib, the judge? Now,
his uncle and my grandfather were cousins," she said. "So you
see, we're related." She smiled a cap-toothed smile, and I noticed
the right side of her mouth drooping a little. Her eyes moved
between Soraya and me again.

I'd asked Baba once why General Taheri's daughter hadn't
married yet. No suitors, Baba said. No suitable suitors, he
amended. But he wouldn't say more—Baba knew how lethal
idle talk could prove to a young woman's prospects of marrying
well. Afghan men, especially those from reputable families, were
fickle creatures. A whisper here, an insinuation there, and they
fled like startled birds. So weddings had come and gone and
no one had sung *ahesta boro* for Soraya, no one had painted her
palms with henna, no one had held a Koran over her headdress,

and it had been General Taheri who'd danced with her at every
wedding.

And now, this woman, this mother, with her heartbreakingly
eager, crooked smile and the barely veiled hope in her eyes. I
cringed a little at the position of power I'd been granted, and all
because I had won at the genetic lottery that had determined
my sex.

I could never read the thoughts in the general's eyes, but I
knew this much about his wife: If I was going to have an adver-
sary in this—whatever *this* was—it would not be her.

"Sit down, Amir jan," she said. "Soraya, get him a chair,
bachem. And wash one of those peaches. They're sweet and fresh."

"Nay, thank you," I said. "I should get going. My father's
waiting."

"Oh?" Khanum Taheri said, clearly impressed that I'd done
the polite thing and declined the offer. "Then here, at least have
this." She threw a handful of kiwis and a few peaches into a
paper bag and insisted I take them. "Carry my *Salaam* to your
father. And come back to see us again."

"I will. Thank you, Khala jan," I said. Out of the corner of my
eye, I saw Soraya looking away.

"I THOUGHT YOU WERE GETTING COKES," Baba said,
taking the bag of peaches from me. He was looking at me
in a simultaneously serious and playful way. I began to make
something up, but he bit into a peach and waved his hand. "Don't
bother, Amir. Just remember what I said."

THAT NIGHT IN BED, I thought of the way dappled sunlight had danced in Soraya's eyes, and of the delicate hollows above her collarbone. I replayed our conversation over and over in my head. Had she said *I heard you write* or *I heard you're a writer?* Which was it? I tossed in my sheets and stared at the ceiling, dismayed at the thought of six laborious, interminable nights of *yelda* until I saw her again.

IT WENT ON LIKE THAT for a few weeks. I'd wait until the general went for a stroll, then I'd walk past the Taheris' stand. If Khanum Taheri was there, she'd offer me tea and a *kolcha* and we'd chat about Kabul in the old days, the people we knew, her arthritis. Undoubtedly, she had noticed that my appearances always coincided with her husband's absences, but she never let on. "Oh you just missed your Kaka," she'd say. I actually liked it when Khanum Taheri was there, and not just because of her amiable ways; Soraya was more relaxed, more talkative with her mother around. As if her presence legitimized whatever was happening between us—though certainly not to the same degree that the general's would have. Khanum Taheri's chaperoning made our meetings, if not gossip-proof, then less gossip-worthy, even if her borderline fawning on me clearly embarrassed Soraya.

One day, Soraya and I were alone at their booth, talking. She was telling me about school, how she too was working on her general education classes, at Ohlone Junior College in Fremont.

"What will you major in?"

"I want to be a teacher," she said.

"Really? Why?"

"I've always wanted to. When we lived in Virginia, I became ESL certified and now I teach at the public library one night a week. My mother was a teacher too, she taught Farsi and history at Zarghoona High School for girls in Kabul."

A potbellied man in a deerstalker hat offered three dollars for a five-dollar set of candlesticks and Soraya let him have it. She dropped the money in a little candy box by her feet. She looked at me shyly. "I want to tell you a story," she said, "but I'm a little embarrassed about it."

"Tell me."

"It's kind of silly."

"Please tell me."

She laughed. "Well, when I was in fourth grade in Kabul, my father hired a woman named Ziba to help around the house. She had a sister in Iran, in Mashad, and, since Ziba was illiterate, she'd ask me to write her sister letters once in a while. And when the sister replied, I'd read her letter to Ziba. One day, I asked her if she'd like to learn to read and write. She gave me this big smile, crinkling her eyes, and said she'd like that very much. So we'd sit at the kitchen table after I was done with my own schoolwork and I'd teach her *Alef-beh*. I remember looking up sometimes in the middle of homework and seeing Ziba in the kitchen, stirring meat in the pressure cooker, then sitting down with a pencil to do the alphabet homework I'd assigned to her the night before.

"Anyway, within a year, Ziba could read children's books. We sat in the yard and she read me the tales of Dara and Sara— slowly but correctly. She started calling me *Moalem* Soraya, Teacher Soraya." She laughed again. "I know it sounds childish, but the first time Ziba wrote her own letter, I knew there was nothing else I'd ever want to be but a teacher. I was so proud of her and I felt I'd done something really worthwhile, you know?"

"Yes," I lied. I thought of how I had used my literacy to ridicule Hassan. How I had teased him about big words he didn't know.

"My father wants me to go to law school, my mother's always throwing hints about medical school, but I'm going to be a teacher. Doesn't pay much here, but it's what I want."

"My mother was a teacher too," I said.

"I know," she said. "My mother told me." Then her face reddened with a blush at what she had blurted, at the implication of her answer, that "Amir Conversations" took place between them when I wasn't there. It took an enormous effort to stop myself from smiling.

"I brought you something." I fished the roll of stapled pages from my back pocket. "As promised." I handed her one of my short stories.

"Oh, you remembered," she said, actually beaming. "Thank you!" I barely had time to register that she'd addressed me with *"tu"* for the first time and not the formal *"shoma,"* because suddenly her smile vanished. The color dropped from her face, and her eyes fixed on something behind me. I turned around. Came face-to-face with General Taheri.

"Amir jan. Our aspiring storyteller. What a pleasure," he said. He was smiling thinly.

"*Salaam,* General Sahib," I said through heavy lips.

He moved past me, toward the booth. "What a beautiful day it is, nay?" he said, thumb hooked in the breast pocket of his vest, the other hand extended toward Soraya. She gave him the pages.

"They say it will rain this week. Hard to believe, isn't it?" He dropped the rolled pages in the garbage can. Turned to me and gently put a hand on my shoulder. We took a few steps together.

"You know, *bachem,* I have grown rather fond of you. You are a decent boy, I really believe that, but—" he sighed and waved a hand "—even decent boys need reminding sometimes. So it's my duty to remind you that you are among peers in this flea market." He stopped. His expressionless eyes bore into mine. "You see, *everyone* here is a storyteller." He smiled, revealing perfectly even teeth. "Do pass my respects to your father, Amir jan."

He dropped his hand. Smiled again.

"WHAT' S WRONG?" Baba said. He was taking an elderly woman's money for a rocking horse.

"Nothing," I said. I sat down on an old TV set. Then I told him anyway.

"Akh, Amir," he sighed.

As it turned out, I didn't get to brood too much over what had happened.

Because later that week, Baba caught a cold.

IT STARTED WITH A HACKING COUGH and the sniffles. He got over the sniffles, but the cough persisted. He'd hack into his handkerchief, stow it in his pocket. I kept after him to get it checked, but he'd wave me away. He hated doctors and hospitals. To my knowledge, the only time Baba had ever gone to a doctor was the time he'd caught malaria in India.

Then, two weeks later, I caught him coughing a wad of bloodstained phlegm into the toilet.

"How long have you been doing that?" I said.

"What's for dinner?" he said.

"I'm taking you to the doctor."

Even though Baba was a manager at the gas station, the owner hadn't offered him health insurance, and Baba, in his recklessness, hadn't insisted. So I took him to the county hospital in San Jose. The sallow, puffy-eyed doctor who saw us introduced himself as a second-year resident. "He looks younger than you and sicker than me," Baba grumbled. The resident sent us down for a chest X ray. When the nurse called us back in, the resident was filling out a form.

"Take this to the front desk," he said, scribbling quickly.

"What is it?" I asked.

"A referral." *Scribble scribble.*

"For what?"

"Pulmonary clinic."

"What's that?"

He gave me a quick glance. Pushed up his glasses. Began scribbling again. "He's got a spot on his right lung. I want them to check it out."

"A spot?" I said, the room suddenly too small.

"Cancer?" Baba added casually.

"Possible. It's suspicious, anyway," the doctor muttered.

"Can't you tell us more?" I asked.

"Not really. Need a CAT scan first, then see the lung doctor." He handed me the referral form. "You said your father smokes, right?"

"Yes."

He nodded. Looked from me to Baba and back again. "They'll call you within two weeks."

I wanted to ask him how I was supposed to live with that word, "suspicious," for two whole weeks. How was I supposed eat, work, study? How could he send me home with that word?

I took the form and turned it in. That night, I waited until Baba fell asleep, and then folded a blanket. I used it as a prayer rug. Bowing my head to the ground, I recited half-forgotten verses from the Koran—verses the mullah had made us commit to memory in Kabul—and asked for kindness from a God I wasn't sure existed. I envied the mullah now, envied his faith and certainty.

Two weeks passed and no one called. And when I called them, they told me they'd lost the referral. Was I sure I had turned it in? They said they would call in another three weeks. I raised hell and bargained the three weeks down to one for the CAT scan, two to see the doctor.

The visit with the pulmonologist, Dr. Schneider, was going well until Baba asked him where he was from. Dr. Schneider said Russia. Baba lost it.

"Excuse us, Doctor," I said, pulling Baba aside. Dr. Schneider smiled and stood back, stethoscope still in hand.

"Baba, I read Dr. Schneider's biography in the waiting room. He was born in Michigan. *Michigan!* He's American, a lot more American than you and I will ever be."

"I don't care where he was born, he's *Roussi*," Baba said, grimacing like it was a dirty word. "His parents were *Roussi*, his grandparents were *Roussi*. I swear on your mother's face I'll break his arm if he tries to touch me."

"Dr. Schneider's parents fled from *Shorawi,* don't you see? They escaped!"

But Baba would hear none of it. Sometimes I think the only

thing he loved as much as his late wife was Afghanistan, his late country. I almost screamed with frustration. Instead, I sighed and turned to Dr. Schneider. "I'm sorry, Doctor. This isn't going to work out."

The next pulmonologist, Dr. Amani, was Iranian and Baba approved. Dr. Amani, a soft-spoken man with a crooked mustache and a mane of gray hair, told us he had reviewed the CAT scan results and that he would have to perform a procedure called a bronchoscopy to get a piece of the lung mass for pathology. He scheduled it for the following week. I thanked him as I helped Baba out of the office, thinking that now I had to live a whole week with this new word, "mass," an even more ominous word than "suspicious." I wished Soraya were there with me.

It turned out that, like Satan, cancer had many names. Baba's was called "Oat Cell Carcinoma." Advanced. Inoperable. Baba asked Dr. Amani for a prognosis. Dr. Amani bit his lip, used the word "grave." "There is chemotherapy, of course," he said. "But it would only be palliative."

"What does that mean?" Baba asked.

Dr. Amani sighed. "It means it wouldn't change the outcome, just prolong it."

"That's a clear answer, Dr. Amani. Thank you for that," Baba said. "But no chemo medication for me." He had the same resolved look on his face as the day he'd dropped the stack of food stamps on Mrs. Dobbins's desk.

"But Baba—"

"Don't you challenge me in public, Amir. Ever. Who do you think you are?"

THE RAIN General Taheri had spoken about at the flea market was a few weeks late, but when we stepped out of Dr. Amani's office, passing cars sprayed grimy water onto the sidewalks. Baba lit a cigarette. He smoked all the way to the car and all the way home.

As he was slipping the key into the lobby door, I said, "I wish you'd give the chemo a chance, Baba."

Baba pocketed the keys, pulled me out of the rain and under the building's striped awning. He kneaded me on the chest with the hand holding the cigarette. "*Bas!* I've made my decision."

"What about me, Baba? What am I supposed to do?" I said, my eyes welling up.

A look of disgust swept across his rain-soaked face. It was the same look he'd give me when, as a kid, I'd fall, scrape my knees, and cry. It was the crying that brought it on then, the crying that brought it on now. "You're twenty-two years old, Amir! A grown man! You …" he opened his mouth, closed it, opened it again, reconsidered. Above us, rain drummed on the canvas awning. "What's going to happen to you, you say? All those years, that's what I was trying to teach you, how to never have to ask that question."

He opened the door. Turned back to me. "And one more thing. No one finds out about this, you hear me? No one. I don't want anybody's sympathy." Then he disappeared into the dim lobby. He chain-smoked the rest of that day in front of the TV. I didn't know what or whom he was defying. Me? Dr. Amani? Or maybe the God he had never believed in.

FOR A WHILE, even cancer couldn't keep Baba from the flea

market. We made our garage sale treks on Saturdays, Baba the driver and me the navigator, and set up our display on Sundays. Brass lamps. Baseball gloves. Ski jackets with broken zippers. Baba greeted acquaintances from the old country and I haggled with buyers over a dollar or two. Like any of it mattered. Like the day I would become an orphan wasn't inching closer with each closing of shop.

Sometimes, General Taheri and his wife strolled by. The general, ever the diplomat, greeted me with a smile and his twohanded shake. But there was a new reticence to Khanum Taheri's demeanor. A reticence broken only by her secret, droopy smiles and the furtive, apologetic looks she cast my way when the general's attention was engaged elsewhere.

I remember that period as a time of many "firsts": The first time I heard Baba moan in the bathroom. The first time I found blood on his pillow. In over three years running the gas station, Baba had never called in sick. Another first.

By Halloween of that year, Baba was getting so tired by mid–Saturday afternoon that he'd wait behind the wheel while I got out and bargained for junk. By Thanksgiving, he wore out before noon. When sleighs appeared on front lawns and fake snow on Douglas firs, Baba stayed home and I drove the VW bus alone up and down the peninsula.

Sometimes at the flea market, Afghan acquaintances made remarks about Baba's weight loss. At first, they were complimentary. They even asked the secret to his diet. But the queries and compliments stopped when the weight loss didn't. When the pounds kept shedding. And shedding. When his cheeks hollowed. And his temples melted. And his eyes receded in their sockets.

Then, one cool Sunday shortly after New Year's Day, Baba was selling a lampshade to a stocky Filipino man while I rummaged in the VW for a blanket to cover his legs with.

"Hey, man, this guy needs help!" the Filipino man said with alarm. I turned around and found Baba on the ground. His arms and legs were jerking.

"*Komak!*" I cried. "Somebody help!" I ran to Baba. He was frothing at the mouth, the foamy spittle soaking his beard. His upturned eyes showed nothing but white.

People were rushing to us. I heard someone say seizure. Someone else yelling, "Call 911!" I heard running footsteps. The sky darkened as a crowd gathered around us.

Baba's spittle turned red. He was biting his tongue. I kneeled beside him and grabbed his arms and said I'm here Baba, I'm here, you'll be all right, I'm right here. As if I could soothe the convulsions out of him. Talk them into leaving my Baba alone. I felt a wetness on my knees. Saw Baba's bladder had let go. *Shhh, Baba jan, I'm here. Your son is right here.*

THE DOCTOR, white-bearded and perfectly bald, pulled me out of the room. "I want to go over your father's CAT scans with you," he said. He put the films up on a viewing box in the hallway and pointed with the eraser end of his pencil to the pictures of Baba's cancer, like a cop showing mug shots of the killer to the victim's family. Baba's brain on those pictures looked like cross sections of a big walnut, riddled with tennis ball–shaped gray things.

"As you can see, the cancer's metastasized," he said. "He'll have to take steroids to reduce the swelling in his brain and antiseizure medications. And I'd recommend palliative radiation. Do you know what that means?"

I said I did. I'd become conversant in cancer talk.

"All right, then," he said. He checked his beeper. "I have to go, but you can have me paged if you have any questions."

"Thank you."

I spent the night sitting on a chair next to Baba's bed.

THE NEXT MORNING, the waiting room down the hall was jammed with Afghans. The butcher from Newark. An engineer who'd worked with Baba on his orphanage. They filed in and paid Baba their respects in hushed tones. Wished him a swift recovery. Baba was awake then, groggy and tired, but awake.

Midmorning, General Taheri and his wife came. Soraya followed. We glanced at each other, looked away at the same time. "How are you, my friend?" General Taheri said, taking Baba's hand. Baba motioned to the IV hanging from his arm. Smiled thinly. The general smiled back.

"You shouldn't have burdened yourselves. All of you," Baba croaked.

"It's no burden," Khanum Taheri said.

"No burden at all. More importantly, do you need anything?" General Taheri said. "Anything at all? Ask me like you'd ask a brother."

I remembered something Baba had said about Pashtuns once. *We may be hardheaded and I know we're far too proud, but, in the hour of need, believe me that there's no one you'd rather have at your side than a Pashtun.*

Baba shook his head on the pillow. "Your coming here has

brightened my eyes." The general smiled and squeezed Baba's hand. "How are you, Amir jan? Do you need anything?"

The way he was looking at me, the kindness in his eyes ... "Nay thank you, General Sahib. I'm ..." A lump shot up in my throat and my eyes teared over. I bolted out of the room.

I wept in the hallway, by the viewing box where, the night before, I'd seen the killer's face.

Baba's door opened and Soraya walked out of his room. She stood near me. She was wearing a gray sweatshirt and jeans. Her hair was down. I wanted to find comfort in her arms.

"I'm so sorry, Amir," she said. "We all knew something was wrong, but we had no idea it was this."

I blotted my eyes with my sleeve. "He didn't want anyone to know."

"Do you need anything?"

"No." I tried to smile. She put her hand on mine. Our first touch. I took it. Brought it to my face. My eyes. I let it go. "You'd better go back inside. Or your father will come after me."

She smiled and nodded. "I should." She turned to go.

"Soraya?"

"Yes?"

"I'm happy you came. It means ... the world to me."

THEY DISCHARGED BABA two days later. They brought in a specialist called a radiation oncologist to talk Baba into getting radiation treatment. Baba refused. They tried to talk me into talking him into it. But I'd seen the look on Baba's face. I thanked them, signed their forms, and took Baba home in my Ford Torino. That night, Baba was lying on the couch, a wool blanket covering him. I brought him hot tea and roasted almonds. Wrapped my arms around his back and pulled him up much too easily. His shoulder blade felt like a bird's wing under my fingers. I pulled the blanket back up to his chest where ribs stretched his thin, sallow skin.

"Can I do anything else for you, Baba?"

"Nay, *bachem*. Thank you."

I sat beside him. "Then I wonder if you'll do something for me. If you're not too exhausted."

"What?"

"I want you to go *khastegari*. I want you to ask General Taheri for his daughter's hand."

Baba's dry lips stretched into a smile. A spot of green on a wilted leaf. "Are you sure?"

"More sure than I've ever been about anything."

"You've thought it over?"

"*Balay*, Baba."

"Then give me the phone. And my little notebook."

I blinked. "Now?"

"Then when?"

I smiled. "Okay." I gave him the phone and the little black notebook where Baba had scribbled his Afghan friends' numbers. He looked up the Taheris. Dialed. Brought the receiver to his ear. My heart was doing pirouettes in my chest.

"Jamila jan? *Salaam alaykum,*" he said. He introduced himself. Paused. "Much better, thank you. It was so gracious of you to come." He listened for a while. Nodded. "I'll remember that, thank you. Is General Sahib home?" Pause. "Thank you."

His eyes flicked to me. I wanted to laugh for some reason. Or scream. I brought the ball of my hand to my mouth and bit on it. Baba laughed softly through his nose.

"General Sahib, *Salaam alaykum* ... Yes, much much better ... *Balay* ... You're so kind. General Sahib, I'm calling to ask if I may pay you and Khanum Taheri a visit tomorrow morning. It's an honorable matter ... Yes ... Eleven o'clock is just fine. Until then. *Khoda hafez.*"

He hung up. We looked at each other. I burst into giggles. Baba joined in.

BABA WET HIS HAIR and combed it back. I helped him into a clean white shirt and knotted his tie for him, noting the two inches of empty space between the collar button and Baba's neck. I thought of all the empty spaces Baba would leave behind when he was gone, and I made myself think of something else. He wasn't gone. Not yet. And this was a day for good thoughts. The jacket of his brown suit, the one he'd worn to my graduation, hung over him—too much of Baba had melted away to fill it anymore. I had to roll up the sleeves. I stooped and tied his shoelaces for him.

The Taheris lived in a flat, one-story house in one of the residential areas in Fremont known for housing a large number of Afghans. It had bay windows, a pitched roof, and an enclosed front porch on which I saw potted geraniums. The general's gray van was parked in the driveway.

I helped Baba out of the Ford and slipped back behind the wheel. He leaned in the passenger window. "Be home, I'll call you in an hour."

"Okay, Baba," I said. "Good luck."

He smiled.

I drove away. In the rearview mirror, Baba was hobbling up the Taheris' driveway for one last fatherly duty.

I PACED THE LIVING ROOM of our apartment waiting for Baba's call. Fifteen paces long. Ten and a half paces wide. What if the general said no? What if he hated me? I kept going to the kitchen, checking the oven clock.

The phone rang just before noon. It was Baba.

"Well?"

"The general accepted."

I let out a burst of air. Sat down. My hands were shaking. "He did?"

"Yes, but Soraya jan is upstairs in her room. She wants to talk to you first."

"Okay."

Baba said something to someone and there was a double click as he hung up.

"Amir?" Soraya's voice.

"Salaam."

"My father said yes."

"I know," I said. I switched hands. I was smiling. "I'm so happy I don't know what to say."

"I'm happy too, Amir. I ... can't believe this is happening."

I laughed. "I know."

"Listen," she said, "I want to tell you something. Something you have to know before ..."

"I don't care what it is."

"You need to know. I don't want us to start with secrets. And I'd rather you hear it from me."

"If it will make you feel better, tell me. But it won't change anything."

There was a long pause at the other end. "When we lived in Virginia, I ran away with an Afghan man. I was eighteen at the time ... rebellious ... stupid, and ... he was into drugs ... We lived together for almost a month. All the Afghans in Virginia were talking about it.

"Padar eventually found us. He showed up at the door and ... made me come home. I was hysterical. Yelling. Screaming. Saying I hated him ...

"Anyway, I came home and—" She was crying. "Excuse me." I heard her put the phone down. Blow her nose. "Sorry," she came back on, sounding hoarse. "When I came home, I saw my mother had had a stroke, the right side of her face was paralyzed and ... I felt so guilty. She didn't deserve that.

"Padar moved us to California shortly after." A silence followed.

"How are you and your father now?" I said.

"We've always had our differences, we still do, but I'm grateful he came for me that day. I really believe he saved me." She paused. "So, does what I told you bother you?"

"A little," I said. I owed her the truth on this one. I couldn't lie to her and say that my pride, my *iftikhar*, wasn't stung at all that she had been with a man, whereas I had never taken a woman to bed. It did bother me a bit, but I had pondered this quite a lot in the weeks before I asked Baba to go *khastegari*. And in the end the question that always came back to me was this: How could I, of all people, chastise someone for their past?

"Does it bother you enough to change your mind?"

"No, Soraya. Not even close," I said. "Nothing you said

changes anything. I want us to marry."

She broke into fresh tears.

I envied her. Her secret was out. Spoken. Dealt with. I opened my mouth and almost told her how I'd betrayed Hassan, lied, driven him out, and destroyed a forty-year relationship between Baba and Ali. But I didn't. I suspected there were many ways in which Soraya Taheri was a better person than me. Courage was just one of them.

THIRTEEN

When we arrived at the Taheris' home the next evening—for *lafz*, the ceremony of "giving word"—I had to park the Ford across the street. Their driveway was already jammed with cars. I wore a navy blue suit I had bought the previous day, after I had brought Baba home from *khastegari*. I checked my tie in the rearview mirror.

"You look *khoshteep*," Baba said. Handsome.

"Thank you, Baba. Are you all right? Do you feel up to this?"

"Up to this? It's the happiest day of my life, Amir," he said, smiling tiredly.

I COULD HEAR CHATTER FROM the other side of the door, laughter, and Afghan music playing softly—it sounded like a classical *ghazal* by Ustad Sarahang. I rang the bell. A face peeked through the curtains of the foyer window and disappeared. "They're here!" I heard a woman's voice say. The chatter stopped. Someone turned off the music.

Khanum Taheri opened the door. *"Salaam alaykum,"* she said, beaming. She'd permed her hair, I saw, and wore an elegant, ankle-length black dress. When I stepped into the foyer, her eyes moistened. "You're barely in the house and I'm crying already, Amir jan," she said. I planted a kiss on her hand, just as Baba had instructed me to do the night before.

She led us through a brightly lit hallway to the living room. On the wood-paneled walls, I saw pictures of the people who would become my new family: A young bouffant-haired Khanum Taheri and the general—Niagara Falls in the background; Khanum Taheri in a seamless dress, the general in a narrow-lapelled jacket and thin tie, his hair full and black; Soraya, about to board a wooden roller coaster, waving and smiling, the sun glinting off the silver wires in her teeth. A photo of the general, dashing in full military outfit, shaking hands with King Hussein of Jordan. A portrait of Zahir Shah.

The living room was packed with about two dozen guests seated on chairs placed along the walls. When Baba entered, everybody stood up. We went around the room, Baba leading slowly, me behind him, shaking hands and greeting the guests. The general—still in his gray suit—and Baba embraced, gently tapping each other on the back. They said their *Salaam*s in respectful hushed tones.

The general held me at arm's length and smiled knowingly, as if saying, "Now, this is the right way—the Afghan way—to do it, *bachem*." We kissed three times on the cheek.

We sat in the crowded room, Baba and I next to each other, across from the general and his wife. Baba's breathing had grown a little ragged, and he kept wiping sweat off his forehead and scalp with his handkerchief. He saw me looking at him and managed a strained grin. "I'm all right," he mouthed.

In keeping with tradition, Soraya was not present.

A few moments of small talk and idle chatter followed until the general cleared his throat. The room became quiet and everyone looked down at their hands in respect. The general nodded toward Baba.

Baba cleared his own throat. When he began, he couldn't speak in complete sentences without stopping to breathe. "General Sahib, Khanum Jamila jan ... it's with great humility that my son and I ... have come to your home today. You are ... honorable people ... from distinguished and reputable families and ... proud lineage. I come with nothing but the utmost *ihtiram* ... and the highest regards for you, your family names, and the memory ... of your ancestors." He stopped. Caught his breath. Wiped his brow. "Amir jan is my only son ... my only child, and he has been a good son to me. I hope he proves... worthy of your kindness. I ask that you honor Amir jan and me ... and accept my son into your family."

The general nodded politely.

"We are honored to welcome the son of a man such as yourself into our family," he said. "Your reputation precedes you. I was your humble admirer in Kabul and remain so today. We are honored that your family and ours will be joined.

"Amir jan, as for you, I welcome you to my home as a son, as the husband of my daughter who is the *noor* of my eye. Your pain will be our pain, your joy our joy. I hope that you will come to see your Khala Jamila and me as a second set of parents, and I pray for your and our lovely Soraya jan's happiness. You both have our blessings."

Everyone applauded, and with that signal, heads turned toward the hallway. The moment I'd waited for.

Soraya appeared at the end. Dressed in a stunning wine-colored traditional Afghan dress with long sleeves and gold trimmings. Baba's hand took mine and tightened. Khanum Taheri burst into fresh tears. Slowly, Soraya came to us, tailed by a procession of young female relatives.

She kissed my father's hands. Sat beside me at last, her eyes downcast.

The applause swelled.

ACCORDING TO TRADITION, Soraya's family would have thrown the engagement party, the *Shirini-khori*—or "Eating of the Sweets" ceremony. Then an engagement period would have followed which would have lasted a few months. Then the wedding, which would be paid for by Baba.

We all agreed that Soraya and I would forgo the *Shirini-khori*. Everyone knew the reason, so no one had to actually say it: that Baba didn't have months to live.

Soraya and I never went out alone together while preparations for the wedding proceeded—since we weren't married yet, hadn't even had a *Shirini-khori,* it was considered improper. So I had to make do with going over to the Taheris with Baba for dinner. Sit across from Soraya at the dinner table. Imagine what it would be like to feel her head on my chest, smell her hair. Kiss her. Make love to her.

Baba spent $35,000, nearly the balance of his life savings, on the *awroussi,* the wedding ceremony. He rented a large Afghan banquet hall in Fremont—the man who owned it knew him from Kabul and gave him a substantial discount. Baba paid for the *chila*s, our matching wedding bands, and for the diamond ring I picked out. He bought my tuxedo, and my traditional green suit for the *nika*—the swearing ceremony.

For all the frenzied preparations that went into the wedding night—most of it, blessedly, by Khanum Taheri and her friends—I remember only a handful of moments from it.

I remember our *nika*. We were seated around a table, Soraya and I dressed in green—the color of Islam, but also the color of spring and new beginnings. I wore a suit, Soraya (the only woman at the table) a veiled long-sleeved dress. Baba, General Taheri (in a tuxedo this time), and several of Soraya's uncles were also present at the table. Soraya and I looked down, solemnly respectful, casting only sideway glances at each other. The mullah questioned the witnesses and read from the Koran. We said our oaths. Signed the certificates. One of Soraya's uncles from Virginia, Sharif jan, Khanum Taheri's brother, stood up and cleared his throat. Soraya had told me that he had lived in the U.S. for more than twenty years. He worked for the INS and had an American wife. He was also a poet. A small man with a birdlike face and fluffy hair, he read a lengthy poem dedicated to Soraya, jotted down on hotel stationery paper. "*Wah wah*, Sharif jan!" everyone exclaimed when he finished.

I remember walking toward the stage, now in my tuxedo, Soraya a veiled *pari* in white, our hands locked. Baba hobbled next to me, the general and his wife beside their daughter. A procession of uncles, aunts, and cousins followed as we made our way through the hall, parting a sea of applauding guests, blinking at flashing cameras. One of Soraya's cousins, Sharif jan's son, held a Koran over our heads as we inched along. The wedding song, *ahesta boro*, blared from the speakers, the same song the Russian soldier at the Mahipar checkpoint had sung the night Baba and

I left Kabul:

Make morning into a key and throw it into the well,
Go slowly, my lovely moon, go slowly.
Let the morning sun forget to rise in the
east, Go slowly, my lovely moon, go slowly.

I remember sitting on the sofa, set on the stage like a throne, Soraya's hand in mine, as three hundred or so faces looked on. We did *Ayena Masshaf,* where they gave us a mirror and threw a veil over our heads, so we'd be alone to gaze at each other's reflection. Looking at Soraya's smiling face in that mirror, in the momentary privacy of the veil, I whispered to her for the first time that I loved her. A blush, red like henna, bloomed on her cheeks.

I picture colorful platters of *chopan* kabob, *sholeh-goshti,* and wild-orange rice. I see Baba between us on the sofa, smiling. I remember sweat-drenched men dancing the traditional *attan* in a circle, bouncing, spinning faster and faster with the feverish tempo of the tabla, until all but a few dropped out of the ring with exhaustion. I remember wishing Rahim Khan were there.

And I remember wondering if Hassan too had married. And if so, whose face he had seen in the mirror under the veil? Whose henna-painted hands had he held?

AROUND 2 A.M., the party moved from the banquet hall to Baba's apartment. Tea flowed once more and music played until the neighbors called the cops. Later that night, the sun less than an hour from rising and the guests finally gone, Soraya and I lay together for the first time. All my life, I'd been around men. That night, I discovered the tenderness of a woman.

IT WAS SORAYA who suggested that she move in with Baba and me.

"I thought you might want us to have our own place," I said.

"With Kaka jan as sick as he is?" she replied. Her eyes told me that was no way to start a marriage. I kissed her. "Thank you."

Soraya dedicated herself to taking care of my father. She made his toast and tea in the morning, and helped him in and out of bed. She gave him his pain pills, washed his clothes, read him the international section of the newspaper every afternoon. She cooked his favorite dish, potato *shorwa,* though he could scarcely eat more than a few spoonfuls, and took him out every day for a brief walk around the block. And when he became bedridden, she turned him on his side every hour so he wouldn't get a bedsore.

One day, I came home from the pharmacy with Baba's morphine pills. Just as I shut the door, I caught a glimpse of Soraya quickly sliding something under Baba's blanket. "Hey, I saw that! What were you two doing?" I said.

"Nothing," Soraya said, smiling.

"Liar." I lifted Baba's blanket. "What's this?" I said, though as soon as I picked up the leather-bound book, I knew. I traced my fingers along the gold-stitched borders. I remembered the fireworks the night Rahim Khan had given it to me, the night of my thirteenth birthday, flares sizzling and exploding into bouquets of red, green, and yellow.

"I can't believe you can write like this," Soraya said.

Baba dragged his head off the pillow. "I put her up to it. I hope you don't mind."

I gave the notebook back to Soraya and left the room. Baba hated it when I cried.

A MONTH AFTER THE WEDDING, the Taheris, Sharif, his wife Suzy, and several of Soraya's aunts came over to our apartment for dinner. Soraya made *sabzi challow*—white rice with spinach and lamb. After dinner, we all had green tea and played cards in groups of four. Soraya and I played with Sharif and Suzy on the coffee table, next to the couch where Baba lay under a wool blanket. He watched me joking with Sharif, watched Soraya and me lacing our fingers together, watched me push back a loose curl of her hair. I could see his internal smile, as wide as the skies of Kabul on nights when the poplars shivered and the sound of crickets swelled in the gardens.

Just before midnight, Baba asked us to help him into bed. Soraya and I placed his arms on our shoulders and wrapped ours around his back. When we lowered him, he had Soraya turn off the bedside lamp. He asked us to lean in, gave us each a kiss.

"I'll come back with your morphine and a glass of water, Kaka jan," Soraya said.

"Not tonight," he said. "There is no pain tonight."

"Okay," she said. She pulled up his blanket. We closed the door. Baba never woke up.

THEY FILLED THE PARKING SPOTS at the mosque in Hayward. On the balding grass field behind the building, cars and SUVs parked in crowded makeshift rows. People had to drive three or four blocks north of the mosque to find a spot.

The men's section of the mosque was a large square room, covered with Afghan rugs and thin mattresses placed in parallel lines. Men filed into the room, leaving their shoes at the entrance, and sat cross-legged on the mattresses. A mullah chanted *surrahs* from the Koran into a microphone. I sat by the door, the customary position for the family of the deceased. General Taheri was seated next to me.

Through the open door, I could see lines of cars pulling in, sunlight winking in their windshields. They dropped off passengers, men dressed in dark suits, women clad in black dresses, their heads covered with traditional white *hijabs*.

As words from the Koran reverberated through the room, I thought of the old story of Baba wrestling a black bear in Baluchistan. Baba had wrestled bears his whole life. Losing his young wife. Raising a son by himself. Leaving his beloved homeland, his *watan*. Poverty. Indignity. In the end, a bear had come that he couldn't best. But even then, he had lost on his own terms.

After each round of prayers, groups of mourners lined up and greeted me on their way out. Dutifully, I shook their hands. Many of them I barely knew. I smiled politely, thanked them for their wishes, listened to whatever they had to say about Baba. "… helped me build the house in Taimani …"

"… bless him …"

"… no one else to turn to and he lent me …"

"… found me a job … barely knew me …"

"… like a brother to me …"

Listening to them, I realized how much of who I was, what I was, had been defined by Baba and the marks he had left on people's lives. My whole life, I had been "Baba's son." Now he was gone. Baba couldn't show me the way anymore; I'd have to find it on my own.

The thought of it terrified me.

Earlier, at the gravesite in the small Muslim section of the cemetery, I had watched them lower Baba into the hole. The mullah and another man got into an argument over which was the correct *ayat* of the Koran to recite at the gravesite. It might have turned ugly had General Taheri not intervened. The mullah chose an *ayat* and recited it, casting the other fellow nasty glances. I watched them toss the first shovelful of dirt into the grave. Then I left. Walked to the other side of the cemetery. Sat in the shade of a red maple.

Now the last of the mourners had paid their respects and the mosque was empty, save for the mullah unplugging the microphone and wrapping his Koran in green cloth. The general and I stepped out into a late-afternoon sun. We walked down the steps, past men smoking in clusters. I heard snippets of their conversations, a soccer game in Union City next weekend, a new Afghan restaurant in Santa Clara. Life moving on already, leaving Baba behind.

"How are you, *bachem*?" General Taheri said.

I gritted my teeth. Bit back the tears that had threatened all day. "I'm going to find Soraya," I said.

"Okay."

I walked to the women's side of the mosque. Soraya was standing on the steps with her mother and a couple of ladies I recognized vaguely from the wedding. I motioned to Soraya. She said something to her mother and came to me.

"Can we walk?" I said.

"Sure." She took my hand.

We walked in silence down a winding gravel path lined by a row of low hedges. We sat on a bench and watched an elderly couple kneeling beside a grave a few rows away and placing a bouquet of daisies by the headstone. "Soraya?"

"Yes?"

"I'm going to miss him."

She put her hand on my lap. Baba's *chila* glinted on her ring finger. Behind her, I could see Baba's mourners driving away on Mission Boulevard. Soon we'd leave too, and for the first time ever, Baba would be all alone.

Soraya pulled me to her and the tears finally came.

BECAUSE SORAYA AND I never had an engagement period, much of what I learned about the Taheris I learned after I married into their family. For example, I learned that, once a month, the general suffered from blinding migraines that lasted almost a week. When the headaches struck, the general went to his room, undressed, turned off the light, locked the door, and didn't come out until the pain subsided. No one was allowed to go in, no one was allowed to knock. Eventually, he would emerge, dressed in his gray suit once more, smelling of sleep and bedsheets, his eyes puffy and bloodshot. I learned from Soraya that he and Khanum Taheri had slept in separate rooms for as long as she could remember. I learned that he could be petty, such as when he'd take a bite of the *qurma* his wife placed before him, sigh, and push it away. "I'll make you something else," Khanum Taheri would say, but he'd ignore her, sulk, and eat bread and onion. This made Soraya angry and her mother cry. Soraya told me he took antidepressants. I learned that he had kept his family on welfare and had never held a job in the U.S., preferring to cash government-issued checks than degrading himself with work unsuitable for a man of his stature—he saw the flea market only as a hobby, a way to socialize with his fellow Afghans. The general believed that, sooner or later, Afghanistan would be freed, the monarchy restored, and his services would once again be called upon. So every day, he donned his gray suit, wound his pocket watch, and waited.

I learned that Khanum Taheri—whom I called Khala Jamila now—had once been famous in Kabul for her enchanting singing voice. Though she had never sung professionally, she had had the talent to—I learned she could sing folk songs, *ghazals*, even raga, which was usually a man's domain. But as much as the general appreciated listening to music—he owned, in fact, a considerable collection of classical *ghazal* tapes by Afghan and Hindi singers— he believed the performing of it best left to those with lesser reputations. That she never sing in public had been one of the general's conditions when they had married. Soraya told me that her mother had wanted to sing at our wedding, only one song, but the general gave her one of his looks and the matter was buried. Khala Jamila played the lotto once a week and watched Johnny Carson every night. She spent her days in the garden, tending to her roses, geraniums, potato vines, and orchids.

When I married Soraya, the flowers and Johnny Carson took a backseat. I was the new delight in Khala Jamila's life. Unlike the general's guarded and diplomatic manners—he didn't correct me when I continued to call him "General Sahib"—Khala Jamila made no secret of how much she adored me. For one thing, I listened to her impressive list of maladies, something the general had long turned a deaf ear to. Soraya told me that, ever since her mother's stroke, every flutter in her chest was a heart attack, every aching joint the onset of rheumatoid arthritis, and every twitch of the eye another stroke. I remember the first time Khala Jamila mentioned a lump in her neck to me. "I'll skip school tomorrow and take you to the doctor," I said, to which the general smiled and said, "Then you might as well turn in your books for good, *bachem*. Your khala's medical charts are like the works of Rumi: They come in volumes."

But it wasn't just that she'd found an audience for her mono- logues of illness. I firmly believed that if I had picked up a rifle and gone on a murdering rampage, I would have still had the benefit of her unblinking love. Because I had rid her heart of its gravest malady. I had relieved her of the greatest fear of every Afghan mother: that no honorable *khastegar* would ask for her daughter's hand. That her daughter would age alone, husbandless, childless. Every woman needed a husband. Even if he did silence the song in her.

And, from Soraya, I learned the details of what had happened in Virginia.

We were at a wedding. Soraya's uncle, Sharif, the one who worked for the INS, was marrying his son to an Afghan girl from Newark. The wedding was at the same hall where, six months prior, Soraya and I had had our *awroussi*. We were standing in a crowd of guests, watching the bride accept rings from the groom's family, when we overheard two middle-aged women talking, their backs to us.

"What a lovely bride," one of them said, "Just look at her. So *maghbool*, like the moon."

"Yes," the other said. "And pure too. Virtuous. No boyfriends."

"I know. I tell you that boy did well not to marry his cousin."

Soraya broke down on the way home. I pulled the Ford off to the curb, parked under a streetlight on Fremont Boulevard.

"It's all right," I said, pushing back her hair. "Who cares?"

"It's so fucking unfair," she barked.

"Just forget it."

"Their sons go out to nightclubs looking for meat and get their girlfriends pregnant, they have kids out of wedlock and no one says a goddamn thing. Oh, they're just men having fun! I make one mistake and suddenly everyone is talking *nang* and *namoos,* and I have to have my face rubbed in it for the rest of my life."

I wiped a tear from her jawline, just above her birthmark, with the pad of my thumb.

"I didn't tell you," Soraya said, dabbing at her eyes, "but my father showed up with a gun that night. He told … him … that he had two bullets in the chamber, one for him and one for himself if I didn't come home. I was screaming, calling my father all kinds of names, saying he couldn't keep me locked up forever, that I wished he were dead." Fresh tears squeezed out between her lids. "I actually said that to him, that I wished he were dead.

"When he brought me home, my mother threw her arms around me and she was crying too. She was saying things but I couldn't understand any of it because she was slurring her words so badly. So my father took me up to my bedroom and sat me in front of the dresser mirror. He handed me a pair of scissors and calmly told me to cut off all my hair. He watched while I did it.

"I didn't step out of the house for weeks. And when I did, I heard whispers or imagined them everywhere I went. That was four years ago and three thousand miles away and I'm still hearing them."

"Fuck 'em," I said.

She made a sound that was half sob, half laugh. "When I told you about this on the phone the night of *khastegari,* I was sure you'd change your mind."

"No chance of that, Soraya."

She smiled and took my hand. "I'm so lucky to have found you. You're so different from every Afghan guy I've met."

"Let's never talk about this again, okay?"

"Okay."

I kissed her cheek and pulled away from the curb. As I drove, I wondered why I was different. Maybe it was because I had been raised by men; I hadn't grown up around women and had never been exposed firsthand to the double standard with which Afghan society sometimes treated them. Maybe it was because Baba had been such an unusual Afghan father, a liberal who had lived by his own rules, a maverick who had disregarded or embraced societal customs as he had seen fit.

But I think a big part of the reason I didn't care about Soraya's past was that I had one of my own. I knew all about regret.

SHORTLY AFTER BABA'S DEATH, Soraya and I moved into a one-bedroom apartment in Fremont, just a few blocks away from the general and Khala Jamila's house. Soraya's parents bought us a brown leather couch and a set of Mikasa dishes as housewarming presents. The general gave me an additional present, a brandnew IBM typewriter. In the box, he had slipped a note written in Farsi:

Amir jan,
I hope you discover many tales on these keys.
                                             General Iqbal Taheri

I sold Baba's VW bus and, to this day, I have not gone back to the flea market. I would drive to his gravesite every Friday, and, sometimes, I'd find a fresh bouquet of freesias by the headstone and know Soraya had been there too.

Soraya and I settled into the routines—and minor wonders—of married life. We shared toothbrushes and socks, passed each other the morning paper. She slept on the right side of the bed, I preferred the left. She liked fluffy pillows, I liked the hard ones. She ate her cereal dry, like a snack, and chased it with milk.

I got my acceptance at San Jose State that summer and declared an English major. I took on a security job, swing shift at a furniture warehouse in Sunnyvale. The job was dreadfully boring, but its saving grace was a considerable one: When everyone left at 6 P.M. and shadows began to crawl between aisles of plasticcovered sofas piled to the ceiling, I took out my books and studied. It was in the Pine-Sol-scented office of that furniture warehouse that I began my first novel.

Soraya joined me at San Jose State the following year and enrolled, to her father's chagrin, in the teaching track.

"I don't know why you're wasting your talents like this," the general said one night over dinner. "Did you know, Amir jan, that she earned nothing but A's in high school?" He turned to her. "An intelligent girl like you could become a lawyer, a political scientist. And, *Inshallah*, when Afghanistan is free, you could help write the new constitution. There would be a need for young talented Afghans like you. They might even offer you a ministry position, given your family name."

I could see Soraya holding back, her face tightening. "I'm not a girl, Padar. I'm a married woman. Besides, they'd need teachers too."

"Anyone can teach."

"Is there any more rice, *Madar*?" Soraya said.

After the general excused himself to meet some friends in Hayward, Khala Jamila tried to console Soraya. "He means well," she said. "He just wants you to be successful."

"So he can boast about his attorney daughter to his friends. Another medal for the general," Soraya said.

"Such nonsense you speak!"

"Successful," Soraya hissed. "At least I'm not like him, sitting around while other people fight the *Shorawi*, waiting for when the dust settles so he can move in and reclaim his posh little government position. Teaching may not pay much, but it's what I want to do! It's what I love, and it's a whole lot better than collecting welfare, by the way."

Khala Jamila bit her tongue. "If he ever hears you saying that, he will never speak to you again."

"Don't worry," Soraya snapped, tossing her napkin on the plate. "I won't bruise his precious ego."

IN THE SUMMER of 1988, about six months before the Soviets withdrew from Afghanistan, I finished my first novel, a father-son story set in Kabul, written mostly with the typewriter the general had given me. I sent query letters to a dozen agencies and was stunned one August day when I opened our mailbox and found a request from a New York agency for the completed manuscript. I mailed it the next day. Soraya kissed the carefully wrapped manuscript and Khala Jamila insisted we pass it under the Koran. She told me that she was going to do *nazr* for me, a vow to have a sheep slaughtered and the meat given to the poor if my book was accepted.

"Please, no *nazr*, Khala jan," I said, kissing her face. "Just do *zakat*, give the money to someone in need, okay? No sheep killing."

Six weeks later, a man named Martin Greenwalt called from New York and offered to represent me. I only told Soraya about it. "But just because I have an agent doesn't mean I'll get published. If Martin sells the novel, then we'll celebrate."

A month later, Martin called and informed me I was going to be a published novelist. When I told Soraya, she screamed.

We had a celebration dinner with Soraya's parents that night. Khala Jamila made *kofta*—meatballs and white rice—and white *ferni*. The general, a sheen of moisture in his eyes, said that he was proud of me. After General Taheri and his wife left, Soraya and I celebrated with an expensive bottle of Merlot I had bought on the way home—the general did not approve of women drinking alcohol, and Soraya didn't drink in his presence.

"I am so proud of you," she said, raising her glass to mine. "Kaka would have been proud too."

"I know," I said, thinking of Baba, wishing he could have seen me.

Later that night, after Soraya fell asleep—wine always made her sleepy—I stood on the balcony and breathed in the cool summer air. I thought of Rahim Khan and the little note of support he had written me after he'd read my first story. And I thought of Hassan. *Some day*, Inshallah, *you will be a great writer,* he had said once, *and people all over the world will read your stories.* There was so much goodness in my life. So much happiness. I wondered whether I deserved any of it.

The novel was released in the summer of that following year, 1989, and the publisher sent me on a five-city book tour. I became a minor celebrity in the Afghan community. That was the year that the *Shorawi* completed their withdrawal from Afghanistan. It should have been a time of glory for Afghans. Instead, the war raged on, this time between Afghans, the *Mujahedin,* against the Soviet puppet government of Najibullah, and Afghan refugees kept flocking to Pakistan. That was the year that the cold war ended, the year the Berlin Wall came down. In the midst of it all, Afghanistan was forgotten. And General Taheri, whose hopes had stirred awake after the Soviets pulled out, went back to winding his pocket watch.

That was also the year that Soraya and I began trying to have a child.

THE IDEA OF FATHERHOOD unleashed a swirl of emotions in me. I found it frightening, invigorating, daunting, and exhilarating all at the same time. What sort of father would I make, I wondered. I wanted to be just like Baba and I wanted to be nothing like him. But a year passed and nothing happened. With each cycle of blood, Soraya grew more frustrated, more impatient, more irritable. By then, Khala Jamila's initially subtle hints had become overt, as in *"Kho dega!"* So! "When am I going to sing *alahoo* for my little *nawasa*?" The general, ever the Pashtun, never made any queries—doing so meant alluding to a sexual act between his daughter and a man, even if the man in question had been married to her for over four years. But his eyes perked up when Khala Jamila teased us about a baby.

"Sometimes, it takes a while," I told Soraya one night.

"A year isn't a while, Amir!" she said, in a terse voice so unlike her. "Something's wrong, I know it."

"Then let's see a doctor."

DR. ROSEN, a round-bellied man with a plump face and small, even teeth, spoke with a faint Eastern European accent, something remotely Slavic. He had a passion for trains—his office was littered with books about the history of railroads, model locomotives, paintings of trains trundling on tracks through green hills and over bridges. A sign above his desk read, LIFE IS A TRAIN. GET ON BOARD.

He laid out the plan for us. I'd get checked first. "Men are easy," he said, fingers tapping on his mahogany desk. "A man's plumbing is like his mind: simple, very few surprises. You ladies, on the other hand ... well, God put a lot of thought into making you." I wondered if he fed that bit about the plumbing to all of his couples.

"Lucky us," Soraya said.

Dr. Rosen laughed. It fell a few notches short of genuine. He gave me a lab slip and a plastic jar, handed Soraya a request for some routine blood tests. We shook hands. "Welcome aboard," he said, as he showed us out.

I PASSED WITH FLYING COLORS.

The next few months were a blur of tests on Soraya: Basal body temperatures, blood tests for every conceivable hormone, urine tests, something called a "Cervical Mucus Test," ultrasounds, more blood tests, and more urine tests. Soraya underwent a procedure called a hysteroscopy—Dr. Rosen inserted a telescope into Soraya's uterus and took a look around. He found nothing. "The plumbing's clear," he announced, snapping off his latex gloves. I wished he'd stop calling it that—we weren't bathrooms. When the tests were over, he explained that he couldn't explain why we couldn't have kids. And, apparently, that wasn't so unusual. It was called "Unexplained Infertility."

Then came the treatment phase. We tried a drug called Clomiphene, and hMG, a series of shots which Soraya gave to herself. When these failed, Dr. Rosen advised in vitro fertilization. We received a polite letter from our HMO, wishing us the best of luck, regretting they couldn't cover the cost.

We used the advance I had received for my novel to pay for it. IVF proved lengthy, meticulous, frustrating, and ultimately unsuccessful. After months of sitting in waiting rooms reading magazines like *Good Housekeeping* and *Reader's Digest,* after endless paper gowns and cold, sterile exam rooms lit by fluorescent lights, the repeated humiliation of discussing every detail of our sex life with a total stranger, the injections and probes and specimen collections, we went back to Dr. Rosen and his trains.

He sat across from us, tapped his desk with his fingers, and used the word "adoption" for the first time. Soraya cried all the way home.

Soraya broke the news to her parents the weekend after our last visit with Dr. Rosen. We were sitting on picnic chairs in the

Taheris' backyard, grilling trout and sipping yogurt *dogh*. It was an early evening in March 1991. Khala Jamila had watered the roses and her new honeysuckles, and their fragrance mixed with the smell of cooking fish. Twice already, she had reached across her chair to caress Soraya's hair and say, "God knows best, *bachem*. Maybe it wasn't meant to be."

Soraya kept looking down at her hands. She was tired, I knew, tired of it all. "The doctor said we could adopt," she murmured.

General Taheri's head snapped up at this. He closed the barbecue lid. "He did?"

"He said it was an option," Soraya said.

We'd talked at home about adoption. Soraya was ambivalent at best. "I know it's silly and maybe vain," she said to me on the way to her parents' house, "but I can't help it. I've always dreamed that I'd hold it in my arms and know my blood had fed it for nine months, that I'd look in its eyes one day and be startled to see you or me, that the baby would grow up and have your smile or mine. Without that … Is that wrong?"

"No," I had said.

"Am I being selfish?"

"No, Soraya."

"Because if you really want to do it …"

"No," I said. "If we're going to do it, we shouldn't have any doubts at all about it, and we should both be in agreement. It wouldn't be fair to the baby otherwise."

She rested her head on the window and said nothing else the rest of the way.

Now the general sat beside her. "*Bachem,* this adoption … thing, I'm not so sure it's for us Afghans." Soraya looked at me tiredly and sighed.

"For one thing, they grow up and want to know who their natural parents are," he said. "Nor can you blame them. Sometimes, they leave the home in which you labored for years to provide for them so they can find the people who gave them life. Blood is a powerful thing, *bachem,* never forget that."

"I don't want to talk about this anymore," Soraya said.

"I'll say one more thing," he said. I could tell he was getting revved up; we were about to get one of the general's little speeches. "Take Amir jan, here. We all knew his father, I know who his grandfather was in Kabul and his great-grandfather before him, I could sit here and trace generations of his ancestors for you if you asked. That's why when his father—God give him peace—came *khastegari,* I didn't hesitate. And believe me, his father wouldn't have agreed to ask for your hand if he didn't know whose descendant you were. Blood is a powerful thing, *bachem,* and when you adopt, you don't know whose blood you're bringing into your house.

"Now, if you were American, it wouldn't matter. People here marry for love, family name and ancestry never even come into the equation. They adopt that way too, as long as the baby is healthy, everyone is happy. But we are Afghans, *bachem.*"

"Is the fish almost ready?" Soraya said. General Taheri's eyeslingered on her. He patted her knee. "Just be happy you have your health and a good husband."

"What do you think, Amir jan?" Khala Jamila said.

I put my glass on the ledge, where a row of her potted geraniums were dripping water. "I think I agree with General Sahib."

Reassured, the general nodded and went back to the grill.

We all had our reasons for not adopting. Soraya had hers, the general his, and I had this: that perhaps something, someone,

somewhere, had decided to deny me fatherhood for the things
I had done. Maybe this was my punishment, and perhaps justly
so. *It wasn't meant to be,* Khala Jamila had said. Or, maybe, it was
meant not to be.

A FEW MONTHS LATER, we used the advance for my
second novel and placed a down payment on a pretty, two-bed-
room Victorian house in San Francisco's Bernal Heights. It had a
peaked roof, hardwood floors, and a tiny backyard which ended
in a sun deck and a fire pit. The general helped me refinish the
deck and paint the walls. Khala Jamila bemoaned us moving
almost an hour away, especially since she thought Soraya needed
all the love and support she could get—oblivious to the fact that
her well-intended but overbearing sympathy was precisely what
was driving Soraya to move.

SOMETIMES, SORAYA SLEEPING NEXT TO ME, I lay
in bed and listened to the screen door swinging open and shut
with the breeze, to the crickets chirping in the yard. And I could
almost feel the emptiness in Soraya's womb, like it was a living,
breathing thing. It had seeped into our marriage, that emptiness,
into our laughs, and our lovemaking. And late at night, in the
darkness of our room, I'd feel it rising from Soraya and settling
between us. Sleeping between us. Like a newborn child.

FOURTEEN

June 2001

I lowered the phone into the cradle and stared at it for a long time. It wasn't until Aflatoon startled me with a bark that I realized how quiet the room had become. Soraya had muted the television.

"You look pale, Amir," she said from the couch, the same one her parents had given us as a housewarming gift for our first apartment. She'd been lying on it with Aflatoon's head nestled on her chest, her legs buried under the worn pillows. She was halfwatching a PBS special on the plight of wolves in Minnesota, half-correcting essays from her summer-school class—she'd been teaching at the same school now for six years. She sat up, and Aflatoon leapt down from the couch. It was the general who had given our cocker spaniel his name, Farsi for "Plato," because, he said, if you looked hard enough and long enough into the dog's filmy black eyes, you'd swear he was thinking wise thoughts.

There was a sliver of fat, just a hint of it, beneath Soraya's chin now. The past ten years had padded the curves of her hips some, and combed into her coal black hair a few streaks of cinder gray. But she still had the face of a Grand Ball princess, with her bird-in-flight eyebrows and nose, elegantly curved like a letter from ancient Arabic writings.

"You look pale," Soraya repeated, placing the stack of papers on the table.

"I have to go to Pakistan."

She stood up now. "Pakistan?"

"Rahim Khan is very sick." A fist clenched inside me with those words.

"Kaka's old business partner?" She'd never met Rahim Khan, but I had told her about him. I nodded.

"Oh," she said. "I'm so sorry, Amir."

"We used to be close," I said. "When I was a kid, he was the first grown-up I ever thought of as a friend." I pictured him and Baba drinking tea in Baba's study, then smoking near the window, a sweetbrier-scented breeze blowing from the garden and bending the twin columns of smoke.

"I remember you telling me that," Soraya said. She paused. "How long will you be gone?"

"I don't know. He wants to see me." "Is it ..."

"Yes, it's safe. I'll be all right, Soraya." It was the question she'd wanted to ask all along—fifteen years of marriage had turned us into mind readers. "I'm going to go for a walk."

"Should I go with you?" "Nay, I'd rather be alone."

I DROVE TO GOLDEN GATE PARK and walked along Spreckels Lake on the northern edge of the park. It was a beautiful Sunday afternoon; the sun sparkled on the water where dozens of miniature boats sailed, propelled by a crisp San Francisco breeze. I sat on a park bench, watched a man toss a football to his son, telling him to not sidearm the ball, to throw over the shoulder. I glanced up and saw a pair of kites, red with long blue tails. They floated high above the trees on the west end of the park, over the windmills.

I thought about a comment Rahim Khan had made just before we hung up. Made it in passing, almost as an afterthought. I closed my eyes and saw him at the other end of the scratchy longdistance line, saw him with his lips slightly parted, head tilted to one side. And again, something in his bottomless black eyes hinted at an unspoken secret between us. Except now I knew he knew. My suspicions had been right all those years. He knew about Assef, the kite, the money, the watch with the lightning bolt hands. He had always known.

Come. There is a way to be good again, Rahim Khan had said on the phone just before hanging up. Said it in passing, almost as an afterthought.

A way to be good again.

WHEN I CAME HOME, Soraya was on the phone with her mother. "Won't be long, Madar jan. A week, maybe two ... Yes, you and Padar can stay with me ..."

Two years earlier, the general had broken his right hip. He'd had one of his migraines again, and emerging from his room, bleary-eyed and dazed, he had tripped on a loose carpet edge. His scream had brought Khala Jamila running from the kitchen. "It sounded like a *jaroo*, a broomstick, snapping in half," she was always fond of saying, though the doctor had said it was unlikely

she'd heard anything of the sort. The general's shattered hip—
and all of the ensuing complications, the pneumonia, blood
poisoning, the protracted stay at the nursing home—ended
Khala Jamila's long-running soliloquies about her own health.
And started new ones about the general's. She'd tell anyone
who would listen that the doctors had told them his kidneys
were failing. "But then they had never seen Afghan kidneys, had
they?" she'd say proudly. What I remember most about the general's hospital stay is how Khala Jamila would wait until he fell
asleep, and then sing to him, songs I remembered from Kabul,
playing on Baba's scratchy old transistor radio.

The general's frailty—and time—had softened things between
him and Soraya too. They took walks together, went to lunch
on Saturdays, and, sometimes, the general sat in on some of her
classes. He'd sit in the back of the room, dressed in his shiny
old gray suit, wooden cane across his lap, smiling. Sometimes he
even took notes.

THAT NIGHT, Soraya and I lay in bed, her back pressed to
my chest, my face buried in her hair. I remembered when we
used to lay forehead to forehead, sharing afterglow kisses and
whispering until our eyes drifted closed, whispering about
tiny, curled toes, first smiles, first words, first steps. We still did
sometimes, but the whispers were about school, my new book, a
giggle over someone's ridiculous dress at a party. Our lovemaking was still good, at times better than good, but some nights all
I'd feel was a relief to be done with it, to be free to drift away
and forget, at least for a while, about the futility of what we'd
just done. She never said so, but I knew sometimes Soraya felt

it too. On those nights, we'd each roll to our side of the bed and let our own savior take us away. Soraya's was sleep. Mine, as always, was a book.

I lay in the dark the night Rahim Khan called and traced with my eyes the parallel silver lines on the wall made by moonlight pouring through the blinds. At some point, maybe just before dawn, I drifted to sleep. And dreamed of Hassan running in the snow, the hem of his green *chapan* dragging behind him, snow crunching under his black rubber boots. He was yelling over his shoulder: *For you, a thousand times over!*

A WEEK LATER, I sat on a window seat aboard a Pakistani International Airlines flight, watching a pair of uniformed airline workers remove the wheel chocks. The plane taxied out of the terminal and, soon, we were airborne, cutting through the clouds. I rested my head against the window. Waited, in vain, for sleep.

FIFTEEN

Three hours after my flight landed in Peshawar, I was sitting on shredded upholstery in the backseat of a smoke-filled taxicab. My driver, a chain-smoking, sweaty little man who introduced himself as Gholam, drove nonchalantly and recklessly, averting collisions by the thinnest of margins, all without so much as a pause in the incessant stream of words spewing from his mouth:

"... terrible what is happening in your country, *yar*. Afghani people and Pakistani people they are like brothers, I tell you. Muslims have to help Muslims so ..."

I tuned him out, switched to a polite nodding mode. I remembered Peshawar pretty well from the few months Baba and I had spent there in 1981. We were heading west now on Jamrud road, past the Cantonment and its lavish, high-walled homes. The bustle of the city blurring past me reminded me of a busier, more crowded version of the Kabul I knew, particularly of the *KochehMorgha,* or Chicken Bazaar, where Hassan and I used to buy chutney-dipped potatoes and cherry water. The streets were clogged with bicycle riders, milling pedestrians, and rickshaws popping blue smoke, all weaving through a maze of narrow lanes and alleys. Bearded vendors draped in thin blankets sold animal-skin lampshades, carpets, embroidered shawls, and copper goods from rows of small, tightly jammed stalls. The city was bursting with sounds; the shouts of vendors rang in my ears mingled with the blare of Hindi music, the sputtering of rickshaws, and the jingling bells of horse-drawn carts. Rich scents, both pleasant and not so pleasant, drifted to me through the passenger window, the spicy aroma of *pakora* and the *nihari* Baba had loved so much blended with the sting of diesel fumes, the stench of rot, garbage, and feces.

A little past the redbrick buildings of Peshawar University, we entered an area my garrulous driver referred to as "Afghan Town." I saw sweetshops and carpet vendors, kabob stalls, kids with dirt-caked hands selling cigarettes, tiny restaurants—maps of Afghanistan painted on their windows—all interlaced with backstreet aid agencies. "Many of your brothers in this area, *yar*. They are opening businesses, but most of them are very poor." He *tsk*'ed his tongue and sighed. "Anyway, we're getting close now."

I thought about the last time I had seen Rahim Khan, in 1981. He had come to say good-bye the night Baba and I had fled Kabul. I remember Baba and him embracing in the foyer, crying softly. When Baba and I arrived in the U.S., he and Rahim Khan kept in touch. They would speak four or five times a year and, sometimes, Baba would pass me the receiver. The last time I had spoken to Rahim Khan had been shortly after Baba's death. The news had reached Kabul and he had called. We'd only spoken for a few minutes and lost the connection.

The driver pulled up to a narrow building at a busy corner where two winding streets intersected. I paid the driver, took my lone suitcase, and walked up to the intricately carved door. The building had wooden balconies with open shutters—from many of them, laundry was hanging to dry in the sun. I walked up the creaky stairs to the second floor, down a dim hallway to the last door on the right. Checked the address on the piece of stationery paper in my palm. Knocked.

Then, a thing made of skin and bones pretending to be Rahim Khan opened the door.

A CREATIVE WRITING TEACHER at San Jose State used to say about clichés: "Avoid them like the plague." Then he'd laugh at his own joke. The class laughed along with him, but I always thought clichés got a bum rap. Because, often, they're dead-on. But the aptness of the clichéd saying is overshadowed by the nature of the saying as a cliché. For example, the "elephant in the room" saying. Nothing could more correctly describe the initial moments of my reunion with Rahim Khan.

We sat on a wispy mattress set along the wall, across the window overlooking the noisy street below. Sunlight slanted in and cast a triangular wedge of light onto the Afghan rug on the floor. Two folding chairs rested against one wall and a small copper samovar sat in the opposite corner. I poured us tea from it.

"How did you find me?" I asked.

"It's not difficult to find people in America. I bought a map of the U.S., and called up information for cities in Northern California," he said. "It's wonderfully strange to see you as a grown man."

I smiled and dropped three sugar cubes in my tea. He liked

his black and bitter, I remembered. "Baba didn't get the chance to tell you but I got married fifteen years ago." The truth was, by then, the cancer in Baba's brain had made him forgetful, negligent.

"You are married? To whom?"

"Her name is Soraya Taheri." I thought of her back home, worrying about me. I was glad she wasn't alone.

"Taheri... whose daughter is she?"

I told him. His eyes brightened. "Oh, yes, I remember now. Isn't General Taheri married to Sharif jan's sister? What was her name ..."

"Jamila jan."

"*Balay!*" he said, smiling. "I knew Sharif jan in Kabul, long time ago, before he moved to America."

"He's been working for the INS for years, handles a lot of Afghan cases."

"*Haiiii,*" he sighed. "Do you and Soraya jan have children?"

"Nay."

"Oh." He slurped his tea and didn't ask more; Rahim Khan had always been one of the most instinctive people I'd ever met.

I told him a lot about Baba, his job, the flea market, and how, at the end, he'd died happy. I told him about my schooling, my books—four published novels to my credit now. He smiled at this, said he had never had any doubt. I told him I had written short stories in the leather-bound notebook he'd given me, but he didn't remember the notebook.

The conversation inevitably turned to the Taliban.

"Is it as bad as I hear?" I said.

"Nay, it's worse. Much worse," he said. "They don't let you be human." He pointed to a scar above his right eye cutting a crooked path through his bushy eyebrow. "I was at a soccer game in Ghazi Stadium in 1998. Kabul against Mazar-i-Sharif, I think, and by the way the players weren't allowed to wear shorts. Indecent exposure, I guess." He gave a tired laugh. "Anyway, Kabul scored a goal and the man next to me cheered loudly. Suddenly this young bearded fellow who was patrolling the aisles, eighteen years old at most by the look of him, he walked up to me and struck me on the forehead with the butt of his Kalashnikov. 'Do that again and I'll cut out your tongue, you old donkey!' he said." Rahim Khan rubbed the scar with a gnarled finger. "I was old enough to be his grandfather and I was sitting there, blood gushing down my face, apologizing to that son of a dog."

I poured him more tea. Rahim Khan talked some more. Much of it I knew already, some not. He told me that, as arranged between Baba and him, he had lived in Baba's house since 1981—this I knew about. Baba had "sold" the house to Rahim Khan shortly before he and I fled Kabul. The way Baba had seen it those days, Afghanistan's troubles were only a temporary interruption of our way of life—the days of parties at the Wazir Akbar Khan house and picnics in Paghman would surely return. So he'd given the house to Rahim Khan to keep watch over until that day.

Rahim Khan told me how, when the Northern Alliance took over Kabul between 1992 and 1996, different factions claimed different parts of Kabul. "If you went from the Shar-e-Nau section to Kerteh-Parwan to buy a carpet, you risked getting shot by a sniper or getting blown up by a rocket—if you got past all the checkpoints, that was. You practically needed a visa to go from one neighborhood to the other. So people just stayed put, prayed the next rocket wouldn't hit their home." He told me how people knocked holes in the walls of their homes so they could bypass the dangerous streets and would move down the block from hole to hole. In other parts, people moved about in underground tunnels.

"Why didn't you leave?" I said.

"Kabul was my home. It still is." He snickered. "Remember the street that went from your house to the *Qishla,* the military barracks next to Istiqlal School?"

"Yes." It was the shortcut to school. I remembered the day Hassan and I crossed it and the soldiers had teased Hassan about his mother. Hassan had cried in the cinema later, and I'd put an arm around him.

"When the Taliban rolled in and kicked the Alliance out of Kabul, I actually danced on that street," Rahim Khan said. "And, believe me, I wasn't alone. People were celebrating at *Chaman,* at *Deh-Mazang,* greeting the Taliban in the streets, climbing their tanks and posing for pictures with them. People were so tired of the constant fighting, tired of the rockets, the gunfire, the explosions, tired of watching Gulbuddin and his cohorts firing on anything that moved. The Alliance did more damage to Kabul than the *Shorawi.* They destroyed your father's orphanage, did you know that?"

"Why?" I said. "Why would they destroy an orphanage?" I remembered sitting behind Baba the day they opened the orphanage. The wind had knocked off his caracul hat and everyone had laughed, then stood and clapped when he'd delivered his speech. And now it was just another pile of rubble. All the money Baba had spent, all those nights he'd sweated over the blueprints, all the visits to the construction site to make sure every brick, every beam, and every block was laid just right ...

"Collateral damage," Rahim Khan said. "You don't want to know, Amir jan, what it was like sifting through the rubble of that orphanage. There were body parts of children ..."

"So when the Taliban came ..."

"They were heroes," Rahim Khan said.

"Peace at last."

"Yes, hope is a strange thing. Peace at last. But at what price?" A violent coughing fit gripped Rahim Khan and rocked his gaunt body back and forth. When he spat into his handkerchief, it immediately stained red. I thought that was as good a time as any to address the elephant sweating with us in the tiny room.

"How are you?" I asked. "I mean *really*, how are you?"

"Dying, actually," he said in a gurgling voice. Another round of coughing. More blood on the handkerchief. He wiped his mouth, blotted his sweaty brow from one wasted temple to the other with his sleeve, and gave me a quick glance. When he nodded, I knew he had read the next question on my face. "Not long," he breathed.

"How long?"

He shrugged. Coughed again. "I don't think I'll see the end of this summer," he said.

"Let me take you home with me. I can find you a good doctor. They're coming up with new treatments all the time. There are new drugs and experimental treatments, we could enroll you in one ..." I was rambling and I knew it. But it was better than crying, which I was probably going to do anyway.

He let out a chuff of laughter, revealed missing lower incisors. It was the most tired laughter I'd ever heard. "I see America has infused you with the optimism that has made her so great. That's very good. We're a melancholic people, we

Afghans, aren't we? Often, we wallow too much in *ghamkhori* and self-pity. We give in to loss, to suffering, accept it as a fact of life, even see it as necessary. *Zendagi migzara,* we say, life goes on. But I am not surrendering to fate here, I am being pragmatic. I have seen several good doctors here and they have given the same answer. I trust them and believe them. There is such a thing as God's will."

"There is only what you do and what you don't do," I said.

Rahim Khan laughed. "You sounded like your father just now. I miss him so much. But it *is* God's will, Amir jan. It really is." He paused. "Besides, there's another reason I asked you to come here. I wanted to see you before I go, yes, but something else too."

"Anything."

"You know all those years I lived in your father's house after you left?"

"Yes."

"I wasn't alone for all of them. Hassan lived there with me."

"Hassan," I said. When was the last time I had spoken his name? Those thorny old barbs of guilt bore into me once more, as if speaking his name had broken a spell, set them free to torment me anew. Suddenly the air in Rahim Khan's little flat was too thick, too hot, too rich with the smell of the street.

"I thought about writing you and telling you before, but I wasn't sure you wanted to know. Was I wrong?"

The truth was no. The lie was yes. I settled for something in between. "I don't know."

He coughed another patch of blood into the handkerchief. When he bent his head to spit, I saw honey-crusted sores on his scalp. "I brought you here because I am going to ask something of you. I'm going to ask you to do something for me. But before I do, I want to tell you about Hassan. Do you understand?"

"Yes," I murmured.

"I want to tell you about him. I want to tell you everything. You will listen?"

I nodded.

Then Rahim Khan sipped some more tea. Rested his head against the wall and spoke.

SIXTEEN

There were a lot of reasons why I went to Hazarajat to find Hassan in 1986. The biggest one, Allah forgive me, was that I was lonely. By then, most of my friends and relatives had either been killed or had escaped the country to Pakistan or Iran. I barely knew anyone in Kabul anymore, the city where I had lived my entire life. Everybody had fled. I would take a walk in the KartehParwan section—where the melon vendors used to hang out in the old days, you remember that spot?—and I wouldn't recognize anyone there. No one to greet, no one to sit down with for *chai,* no one to share stories with, just *Roussi* soldiers patrolling the streets. So eventually, I stopped going out to the city. I would spend my days in your father's house, up in the study, reading your mother's old books, listening to the news, watching the propaganda on television. Then I would pray *namaz,* cook something, eat, read some more, pray again, and go to bed. I would rise in the morning, pray, do it all over again.

And with my arthritis, it was getting harder for me to maintain the house. My knees and back were always aching—I would get up in the morning and it would take me at least an hour to shake the stiffness from my joints, especially in the wintertime. I did not want to let your father's house go to rot; we had all had many good times in that house, so many memories, Amir jan. It was not right—your father had designed that house himself; it had meant so much to him, and besides, I had promised him I would care for it when he and you left for Pakistan. Now it was just me and the house and ...I did my best. I tried to water the trees every few days, cut the lawn, tend to the flowers, fix things that needed fixing, but, even then, I was not a young man anymore.

But even so, I might have been able to manage. At least for a while longer. But when news of your father's death reached me ... for the first time, I felt a terrible loneliness in that house. An unbearable emptiness.

So one day, I fueled up the Buick and drove up to Hazarajat. I remembered that, after Ali dismissed himself from the house, your father told me he and Hassan had moved to a small village just outside Bamiyan. Ali had a cousin there as I recalled. I had no idea if Hassan would still be there, if anyone would even know of him or his whereabouts. After all, it had been ten years since Ali and Hassan had left your father's house. Hassan would have been a grown man in 1986, twenty-two, twenty-three years old. If he was even alive, that is—the *Shorawi*, may they rot in hell for what they did to our *watan*, killed so many of our young men. I don't have to tell you that.

But, with the grace of God, I found him there. It took very little searching—all I had to do was ask a few questions in Bamiyan and people pointed me to his village. I do not even recall its name, or whether it even had one. But I remember it was a scorching summer day and I was driving up a rutted dirt road, nothing on either side but sunbaked bushes, gnarled, spiny tree trunks, and dried grass like pale straw. I passed a dead donkey rotting on the side of the road. And then I turned a corner and, right in the middle of that barren land, I saw a cluster of mud houses, beyond them nothing but broad sky and mountains like jagged teeth.

The people in Bamiyan had told me I would find him easily— he lived in the only house in the village that had a walled garden. The mud wall, short and pocked with holes, enclosed the tiny house—which was really not much more than a glorified hut. Barefoot children were playing on the street, kicking a ragged tennis ball with a stick, and they stared when I pulled up and killed the engine. I knocked on the wooden door and stepped through into a yard that had very little in it save for a parched strawberry patch and a bare lemon tree. There was a *tandoor* in the corner in the shadow of an acacia tree and I saw a man squatting beside it. He was placing dough on a large wooden spatula and slapping it against the walls of the *tandoor*. He dropped the dough when he saw me. I had to make him stop kissing my hands.

"Let me look at you," I said. He stepped away. He was so tall now—I stood on my toes and still just came up to his chin. The Bamiyan sun had toughened his skin, and turned it several shades darker than I remembered, and he had lost a few of his front teeth. There were sparse strands of hair on his chin. Other than that, he had those same narrow green eyes, that scar on his upper lip, that round face, that affable smile. You would have recognized him, Amir jan. I am sure of it.

We went inside. There was a young light-skinned Hazara

woman sewing a shawl in a corner of the room. She was visibly expecting. "This is my wife, Rahim Khan," Hassan said proudly. "Her name is Farzana jan." She was a shy woman, so courteous she spoke in a voice barely higher than a whisper and she would not raise her pretty hazel eyes to meet my gaze. But the way she was looking at Hassan, he might as well have been sitting on the throne at the *Arg*.

"When is the baby coming?" I said after we all settled around the adobe room. There was nothing in the room, just a frayed rug, a few dishes, a pair of mattresses, and a lantern.

"*Inshallah,* this winter," Hassan said. "I am praying for a boy to carry on my father's name."

"Speaking of Ali, where is he?"

Hassan dropped his gaze. He told me that Ali and his cousin—who had owned the house—had been killed by a land mine two years before, just outside of Bamiyan. A land mine. Is there a more Afghan way of dying, Amir jan? And for some crazy reason, I became absolutely certain that it had been Ali's right leg—his twisted polio leg—that had finally betrayed him and stepped on that land mine. I was deeply saddened to hear Ali had died. Your father and I grew up together, as you know, and Ali had been with him as long as I could remember. I remember when we were all little, the year Ali got polio and almost died. Your father would walk around the house all day crying.

Farzana made us *shorwa* with beans, turnips, and potatoes. We washed our hands and dipped fresh *naan* from the *tandoor* into the *shorwa*—it was the best meal I had had in months. It was then that I asked Hassan to move to Kabul with me. I told him about the house, how I could not care for it by myself anymore. I told him I would pay him well, that he and his *khanum* would be comfortable. They looked to each other and did not say anything. Later, after we had washed our hands and Farzana had served us grapes, Hassan said the village was his home now; he and Farzana had made a life for themselves there.

"And Bamiyan is so close. We know people there. Forgive me, Rahim Khan. I pray you understand."

"Of course," I said. "You have nothing to apologize for. I understand."

It was midway through tea after *shorwa* that Hassan asked about you. I told him you were in America, but that I did not know much more. Hassan had so many questions about you. Had you married? Did you have children? How tall were you? Did you still fly kites and go to the cinema? Were you happy? He said he had befriended an old Farsi teacher in Bamiyan who had taught him to read and write. If he wrote you a letter, would I pass it on to you? And did I thinkyou would write back? I told him what I knew of you from the few phone conversations I had had with your father, but mostly I did not know how to answer him. Then he asked me about your father. When I told him, Hassan buried his face in his hands and broke into tears. He wept like a child for the rest of that night. They insisted that I spend the night there. Farzana fixed a cot for me and left me a glass of well water in case I got thirsty. All night, I heard her whispering to Hassan, and heard him sobbing.

In the morning, Hassan told me he and Farzana had decided to move to Kabul with me.

"I should not have come here," I said. "You were right, Hassan jan. You have a *zendagi*, a life here. It was presumptuous of me to just show up and ask you to drop everything. It is me who needs to be forgiven."

"We don't have that much to drop, Rahim Khan," Hassan said. His eyes were still red and puffy. "We'll go with you. We'll help you take care of the house."

"Are you absolutely sure?"

He nodded and dropped his head. "Agha sahib was like my second father ... God give him peace."

They piled their things in the center of a few worn rags and tied the corners together. We loaded the bundle into the Buick. Hassan stood in the threshold of the house and held the Koran as we all kissed it and passed under it. Then we left for Kabul. I remember as I was pulling away, Hassan turned to take a last look at their home.

When we got to Kabul, I discovered that Hassan had no intention of moving *into* the house. "But all these rooms are empty, Hassan jan. No one is going to live in them," I said.

But he would not. He said it was a matter of *ihtiram,* a matter of respect. He and Farzana moved their things into the hut in the backyard, where he was born. I pleaded for them to move into one of the guest bedrooms upstairs, but Hassan would hear nothing of it. "What will Amir agha think?" he said to me. "What will he think when he comes back to Kabul after the war and finds that I have assumed his place in the house?" Then, in mourning for your father, Hassan wore black for the next forty days.

I did not want them to, but the two of them did all the cooking, all the cleaning. Hassan tended to the flowers in the garden, soaked the roots, picked off yellowing leaves, and planted rosebushes. He painted the walls. In the house, he swept rooms no one had slept in for years, and cleaned bathrooms no one had bathed in. Like he was preparing the house for someone's return.

Do you remember the wall behind the row of corn your father had planted, Amir jan? What did you and Hassan call it, "the Wall of Ailing Corn"? A rocket destroyed a whole section of that wall in the middle of the night early that fall. Hassan rebuilt the wall with his own hands, brick by brick, until it stood whole again. I do not know what I would have done if he had not been there.

Then late that fall, Farzana gave birth to a stillborn baby girl. Hassan kissed the baby's lifeless face, and we buried her in the backyard, near the sweetbrier bushes. We covered the little mound with leaves from the poplar trees. I said a prayer for her. Farzana stayed in the hut all day and wailed—it is a heartbreaking sound, Amir jan, the wailing of a mother. I pray to Allah you never hear it.

Outside the walls of that house, there was a war raging. But the three of us, in your father's house, we made our own little haven from it. My vision started going by the late 1980s, so I had Hassan read me your mother's books. We would sit in the foyer, by the stove, and Hassan would read me from Masnawi or Khayyám, as Farzana cooked in the kitchen. And every morning, Hassan placed a flower on the little mound by the sweetbrier bushes.

In early 1990, Farzana became pregnant again. It was that same year, in the middle of the summer, that a woman covered in a sky blue *burqa* knocked on the front gates one morning. When I walked up to the gates, she was swaying on her feet, like she was too weak to even stand. I asked her what she wanted, but she would not answer.

"Who are you?" I said. But she just collapsed right there in the driveway. I yelled for Hassan and he helped me carry her into the house, to the living room. We lay her on the sofa and took off her *burqa*. Beneath it, we found a toothless woman with stringy graying hair and sores on her arms. She looked like she had not eaten for days. But the worst of it by far was her face. Someone had taken a knife to it and ... Amir jan, the slashes cut this way and that way. One of the cuts went from cheekbone to hairline and it had not spared her left eye on the way. It was grotesque. I patted her brow with a wet cloth and she opened her eyes. "Where is Hassan?" she whispered.

"I'm right here," Hassan said. He took her hand and squeezed it.

Her good eye rolled to him. "I have walked long and far to see if you are as beautiful in the flesh as you are in my dreams. And you are. Even more." She pulled his hand to her scarred face. "Smile for me. Please."

Hassan did and the old woman wept. "You smiled coming out of me, did anyone ever tell you? And I wouldn't even hold you. Allah forgive me, I wouldn't even hold you."

None of us had seen Sanaubar since she had eloped with a band of singers and dancers in 1964, just after she had given birth to Hassan. You never saw her, Amir, but in her youth, she was a vision. She had a dimpled smile and a walk that drove men crazy. No one who passed her on the street, be it a man or a woman, could look at her only once. And now ...

Hassan dropped her hand and bolted out of the house. I went after him, but he was too fast. I saw him running up the hill where you two used to play, his feet kicking up plumes of dust. I let him go. I sat with Sanaubar all day as the sky went from bright blue to purple. Hassan still had not come back when night fell and moonlight bathed the clouds. Sanaubar cried that coming back had been a mistake, maybe even a worse one than leaving. But I made her stay. Hassan would return, I knew.

He came back the next morning, looking tired and weary, like he had not slept all night. He took Sanaubar's hand in both of his and told her she could cry if she wanted to but she needn't, she was home now, he said, home with her family. He touched the scars on her face, and ran his hand through her hair.

Hassan and Farzana nursed her back to health. They fed her and washed her clothes. I gave her one of the guest rooms upstairs. Sometimes, I would look out the window into the yard and watch Hassan and his mother kneeling together, picking tomatoes or trimming a rosebush, talking. They were catching up on all the lost years, I suppose. As far as I know, he never asked where she had been or why she had left and she never told. I guess some stories do not need telling.

It was Sanaubar who delivered Hassan's son that winter of 1990. It had not started snowing yet, but the winter winds were blowing through the yards, bending the flowerbeds and rustling the leaves. I remember Sanaubar came out of the hut holding her grandson, had him wrapped in a wool blanket. She stood beaming under a dull gray sky, tears streaming down her cheeks, the needle-cold wind blowing her hair, and clutching that baby in her arms like she never wanted to let go. Not this time. She handed him to Hassan and he handed him to me and I sang the prayer of *Ayat-ul-kursi* in that little boy's ear.

They named him Sohrab, after Hassan's favorite hero from the *Shahnamah,* as you know, Amir jan. He was a beautiful little boy, sweet as sugar, and had the same temperament as his father. You should have seen Sanaubar with that baby, Amir jan. He became the center of her existence. She sewed clothes for him, built him toys from scraps of wood, rags, and dried grass. When he caught a fever, she stayed up all night, and fasted for three days. She burned *isfand* for him on a skillet to cast out *nazar,* the evil eye. By the time Sohrab was two, he was calling her *Sasa.* The two of them were inseparable.

She lived to see him turn four, and then, one morning, she just did not wake up. She looked calm, at peace, like she did not mind dying now. We buried her in the cemetery on the hill, the one by the pomegranate tree, and I said a prayer for her too. The loss was hard on Hassan—it always hurts more to have and lose than to not have in the first place. But it was even harder on little Sohrab. He kept walking around the house, looking for *Sasa,* but you know how children are, they forget so quickly.

By then—that would have been 1995—the *Shorawi* were defeated and long gone and Kabul belonged to Massoud, Rabbani, and the *Mujahedin.* The infighting between the factions was fierce and no one knew if they would live to see the end of the day. Our ears became accustomed to the whistle of falling shells, to the rumble of gunfire, our eyes familiar with the sight of men digging bodies out of piles of rubble. Kabul in those days, Amir jan, was as close as you could get to that proverbial hell on earth. Allah was kind to us, though. The Wazir Akbar Khan area was not attacked as much, so we did not have it as bad as some of the other neighborhoods.

On those days when the rocket fire eased up a bit and the gunfighting was light, Hassan would take Sohrab to the zoo to see Marjan the lion, or to the cinema. Hassan taught him how to shoot the slingshot, and, later, by the time he was eight, Sohrab had become deadly with that thing: He could stand on the terrace and hit a pinecone propped on a pail halfway across the yard. Hassan taught him to read and write—his son was not going to grow up illiterate like he had. I grew very attached to that little boy—I had seen him take his first step, heard him utter his first word. I bought children's books for Sohrab from the bookstore by Cinema Park—they have destroyed that too now—and Sohrab read them as quickly as I could get them to him. He reminded me of you, how you loved to read when you were little, Amir jan. Sometimes, I read to him at night, played riddles with him, taught him card tricks. I miss him terribly.

In the wintertime, Hassan took his son kite running. There were not nearly as many kite tournaments as in the old days—no one felt safe outside for too long—but there were still a few scattered tournaments. Hassan would prop Sohrab on his shoulders and they would go trotting through the streets, running kites, climbing trees where kites had dropped. You remember, Amir jan, what a good kite runner Hassan was? He was still just as good. At the end of winter, Hassan and Sohrab would hang the kites they had run all winter on the walls of the main hallway. They would put them up like paintings.

I told you how we all celebrated in 1996 when the Taliban rolled in and put an end to the daily fighting. I remember coming home that night and finding Hassan in the kitchen, listening to the radio. He had a sober look in his eyes. I asked him what was wrong, and he just shook his head. "God help the Hazaras now, Rahim Khan sahib," he said.

"The war is over, Hassan," I said. "There's going to be peace, *Inshallah,* and happiness and calm. No more rockets, no more killing, no more funerals!" But he just turned off the radio and asked if he could get me anything before he went to bed.

A few weeks later, the Taliban banned kite fighting. And two years later, in 1998, they massacred the Hazaras in Mazar-i-Sharif.

SEVENTEEN

Rahim Khan slowly uncrossed his legs and leaned against the bare wall in the wary, deliberate way of a man whose every movement triggers spikes of pain. Outside, a donkey was braying and someone was shouting something in Urdu. The sun was beginning to set, glittering red through the cracks between the ramshackle buildings.

It hit me again, the enormity of what I had done that winter and that following summer. The names rang in my head: Hassan, Sohrab, Ali, Farzana, and Sanaubar. Hearing Rahim Khan speak Ali's name was like finding an old dusty music box that hadn't been opened in years; the melody began to play immediately: *Who did you eat today, Babalu? Who did you eat, you slant-eyed Babalu?* I tried to conjure Ali's frozen face, to *really* see his tranquil eyes, but time can be a greedy thing—sometimes it steals all the details for itself.

"Is Hassan still in that house now?" I asked.

Rahim Khan raised the teacup to his parched lips and took a sip. He then fished an envelope from the breast pocket of his vest and handed it to me. "For you."

I tore the sealed envelope. Inside, I found a Polaroid photograph and a folded letter. I stared at the photograph for a full
minute.

A tall man dressed in a white turban and a green-striped
chapan stood with a little boy in front of a set of wrought-iron
gates. Sunlight slanted in from the left, casting a shadow on half
of his rotund face. He was squinting and smiling at the camera,
showing a pair of missing front teeth. Even in this blurry Polaroid, the man in the *chapan* exuded a sense of self-assuredness, of
ease. It was in the way he stood, his feet slightly apart, his arms
comfortably crossed on his chest, his head titled a little toward
the sun. Mostly, it was in the way he smiled. Looking at the photo, one might have concluded that this was a man who thought
the world had been good to him. Rahim Khan was right: I
would have recognized him if I had bumped into him on the
street. The little boy stood barefoot, one arm wrapped around
the man's thigh, his shaved head resting against his father's hip.
He too was grinning and squinting. I unfolded the letter. It was
written in Farsi. No dots were omitted, no crosses forgotten, no
words blurred together—the handwriting was almost childlike
in its neatness. I began to read:

In the name of Allah the most beneficent,
the most merciful,
Amir agha, with my deepest respects,
   Farzana jan, Sohrab, and I pray that this latest letter finds
you in good health and in the light of Allah's good graces.
Please offer my warmest thanks to Rahim Khan sahib for
carrying it to you. I am hopeful that one day I will hold

one of your letters in my hands and read of your life in America. Perhaps a photograph of you will even grace our eyes. I have told much about you to Farzana jan and Sohrab, about us growing up together and playing games and running in the streets. They laugh at the stories of all the mischief you and I used to cause!

Amir agha,

Alas the Afghanistan of our youth is long dead. Kindness is gone from the land and you cannot escape the killings. Always the killings. In Kabul, fear is everywhere, in the streets, in the stadium, in the markets, it is a part of our lives here, Amir agha. The savages who rule our *watan* don't care about human decency. The other day, I accompanied Farzana jan to the bazaar to buy some potatoes and *naan*. She asked the vendor how much the potatoes cost, but he did not hear her, I think he had a deaf ear. So she asked louder and suddenly a young Talib ran over and hit her on the thighs with his wooden stick. He struck her so hard she fell down. He was screaming at her and cursing and saying the Ministry of Vice and Virtue does not allow women to speak loudly. She had a large purple bruise on her leg for days but what could I do except stand and watch my wife get beaten? If I fought, that dog would have surely put a bullet in me, and gladly! Then what would happen to my Sohrab? The streets are full enough already of hungry orphans and every day I thank Allah that I am alive, not because I fear death, but because my wife has a husband and my son is not an orphan.

I wish you could see Sohrab. He is a good boy. Rahim

Khan sahib and I have taught him to read and write so he does not grow up stupid like his father. And can he shoot with that slingshot! I take Sohrab around Kabul sometimes and buy him candy. There is still a monkey man in Share-Nau and if we run into him, I pay him to make his monkey dance for Sohrab. You should see how he laughs! The two of us often walk up to the cemetery on the hill. Do you remember how we used to sit under the pomegranate tree there and read from the *Shahnamah*? The droughts have dried the hill and the tree hasn't borne fruit in years, but Sohrab and I still sit under its shade and I read to him from the *Shahnamah*. It is not necessary to tell you that his favorite part is the one with his namesake, Rostam and Sohrab. Soon he will be able to read from the book himself. I am a very proud and very lucky father.

Amir agha,

Rahim Khan sahib is quite ill. He coughs all day and I see blood on his sleeve when he wipes his mouth. He has lost much weight and I wish he would eat a little of the *shorwa* and rice that Farzana jan cooks for him. But he only takes a bite or two and even that I think is out of courtesy to Farzana jan. I am so worried about this dear man I pray for him every day. He is leaving for Pakistan in a few days to consult some doctors there and, *Inshallah*, he will return with good news. But in my heart I fear for him. Farzana jan and I have told little Sohrab that Rahim Khan sahib is going to be well. What can we do? He is only ten and he adores Rahim Khan sahib. They have grown so close to each other. Rahim Khan sahib used to take him to the bazaar for balloons and biscuits but he is too weak for that now.

I have been dreaming a lot lately, Amir agha. Some of them are nightmares, like hanged corpses rotting in soccer fields with bloodred grass. I wake up from those short of breath and sweaty. Mostly, though, I dream of good things, and praise Allah for that. I dream that Rahim Khan sahib will be well. I dream that my son will grow up to be a good person, a free person, and an important person. I dream that *lawla* flowers will bloom in the streets of Kabul again and *rubab* music will play in the samovar houses and kites will fly in the skies. And I dream that someday you will return to Kabul to revisit the land of our childhood. If you do, you will find an old faithful friend waiting for you.

May Allah be with you always.

Hassan

I read the letter twice. I folded the note and looked at the photograph for another minute. I pocketed both. "How is he?" I asked.

"That letter was written six months ago, a few days before I left for Peshawar," Rahim Khan said. "I took the Polaroid the day before I left. A month after I arrived in Peshawar, I received a telephone call from one of my neighbors in Kabul. He told me this story: Soon after I took my leave, a rumor spread that a Hazara family was living alone in the big house in Wazir Akbar Khan, or so the Taliban claim. A pair of Talib officials came to investigate and interrogated Hassan. They accused him of lying when Hassan told them he was living with me even though many of the neighbors, including the one who called me, supported Hassan's story. The Talibs said he was a liar and a thief like all Hazaras and ordered him to get his family out of the house by sundown. Has-san protested. But my neighbor said the Talibs were looking at the big house like—how did he say it?— yes, like 'wolves looking at a flock of sheep.' They told Hassan they would be moving in to supposedly keep it safe until I return. Hassan protested again. So they took him to the street—"

"No," I breathed.

"—and order him to kneel—"

"No. God, no."

"—and shot him in the back of the head."

"No."

"—Farzana came screaming and attacked them—"

"No."

"—shot her too. Self-defense, they claimed later—"

But all I could manage was to whisper "No. No. No" over and over again.

I KEPT THINKING OF THAT DAY IN 1974, in the hospital room, just after Hassan's harelip surgery. Baba, Rahim Khan, Ali, and I had huddled around Hassan's bed, watched him examine his new lip in a handheld mirror. Now everyone in that room was either dead or dying. Except for me.

Then I saw something else: a man dressed in a herringbone vest pressing the muzzle of his Kalashnikov to the back of Hassan's head. The blast echoes through the street of my father's house. Hassan slumps to the asphalt, his life of unrequited loyalty drifting from him like the windblown kites he used to chase.

"The Taliban moved into the house," Rahim Khan said. "The

pretext was that they had evicted a trespasser. Hassan's and Far-zana's murders were dismissed as a case of self-defense. No one said a word about it. Most of it was fear of the Taliban, I think. But no one was going to risk anything for a pair of Hazara servants."

"What did they do with Sohrab?" I asked. I felt tired, drained. A coughing fit gripped Rahim Khan and went on for a long time. When he finally looked up, his face was flushed and his eyes bloodshot. "I heard he's in an orphanage somewhere in KartehSeh. Amir jan—" then he was coughing again. When he stopped, he looked older than a few moments before, like he was aging with each coughing fit. "Amir jan, I summoned you here because I wanted to see you before I die, but that's not all."

I said nothing. I think I already knew what he was going to say. "I want you to go to Kabul. I want you to bring Sohrab here,"he said.

I struggled to find the right words. I'd barely had time to deal with the fact that Hassan was dead.

"Please hear me. I know an American pair here in Peshawar, a husband and wife named Thomas and Betty Caldwell. They are Christians and they run a small charity organization that they manage with private donations. Mostly they house and feed Afghan children who have lost their parents. I have seen the place. It's clean and safe, the children are well cared for, and Mr. and Mrs. Caldwell are kind people. They have already told me that Sohrab would be welcome to their home and—"

"Rahim Khan, you can't be serious."

"Children are fragile, Amir jan. Kabul is already full of broken children and I don't want Sohrab to become another."

"Rahim Khan, I don't want to go to Kabul. I can't!" I said.

"Sohrab is a gifted little boy. We can give him a new life here, new hope, with people who would love him. Thomas agha is a good man and Betty khanum is so kind, you should see how she treats those orphans."

"Why me? Why can't you pay someone here to go? I'll pay for it if it's a matter of money."

"It isn't about money, Amir!" Rahim Khan roared. "I'm a dying man and I will not be insulted! It has *never* been about money with me, you know that. And why you? I think we both know why it has to be you, don't we?"

I didn't want to understand that comment, but I did. I understood it all too well. "I have a wife in America, a home, a career, and a family. Kabul is a dangerous place, you know that, and you'd have me risk everything for ..." I stopped.

"You know," Rahim Khan said, "one time, when you weren't around, your father and I were talking. And you know how he always worried about you in those days. I remember he said to me, 'Rahim, a boy who won't stand up for himself becomes a man who can't stand up to anything.' I wonder, is that what you've become?"

I dropped my eyes.

"What I'm asking from you is to grant an old man his dying wish," he said gravely.

He had gambled with that comment. Played his best card. Or so I thought then. His words hung in limbo between us, but at least he'd known what to say. I was still searching for the right words, and I was the writer in the room. Finally, I settled for this: "Maybe Baba was right."

"I'm sorry you think that, Amir."

I couldn't look at him. "And you don't?"

"If I did, I would not have asked you to come here."

I toyed with my wedding ring. "You've always thought too highly of me, Rahim Khan."

"And you've always been far too hard on yourself." He hesitated. "But there's something else. Something you don't know."

"Please, Rahim Khan—""Sanaubar wasn't Ali's first wife." Now I looked up.

"He was married once before, to a Hazara woman from the Jaghori area. This was long before you were born. They were married for three years."

"What does this have to do with anything?"

"She left him childless after three years and married a man in Khost. She bore *him* three daughters. That's what I am trying to tell you."

I began to see where he was going. But I didn't want to hear the rest of it. I had a good life in California, pretty Victorian home with a peaked roof, a good marriage, a promising writing career, in-laws who loved me. I didn't need any of this shit.

"Ali was sterile," Rahim Khan said.

"No he wasn't. He and Sanaubar had Hassan, didn't they? They had Hassan—"

"No they didn't," Rahim Khan said. "Yes they did!"

"No they didn't, Amir." "Then who—"

"I think you know who."

I felt like a man sliding down a steep cliff, clutching at shrubs and tangles of brambles and coming up empty-handed. The room was swooping up and down, swaying side to side. "Did Hassan know?" I said through lips that didn't feel like my own. Rahim Khan closed his eyes. Shook his head.

"You bastards," I muttered. Stood up. "You goddamn bastards!"

I screamed. "All of you, you bunch of lying goddamn bastards!"

"Please sit down," Rahim Khan said.

"How could you hide this from me? From *him*?" I bellowed.

"Please think, Amir jan. It was a shameful situation. People would talk. All that a man had back then, all that he was, was his honor, his name, and if people talked … We couldn't tell anyone, surely you can see that." He reached for me, but I shed his hand. Headed for the door.

"Amir jan, please don't leave."

I opened the door and turned to him. "Why? What can you possibly say to me? I'm thirty-eight years old and I've just found out my whole life is one big fucking lie! What can you possibly say to make things better? Nothing. Not a goddamn thing!"

And with that, I stormed out of the apartment.

EIGHTEEN

The sun had almost set and left the sky swathed in smothers of purple and red. I walked down the busy, narrow street that led away from Rahim Khan's building. The street was a noisy lane in a maze of alleyways choked with pedestrians, bicycles, and rickshaws. Billboards hung at its corners, advertising Coca-Cola and cigarettes; Lollywood movie posters displayed sultry actresses dancing with handsome, brown-skinned men in fields of marigolds.

I walked into a smoky little samovar house and ordered a cup of tea. I tilted back on the folding chair's rear legs and rubbed my face. That feeling of sliding toward a fall was fading. But in its stead, I felt like a man who awakens in his own house and finds all the furniture rearranged, so that every familiar nook and cranny looks foreign now. Disoriented, he has to reevaluate his surroundings, reorient himself.

How could I have been so blind? The signs had been there for me to see all along; they came flying back at me now: Baba hiring Dr. Kumar to fix Hassan's harelip. Baba never missing Hassan's birthday. I remembered the day we were planting tulips, when I had asked Baba if he'd ever consider getting new servants. *Hassan's not going anywhere,* he'd barked. *He's staying right here with us, where he belongs. This is his home and we're his family.* He had wept, *wept,* when Ali announced he and Hassan were leaving us.

The waiter placed a teacup on the table before me. Where the table's legs crossed like an *X,* there was a ring of brass balls, each walnut-sized. One of the balls had come unscrewed. I stooped and tightened it. I wished I could fix my own life as easily. I took a gulp of the blackest tea I'd had in years and tried to think of Soraya, of the general and Khala Jamila, of the novel that needed finishing. I tried to watch the traffic bolting by on the street, the people milling in and out of the little sweetshops. Tried to listen to the *Qawali* music playing on the transistor radio at the next table. Anything. But I kept seeing Baba on the night of my graduation, sitting in the Ford he'd just given me, smelling of beer and saying, *I wish Hassan had been with us today.*

How could he have lied to me all those years? To Hassan? He had sat me on his lap when I was little, looked me straight in the eyes, and said, *There is only one sin. And that is theft ... When you tell a lie, you steal someone's right to the truth.* Hadn't he said those words to me? And now, fifteen years after I'd buried him, I was learning that Baba had been a thief. And a thief of the worst kind, because the things he'd stolen had been sacred: from me the right to know I had a brother, from Hassan his identity, and from Ali his honor. His *nang.* His *namoos.*

The questions kept coming at me: How had Baba brought himself to look Ali in the eye? How had Ali lived in that house, day in and day out, knowing he had been dishonored by his master in the single worst way an Afghan man can be dishonored? And how was I going to reconcile this new image of Baba with the one that had been imprinted on my mind for so long, that of him in his old brown suit, hobbling up the Taheris' driveway to askfor Soraya's hand?

Here is another cliché my creative writing teacher would have scoffed at; like father, like son. But it was true, wasn't it? As it turned out, Baba and I were more alike than I'd ever known. We had both betrayed the people who would have given their lives for us. And with that came this realization: that Rahim Khan had summoned me here to atone not just for my sins but for Baba's too. Rahim Khan said I'd always been too hard on myself. But I wondered. True, I hadn't made Ali step on the land mine, and I hadn't brought the Taliban to the house to shoot Hassan. But I had driven Hassan and Ali out of the house. Was it too far-fetched to imagine that things might have turned out differently if I hadn't? Maybe Baba would have brought them along to America. Maybe Hassan would have had a home of his own now, a job, a family, a life in a country where no one cared that he was a Hazara, where most people didn't even know what a Hazara was. Maybe not. But maybe so.

I can't go to Kabul, I had said to Rahim Khan. *I have a wife in America, a home, a career, and a family.* But how could I pack up and go back home when my actions may have cost Hassan a chance at those very same things?

I wished Rahim Khan hadn't called me. I wished he had let me live on in my oblivion. But he had called me. And what Rahim Khan revealed to me changed things. Made me see how my entire life, long before the winter of 1975, dating back to when that singing Hazara woman was still nursing me, had been a cycle of lies, betrayals, and secrets.

There is a way to be good again, he'd said.

A way to end the cycle.

With a little boy. An orphan. Hassan's son. Somewhere in Kabul.

ON THE RICKSHAW RIDE back to Rahim Khan's apartment, I remembered Baba saying that my problem was that someone had always done my fighting for me. I was thirty-eight now. My hair was receding and streaked with gray, and lately I'd traced little crow's-feet etched around the corners of my eyes. I was older now, but maybe not yet too old to start doing my own fighting. Baba had lied about a lot of things as it turned out but he hadn't lied about that.

I looked at the round face in the Polaroid again, the way the sun fell on it. My brother's face. Hassan had loved me once, loved me in a way that no one ever had or ever would again. He was gone now, but a little part of him lived on. It was in Kabul.

Waiting.

I FOUND RAHIM KHAN praying *namaz* in a corner of the room. He was just a dark silhouette bowing eastward against a bloodred sky. I waited for him to finish.

Then I told him I was going to Kabul. Told him to call the Caldwells in the morning.

"I'll pray for you, Amir jan," he said.

N I N E T E E N

Again, the car sickness. By the time we drove past the bulletrid-
dled sign that read THE KHYBER PASS WELCOMES YOU,
my mouth had begun to water. Something inside my stomach
churned and twisted. Farid, my driver, threw me a cold glance.
There was no empathy in his eyes.

"Can we roll down the window?" I asked.

He lit a cigarette and tucked it between the remaining two
fingers of his left hand, the one resting on the steering wheel.
Keeping his black eyes on the road, he stooped forward, picked
up the screwdriver lying between his feet, and handed it to me. I
stuck it in the small hole in the door where the handle belonged
and turned it to roll down my window.

Farid gave me another dismissive look, this one with a hint
of barely suppressed animosity, and went back to smoking his
cigarette. He hadn't said more than a dozen words since we'd
departed from Jamrud Fort.

"*Tashakor,*" I muttered. I leaned my head out of the window
and let the cold midafternoon air rush past my face. The drive
through the tribal lands of the Khyber Pass, winding between

cliffs of shale and limestone, was just as I remembered it—
Baba and I had driven through the broken terrain back in
1974. The arid, imposing mountains sat along deep gorges and
soared to jagged peaks. Old fortresses, adobe-walled and crumbling, topped the crags. I tried to keep my eyes glued to the
snowcapped Hindu Kush on the north side, but each time my
stomach settled even a bit, the truck skidded around yet another
turn, rousing a fresh wave of nausea.

"Try a lemon." "What?"

"Lemon. Good for the sickness," Farid said. "I always bring
one for this drive."

"Nay, thank you," I said. The mere thought of adding acidity
to my stomach stirred more nausea. Farid snickered. "It's not
fancy like American medicine, I know, just an old remedy my
mother taught me."

I regretted blowing my chance to warm up to him. "In that
case, maybe you should give me some."

He grabbed a paper bag from the backseat and plucked a half
lemon out of it. I bit down on it, waited a few minutes. "You
were right. I feel better," I lied. As an Afghan, I knew it was
better to be miserable than rude. I forced a weak smile.

"Old *watani* trick, no need for fancy medicine," he said. His
tone bordered on the surly. He flicked the ash off his cigarette
and gave himself a self-satisfied look in the rearview mirror.
He was a Tajik, a lanky, dark man with a weather-beaten face,
narrow shoulders, and a long neck punctuated by a protruding
Adam's apple that only peeked from behind his beard when
he turned his head. He was dressed much as I was, though I
suppose it was really the other way around: a rough-woven wool
blanket wrapped over a gray *pirhan-tumban* and a vest. On his

head, he wore a brown *pakol,* tilted slightly to one side, like the
Tajik hero Ahmad Shah Massoud—referred to by Tajiks as "the
Lion of Panjsher."

It was Rahim Khan who had introduced me to Farid in
Peshawar. He told me Farid was twenty-nine, though he had
the wary, lined face of a man twenty years older. He was born in
Mazar-i-Sharif and lived there until his father moved the family
to Jalalabad when Farid was ten. At fourteen, he and his father
had joined the jihad against the *Shorawi.* They had fought in the
Panjsher Valley for two years until helicopter gunfire had torn
the older man to pieces. Farid had two wives and five children.
"He used to have seven," Rahim Khan said with a rueful look,
but he'd lost his two youngest girls a few years earlier in a land
mine blast just outside Jalalabad, the same explosion that had
severed toes from his feet and three fingers from his left hand.
After that, he had moved his wives and children to Peshawar.

"Checkpoint," Farid grumbled. I slumped a little in my seat,
arms folded across my chest, forgetting for a moment about
the nausea. But I needn't have worried. Two Pakistani militia
approached our dilapidated Land Cruiser, took a cursory glance
inside, and waved us on.

Farid was first on the list of preparations Rahim Khan and
I made, a list that included exchanging dollars for Kaldar and
Afghani bills, my garment and *pakol*—ironically, I'd never worn
either when I'd actually lived in Afghanistan—the Polaroid of
Hassan and Sohrab, and, finally, perhaps the most important
item: an artificial beard, black and chest length, *Shari'a*friendly—
or at least the Taliban version of *Shari'a.* Rahim Khan knew of a
fellow in Peshawar who specialized in weaving them, sometimes
for Western journalists who covered the war.

Rahim Khan had wanted me to stay with him a few more days, to plan more thoroughly. But I knew I had to leave as soon as possible. I was afraid I'd change my mind. I was afraid I'd deliberate, ruminate, agonize, rationalize, and talk myself into not going. I was afraid the appeal of my life in America would draw me back, that I would wade back into that great, big river and let myself forget, let the things I had learned these last few days sink to the bottom. I was afraid that I'd let the waters carry me away from what I had to do. From Hassan. From the past that had come calling. And from this one last chance at redemption. So I left before there was any possibility of that happening. As for Soraya, telling her I was going back to Afghanistan wasn't an option. If I had, she would have booked herself on the next flight to Pakistan.

We had crossed the border and the signs of poverty were everywhere. On either side of the road, I saw chains of little villages sprouting here and there, like discarded toys among the rocks, broken mud houses and huts consisting of little more than four wooden poles and a tattered cloth as a roof. I saw children dressed in rags chasing a soccer ball outside the huts. A few miles later, I spotted a cluster of men sitting on their haunches, like a row of crows, on the carcass of an old burned-out Soviet tank, the wind fluttering the edges of the blankets thrown around them. Behind them, a woman in a brown *burqa* carried a large clay pot on her shoulder, down a rutted path toward a string of mud houses.

"Strange," I said. "What?"

"I feel like a tourist in my own country," I said, taking in a goatherd leading a half-dozen emaciated goats along the side of the road.

Farid snickered. Tossed his cigarette. "You still think of this place as your country?"

"I think a part of me always will," I said, more defensively than I had intended.

"After twenty years of living in America," he said, swerving the truck to avoid a pothole the size of a beach ball.

I nodded. "I grew up in Afghanistan." Farid snickered again. "Why do you do that?" "Never mind," he murmured.

"No, I want to know. Why do you do that?"

In his rearview mirror, I saw something flash in his eyes. "You want to know?" he sneered. "Let me imagine, Agha sahib. You probably lived in a big twoor three-story house with a nice backyard that your gardener filled with flowers and fruit trees. All gated, of course. Your father drove an American car. You had servants, probably Hazaras. Your parents hired workers to decorate the house for the fancy *mehmanis* they threw, so their friends would come over to drink and boast about their travels to Europe or America. And I would bet my first son's eyes that this is the first time you've ever worn a *pakol*." He grinned at me, revealing a mouthful of prematurely rotting teeth. "Am I close?"

"Why are you saying these things?" I said.

"Because you wanted to know," he spat. He pointed to an old man dressed in ragged clothes trudging down a dirt path, a large burlap pack filled with scrub grass tied to his back. "That's the real Afghanistan, Agha sahib. That's the Afghanistan I know. You? You've *always* been a tourist here, you just didn't know it."

Rahim Khan had warned me not to expect a warm welcome in Afghanistan from those who had stayed behind and fought the wars. "I'm sorry about your father," I said. "I'm sorry about your daughters, and I'm sorry about your hand."

"That means nothing to me," he said. He shook his head. "Why are you coming back here anyway? Sell off your Baba's land? Pocket the money and run back to your mother in America?"

"My mother died giving birth to me," I said.

He sighed and lit another cigarette. Said nothing. "Pull over."

"What?"

"Pull over, goddamn it!" I said. "I'm going to be sick." I tumbled out of the truck as it was coming to a rest on the gravel alongside the road.

BY LATE AFTERNOON, the terrain had changed from one of sun-beaten peaks and barren cliffs to a greener, more rural landscape. The main pass had descended from Landi Kotal through Shinwari territory to Landi Khana. We'd entered Afghanistan at Torkham. Pine trees flanked the road, fewer than I remembered and many of them bare, but it was good to see trees again after the arduous drive through the Khyber Pass. We were getting closer to Jalalabad, where Farid had a brother who would take us in for the night.

The sun hadn't quite set when we drove into Jalalabad, capital of the state of Nangarhar, a city once renowned for its fruit and warm climate. Farid drove past the buildings and stone houses of the city's central district. There weren't as many palm trees there as I remembered, and some of the homes had been reduced to roofless walls and piles of twisted clay.

Farid turned onto a narrow unpaved road and parked the Land Cruiser along a dried-up gutter. I slid out of the truck, stretched, and took a deep breath. In the old days, the winds swept through the irrigated plains around Jalalabad where farmers grew sugarcane, and impregnated the city's air with a sweet scent. I closed my eyes and searched for the sweetness. I didn't find it.

"Let's go," Farid said impatiently. We walked up the dirt road past a few leafless poplars along a row of broken mud walls. Farid led me to a dilapidated one-story house and knocked on the woodplank door.

A young woman with ocean-green eyes and a white scarf draped around her face peeked out. She saw me first, flinched, spotted Farid and her eyes lit up. "*Salaam alaykum,* Kaka Farid!"

"*Salaam,* Maryam jan," Farid replied and gave her something he'd denied me all day: a warm smile. He planted a kiss on the top of her head. The young woman stepped out of the way, eyeing me a little apprehensively as I followed Farid into the small house.

The adobe ceiling was low, the dirt walls entirely bare, and the only light came from a pair of lanterns set in a corner. We took off our shoes and stepped on the straw mat that covered the floor. Along one of the walls sat three young boys, cross-legged, on a mattress covered with a blanket with shredded borders. A tall bearded man with broad shoulders stood up to greet us. Farid and he hugged and kissed on the cheek. Farid introduced him to me as Wahid, his older brother. "He's from America," he said to Wahid, flicking his thumb toward me. He left us alone and went to greet the boys.

Wahid sat with me against the wall across from the boys, who had ambushed Farid and climbed his shoulders. Despite my protests, Wahid ordered one of the boys to fetch another blanket so I'd be more comfortable on the floor, and asked Maryam to bring me some tea. He asked about the ride from Peshawar, the drive over the Khyber Pass.

"I hope you didn't come across any *dozd*s," he said. The Khyber Pass was as famous for its terrain as for the bandits who used that terrain to rob travelers. Before I could answer, he winked and said in a loud voice, "Of course no *dozd* would waste his time on a car as ugly as my brother's."

Farid wrestled the smallest of the three boys to the floor and tickled him on the ribs with his good hand. The kid giggled and kicked. "At least I have a car," Farid panted. "How is your donkey these days?"

"My donkey is a better ride than your car."

"*Khar khara mishnassah,*" Farid shot back. *Takes a donkey to know a donkey.* They all laughed and I joined in. I heard female voices from the adjoining room. I could see half of the room from where I sat. Maryam and an older woman wearing a brown *hijab*—presumably her mother—were speaking in low voices and pouring tea from a kettle into a pot.

"So what do you do in America, Amir agha?" Wahid asked.

"I'm a writer," I said. I thought I heard Farid chuckle at that.

"A writer?" Wahid said, clearly impressed. "Do you write about Afghanistan?"

"Well, I have. But not currently," I said. My last novel, *A Season for Ashes,* had been about a university professor who joins a clan of gypsies after he finds his wife in bed with one of his students. It wasn't a bad book. Some reviewers had called it a "good" book, and one had even used the word "riveting." But suddenly I was embarrassed by it. I hoped Wahid wouldn't ask what it was about.

"Maybe you should write about Afghanistan again," Wahid

said. "Tell the rest of the world what the Taliban are doing to our country."

"Well, I'm not ... I'm not quite that kind of writer."

"Oh," Wahid said, nodding and blushing a bit. "You know best, of course. It's not for me to suggest ..."

Just then, Maryam and the other woman came into the room with a pair of cups and a teapot on a small platter. I stood up in respect, pressed my hand to my chest, and bowed my head. "*Salaam alaykum,*" I said.

The woman, who had now wrapped her *hijab* to conceal her lower face, bowed her head too. "*Salaam,*" she replied in a barely audible voice. We never made eye contact. She poured the tea while I stood.

The woman placed the steaming cup of tea before me and exited the room, her bare feet making no sound at all as she disappeared. I sat down and sipped the strong black tea. Wahid finally broke the uneasy silence that followed.

"So what brings you back to Afghanistan?"

"What brings them *all* back to Afghanistan, dear brother?" Farid said, speaking to Wahid but fixing me with a contemptuous gaze.

"*Bas!*" Wahid snapped.

"It's always the same thing," Farid said. "Sell this land, sell that house, collect the money, and run away like a mouse. Go back to America, spend the money on a family vacation to Mexico."

"Farid!" Wahid roared. His children, and even Farid, flinched. "Have you forgotten your manners? This is *my* house! Amir agha is my guest tonight and I will not allow you to dishonor me like this!" Farid opened his mouth, almost said something, reconsidered and said nothing. He slumped against the wall, muttered something under his breath, and crossed his mutilated foot over the good one. His accusing eyes never left me.

"Forgive us, Amir agha," Wahid said. "Since childhood, my brother's mouth has been two steps ahead of his head."

"It's my fault, really," I said, trying to smile under Farid's intense gaze. "I am not offended. I should have explained to him my business here in Afghanistan. I am not here to sell property. I'm going to Kabul to find a boy."

"A boy," Wahid repeated.

"Yes." I fished the Polaroid from the pocket of my shirt. Seeing Hassan's picture again tore the fresh scab off his death. I had to turn my eyes away from it. I handed it to Wahid. He studied the photo. Looked from me to the photo and back again. "This boy?"

I nodded.

"This Hazara boy." "Yes."

"What does he mean to you?"

"His father meant a lot to me. He is the man in the photo. He's dead now."

Wahid blinked. "He was a friend of yours?"

My instinct was to say yes, as if, on some deep level, I too wanted to protect Baba's secret. But there had been enough lies already. "He was my half-brother." I swallowed. Added, "My illegitimate half brother." I turned the teacup. Toyed with the handle.

"I didn't mean to pry." "You're not prying," I said. "What will you do with him?"

"Take him back to Peshawar. There are people there who will take care of him."

Wahid handed the photo back and rested his thick hand on

my shoulder. "You are an honorable man, Amir agha. A true Afghan."

I cringed inside.

"I am proud to have you in our home tonight," Wahid said. I thanked him and chanced a glance over to Farid. He was looking down now, playing with the frayed edges of the straw mat.

A SHORT WHILE LATER, Maryam and her mother brought two steaming bowls of vegetable *shorwa* and two loaves of bread. "I'm sorry we can't offer you meat," Wahid said. "Only the Taliban can afford meat now."

"This looks wonderful," I said. It did too. I offered some to him, to the kids, but Wahid said the family had eaten before we arrived. Farid and I rolled up our sleeves, dipped our bread in the *shorwa,* and ate with our hands.

As I ate, I noticed Wahid's boys, all three thin with dirt-caked faces and short-cropped brown hair under their skullcaps, stealing furtive glances at my digital wristwatch. The youngest whispered something in his brother's ear. The brother nodded, didn't take his eyes off my watch. The oldest of the boys—I guessed his age at about twelve—rocked back and forth, his gaze glued to my wrist. After dinner, after I'd washed my hands with the water Maryam poured from a clay pot, I asked for Wahid's permission to give his boys a *hadia,* a gift. He said no, but, when I insisted, he reluctantly agreed. I unsnapped the wristwatch and gave it to the youngest of the three boys. He muttered a sheepish *"Tashakor."*

"It tells you the time in any city in the world," I told him. The boys nodded politely, passing the watch between them, taking turns trying it on. But they lost interest and, soon, the watch sat abandoned on the straw mat.

"YOU COULD HAVE TOLD ME," Farid said later. The two of us were lying next to each other on the straw mats Wahid's wife had spread for us.

"Told you what?"

"Why you've come to Afghanistan." His voice had lost the rough edge I'd heard in it since the moment I had met him.

"You didn't ask," I said. "You should have told me." "You didn't ask."

He rolled to face me. Curled his arm under his head. "Maybe I will help you find this boy."

"Thank you, Farid," I said.

"It was wrong of me to assume."

I sighed. "Don't worry. You were more right than you know."

HIS HANDS ARE TIED BEHIND HIM with roughly woven rope cutting through the flesh of his wrists. He is blindfolded with black cloth. He is kneeling on the street, on the edge of a gutter filled with still water, his head drooping between his shoulders. His knees roll on the hard ground and bleed through his pants as he rocks in prayer. It is late afternoon and his long shadow sways back and forth on the gravel. He is muttering something under his breath. I step closer. A thousand times over, he mutters. For you a thousand times over. Back and forth he rocks. He lifts his face. I see a faint scar above his upper lip.

We are not alone.

I see the barrel first. Then the man standing behind him. He is tall, dressed in a herringbone vest and a black turban. He looks down at the blindfolded man before him with eyes that show nothing but a vast, cavernous emptiness. He takes a step back and raises the barrel. Places it on the back of the kneeling man's head. For a moment, fading sunlight catches in the metal and twinkles.

The rifle roars with a deafening crack.

I follow the barrel on its upward arc. I see the face behind the plume of smoke swirling from the muzzle. I am the man in the herringbone vest.

I woke up with a scream trapped in my throat.

I STEPPED OUTSIDE. Stood in the silver tarnish of a half-moon and glanced up to a sky riddled with stars. Crickets chirped in the shuttered darkness and a wind wafted through the trees. The ground was cool under my bare feet and suddenly, for the first time since we had crossed the border, I felt like I was back. After all these years, I was home again, standing on the soil of my ancestors. This was the soil on which my great-grandfather had married his third wife a year before dying in the cholera epidemic that hit Kabul in 1915. She'd borne him what his first two wives had failed to, a son at last. It was on this soil that my grandfather had gone on a hunting trip with King Nadir Shah and shot a deer. My mother had died on this soil. And on this soil, I had fought for my father's love. I sat against one of the house's clay walls. The kinship I felt suddenly for the old land ... it surprised me. I'd been gone long enough to forget and be forgotten. I had a home in a land that might as well be in another galaxy to the people sleeping on the other side of the wall I leaned against. I thought I had forgotten about this land.

But I hadn't. And, under the bony glow of a halfmoon, I sensed Afghanistan humming under my feet. Maybe Afghanistan hadn't forgotten me either.

I looked westward and marveled that, somewhere over those mountains, Kabul still existed. It really existed, not just as an old memory, or as the heading of an AP story on page 15 of the *San Francisco Chronicle*. Somewhere over those mountains in the west slept the city where my harelipped brother and I had run kites. Somewhere over there, the blindfolded man from my dream had died a needless death. Once, over those mountains, I had made a choice. And now, a quarter of a century later, that choice had landed me right back on this soil.

I was about to go back inside when I heard voices coming from the house. I recognized one as Wahid's.

"—nothing left for the children."

"We're hungry but we're not savages! He is a guest! What was I supposed to do?" he said in a strained voice.

"—to find something tomorrow." She sounded near tears. "What do I feed—"

I tiptoed away. I understood now why the boys hadn't shown any interest in the watch. They hadn't been staring at the watch at all. They'd been staring at my food.

WE SAID OUR GOOD-BYES early the next morning. Just before I climbed into the Land Cruiser, I thanked Wahid for his hospitality. He pointed to the little house behind him. "This is your home," he said. His three sons were standing in the doorway watching us. The little one was wearing the watch—it dangled around his twiggy wrist.

I glanced in the side-view mirror as we pulled away. Wahid stood surrounded by his boys in a cloud of dust whipped up by the truck. It occurred to me that, in a different world, those boys wouldn't have been too hungry to chase after the car.

Earlier that morning, when I was certain no one was looking, I did something I had done twenty-six years earlier: I planted a fistful of crumpled money under a mattress.

TWENTY

Farid had warned me. He had. But, as it turned out, he had wasted his breath.

We were driving down the cratered road that winds from Jalalabad to Kabul. The last time I'd traveled that road was in a tarpaulin-covered truck going the other way. Baba had nearly gotten himself shot by a singing, stoned *Roussi* officer—Baba had made me so mad that night, so scared, and, ultimately, so proud. The trek between Kabul and Jalalabad, a bone-jarring ride down a teetering pass snaking through the rocks, had become a relic now, a relic of two wars. Twenty years earlier, I had seen some of the first war with my own eyes. Grim reminders of it were strewn along the road: burned carcasses of old Soviet tanks, overturned military trucks gone to rust, a crushed Russian jeep that had plunged over the mountainside. The second war, I had watched on my TV screen. And now I was seeing it through Farid's eyes.

Swerving effortlessly around potholes in the middle of the broken road, Farid was a man in his element. He had become much chattier since our overnight stay at Wahid's house. He had me sit in the passenger seat and looked at me when he spoke. He even smiled once or twice. Maneuvering the steering wheel with his mangled hand, he pointed to mud-hut villages along the way where he'd known people years before. Most of those people, he said, were either dead or in refugee camps in Pakistan. "And sometimes the dead are luckier," he said.

He pointed to the crumbled, charred remains of a tiny village. It was just a tuft of blackened, roofless walls now. I saw a dog sleeping along one of the walls. "I had a friend there once," Farid said. "He was a very good bicycle repairman. He played the tabla well too. The Taliban killed him and his family and burned the village."

We drove past the burned village, and the dog didn't move.

IN THE OLD DAYS, the drive from Jalalabad to Kabul took two hours, maybe a little more. It took Farid and me over four hours to reach Kabul. And when we did ... Farid warned me just after we passed the Mahipar dam.

"Kabul is not the way you remember it," he said. "So I hear."

Farid gave me a look that said hearing is not the same as seeing. And he was right. Because when Kabul finally did unroll before us, I was certain, absolutely certain, that he had taken a wrong turn somewhere. Farid must have seen my stupefied expression; shuttling people back and forth to Kabul, he would have become familiar with that expression on the faces of those who hadn't seen Kabul for a long time.

He patted me on the shoulder. "Welcome back," he said morosely.

. . .

Rubble and beggars. Everywhere I looked, that was what I saw. I remembered beggars in the old days too—Baba always carried an extra handful of Afghani bills in his pocket just for them; I'd never seen him deny a peddler. Now, though, they squatted at every street corner, dressed in shredded burlap rags, mud-caked hands held out for a coin. And the beggars were mostly children now, thin and grim-faced, some no older than five or six. They sat in the laps of their *burqa*-clad mothers alongside gutters at busy street corners and chanted *"Bakhshesh, bakhshesh!"* And something else, something I hadn't noticed right away: Hardly any of them sat with an adult male—the wars had made fathers a rare commodity in Afghanistan.

We were driving westbound toward the Karteh-Seh district on what I remembered as a major thoroughfare in the seventies: Jadeh Maywand. Just north of us was the bone-dry Kabul River. On the hills to the south stood the broken old city wall. Just east of it was the Bala Hissar Fort—the ancient citadel that the warlord Dostum had occupied in 1992—on the Shirdarwaza mountain range, the same mountains from which *Mujahedin* forces had showered Kabul with rockets between 1992 and 1996, inflicting much of the damage I was witnessing now. The Shirdarwaza range stretched all the way west. It was from those mountains that I remember the firing of the *Topeh chasht,* the "noon cannon." It went off every day to announce noontime, and also to signal the end of daylight fasting during the month of Ramadan. You'd hear the roar of that cannon all through the city in those days.

"I used to come here to Jadeh Maywand when I was a kid," I

mumbled. "There used to be shops here and hotels. Neon lights and restaurants. I used to buy kites from an old man named Saifo. He ran a little kite shop by the old police headquarters."

"The police headquarters is still there," Farid said. "No shortage of police in this city. But you won't find kites or kite shops on Jadeh Maywand or anywhere else in Kabul. Those days are over."

Jadeh Maywand had turned into a giant sand castle. The buildings that hadn't entirely collapsed barely stood, with caved in roofs and walls pierced with rockets shells. Entire blocks had been obliterated to rubble. I saw a bullet-pocked sign half buried at an angle in a heap of debris. It read DRINK COCA CO—. I saw children playing in the ruins of a windowless building amid jagged stumps of brick and stone. Bicycle riders and mule-drawn carts swerved around kids, stray dogs, and piles of debris. A haze of dust hovered over the city and, across the river, a single plume of smoke rose to the sky.

"Where are the trees?" I said.

"People cut them down for firewood in the winter," Farid said. "The *Shorawi* cut a lot of them down too."

"Why?"

"Snipers used to hide in them."

A sadness came over me. Returning to Kabul was like running into an old, forgotten friend and seeing that life hadn't been good to him, that he'd become homeless and destitute.

"My father built an orphanage in Shar-e-Kohna, the old city, south of here," I said.

"I remember it," Farid said. "It was destroyed a few years ago."

"Can you pull over?" I said. "I want to take a quick walk here."

Farid parked along the curb on a small backstreet next to a

ramshackle, abandoned building with no door. "That used to be a pharmacy," Farid muttered as we exited the truck. We walked back to Jadeh Maywand and turned right, heading west. "What's that smell?" I said. Something was making my eyes water.

"Diesel," Farid replied. "The city's generators are always going down, so electricity is unreliable, and people use diesel fuel."

"Diesel. Remember what this street smelled like in the old days?"

Farid smiled.

"Kabob." "Lamb kabob," I said.

"Lamb," Farid said, tasting the word in his mouth. "The only people in Kabul who get to eat lamb now are the Taliban." He pulled on my sleeve. "Speaking of which …"

A vehicle was approaching us. "Beard Patrol," Farid murmured. That was the first time I saw the Taliban. I'd seen them on TV,

on the Internet, on the cover of magazines, and in newspapers. But here I was now, less than fifty feet from them, telling myself that the sudden taste in my mouth wasn't unadulterated, naked fear. Telling myself my flesh hadn't suddenly shrunk against my bones and my heart wasn't battering. Here they came. In all their glory.

The red Toyota pickup truck idled past us. A handful of stern-faced young men sat on their haunches in the cab, Kalashnikovs slung on their shoulders. They all wore beards and black turbans. One of them, a dark-skinned man in his early twenties with thick, knitted eyebrows twirled a whip in his hand and rhythmically swatted the side of the truck with it. His roaming eyes fell on me. Held my gaze. I'd never felt so naked in my entire life. Then the Talib spat tobacco-stained spittle and looked

away. I found I could breathe again. The truck rolled down
Jadeh Maywand, leaving in its trail a cloud of dust.

"What is the matter with you?" Farid hissed.

"What?"

"Don't ever stare at them! Do you understand me? Never!" "I
didn't mean to," I said.

"Your friend is quite right, Agha. You might as well poke a
rabid dog with a stick," someone said. This new voice belonged
to an old beggar sitting barefoot on the steps of a bullet-scarred
building. He wore a threadbare *chapan* worn to frayed shreds
and a dirt-crusted turban. His left eyelid drooped over an empty
socket. With an arthritic hand, he pointed to the direction the
red truck had gone. "They drive around looking. Looking and
hoping that someone will provoke them. Sooner or later, someone always obliges. Then the dogs feast and the day's boredom
is broken at last and everyone says '*Allah-u-akbar!*' And on those
days when no one offends, well, there is always random violence,
isn't there?"

"Keep your eyes on your feet when the Talibs are near," Farid
said.

"Your friend dispenses good advice," the old beggar chimed
in. He barked a wet cough and spat in a soiled handkerchief.
"Forgive me, but could you spare a few Afghanis?" he breathed.

"*Bas.* Let's go," Farid said, pulling me by the arm.

I handed the old man a hundred thousand Afghanis, or the
equivalent of about three dollars. When he leaned forward to
take the money, his stench—like sour milk and feet that hadn't
been washed in weeks—flooded my nostrils and made my gorge
rise. He hurriedly slipped the money in his waist, his lone eye
darting side to side. "A world of thanks for your benevolence,

Agha sahib." "Do you know where the orphanage is in Karteh-Seh?" I said. "It's not hard to find, it's just west of Darulaman Boulevard,"he said. "The children were moved from here to Karteh-Seh after the rockets hit the old orphanage. Which is like saving someone from the lion's cage and throwing them in the tiger's."

"Thank you, Agha," I said. I turned to go. "That was your first time, nay?"

"I'm sorry?"

"The first time you saw a Talib."

I said nothing. The old beggar nodded and smiled. Revealed a handful of remaining teeth, all crooked and yellow. "I remember the first time I saw them rolling into Kabul. What a joyous day that was!" he said. "An end to the killing! *Wah wah!* But like the poet says: 'How seamless seemed love and then came trouble!'"

A smile sprouted on my face. "I know that *ghazal*. That's Hafez."

"Yes it is. Indeed," the old man replied. "I should know. I used to teach it at the university."

"You did?"

The old man coughed. "From 1958 to 1996. I taught Hãfez, Khayyám, Rumi, Beydel, Jami, Saadi. Once, I was even a guest lecturer in Tehran, 1971 that was. I gave a lecture on the mystic Beydel. I remember how they all stood and clapped. Ha!" He shook his head. "But you saw those young men in the truck. What value do you think they see in Sufism?"

"My mother taught at the university," I said. "And what was her name?"

"Sofia Akrami."

His eye managed to twinkle through the veil of cataracts. "'The desert weed lives on, but the flower of spring blooms and wilts.' Such grace, such dignity, such a tragedy."

"You knew my mother?" I asked, kneeling before the old man. "Yes indeed," the old beggar said. "We used to sit and talk after class. The last time was on a rainy day just before final exams when we shared a marvelous slice of almond cake together. Almond cake with hot tea and honey. She was rather obviously pregnant by then, and all the more beautiful for it. I will never forget what she said to me that day."

"What? Please tell me." Baba had always described my mother to me in broad strokes, like, "She was a great woman." But what I had always thirsted for were the details: the way her hair glinted in the sunlight, her favorite ice cream flavor, the songs she liked to hum, did she bite her nails? Baba took his memories of her to the grave with him. Maybe speaking her name would have reminded him of his guilt, of what he had done so soon after she had died. Or maybe his loss had been so great, his pain so deep, he couldn't bear to talk about her. Maybe both.

"She said, 'I'm so afraid.' And I said, 'Why?,' and she said, 'Because I'm so profoundly happy, Dr. Rasul. Happiness like this is frightening.' I asked her why and she said, 'They only let you be this happy if they're preparing to take something from you,' and I said, 'Hush up, now. Enough of this silliness.'"

Farid took my arm. "We should go, Amir agha," he said softly. I snatched my arm away. "What else? What else did she say?"

The old man's features softened. "I wish I remembered for you. But I don't. Your mother passed away a long time ago and my memory is as shattered as these buildings. I am sorry."

"But even a small thing, anything at all."

The old man smiled. "I'll try to remember and that's a

promise. Come back and find me."

"Thank you," I said. "Thank you so much." And I meant it. Now I knew my mother had liked almond cake with honey and hot tea, that she'd once used the word "profoundly," that she'd fretted about her happiness. I had just learned more about my mother from this old man on the street than I ever did from Baba.

Walking back to the truck, neither one of us commented about what most non-Afghans would have seen as an improbable coincidence, that a beggar on the street would happen to know my mother. Because we both knew that in Afghanistan, and particularly in Kabul, such absurdity was commonplace. Baba used to say, "Take two Afghans who've never met, put them in a room for ten minutes, and they'll figure out how they're related."

We left the old man on the steps of that building. I meant to take him up on his offer, come back and see if he'd unearthed any more stories about my mother. But I never saw him again.

WE FOUND THE NEW ORPHANAGE in the northern part of Karteh-Seh, along the banks of the dried-up Kabul River. It was a flat, barracks-style building with splintered walls and windows boarded with planks of wood. Farid had told me on the way there that Karteh-Seh had been one of the most war-ravaged neighborhoods in Kabul, and, as we stepped out of the truck, the evidence was overwhelming. The cratered streets were flanked by little more than ruins of shelled buildings and abandoned homes. We passed the rusted skeleton of an overturned car, a TV set with no screen half-buried in rubble, a wall with the words ZENDA BAD TALIBAN! (Long live the Taliban!) sprayed in black.

A short, thin, balding man with a shaggy gray beard opened the door. He wore a ragged tweed jacket, a skullcap, and a pair of eyeglasses with one chipped lens resting on the tip of his nose. Behind the glasses, tiny eyes like black peas flitted from me to Farid. *"Salaam alaykum,"* he said.

"Salaam alaykum," I said. I showed him the Polaroid. "We're searching for this boy."

He gave the photo a cursory glance. "I am sorry. I have never seen him."

"You barely looked at the picture, my friend," Farid said. "Why not take a closer look?"

"Lotfan," I added. Please.

The man behind the door took the picture. Studied it. Handed it back to me. "Nay, sorry. I know just about every single child in this institution and that one doesn't lookfamiliar. Now, if you'll permit me, I have work to do." He closed the door. Locked the bolt.

I rapped on the door with my knuckles. "Agha! Agha, please open the door. We don't mean him any harm."

"I told you. He's not here," his voice came from the other side. "Now, please go away."

Farid stepped up to the door, rested his forehead on it. "Friend, we are not with the Taliban," he said in a low, cautious voice. "The man who is with me wants to take this boy to a safe place."

"I come from Peshawar," I said. "A good friend of mine knows an American couple there who run a charity home for children." I felt the man's presence on the other side of the door. Sensed him standing there, listening, hesitating, caught between suspicion and hope. "Look, I knew Sohrab's father," I said. "His name was Hassan. His mother's name was Farzana. He called his grandmother *Sasa*. He knows how to read and write. And he's good with the slingshot. There's hope for this boy, Agha, a way out. Please open the door."

From the other side, only silence. "I'm his half uncle," I said.

A moment passed. Then a key rattled in the lock. The man's narrow face reappeared in the crack. He looked from me to Farid and back. "You were wrong about one thing."

"What?"

"He's *great* with the slingshot." I smiled.

"He's inseparable from that thing. He tucks it in the waist of his pants everywhere he goes."

THE MAN WHO LET US IN introduced himself as Zaman, the director of the orphanage. "I'll take you to my office," he said.

We followed him through dim, grimy hallways where barefoot children dressed in frayed sweaters ambled around. We walked past rooms with no floor covering but matted carpets and windows shuttered with sheets of plastic. Skeleton frames of steel beds, most with no mattress, filled the rooms.

"How many orphans live here?" Farid asked.

"More than we have room for. About two hundred and fifty," Zaman said over his shoulder. "But they're not all *yateem*. Many of them have lost their fathers in the war, and their mothers can't feed them because the Taliban don't allow them to work. So they bring their children here." He made a sweeping gesture with his hand and added ruefully, "This place is better than the street, but not that much better. This building was never meant to be lived in—it used to be a storage warehouse for a carpet manufacturer. So there's no water heater and they've let the well go dry." He dropped his voice. "I've asked the Taliban for money to dig a new well more times than I remember and they just twirl their rosaries and tell me there is no money. No money." He snickered.

He pointed to a row of beds along the wall. "We don't have enough beds, and not enough mattresses for the beds we do have. Worse, we don't have enough blankets." He showed us a little girl skipping rope with two other kids. "You see that girl? This past winter, the children had to share blankets. Her brother died of exposure." He walked on. "The last time I checked, we have less than a month's supply of rice left in the warehouse, and, when that runs out, the children will have to eat bread and tea for breakfast *and* dinner." I noticed he made no mention of lunch.

He stopped and turned to me. "There is very little shelter here, almost no food, no clothes, no clean water. What I have in ample supply here is children who've lost their childhood. But the tragedy is that these are the lucky ones. We're filled beyond capacity and every day I turn away mothers who bring their children." He took a step toward me. "You say there is hope for Sohrab? I pray you don't lie, Agha. But… you may well be too late."

"What do you mean?"

Zaman's eyes shifted. "Follow me."

WHAT PASSED FOR THE DIRECTOR'S OFFICE was four

bare, cracked walls, a mat on the floor, a table, and two folding chairs. As Zaman and I sat down, I saw a gray rat poke its head from a burrow in the wall and flit across the room. I cringed when it sniffed at my shoes, then Zaman's, and scurried through the open door.

"What did you mean it may be too late?" I said. "Would you like some *chai*? I could make some." "Nay, thank you. I'd rather we talk."

Zaman tilted back in his chair and crossed his arms on his chest. "What I have to tell you is not pleasant. Not to mention that it may be very dangerous."

"For whom?"

"You. Me. And, of course, for Sohrab, if it's not too late already."

"I need to know," I said.

He nodded. "So you say. But first I want to ask you a question: How badly do you want to find your nephew?"

I thought of the street fights we'd get into when we were kids, all the times Hassan used to take them on for me, two against one, sometimes three against one. I'd wince and watch, tempted to step in, but always stopping short, always held back by something.

I looked at the hallway, saw a group of kids dancing in a circle. A little girl, her left leg amputated below the knee, sat on a ratty mattress and watched, smiling and clapping along with the other children. I saw Farid watching the children too, his own mangled hand hanging at his side. I remembered Wahid's boys and ...I realized something: I would not leave Afghanistan without finding Sohrab. "Tell me where he is," I said.

Zaman's gaze lingered on me. Then he nodded, picked up a

pencil, and twirled it between his fingers. "Keep my name out of it."

"I promise."

He tapped the table with the pencil. "Despite your promise, I think I'll live to regret this, but perhaps it's just as well. I'm damned anyway. But if something can be done for Sohrab ... I'll tell you because I believe you. You have the look of a desperate man." He was quiet for a long time. "There is a Talib official," he muttered. "He visits once every month or two. He brings cash with him, not a lot, but better than nothing at all." His shifty eyes fell on me, rolled away. "Usually he'll take a girl. But not always."

"And you allow this?" Farid said behind me. He was going around the table, closing in on Zaman.

"What choice do I have?" Zaman shot back. He pushed himself away from the desk.

"You're the director here," Farid said. "Your job is watch over these children."

"There's nothing I can do to stop it." "You're selling children!" Farid barked.

"Farid, sit down! Let it go!" I said. But I was too late. Because suddenly Farid was leaping over the table. Zaman's chair went flying as Farid fell on him and pinned him to the floor. The director thrashed beneath Farid and made muffled screaming sounds. His legs kicked a desk drawer free and sheets of paper spilled to the floor.

I ran around the desk and saw why Zaman's screaming was muffled: Farid was strangling him. I grasped Farid's shoulders with both hands and pulled hard. He snatched away from me. "That's enough!" I barked. But Farid's face had flushed red, his lips pulled back in a snarl. "I'm killing him! You can't stop me! I'm killing him," he sneered.

"Get off him!"

"I'm killing him!" Something in his voice told me that if I didn't do something quickly I'd witness my first murder.

"The children are watching, Farid. They're watching," I said. His shoulder muscles tightened under my grip and, for a moment, I thought he'd keep squeezing Zaman's neck anyway. Then he turned around, saw the children. They were standing silently by the door, holding hands, some of them crying. I felt Farid's muscles slacken. He dropped his hands, rose to his feet. He looked down on Zaman and dropped a mouthful of spit on his face. Then he walked to the door and closed it.

Zaman struggled to his feet, blotted his bloody lips with his sleeve, wiped the spit off his cheek. Coughing and wheezing, he put on his skullcap, his glasses, saw both lenses had cracked, and took them off. He buried his face in his hands. None of us said anything for a long time.

"He took Sohrab a month ago," Zaman finally croaked, hands still shielding his face.

"You call yourself a director?" Farid said.

Zaman dropped his hands. "I haven't been paid in over six months. I'm broke because I've spent my life's savings on this orphanage. Everything I ever owned or inherited I sold to run this godforsaken place. You think I don't have family in Pakistan and Iran? I could have run like everyone else. But I didn't. I stayed. I stayed because of *them*." He pointed to the door. "If I deny him one child, he takes ten. So I let him take one and leave the judging to Allah. I swallow my pride and take his goddamn filthy ... dirty money. Then I go to the bazaar and buy food for the children."

Farid dropped his eyes.

"What happens to the children he takes?" I asked.

Zaman rubbed his eyes with his forefinger and thumb. "Sometimes they come back."

"Who is he? How do we find him?" I said.

"Go to Ghazi Stadium tomorrow. You'll see him at halftime. He'll be the one wearing black sunglasses." He picked up his broken glasses and turned them in his hands. "I want you to go now. The children are frightened."

He escorted us out.

As the truck pulled away, I saw Zaman in the side-view mirror, standing in the doorway. A group of children surrounded him, clutching the hem of his loose shirt. I saw he had put on his broken glasses.

TWENTY ONE

We crossed the river and drove north through the crowded Pashtunistan Square. Baba used to take me to Khyber Restaurant there for kabob. The building was still standing, but its doors were padlocked, the windows shattered, and the letters *K* and *R* missing from its name.

I saw a dead body near the restaurant. There had been a hanging. A young man dangled from the end of a rope tied to a beam, his face puffy and blue, the clothes he'd worn on the last day of his life shredded, bloody. Hardly anyone seemed to notice him.

We rode silently through the square and headed toward the Wazir Akbar Khan district. Everywhere I looked, a haze of dust covered the city and its sun-dried brickbuildings. A few blocks north of Pashtunistan Square, Farid pointed to two men talking animatedly at a busy street corner. One of them was hobbling on one leg, his other leg amputated below the knee. He cradled an artificial leg in his arms. "You know what they're doing? Haggling over the leg."

"He's selling his leg?"

Farid nodded. "You can get good money for it on the black market. Feed your kids for a couple of weeks."

TO MY SURPRISE, most of the houses in the Wazir Akbar Khan district still had roofs and standing walls. In fact, they were in pretty good shape. Trees still peeked over the walls, and the streets weren't nearly as rubble-strewn as the ones in Karteh-Seh. Faded streets signs, some twisted and bullet-pocked, still pointed the way.

"This isn't so bad," I remarked.

"No surprise. Most of the important people live here now."

"Taliban?"

"Them too," Farid said. "Who else?"

He drove us into a wide street with fairly clean sidewalks and walled homes on either side. "The people behind the Taliban. The real brains of this government, if you can call it that: Arabs, Chechens, Pakistanis," Farid said. He pointed northwest. "Street 15, that way, is called Sarak-e-Mehmana." Street of the Guests. "That's what they call them here, guests. I think someday these guests are going to pee all over the carpet."

"I think that's it!" I said. "Over there!" I pointed to the landmark that used to serve as a guide for me when I was a kid. *If you ever get lost,* Baba used to say, *remember that our street is the one with the pink house at the end of it.* The pink house with the steeply pitched roof had been the neighborhood's only house of that color in the old days. It still was.

Farid turned onto the street. I saw Baba's house right away.

.　.　.

WE FIND THE LITTLE TURTLE behind tangles of sweetbrier in the yard. We don't know how it got there and we're too excited to care. We paint its shell a bright red, Hassan's idea, and a good one: This way, we'll never lose it in the bushes. We pretend we're a pair of daredevil explorers who've discovered a giant prehistoric monster in some distant jungle and we've brought it back for the world to see. We set it down in the wooden wagon Ali built Hassan last winter for his birthday, pretend it's a giant steel cage. Behold the firebreathing monstrosity! We march on the grass and pull the wagon behind us, around apple and cherry trees, which become skyscrapers soaring into clouds, heads poking out of thousands of windows to watch the spectacle passing below. We walk over the little semilunar bridge Baba has built near a cluster of fig trees; it becomes a great suspension bridge joining cities, and the little pond below, a foamy sea. Fireworks explode above the bridge's massive pylons and armed soldiers salute us on both sides as gigantic steel cables shoot to the sky. The little turtle bouncing around in the cab, we drag the wagon around the circular redbrick driveway outside the wroughtiron gates and return the salutes of the world's leaders as they stand and applaud. We are Hassan and Amir, famed adventurers and the world's greatest explorers, about to receive a medal of honor for our courageous feat …

GINGERLY, I WALKED up the driveway where tufts of weed now grew between the sun-faded bricks. I stood outside the gates of my father's house, feeling like a stranger. I set my hands on the rusty bars, remembering how I'd run through these same gates thousands of times as a child, for things that mattered not at all now and yet had seemed so important then. I peered in.

The driveway extension that led from the gates to the yard,

where Hassan and I took turns falling the summer we learned to ride a bike, didn't look as wide or as long as I remembered it. The asphalt had split in a lightning-streak pattern, and more tangles of weed sprouted through the fissures. Most of the poplar trees had been chopped down—the trees Hassan and I used to climb to shine our mirrors into the neighbors' homes. The ones still standing were nearly leafless. The Wall of Ailing Corn was still there, though I saw no corn, ailing or otherwise, along that wall now. The paint had begun to peel and sections of it had sloughed off altogether. The lawn had turned the same brown as the haze of dust hovering over the city, dotted by bald patches of dirt where nothing grew at all.

A jeep was parked in the driveway and that looked all wrong: Baba's black Mustang belonged there. For years, the Mustang's eight cylinders roared to life every morning, rousing me from sleep. I saw that oil had spilled under the jeep and stained the driveway like a big Rorschach inkblot. Beyond the jeep, an empty wheelbarrow lay on its side. I saw no sign of the rosebushes that Baba and Ali had planted on the left side of the driveway, only dirt that spilled onto the asphalt. And weeds.

Farid honked twice behind me. "We should go, Agha. We'll draw attention," he called.

"Just give me one more minute," I said.

The house itself was far from the sprawling white mansion I remembered from my childhood. It looked smaller. The roof sagged and the plaster was cracked. The windows to the living room, the foyer, and the upstairs guest bathroom were broken, patched haphazardly with sheets of clear plastic or wooden boards nailed across the frames. The paint, once sparkling white, had faded to ghostly gray and eroded in parts, revealing the layered bricks beneath. The front steps had crumbled. Like so much else in Kabul, my father's house was the picture of fallen splendor.

I found the window to my old bedroom, second floor, third window south of the main steps to the house. I stood on tiptoes, saw nothing behind the window but shadows. Twenty-five years earlier, I had stood behind that same window, thick rain dripping down the panes and my breath fogging up the glass. I had watched Hassan and Ali load their belongings into the trunk of my father's car.

"Amir agha," Farid called again. "I'm coming," I shot back.

Insanely, I wanted to go in. Wanted to walk up the front steps where Ali used to make Hassan and me take off our snow boots. I wanted to step into the foyer, smell the orange peel Ali always tossed into the stove to burn with sawdust. Sit at the kitchen table, have tea with a slice of *naan,* listen to Hassan sing old Hazara songs.

Another honk. I walked back to the Land Cruiser parked along the sidewalk. Farid sat smoking behind the wheel.

"I have to look at one more thing," I told him. "Can you hurry?"

"Give me ten minutes."

"Go, then." Then, just as I was turning to go: "Just forget it all. Makes it easier." "To what?"

"To go on," Farid said. He flicked his cigarette out of the window. "How much more do you need to see? Let me save you the trouble: Nothing that you remember has survived. Best to forget." "I don't want to forget anymore," I said. "Give me ten minutes."

WE HARDLY BROKE A SWEAT, Hassan and I, when we hiked up the hill just north of Baba's house. We scampered about the hilltop chasing each other or sat on a sloped ridge where there was a good view of the airport in the distance. We'd watch airplanes take off and land. Go running again.

Now, by the time I reached the top of the craggy hill, each ragged breath felt like inhaling fire. Sweat trickled down my face. I stood wheezing for a while, a stitch in my side. Then I went looking for the abandoned cemetery. It didn't take me long to find it. It was still there, and so was the old pomegranate tree.

I leaned against the gray stone gateway to the cemetery where Hassan had buried his mother. The old metal gates hanging off the hinges were gone, and the headstones were barely visible through the thick tangles of weeds that had claimed the plot. A pair of crows sat on the low wall that enclosed the cemetery.

Hassan had said in his letter that the pomegranate tree hadn't borne fruit in years. Looking at the wilted, leafless tree, I doubted it ever would again. I stood under it, remembered all the times we'd climbed it, straddled its branches, our legs swinging, dappled sunlight flickering through the leaves and casting on our faces a mosaic of light and shadow. The tangy taste of pomegranate crept into my mouth.

I hunkered down on my knees and brushed my hands against the trunk. I found what I was looking for. The carving had dulled, almost faded altogether, but it was still there: "Amir and Hassan. The Sultans of Kabul." I traced the curve of each letter with my fingers. Picked small bits of bark from the tiny crevasses.

I sat cross-legged at the foot of the tree and looked south on the city of my childhood. In those days, treetops poked behind the walls of every house. The sky stretched wide and blue, and laundry drying on clotheslines glimmered in the sun. If you listened hard, you might even have heard the call of the fruit seller passing through Wazir Akbar Khan with his donkey: *Cherries! Apricots!Grapes!* In the early evening, you would have heard *azan*, the *mueszzin*'s call to prayer from the mosque in Shar-e-Nau.

I heard a honk and saw Farid waving at me. It was time to go.

WE DROVE SOUTH AGAIN, back toward Pashtunistan Square. We passed several more red pickup trucks with armed, bearded young men crammed into the cabs. Farid cursed under his breath every time we passed one.

I paid for a room at a small hotel near Pashtunistan Square. Three little girls dressed in identical black dresses and white scarves clung to the slight, bespectacled man behind the counter. He charged me $75, an unthinkable price given the run-down appearance of the place, but I didn't mind. Exploitation to finance a beach house in Hawaii was one thing. Doing it to feed your kids was another.

There was no hot running water and the cracked toilet didn't flush. Just a single steel-frame bed with a worn mattress, a ragged blanket, and a wooden chair in the corner. The window overlooking the square had broken, hadn't been replaced. As I lowered my suitcase, I noticed a dried bloodstain on the wall behind the bed. I gave Farid some money and he went out to get food. He returned with four sizzling skewers of kabob, fresh *naan,* and a bowl of white rice. We sat on the bed and all but devoured the food. There *was* one thing that hadn't changed in Kabul after all: The kabob was as succulent and delicious as I remembered.

That night, I took the bed and Farid lay on the floor, wrapped himself with an extra blanket for which the hotel owner charged me an additional fee. No light came into the room except for the moonbeams streaming through the broken window. Farid said the owner had told him that Kabul had been without electricity for two days now and his generator needed fixing. We talked for a while. He told me about growing up in Mazar-i-Sharif, in Jalalabad. He told me about a time shortly after he and his father joined the jihad and fought the *Shorawi* in the Panjsher Valley. They were stranded without food and ate locust to survive. He told me of the day helicopter gunfire killed his father, of the day the land mine took his two daughters. He asked me about America. I told him that in America you could step into a grocery store and buy any of fifteen or twenty different types of cereal. The lamb was always fresh and the milk cold, the fruit plentiful and the water clear. Every home had a TV, and every TV a remote, and you could get a satellite dish if you wanted. Receive over five hundred channels.

"Five hundred?" Farid exclaimed. "Five hundred."

We fell silent for a while. Just when I thought he had fallen asleep, Farid chuckled. "Agha, did you hear what Mullah Nasruddin did when his daughter came home and complained that her husband had beaten her?" I could feel him smiling in the dark and a smile of my own formed on my face. There wasn't an Afghan in the world who didn't know at least a few jokes about the bumbling mullah.

"What?"

"He beat her too, then sent her back to tell the husband that Mullah was no fool: If the bastard was going to beat his daughter, then Mullah would beat his wife in return."

I laughed. Partly at the joke, partly at how Afghan humor never changed. Wars were waged, the Internet was invented, and a robot had rolled on the surface of Mars, and in Afghanistan we were still telling Mullah Nasruddin jokes. "Did you hear about the boy?" "For the boy."

Farid shifted on the ground. "It's hard to believe." "Sometimes I myself can hardly believe I'm here."

"No ... What I mean to ask is why *that* boy? You come all the way from America for ... a Shi'a?"

That killed all the laughter in me. And the sleep. "I am tired," I said. "Let's just get some sleep."

Farid's snoring soon echoed through the empty room. I stayed awake, hands crossed on my chest, staring into the starlit night through the broken window, and thinking that maybe what people said about Afghanistan was true. Maybe it *was* a hopeless place.

A BUSTLING CROWD was filling Ghazi Stadium when we walked through the entrance tunnels. Thousands of people milled about the tightly packed concrete terraces. Children played in the aisles and chased each other up and down the steps. The scent of garbanzo beans in spicy sauce hung in the air, mixed with the smell of dung and sweat. Farid and I walked past street peddlers selling cigarettes, pine nuts, and biscuits.

A scrawny boy in a tweed jacket grabbed my elbow and spoke

into my ear. Asked me if I wanted to buy some "sexy pictures."

"Very sexy, Agha," he said, his alert eyes darting side to side—reminding me of a girl who, a few years earlier, had tried to sell me crack in the Tenderloin district in San Francisco. The kid peeled one side of his jacket open and gave me a fleeting glance of his sexy pictures: postcards of Hindi movies showing doe-eyed sultry actresses, fully dressed, in the arms of their leading men. "So sexy," he repeated.

"Nay, thanks," I said, pushing past him.

"He gets caught, they'll give him a flogging that will waken his father in the grave," Farid muttered.

There was no assigned seating, of course. No one to show us politely to our section, aisle, row, and seat. There never had been, even in the old days of the monarchy. We found a decent spot to sit, just left of midfield, though it took some shoving and elbowing on Farid's part.

I remembered how green the playing field grass had been in the '70s when Baba used to bring me to soccer games here. Now the pitch was a mess. There were holes and craters everywhere, most notably a pair of deep holes in the ground behind the southend goalposts. And there was no grass at all, just dirt. When the two teams finally took the field—all wearing long pants despite the heat—and play began, it became difficult to follow the ball in the clouds of dust kicked up by the players. Young, whip-toting Talibs roamed the aisles, striking anyone who cheered too loudly.

They brought them out shortly after the halftime whistle blew. A pair of dusty red pickup trucks, like the ones I'd seen around town since I'd arrived, rode into the stadium through the gates. The crowd rose to its feet. A woman dressed in a green *burqa* sat in the cab of one truck, a blindfolded man in the other. The trucks drove around the track, slowly, as if to let the crowd get a long look. It had the desired effect: People craned their necks, pointed, stood on tiptoes. Next to me, Farid's Adam's apple bobbed up and down as he mumbled a prayer under his breath.

The red trucks entered the playing field, rode toward one end in twin clouds of dust, sunlight reflecting off their hubcaps. A third truck met them at the end of the field. This one's cab was filled with something and I suddenly understood the purpose of those two holes behind the goalposts. They unloaded the third truck. The crowd murmured in anticipation.

"Do you want to stay?" Farid said gravely.

"No," I said. I had never in my life wanted to be away from a place as badly as I did now. "But we have to stay."

Two Talibs with Kalashnikovs slung across their shoulders helped the blindfolded man from the first truck and two others helped the *burqa*-clad woman. The woman's knees buckled under her and she slumped to the ground. The soldiers pulled her up and she slumped again. When they tried to lift her again, she screamed and kicked. I will never, as long as I draw breath, forget the sound of that scream. It was the cry of a wild animal trying to pry its mangled leg free from the bear trap. Two more Talibs joined in and helped force her into one of the chest-deep holes. The blindfolded man, on the other hand, quietly allowed them to lower him into the hole dug for him. Now only the accused pair's torsos protruded from the ground.

A chubby, white-bearded cleric dressed in gray garments stood near the goalposts and cleared his throat into a handheld microphone. Behind him the woman in the hole was still screaming. He recited a lengthy prayer from the Koran, his nasal voice undulating through the sudden hush of the stadium's crowd. I remembered something Baba had said to me a long time ago: *Piss on the beards of all those self-righteous monkeys. They do nothing but thumb their rosaries and recite a book written in a tongue they don't even understand. God help us all if Afghanistan ever falls into their hands.*

When the prayer was done, the cleric cleared his throat. "Brothers and sisters!" he called, speaking in Farsi, his voice booming through the stadium. "We are here today to carry out *Shari'a.* We are here today to carry out justice. We are here today because the will of Allah and the word of the Prophet Muhammad, peace be upon him, are alive and well here in Afghanistan, our beloved homeland. We listen to what God says and we obey because we are nothing but humble, powerless creatures before God's greatness. And what does God say? I askyou! WHAT DOES GOD SAY? God says that every sinner must be punished in a manner befitting his sin. Those are not my words, nor the words of my brothers. Those are the words of GOD!" He pointed with his free hand to the sky. My head was pounding and the sun felt much too hot.

"Every sinner must be punished in a manner befitting his sin!" the cleric repeated into the mike, lowering his voice, enunciating each word slowly, dramatically. "And what manner of punishment, brothers and sisters, befits the adulterer? How shall we punish those who dishonor the sanctity of marriage? How shall we deal with those who spit in the face of God? How shall we answer those who throw stones at the windows of God's house? WE SHALL THROW THE STONES BACK!" He shut off the microphone. A low-pitched murmur spread through the crowd.

Next to me, Farid was shaking his head. "And they call them-selves Muslims," he whispered.

Then a tall, broad-shouldered man stepped out of the pickup truck. The sight of him drew cheers from a few spectators. This time, no one was struckwith a whip for cheering too loudly. The tall man's sparkling white garment glimmered in the afternoon sun. The hem of his loose shirt fluttered in the breeze, his arms spread like those of Jesus on the cross. He greeted the crowd by turning slowly in a full circle. When he faced our section, I saw he was wearing dark round sunglasses like the ones John Lennon wore.

"That must be our man," Farid said.

The tall Talib with the black sunglasses walked to the pile of stones they had unloaded from the third truck. He picked up a rock and showed it to the crowd. The noise fell, replaced by a buzzing sound that rippled through the stadium. I looked around me and saw that everyone was *tsk*'ing. The Talib, looking absurdly like a baseball pitcher on the mound, hurled the stone at the blindfolded man in the hole. It struck the side of his head. The woman screamed again. The crowd made a startled "OH!" sound. I closed my eyes and covered my face with my hands. The spectators' "OH!" rhymed with each flinging of the stone, and that went on for a while. When they stopped, I asked Farid if it was over. He said no. I guessed the people's throats had tired. I don't know how much longer I sat with my face in my hands. I know that I reopened my eyes when I heard people around me asking, *"Mord? Mord? Is he dead?"*

The man in the hole was now a mangled mess of blood and shredded rags. His head slumped forward, chin on chest. The

Talib in the John Lennon sunglasses was looking down at another man squatting next to the hole, tossing a rock up and down
in his hand. The squatting man had one end of a stethoscope
to his ears and the other pressed on the chest of the man in the
hole. He removed the stethoscope from his ears and shook his
head no at the Talib in the sunglasses. The crowd moaned.

John Lennon walked back to the mound.

When it was all over, when the bloodied corpses had been
unceremoniously tossed into the backs of red pickup trucks—
separate ones—a few men with shovels hurriedly filled the
holes. One of them made a passing attempt at covering up the
large bloodstains by kicking dirt over them. A few minutes later,
the teams took the field. Second half was under way.

Our meeting was arranged for three o'clock that afternoon.
The swiftness with which the appointment was set surprised
me. I'd expected delays, a round of questioning at least, perhaps
a check of our papers. But I was reminded of how unofficial
even official matters still were in Afghanistan: all Farid had
to do was tell one of the whip-carrying Talibs that we had
personal business to discuss with the man in white. Farid and
he exchanged words. The guy with the whip then nodded and
shouted something in Pashtu to a young man on the field, who
ran to the southend goalposts where the Talib in the sunglasses
was chatting with the plump cleric who'd given the sermon.
The three spoke. I saw the guy in the sunglasses look up. He
nodded. Said something in the messenger's ear. The young man
relayed the message back to us.

It was set, then. Three o'clock.

T W E N T Y T W O

Farid eased the Land Cruiser up the driveway of a big house in Wazir Akbar Khan. He parked in the shadows of willow trees that spilled over the walls of the compound located on Street 15, Sarak-e-Mehmana, Street of the Guests. He killed the engine and we sat for a minute, listening to the *tink-tink* of the engine cooling off, neither one of us saying anything. Farid shifted on his seat and toyed with the keys still hanging from the ignition switch. I could tell he was readying himself to tell me something.

"I guess I'll wait in the car for you," he said finally, his tone a little apologetic. He wouldn't look at me. "This is your business now. I—"

I patted his arm. "You've done much more than I've paid you for. I don't expect you to go with me." But I wished I didn't have to go in alone. Despite what I had learned about Baba, I wished he were standing alongside me now. Baba would have busted through the front doors and demanded to be taken to the man in charge, piss on the beard of anyone who stood in his way. But Baba was long dead, buried in the Afghan section of a little cemetery in Hayward. Just last month, Soraya and I had placed a bouquet of daisies and freesias beside his headstone. I was on my own.

I stepped out of the car and walked to the tall, wooden front gates of the house. I rang the bell but no buzz came—still no electricity—and I had to pound on the doors. A moment later, I heard terse voices from the other side and a pair of men toting Kalashnikovs answered the door.

I glanced at Farid sitting in the car and mouthed, *I'll be back,* not so sure at all that I would be.

The armed men frisked me head to toe, patted my legs, felt my crotch. One of them said something in Pashtu and they both chuckled. We stepped through the front gates. The two guards escorted me across a well-manicured lawn, past a row of geraniums and stubby bushes lined along the wall. An old hand-pump water well stood at the far end of the yard. I remembered how Kaka Homayoun's house in Jalalabad had had a water well like that—the twins, Fazila and Karima, and I used to drop pebbles in it, listen for the *plink.*

We climbed a few steps and entered a large, sparsely decorated house. We crossed the foyer—a large Afghan flag draped one of the walls—and the men took me upstairs to a room with twin mint green sofas and a big-screen TV in the far corner. A prayer rug showing a slightly oblong Mecca was nailed to one of the walls. The older of the two men motioned toward the sofa with the barrel of his weapon. I sat down. They left the room.

I crossed my legs. Uncrossed them. Sat with my sweaty hands on my knees. Did that make me look nervous? I clasped them together, decided that was worse and just crossed my arms on my chest. Blood thudded in my temples. I felt utterly alone. Thoughts were flying around in my head, but I didn't want to think at all, because a sober part of me knew that what I had managed to get myself into was insanity. I was thousands of miles from my wife, sitting in a room that felt like a holding cell, waiting for a man I had seen murder two people that same day. It *was* insanity. Worse yet, it was irresponsible. There was a very realistic chance that I was going to render Soraya a *biwa,* a widow, at the age of thirty-six. *This isn't you, Amir,* part of me said. *You're gutless. It's how you were made. And that's not such a bad thing because your saving grace is that you've never lied to yourself about it. Not about that. Nothing wrong with cowardice as long as it comes with prudence. But when a coward stops remembering who he is … God help him.*

There was a coffee table by the sofa. The base was X-shaped, walnut-sized brass balls studding the ring where the metallic legs crossed. I'd seen a table like that before. Where? And then it came to me: at the crowded tea shop in Peshawar, that night I'd gone for a walk. On the table sat a bowl of red grapes. I plucked one and tossed it in my mouth. I had to preoccupy myself with something, anything, to silence the voice in my head. The grape was sweet. I popped another one in, unaware that it would be the last bit of solid food I would eat for a long time.

The door opened and the two armed men returned, between them the tall Talib in white, still wearing his dark John Lennon glasses, looking like some broad-shouldered, New Age mystic guru. He took a seat across from me and lowered his hands on the armrests. For a long time, he said nothing. Just sat there, watching me, one hand drumming the upholstery, the other twirling turquoise blue prayer beads. He wore a black vest over the white shirt now, and a gold watch. I saw a splotch of dried blood on his left sleeve. I found it morbidly fascinating that he hadn't changed clothes after the executions earlier that day.

Periodically, his free hand floated up and his thick fingers batted at something in the air. They made slow stroking motions, up and down, side to side, as if he were caressing an invisible pet. One of his sleeves retracted and I saw marks on his forearm—I'd seen those same tracks on homeless people living in grimy alleys in San Francisco.

His skin was much paler than the other two men's, almost sallow, and a crop of tiny sweat beads gleamed on his forehead just below the edge of his black turban. His beard, chest-length like the others, was lighter in color too.

"Salaam alaykum," he said.

"Salaam."

"You can do away with that now, you know," he said. "Pardon?"

He turned his palm to one of the armed men and motioned. *Rrrriiiip.* Suddenly my cheeks were stinging and the guard was tossing my beard up and down in his hand, giggling. The Talib grinned. "One of the better ones I've seen in a while. But it really is so much better this way, I think. Don't you?" He twirled his fingers, snapped them, fist opening and closing. "So, *Inshallah,* you enjoyed the show today?"

"Was that what it was?" I said, rubbing my cheeks, hoping my voice didn't betray the explosion of terror I felt inside.

"Public justice is the greatest kind of show, my brother. Drama. Suspense. And, best of all, education en masse." He snapped his fingers. The younger of the two guards lit him a cigarette. The Talib laughed. Mumbled to himself. His hands were shaking and he almost dropped the cigarette. "But you want a real show, you should have been with me in Mazar. August 1998, that was."

"I'm sorry?"

"We left them out for the dogs, you know." I saw what he was getting at.

He stood up, paced around the sofa once, twice. Sat down again. He spoke rapidly. "Door to door we went, calling for the men and the boys. We'd shoot them right there in front of their families. Let them see. Let them remember who they were, where they belonged." He was almost panting now. "Sometimes, we broke down their doors and went inside their homes. And ... I'd ... I'd sweep the barrel of my machine gun around the room and fire and fire until the smoke blinded me." He leaned toward me, like a man about to share a great secret. "You don't know the meaning of the word 'liberating' until you've done that, stood in a roomful of targets, let the bullets fly, free of guilt and remorse, knowing you are virtuous, good, and decent. Knowing you're doing God's work. It's breathtaking." He kissed the prayer beads, tilted his head. "You remember that, Javid?"

"Yes, Agha sahib," the younger of the guards replied. "How could I forget?"

I had read about the Hazara massacre in Mazar-i-Sharif in the papers. It had happened just after the Taliban took over Mazar, one of the last cities to fall. I remembered Soraya handing me the article over breakfast, her face bloodless.

"Door-to-door. We only rested for food and prayer," the Talib said. He said it fondly, like a man telling of a great party he'd attended. "We left the bodies in the streets, and if their families tried to sneak out to drag them back into their homes, we'd shoot them too. We left them in the streets for days. We left them for the dogs. Dog meat for dogs." He crushed his cigarette. Rubbed his eyes with tremulous hands. "You come from America?"

"Yes."

"How is that whore these days?"

I had a sudden urge to urinate. I prayed it would pass. "I'm looking for a boy."

"Isn't everyone?" he said. The men with the Kalashnikovs laughed. Their teeth were stained green with *naswar.*

"I understand he is here, with you," I said. "His name is Sohrab."

"I'll ask you something: What are you doing with that whore? Why aren't you here, with your Muslim brothers, serving your country?"

"I've been away a long time," was all I could think of saying. My head felt so hot. I pressed my knees together, held my bladder.

The Talib turned to the two men standing by the door. "That's an answer?" he asked them.

"Nay, Agha sahib," they said in unison, smiling.

He turned his eyes to me. Shrugged. "Not an answer, they say." He took a drag of his cigarette. "There are those in my circle who believe that abandoning *watan* when it needs you the most is the same as treason. I could have you arrested for treason, have you shot for it even. Does that frighten you?"

"I'm only here for the boy." "Does that frighten you?" "Yes."

"It should," he said. He leaned back in the sofa. Crushed the cigarette.

I thought about Soraya. It calmed me. I thought of her sickle-shaped birthmark, the elegant curve of her neck, her luminous eyes. I thought of our wedding night, gazing at each other's reflection in the mirror under the green veil, and how her cheeks blushed when I whispered that I loved her. I remembered the two of us dancing to an old Afghan song, round and round, everyone watching and clapping, the world a blur of flowers, dresses, tuxedos, and smiling faces.

The Talib was saying something. "Pardon?"

"I said would you like to see him? Would you like to see my boy?" His upper lip curled up in a sneer when he said those last two words.

"Yes."

The guard left the room. I heard the creak of a door swinging open. Heard the guard say something in Pashtu, in a hard voice. Then, footfalls, and the jingle of bells with each step. It reminded me of the Monkey Man Hassan and I used to chase down in Share-Nau. We used to pay him a *rupia* of our allowance for a dance. The bell around his monkey's neck had made that same jingling sound.

Then the door opened and the guard walked in. He carried a stereo—a boom box—on his shoulder. Behind him, a boy dressed in a loose, sapphire blue *pirhan-tumban* followed.

The resemblance was breathtaking. Disorienting. Rahim Khan's Polaroid hadn't done justice to it.

The boy had his father's round moon face, his pointy stub of a chin, his twisted, seashell ears, and the same slight frame. It was the Chinese doll face of my childhood, the face peering above fanned-out playing cards all those winter days, the face behind the mosquito net when we slept on the roof of my father's house in the summer. His head was shaved, his eyes darkened with mascara, and his cheeks glowed with an unnatural red. When he stopped in the middle of the room, the bells strapped around his anklets stopped jingling.

His eyes fell on me. Lingered. Then he looked away. Looked

down at his naked feet.

One of the guards pressed a button and Pashtu music filled the room. Tabla, harmonium, the whine of a *dil-roba*. I guessed music wasn't sinful as long as it played to Taliban ears. The three men began to clap.

"Wah wah! Mashallah!" they cheered.

Sohrab raised his arms and turned slowly. He stood on tiptoes, spun gracefully, dipped to his knees, straightened, and spun again. His little hands swiveled at the wrists, his fingers snapped, and his head swung side to side like a pendulum. His feet pounded the floor, the bells jingling in perfect harmony with the beat of the tabla. He kept his eyes closed.

"Mashallah!" they cheered. *"Shahbas!* Bravo!" The two guards whistled and laughed. The Talib in white was tilting his head back and forth with the music, his mouth half-open in a leer.

Sohrab danced in a circle, eyes closed, danced until the music stopped. The bells jingled one final time when he stomped his foot with the song's last note. He froze in midspin.

"Bia, bia, my boy," the Talib said, calling Sohrab to him. Sohrab went to him, head down, stood between his thighs. The Talib wrapped his arms around the boy. "How talented he is, nay, my Hazara boy!" he said. His hands slid down the child's back, then up, felt under his armpits. One of the guards elbowed the other and snickered. The Talib told them to leave us alone.

"Yes, Agha sahib," they said as they exited.

The Talib spun the boy around so he faced me. He locked his arms around Sohrab's belly, rested his chin on the boy's shoulder. Sohrab looked down at his feet, but kept stealing shy, furtive glances at me. The man's hand slid up and down the boy's belly. Up and down, slowly, gently.

"I've been wondering," the Talib said, his bloodshot eyes peering at me over Sohrab's shoulder. "Whatever happened to old *Babalu,* anyway?"

The question hit me like a hammer between the eyes. I felt the color drain from my face. My legs went cold. Numb.

He laughed. "What did you think? That you'd put on a fake beard and I wouldn't recognize you? Here's something I'll bet you never knew about me: I never forget a face. Not ever." He brushed his lips against Sohrab's ear, kept his eye on me. "I heard your father died. *Tsk-tsk.* I always did want to take him on. Looks like I'll have to settle for his weakling of a son." Then he took off his sunglasses and locked his bloodshot blue eyes on mine.

I tried to take a breath and couldn't. I tried to blink and couldn't. The moment felt surreal—no, not surreal, *absurd*—it had knocked the breath out of me, brought the world around me to a standstill. My face was burning. What was the old saying about the bad penny? My past was like that, always turning up. His name rose from the deep and I didn't want to say it, as if uttering it might conjure him. But he was already here, in the flesh, sitting less than ten feet from me, after all these years. His name escaped my lips: "Assef."

"Amir jan."

"What are you doing here?" I said, knowing how utterly foolish the question sounded, yet unable to think of anything else to say. "Me?" Assef arched an eyebrow. "I'm in my element. The question is what are you doing here?"

"I already told you," I said. My voice was trembling. I wished it wouldn't do that, wished my flesh wasn't shrinking against my bones.

"The boy?"

"Yes."

"Why?"

"I'll pay you for him," I said. "I can have money wired."

"Money?" Assef said. He tittered. "Have you ever heard of Rockingham? Western Australia, a slice of heaven. You should see it, miles and miles of beach. Green water, blue skies. My parents live there, in a beachfront villa. There's a golf course behind the villa and a little lake. Father plays golf every day. Mother, she prefers tennis—Father says she has a wicked backhand. They own an Afghan restaurant and two jewelry stores; both businesses are doing spectacularly." He plucked a red grape. Put it, lovingly, in Sohrab's mouth. "So if I need money, I'll have *them* wire it to me." He kissed the side of Sohrab's neck. The boy flinched a little, closed his eyes again. "Besides, I didn't fight the *Shorawi* for money. Didn't join the Taliban for money either. Do you want to know why I joined them?"

My lips had gone dry. I licked them and found my tongue had dried too.

"Are you thirsty?" Assef said, smirking. "No."

"I think you're thirsty."

"I'm fine," I said. The truth was, the room felt too hot suddenly—sweat was bursting from my pores, prickling my skin. And was this really happening? Was I really sitting across from Assef? "As you wish," he said. "Anyway, where was I? Oh yes, how I joined the Taliban. Well, as you may remember, I wasn't much of a religious type. But one day I had an epiphany. I had it in jail. Do you want to hear?" I said nothing.

"Good. I'll tell you," he said. "I spent some time in jail, at Poleh-Charkhi, just after Babrak Karmal took over in 1980. I ended up there one night, when a group of *Parchami* soldiers marched into our house and ordered my father and me at gunpoint to follow them. The bastards didn't give a reason, and they wouldn't answer my mother's questions. Not that it was a mystery; everyone knew the communists had no class. They came from poor families with no name. The same dogs who weren't fit to lick my shoes before the *Shorawi* came were now ordering me at gunpoint, *Parchami* flag on their lapels, making their little point about the fall of the bourgeoisie and acting like they were the ones with class. It was happening all over: Round up the rich, throw them in jail, make an example for the comrades.

"Anyway, we were crammed in groups of six in these tiny cells each the size of a refrigerator. Every night the commandant, a half-Hazara, half-Uzbek thing who smelled like a rotting donkey, would have one of the prisoners dragged out of the cell and he'd beat him until sweat poured from his fat face. Then he'd light a cigarette, crack his joints, and leave. The next night, he'd pick someone else. One night, he picked me. It couldn't have come at a worse time. I'd been peeing blood for three days. Kidney stones. And if you've never had one, believe me when I say it's the worst imaginable pain. My mother used to get them too, and I remember she told me once she'd rather give birth than pass a kidney stone. Anyway, what could I do? They dragged me out and he started kicking me. He had knee-high boots with steel toes that he wore every night for his little kicking game, and he used them on me. I was screaming and screaming and he kept kicking me and then, suddenly, he kicked me on the left kidney and the stone passed. Just like that! Oh, the relief!" Assef laughed. "And I yelled *'Allah-uakbar'* and he kicked me even harder and I started laughing. He got mad and hit me harder, and the harder he kicked me, the harder I laughed. They threw me back in the cell laughing. I kept laughing and laughing because suddenly I knew that had been a message from God: He was on *my* side. He wanted me to live for a reason.

"You know, I ran into that commandant on the battlefield a few years later—funny how God works. I found him in a trench just outside Meymanah, bleeding from a piece of shrapnel in his chest. He was still wearing those same boots. I asked him if he remembered me. He said no. I told him the same thing I just told you, that I never forget a face. Then I shot him in the balls. I've been on a mission since."

"What mission is that?" I heard myself say. "Stoning adulterers? Raping children? Flogging women for wearing high heels? Massacring Hazaras? All in the name of Islam?" The words spilled suddenly and unexpectedly, came out

before I could yank the leash. I wished I could take them back. Swallow them. But they were out. I had crossed a line, and whatever little hope I had of getting out alive had vanished with those words.

A look of surprise passed across Assef's face, briefly, and disappeared. "I see this may turn out to be enjoyable after all," he said, snickering. "But there are things traitors like you don't understand."

"Like what?"

Assef's brow twitched. "Like pride in your people, your customs, your language. Afghanistan is like a beautiful mansion littered with garbage, and someone has to take out the garbage."

"That's what you were doing in Mazar, going door-to-door? Taking out the garbage?" "Precisely."

"In the west, they have an expression for that," I said. "They call it ethnic cleansing."

"Do they?" Assef's face brightened. "Ethnic cleansing. I like it. I like the sound of it." "All I want is the boy."

"Ethnic cleansing," Assef murmured, tasting the words.

"I want the boy," I said again. Sohrab's eyes flicked to me. They were slaughter sheep's eyes. They even had the mascara— I remembered how, on the day of *Eid* of *qorban,* the mullah in our backyard used to apply mascara to the eyes of the sheep and feed it a cube of sugar before slicing its throat. I thought I saw pleading in Sohrab's eyes.

"Tell me why," Assef said. He pinched Sohrab's earlobe between his teeth. Let go. Sweat beads rolled down his brow.

"That's my business."

"What do you want to do with him?" he said. Then a coy smile. "Or *to* him."

"That's disgusting," I said.

"How would you know? Have you tried it?" "I want to take him to a better place." "Tell me why."

"That's my business," I said. I didn't know what had emboldened me to be so curt, maybe the fact that I thought I was going to die anyway.

"I wonder," Assef said. "I wonder why you've come all this way, Amir, come all this way for a Hazara? Why are you here? Why are you *really* here?"

"I have my reasons," I said.

"Very well then," Assef said, sneering. He shoved Sohrab in the back, pushed him right into the table. Sohrab's hips struck the table, knocking it upside down and spilling the grapes. He fell on them, face first, and stained his shirt purple with grape juice. The table's legs, crossing through the ring of brass balls, were now pointing to the ceiling.

"Take him, then," Assef said. I helped Sohrab to his feet, swatted the bits of crushed grape that had stuck to his pants like barnacles to a pier.

"Go, take him," Assef said, pointing to the door.

I took Sohrab's hand. It was small, the skin dry and calloused. His fingers moved, laced themselves with mine. I saw Sohrab in that Polaroid again, the way his arm was wrapped around Hassan's leg, his head resting against his father's hip. They'd both been smiling. The bells jingled as we crossed the room.

We made it as far as the door.

"Of course," Assef said behind us, "I didn't say you could take him for free."

I turned. "What do you want?" "You have to earn him." "What do you want?"

"We have some unfinished business, you and I," Assef said. "You remember, don't you?"

He needn't have worried. I would never forget the day after Daoud Khan overthrew the king. My entire adult life, whenever I heard Daoud Khan's name, what I saw was Hassan with his slingshot pointed at Assef's face, Hassan saying that they'd have to start calling him One-Eyed Assef instead of Assef *Goshkhor*. I remember how envious I'd been of Hassan's bravery. Assef had backed down, promised that in the end he'd get us both. He'd kept that promise with Hassan. Now it was my turn.

"All right," I said, not knowing what else there was to say. I wasn't about to beg; that would have only sweetened the moment for him.

Assef called the guards backinto the room. "I want you to listen to me," he said to them. "In a moment, I'm going to close the door. Then he and I are going to finish an old bit of business. No matter what you hear, don't come in! Do you hear me? Don't come in!"

The guards nodded. Looked from Assef to me. "Yes, Agha sahib."

"When it's all done, only one of us will walk out of this room alive," Assef said. "If it's him, then he's earned his freedom and you let him pass, do you understand?"

The older guard shifted on his feet. "But Agha sahib—"

"If it's him, you let him pass!" Assef screamed. The two men flinched but nodded again. They turned to go. One of them reached for Sohrab.

"Let him stay," Assef said. He grinned. "Let him watch. Lessons are good things for boys."

The guards left. Assef put down his prayer beads. Reached in the breast pocket of his black vest. What he fished out of that pocket didn't surprise me one bit: stainless-steel brass knuckles.

HE HAS GEL IN HIS HAIR and a Clark Gable mustache above his thick lips. The gel has soaked through the green paper surgical cap, made a dark stain the shape of Africa. I remember that about him. That, and the gold Allah chain around his dark neck. He is peering down at me, speaking rapidly in a language I don't understand, Urdu, I think. My eyes keep going to his Adam's apple bobbing up and down, up and down, and I want to ask him how old he is anyway—he looks far too young, like an actor from some foreign soap opera—but all I can mutter is, I think I gave him a good fight. I think I gave him a good fight.

I DON'T KNOW if I gave Assef a good fight. I don't think I did. How could I have? That was the first time I'd fought any-one. I had never so much as thrown a punch in my entire life.

My memory of the fight with Assef is amazingly vivid in stretches: I remember Assef turning on the music before slipping on his brass knuckles. The prayer rug, the one with the oblong, woven Mecca, came loose from the wall at one point and landed on my head; the dust from it made me sneeze. I remember Assef shoving grapes in my face, his snarl all spit-shining teeth, his bloodshot eyes rolling. His turban fell at some point, let loose curls of shoulder-length blond hair.

And the end, of course. That, I still see with perfect clarity. I always will.

Mostly, I remember this: His brass knuckles flashing in the afternoon light; how cold they felt with the first few blows and how quickly they warmed with my blood. Getting thrown against the wall, a nail where a framed picture may have hung once jabbing at my back. Sohrab screaming. Tabla, harmonium, a *dil-roba*. Getting hurled against the wall. The knuckles shattering my jaw. Choking on my own teeth, swallowing them, thinking about all the countless hours I'd spent flossing and brushing. Getting hurled against the wall. Lying on the floor, blood from my split upper lip staining the mauve carpet, pain ripping through my belly, and wondering when I'd be able to breathe again. The sound of my ribs snapping like the tree branches Hassan and I used to break to swordfight like Sinbad in those old movies. Sohrab screaming. The side of my face slamming against the corner of the television stand. That snapping sound again, this time just under my left eye. Music. Sohrab screaming.

Fingers grasping my hair, pulling my head back, the twinkle of stainless steel. Here they come. That snapping sound yet again, now my nose. Biting down in pain, noticing how my teeth didn't align like they used to. Getting kicked. Sohrab screaming.

I don't know at what point I started laughing, but I did. It hurt to laugh, hurt my jaws, my ribs, my throat. But I was laughing and laughing. And the harder I laughed, the harder he kicked me, punched me, scratched me.

"WHAT'S SO FUNNY?" Assef kept roaring with each blow.

His spittle landed in my eye. Sohrab screamed.

"WHAT'S SO FUNNY?" Assef bellowed. Another rib snapped, this time left lower. What was so funny was that, for the first time since the winter of 1975, I felt at peace. I laughed because I saw that, in some hidden nook in a corner of my mind, I'd even been looking forward to this. I remembered the day on the hill I had pelted Hassan with pomegranates and tried to provoke him. He'd just stood there, doing nothing, red juice soaking through his shirt like blood. Then he'd taken the pomegranate from my hand, crushed it against his forehead. *Are you satisfied now?* he'd hissed. *Do you feel better?* I hadn't been happy and I hadn't felt better, not at all. But I did now. My body was broken—just how badly I wouldn't find out until later—but I felt *healed*. Healed at last. I laughed.

Then the end. That, I'll take to my grave:

I was on the ground laughing, Assef straddling my chest, his face a mask of lunacy, framed by snarls of his hair swaying inches from my face. His free hand was locked around my throat. The other, the one with the brass knuckles, cocked above his shoulder. He raised his fist higher, raised it for another blow.

Then: *"Bas."* A thin voice. We both looked.

"Please, no more."

I remembered something the orphanage director had said when he'd opened the door to me and Farid. What had been his name? Zaman? *He's inseparable from that thing,* he had said. *He tucks it in the waist of his pants everywhere he goes.*

"No more."

Twin trails of black mascara, mixed with tears, had rolled down his cheeks, smeared the rouge. His lower lip trembled. Mucus seeped from his nose. *"Bas,"* he croaked.

His hand was cocked above his shoulder, holding the cup of the slingshot at the end of the elastic band which was pulled all the way back. There was something in the cup, something shiny and yellow. I blinked the blood from my eyes and saw it was one of the brass balls from the ring in the table base. Sohrab had the slingshot pointed to Assef's face.

"No more, Agha. Please," he said, his voice husky and trembling. "Stop hurting him."

Assef's mouth moved wordlessly. He began to say something, stopped. "What do you think you're you doing?" he finally said.

"Please stop," Sohrab said, fresh tears pooling in his green eyes, mixing with mascara.

"Put it down, Hazara," Assef hissed. "Put it down or what I'm doing to him will be a gentle ear twisting compared to what I'll do to you."

The tears broke free. Sohrab shook his head. "Please, Agha," he said. "Stop."

"Put it down."

"Don't hurt him anymore."

"Put it down."

"Please."

"PUT IT DOWN!"

"Bas."

"PUT IT DOWN!" Assef let go of my throat. Lunged at Sohrab.

The slingshot made a *thwiiiiit* sound when Sohrab released the cup. Then Assef was screaming. He put his hand where his left eye had been just a moment ago. Blood oozed between his fingers. Blood and something else, something white and gel-like. *That's called vitreous fluid,* I thought with clarity. *I've read that somewhere. Vitreous fluid.*

Assef rolled on the carpet. Rolled side to side, shrieking, his hand still cupped over the bloody socket.

"Let's go!" Sohrab said. He took my hand. Helped me to my feet. Every inch of my battered body wailed with pain. Behind us, Assef kept shrieking.

"OUT! GET IT OUT!" he screamed.

Teetering, I opened the door. The guards' eyes widened when they saw me and I wondered what I looked like. My stomach hurt with each breath. One of the guards said something in Pashtu and then they blew past us, running into the room where Assef was still screaming. "OUT!"

"Bia," Sohrab said, pulling my hand. "Let's go!"

I stumbled down the hallway, Sohrab's little hand in mine. I took a final look over my shoulder. The guards were huddled over Assef, doing something to his face. Then I understood: The brass ball was still stuck in his empty eye socket.

The whole world rocking up and down, swooping side to side, I hobbled down the steps, leaning on Sohrab. From above, Assef's screams went on and on, the cries of a wounded animal. We made it outside, into daylight, my arm around Sohrab's shoulder, and I saw Farid running toward us.

"Bismillah! Bismillah!" he said, eyes bulging at the sight of me. He slung my arm around his shoulder and lifted me. Carried me to the truck, running. I think I screamed. I watched the way his sandals pounded the pavement, slapped his black, calloused heels. It hurt to breathe. Then I was looking up at the roof of the Land Cruiser, in the backseat, the upholstery beige and ripped, listening to the *ding-ding-ding* signaling an open door. Running footsteps around the truck. Farid and Sohrab exchanging quick words. The truck's doors slammed shut and the engine roared to life. The car jerked forward and I felt a tiny hand on my forehead. I heard voices on the street, some shouting, and saw trees blurring past in the window. Sohrab was sobbing. Farid was still repeating, *"Bismillah! Bismillah!"*

It was about then that I passed out.

TWENTYTHREE

Faces poke through the haze, linger, fade away. They peer down, ask me questions. They all ask questions. Do I know who I am? Do I hurt anywhere? I know who I am and I hurt everywhere. I want to tell them this but talking hurts. I know this because some time ago, maybe a year ago, maybe two, maybe ten, I tried to talk to a child with rouge on his cheeks and eyes smeared black. The child. Yes, I see him now. We are in a car of sorts, the child and I, and I don't think Soraya's driving because Soraya never drives this fast. I want to say something to this child—it seems very important that I do. But I don't remember what I want to say, or why it might have been important. Maybe I want to tell him to stop crying, that everything will be all right now. Maybe not. For some reason I can't think of, I want to thank the child.

Faces. They're all wearing green hats. They slip in and out of view. They talk rapidly, use words I don't understand. I hear other voices, other noises, beeps and alarms. And always more faces. Peering down. I don't remember any of them, except for the one with the gel in his hair and the Clark Gable mustache,

the one with the Africa stain on his cap. Mister Soap Opera Star.
That's funny. I want to laugh now. But laughing hurts too.

I fade out.

SHE SAYS HER NAME IS AISHA, "like the prophet's wife."
Her graying hair is parted in the middle and tied in a ponytail,
her nose pierced with a stud shaped like the sun. She wears
bifocals that make her eyes bug out. She wears green too and
her hands are soft. She sees me looking at her and smiles. Says
something in English. Something is jabbing at the side of my
chest.

I fade out.

A MAN IS STANDING at my bedside. I know him. He is dark
and lanky, has a long beard. He wears a hat—what are those hats
called? *Pakols?* Wears it tilted to one side like a famous person
whose name escapes me now. I know this man. He drove me
somewhere a few years ago. I know him. There is something
wrong with my mouth. I hear a bubbling sound.

I fade out.

MY RIGHT ARM BURNS. The woman with the bifocals and
sun-shaped stud is hunched over my arm, attaching a clear plastic tubing to it. She says it's "the Potassium." "It stings like a bee,
no?" she says. It does. What's her name? Something to do with a
prophet. I know her too from a few years ago. She used to wear
her hair in a ponytail. Now it's pulled back, tied in a bun. Soraya

wore her hair like that the first time we spoke. When was that? Last week?

Aisha! Yes.

There is something wrong with my mouth. And that thing jabbing at my chest.

I fade out.

WE ARE IN THE SULAIMAN MOUNTAINS OF Baluchistan and Baba is wrestling the black bear. He is the Baba of my childhood, *Toophan agha,* the towering specimen of Pashtun might, not the withered man under the blankets, the man with the sunken cheeks and hollow eyes. They roll over a patch of green grass, man and beast, Baba's curly brown hair flying. The bear roars, or maybe it's Baba. Spittle and blood fly; claw and hand swipe. They fall to the ground with a loud thud and Baba is sitting on the bear's chest, his fingers digging in its snout. He looks up at me and I see. He's me. I am wrestling the bear.

I wake up. The lanky, dark man is back at my bedside. His name is Farid, I remember now. And with him is the child from the car. His face reminds me of the sound of bells. I am thirsty.

I fade out.

I keep fading in and out.

THE NAME OF THE MAN with the Clark Gable mustache turned out to be Dr. Faruqi. He wasn't a soap opera star at all, but a head-and-neck surgeon, though I kept thinking of him as someone named Armand in some steamy soap set on a tropical island.

Where am I? I wanted to ask. But my mouth wouldn't open. I frowned. Grunted. Armand smiled; his teeth were blinding white. "Not yet, Amir," he said, "but soon. When the wires are out."

He spoke English with a thick, rolling Urdu accent.

Wires?

Armand crossed his arms; he had hairy forearms and wore a gold wedding band. "You must be wondering where you are, what happened to you. That's perfectly normal, the postsurgical state is always disorienting. So I'll tell you what I know."

I wanted to ask him about the wires. Postsurgical? Where was Aisha? I wanted her to smile at me, wanted her soft hands in mine. Armand frowned, cocked one eyebrow in a slightly selfimportant way. "You are in a hospital in Peshawar. You've been here two days. You have suffered some very significant injuries, Amir, I should tell you. I would say you're very lucky to be alive, my friend." He swayed his index finger back and forth like a pendulum when he said this. "Your spleen had ruptured, probably—and fortunately for you—a delayed rupture, because you had signs of early hemorrhage into your abdominal cavity. My colleagues from the general surgery unit had to perform an emergency splenectomy. If it had ruptured earlier, you would have bled to death." He patted me on the arm, the one with the IV, and smiled. "You also suffered seven broken ribs. One of them caused a pneumothorax."

I frowned. Tried to open my mouth. Remembered about the wires.

"That means a punctured lung," Armand explained. He tugged at a clear plastic tubing on my left side. I felt the jabbing again in my chest. "We sealed the leak with this chest tube." I followed the tube poking through bandages on my chest to a container half-filled with columns of water. The bubbling sound came from there. "You had also suffered various lacerations. That means 'cuts.' "

I wanted to tell him I knew what the word meant; I was a writer. I went to open my mouth. Forgot about the wires again.

"The worst laceration was on your upper lip," Armand said. "The impact had cut your upper lip in two, clean down the middle. But not to worry, the plastics guys sewed it back together and they think you will have an excellent result, though there will be a scar. That is unavoidable.

"There was also an orbital fracture on the left side; that's the eye socket bone, and we had to fix that too. The wires in your jaws will come out in about six weeks," Armand said. "Until then it's liquids and shakes. You will lose some weight and you will be talking like Al Pacino from the first *Godfather* movie for a little while." He laughed. "But you have a job to do today. Do you know what it is?"

I shook my head.

"Your job today is to pass gas. You do that and we can start feeding you liquids. No fart, no food." He laughed again.

Later, after Aisha changed the IV tubing and raised the head of the bed like I'd asked, I thought about what had happened to me. Ruptured spleen. Broken teeth. Punctured lung. Busted eye socket. But as I watched a pigeon peck at a bread crumb on the windowsill, I kept thinking of something else Armand/Dr. Faruqi had said: *The impact had cut your upper lip in two,* he had said, *clean down the middle.* Clean down the middle. Like a harelip.

FARID AND SOHRAB came to visit the next day. "Do you know who we are today? Do you remember?" Farid said, only halfjokingly. I nodded.

"*Al hamdullellah!*" he said, beaming. "No more talking nonsense."

"Thank you, Farid," I said through jaws wired shut. Armand was right—I did sound like Al Pacino from *The Godfather.* And my tongue surprised me every time it poked in one of the empty spaces left by the teeth I had swallowed. "I mean, thank you. For everything."

He waved a hand, blushed a little. "*Bas,* it's not worthy of thanks," he said. I turned to Sohrab. He was wearing a new outfit, light brown *pirhan-tumban* that looked a bit big for him, and a black skullcap. He was looking down at his feet, toying with the IV line coiled on the bed.

"We were never properly introduced," I said. I offered him my hand. "I am Amir."

He looked at my hand, then to me. "You are the Amir agha Father told me about?" he said.

"Yes." I remembered the words from Hassan's letter. *I have told much about you to Farzana jan and Sohrab, about us growing up together and playing games and running in the streets. They laugh at the stories of all the mischief you and I used to cause!* "I owe you thanks too, Sohrab jan," I said. "You saved my life."

He didn't say anything. I dropped my hand when he didn't take it. "I like your new clothes," I mumbled.

"They're my son's," Farid said. "He has outgrown them. They fit Sohrab pretty well, I would say." Sohrab could stay with him, he said, until we found a place for him. "We don't have a lot of room, but what can I do? I can't leave him to the streets. Besides, my children have taken a liking to him. *Ha,* Sohrab?" But the boy just kept looking down, twirling the line with his finger.

"I've been meaning to ask," Farid said, a little hesitantly. "What happened in that house? What happened between you and the Talib?"

"Let's just say we both got what we deserved," I said.

Farid nodded, didn't push it. It occurred to me that somewhere between the time we had left Peshawar for Afghanistan and now, we had become friends. "I've been meaning to ask something too."

"What?"

I didn't want to ask. I was afraid of the answer. "Rahim Khan," I said.

"He's gone."

My heart skipped. "Is he—"

"No, just ... gone." He handed me a folded piece of paper and a small key. "The landlord gave me this when I went looking for him. He said Rahim Khan left the day after we did."

"Where did he go?"

Farid shrugged. "The landlord didn't know. He said Rahim Khan left the letter and the key for you and took his leave." He checked his watch. "I'd better go. *Bia,* Sohrab."

"Could you leave him here for a while?" I said. "Pick him up later?" I turned to Sohrab. "Do you want to stay here with me for a little while?"

He shrugged and said nothing.

"Of course," Farid said. "I'll pick him up just before evening *namaz.*"

THERE WERE THREE OTHER PATIENTS in my room. Two older men, one with a cast on his leg, the other wheezing with asthma, and a young man of fifteen or sixteen who'd had appendix surgery. The old guy in the cast stared at us without blinking, his eyes switching from me to the Hazara boy sitting on a stool. My roommates' families—old women in bright *shalwar-kameez*es, children, men wearing skullcaps—shuffled noisily in and out of the room. They brought with them *pakoras, naan, samosas, biryani*. Sometimes people just wandered into the room, like the tall, bearded man who walked in just before Farid and Sohrab arrived. He wore a brown blanket wrapped around him. Aisha asked him something in Urdu. He paid her no attention and scanned the room with his eyes. I thought he looked at me a little longer than necessary. When the nurse spoke to him again, he just spun around and left.

"How are you?" I asked Sohrab. He shrugged, looked at his hands.

"Are you hungry? That lady there gave me a plate of *biryani*, but I can't eat it," I said. I didn't know what else to say to him. "You want it?"

He shook his head. "Do you want to talk?"

He shook his head again.

We sat there like that for a while, silent, me propped up in bed, two pillows behind my back, Sohrab on the three-legged stool next to the bed. I fell asleep at some point, and, when I woke up, daylight had dimmed a bit, the shadows had stretched, and Sohrab was still sitting next to me. He was still looking down at his hands.

THAT NIGHT, after Farid picked up Sohrab, I unfolded Rahim Khan's letter. I had delayed reading it as long as possible. It read:

Amir jan,
Inshallah, you have reached this letter safely. I pray that I have not put you in harm's way and that Afghanistan has not been too unkind to you. You have been in my prayers since the day you left.

You were right all those years to suspect that I knew. I did know. Hassan told me shortly after it happened. What you did was wrong, Amir jan, but do not forget that you were a boy when it happened. A troubled little boy. You were too hard on yourself then, and you still are—I saw it in your eyes in Peshawar. But I hope you will heed this: A man who has no conscience, no goodness, does not suffer. I hope your suffering comes to an end with this journey to Afghanistan.

Amir jan, I am ashamed for the lies we told you all those years. You were right to be angry in Peshawar. You had a right to know. So did Hassan. I know it doesn't absolve anyone of anything, but the Kabul we lived in in those days was a strange world, one in which some things mattered more than the truth.

Amir jan, I know how hard your father was on you when you were growing up. I saw how you suffered and yearned for his affections, and my heart bled for you. But your father was a man torn between two halves, Amir jan: you and Hassan. He loved you both, but he could not love Hassan the way he longed to, openly, and as a father. So he took it out on you instead—Amir, the socially legitimate half, the half that represented the riches he had inherited and the sin-with-impunity privileges that came with them. When he saw you, he saw himself. And his guilt. You are still angry and I realize it is far too early to expect you to accept this, but maybe someday you will see that when your father was hard on you, he was also being hard on himself. Your father, like you, was a tortured soul, Amir jan. I cannot describe to you the depth and blackness of the sorrow that came over me when I learned of his passing. I loved him because he was my friend, but also because he was a good man, maybe even a great man. And this is what I want you to understand, that good, *real* good, was born out of your father's remorse. Sometimes, I think everything he did, feeding the poor on the streets, building the orphanage, giving money to friends in need, it was all his way of redeeming himself. And that, I believe, is what true redemption is, Amir jan, when guilt leads to good.

I know that in the end, God will forgive. He will forgive your father, me, and you too. I hope you can do the same. Forgive your father if you can. Forgive me if you wish. But, most important, forgive yourself.

I have left you some money, most of what I have left, in fact. I think you may have some expenses when you return here, and the money should be enough to cover them. There is a bank in Peshawar; Farid knows the location. The money is in a safe-deposit box. I have given you the key.

As for me, it is time to go. I have little time left and I wish to spend it alone. Please do not look for me. That is my final request of you.

I leave you in the hands of God.

Your friend always,

Rahim

I dragged the hospital gown sleeve across my eyes. I folded the letter and put it under my mattress.

Amir, the socially legitimate half, the half that represented the riches he had inherited and the sin-with-impunity privileges that came with them. Maybe that was why Baba and I had been on such better terms in the U.S., I wondered. Selling junk for petty cash, our menial jobs, our grimy apartment—the American version of a hut; maybe in America, when Baba looked at me, he saw a little bit of Hassan.

Your father, like you, was a tortured soul, Rahim Khan had written. Maybe so. We had both sinned and betrayed. But Baba had found a way to create good out of his remorse. What had I done, other than take my guilt out on the very same people I had betrayed, and then try to forget it all? What had I done, other than become an insomniac?

What had I ever done to right things?

When the nurse—not Aisha but a red-haired woman whose name escapes me—walked in with a syringe in hand and asked me if I needed a morphine injection, I said yes.

THEY REMOVED THE CHEST TUBE early the next morning, and Armand gave the staff the go-ahead to let me sip apple juice. I asked Aisha for a mirror when she placed the cup of juice on the dresser next to my bed. She lifted her bifocals to her forehead as she pulled the curtain open and let the morning sun flood the room. "Remember, now," she said over her shoulder, "it will look better in a few days. My son-in-law was in a moped accident last year. His handsome face was dragged on the asphalt and became purple like an eggplant. Now he is beautiful again, like a Lollywood movie star."

Despite her reassurances, looking in the mirror and seeing the thing that insisted it was my face left me a little breathless. It looked like someone had stuck an air pump nozzle under my skin and had pumped away. My eyes were puffy and blue. The worst of it was my mouth, a grotesque blob of purple and red, all bruise and stitches. I tried to smile and a bolt of pain ripped through my lips. I wouldn't be doing that for a while. There were stitches across my left cheek, just under the chin, on the forehead just below the hairline.

The old guy with the leg cast said something in Urdu. I gave him a shrug and shook my head. He pointed to his face, patted it, and grinned a wide, toothless grin. "Very good," he said in English. *"Inshallah."*

"Thank you," I whispered.

Farid and Sohrab came in just as I put the mirror away. Sohrab took his seat on the stool, rested his head on the bed's side rail.

"You know, the sooner we get you out of here the better," Farid said.

"Dr. Faruqi says—"

"I don't mean the hospital. I mean Peshawar." "Why?"

"I don't think you'll be safe here for long," Farid said. He lowered his voice. "The Taliban have friends here. They will start looking for you."

"I think they already may have," I murmured. I thought suddenly of the bearded man who'd wandered into the room and just stood there staring at me.

Farid leaned in. "As soon as you can walk, I'll take you to Islamabad. Not entirely safe there either, no place in Pakistan is, but it's better than here. At least it will buy you some time."

"Farid jan, this can't be safe for you either. Maybe you shouldn't be seen with me. You have a family to take care of."

Farid made a waving gesture. "My boys are young, but they are very shrewd. They know how to take care of their mothers and sisters." He smiled. "Besides, I didn't say I'd do it for free."

"I wouldn't let you if you offered," I said. I forgot I couldn't smile and tried. A tiny streak of blood trickled down my chin. "Can I ask you for one more favor?"

"For you a thousand times over," Farid said.

And, just like that, I was crying. I hitched gusts of air, tears gushing down my cheeks, stinging the raw flesh of my lips.

"What's the matter?" Farid said, alarmed.

I buried my face in one hand and held up the other. I knew the whole room was watching me. After, I felt tired, hollow. "I'm sorry," I said. Sohrab was looking at me with a frown creasing his brow.

When I could talk again, I told Farid what I needed. "Rahim Khan said they live here in Peshawar."

"Maybe you should write down their names," Farid said, eyeing me cautiously, as if wondering what might set me off next. I scribbled their names on a scrap of paper towel. "John and Betty Caldwell."

Farid pocketed the folded piece of paper. "I will look for them as soon as I can," he said. He turned to Sohrab. "As for you, I'll pick you up this evening. Don't tire Amir agha too much."

But Sohrab had wandered to the window, where a half-dozen pigeons strutted back and forth on the sill, pecking at wood and scraps of old bread.

IN THE MIDDLE DRAWER of the dresser beside my bed, I had found an old *National Geographic* magazine, a chewed-up pencil, a comb with missing teeth, and what I was reaching for now, sweat pouring down my face from the effort: a deck of cards. I had counted them earlier and, surprisingly, found the deck complete. I asked Sohrab if he wanted to play. I didn't expect him to answer, let alone play. He'd been quiet since we had fled Kabul. But he turned from the window and said, "The only game I know is panjpar."

"I feel sorry for you already, because I am a grand master at panjpar. World renowned."

He took his seat on the stool next to me. I dealt him his five cards. "When your father and I were your age, we used to play this game. Especially in the winter, when it snowed and we couldn't go outside. We used to play until the sun went down."

He played me a card and picked one up from the pile. I stole looks at him as he pondered his cards. He was his father in so many ways: the way he fanned out his cards with both hands, the way he squinted while reading them, the way he rarely looked a person in the eye.

We played in silence. I won the first game, let him win the next one, and lost the next five fair and square. "You're as good as your father, maybe even better," I said, after my last loss. "I used to beat him sometimes, but I think he let me win." I paused before saying, "Your father and I were nursed by the same woman."

"I know."

"What ... what did he tell you about us?"

"That you were the best friend he ever had," he said.

I twirled the jack of diamonds in my fingers, flipped it back and forth. "I wasn't such a good friend, I'm afraid," I said. "But I'd like to be your friend. I think I could be a good friend to you. Would that be all right? Would you like that?" I put my hand on his arm, gingerly, but he flinched. He dropped his cards and pushed away on the stool. He walked back to the window. The sky was awash with streaks of red and purple as the sun set on Peshawar. From the street below came a succession of honks and the braying of a donkey, the whistle of a policeman. Sohrab stood in that crimson light, forehead pressed to the glass, fists buried in his armpits.

AISHA HAD A MALE ASSISTANT help me take my first steps that night. I only walked around the room once, one hand clutching the wheeled IV stand, the other clasping the assistant's forearm. It took me ten minutes to make it back to bed, and, by then, the incision on my stomach throbbed and I'd broken out in a drenching sweat. I lay in bed, gasping, my heart hammering in my ears, thinking how much I missed my wife.

Sohrab and I played panjpar most of the next day, again in silence. And the day after that. We hardly spoke, just played panjpar, me propped in bed, he on the three-legged stool, our routine broken only by my taking a walk around the room, or going to the bathroom down the hall. I had a dream later that night. I dreamed Assef was standing in the doorway of my hospital room, brass ball still in his eye socket. "We're the same, you and I," he was saying. "You nursed with him, but you're *my* twin."

I TOLD ARMAND early that next day that I was leaving.

"It's still early for discharge," Armand protested. He wasn't dressed in surgical scrubs that day, instead in a button-down navy blue suit and yellow tie. The gel was back in the hair. "You are still in intravenous antibiotics and—"

"I have to go," I said. "I appreciate everything you've done for me, all of you. Really. But I have to leave."

"Where will you go?" Armand said. "I'd rather not say."

"You can hardly walk."

"I can walk to the end of the hall and back," I said. "I'll be fine." The plan was this: Leave the hospital. Get the money from the safe-deposit box and pay my medical bills. Drive to the orphanage and drop Sohrab off with John and Betty Caldwell. Then get a ride to Islamabad and change travel plans. Give myself a few more days to get better. Fly home.

That was the plan, anyway. Until Farid and Sohrab arrived that morning. "Your friends, this John and Betty Caldwell, they aren't in Peshawar," Farid said.

It had taken me ten minutes just to slip into my *pirhantumban*. My chest, where they'd cut me to insert the chest tube, hurt when I raised my arm, and my stomach throbbed every time I leaned over. I was drawing ragged breaths just from the effort of packing a few of my belongings into a brown paper bag. But I'd managed to get ready and was sitting on the edge of the bed when Farid came in with the news. Sohrab sat on the bed next to me.

"Where did they go?" I asked.

Farid shook his head. "You don't understand—" "Because Rahim Khan said—"

"I went to the U.S. consulate," Farid said, picking up my bag. "There never was a John and Betty Caldwell in Peshawar. According to the people at the consulate, they never existed. Not here in Peshawar, anyhow."

Next to me, Sohrab was flipping through the pages of the old *National Geographic.*

WE GOT THE MONEY from the bank. The manager, a paunchy man with sweat patches under his arms, kept flashing smiles and telling me that no one in the bank had touched the money. "Absolutely nobody," he said gravely, swinging his index finger the same way Armand had.

Driving through Peshawar with so much money in a paper bag was a slightly frightening experience. Plus, I suspected every bearded man who stared at me to be a Talib killer, sent by Assef. Two things compounded my fears: There are a lot of bearded men in Peshawar, and everybody stares.

"What do we do with him?" Farid said, walking me slowly from the hospital accounting office back to the car. Sohrab was in the backseat of the Land Cruiser, looking at traffic through the rolled-down window, chin resting on his palms.

"He can't stay in Peshawar," I said, panting.

"Nay, Amir agha, he can't," Farid said. He'd read the question in my words. "I'm sorry. I wish I—"

"That's all right, Farid," I said. I managed a tired smile. "You have mouths to feed." A dog was standing next to the truck now, propped on its rear legs, paws on the truck's door, tail wagging. Sohrab was petting the dog. "I guess he goes to Islamabad for now," I said.

I SLEPT THROUGH almost the entire four-hour ride to Islamabad. I dreamed a lot, and most of it I only remember as a hodgepodge of images, snippets of visual memory flashing in my head like cards in a Rolodex: Baba marinating lamb for my thirteenth birthday party. Soraya and I making love for the first time, the sun rising in the east, our ears still ringing from the wedding music, her henna-painted hands laced in mine. The time Baba had taken Hassan and me to a strawberry field in Jalalabad— the owner had told us we could eat as much as we wanted to as long as we bought at least four kilos—and how we'd both ended up with bellyaches. How dark, almost black, Hassan's blood had looked on the snow, dropping from the seat of his pants. *Blood is a powerful thing, bachem.* Khala Jamila patting Soraya's knee and saying, *God knows best, maybe it wasn't meant to be.* Sleeping on the roof of my father's house. Baba saying that the only sin that mattered was theft. *When you tell a lie, you steal a man's right to the truth.* Rahim Khan on the phone, telling me there was a way to be good again. *A way to be good again ...*

TWENTY FOUR

If Peshawar was the city that reminded me of what Kabul used to be, then Islamabad was the city Kabul could have become someday. The streets were wider than Peshawar's, cleaner, and lined with rows of hibiscus and flame trees. The bazaars were more organized and not nearly as clogged with rickshaws and pedestrians. The architecture was more elegant too, more modern, and I saw parks where roses and jasmine bloomed in the shadows of trees.

Farid found a small hotel on a side street running along the foot of the Margalla Hills. We passed the famous Shah Faisal Mosque on the way there, reputedly the biggest mosque in the world, with its giant concrete girders and soaring minarets. Sohrab perked up at the sight of the mosque, leaned out of the window and looked at it until Farid turned a corner.

THE HOTEL ROOM was a vast improvement over the one in Kabul where Farid and I had stayed. The sheets were clean, the carpet vacuumed, and the bathroom spotless. There was shampoo, soap, razors for shaving, a bathtub, and towels that smelled like lemon. And no bloodstains on the walls. One other thing: a television set sat on the dresser across from the two single beds.

"Look!" I said to Sohrab. I turned it on manually—no remote—and turned the dial. I found a children's show with two fluffy sheep puppets singing in Urdu. Sohrab sat on one of the beds and drew his knees to his chest. Images from the TV reflected in his green eyes as he watched, stone-faced, rocking back and forth. I remembered the time I'd promised Hassan I'd buy his family a color TV when we both grew up.

"I'll get going, Amir agha," Farid said.

"Stay the night," I said. "It's a long drive. Leave tomorrow."

"*Tashakor*," he said. "But I want to get back tonight. I miss my children." On his way out of the room, he paused in the doorway. "Good-bye, Sohrab jan," he said. He waited for a reply, but Sohrab paid him no attention. Just rocked back and forth, his face lit by the silver glow of the images flickering across the screen.

Outside, I gave him an envelope. When he tore it, his mouth opened.

"I didn't know how to thank you," I said. "You've done so much for me."

"How much is in here?" Farid said, slightly dazed. "A little over two thousand dollars."

"Two thou—" he began. His lower lip was quivering a little. Later, when he pulled away from the curb, he honked twice and waved. I waved back. I never saw him again.

I returned to the hotel room and found Sohrab lying on the bed, curled up in a big *C*. His eyes were closed but I couldn't

tell if he was sleeping. He had shut off the television. I sat on my
bed and grimaced with pain, wiped the cool sweat off my brow.
I wondered how much longer it would hurt to get up, sit down,
roll over in bed. I wondered when I'd be able to eat solid food. I
wondered what I'd do with the wounded little boy lying on the
bed, though a part of me already knew.

There was a carafe of water on the dresser. I poured a glass
and took two of Armand's pain pills. The water was warm and
bitter. I pulled the curtains, eased myself back on the bed, and
lay down. I thought my chest would rip open. When the pain
dropped a notch and I could breathe again, I pulled the blanket
to my chest and waited for Armand's pills to work.

WHEN I WOKE UP, the room was darker. The slice of sky
peeking between the curtains was the purple of twilight turning
into night. The sheets were soaked and my head pounded. I'd
been dreaming again, but I couldn't remember what it had been
about. My heart gave a sick lurch when I looked to Sohrab's
bed and found it empty. I called his name. The sound of my
voice startled me. It was disorienting, sitting in a dark hotel
room, thousands of miles from home, my body broken, calling
the name of a boy I'd only met a few days ago. I called his name
again and heard nothing. I struggled out of bed, checked the
bathroom, looked in the narrow hallway outside the room. He
was gone.

I locked the door and hobbled to the manager's office in
the lobby, one hand clutching the rail along the walkway for
support. There was a fake, dusty palm tree in the corner of the
lobby and flying pink flamingos on the wallpaper. I found the

hotel manager reading a newspaper behind the Formica-topped check-in counter. I described Sohrab to him, asked if he'd seen him. He put down his paper and took off his reading glasses. He had greasy hair and a square-shaped little mustache speckled with gray. He smelled vaguely of some tropical fruit I couldn't quite recognize.

"Boys, they like to run around," he said, sighing. "I have three of them. All day they are running around, troubling their mother." He fanned his face with the newspaper, staring at my jaws.

"I don't think he's out running around," I said. "And we're not from here. I'm afraid he might get lost."

He bobbed his head from side to side. "Then you should have kept an eye on the boy, mister."

"I know," I said. "But I fell asleep and when I woke up, he was gone."

"Boys must be tended to, you know."

"Yes," I said, my pulse quickening. How could he be so oblivious to my apprehension? He shifted the newspaper to his other hand, resumed the fanning. "They want bicycles now."

"Who?"

"My boys," he said. "They're saying, 'Daddy, Daddy, please buy us bicycles and we'll not trouble you. Please, Daddy!'" He gave a short laugh through his nose. "Bicycles. Their mother will kill me, I swear to you."

I imagined Sohrab lying in a ditch. Or in the trunk of some car, bound and gagged. I didn't want his blood on my hands. Not his too. "Please ..." I said. I squinted. Read his name tag on the lapel of his short-sleeve blue cotton shirt. "Mr. Fayyaz, have you seen him?"

"The boy?"

I bit down. "Yes, the boy! The boy who came with me. Have
you seen him or not, for God's sake?"

The fanning stopped. His eyes narrowed. "No getting smart
with me, my friend. I am not the one who lost him."

That he had a point did not stop the blood from rushing to
my face. "You're right. I'm wrong. My fault. Now, have you seen
him?"

"Sorry," he said curtly. He put his glasses back on. Snapped his
newspaper open. "I have seen no such boy."

I stood at the counter for a minute, trying not to scream. As
I was exiting the lobby, he said, "Any idea where he might have
wandered to?"

"No," I said. I felt tired. Tired and scared.

"Does he have any interests?" he said. I saw he had folded the
paper. "My boys, for example, they will do anything for American action films, especially with that Arnold Whatsanegger—"

"The mosque!" I said. "The big mosque." I remembered the
way the mosque had jolted Sohrab from his stupor when we'd
driven by it, how he'd leaned out of the window looking at it.

"Shah Faisal?"

"Yes. Can you take me there?"

"Did you know it's the biggest mosque in the world?" he
asked. "No, but—"

"The courtyard alone can fit forty thousand people." "Can
you take me there?"

"It's only a kilometer from here," he said. But he was already
pushing away from the counter.

"I'll pay you for the ride," I said.

He sighed and shook his head. "Wait here." He disappeared
into the back room, returned wearing another pair of eyeglasses,

a set of keys in hand, and with a short, chubby woman in an orange sari trailing him. She took his seat behind the counter. "I don't take your money," he said, blowing by me. "I will drive you because I am a father like you."

I THOUGHT WE'D END UP DRIVING around the city until night fell. I saw myself calling the police, describing Sohrab to them under Fayyaz's reproachful glare. I heard the officer, his voice tired and uninterested, asking his obligatory questions. And beneath the official questions, an unofficial one: Who the hell cared about another dead Afghan kid?

But we found him about a hundred yards from the mosque, sitting in the half-full parking lot, on an island of grass. Fayyaz pulled up to the island and let me out. "I have to get back," he said. "That's fine. We'll walk back," I said. "Thank you, Mr. Fayyaz. Really."

He leaned across the front seat when I got out. "Can I say something to you?"

"Sure."

In the dark of twilight, his face was just a pair of eyeglasses reflecting the fading light. "The thing about you Afghanis is that ... well, you people are a little reckless."

I was tired and in pain. My jaws throbbed. And those damn wounds on my chest and stomach felt like barbed wire under my skin. But I started to laugh anyway.

"What ... what did I ..." Fayyaz was saying, but I was cackling by then, full-throated bursts of laughter spilling through my wired mouth.

"Crazy people," he said. His tires screeched when he peeled away, his taillights blinking red in the dimming light.

"YOU GAVE ME A GOOD SCARE," I said. I sat beside him, wincing with pain as I bent.

He was looking at the mosque. Shah Faisal Mosque was shaped like a giant tent. Cars came and went; worshipers dressed in white streamed in and out. We sat in silence, me leaning against the tree, Sohrab next to me, knees to his chest. We listened to the call to prayer, watched the building's hundreds of lights come on as daylight faded. The mosque sparkled like a diamond in the dark. It lit up the sky, Sohrab's face.

"Have you ever been to Mazar-i-Sharif?" Sohrab said, his chin resting on his kneecaps.

"A long time ago. I don't remember it much."

"Father took me there when I was little. Mother and Sasa came along too. Father bought me a monkey from the bazaar. Not a real one but the kind you have to blow up. It was brown and had a bow tie."

"I might have had one of those when I was a kid."

"Father took me to the Blue Mosque," Sohrab said. "I remember there were so many pigeons outside the *masjid,* and they weren't afraid of people. They came right up to us. Sasa gave me little pieces of *naan* and I fed the birds. Soon, there were pigeons cooing all around me. That was fun."

"You must miss your parents very much," I said. I wondered if he'd seen the Taliban drag his parents out into the street. I hoped he hadn't.

"Do you miss your parents?" he aked, resting his cheek on his knees, looking up at me.

"Do I miss my parents? Well, I never met my mother. My father died a few years ago, and, yes, I do miss him. Sometimes a lot."

"Do you remember what he looked like?"

I thought of Baba's thick neck, his black eyes, his unruly brown hair. Sitting on his lap had been like sitting on a pair of tree trunks. "I remember what he looked like," I said. "What he smelled like too."

"I'm starting to forget their faces," Sohrab said. "Is that bad?"

"No," I said. "Time does that." I thought of something. I looked in the front pocket of my coat. Found the Polaroid snapshot of Hassan and Sohrab. "Here," I said.

He brought the photo to within an inch of his face, turned it so the light from the mosque fell on it. He looked at it for a long time. I thought he might cry, but he didn't. He just held it in both hands, traced his thumb over its surface. I thought of a line I'd read somewhere, or maybe I'd heard someone say it: There are a lot of children in Afghanistan, but little childhood. He stretched his hand to give it back to me.

"Keep it," I said. "It's yours."

"Thank you." He looked at the photo again and stowed it in the pocket of his vest. A horse-drawn cart *clip-clopped* by in the parking lot. Little bells dangled from the horse's neck and jingled with each step.

"I've been thinking a lot about mosques lately," Sohrab said.

"You have? What about them?"

He shrugged. "Just thinking about them." He lifted his face, looked straight at me. Now he was crying, softly, silently. "Can I ask you something, Amir agha?"

"Of course."

"Will God ..." he began, and choked a little. "Will God put me in hell for what I did to that man?"

I reached for him and he flinched. I pulled back. "Nay. Of course not," I said. I wanted to pull him close, hold him, tell him the world had been unkind to *him,* not the other way around.

His face twisted and strained to stay composed. "Father used to say it's wrong to hurt even bad people. Because they don't know any better, and because bad people sometimes become good."

"Not always, Sohrab."

He looked at me questioningly.

"The man who hurt you, I knew him from many years ago," I said. "I guess you figured that out that from the conversation he and I had. He ... he tried to hurt me once when I was your age, but your father saved me. Your father was very brave and he was always rescuing me from trouble, standing up for me. So one day the bad man hurt your father instead. He hurt him in a very bad way, and I ... I couldn't save your father the way he had saved me." "Why did people want to hurt my father?" Sohrab said in a wheezy little voice. "He was never mean to anyone."

"You're right. Your father was a good man. But that's what I'm trying to tell you, Sohrab jan. That there are bad people in this world, and sometimes bad people stay bad. Sometimes you have to stand up to them. What you did to that man is what I should have done to him all those years ago. You gave him what he deserved, and he deserved even more."

"Do you think Father is disappointed in me?"

"I know he's not," I said. "You saved my life in Kabul. I know he is very proud of you for that."

He wiped his face with the sleeve of his shirt. It burst a bubble of spittle that had formed on his lips. He buried his face in his hands and wept a long time before he spoke again. "I miss Father, and Mother too," he croaked. "And I miss Sasa and Rahim Khan sahib. But sometimes I'm glad they're not ... they're not here anymore."

"Why?" I touched his arm. He drew back.

"Because—" he said, gasping and hitching between sobs, "because I don't want them to see me ... I'm so dirty." He sucked in his breath and let it out in a long, wheezy cry. "I'm so dirty and full of sin."

"You're not dirty, Sohrab," I said. "Those men—"

"You're not dirty at all."

"—they did things ... the bad man and the other two ... they did things ... did things to me."

"You're not dirty, and you're not full of sin." I touched his arm again and he drew away. I reached again, gently, and pulled him to me. "I won't hurt you," I whispered. "I promise." He resisted a little. Slackened. He let me draw him to me and rested his head on my chest. His little body convulsed in my arms with each sob.

A kinship exists between people who've fed from the same breast. Now, as the boy's pain soaked through my shirt, I saw that a kinship had taken root between us too. What had happened in that room with Assef had irrevocably bound us.

I'd been looking for the right time, the right moment, to ask the question that had been buzzing around in my head and keeping me up at night. I decided the moment was now, right here, right now, with the bright lights of the house of God shining on us. "Would you like to come live in America with me and my wife?"

He didn't answer. He sobbed into my shirt and I let him.

FOR A WEEK, neither one of us mentioned what I had asked him, as if the question hadn't been posed at all. Then one day, Sohrab and I took a taxicab to the Daman-e-Koh Viewpoint— or "the hem of the mountain." Perched midway up the Margalla Hills, it gives a panoramic view of Islamabad, its rows of clean, tree-lined avenues and white houses. The driver told us we could see the presidential palace from up there. "If it has rained and the air is clear, you can even see past Rawalpindi," he said. I saw his eyes in his rearview mirror, skipping from Sohrab to me, back and forth, back and forth. I saw my own face too. It wasn't as swollen as before, but it had taken on a yellow tint from my assortment of fading bruises.

We sat on a bench in one of the picnic areas, in the shade of a gum tree. It was a warm day, the sun perched high in a topaz blue sky. On benches nearby, families snacked on *samosa*s and *pakora*s. Somewhere, a radio played a Hindi song I thought I remembered from an old movie, maybe *Pakeeza*. Kids, many of them Sohrab's age, chased soccer balls, giggling, yelling. I thought about the orphanage in Karteh-Seh, thought about the rat that had scurried between my feet in Zaman's office. My chest tightened with a surge of unexpected anger at the way my countrymen were destroying their own land.

"What?" Sohrab asked. I forced a smile and told him it wasn't important.

We unrolled one of the hotel's bathroom towels on the picnic table and played panjpar on it. It felt good being there, with my half brother's son, playing cards, the warmth of the sun patting the back of my neck. The song ended and another one started, one I didn't recognize.

"Look," Sohrab said. He was pointing to the sky with his cards. I looked up, saw a hawk circling in the broad seamless sky. "Didn't know there were hawks in Islamabad," I said.

"Me neither," he said, his eyes tracing the bird's circular flight. "Do they have them where you live?"

"San Francisco? I guess so. I can't say I've seen too many, though."

"Oh," he said. I was hoping he'd ask more, but he dealt another hand and asked if we could eat. I opened the paper bag and gave him his meatball sandwich. My lunch consisted of yet another cup of blended bananas and oranges—I'd rented Mrs. Fayyaz's blender for the week. I sucked through the straw and my mouth filled with the sweet, blended fruit. Some of it dripped from the corner of my lips. Sohrab handed me a napkin and watched me dab at my lips. I smiled and he smiled back.

"Your father and I were brothers," I said. It just came out. I had wanted to tell him the night we had sat by the mosque, but I hadn't. But he had a right to know; I didn't want to hide anything anymore. "Half brothers, really. We had the same father."

Sohrab stopped chewing. Put the sandwich down. "Father never said he had a brother."

"That's because he didn't know." "Why didn't he know?"

"No one told him," I said. "No one told me either. I just found out recently."

Sohrab blinked. Like he was looking at me, *really* looking at me, for the very first time. "But why did people hide it from Father and you?"

"You know, I asked myself that same question the other day. And there's an answer, but not a good one. Let's just say they didn't tell us because your father and I … we weren't supposed to be brothers."

"Because he was a Hazara?"

I willed my eyes to stay on him. "Yes."

"Did your father," he began, eyeing his food, "did your father love you and my father equally?"

I thought of a long ago day at Ghargha Lake, when Baba had allowed himself to pat Hassan on the back when Hassan's stone had outskipped mine. I pictured Baba in the hospital room, beaming as they removed the bandages from Hassan's lips. "I think he loved us equally but differently."

"Was he ashamed of my father?"

"No," I said. "I think he was ashamed of himself." He picked up his sandwich and nibbled at it silently.

WE LEFT LATE THAT AFTERNOON, tired from the heat, but tired in a pleasant way. All the way back, I felt Sohrab watching me. I had the driver pull over at a store that sold calling cards. I gave him the money and a tip for running in and buying me one.

That night, we were lying on our beds, watching a talk show on TV. Two clerics with pepper gray long beards and white turbans were taking calls from the faithful all over the world. One caller from Finland, a guy named Ayub, asked if his teenaged son could go to hell for wearing his baggy pants so low the seam of his underwear showed.

"I saw a picture of San Francisco once," Sohrab said. "Really?"

"There was a red bridge and a building with a pointy top."
"You should see the streets," I said.

"What about them?" He was looking at me now. On the TV screen, the two mullahs were consulting each other.

"They're so steep, when you drive up all you see is the hood of your car and the sky," I said.

"It sounds scary," he said. He rolled to his side, facing me, his back to the TV.

"It is the first few times," I said. "But you get used to it." "Does it snow there?"

"No, but we get a lot of fog. You know that red bridge you saw?" "Yes."

"Sometimes the fog is so thick in the morning, all you see is the tip of the two towers poking through."

There was wonder in his smile. "Oh."

"Sohrab?"

"Yes."

"Have you given any thought to what I asked you before?"

His smiled faded. He rolled to his back. Laced his hands under his head. The mullahs decided that Ayub's son would go to hell after all for wearing his pants the way he did. They claimed it was in the *Haddith*. "I've thought about it," Sohrab said.

"And?"

"It scares me."

"I know it's a little scary," I said, grabbing onto that loose thread of hope. "But you'll learn English so fast and you'll get used to—"

"That's not what I mean. That scares me too, but..." "But what?"

He rolled toward me again. Drew his knees up. "What if you

get tired of me? What if your wife doesn't like me?"

I struggled out of bed and crossed the space between us. I sat beside him. "I won't ever get tired of you, Sohrab," I said. "Not ever. That's a promise. You're my nephew, remember? And Soraya jan, she's a very kind woman. Trust me, she's going to love you. I promise that too." I chanced something. Reached down and took his hand. He tightened up a little but let me hold it.

"I don't want to go to another orphanage," he said.

"I won't ever let that happen. I promise you that." I cupped his hand in both of mine. "Come home with me."

His tears were soaking the pillow. He didn't say anything for a long time. Then his hand squeezed mine back. And he nodded. He nodded.

THE CONNECTION WENT THROUGH on the fourth try. The phone rang three times before she picked it up. "Hello?" It was 7:30 in the evening in Islamabad, roughly about the same time in the morning in California. That meant Soraya had been up for an hour, getting ready for school.

"It's me," I said. I was sitting on my bed, watching Sohrab sleep.

"Amir!" she almost screamed. "Are you okay? Where are you?" "I'm in Pakistan."

"Why didn't you call earlier? I've been sick with *tashweesh!* My mother's praying and doing *nazr* every day."

"I'm sorry I didn't call. I'm fine now." I had told her I'd be away a week, two at the most. I'd been gone for nearly a month. I smiled. "And tell Khala Jamila to stop killing sheep."

"What do you mean 'fine now'? And what's wrong with your

voice?"

"Don't worry about that for now. I'm fine. Really. Soraya, I have a story to tell you, a story I should have told you a long time ago, but first I need to tell you one thing."

"What is it?" she said, her voice lower now, more cautious. "I'm not coming home alone. I'm bringing a little boy with me." I paused. "I want us to adopt him."

"What?"

I checked my watch. "I have fifty-seven minutes left on this stupid calling card and I have so much to tell you. Sit somewhere." I heard the legs of a chair dragged hurriedly across the wooden floor.

"Go ahead," she said.

Then I did what I hadn't done in fifteen years of marriage: I told my wife everything. Everything. I had pictured this moment so many times, dreaded it, but, as I spoke, I felt something lifting off my chest. I imagined Soraya had experienced something very similar the night of our *khastegari,* when she'd told me about her past.

By the time I was done with my story, she was weeping. "What do you think?" I said.

"I don't know what to think, Amir. You've told me so much all at once."

"I realize that."

I heard her blowing her nose. "But I know this much: You have to bring him home. I want you to."

"Are you sure?" I said, closing my eyes and smiling.

"Am I sure?" she said. "Amir, he's your *qaom,* your family, so he's my *qaom* too. Of course I'm sure. You can't leave him to the streets." There was a short pause. "What's he like?"

I looked over at Sohrab sleeping on the bed. "He's sweet, in a solemn kind of way."

"Who can blame him?" she said. "I want to see him, Amir. I really do."

"Soraya?"

"Yeah."

"Dostet darum." I love you.

"I love you back," she said. I could hear the smile in her words. "And be careful."

"I will. And one more thing. Don't tell your parents who he is.

If they need to know, it should come from me." "Okay."

We hung up.

THE LAWN OUTSIDE the American embassy in Islamabad was neatly mowed, dotted with circular clusters of flowers, bordered by razor-straight hedges. The building itself was like a lot of buildings in Islamabad: flat and white. We passed through several roadblocks to get there and three different security officials conducted a body search on me after the wires in my jaws set off the metal detectors. When we finally stepped in from the heat, the airconditioning hit my face like a splash of ice water. The secretary in the lobby, a fifty-something, lean-faced blond woman, smiled when I gave her my name. She wore a beige blouse and black slacks—the first woman I'd seen in weeks dressed in something other than a *burqa* or a *shalwar-kameez*. She looked me up on the appointment list, tapping the eraser end of her pencil on the desk. She found my name and asked me to take a seat.

"Would you like some lemonade?" she asked. "None for me, thanks," I said.

"How about your son?" "Excuse me?"

"The handsome young gentleman," she said, smiling at Sohrab.

"Oh. That'd be nice, thank you."

Sohrab and I sat on the black leather sofa across the reception desk, next to a tall American flag. Sohrab picked up a magazine from the glass-top coffee table. He flipped the pages, not really looking at the pictures.

"What?" Sohrab said. "Sorry?"

"You're smiling."

"I was thinking about you," I said.

He gave a nervous smile. Picked up another magazine and flipped through it in under thirty seconds.

"Don't be afraid," I said, touching his arm. "These people are friendly. Relax." I could have used my own advice. I kept shifting in my seat, untying and retying my shoelaces. The secretary placed a tall glass of lemonade with ice on the coffee table. "There you go."

Sohrab smiled shyly. "Thank you very much," he said in English. It came out as "Tank you wery match." It was the only English he knew, he'd told me, that and "Have a nice day."

She laughed. "You're most welcome." She walked back to her desk, high heels clicking on the floor.

"Have a nice day," Sohrab said.

RAYMOND ANDREWS was a short fellow with small hands, nails perfectly trimmed, wedding band on the ring finger. He gave me a curt little shake; it felt like squeezing a sparrow. *Those are the hands that hold our fates,* I thought as Sohrab and I seated ourselves across from his desk. A *Les Misérables* poster was nailed to the wall behind Andrews next to a topographical map of the U.S. A pot of tomato plants basked in the sun on the windowsill.

"Smoke?" he asked, his voice a deep baritone that was at odds with his slight stature.

"No thanks," I said, not caring at all for the way Andrews's eyes barely gave Sohrab a glance, or the way he didn't look at me when he spoke. He pulled open a desk drawer and lit a cigarette from a half-empty pack. He also produced a bottle of lotion from the same drawer. He looked at his tomato plants as he rubbed lotion into his hands, cigarette dangling from the corner of his mouth. Then he closed the drawer, put his elbows on the desktop, and exhaled. "So," he said, crinkling his gray eyes against the smoke, "tell me your story."

I felt like Jean Valjean sitting across from Javert. I reminded myself that I was on American soil now, that this guy was on my side, that he got paid for helping people like me. "I want to adopt this boy, take him back to the States with me," I said.

"Tell me your story," he repeated, crushing a flake of ash on the neatly arranged desk with his index finger, flicking it into the trash can.

I gave him the version I had worked out in my head since I'd hung up with Soraya. I had gone into Afghanistan to bring back my half brother's son. I had found the boy in squalid conditions, wasting away in an orphanage. I had paid the orphanage director a sum of money and withdrawn the boy. Then I had brought him to Pakistan.

"You are the boy's half uncle?" "Yes."

He checked his watch. Leaned and turned the tomato plants on the sill. "Know anyone who can attest to that?"

"Yes, but I don't know where he is now."

He turned to me and nodded. I tried to read his face and couldn't. I wondered if he'd ever tried those little hands of his at poker.

"I assume getting your jaws wired isn't the latest fashion statement," he said. We were in trouble, Sohrab and I, and I knew it then. I told him I'd gotten mugged in Peshawar.

"Of course," he said. Cleared his throat. "Are you Muslim?"

"Yes."

"Practicing?"

"Yes." In truth, I didn't remember the last time I had laid my forehead to the ground in prayer. Then I did remember: the day Dr. Amani gave Baba his prognosis. I had kneeled on the prayer rug, remembering only fragments of verses I had learned in school. "Helps your case some, but not much," he said, scratching a spot on the flawless part in his sandy hair.

"What do you mean?" I asked. I reached for Sohrab's hand, intertwined my fingers with his. Sohrab looked uncertainly from me to Andrews.

"There's a long answer and I'm sure I'll end up giving it to you.

You want the short one first?" "I guess," I said.

Andrews crushed his cigarette, his lips pursed. "Give it up." "I'm sorry?"

"Your petition to adopt this young fellow. Give it up. That's my advice to you."

"Duly noted," I said. "Now, perhaps you'll tell me why."

"That means you want the long answer," he said, his voice

impassive, not reacting at all to my curt tone. He pressed his hands palm to palm, as if he were kneeling before the Virgin Mary. "Let's assume the story you gave me is true, though I'd bet my pension a good deal of it is either fabricated or omitted. Not that I care, mind you. You're here, he's here, that's all that matters. Even so, your petition faces significant obstacles, not the least of which is that this child is not an orphan."

"Of course he is." "Not legally he isn't."

"His parents were executed in the street. The neighbors saw it," I said, glad we were speaking in English.

"You have death certificates?"

"*Death certificates?* This is Afghanistan we're talking about.

Most people there don't have *birth* certificates."

His glassy eyes didn't so much as blink. "I don't make the laws, sir. Your outrage notwithstanding, you still need to prove the parents are deceased. The boy has to be declared a legal orphan."

"But—"

"You wanted the long answer and I'm giving it to you. Your next problem is that you need the cooperation of the child's country of origin. Now, that's difficult under the best of circumstances, and, to quote you, this *is* Afghanistan we're talking about. We don't have an American embassy in Kabul. That makes things extremely complicated. Just about impossible."

"What are you saying, that I should throw him back on the streets?" I said.

"I didn't say that."

"He was sexually abused," I said, thinking of the bells around Sohrab's ankles, the mascara on his eyes.

"I'm sorry to hear that," Andrews's mouth said. The way he was looking at me, though, we might as well have been talking about the weather. "But that is not going to make the INS issue this young fellow a visa."

"What are you saying?"

"I'm saying that if you want to help, send money to a reputable relief organization. Volunteer at a refugee camp. But at this point in time, we strongly discourage U.S. citizens from attempting to adopt Afghan children."

I got up. "Come on, Sohrab," I said in Farsi. Sohrab slid next to me, rested his head on my hip. I remembered the Polaroid of him and Hassan standing that same way. "Can I ask you something, Mr. Andrews?"

"Yes."

"Do you have children?"

For the first time, he blinked.

"Well, do you? It's a simple question." He was silent.

"I thought so," I said, taking Sohrab's hand. "They ought to put someone in your chair who knows what it's like to want a child." I turned to go, Sohrab trailing me.

"Can I ask *you* a question?" Andrews called. "Go ahead."

"Have you promised this child you'll take him with you?"

"What if I have?"

He shook his head. "It's a dangerous business, making promises to kids." He sighed and opened his desk drawer again. "You mean to pursue this?" he said, rummaging through papers.

"I mean to pursue this."

He produced a business card. "Then I advise you to get a good immigration lawyer. Omar Faisal works here in Islamabad. You can tell him I sent you."

I took the card from him. "Thanks," I muttered.

"Good luck," he said. As we exited the room, I glanced over

my shoulder. Andrews was standing in a rectangle of sunlight, absently staring out the window, his hands turning the potted tomato plants toward the sun, petting them lovingly.

"TAKE CARE," the secretary said as we passed her desk.

"Your boss could use some manners," I said. I expected her to roll her eyes, maybe nod in that "I know, everybody says that," kind of way. Instead, she lowered her voice. "Poor Ray. He hasn't been the same since his daughter died."

I raised an eyebrow.

"Suicide," she whispered.

ON THE TAXI RIDE back to the hotel, Sohrab rested his head on the window, kept staring at the passing buildings, the rows of gum trees. His breath fogged the glass, cleared, fogged it again. I waited for him to ask me about the meeting but he didn't.

ON THE OTHER SIDE of the closed bathroom door the water was running. Since the day we'd checked into the hotel, Sohrab took a long bath every night before bed. In Kabul, hot running water had been like fathers, a rare commodity. Now Sohrab spent almost an hour a night in the bath, soaking in the soapy water, scrubbing. Sitting on the edge of the bed, I called Soraya. I glanced at the thin line of light under the bathroom door. *Do you feel clean yet, Sohrab?*

I passed on to Soraya what Raymond Andrews had told me. "So what do you think?" I said.

"We have to think he's wrong." She told me she had called a few adoption agencies that arranged international adoptions. She hadn't yet found one that would consider doing an Afghan adoption, but she was still looking.

"How are your parents taking the news?"

"Madar is happy for us. You know how she feels about you, Amir, you can do no wrong in her eyes. Padar ... well, as always, he's a little harder to read. He's not saying much."

"And you? Are you happy?"

I heard her shifting the receiver to her other hand. "I think we'll be good for your nephew, but maybe that little boy will be good for us too."

"I was thinking the same thing."

"I know it sounds crazy, but I find myself wondering what his favorite *qurma* will be, or his favorite subject in school. I picture myself helping him with homework ..." She laughed. In the bathroom, the water had stopped running. I could hear Sohrab in there, shifting in the tub, spilling water over the sides.

"You're going to be great," I said.

"Oh, I almost forgot! I called Kaka Sharif."

I remembered him reciting a poem at our *nika* from a scrap of hotel stationery paper. His son had held the Koran over our heads as Soraya and I had walked toward the stage, smiling at the flashing cameras. "What did he say?"

"Well, he's going to stir the pot for us. He'll call some of his INS buddies," she said.

"That's really great news," I said. "I can't wait for you to see Sohrab."

"I can't wait to see you," she said. I hung up smiling.

Sohrab emerged from the bathroom a few minutes later. He

had barely said a dozen words since the meeting with Raymond Andrews and my attempts at conversation had only met with a nod or a monosyllabic reply. He climbed into bed, pulled the blanket to his chin. Within minutes, he was snoring.

I wiped a circle on the fogged-up mirror and shaved with one of the hotel's old-fashioned razors, the type that opened and you slid the blade in. Then I took my own bath, lay there until the steaming hot water turned cold and my skin shriveled up. I lay there drifting, wondering, imagining …

OMAR FAISAL WAS CHUBBY, dark, had dimpled cheeks, black button eyes, and an affable, gap-toothed smile. His thinning gray hair was tied back in a ponytail. He wore a brown corduroy suit with leather elbow patches and carried a worn, overstuffed briefcase. The handle was missing, so he clutched the briefcase to his chest. He was the sort of fellow who started a lot of sentences with a laugh and an unnecessary apology, like *I'm sorry, I'll be there at five.* Laugh. When I had called him, he had insisted on coming out to meet us. "I'm sorry, the cabbies in this town are sharks," he said in perfect English, without a trace of an accent. "They smell a foreigner, they triple their fares."

He pushed through the door, all smiles and apologies, wheezing a little and sweating. He wiped his brow with a handkerchief and opened his briefcase, rummaged in it for a notepad and apologized for the sheets of paper that spilled on the bed. Sitting crosslegged on his bed, Sohrab kept one eye on the muted television, the other on the harried lawyer. I had told him in the morning that Faisal would be coming and he had nodded, almost asked something, and had just gone on watching a show with talking animals. "Here we are," Faisal said, flipping open a yellow legal notepad. "I hope my children take after their mother when it comes to organization. I'm sorry, probably not the sort of thing you want to hear from your prospective lawyer, heh?" He laughed. "Well, Raymond Andrews thinks highly of you."

"Mr. Andrews. Yes, yes. Decent fellow. Actually, he rang me and told me about you."

"He did?"

"Oh yes."

"So you're familiar with my situation."

Faisal dabbed at the sweat beads above his lips. "I'm familiar with the version of the situation you gave Mr. Andrews," he said. His cheeks dimpled with a coy smile. He turned to Sohrab. "This must be the young man who's causing all the trouble," he said in Farsi.

"This is Sohrab," I said. "Sohrab, this is Mr. Faisal, the lawyer I told you about."

Sohrab slid down the side of his bed and shook hands with Omar Faisal. *"Salaam alaykum,"* he said in a low voice.

"Alaykum salaam, Sohrab," Faisal said. "Did you know you are named after a great warrior?"

Sohrab nodded. Climbed back onto his bed and lay on his side to watch TV.

"I didn't know you spoke Farsi so well," I said in English. "Did you grow up in Kabul?"

"No, I was born in Karachi. But I did live in Kabul for a number of years. Shar-e-Nau, near the Haji Yaghoub Mosque," Faisal said. "I grew up in Berkeley, actually. My father opened a music store there in the late sixties. Free love, headbands, tie-dyed shirts, you name it." He leaned forward. "I was at Woodstock."

"Groovy," I said, and Faisal laughed so hard he started sweating all over again. "Anyway," I continued, "what I told Mr. Andrews was pretty much it, save for a thing or two. Or maybe three. I'll give you the uncensored version."

He licked a finger and flipped to a blank page, uncapped his pen. "I'd appreciate that, Amir. And why don't we just keep it in English from here on out?"

"Fine."

I told him everything that had happened. Told him about my meeting with Rahim Khan, the trek to Kabul, the orphanage, the stoning at Ghazi Stadium.

"God," he whispered. "I'm sorry, I have such fond memories of Kabul. Hard to believe it's the same place you're telling me about."

"Have you been there lately?" "God no."

"It's not Berkeley, I'll tell you that," I said. "Go on."

I told him the rest, the meeting with Assef, the fight, Sohrab and his slingshot, our escape back to Pakistan. When I was done, he scribbled a few notes, breathed in deeply, and gave me a sober look. "Well, Amir, you've got a tough battle ahead of you."

"One I can win?"

He capped his pen. "At the risk of sounding like Raymond Andrews, it's not likely. Not impossible, but hardly likely." Gone was the affable smile, the playful look in his eyes.

"But it's kids like Sohrab who need a home the most," I said. "These rules and regulations don't make any sense to me."

"You're preaching to the choir, Amir," he said. "But the fact is, take current immigration laws, adoption agency policies, and the political situation in Afghanistan, and the deck is stacked against you."

"I don't get it," I said. I wanted to hit something. "I mean, I get it but I don't get it."

Omar nodded, his brow furrowed. "Well, it's like this. In the aftermath of a disaster, whether it be natural or man-made—and the Taliban are a disaster, Amir, believe me—it's always difficult to ascertain that a child is an orphan. Kids get displaced in refugee camps, or parents just abandon them because they can't take care of them. Happens all the time. So the INS won't grant a visa unless it's clear the child meets the definition of an eligible orphan. I'm sorry, I know it sounds ridiculous, but you need death certificates." "You've been to Afghanistan," I said. "You know how improbable that is."

"I know," he said. "But let's suppose it's clear that the child has no surviving parent. Even then, the INS thinks it's good adoption practice to place the child with someone in his own country so his heritage can be preserved."

"What heritage?" I said. "The Taliban have destroyed what heritage Afghans had. You saw what they did to the giant Buddhas in Bamiyan."

"I'm sorry, I'm telling you how the INS works, Amir," Omar said, touching my arm. He glanced at Sohrab and smiled. Turned back to me. "Now, a child has to be legally adopted according to the laws and regulations of his own country. But when you have a country in turmoil, say a country like Afghanistan, government offices are busy with emergencies, and processing adoptions won't be a top priority."

I sighed and rubbed my eyes. A pounding headache was settling in just behind them.

"But let's suppose that somehow Afghanistan gets its act

together," Omar said, crossing his arms on his protruding belly. "It still may not permit this adoption. In fact, even the more moderate Muslim nations are hesitant with adoptions because in many of those countries, Islamic law, *Shari'a,* doesn't recognize adoption."

"You're telling me to give it up?" I asked, pressing my palm to my forehead.

"I grew up in the U.S., Amir. If America taught me anything, it's that quitting is right up there with pissing in the Girl Scouts' lemonade jar. But, as your lawyer, I have to give you the facts," he said. "Finally, adoption agencies routinely send staff members to evaluate the child's milieu, and no reasonable agency is going to send an agent to Afghanistan."

I looked at Sohrab sitting on the bed, watching TV, watching us. He was sitting the way his father used to, chin resting on one knee.

"I'm his half uncle, does that count for anything?"

"It does if you can prove it. I'm sorry, do you have any papers or anyone who can support you?"

"No papers," I said, in a tired voice. "No one knew about it. Sohrab didn't know until I told him, and I myself didn't find out until recently. The only other person who knows is gone, maybe dead."

"Hmm."

"What are my options, Omar?"

"I'll be frank. You don't have a lot of them." "Well, Jesus, what can I do?"

Omar breathed in, tapped his chin with the pen, let his breath out. "You could still file an orphan petition, hope for the best. You could do an independent adoption. That means you'd have to live with Sohrab here in Pakistan, day in and day out, for the next two years. You could seek asylum on his behalf. That's a lengthy process and you'd have to prove political persecution. You could request a humanitarian visa. That's at the discretion of the attorney general and it's not easily given." He paused. "There is another option, probably your best shot."

"What?" I said, leaning forward.

"You could relinquish him to an orphanage here, then file an orphan petition. Start your I-600 form and your home study while he's in a safe place."

"What are those?"

"I'm sorry, the I-600 is an INS formality. The home study is done by the adoption agency you choose," Omar said. "It's, you know, to make sure you and your wife aren't raving lunatics."

"I don't want to do that," I said, looking again at Sohrab. "I promised him I wouldn't send him back to an orphanage."

"Like I said, it may be your best shot."

We talked a while longer. Then I walked him out to his car, an old VW Bug. The sun was setting on Islamabad by then, a flaming red nimbus in the west. I watched the car tilt under Omar's weight as he somehow managed to slide in behind the wheel. He rolled down the window. "Amir?"

"Yes."

"I meant to tell you in there, about what you're trying to do? I think it's pretty great."

He waved as he pulled away. Standing outside the hotel room and waving back, I wished Soraya could be there with me.

SOHRAB HAD TURNED OFF THE TV when I went back

into the room. I sat on the edge of my bed, asked him to sit next to me. "Mr. Faisal thinks there is a way I can take you to America with me," I said.

"He does?" Sohrab said, smiling faintly for the first time in days. "When can we go?"

"Well, that's the thing. It might take a little while. But he said it can be done and he's going to help us." I put my hand on the back of his neck. From outside, the call to prayer blared through the streets.

"How long?" Sohrab asked. "I don't know. A while."

Sohrab shrugged and smiled, wider this time. "I don't mind. I can wait. It's like the sour apples."

"Sour apples?"

"One time, when I was really little, I climbed a tree and ate these green, sour apples. My stomach swelled and became hard like a drum, it hurt a lot. Mother said that if I'd just waited for the apples to ripen, I wouldn't have become sick. So now, whenever I really want something, I try to remember what she said about the apples."

"Sour apples," I said. "*Mashallah,* you're just about the smartest little guy I've ever met, Sohrab jan." His ears reddened with a blush.

"Will you take me to that red bridge? The one with the fog?" he said.

"Absolutely," I said. "Absolutely."

"And we'll drive up those streets, the ones where all you see is the hood of the car and the sky?"

"Every single one of them," I said. My eyes stung with tears and I blinked them away.

"Is English hard to learn?"

"I say, within a year, you'll speak it as well as Farsi." "Really?"

"Yes." I placed a finger under his chin, turned his face up to mine. "There *is* one other thing, Sohrab."

"What?"

"Well, Mr. Faisal thinks that it would really help if we could ... if we could ask you to stay in a home for kids for a while."

"Home for kids?" he said, his smile fading. "You mean an orphanage?"

"It would only be for a little while." "No," he said. "No, please."

"Sohrab, it would be for just a little while. I promise."

"You promised you'd never put me in one of those places, Amir agha," he said. His voice was breaking, tears pooling in his eyes. I felt like a prick.

"This is different. It would be here, in Islamabad, not in Kabul. And I'd visit you all the time until we can get you out and take you to America."

"Please! Please, no!" he croaked. "I'm scared of that place. They'll hurt me! I don't want to go."

"No one is going to hurt you. Not ever again."

"Yes they will! They always say they won't but they lie. They lie! Please, God!"

I wiped the tear streaking down his cheek with my thumb. "Sour apples, remember? It's just like the sour apples," I said softly.

"No it's not. Not that place. God, oh God. Please, no!" He was trembling, snot and tears mixing on his face.

"*Shhh.*" I pulled him close, wrapped my arms around his shaking little body. "*Shhh.* It'll be all right. We'll go home together. You'll see, it'll be all right."

His voice was muffled against my chest, but I heard the panic in it. "Please promise you won't! Oh God, Amir agha! Please promise you won't!"

How could I promise? I held him against me, held him tightly, and rocked back and forth. He wept into my shirt until his tears dried, until his shaking stopped and his frantic pleas dwindled to indecipherable mumbles. I waited, rocked him until his breathing slowed and his body slackened. I remembered something I had read somewhere a long time ago: *That's how children deal with terror. They fall asleep.*

I carried him to his bed, set him down. Then I lay in my own bed, looking out the window at the purple sky over Islamabad.

THE SKY WAS A DEEP BLACK when the phone jolted me from sleep. I rubbed my eyes and turned on the bedside lamp. It was a little past 10:30 P.M.; I'd been sleeping for almost three hours. I picked up the phone. "Hello?"

"Call from America." Mr. Fayyaz's bored voice.

"Thank you," I said. The bathroom light was on; Sohrab was taking his nightly bath. A couple of clicks and then Soraya: *"Salaam!"* She sounded excited.

"Hi."

"How did the meeting go with the lawyer?"

I told her what Omar Faisal had suggested. "Well, you can forget about it," she said. "We won't have to do that."

I sat up. *"Rawsti?* Why, what's up?"

"I heard back from Kaka Sharif. He said the key was getting Sohrab into the country. Once he's in, there are ways of keeping him here. So he made a few calls to his INS friends. He called me back tonight and said he was almost certain he could get Sohrab a humanitarian visa."

"No kidding?" I said. "Oh thank God! Good ol' Sharif jan!"

"I know. Anyway, we'll serve as the sponsors. It should all happen pretty quickly. He said the visa would be good for a year, plenty of time to apply for an adoption petition."

"It's really going to happen, Soraya, huh?"

"It looks like it," she said. She sounded happy. I told her I loved her and she said she loved me back. I hung up.

"Sohrab!" I called, rising from my bed. "I have great news." I knocked on the bathroom door. "Sohrab! Soraya jan just called from California. We won't have to put you in the orphanage, Sohrab. We're going to America, you and I. Did you hear me? We're going to America!"

I pushed the door open. Stepped into the bathroom.

Suddenly I was on my knees, screaming. Screaming through my clenched teeth. Screaming until I thought my throat would rip and my chest explode.

Later, they said I was still screaming when the ambulance arrived.

TWENTY·FIVE

They won't let me in.

I see them wheel him through a set of double doors and I follow. I burst through the doors, the smell of iodine and peroxide hits me, but all I have time to see is two men wearing surgical caps and a woman in green huddling over a gurney. A white sheet spills over the side of the gurney and brushes against grimy checkered tiles. A pair of small, bloody feet poke out from under the sheet and I see that the big toenail on the left foot is chipped. Then a tall, thickset man in blue presses his palm against my chest and he's pushing me back out through the doors, his wedding band cold on my skin. I shove forward and I curse him, but he says you cannot be here, he says it in English, his voice polite but firm. "You must wait," he says, leading me back to the waiting area, and now the double doors swing shut behind him with a sigh and all I see is the top of the men's surgical caps through the doors' narrow rectangular windows.

He leaves me in a wide, windowless corridor crammed with people sitting on metallic folding chairs set along the walls, others on the thin frayed carpet. I want to scream again, and

I remember the last time I felt this way, riding with Baba in the tank of the fuel truck, buried in the dark with the other refugees. I want to tear myself from this place, from this reality, rise up like a cloud and float away, melt into this humid summer night and dissolve somewhere far, over the hills. But I am here, my legs blocks of concrete, my lungs empty of air, my throat burning. There will be no floating away. There will be no other reality tonight. I close my eyes and my nostrils fill with the smells of the corridor, sweat and ammonia, rubbing alcohol and curry. On the ceiling, moths fling themselves at the dull gray light tubes running the length of the corridor and I hear the papery flapping of their wings. I hear chatter, muted sobbing, sniffling, someone moaning, someone else sighing, elevator doors opening with a *bing,* the operator paging someone in Urdu.

I open my eyes again and I know what I have to do. I look around, my heart a jackhammer in my chest, blood thudding in my ears. There is a dark little supply room to my left. In it, I find what I need. It will do. I grab a white bedsheet from the pile of folded linens and carry it back to the corridor. I see a nurse talking to a policeman near the restroom. I take the nurse's elbow and pull, I want to know which way is west. She doesn't understand and the lines on her face deepen when she frowns. My throat aches and my eyes sting with sweat, each breath is like inhaling fire, and I think I am weeping. I ask again. I beg. The policeman is the one who points.

I throw my makeshift *jai-namaz,* my prayer rug, on the floor and I get on my knees, lower my forehead to the ground, my tears soaking through the sheet. I bow to the west. Then I remember I haven't prayed for over fifteen years. I have long forgotten the words. But it doesn't matter, I will utter those few

words I still remember: *La illaha il Allah, Muhammad u rasul ullah.*
There is no God but Allah and Muhammad is His messenger. I
see now that Baba was wrong, there is a God, there always had
been. I see Him here, in the eyes of the people in this corridor
of desperation. This is the real house of God, this is where
those who have lost God will find Him, not the white *masjid*
with its bright diamond lights and towering minarets. There is
a God, there has to be, and now I will pray, I will pray that He
forgive that I have neglected Him all of these years, forgive that
I have betrayed, lied, and sinned with impunity only to turn
to Him now in my hour of need, I pray that He is as merciful,
benevolent, and gracious as His book says He is. I bow to the
west and kiss the ground and promise that I will do *zakat,* I will
do *namaz,* I will fast during Ramadan and when Ramadan has
passed I will go on fasting, I will commit to memory every last
word of His holy book, and I will set on a pilgrimage to that
sweltering city in the desert and bow before the Ka'bah too. I
will do all of this and I will think of Him every day from this
day on if He only grants me this one wish: My hands are stained
with Hassan's blood; I pray God doesn't let them get stained
with the blood of his boy too.

I hear a whimpering and realize it is mine, my lips are salty
with the tears trickling down my face. I feel the eyes of everyone in this corridor on me and still I bow to the west. I pray. I
pray that my sins have not caught up with me the way I'd always
feared they would.

A STARLESS, BLACK NIGHT falls over Islamabad. It's a few
hours later and I am sitting now on the floor of a tiny lounge

off the corridor that leads to the emergency ward. Before me is a dull brown coffee table cluttered with newspapers and dog-eared magazines—an April 1996 issue of *Time;* a Pakistani newspaper showing the face of a young boy who was hit and killed by a train the week before; an entertainment magazine with smiling Lollywood actors on its glossy cover. There is an old woman wearing a jade green *shalwar-kameez* and a crocheted shawl nodding off in a wheelchair across from me. Every once in a while, she stirs awake and mutters a prayer in Arabic. I wonder tiredly whose prayers will be heard tonight, hers or mine. I picture Sohrab's face, the pointed meaty chin, his small seashell ears, his slanting bamboo-leaf eyes so much like his father's. A sorrow as black as the night outside invades me, and I feel my throat clamping.

I need air.

I get up and open the windows. The air coming through the screen is musty and hot—it smells of overripe dates and dung. I force it into my lungs in big heaps, but it doesn't clear the clamping feeling in my chest. I drop back on the floor. I pick up the *Time* magazine and flip through the pages. But I can't read, can't focus on anything. So I toss it on the table and go back to staring at the zigzagging pattern of the cracks on the cement floor, at the cobwebs on the ceiling where the walls meet, at the dead flies littering the windowsill. Mostly, I stare at the clock on the wall. It's just past 4 A.M. and I have been shut out of the room with the swinging double doors for over five hours now. I still haven't heard any news.

The floor beneath me begins to feel like part of my body, and my breathing is growing heavier, slower. I want to sleep, shut my eyes and lie my head down on this cold, dusty floor. Drift off.

When I wake up, maybe I will discover that everything I saw in the hotel bathroom was part of a dream: the water drops dripping from the faucet and landing with a *plink* into the bloody bathwater; the left arm dangling over the side of the tub, the blood-soaked razor sitting on the toilet tank—the same razor I had shaved with the day before—and his eyes, still half open but lightless. That more than anything. I want to forget the eyes.

Soon, sleep comes and I let it take me. I dream of things I can't remember later.

SOMEONE IS TAPPING ME on the shoulder. I open my eyes. There is a man kneeling beside me. He is wearing a cap like the men behind the swinging double doors and a paper surgical mask over his mouth—my heart sinks when I see a drop of blood on the mask. He has taped a picture of a doe-eyed little girl to his beeper. He unsnaps his mask and I'm glad I don't have to look at Sohrab's blood anymore. His skin is dark like the imported Swiss chocolate Hassan and I used to buy from the bazaar in Shar-e-Nau; he has thinning hair and hazel eyes topped with curved eyelashes. In a British accent, he tells me his name is Dr. Nawaz, and suddenly I want to be away from this man, because I don't think I can bear to hear what he has come to tell me. He says the boy had cut himself deeply and had lost a great deal of blood and my mouth begins to mutter that prayer again:

La illaha il Allah, Muhammad u rasul ullah. They had to transfuse several units of red cells—

How will I tell Soraya?

Twice, they had to revive him—

I will do namaz, I will do zakat.

They would have lost him if his heart hadn't been young and strong—

I will fast.

He is alive.

Dr. Nawaz smiles. It takes me a moment to register what he has just said. Then he says more but I don't hear him. Because I have taken his hands and I have brought them up to my face. I weep my relief into this stranger's small, meaty hands and he says nothing now. He waits.

THE INTENSIVE CARE UNIT is *L*-shaped and dim, a jumble of bleeping monitors and whirring machines. Dr. Nawaz leads me between two rows of beds separated by white plastic curtains. Sohrab's bed is the last one around the corner, the one nearest the nurses' station where two nurses in green surgical scrubs are jotting notes on clipboards, chatting in low voices. On the silent ride up the elevator with Dr. Nawaz, I had thought I'd weep again when I saw Sohrab. But when I sit on the chair at the foot of his bed, looking at his white face through the tangle of gleaming plastic tubes and IV lines, I am dry-eyed. Watching his chest rise and fall to the rhythm of the hissing ventilator, a curious numbness washes over me, the same numbness a man might feel seconds after he has swerved his car and barely avoided a head-on collision.

I doze off, and, when I wake up, I see the sun rising in a buttermilk sky through the window next to the nurses' station. The light slants into the room, aims my shadow toward Sohrab. He hasn't moved.

"You'd do well to get some sleep," a nurse says to me. I don't

recognize her—there must have been a shift change while I'd
napped. She takes me to another lounge, this one just outside
the ICU. It's empty. She hands me a pillow and a hospital-issue
blanket. I thank her and lie on the vinyl sofa in the corner of
the lounge. I fall asleep almost immediately.

I dream I am back in the lounge downstairs. Dr. Nawaz walks
in and I rise to meet him. He takes off his paper mask, his hands
suddenly whiter than I remembered, his nails manicured, he
has neatly parted hair, and I see he is not Dr. Nawaz at all but
Raymond Andrews, the little embassy man with the potted
tomatoes. Andrews cocks his head. Narrows his eyes.

IN THE DAYTIME, the hospital was a maze of teeming, angled
hallways, a blur of blazing-white overhead fluorescence. I came
to know its layout, came to know that the fourth-floor button in
the east wing elevator didn't light up, that the door to the men's
room on that same floor was jammed and you had to ram your
shoulder into it to open it. I came to know that hospital life has
a rhythm, the flurry of activity just before the morning shift
change, the midday hustle, the stillness and quiet of the late-
night hours interrupted occasionally by a blur of doctors and
nurses rushing to revive someone. I kept vigil at Sohrab's bedside
in the daytime and wandered through the hospital's serpentine
corridors at night, listening to my shoe heels clicking on the
tiles, thinking of what I would say to Sohrab when he woke up.
I'd end up back in the ICU, by the whooshing ventilator beside
his bed, and I'd be no closer to knowing.

After three days in the ICU, they withdrew the breathing tube
and transferred him to a ground-level bed. I wasn't there when

they moved him. I had gone back to the hotel that night to get some sleep and ended up tossing around in bed all night. In the morning, I tried to not look at the bathtub. It was clean now, someone had wiped off the blood, spread new floor mats on the floor, and scrubbed the walls. But I couldn't stop myself from sitting on its cool, porcelain edge. I pictured Sohrab filling it with warm water. Saw him undressing. Saw him twisting the razor handle and opening the twin safety latches on the head, sliding the blade out, holding it between his thumb and forefinger. I pictured him lowering himself into the water, lying there for a while, his eyes closed. I wondered what his last thought had been as he had raised the blade and brought it down.

I was exiting the lobby when the hotel manager, Mr. Fayyaz, caught up with me. "I am very sorry for you," he said, "but I am asking for you to leave my hotel, please. This is bad for my business, very bad."

I told him I understood and I checked out. He didn't charge me for the three days I'd spent at the hospital. Waiting for a cab outside the hotel lobby, I thought about what Mr. Fayyaz had said to me that night we'd gone looking for Sohrab: *The thing about you Afghanis is that ... well, you people are a little reckless.* I had laughed at him, but now I wondered. Had I actually gone to sleep after I had given Sohrab the news he feared most?

When I got in the cab, I asked the driver if he knew any Persian bookstores. He said there was one a couple of kilometers south. We stopped there on the way to the hospital.

SOHRAB'S NEW ROOM had cream-colored walls, chipped, dark gray moldings, and glazed tiles that might have once been white. He shared the room with a teenaged Punjabi boy who, I later learned from one of the nurses, had broken his leg when he had slipped off the roof of a moving bus. His leg was in a cast, raised and held by tongs strapped to several weights.

Sohrab's bed was next to the window, the lower half lit by the late-morning sunlight streaming through the rectangular panes. A uniformed security guard was standing at the window, munching on cooked watermelon seeds—Sohrab was under twenty-four-hours-a-day suicide watch. Hospital protocol, Dr. Nawaz had informed me. The guard tipped his hat when he saw me and left the room.

Sohrab was wearing short-sleeved hospital pajamas and lying on his back, blanket pulled to his chest, face turned to the window. I thought he was sleeping, but when I scooted a chair up to his bed his eyelids fluttered and opened. He looked at me, then looked away. He was so pale, even with all the blood they had given him, and there was a large purple bruise in the crease of his right arm.

"How are you?" I said.

He didn't answer. He was looking through the window at a fenced-in sandbox and swing set in the hospital garden. There was an arch-shaped trellis near the playground, in the shadow of a row of hibiscus trees, a few green vines climbing up the timber lattice. A handful of kids were playing with buckets and pails in the sandbox. The sky was a cloudless blue that day, and I saw a tiny jet leaving behind twin white trails. I turned back to Sohrab. "I spoke to Dr. Nawaz a few minutes ago and he thinks you'll be discharged in a couple of days. That's good news, nay?"

Again I was met by silence. The Punjabi boy at the other end of the room stirred in his sleep and moaned something. "I like your room," I said, trying not to look at Sohrab's bandaged wrists. "It's bright, and you have a view." Silence. A few more awkward minutes passed, and a light sweat formed on my brow, my upper lip. I pointed to the untouched bowl of green pea *aush* on his nightstand, the unused plastic spoon. "You should try to eat something. Gain your *quwat* back, your strength. Do you want me to help you?"

He held my glance, then looked away, his face set like stone. His eyes were still lightless, I saw, vacant, the way I had found them when I had pulled him out of the bathtub. I reached into the paper bag between my feet and took out the used copy of the *Shahnamah* I had bought at the Persian bookstore. I turned the cover so it faced Sohrab. "I used to read this to your father when we were children. We'd go up the hill by our house and sit beneath the pomegranate ..." I trailed off. Sohrab was looking through the window again. I forced a smile. "Your father's favorite was the story of Rostam and Sohrab and that's how you got your name, I know you know that." I paused, feeling a bit like an idiot. "Anyway, he said in his letter that it was your favorite too, so I thought I'd read you some of it. Would you like that?"

Sohrab closed his eyes. Covered them with his arm, the one with the bruise.

I flipped to the page I had bent in the taxicab. "Here we go," I said, wondering for the first time what thoughts had passed through Hassan's head when he had finally read the *Shahnamah* for himself and discovered that I had deceived him all those times. I cleared my throat and read. "'Give ear unto the combat of Sohrab against Rostam, though it be a tale replete with tears,'" I began. "'It came about that on a certain day Rostam rose from his couch and his mind was filled with forebodings.

He bethought him …'" I read him most of chapter 1, up to the part where the young warrior Sohrab comes to his mother, Tahmineh, the princess of Samengan, and demands to know the identity of his father. I closed the book. "Do you want me to go on? There are battles coming up, remember? Sohrab leading his army to the White Castle in Iran? Should I read on?"

He shook his head slowly. I dropped the book back in the paper bag. "That's fine," I said, encouraged that he had responded at all. "Maybe we can continue tomorrow. How do you feel?"

Sohrab's mouth opened and a hoarse sound came out. Dr. Nawaz had told me that would happen, on account of the breathing tube they had slid through his vocal cords. He licked his lips and tried again. "Tired."

"I know. Dr. Nawaz said that was to be expected—"

He was shaking his head. "What, Sohrab?"

He winced when he spoke again in that husky voice, barely above a whisper. "Tired of everything."

I sighed and slumped in my chair. There was a band of sunlight on the bed between us, and, for just a moment, the ashen gray face looking at me from the other side of it was a dead ringer for Hassan's, not the Hassan I played marbles with until the mullah belted out the evening *azan* and Ali called us home, not the Hassan I chased down our hill as the sun dipped behind clay rooftops in the west, but the Hassan I saw alive for the last time, dragging his belongings behind Ali in a warm summer downpour, stuffing them in the trunk of Baba's car while I watched through the rain-soaked window of my room.

He gave a slow shake of his head. "Tired of everything," he repeated.

"What can I do, Sohrab? Please tell me."

"I want—" he began. He winced again and brought his hand to his throat as if to clear whatever was blocking his voice. My eyes were drawn again to his wrist wrapped tightly with white gauze bandages. "I want my old life back," he breathed.

"Oh, Sohrab."

"I want Father and Mother jan. I want Sasa. I want to play with Rahim Khan sahib in the garden. I want to live in our house again." He dragged his forearm across his eyes. "I want my old life back."

I didn't know what to say, where to look, so I gazed down at my hands. *Your old life,* I thought. *My old life too. I played in the same yard, Sohrab. I lived in the same house. But the grass is dead and a stranger's jeep is parked in the driveway of our house, pissing oil all over the asphalt. Our old life is gone, Sohrab, and everyone in it is either dead or dying. It's just you and me now. Just you and me.*

"I can't give you that," I said. "I wish you hadn't—" "Please don't say that."

"—wish you hadn't …I wish you had left me in the water." "Don't ever say that, Sohrab," I said, leaning forward. "I can't bear to hear you talk like that." I touched his shoulder and he flinched. Drew away. I dropped my hand, remembering ruefully how in the last days before I'd broken my promise to him he had finally become at ease with my touch. "Sohrab, I can't give you your old life back, I wish to God I could. But I can take you with me. That was what I was coming in the bathroom to tell you. You have a visa to go to America, to live with me and my wife. It's true. I promise."

He sighed through his nose and closed his eyes. I wished I hadn't said those last two words. "You know, I've done a lot of things I regret in my life," I said, "and maybe none more than going back on the promise I made you. But that will never happen again, and I am so very profoundly sorry. I ask for your *bakhshesh,* your forgiveness. Can you do that? Can you forgive me? Can you believe me?" I dropped my voice. "Will you come with me?"

As I waited for his reply, my mind flashed back to a winter day from long ago, Hassan and I sitting on the snow beneath a leafless sour cherry tree. I had played a cruel game with Hassan that day, toyed with him, asked him if he would chew dirt to prove his loyalty to me. Now I was the one under the microscope, the one who had to prove my worthiness. I deserved this.

Sohrab rolled to his side, his back to me. He didn't say anything for a long time. And then, just as I thought he might have drifted to sleep, he said with a croak, "I am so *khasta.*" So very tired.

I sat by his bed until he fell asleep. Something was lost between Sohrab and me. Until my meeting with the lawyer, Omar Faisal, a light of hope had begun to enter Sohrab's eyes like a timid guest. Now the light was gone, the guest had fled, and I wondered when it would dare return. I wondered how long before Sohrab smiled again. How long before he trusted me. If ever.

So I left the room and went looking for another hotel, unaware that almost a year would pass before I would hear Sohrab speak another word.

IN THE END, Sohrab never accepted my offer. Nor did he decline it. But he knew that when the bandages were removed and the hospital garments returned, he was just another homeless

Hazara orphan. What choice did he have? Where could he go? So what I took as a yes from him was in actuality more of a quiet surrender, not so much an acceptance as an act of relinquishment by one too weary to decide, and far too tired to believe. What he yearned for was his old life. What he got was me and America. Not that it was such a bad fate, everything considered, but I couldn't tell him that. Perspective was a luxury when your head was constantly buzzing with a swarm of demons.

And so it was that, about a week later, we crossed a strip of warm, black tarmac and I brought Hassan's son from Afghanistan to America, lifting him from the certainty of turmoil and dropping him in a turmoil of uncertainty.

ONE DAY, maybe around 1983 or 1984, I was at a video store in Fremont. I was standing in the Westerns section when a guy next to me, sipping Coke from a 7-Eleven cup, pointed to *The Magnificent Seven* and asked me if I had seen it. "Yes, thirteen times," I said. "Charles Bronson dies in it, so do James Coburn and Robert Vaughn." He gave me a pinch-faced look, as if I had just spat in his soda. "Thanks a lot, man," he said, shaking his head and muttering something as he walked away. That was when I learned that, in America, you don't reveal the ending of the movie, and if you do, you will be scorned and made to apologize profusely for having committed the sin of Spoiling the End.

In Afghanistan, the ending was all that mattered. When Hassan and I came home after watching a Hindi film at Cinema Zainab, what Ali, Rahim Khan, Baba, or the myriad of Baba's friends—second and third cousins milling in and out of the house—wanted to know was this: Did the Girl in the film find happiness? Did the *bacheh film,* the Guy in the film, become *kamyab* and fulfill his dreams, or was he *nah-kam,* doomed to wallow in failure?

Was there happiness at the end, they wanted to know.

If someone were to ask me today whether the story of Hassan, Sohrab, and me ends with happiness, I wouldn't know what to say.

Does anybody's?

After all, life is not a Hindi movie. *Zendagi migzara,* Afghans like to say: Life goes on, unmindful of beginning, end, *kamyab, nah-kam,* crisis or catharsis, moving forward like a slow, dusty caravan of *kochis.*

I wouldn't know how to answer that question. Despite the matter of last Sunday's tiny miracle.

WE ARRIVED HOME about seven months ago, on a warm day in August 2001. Soraya picked us up at the airport. I had never been away from Soraya for so long, and when she locked her arms around my neck, when I smelled apples in her hair, I realized how much I had missed her. "You're still the morning sun to my *yelda,*" I whispered.

"What?"

"Never mind." I kissed her ear.

After, she knelt to eye level with Sohrab. She took his hand and smiled at him. "*Salaam,* Sohrab jan, I'm your Khala Soraya. We've all been waiting for you."

Looking at her smiling at Sohrab, her eyes tearing over a little, I had a glimpse of the mother she might have been, had her own womb not betrayed her.

Sohrab shifted on his feet and looked away.

SORAYA HAD TURNED THE STUDY upstairs into a bedroom for Sohrab. She led him in and he sat on the edge of the bed. The sheets showed brightly colored kites flying in indigo blue skies. She had made inscriptions on the wall by the closet, feet and inches to measure a child's growing height. At the foot of the bed, I saw a wicker basket stuffed with books, a locomotive, a watercolor set.

Sohrab was wearing the plain white T-shirt and new denims I had bought him in Islamabad just before we'd left—the shirt hung loosely over his bony, slumping shoulders. The color still hadn't seeped back into his face, save for the halo of dark circles around his eyes. He was looking at us now in the impassive way he looked at the plates of boiled rice the hospital orderly placed before him. Soraya asked if he liked his room and I noticed that she was trying to avoid looking at his wrists and that her eyes kept swaying back to those jagged pink lines. Sohrab lowered his head. Hid his hands under his thighs and said nothing. Then he simply lay his head on the pillow. Less than five minutes later, Soraya and I watching from the doorway, he was snoring.

We went to bed, and Soraya fell asleep with her head on my chest. In the darkness of our room, I lay awake, an insomniac once more. Awake. And alone with demons of my own.

Sometime in the middle of the night, I slid out of bed and went to Sohrab's room. I stood over him, looking down, and saw something protruding from under his pillow. I picked it up. Saw it was Rahim Khan's Polaroid, the one I had given to Sohrab the night we had sat by the Shah Faisal Mosque. The one of Hassan and Sohrab standing side by side, squinting in the light of the sun, and smiling like the world was a good and just place. I wondered how long Sohrab had lain in bed staring at the photo, turning it in his hands. I looked at the photo. *Your father was a man torn between two halves,* Rahim Khan had said in his letter. I had been the entitled half, the society-approved, legitimate half, the unwitting embodiment of Baba's guilt. I looked at Hassan, showing those two missing front teeth, sunlight slanting on his face. Baba's other half. The unentitled, unprivileged half. The half who had inherited what had been pure and noble in Baba. The half that, maybe, in the most secret recesses of his heart, Baba had thought of as his true son.

I slipped the picture back where I had found it. Then I realized something: That last thought had brought no sting with it. Closing Sohrab's door, I wondered if that was how forgiveness budded, not with the fanfare of epiphany, but with pain gathering its things, packing up, and slipping away unannounced in the middle of the night.

THE GENERAL AND KHALA JAMILA came over for dinner the following night. Khala Jamila, her hair cut short and a darker shade of red than usual, handed Soraya the plate of almond-topped *maghout* she had brought for dessert. She saw Sohrab and beamed. *"Mashallah!* Soraya jan told us how *khoshteep* you were, but you are even more handsome in person, Sohrab jan." She handed him a blue turtleneck sweater. "I knitted this for you," she said. "For next winter. *Inshallah,* it will fit you."

Sohrab took the sweater from her.

"Hello, young man," was all the general said, leaning with both hands on his cane, looking at Sohrab the way one might study a bizarre decorative item at someone's house.

I answered, and answered again, Khala Jamila's questions about my injuries—I'd asked Soraya to tell them I had been mugged—reassuring her that I had no permanent damage, that the wires would come out in a few weeks so I'd be able to eat her cooking again, that, yes, I would try rubbing rhubarb juice and sugar on my scars to make them fade faster.

The general and I sat in the living room and sipped wine while Soraya and her mother set the table. I told him about Kabul and the Taliban. He listened and nodded, his cane on his lap, and *tsk*'ed when I told him of the man I had spotted selling his artificial leg. I made no mention of the executions at Ghazi Stadium and Assef. He asked about Rahim Khan, whom he said he had met in Kabul a few times, and shook his head solemnly when I told him of Rahim Khan's illness. But as we spoke, I caught his eyes drifting again and again to Sohrab sleeping on the couch. As if we were skirting around the edge of what he really wanted to know.

The skirting finally came to an end over dinner when the general put down his fork and said, "So, Amir jan, you're going to tell us why you have brought back this boy with you?"

"Iqbal jan! What sort of question is that?" Khala Jamila said.

"While you're busy knitting sweaters, my dear, I have to deal with the community's perception of our family. People will ask. They will want to know why there is a Hazara boy living with our daughter. What do I tell them?"

Soraya dropped her spoon. Turned on her father. "You can tell them—"

"It's okay, Soraya," I said, taking her hand. "It's okay. General Sahib is quite right. People *will* ask."

"Amir—" she began.

"It's all right." I turned to the general. "You see, General Sahib, my father slept with his servant's wife. She bore him a son named Hassan. Hassan is dead now. That boy sleeping on the couch is Hassan's son. He's my nephew. That's what you tell people when they ask."

They were all staring at me.

"And one more thing, General Sahib," I said. "You will never again refer to him as 'Hazara boy' in my presence. He has a name and it's Sohrab."

No one said anything for the remainder of the meal.

IT WOULD BE ERRONEOUS to say Sohrab was quiet. Quiet is peace. Tranquillity. Quiet is turning down the VOLUME knob on life.

Silence is pushing the OFF button. Shutting it down. All of it.

Sohrab's silence wasn't the self-imposed silence of those with convictions, of protesters who seek to speak their cause by not speaking at all. It was the silence of one who has taken cover in a dark place, curled up all the edges and tucked them under.

He didn't so much live with us as occupy space. And precious little of it. Sometimes, at the market, or in the park, I'd notice how other people hardly seemed to even see him, like he wasn't there at all. I'd look up from a book and realize Sohrab had entered the room, had sat across from me, and I hadn't noticed. He walked like he was afraid to leave behind footprints. He moved as if not to stir the air around him. Mostly, he slept.

Sohrab's silence was hard on Soraya too. Over that long-distance line to Pakistan, Soraya had told me about the things she was planning for Sohrab. Swimming classes. Soccer. Bowling league. Now she'd walk past Sohrab's room and catch a glimpse of books sitting unopened in the wicker basket, the growth chart unmarked, the jigsaw puzzle unassembled, each item a reminder of a life that could have been. A reminder of a dream that was wilting even as it was budding. But she hadn't been alone. I'd had my own dreams for Sohrab.

While Sohrab was silent, the world was not. One Tuesday morning last September, the Twin Towers came crumbling down and, overnight, the world changed. The American flag suddenly appeared everywhere, on the antennae of yellow cabs weaving around traffic, on the lapels of pedestrians walking the sidewalks in a steady stream, even on the grimy caps of San Francisco's panhandlers sitting beneath the awnings of small art galleries and open-fronted shops. One day I passed Edith, the homeless woman who plays the accordion every day on the corner of Sutter and Stockton, and spotted an American flag sticker on the accordion case at her feet.

Soon after the attacks, America bombed Afghanistan, the Northern Alliance moved in, and the Taliban scurried like rats into the caves. Suddenly, people were standing in grocery store lines and talking about the cities of my childhood, Kandahar, Herat, Mazar-i-Sharif. When I was very little, Baba took Hassan and me to Kunduz. I don't remember much about the trip, except sitting in the shade of an acacia tree with Baba and Hassan, taking turns sipping fresh watermelon juice from a clay pot and seeing who could spit the seeds farther. Now Dan Rather, Tom Brokaw, and people sipping lattes at Starbucks were talking about the battle for Kunduz, the Taliban's last stronghold in the north. That December, Pashtuns, Tajiks, Uzbeks, and Hazaras gathered in Bonn and, under the watchful eye of the UN, began the process that might someday end over twenty years of unhappiness in their *watan*. Hamid Karzai's caracul hat and green *chapan* became famous.

Sohrab sleepwalked through it all.

Soraya and I became involved in Afghan projects, as much out of a sense of civil duty as the need for something—anything—to fill the silence upstairs, the silence that sucked everything in like a black hole. I had never been the active type before, but when a man named Kabir, a former Afghan ambassador to Sofia, called and asked if I wanted to help him with a hospital project, I said yes. The small hospital had stood near the Afghan-Pakistani border and had a small surgical unit that treated Afghan refugees with land mine injuries. But it had closed down due to a lack of funds. I became the project manager, Soraya my comanager. I spent most of my days in the study, e-mailing people around the world, applying for grants, organizing fund-raising events. And telling myself that bringing Sohrab here had been the right thing to do.

The year ended with Soraya and me on the couch, blanket spread over our legs, watching Dick Clark on TV. People cheered and kissed when the silver ball dropped, and confetti whitened the screen. In our house, the new year began much the same way the last one had ended. In silence.

THEN, FOUR DAYS AGO, on a cool rainy day in March 2002, a small, wondrous thing happened.

I took Soraya, Khala Jamila, and Sohrab to a gathering of Afghans at Lake Elizabeth Park in Fremont. The general had finally been summoned to Afghanistan the month before for a ministry position, and had flown there two weeks earlier—he had left behind his gray suit and pocket watch. The plan was for Khala Jamila to join him in a few months once he had settled. She missed him terribly—and worried about his health there—and we had insisted she stay with us for a while.

The previous Thursday, the first day of spring, had been the Afghan New Year's Day—the *Sawl-e-Nau*—and Afghans in the Bay Area had planned celebrations throughout the East Bay and the peninsula. Kabir, Soraya, and I had an additional reason to rejoice: Our little hospital in Rawalpindi had opened the week before, not the surgical unit, just the pediatric clinic. But it was a good start, we all agreed.

It had been sunny for days, but Sunday morning, as I swung my legs out of bed, I heard raindrops pelting the window. *Afghan luck,* I thought. Snickered. I prayed morning *namaz* while Soraya slept—I didn't have to consult the prayer pamphlet I had obtained from the mosque anymore; the verses came naturally now, effortlessly.

We arrived around noon and found a handful of people taking cover under a large rectangular plastic sheet mounted on six poles spiked to the ground. Someone was already frying *bolani;* steam rose from teacups and a pot of cauliflower *aush*. A scratchy old Ahmad Zahir song was blaring from a cassette player. I smiled a little as the four of us rushed across the soggy grass field, Soraya and I in the lead, Khala Jamila in the middle, Sohrab behind us, the hood of his yellow raincoat bouncing on his back.

"What's so funny?" Soraya said, holding a folded newspaper

over her head.

"You can take Afghans out of Paghman, but you can't take Paghman out of Afghans," I said.

We stooped under the makeshift tent. Soraya and Khala Jamila drifted toward an overweight woman frying spinach *bolani*. Sohrab stayed under the canopy for a moment, then stepped back out into the rain, hands stuffed in the pockets of his raincoat, his hair—now brown and straight like Hassan's—plastered against his scalp. He stopped near a coffee-colored puddle and stared at it. No one seemed to notice. No one called him back in. With time, the queries about our adopted—and decidedly eccentric— little boy had mercifully ceased, and, considering how tactless Afghan queries can be sometimes, that was a considerable relief. People stopped asking why he never spoke. Why he didn't play with the other kids. And best of all, they stopped suffocating us with their exaggerated empathy, their slow head shaking, their *tsktsks*, their "*Oh gung bichara.*" Oh, poor little mute one. The novelty had worn off. Like dull wallpaper, Sohrab had blended into the background.

I shook hands with Kabir, a small, silver-haired man. He introduced me to a dozen men, one of them a retired teacher, another an engineer, a former architect, a surgeon who was now running a hot dog stand in Hayward. They all said they'd known Baba in Kabul, and they spoke about him respectfully. In one way or another, he had touched all their lives. The men said I was lucky to have had such a great man for a father.

We chatted about the difficult and maybe thankless job Karzai had in front of him, about the upcoming *Loya jirga,* and the king's imminent return to his homeland after twenty-eights years of exile. I remembered the night in 1973, the night Zahir

Shah's cousin overthrew him; I remembered gunfire and the sky lighting up silver—Ali had taken me and Hassan in his arms, told us not to be afraid, that they were just shooting ducks.

Then someone told a Mullah Nasruddin joke and we were all laughing. "You know, your father was a funny man too," Kabir said.

"He was, wasn't he?" I said, smiling, remembering how, soon after we arrived in the U.S., Baba started grumbling about American flies. He'd sit at the kitchen table with his flyswatter, watch the flies darting from wall to wall, buzzing here, buzzing there, harried and rushed. "In this country, even flies are pressed for time," he'd groan. How I had laughed. I smiled at the memory now. By three o'clock, the rain had stopped and the sky was a curdled gray burdened with lumps of clouds. A cool breeze blew through the park. More families turned up. Afghans greeted each other, hugged, kissed, exchanged food. Someone lighted coal in a barbecue and soon the smell of garlic and *morgh* kabob flooded my senses. There was music, some new singer I didn't know, and the giggling of children. I saw Sohrab, still in his yellow raincoat, leaning against a garbage pail, staring across the park at the empty batting cage.

A little while later, as I was chatting with the former surgeon, who told me he and Baba had been classmates in eighth grade, Soraya pulled on my sleeve. "Amir, look!"

She was pointing to the sky. A half-dozen kites were flying high, speckles of bright yellow, red, and green against the gray sky. "Check it out," Soraya said, and this time she was pointing to a guy selling kites from a stand nearby.

"Hold this," I said. I gave my cup of tea to Soraya. I excused myself and walked over to the kite stand, my shoes squishing on the wet grass. I pointed to a yellow *seh-parcha*. *"Sawl-e-nau mubabrak,"* the kite seller said, taking the twenty and handing me the kite and a wooden spool of glass *tar.* I thanked him and wished him a Happy New Year too. I tested the string the way Hassan and I used to, by holding it between my thumb and forefinger and pulling it. It reddened with blood and the kite seller smiled. I smiled back.

I took the kite to where Sohrab was standing, still leaning against the garbage pail, arms crossed on his chest. He was looking up at the sky.

"Do you like the *seh-parcha?*" I said, holding up the kite by the ends of the cross bars. His eyes shifted from the sky to me, to the kite, then back. A few rivulets of rain trickled from his hair, down his face.

"I read once that, in Malaysia, they use kites to catch fish," I said. "I'll bet you didn't know that. They tie a fishing line to it and fly it beyond the shallow waters, so it doesn't cast a shadow and scare the fish. And in ancient China, generals used to fly kites over battlefields to send messages to their men. It's true. I'm not slipping you a trick." I showed him my bloody thumb. "Nothing wrong with the *tar* either."

Out of the corner of my eye, I saw Soraya watching us from the tent. Hands tensely dug in her armpits. Unlike me, she'd gradually abandoned her attempts at engaging him. The unanswered questions, the blank stares, the silence, it was all too painful. She had shifted to "Holding Pattern," waiting for a green light from Sohrab. Waiting.

I wet my index finger and held it up. "I remember the way your father checked the wind was to kick up dust with his sandal, see which way the wind blew it. He knew a lot of little tricks like that," I said. Lowered my finger. "West, I think."

Sohrab wiped a raindrop from his earlobe and shifted on his feet. Said nothing. I thought of Soraya asking me a few months ago what his voice sounded like. I'd told her I didn't remember anymore.

"Did I ever tell you your father was the best kite runner in Wazir Akbar Khan? Maybe all of Kabul?" I said, knotting the loose end of the spool *tar* to the string loop tied to the center spar. "How jealous he made the neighborhood kids. He'd run kites and never look up at the sky, and people used to say he was chasing the kite's shadow. But they didn't know him like I did. Your father wasn't chasing any shadows. He just ... knew."

Another half-dozen kites had taken flight. People had started to gather in clumps, teacups in hand, eyes glued to the sky.

"Do you want to help me fly this?" I said.

Sohrab's gaze bounced from the kite to me. Back to the sky. "Okay." I shrugged. "Looks like I'll have to fly it *tanhaii*." Solo.

I balanced the spool in my left hand and fed about three feet of *tar*. The yellow kite dangled at the end of it, just above the wet grass. "Last chance," I said. But Sohrab was looking at a pair of kites tangling high above the trees.

"All right. Here I go." I took off running, my sneakers splashing rainwater from puddles, the hand clutching the kite end of the string held high above my head. It had been so long, so many years since I'd done this, and I wondered if I'd make a spectacle of myself. I let the spool roll in my left hand as I ran, felt the string cut my right hand again as it fed through. The kite was lifting behind my shoulder now, lifting, wheeling, and I ran harder. The spool spun faster and the glass string tore another gash in my right palm. I stopped and turned. Looked up. Smiled. High above, my kite was tilting side to side like a pendulum, making that old paper-bird-flapping-its-wings sound I always associated with winter mornings in Kabul. I hadn't flown a kite in a quarter of a century, but suddenly I was twelve again and all the old instincts came rushing back.

I felt a presence next to me and looked down. It was Sohrab. Hands dug deep in the pockets of his raincoat. He had followed me.

"Do you want to try?" I asked. He said nothing. But when I held the string out for him, his hand lifted from his pocket. Hesitated. Took the string. My heart quickened as I spun the spool to gather the loose string. We stood quietly side by side. Necks bent up.

Around us, kids chased each other, slid on the grass. Someone was playing an old Hindi movie soundtrack now. A line of elderly men were praying afternoon *namaz* on a plastic sheet spread on the ground. The air smelled of wet grass, smoke, and grilled meat. I wished time would stand still.

Then I saw we had company. A green kite was closing in. I traced the string to a kid standing about thirty yards from us. He had a crew cut and a T-shirt that read THE ROCK RULES in bold block letters. He saw me looking at him and smiled. Waved. I waved back.

Sohrab was handing the string back to me. "Are you sure?" I said, taking it.

He took the spool from me.

"Okay," I said. "Let's give him a *sabagh*, teach him a lesson, nay?" I glanced over at him. The glassy, vacant look in his eyes was gone. His gaze flitted between our kite and the green one. His face was a little flushed, his eyes suddenly alert. Awake. Alive. I wondered when I had forgotten that, despite everything, he was still just a child.

The green kite was making its move. "Let's wait," I said. "We'll let him get a little closer." It dipped twice and crept toward us. "Come on. Come to me," I said.

The green kite drew closer yet, now rising a little above us, unaware of the trap I'd set for it. "Watch, Sohrab. I'm going to show you one of your father's favorite tricks, the old lift-and-dive." Next to me, Sohrab was breathing rapidly through his nose.

The spool rolled in his palms, the tendons in his scarred wrists like *rubab* strings. Then I blinked and, for just a moment, the hands holding the spool were the chipped-nailed, calloused hands of a harelipped boy. I heard a crow cawing somewhere and I looked up. The park shimmered with snow so fresh, so dazzling white, it burned my eyes. It sprinkled soundlessly from the branches of white-clad trees. I smelled turnip *qurma* now. Dried mulberries. Sour oranges. Sawdust and walnuts. The muffled quiet, snow-quiet, was deafening. Then far away, across the stillness, a voice calling us home, the voice of a man who dragged his right leg.

The green kite hovered directly above us now. "He's going for it. Anytime now," I said, my eyes flicking from Sohrab to our kite. The green kite hesitated. Held position. Then shot down.

"Here he comes!" I said.

I did it perfectly. After all these years. The old lift-and-dive trap. I loosened my grip and tugged on the string, dipping and dodging the green kite. A series of quick sidearm jerks and our kite shot up counterclockwise, in a half circle. Suddenly I was on top. The green kite was scrambling now, panic-stricken. But it was too late. I'd already slipped him Hassan's trick. I pulled hard and our kite plummeted. I could almost feel our string sawing his. Almost heard the snap.

Then, just like that, the green kite was spinning and wheeling out of control.

Behind us, people cheered. Whistles and applause broke out. I was panting. The last time I had felt a rush like this was that day in the winter of 1975, just after I had cut the last kite, when I spotted Baba on our rooftop, clapping, beaming.

I looked down at Sohrab. One corner of his mouth had curled up just so.

A smile.

Lopsided.

Hardly there. But there.

Behind us, kids were scampering, and a melee of screaming kite runners was chasing the loose kite drifting high above the trees. I blinked and the smile was gone. But it had been there. I had seen it.

"Do you want me to run that kite for you?"

His Adam's apple rose and fell as he swallowed. The wind lifted his hair. I thought I saw him nod.

"For you, a thousand times over," I heard myself say. Then I turned and ran.

It was only a smile, nothing more. It didn't make everything all right. It didn't make *anything* all right. Only a smile. A tiny thing. A leaf in the woods, shaking in the wake of a startled bird's flight. But I'll take it. With open arms. Because when spring comes, it melts the snow one flake at a time, and maybe I just witnessed the first flake melting.

I ran. A grown man running with a swarm of screaming children. But I didn't care. I ran with the wind blowing in my face, and a smile as wide as the Valley of Panjsher on my lips.

I ran.